SECOND EDITION

MARK TWAIN
Adventures of Huckleberry Finn

A Case Study in Critical Controversy

EDITED BY

Gerald Graff
University of Chicago

James Phelan
The Ohio State University

Bedford/St. Martin's
BOSTON • NEW YORK

For Bedford/St. Martin's

Executive Editor: Stephen A. Scipione
Editorial Assistant: Anne Noyes
Assistant Editor, Publishing Services: Maria Burwell
Senior Production Supervisor: Dennis J. Conroy
Production Associate: Christie Gross
Marketing Manager: Jenna Bookin Barry
Project Management: Stratford Publishing Services, Inc.
Cover Design: Diane Levy
Cover Art: Thomas Hart Benton, *A Social History of the State
of Missouri: Huckleberry Finn* (detail of the north wall), 1936. Courtesy of
Missouri Department of Natural Resources, Missouri State Museum.
Composition: Stratford Publishing Services, Inc.
Printing and Binding: RR Donnelley & Sons Company

President: Joan E. Feinberg
Editorial Director: Denise B. Wydra
Director of Marketing: Karen Melton Soeltz
Director of Editing, Design, and Production: Marcia Cohen
Manager, Publishing Services: Emily Berleth

Library of Congress Control Number: 2003108335

Manufactured in the United States of America.

9 8 7 6 5 4
f e d c b a

For information, write: Bedford/St. Martin's,
75 Arlington Street, Boston, MA 02116   (617-399-4000)

ISBN: 0-312-40029-2

Acknowledgments

*Acknowledgments and copyrights appear at the back of the book on pp. 548–50, which consti-
tute an extension of the copyright page.*

Published and distributed outside North America by

PALGRAVE MACMILLAN
Houndmills, Basingstoke, Hampshire RG21 2XS and London
Companies and representatives throughout the world.

ISBN: 0-4039-0506-1

A catalog record for this book is available from the British Library

Preface

Is *Huckleberry Fir...* ...sm?
Did Mark Twain bot... ...g to
say about the politic... ...ing
students participate i... ...ated
by such questions is... *inn:*
A Case Study in Crit... ...f the
complete 1885 text ...ding
to three important c ...dito-
rial commentary tha ...*nn* in
the context of critic ...t discusses principles and ...sy.

LEARNING BY

This case study ...eading
with absorption ar ...others
about what we rea ...endent
activities. All of us ...ok at a
painting, or, inde ...ntion is
directed and inte ...In fact,
we would argue ...nses to

inspire us to make our own contributions to the ongoing discussion. Thus, this case study emphasizes controversy — not just conversation — because controversy, increasingly, is the form contemporary discourse about books and culture takes.

Our approach as editors of this volume grows out of our own undergraduate experiences, coming to college from families and neighborhoods where book talk and intellectual discussions were not everyday events. Like many of our students today, we wondered why the academy put so much emphasis on reading literature for its "hidden meanings" when, from our perspectives, literature was something primarily to be enjoyed, not elaborately analyzed. We each eventually found that exposure to pertinent critical controversies in the classroom helped greatly to dispel our initial fear and confusion and to show us why the "meanings" of texts, and the debates about those meanings, can indeed matter.[1]

The problems we had in getting socialized into the conversations of literary study are as typical now as then. When students in literature courses are shy and silent in class discussions and find critical essays a struggle to write, the reason often lies in the mysterious and intimidating nature of literary critical discourse.

To be sure, an instructor can alleviate the problem by telling such students to forget academic intellectual talk and just respond in their own voices: "Never mind how the critical elite says you should feel about *Huckleberry Finn;* tell us how you feel." Though such a tactic is understandable — perhaps even essential — at the beginning stages of literary study, it represents a poor solution. It widens rather than closes the already large gulf between the discourse of the teacher and that of the student. More important, it deepens the gulf between those students who "talk the talk" of the academy — the ones who get the A's and are destined for professional career tracks — and those who settle for lesser rewards and ambitions.

Closing the gap between literary critical discourse and student discourse is important if higher education in the humanities is to be effective. And the best way to close this gap is to think of reading, discussing, and writing about literature as a process of entering into a critical conversation about it. Learning by controversy offers not only a

---

[1] See Gerald Graff's *Beyond the Culture Wars* (New York: Norton, 1992) 67–68 for an account of how his awareness of controversies about *Huckleberry Finn* helped him begin to like books. Graff reflects back on this account in his more recent book, *Clueless in Academe: How Schooling Obscures the Life of the Mind* (New Haven: Yale UP, 2003).

practical classroom solution to the "hidden meaning" problem but also an effective response to the angrily polarized debates of our time. Indeed, this strategy presents a model of how the quality of cultural debate in our society at large might be improved. It is a common prediction that our twenty-first-century culture will continue to put a premium on our ability to deal productively with conflict and cultural difference and especially on our ability to listen to those whose views differ greatly from our own. Learning by controversy is sound training for responsible citizenship.

THE CASE OF *HUCKLEBERRY FINN*

Part One of this edition contains the 1885 text of *Adventures of Huckleberry Finn,* the one most commonly read and taught. We do not include the raftsmen's passage, which was not part of the 1885 text and is not directly relevant to any of our three controversies. We do include a portfolio of seventeen of E. W. Kemble's illustrations from the 1885 edition, each of which bears on one or more of the controversies. In Part One, we also include a biographical essay on Samuel Clemens that locates *Huckleberry Finn* in the larger context of his paradoxical life and career, which, as the latter part of that essay indicates, has also been a subject of debate. Preceding Part One, we offer "Why Study Critical Controversies?" an introductory essay addressed directly to students that explains the pedagogical principles underlying this book's design.

Part Two of this case study presents twenty readings on three crucial controversies swirling around *Huckleberry Finn:* on the ending, on Twain's representation of race, and on the novel's treatment of gender and sexuality. In order to orient students to the larger critical and cultural issues at stake in the controversies, we have written introductions to each one. The most widely debated of the three controversies has been whether the book's language and its characterization of Jim are racist and, therefore, so offensive as to merit being banned from school libraries and reading lists. The ensuing debates about the pros and cons of censorship have revived ancient questions about the moral effects of literature and have sparked relatively new ones about the racial subtexts of many literary works. The controversy about the ending is the earliest of the major controversies surrounding the novel, and one that has received considerable new attention within the last several years. The controversy about gender and sexuality is the one that has most recently emerged as being important. Believing that the histories of the controversies are important, we have included both older and more recent contributions to them, thus enabling students to make intelligent choices between traditional literary analysis and more recent approaches such as feminism and gay studies. We think that students will better understand such new approaches to literature if they encounter them in dialogue with the more traditional approaches. The volume concludes with an Appendix containing "Writing about Critical Controversy," which suggests some step-by-step guidelines on how to write essays that contribute to the conversations among the critics in this book. Throughout, the essays have been cross-referenced to each other and to the pagination of the text of *Huckleberry Finn* that appears in this volume.

NEW TO THIS EDITION

Since the publication of the first edition in 1995, *Huckleberry Finn* has continued to be a source of controversy, and this edition includes three new contributions to the debates about the ending (by Toni Morrison, Stacey Margolis, and Sacvan Bercovitch) and three new contributions to the debates about race (by Jonathan Arac, Jane Smiley, and Seymour Chwast). We have also added our own essay on "Writing about Critical Controversy" because we wanted not merely to exhort students to enter the controversies but also to offer them some specific advice for doing so. In addition, we have revised the introductions to the controversies and made other small changes such as expanding the introduction to the portfolio of illustrations. As always, we welcome comments on our work and suggestions for improving a future edition.

ACKNOWLEDGMENTS

The collaboration necessary to bring this book into existence extends beyond that between the editors, and we would like to express our thanks to some of our other collaborators: to David Richter, whose *Falling into Theory* provided a model of how to turn the theory of learning by controversy into an effective textbook. To Martha Banta, Christoph K. Lohmann, Steven Mailloux, Thomas Riggio, and Nancy A. Walker, who wrote helpful reviews of our prospectus and materials for the first edition, and to Jonathan Arac, whose trenchant criticisms of an early draft of "Why Study Critical Controversies?" proved to be invaluable. To Elizabeth Addison, Mark Altschuler, Phillip Barish,

Peter J. Bellis, Brian A. Bremen, David A. Brewer, Deborah K. Chappel, Jeffrey R. DiLeo, Glenn Hendler, Thomas Kaplan-Maxfield, Margaret Karsten, Alan Kaufman, Frank J. McGill, Chris Mott, Caren J. Town, Sarah Wadsworth, Mark Walhout, Annette Wannemaker, and Gary Williams, who provided helpful reviews of the first edition based on their experiences teaching it. To Alfred Bendixen, Nancy Cook, Robert Levine, Bruce Michelson, and Brook Thomas, who provided valuable advice on our proposal for this second edition. To Chuck Christensen and Joan Feinberg of Bedford/St. Martin's, who provided crucial encouragement and support that have made both editions possible. To Lori Chong and Mark Reimold of Bedford/St. Martin's, who did important nitty-gritty work under the pressure of deadlines for the first edition, and to Anne Noyes, who played a similar role for this one. To Jane Greer and Susan Swinford, Jim Phelan's research assistants, who provided abundant and invaluable assistance in the preparation of the first edition, and to James Weaver, who provided similar assistance in the preparation of this one. And above all to Steve Scipione of Bedford/St. Martin's, who guided us through the process of converting our initial idea into the first edition with remarkable diligence, intelligence, and sensitivity, and whose encouragement, energy, and advice were essential to our completion of this edition.

Any remaining stretchers or low-down humbug are the sole responsibility of the editors.

Gerald Graff
University of Chicago

James Phelan
The Ohio State University

Contents

Why Study Critical Controversies?

THE HIDDEN-MEANING PROBLEM; OR, WHY CRITICISM AND THEORY ARE UNAVOIDABLE

If you are a literature major, you may have been asked by friends or relatives, "Why do you people always have to look for hidden meaning in literary works?" Whether you are a literature major or not, you may have wondered why it is always necessary to analyze — and over-analyze — literature. Why not read books just for the fun of it?

The question assumes that the search for meanings supposedly "hidden" under the surface of a text spoils the pleasure of reading literature. If you are like us, your answer will be that the opposition between enjoying and analyzing books is a false one, that the more conscious and reflective our understanding of a text, the deeper our enjoyment of it is likely to be. If you are not used to doing literary analysis, however, you may feel there is a gap between your reading experience and the things literary critics, professors, and some other students do with texts.

If you feel this gap, you may not be comfortable admitting it in class or after, and so your teacher may not realize that you are experiencing it. As literature courses go about their business of analyzing texts, they tacitly assume that everyone knows the justification for the analysis, a situation that can widen the gap between students who eagerly talk

1

the talk of literary analysis and students who remain silent, bored, and alienated.

For teachers these silent students present a great challenge: How can such students be persuaded that enjoyment and analysis do go together, that academic interpretation is worth doing? We think the first step toward an answer is to bring the issue right out into the open and ask: *Why* do criticism anyway? Why not just read the books?

We have two main replies. First, since most literature classes demand that you *write* and *speak* literary criticism and will reward or penalize you according to your fluency, it is only reasonable to ask you to *read* examples of the kind of discourse you will be expected to produce. In fact, *not* to encourage you to read criticism would be to keep you in the dark about the discourse you are expected to write, thereby making criticism all the more mysterious.

A broader reply is that you are always inevitably doing criticism of a kind in your day-to-day activities, and it is better to do it well than poorly. Criticism is not the optional matter that the distinction between enjoyment and analysis seems to suggest. In an important sense, you are *already* doing criticism the moment you begin to talk about a book, film, television show, rock concert, ball game, court case, or political campaign speech — indeed, about any of the various kinds of texts or performances we participate in, experience, or witness in our classes, our jobs, and our relationships with other people. This book focuses on a literary text, but these remarks also apply to any kind of text or performance. Even the most modest assertions about a text carry implicit claims about its meaning, value, or consequences in the world. Merely in saying to a classmate that a book "is a cool read" or that "it's boring," you are performing a rudimentary act of criticism. If you go on and give a *reason* or two for your judgment — "Huck expresses a lot of my dissatisfactions with conventional morality" — you are moving toward a more sophisticated critical act.

Furthermore, in making such critical judgments, you are beginning to do what has come to be called "literary theory." Articulating the underlying reasons for your likes and dislikes adds another layer of abstraction to literary discussion and risks deepening the hidden-meaning problem. Being theoretically explicit, however, better enables you, your classmates, and your teachers to compare and discuss your often very different reasons for liking or disliking books.

Don't be intimidated by the critics and theorists. Remember that even the most sophisticated and complicated critical discourses often have their roots in the kind of responses you yourself have to texts. Academic criticism and theory, in other words, are formalized book-talk, commentary on books elevated to the level of rigorous argumentation.

Students (and some teachers) who resist bringing academic criticism into class discussion may be reacting to earlier encounters with the overly abstruse, arid, or jargon-ridden forms of theory or textual analysis that pervade academic discourse. Or they may be reacting to criticism or theory that is written clearly enough but fails to answer the reader's question, "So what?" — analysis that fails to make clear to the reader why it is informative and worthwhile. As we hope our selections in this volume will show, the most useful critical essays do not hesitate to spell out their main point clearly, even bluntly, though they may go on to complicate that point at some length.

To all the preceding arguments, however, readers who remain skeptical about the benefits of analyzing hidden meanings might reply:

> What you say so far is all well and good, but there still is a problem. Didn't Mark Twain himself warn us against grubbing for hidden meaning in *Adventures of Huckleberry Finn*? After all, in his opening "Notice," Twain wrote: "Persons attempting to find a motive in this narrative will be prosecuted; persons attempting to find a moral in it will be banished; persons attempting to find a plot in it will be shot." Furthermore, by using Huck's voice to narrate the book, by including a range of other colloquial dialects, and by sometimes satirizing the pretensions of genteel speech, Twain sets up an apparent obstacle to the application of ponderous analysis.

This objection is a good one. If you react to the novel as a pleasurable story and resist looking for complicated significance in it, you may be closer than we academic critics and teachers are to the kind of response Twain meant to elicit. If Twain could have foreseen the massive institution of "Twain Studies" that has evolved to pick over every minute aspect of his work, would he have laughed or cried?

In fact, some academic critics themselves chide their colleagues for overdissecting the novel. One such critic, Richard Hill, argues that

> all of us, even the most solemn and ideologically lockstep among us, know in our hearts that Huck's story was written especially for children. . . . Adults who attempt to fit it into sophisticated aesthetic, intellectual, or ideological agendas will never be quite satisfied with the mixed-up and splendid ambuscade that is *Huckleberry Finn*. (509)

Though he stops short of recommending any actual shooting, Hill has certainly caught the spirit of Twain's "Notice" on page 27 — and his words should give pause to those of us who pride ourselves on our sophisticated analyses.

On the other hand, don't we have to ask how seriously readers should take Twain's warning "Notice"? A writer who has his main character wrestle with his conscience at a climactic moment and decide, "All right, then, I'll *go* to hell" is apparently inviting readers to treat his text as something more than a good story, whatever his "Notice" may say. Despite Twain's threat to banish anyone finding a moral in his book, any reader who does *not* detect some engagement with important moral issues in the narrative would seem to be missing the point. It is hard to disagree with Lionel Trilling's view that *Huckleberry Finn* expresses a deep "moral passion; it deals directly with the virtue and depravity of man's heart" (vii). Trilling concludes that though the novel succeeds "as a boys' book" that can be read at age ten, each rereading at a later age will add "a new growthring of meaning" (vii).

Even writers such as Hill, who think critics of *Huckleberry Finn* should lighten up, concedes that the novel "is concerned not only with adventure and hilarity but also with 'respectable' morality and societal hypocrisy" (509). Furthermore, Hill's own essay is just as intellectual and analytical as the essays he objects to. For that matter, even Twain's "Notice," with its implicit argument that the book should be enjoyed rather than analyzed too closely, is a kind of criticism: it makes a claim about how the book should, and should not, be read.

Of course it is one thing to discuss deep meanings that Twain himself seems manifestly to have *intended* — such as the implications of Huck's wrestling with his conscience or Twain's views on the morality of slavery. It seems to be quite another thing, though, for critics and teachers and literature majors to claim that *Huckleberry Finn* "problematizes" traditional gender roles (as Myra Jehlen argues in her essay reprinted in this book) or that Jim and Huck's camaraderie on the raft involves homosexual desire (as Leslie Fiedler and Christopher Looby suggest in their essays). Wouldn't Huck say that these interpretations are "stretchers"? Frederick Crews suggests as much in his critique of Jehlen's essay, as he argues that Jehlen is so interested in advancing her political cause that she imposes a feminist message on the book that Twain does not in fact send.

Such interpretations as Jehlen's, Fiedler's, and Looby's do raise the question of whether what we say ever means things we don't intend or want to acknowledge. Since this issue is fundamental to several of the debates in this book, let's not prejudge it here. It is useful, however, to think about whether a text may convey assumptions or implications about, say, gender or sexual orientation, even though it is not directly addressing these matters and even though its author might not recognize the implications that a subsequent critic finds in the text. Since literary works deal with men and women in interaction, do they not *inevitably* convey assumptions and attitudes about gender and desire (and language and power and culture and many other things that go hand-in-hand with representing human life)?

At some point in our everyday interactions, all of us confront this question of the relation between conscious intentions and hidden meanings. Sometimes when we say X, we are shocked to discover that our listeners hear us meaning Y; at other times, when we hear someone say P, we cannot believe her subsequent claim that she meant Q. Sometimes these misunderstandings can be easily cleared up, but sometimes they become matters of debate. Such debates typically focus not on what was explicitly said but on what was assumed to go without saying and on the attitudes and meanings attached to those assumptions. Most of the psychoanalytic and cultural interpretations that some of you find far-fetched are trying to identify the kind of hidden meaning that is carried in the unspoken assumptions and attitudes of texts. In everyday interactions our decisions, say, about what counts as racist, sexist, or homophobic speech typically turn on how we resolve this question of the relations among assumptions, attitudes, and meanings. Any time we conclude that "he just doesn't get it," we are concluding that the speaker cannot see the hidden meanings in what he has said — does not, that is, recognize his own assumptions and attitudes. Again the larger point is that efforts to clear up misunderstandings or to decide whether given remarks are racist, sexist, or homophobic require all of us to practice a kind of textual criticism whether we give that name to our activity or not.

Another reason there is finally no choice about whether to do criticism is that practical decisions arise about such matters as what to publish, what to teach, what courses to take — and these decisions require us to judge some texts as better or more important than others. Take the question of which texts will be assigned in an American literature survey course. Any text on the syllabus is there only because decisions have been made about the value of that text in comparison with other candidates for inclusion. These value judgments are made not just by the teacher of the course but by the larger community, including scholars studying American literature. However, once a text like *Huckleberry*

Finn becomes part of the canon of American literature — accepted as a standard item in courses that introduce or survey American literature — we tend to regard its presence on the syllabus as natural and beyond question. That is, we forget that the book had to acquire canonical status through a complicated interplay of interpretations, evaluations, and debates.

Typically, we become aware of such critical intervention when somebody comes along and questions a book's generally accepted value and meaning. As you will see in the unit in Part Two devoted to the debate over race in *Huckleberry Finn,* those who would remove the novel from high school curricula on the ground that its representation of African Americans is offensive maintain, in effect, that the novel has a different and more sinister set of meanings than mainstream white readers have been willing to see. Some go even further, arguing that the novel's very celebrity rests on these sinister, but not officially acknowledged, meanings. Faced with such arguments for banning the book, school boards and individual citizens must in turn make their own critical decisions about its meaning and value.

We would not be editing this book if we agreed with those who would ban it. However, we think that the controversy their arguments have provoked is not only immensely fruitful for investigating the novel's treatment of race but can also be an invaluable way to interest all of us in reading and analyzing the book. One of us was told by an African American undergraduate from Mississippi that he was provoked to read *Huckleberry Finn* by the controversy over banning it that erupted in his community. This and other controversies force readers to become more aware of their own critical decisions about the book's meaning and value. This principle — that controversy among critics can be a helpful part of your reading and discussion of literature — is the key premise on which this edition of *Huckleberry Finn* is based.

CRITICISM, CONFLICT, AND LEARNING BY CONTROVERSY; OR, THE ENDLESS-QUARREL PROBLEM

In addition to the hidden-meaning problem, another aspect of literary critical activity often seems strange or off-putting to nonprofessionals. Critics have the notorious habit of engaging in seemingly interminable *quarrels* about the merits of different elaborate analyses of hidden meaning. To illustrate how absurd such quibbling can be when it is applied to such a down-to-earth book as *Huckleberry Finn,* one critic, John Seelye, has published a "rewritten" version of the novel in which Huck actually talks about the disputes of the critics, or "crickits," as Seelye's Huck calls them. Referring to the dispute over the ending of the novel, "Huck" writes:

> Well, there was this crickit named Mr Henry Seidel Canby, and he got hopping mad. He said that there warn't no ending *worse* than [Twain's] ending, and that Mark Twain had ought to be shot for writing it, but he had died anyway so nobody took him up on it. Then along comes Mr Leo Marx, and give both Mr Eliot and Mr Trilling hell. 'Cording to him, that ending warn't moral, and it was because Mark Twain couldn't face up to his own story — by which he meant mine. . . . (vii)

To those outside academia and to some inside, the intricate and often acrimonious squabbles of academic critics sometimes are reminiscent of the legendary disputes among medieval monks about how many angels could dance on the head of a pin.

Even if they never arrive at a clear-cut resolution, however, disagreements among critics can help you understand not only literature but life. The recent, heated debates about multicultural, feminist, postcolonial, and other "ideological" approaches to literature and the humanities often overlap with the battles erupting on many campuses, including perhaps your own, over issues such as affirmative action, hate speech, and sexual harassment. Suddenly the controversies of academic "crickits" are intersecting with those of real life.

Some teachers will prefer to shelter your study of literature from these controversies, saying that you should "just read the books" closely and well and not be distracted by contemporary disputes that, in their view, will soon pass from the scene. These teachers will not let on, in other words, that with respect to any particular controversy, their own argument itself constitutes one of the available positions. Other teachers may try to recruit you to their "side" in a controversy, or they may address you as one who, like any sensible person, is already on this correct side. We would not deny that each of these approaches has led to some good courses. But we also believe that a better approach is to tap the energy and vitality of the controversies themselves by bringing them into the classroom. We call this strategy "teaching by controversy."

Studying critical controversies draws on the productive potential of cultural and academic conflicts to investigate, clarify, and even, perhaps, solve the problem of meaning. Given the increasingly diverse nature of academia and society today, with each topic you study, you are probably confronted by a conflicting array of views, approaches, and interpretations. In today's college or university you can go from one class in which it is taken for granted (and therefore never explicitly stated) that traditional Western culture is a heritage whose value is beyond question to another class the next hour in which it is equally taken for granted (and therefore again left unstated) that Western culture is seriously compromised by sexism, racism, and imperialism. The process of constructing a conversation for yourself out of such different courses can be the most exciting part of your education. If, however, you don't experience any dialogue between their viewpoints, you may need help in making sense of them.

The vocabularies used by different instructors often add to the problem. When Professor Jones refers to "the great tradition" and Professor Smith refers to "hegemonic discursive practices," it may not be immediately obvious that the two are referring to the same body of works. And when Professor Jones speaks of the "self," while Professor Smith speaks of the "subject," you may not immediately recognize that the two are talking in significantly different ways about the same thing — much less be sufficiently prepared to enter the discussion with either of them. Furthermore, what counts as evidence for the greatness of the Western tradition in Dr. Jones's class may not be admissible as evidence in Dr. Smith's — or, indeed, it may be evidence for the bankruptcy of the tradition. Faced with confusingly different views and terminologies, you may, not surprisingly, simply begin to tune out the underlying controversy between professors and give each what he or she seems to want, even if their wants are contradictory.[1]

The mixed messages you are likely to receive from teachers go beyond the subject matter of courses to styles of teaching, learning, and classroom authority. You have probably already discovered that certain codes and buzzwords, such as "empowerment," "excellence," or "dialogue," often betray a given teacher's allegiance to one or another of the diverse theories of pedagogy — and that failing to decode the signals can have unfortunate consequences. For some professors, your role as their student is to master the knowledge they present and to reproduce that knowledge in examinations. For other instructors, who reject this "banking" model of education (as it is often called), with its assumption that knowledge is a substance to be deposited in and then

---

[1]We draw on David Richter's nice discussion of this problem in *Falling into Theory*.

withdrawn from the student's brain, your role is to be an active *constructor* of knowledge. In class, these teachers may try to get out of your way, intervening little in the discussion in order to "empower" you and your classmates to take control over your own learning. Still other professors see the best teacher as a passionate activist who tries to transform your presumably not yet enlightened consciousness, turning you against the patriarchal, racist, or homophobic attitudes that you presumably brought to the classroom, and converting you into an agent of social change. Yet another set of instructors may view this last group as an unprofessional and intolerant cadre of ideologues bent on coercing you into political correctness.

Just as diversity of views is a good thing for education, so too is diversity of teaching theories and styles. There is no magic formula for teaching and learning, no single right way for all teachers and all students to follow. Just as you should be invited to participate in the controversies over subject matters and interpretations, you should also be brought into the controversies about authority and pedagogy.

By now you may be thinking, "Yes, studying controversy may be all well and good, but what about the truth? What about the conclusions and results that controversy is supposed to be the means to? As you two describe it so far, learning by controversy seems to assume that all values, interpretations, and teaching methods are equally valid — is that its guiding assumption?"

By no means. We would not be offering this edition of *Huckleberry Finn* if we thought that the literary value of Twain's text and that of, say, X-Men comics were indistinguishable. And we would have been unable to select from the mass of critical writing on the book if we thought that all interpretations (and debates) were equally productive. Literary value and interpretive truth are not merely arbitrary matters of opinion, and debates should not proliferate without ever reaching resolution. Our premise is that the process of reasoned and passionate debate about questions of value and truth is an essential means to resolving such questions. In other words, controversy is not the opposite of reaching resolution but a precondition of doing so.

Moreover, studying and engaging in debate over significant controversies will help you to gain control over the initially mysterious conventions, formulas, and idioms of critical discourse in various academic disciplines. As in learning a foreign language, you are more likely to achieve fluency by conversing directly with native speakers than by memorizing grammar rules or phrasebook sentences.

We do acknowledge the risk in teaching by controversy that paying so much attention to critical debates will divert your attention from a literary work itself. It is possible to go on for whole class periods arguing about the hidden-meaning issue and never get back to *Huckleberry Finn*. Though this development would not always be disastrous in our view, we think training in critical reading and analysis must involve the application of general arguments and analyses to particular texts. Critical dialogues that are clear, pointed, and well-focused — as we believe the ones chosen for this book are — should lead you *into* the intricacies of literary works rather than away from them.

The view that reading the critical debate about *Huckleberry Finn* necessarily competes with reading the text itself fails to recognize that our responses to texts do not take place in a vacuum but are inevitably formed in relation to the responses of other readers. Critic Robert Scholes has argued that a reader's response to a literary text is always "a statement in dialogue with other interpretations" (30–31). You may find it hard to see this point because you usually read in the privacy of your room, and outside of class you may rarely talk about a book with other people. But isn't your reading influenced by your sense of the book's reputation, comments about a book made by your friends and teachers, even the book's cover and the blurbs printed on the back? We all carry other people's opinions and ideas around in our heads, and our sense of what others think provides a necessary and helpful starting point for the formulation of our own opinions and ideas.

Far from contaminating the purity of your reading experience, then, your knowledge of the reactions of other readers — for example, knowing that some people want to ban *Huckleberry Finn* — provides a conceptual handle on the book. Without some such handle, books may become virtually unreadable masses of detail, since you as reader have no way of knowing where to focus your attention. Although the text itself guides your focus, texts contain so many potential focal points that the choice of any one or two is far from obvious. Beginning students may have no way to predict which details will be emphasized in class. They may not only focus on other details but also may have difficulty clearly remembering the scenes their teachers emphasize.

This book provides three focal points for studying *Huckleberry Finn*: the ending, race, and gender and sexuality. We believe that these topics are central to reading the book in the current literary and cultural climate, but we also acknowledge that it is the nature of controversy itself for some readers to object that certain issues have been excluded or marginalized while others have been unduly privileged. We welcome this kind of criticism and invite suggestions for improving this edition.

We also recognize that conflict and controversy are not themselves neutral terms or activities and may seem to promote a masculinist mode of critical combat. But learning by controversy need not reward critical John Waynes who excel in shoot-outs with rival critics and critical schools. Nor need it bring to literature the aridly legalistic feel of a judicial court's proceedings. The aim of literary education is not to determine who is the best critical prosecuting attorney or fastest critical gunslinger but to help you excel in the kind of analysis and reasoned argument that will make you an effective citizen as well as a good student.

CRITICAL APPROACHES, NEW AND OLD

Teaching by controversy accords in spirit with the revisionist impulses underlying attempts both to create a broader and more inclusive canon and to develop new theoretical approaches to literature. We identify ourselves with those working to revise the canon, and we regard the new approaches to literature — approaches that stress issues of race, gender, class, sexuality, and power — as a very positive force, not least because they have aroused controversy.

The new texts and approaches promise to bring literature closer to people's experiences and to bridge the gulfs between students and teachers and between different groups of students. If you have felt alienated from traditional, impersonal academic criticism, your alienation may be reduced by the recent insistence that we all read from particular "subject positions" and perspectives rather than as objective minds contemplating universal values.

At the same time, introducing new texts or approaches may cure one kind of alienation only to replace it with another — or it may cure yours only to deepen the kind experienced by some of your classmates. In our classes, we have noticed that while some of our students become so energized by these new texts and approaches that they seem to undergo a conversion experience, others regard the new texts and approaches as the imposition of a special-interest agenda on literary study. If you belong to this latter group, you may believe that issues of race, class, gender, sexuality, and power are more properly taken up in the social sciences or in a women's studies or ethnic studies program, and you may want to make some version of the objection one woman voiced to one of us in response to a feminist critique of Ernest Hemingway: "I'm a feminist myself, but I just don't see what this has to do with *literature*."

Then, too, if you are a student unfamiliar with the terms and conventions of literary critical discourse, you may find newly emphasized ideas like "ethnicity," "ideology," and "dominant discourse" to be no less off-putting and mysterious than more old-fashioned terms such as "thematic center" or "transcendent truths." For you it is academic discourse as such that seems estranging, whether this discourse has radical or conservative designs on you, whether it carries the weight of tradition or the sparkle of the contemporary. If you are one of these students, the new approaches may seem like the same old thing in a new guise, ye olde academic jargon decked out in a new wardrobe from Calvin Kleincritic.

Consider the following comment by the feminist critic, Nancy A. Walker, from an essay we have included in Part Two's third unit, on gender and sexuality in *Huckleberry Finn:*

> Twain's use of nineteenth-century stereotypes of women as the basis for his female characters in *Huck Finn* allows the reader to understand some of the ways a male-dominated culture perceived woman's place and function. (p. 495 in this volume)

If you have read *Huckleberry Finn* primarily as a good story, or if you have been taught to read literary narratives as aesthetic objects, Walker's point may seem puzzling or alienating. Why, you may wonder, are questions of gender being "imposed" on literature? Or you may find Walker's gender reading as obscure as any reading identifying universal themes.

If you are unsympathetic to feminist criticism, we think you will benefit from encountering an approach such as Walker's, and if you are sympathetic to feminist criticism, we think you will benefit from encountering reservations about that approach. The same holds true for the adherents and detractors of any new approach. Indeed, the benefits to each group of students increase the more they discuss the powers and limits of the approach. Representing strong feminist work, such as Walker's and Myra Jehlen's in this book, and serious reservations about some of it, such as the selection here from Frederick Crews, should make clearer just what is at stake in adopting a feminist critical approach. Giving voice to the reservations helps the approach clarify itself and make the case for its value.

When approaches such as those of feminism are not openly discussed, the classroom atmosphere may become nervous and uncomfortable. Some students may be reluctant to espouse their views not knowing how they'll be received; others may believe that any discussion of gender or race amounts to forcing an alien agenda on the literature. Addressing the controversy will, by contrast, facilitate debate while also providing models of argumentation on different sides of the question.

In this edition, then, we have presented examples not only of new feminist and racial readings but also of reservations about these readings as well as examples of more traditional approaches. This range and contrast should help you make the fullest sense of all the approaches and help you make informed choices among them.

LEARNING BY CONTROVERSY: ACADEMIC AND NONACADEMIC READERS

Huckleberry Finn is one of the few American literary classics that has consistently appealed to both academic and nonacademic readers. At the same time, critical disagreements about the novel have frequently reflected the split we described earlier between academics and nonacademics. This split is especially apparent in the controversy caused by recent pressures to remove *Huckleberry Finn* from high school and college reading lists on the grounds that its depiction of African Americans in general, and Jim in particular, is offensive and racist. (There is historical irony here: on its first publication in 1885, Twain's novel was removed from the Concord, Massachusetts, public library for its "trashy and vicious" offenses to conventional taste; by contrast, those who would ban it today claim that it reflects an all too conventional racist taste.) As Peaches Henry observes in the unit on race, the citizens' groups that would censor the book "regard academics as inhabitants of ivory towers who pontificate on the virtue of *Huck Finn* without recognizing its potential for harm" (p. 386). The academics and intellectuals, on their side, often dismiss attempts to ban the book as "misguided rantings" by unsophisticated " 'know nothings and noise makers' " (p. 385) or as " 'neurotics' who have fallen prey to personal racial insecurities or have failed to grasp Twain's underlying truth" (p. 386).

Henry cogently argues that such dismissals by academics simply ignore the serious pain that has been inflicted on some students, vividly testified to by a former student, who wrote of the anger he felt

> as my white classmates read aloud the word "nigger." . . . I can recall nothing of the literary merits of this work that [is labeled] "the greatest of all American novels." I only recall the sense of relief I felt when I would flip ahead a few pages and see that the word "nigger" would not be read that hour. (pp. 386–87)

Here the discrepancy between personal experience and academic criticism is extreme. Henry comments that in this "contest between lay readers and so-called scholarly experts," the opponents do not "appear to *hear* each other" (p. 386).

We agree with Henry, and we think the failure of academics and nonacademics (and of whites and nonwhites in both groups) to hear each other is related to the fact that these groups rarely communicate or share the same forums. Certainly the increasing urgency of the issues in our present climate of interracial conflict makes it important to create a dialogue between academics and nonacademics, and in fact, Henry's essay begins to construct that dialogue for teachers and students.

We recognize the pain Twain's book may inflict, but again we believe that the best way to deal with the issue of racism and censorship is to make it part of the reading and discussion. Whereas banning the book keeps the pain felt by some readers from being spoken, teaching the book and debating its representation of race enable those painful experiences to be expressed and compared to other readers' more positive experiences. This juxtaposition of different experiences creates the chance that opposing sides will come more fully to understand one another as well as the complexities of Twain's book.

Like the debates over the ending and over the role of gender and sexuality in the book, the debate over Twain's treatment of race poses once again the question of the relation between literature and the reader's moral and political convictions: Are those who find the novel racially offensive "imposing" an alien moral and political agenda on a work of literature? Or does the work invite and support the objection? Whatever answer you wish to give in this particular case, the general issue of how literature relates to our beliefs and convictions is arguably the central point of contention in the current battles over the canon and over some of the new approaches to interpretation. The question, interestingly, is as old as Plato, who wanted to banish poets from his ideal republic because they violated his standards of truth and morality. As you enter the debates about race, gender, and the ending in *Huckleberry Finn*, you will, in a sense, be contributing your voice to literary criticism's longest ongoing controversy. We believe that informing yourself about the current state of such controversies will best prepare you to make your voice heard.

WORKS CITED

Hill, Richard. "Overreaching: Critical Agenda and the Ending of *Adventures of Huckleberry Finn*." *Texas Studies in Literature and Language* 33 (1991): 492–513.

Richter, David H. "Introduction." *Falling into Theory: Conflicting Views on Reading Literature*. Boston: Bedford, 1995. 1–11.

Scholes, Robert. *Textual Power: Literary Theory and the Teaching of English*. New Haven: Yale UP, 1985.

Seelye, John. *The True Adventures of Huckleberry Finn*. Champaign: U of Illinois P, 1987.

Trilling, Lionel. "Introduction." *Adventures of Huckleberry Finn*. New York: Holt, 1948. v–xviii.

PART ONE

Mark Twain
and
Adventures of Huckleberry Finn

The Life of Samuel Clemens and the Reception of *Huckleberry Finn*

White hair, curling mustache, sharp wit, down-home wisdom: Most Americans associate these benign features with the name "Mark Twain" regardless of whether they have read *Huckleberry Finn* or anything else he wrote. Twain is the American writer with the greatest name recognition (eclipsing even Ernest Hemingway, the twentieth century's contender), the one who has most deeply entered into the American cultural imagination, the one whose image and influence have been most widely disseminated across high and popular culture. (To pick just one of many signs of this phenomenon, Kool-Aid has a flavor called Sharkleberry Fin.) But who was the man himself?

A clear and definitive answer does not easily emerge from the biographical record; indeed, the only clear picture is that Twain was a man of paradoxes, one whose life has been as much a subject of debate as has his most famous novel.

Twain's writing career began in the rough-and-tumble environment of the American West, but he courted and married the genteel daughter of a wealthy eastern family. He often satirized the pretensions and greed of the Gilded Age of the 1870s, a period he and Charles Dudley Warner named in the title of their 1873 novel, but he had a lifelong desire to be rich. His most appealing characters were in close touch with the land, with nature, and with the simple things of life (such as rafting down the Mississippi), but for many years he himself lived in one of the most lavish and ostentatious houses in the state of Connecticut. He had a long nose for hypocrisy, but he successfully created and managed a public persona quite different from his private self. Though he ended his life a misanthrope, he had an increasingly adoring public.

Not surprisingly, some critics have seen the paradoxes of Twain's life reflected in *Huckleberry Finn,* especially the ambivalence about whether he wanted to criticize conventional society or succeed in it. In this view, Twain's desire to be a social critic is evident in his satiric treatment of the society along the Mississippi shore, while his desire for acceptance is revealed in his granting Tom Sawyer considerable influence over Huck; furthermore, pointing to Twain's ambivalence provides an explanation of the problematic ending.

Some, though perhaps not all, of Twain's paradoxes become more understandable in the context of the complex trajectory of his life. Mark Twain was born Samuel Langhorne Clemens on November 30, 1835, in Florida, Missouri, the sixth of seven children born to John Marshall Clemens and Jane Lampton Clemens. Marshall and Jane were both from genteel Virginia families who were proud of their British ancestors: The Clemens clan could find a branch on the family tree identifying one of the judges who sentenced Charles I to death; the Lamptons could trace their connection to the earls of Dunham. Neither family, however, was well-off when Marshall and Jane wed in 1823, and their union did nothing to reverse the downward trend of their families' fortunes. Marshall, a storekeeper, a lawyer, and at the time of his death, a justice of the peace, always hoped to be a prosperous man but never was. His chief hope arose from his investment in Tennessee land that he mistakenly believed to contain coal, copper, and iron ore. Marshall's unfulfilled ambitions made him a gloomy man and a distant father; they also seemed to instill in Samuel a similar desire for riches in his own life. Jane, the model for Aunt Polly in *The Adventures of Tom Sawyer,* was a loving and expressive mother, but she was also a strict disciplinarian who preached Christian morality — including the tenets on sin, hell, and damnation — to her children. Three of the seven Clemens children died before the age of ten; Samuel's older brother Orion is the only sibling who seems to have played an important role in his life. With Marshall and Jane as his parents, it is not surprising that Clemens later sought the love and approval of a woman from an established and correct family.

In 1839, Marshall and Jane moved the family to Hannibal, Missouri, a town on the banks of the Mississippi River where Samuel spent the next thirteen and a half years of his life. Although Clemens rarely visited Hannibal after he left in 1853, his experiences there played a large role in his writing and, indeed, strongly shaped his best-known works, *Huckleberry Finn* and *The Adventures of Tom Sawyer.* The St. Petersburg of these novels is a largely faithful rendition of Hannibal in the 1840s.

In the spring of 1847, Marshall Clemens died of pneumonia, an event that effectively meant the end of Samuel's boyhood. His father's death also marked the beginning of Samuel's circuitous route toward his eventual career. To help support his family, he began to work for a printer: first, after school; next, as a full-time apprentice; and then, for several years, as an assistant to Orion, who was trying to establish him- self as a printer and a newspaper man. In 1853, at the age of seventeen, Samuel set out on his own and, over the next four years, crisscrossed the East and Midwest, working, among other places, in St. Louis, Phila- delphia, and Cincinnati. Though Clemens's formal schooling ended when he was only thirteen, his work honed his skills as a reader and a writer. As he said in 1909, "One isn't a printer ten years without setting up acres of good and bad literature, and learning — unconsciously at first, consciously later — to discriminate between the two, within his mental limitations; and meanwhile, he is consciously acquiring what is called a 'style.'"

Dissatisfied with his abilities and his prospects in the printing trade, Clemens decided at age twenty-one in 1857 to head to South America, where he hoped to become rich selling cocaine (the drug was not well- known in America — or illegal — at the time). He never made it. On the steamboat ride down the Mississippi to New Orleans, he got to talking with the pilot, Horace Bixby, and ended up persuading Bixby to let him become an apprentice. The next four years may well have been the happiest of Clemens's life. He learned the river, got his own license in 1859, and immersed himself in the challenges and the variety of the pilot's life, which was in many ways preparation for his later career. The challenges of reading the Mississippi with sufficient skill to guide a steamboat safely through it provided Clemens with a model for the dif- ficulties and satisfactions of writing, and the variety of life along the river gave him a rich diversity of experience. "When I find a well-drawn character in fiction or biography," he later said, "I generally take a warm, personal interest in him, for the reason that I have known him before — met him on the river." In the 1870s, Clemens imaginatively relived the experiences of these years as he wrote the first half of *Life on the Mississippi.*

The outbreak of the Civil War in 1861 put an end to commerce along the Mississippi and, thus, to Clemens's career as a steamboat pilot. After an uneasy two-week stint as a volunteer in the Marion Rangers of the Confederate Army, Clemens accompanied Orion to Nevada, where his brother assumed his new duties as Secretary of the Nevada Territory. Samuel's mind, characteristically, was set on striking it rich, but in July 1862, after failing to find gold or silver in the Nevada mines, he took a job as a reporter for the Virginia City *Territorial Enterprise*. Clemens was to be a writer for the rest of his life, though he did not know this at the time — he was not fulfilling a lifelong ambition or a natural inclination but simply finding a way to support himself. As his skills and his success grew, he developed other more artistic ambitions, but he never stopped thinking of the relationships among his writing, his income, and his reputation. This habit of mind helps explain the occasional conflicts in Clemens's life and work between artistic conscience and commercial success.

In writing for the *Enterprise,* he had an opportunity to try a range of modes and styles — everything from straight news to comic satire, editorials to travel correspondence. In a comic travel piece he filed from Carson City in February 1863, Clemens first signed his name as "Mark Twain." Clemens later said that he took the name, which on the Mississippi meant "two fathoms," from an old writer-pilot named Isaiah Sellers; in Nevada, however, the term meant two drinks bought on credit, so Clemens may have wanted his readers to think of this meaning as well. In any case, at the age of twenty-seven, Samuel Clemens had found the persona he would use and develop for the rest of his career.

Clemens stayed out west till December 1866, becoming part of a group of writers and humorists that included Bret Harte and earning a reputation as a humorist. By the time he came east, he had published his first mature story, "The Celebrated Jumping Frog of Calaveras County," and he had tested his skills at public speaking. More generally, he had transferred his initial desire to find wealth in the mines to an ambition to become a nationally recognized writer. Taking a job as the traveling correspondent for the San Francisco *Alta California,* Clemens arrived in New York in January 1867 and soon set out to fulfill his ambitions. He published his first book, *The Celebrated Jumping Frog of Calaveras County and Other Sketches,* and he gave his first public lecture in New York. More important, after his five-month trip to Europe and the Middle East on the steamship *Quaker City,* duly reported for the *Alta California,* Clemens began to write *The Innocents Abroad.* The book, in which the character-narrator Mark Twain is the guiding presence, was his first major success, selling one hundred thousand copies within the first two years of its publication in 1869.

The trip aboard the *Quaker City* was also eventful in another way. As Twain later wrote about Olivia Langdon, the woman who was to become his wife, "I saw her first in the form of an ivory miniature in her brother Charley's stateroom in the steamer *Quaker City*, in the Bay of Smyrna, in the summer of 1867, when she was in her twenty-second year." He met her in New York in December 1867, and they spent their first evening together listening to Charles Dickens read from *David Copperfield* (Clemens was unimpressed). The following summer, he visited "Livy" at her home in Elmira, New York, and during this period fell in love. Clemens had, however, to court both Livy and her parents, who initially judged Clemens and his roughneck Western ways as beneath their daughter. He had immediate success with neither party, though Livy came round a lot more easily than her parents. They did eventually accept him completely, and, indeed, when Samuel and Olivia were married on February 2, 1870, the Langdons gave the newlyweds a substantial present: a mansion in Buffalo, New York. Soon, however, the crest of happiness and success Clemens was riding broke: In October, Livy had a near miscarriage and had to be confined to the downstairs library; in November, she gave birth to a premature, sickly boy, Langdon, who lived only nineteen months; in the spring of 1871, she came down with typhoid fever. Although Clemens was able to work on *Roughing It* during some of this time, he became anxious to leave Buffalo.

In October of 1871, Clemens moved with his family to Hartford, Connecticut; from then until 1885, he entered the most productive period of his life, publishing *Roughing It* (1872), *The Gilded Age* (1873, cowritten with Charles Dudley Warner), *Sketches, New and Old* (1875), *The Adventures of Tom Sawyer* (1876), *A Tramp Abroad* (1880), *The Prince and the Pauper* (1882), and *Life on the Mississippi* (1883). In 1876, he began work on *Huckleberry Finn* but did not complete the book until 1884. During this major phase of his career, Clemens sharpened his skills as humorist and social critic, a thinker whose wit was rooted in his understanding of a considerable range of American characters and his mastery of numerous narrative and stylistic techniques. Clemens's steady productivity during these years was matched by a steady growth in the celebrity of Mark Twain both at home and abroad.

At the same time, the lavishly respectable life Clemens was living was in marked contrast to the lives he was writing about and the artistic values his work was expressing. This discrepancy has led some critics to see a radical split in Twain's life and work between the iconoclastic artist who refuses to compromise with genteel morality and the respectable popular entertainer who pulls his most satiric punches.

Within a few years after moving to Hartford, Clemens purchased a mansion greater than the one his father-in-law had given him in Buffalo — a purchase that, however much it symbolized his success, was also a constant drain on his income. In 1872, shortly after the death of their son Langdon, the Clemenses' daughter, Susy, was born; in 1874, Livy gave birth to Clara, the only child who would outlive both of them; and in 1880, Jean, the last child, arrived. Though Clemens's marriage was generally happy, Livy, whose role as his "censor" he probably overstated, was frequently ill. Though Clemens loved his daughters, he was a difficult father, one who did not find it easy to grant them anything like the independence he valued in Huck.

Even while Clemens was writing regularly and successfully, he continued to hope he would find the investment that would make him rich. In 1880, he thought he had found it and made an initial investment in James Paige's automatic typesetting machine. Throughout the next decade, Clemens continued to pour money into Paige's unwieldy machine until, by 1891, he was deeply in debt. Meanwhile, after *Huckleberry Finn,* the quality of his work slowly declined. He published the worthy *Connecticut Yankee in King Arthur's Court* in 1889 and the intriguing *Tragedy of Pudd'nhead Wilson* in 1894, but his efforts to do more with Tom and Huck in such books as *Tom Sawyer Abroad* (1894) and *Tom Sawyer, Detective* (1896) were dismal failures. His second foray into the medieval world, *The Personal Recollections of Joan of Arc* (1896), which he curiously identified as his favorite book, is largely neglected today. In 1895, Clemens began a grueling but ultimately successful, yearlong, round-the-world lecture tour to raise money to pay off his debts. Shortly after the tour, when he had settled in England to write what was to become his book about the experience, *Following the Equator,* he received the news that Susy, then twenty-four, had died of meningitis in Hartford.

This news, coupled with his financial losses, deepened the pessimism that had been growing in him since the latter half of the 1880s. At this point, we see perhaps the most poignant paradox of Clemens's life. He was held in increasingly high esteem by critical and popular audiences: William Dean Howells, one of the most influential literary figures of the period, consistently praised his work (after Clemens's death, Howells called him "the Lincoln of our literature"), and his return from financial ruin was hailed by the public as a magnificent achievement. Yet Clemens could not really savor this acclaim, as he became increasingly bitter and misanthropic. His attitude is clearly evident in such writings as *The Man Who Corrupted Hadleyburg* (1900), *What Is Man?* (1905), and *The Mysterious Stranger* (1916). In 1902, Livy began a long, slow decline toward death; despite leaving America for the milder climate of Italy in 1903, she did not substantially improve, and during this time, Clemens was frequently unable to visit her. In June 1909, Livy passed away; in December, Jean, an epileptic, died during a seizure. On April 21, 1910, at the age of seventy-four, Clemens followed them to the grave.

During Clemens's lifetime, *Huckleberry Finn* had an initially controversial but eventually enthusiastic reception. Interestingly, it was most unequivocally praised in England, where one reviewer, Andrew Lang, called it "*the* great American novel" (emphasis added). In the United States, the first major debate was sparked when the Concord, Massachusetts, public library banned the book on the grounds that prolonged exposure to the lower-class Huck, his vernacular dialect, and his doubts about "sivilization" would have an unhealthy effect on young readers. Many people, both in New England and beyond, rushed to the book's defense, but many others supported the library. The controversy helped fuel sales of the book, and by 1900 it had established itself as a popular success, if not an unqualified critical triumph.

From 1900 to 1925, *Huckleberry Finn* slowly grew out of the shadow of *Tom Sawyer* and came to be regarded as Twain's best book. *Huck* was championed not only by Howells but also by the influential H. L. Mencken, who described the book as "one of the great masterpieces of the world" (1913) and as a "truly stupendous piece of work — perhaps the greatest novel ever written in English" (1919). Mencken's voice was echoed by such academic critics as Stuart Sherman, who called *Huck* "imperishably substantial" and William Lyon Phelps, who declared that "*Huckleberry Finn* is not only the great American novel. It is America."

Yet even as *Huckleberry Finn* was being canonized, Clemens's career came in for its first, sharp, academic critique in Van Wyck Brooks's *The Ordeal of Mark Twain* (1920). Brooks's thesis is that Clemens, for all his talent, is finally a failure, a case of "arrested development" whose ties to the genteel tradition — represented by his mother, his wife, and his lifestyle in Hartford — prevented him from realizing his potential. Though Brooks himself exempted *Huckleberry Finn* from his general indictment, many others who found his thesis persuasive did not. Brooks's book and its influence provoked Bernard De Voto to come to Clemens's defense in *Mark Twain's America* (1932). De Voto gave greater emphasis to Clemens's experience in the West than to his genteel family life, and he turned to *Huckleberry Finn* as the best example of Clemens's greatness. The book, argued De Voto, captures something quintessential about America.

By the 1940s the debate over Clemens's claim to greatness had become a debate over *Huckleberry Finn*'s claim to that status. With the rise of formal criticism during this decade, the key issue became the book's ending. More recently, the chief topic of debate has been Twain's representation of race, and it now seems likely that the debate about race will become intertwined with newly emerging debates about gender and sexuality (though it should be pointed out that Leslie Fiedler first pointed to a homoerotic element in the book in 1949). In any case, like any good book, *Huckleberry Finn* has been the occasion of disagreement and debate since its publication, yet these controversies have increased rather than decreased its value over time. We are confident that, though the topics of the debates may change, *Huckleberry Finn* will remain a worthy object of controversy for a long time to come.

WORKS CONSULTED

Budd, Louis J. "Introduction." *New Essays on "Adventures of Huckleberry Finn,"* 1–33. Ed. Louis J. Budd. New York: Cambridge UP, 1985.

———. *Our Mark Twain.* Philadelphia: U of Pennsylvania P, 1983.

Hill, Hamlin. *Mark Twain, God's Fool.* New York: Harper, 1973.

Kaplan, Justin. *Mark Twain and His World.* New York: Simon, 1974.

Adventures of Huckleberry Finn

(TOM SAWYER'S COMRADE)

THE 1885 TEXT

SCENE: THE MISSISSIPPI VALLEY
TIME: FORTY TO FIFTY YEARS AGO

NOTICE

PERSONS attempting to find a motive in this narrative will be prosecuted; persons attempting to find a moral in it will be banished; persons attempting to find a plot in it will be shot.

BY ORDER OF THE AUTHOR
PER G. G., CHIEF OF ORDNANCE.

EXPLANATORY

IN this book a number of dialects are used, to wit: the Missouri negro dialect; the extremest form of the backwoods South-Western dialect; the ordinary "Pike-County" dialect; and four modified varieties of this last. The shadings have not been done in a hap-hazard fashion, or by guess-work; but pains-takingly, and with the trustworthy guidance and support of personal familiarity with these several forms of speech.

I make this explanation for the reason that without it many readers would suppose that all these characters were trying to talk alike and not succeeding.

THE AUTHOR.

CONTENTS

Adventures of Huckleberry Finn

Chapter I

You don't know about me, without you have read a book by the name of "The Adventures of Tom Sawyer," but that ain't no matter. That book was made by Mr. Mark Twain, and he told the truth, mainly. There was things which he stretched, but mainly he told the truth. That is nothing. I never seen anybody but lied, one time or another, without it was Aunt Polly, or the widow, or maybe Mary. Aunt Polly — Tom's Aunt Polly, she is — and Mary, and the Widow Douglas, is all told about in that book — which is mostly a true book; with some stretchers, as I said before.

Now the way that the book winds up, is this: Tom and me found the money that the robbers hid in the cave, and it made us rich. We got six thousand dollars apiece — all gold. It was an awful sight of money when it was piled up. Well, Judge Thatcher, he took it and put it out at interest, and it fetched us a dollar a day apiece, all the year round — more than a body could tell what to do with. The Widow Douglas, she took me for her son, and allowed she would sivilize me; but it was rough living in the house all the time, considering how dismal regular and decent the widow was in all her ways; and so when I couldn't stand it no longer, I lit out. I got into my old rags, and my sugar-hogshead° again, and was free and satisfied. But Tom Sawyer, he hunted me up and said he was going to start a band of robbers, and I might join if I would go back to the widow and be respectable. So I went back.

The widow she cried over me, and called me a poor lost lamb, and she called me a lot of other names, too, but she never meant no harm by it. She put me in them new clothes again, and I couldn't do nothing but sweat and sweat, and feel all cramped up. Well, then, the old thing commenced again. The widow rung a bell for supper, and you had to

---

sugar-hogshead: A large cask in which sugar had been stored.

come to time. When you got to the table you couldn't go right to eating, but you had to wait for the widow to tuck down her head and grumble a little over the victuals, though there warn't really anything the matter with them. That is, nothing only everything was cooked by itself. In a barrel of odds and ends it is different; things get mixed up, and the juice kind of swaps around, and the things go better.

After supper she got out her book and learned me about Moses and the Bulrushers; and I was in a sweat to find out all about him; but by-and-by she let it out that Moses had been dead a considerable long time; so then I didn't care no more about him; because I don't take no stock in dead people.

Pretty soon I wanted to smoke, and asked the widow to let me. But she wouldn't. She said it was a mean practice and wasn't clean, and I must try to not do it any more. That is just the way with some people. They get down on a thing when they don't know nothing about it. Here she was a bothering about Moses, which was no kin to her, and no use to anybody, being gone, you see, yet finding a power of fault with me for doing a thing that had some good in it. And she took snuff too; of course that was all right, because she done it herself.

Her sister, Miss Watson, a tolerable slim old maid, with goggles on, had just come to live with her, and took a set at me now, with a spelling-book. She worked me middling hard for about an hour, and then the widow made her ease up. I couldn't stood it much longer. Then for an hour it was deadly dull, and I was fidgety. Miss Watson would say, "Dont put your feet up there, Huckleberry;" and "dont scrunch up like that, Huckleberry — set up straight;" and pretty soon she would say, "Don't gap and stretch like that, Huckleberry — why don't you try to behave?" Then she told me all about the bad place, and I said I wished I was there. She got mad, then, but I didn't mean no harm. All I wanted was to go somewheres; all I wanted was a change, I warn't particular. She said it was wicked to say what I said; said she wouldn't say it for the whole world; *she* was going to live so as to go to the good place. Well, I couldn't see no advantage in going where she was going, so I made up my mind I wouldn't try for it. But I never said so, because it would only make trouble, and wouldn't do no good.

Now she had got a start, and she went on and told me all about the good place. She said all a body would have to do there was to go around all day long with a harp and sing, forever and ever. So I didn't think much of it. But I never said so. I asked her if she reckoned Tom Sawyer would go there, and, she said, not by a considerable sight. I was glad about that, because I wanted him and me to be together.

Miss Watson she kept pecking at me, and it got tiresome and lonesome. By-and-by they fetched the niggers in and had prayers, and then everybody was off to bed. I went up to my room with a piece of candle and put it on the table. Then I set down in a chair by the window and tried to think of something cheerful, but it warn't no use. I felt so lonesome I most wished I was dead. The stars was shining, and the leaves rustled in the woods ever so mournful; and I heard an owl, away off, who-whooing about somebody that was dead, and a whippowill and a dog crying about somebody that was going to die; and the wind was trying to whisper something to me and I couldn't make out what it was, and so it made the cold shivers run over me. Then away out in the woods I heard that kind of a sound that a ghost makes when it wants to tell about something that's on its mind and can't make itself understood, and so can't rest easy in its grave and has to go about that way every night grieving. I got so down-hearted and scared, I did wish I had some company. Pretty soon a spider went crawling up my shoulder, and I flipped it off and it lit in the candle; and before I could budge it was all shriveled up. I didn't need anybody to tell me that that was an awful bad sign and would fetch me some bad luck, so I was scared and most shook the clothes off of me. I got up and turned around in my tracks three times and crossed my breast every time; and then I tied up a little lock of my hair with a thread to keep witches away. But I hadn't no confidence. You do that when you've lost a horse-shoe that you've found, instead of nailing it up over the door, but I hadn't ever heard anybody say it was any way to keep off bad luck when you'd killed a spider.

I set down again, a shaking all over, and got out my pipe for a smoke; for the house was all as still as death, now, and so the widow wouldn't know. Well, after a long time I heard the clock away off in the town go boom — boom — boom — twelve licks — and all still again — stiller than ever. Pretty soon I heard a twig snap, down in the dark amongst the trees — something was a stirring. I set still and listened. Directly I could just barely hear a *"me-yow! me-yow!"* down there. That was good! Says I, *"me-yow! me-yow!"* as soft as I could, and then I put out the light and scrambled out of the window onto the shed. Then I slipped down to the ground and crawled in amongst the trees, and sure enough there was Tom Sawyer waiting for me.

Chapter II

We went tip-toeing along a path amongst the trees back towards the end of the widow's garden, stooping down so as the branches wouldn't scrape our heads. When we was passing by the kitchen I fell over a root and made a noise. We scrouched down and laid still. Miss Watson's big nigger, named Jim, was setting in the kitchen door; we could see him pretty clear, because there was a light behind him. He got up and stretched his neck out about a minute, listening. Then he says,

"Who dah?"

He listened some more; then he come tip-toeing down and stood right between us; we could a touched him, nearly. Well, likely it was minutes and minutes that there warn't a sound, and we all there so close together. There was a place on my ankle that got to itching; but I dasn't scratch it; and then my ear begun to itch; and next my back, right between my shoulders. Seemed like I'd die if I couldn't scratch. Well, I've noticed that thing plenty of times since. If you are with the quality, or at a funeral, or trying to go to sleep when you ain't sleepy — if you are anywheres where it won't do for you to scratch, why you will itch all over in upwards of a thousand places. Pretty soon Jim says:

"Say — who is you? Whar is you? Dog my cats ef I didn' hear sumf'n. Well, I knows what I's gwyne to do. I's gwyne to set down here and listen tell I hears it agin."

So he set down on the ground betwixt me and Tom. He leaned his back up against a tree, and stretched his legs out till one of them most touched one of mine. My nose begun to itch. It itched till the tears come into my eyes. But I dasn't scratch. Then it begun to itch on the inside. Next I got to itching underneath. I didn't know how I was going to set still. This miserableness went on as much as six or seven minutes; but it seemed a sight longer than that. I was itching in eleven different places now. I reckoned I couldn't stand it more'n a minute longer, but I set my teeth hard and got ready to try. Just then Jim begun to breathe heavy; next he begun to snore — and then I was pretty soon comfortable again.

Tom he made a sign to me — kind of a little noise with his mouth — and we went creeping away on our hands and knees. When we was ten foot off, Tom whispered to me and wanted to tie Jim to the tree for fun; but I said no; he might wake and make a disturbance, and then they'd find out I warn't in. Then Tom said he hadn't got candles enough, and he would slip in the kitchen and get some more. I didn't want him to try. I said Jim might wake up and come. But Tom wanted to resk it; so we slid in there and got three candles, and Tom laid five cents on the table for pay. Then we got out, and I was in a sweat to get away; but nothing would do Tom but he must crawl to where Jim was, on his hands and knees, and play something on him. I waited, and it seemed a good while, everything was so still and lonesome.

As soon as Tom was back, we cut along the path, around the garden fence, and by-and-by fetched up on the steep top of the hill at the other side of the house. Tom said he slipped Jim's hat off of his head and hung it on a limb right over him, and Jim stirred a little, but he didn't wake. Afterwards Jim said the witches bewitched him and put him in a trance, and rode him all over the State, and then set him under the trees again and hung his hat on a limb to show who done it. And next time Jim told it he said they rode him down to New Orleans: and after that, every time he told it he spread it more and more, till by-and-by he said they rode him all over the world, and tired him most to death, and his back was all over saddle-boils. Jim was monstrous proud about it, and he got so he wouldn't hardly notice the other niggers. Niggers would come miles to hear Jim tell about it, and he was more looked up to than any nigger in that country. Strange niggers would stand with their mouths open and look him all over, same as if he was a wonder. Niggers is always talking about witches in the dark by the kitchen fire; but whenever one was talking and letting on to know all about such things, Jim would happen in and say, "Hm! What you know 'bout witches?" and that nigger was corked up and had to take a back seat. Jim always kept that five-center piece around his neck with a string and said it was a charm the devil give to him with his own hands and told him he could cure anybody with it and fetch witches whenever he wanted to, just by saying something to it; but he never told what it was he said to it. Niggers would come from all around there and give Jim anything they had, just for a sight of that five-center piece; but they wouldn't touch it, because the devil had had his hands on it. Jim was most ruined, for a servant, because he got so stuck up on account of having seen the devil and been rode by witches.

Well, when Tom and me got to the edge of the hill-top, we looked away down into the village and could see three or four lights twinkling, where there was sick folks, may be; and the stars over us was sparkling ever so fine; and down by the village was the river, a whole mile broad, and awful still and grand. We went down the hill and found Jo Harper, and Ben Rogers, and two or three more of the boys, hid in the old tan-yard. So we unhitched a skiff and pulled down the river two mile and a half, to the big scar on the hillside, and went ashore.

We went to a clump of bushes, and Tom made everybody swear to keep the secret, and then showed them a hole in the hill, right in the thickest part of the bushes. Then we lit the candles and crawled in on our hands and knees. We went about two hundred yards, and then the cave opened up. Tom poked about amongst the passages and pretty soon ducked under a wall where you wouldn't a noticed that there was a hole. We went along a narrow place and got into a kind of room, all damp and sweaty and cold, and there we stopped. Tom says:

"Now we'll start this band of robbers and call it Tom Sawyer's Gang. Everybody that wants to join has got to take an oath, and write his name in blood."

Everybody was willing. So Tom got out a sheet of paper that he had wrote the oath on, and read it. It swore every boy to stick to the band, and never tell any of the secrets; and if anybody done anything to any boy in the band, whichever boy was ordered to kill that person and his family must do it, and he mustn't eat and he mustn't sleep till he had killed them and hacked a cross in their breasts, which was the sign of the band. And nobody that didn't belong to the band could use that mark, and if he did he must be sued; and if he done it again he must be killed. And if anybody that belonged to the band told the secrets, he must have his throat cut, and then have his carcass burnt up and the ashes scattered all around, and his name blotted off of the list with blood and never mentioned again by the gang, but have a curse put on it and be forgot, forever.

Everybody said it was a real beautiful oath, and asked Tom if he got it out of his own head. He said, some of it, but the rest was out of pirate books, and robber books, and every gang that was high-toned had it.

Some thought it would be good to kill the *families* of boys that told the secrets. Tom said it was a good idea, so he took a pencil and wrote it in. Then Ben Rogers says:

"Here's Huck Finn, he hain't got no family — what you going to do 'bout him?"

"Well, hain't he got a father?" says Tom Sawyer.

"Yes, he's got a father, but you can't never find him, these days. He used to lay drunk with the hogs in the tanyard, but he hain't been seen in these parts for a year or more."

They talked it over, and they was going to rule me out, because they said every boy must have a family or somebody to kill, or else it wouldn't be fair and square for the others. Well, nobody could think of anything to do — everybody was stumped, and set still. I was most ready to cry; but all at once I thought of a way, and so I offered them Miss Watson — they could kill her. Everybody said:

"Oh, she'll do, she'll do. That's all right. Huck can come in."

Then they all stuck a pin in their fingers to get blood to sign with, and I made my mark on the paper.

"Now," says Ben Rogers, "what's the line of business of this Gang?"

"Nothing only robbery and murder," Tom said.

"But who are we going to rob? houses — or cattle — or —"

"Stuff! stealing cattle and such things ain't robbery, it's burglary," says Tom Sawyer. "We ain't burglars. That ain't no sort of style. We are highwaymen. We stop stages and carriages on the road, with masks on, and kill the people and take their watches and money."

"Must we always kill the people?"

"Oh, certainly. It's best. Some authorities think different, but mostly it's considered best to kill them. Except some that you bring to the cave here and keep till they're ransomed."

"Ransomed? What's that?"

"I don't know. But that's what they do. I've seen it in books; and so of course that's what we've got to do."

"But how can we do it if we don't know what it is?"

"Why blame it all, we've *got* to do it. Don't I tell you it's in the books? Do you want to go to doing different from what's in the books, and get things all muddled up?"

"Oh, that's all very fine to *say*, Tom Sawyer, but how in the nation are these fellows going to be ransomed if we don't know how to do it to them? that's the thing *I* want to get at. Now what do you *reckon* it is?"

"Well I don't know. But per'aps if we keep them till they're ransomed, it means that we keep them till they're dead."

"Now, that's something *like*. That'll answer. Why couldn't you said that before? We'll keep them till they're ransomed to death — and a bothersome lot they'll be, too, eating up everything and always trying to get loose."

"How you talk, Ben Rogers. How can they get loose when there's a guard over them, ready to shoot them down if they move a peg?"

"A guard. Well, that *is* good. So somebody's got to set up all night and never get any sleep, just so as to watch them. I think that's foolishness. Why can't a body take a club and ransom them as soon as they get here?"

"Because it ain't in the books so — that's why. Now Ben Rogers, do you want to do things regular, or don't you? — that's the idea. Don't you reckon that the people that made the books knows what's the correct thing to do? Do you reckon *you* can learn 'em anything?

Not by a good deal. No, sir, we'll just go on and ransom them in the regular way."

"All right. I don't mind; but I say it's a fool way, anyhow. Say — do we kill the women, too?"

"Well, Ben Rogers, if I was as ignorant as you I wouldn't let on. Kill the women? No — nobody ever saw anything in the books like that. You fetch them to the cave, and you're always as polite as pie to them; and by-and-by they fall in love with you and never want to go home any more."

"Well, if that's the way, I'm agreed, but I don't take no stock in it. Mighty soon we'll have the cave so cluttered up with women, and fellows waiting to be ransomed, that there won't be no place for the robbers. But go ahead, I ain't got nothing to say."

Little Tommy Barnes was asleep, now, and when they waked him up he was scared, and cried, and said he wanted to go home to his ma, and didn't want to be a robber any more.

So they all made fun of him, and called him cry-baby, and that made him mad, and he said he would go straight and tell all the secrets. But Tom give him five cents to keep quiet, and said we would all go home and meet next week and rob somebody and kill some people.

Ben Rogers said he couldn't get out much, only Sundays, and so he wanted to begin next Sunday; but all the boys said it would be wicked to do it on Sunday, and that settled the thing. They agreed to get together and fix a day as soon as they could, and then we elected Tom Sawyer first captain and Jo Harper second captain of the Gang, and so started home.

I clumb up the shed and crept into my window just before day was breaking. My new clothes was all greased up and clayey, and I was dog-tired.

Chapter III

Well, I got a good going-over in the morning, from old Miss Watson, on account of my clothes; but the widow she didn't scold, but only cleaned off the grease and clay and looked so sorry that I thought I would behave a while if I could. Then Miss Watson she took me in the closet and prayed, but nothing come of it. She told me to pray every day, and whatever I asked for I would get it. But it warn't so. I tried it. Once I got a fish-line, but no hooks. It warn't any good to me without hooks. I tried for the hooks three or four times, but somehow I couldn't make it work. By-and-by, one day, I asked Miss Watson to try for me, but she said I was a fool. She never told me why, and I couldn't make it out no way.

I set down, one time, back in the woods, and had a long think about it. I says to myself, if a body can get anything they pray for, why don't Deacon Winn get back the money he lost on pork? Why can't the widow get back her silver snuff-box that was stole? Why can't Miss Watson fat up? No, says I to myself, there ain't nothing in it. I went and told the widow about it, and she said the thing a body could get by praying for it was "spiritual gifts." This was too many for me, but she told me what she meant — I must help other people, and do everything I could for other people, and look out for them all the time, and never think about myself. This was including Miss Watson, as I took it. I went out in the woods and turned it over in my mind a long time, but I couldn't see no advantage about it — except for the other people — so at last I reckoned I wouldn't worry about it any more, but just let it go. Sometimes the widow would take me one side and talk about Providence in a way to make a body's mouth water; but maybe next day Miss Watson would take hold and knock it all down again. I judged I could see that there was two Providences, and a poor chap would stand considerable show with the widow's Providence, but if Miss Watson's got him there warn't no help for him any more. I thought it all out, and reckoned I would belong to the widow's, if he wanted me, though I couldn't make out how he was agoing to be any better off then than what he was before, seeing I was so ignorant and so kind of low-down and ornery.

Pap he hadn't been seen for more than a year, and that was comfortable for me; I didn't want to see him no more. He used to always whale me when he was sober and could get his hands on me; though I used to take to the woods most of the time when he was around. Well, about this time he was found in the river drowned, about twelve mile above town, so people said. They judged it was him, anyway; said this drowned man was just his size, and was ragged, and had uncommon long hair — which was all like pap — but they couldn't make nothing out of the face, because it had been in the water so long it warn't much like a face at all. They said he was floating on his back in the water. They took him and buried him on the bank. But I warn't comfortable long, because I happened to think of something. I knowed mighty well that a drownded man don't float on his back, but on his face. So I knowed, then, that this warn't pap, but a woman dressed up in a man's clothes. So I was uncomfortable again. I judged the old man would turn up again by-and-by, though I wished he wouldn't.

We played robber now and then about a month, and then I resigned. All the boys did. We hadn't robbed nobody, we hadn't killed any people, but only just pretended. We used to hop out of the woods and go charging down on hog-drovers and women in carts taking garden stuff to market, but we never hived any of them. Tom Sawyer called the hogs "ingots," and he called the turnips and stuff "julery" and we would go to the cave and pow-wow over what we had done and how many people we had killed and marked. But I couldn't see no profit in it. One time Tom sent a boy to run about town with a blazing stick, which he called a slogan (which was the sign for the Gang to get together), and then he said he had got secret news by his spies that next day a whole parcel of Spanish merchants and rich A-rabs was going to camp in Cave Hollow with two hundred elephants, and six hundred camels, and over a thousand "sumter" mules, all loaded down with di'monds, and they didn't have only a guard of four hundred soldiers, and so we would lay in ambuscade, as he called it, and kill the lot and scoop the things. He said we must slick up our swords and guns, and get ready. He never could go after even a turnip-cart but he must have the swords and guns all scoured up for it; though they was only lath and broom-sticks, and you might scour at them till you rotted and then they warn't worth a mouthful of ashes more than what they was before. I didn't believe we could lick such a crowd of Spaniards and A-rabs, but I wanted to see the camels and elephants, so I was on hand next day, Saturday, in the ambuscade; and when we got the word, we rushed out of the woods and down the hill. But there warn't no Spaniards and A-rabs, and there warn't no camels nor no elephants. It warn't anything but a Sunday-school picnic, and only a primer-class at that. We busted it up, and chased the children up the hollow; but we never got anything but some doughnuts and jam, though Ben Rogers got a rag doll, and Jo Harper got a hymn-book and a tract; and then the teacher charged in and made us drop everything and cut. I didn't see no di'monds, and I told Tom Sawyer so. He said there was loads of them there, anyway; and he said there was A-rabs there, too, and elephants and things. I said, why couldn't we see them, then? He said if I warn't so ignorant, but had read a book called "Don Quixote," I would know without asking. He said it was all done by enchantment. He said there was hundreds of soldiers there, and elephants and treasure, and so on, but we had enemies which he called magicians, and they had turned the whole thing into an infant Sunday school, just out of spite. I said, all right, then the thing for us to do was to go for the magicians. Tom Sawyer said I was a numskull.

"Why," says he, "a magician could call up a lot of genies, and they would hash you up like nothing before you could say Jack Robinson. They are as tall as a tree and as big around as a church."

"Well," I says, "s'pose we got some genies to help *us* — can't we lick the other crowd then?"

"How you going to get them?"

"I don't know. How do *they* get them?"

"Why they rub an old tin lamp or an iron ring, and then the genies come tearing in, with the thunder and lightning a-ripping around and the smoke a-rolling, and everything they're told to do they up and do it. They don't think nothing of pulling a shot tower up by the roots, and belting a Sunday-school superintendent over the head with it — or any other man."

"Who makes them tear around so?"

"Why, whoever rubs the lamp or the ring. They belong to whoever rubs the lamp or the ring, and they've got to do whatever he says. If he tells them to build a palace forty miles long, out of di'monds, and fill it full of chewing gum, or whatever you want, and fetch an emperor's daughter from China for you to marry, they've got to do it — and they've got to do it before sun-up next morning, too. And more — they've got to waltz that palace around over the country wherever you want it, you understand."

"Well," says I, "I think they are a pack of flatheads for not keeping the palace themselves 'stead of fooling them away like that. And what's more — if I was one of them I would see a man in Jericho before I would drop my business and come to him for the rubbing of an old tin lamp."

"How you talk, Huck Finn. Why, you'd *have* to come when he rubbed it, whether you wanted to or not."

"What, and I as high as a tree and as big as a church? All right, then; I *would* come; but I lay I'd make that man climb the highest tree there was in the country."

"Shucks, it ain't no use to talk to you, Huck Finn. You don't seem to know anything, somehow — perfect sap-head."

I thought all this over for two or three days, and then I reckoned I would see if there was anything in it. I got an old tin lamp and an iron ring and went out in the woods and rubbed and rubbed till I sweat like an Injun, calculating to build a palace and sell it; but it warn't no use, none of the genies come. So then I judged that all that stuff was only just one of Tom Sawyer's lies. I reckoned he believed in the A-rabs and the elephants, but as for me I think different. It had all the marks of a Sunday school.

Chapter IV

Well, three or four months run along, and it was well into the winter, now. I had been to school most all the time, and could spell, and read, and write just a little, and could say the multiplication table up to six times seven is thirty-five, and I don't reckon I could ever get any further than that if I was to live forever. I don't take no stock in mathematics, anyway.

At first I hated the school, but by-and-by I got so I could stand it. Whenever I got uncommon tired I played hookey, and the hiding I got next day done me good and cheered me up. So the longer I went to school the easier it got to be. I was getting sort of used to the widow's ways, too, and they warn't so raspy on me. Living in a house, and sleeping in a bed, pulled on me pretty tight, mostly, but before the cold weather I used to slide out and sleep in the woods, sometimes, and so that was a rest to me. I liked the old ways best, but I was getting so I liked the new ones, too, a little bit. The widow said I was coming along slow but sure, and doing very satisfactory. She said she warn't ashamed of me.

One morning I happened to turn over the salt-cellar at breakfast. I reached for some of it as quick as I could, to throw over my left shoulder and keep off the bad luck, but Miss Watson was in ahead of me, and crossed me off. She says, "Take your hands away, Huckleberry — what a mess you are always making." The widow put in a good word for me, but that warn't going to keep off the bad luck, I knowed that well enough. I started out, after breakfast, feeling worried and shaky, and wondering where it was going to fall on me, and what it was going to be. There is ways to keep off some kinds of bad luck, but this wasn't one of them kind; so I never tried to do anything, but just poked along low-spirited and on the watch-out.

I went down the front garden and clumb over the stile, where you go through the high board fence. There was an inch of new snow on the ground, and I seen somebody's tracks. They had come up from the quarry and stood around the stile a while, and then went on around the garden fence. It was funny they hadn't come in, after standing around so. I couldn't make it out. It was very curious, somehow. I was going to follow around, but I stooped down to look at the tracks first. I didn't

*Father super st.3:00

notice anything at first, but next I did. There was a cross in the left boot-heel made with big nails, to keep off the devil.

I was up in a second and shinning down the hill. I looked over my shoulder every now and then, but I didn't see nobody. I was at Judge Thatcher's as quick as I could get there. He said:

"Why, my boy, you are all out of breath. Did you come for your interest?"

"No sir," I says; "is there some for me?"

"Oh, yes, a half-yearly is in, last night. Over a hundred and fifty dollars. Quite a fortune for you. You better let me invest it along with your six thousand, because if you take it you'll spend it."

"No sir," I says, "I don't want to spend it. I don't want it at all — nor the six thousand, nuther. I want you to take it; I want to give it to you — the six thousand and all."

He looked surprised. He couldn't seem to make it out. He says:

"Why, what can you mean, my boy?"

I says, "Don't you ask me no questions about it, please. You'll take it — won't you?"

He says:

"Well I'm puzzled. Is something the matter?"

"Please take it," says I, "and don't ask me nothing — then I won't have to tell no lies."

He studied a while, and then he says:

"Oho-o. I think I see. You want to *sell* all your property to me — not give it. That's the correct idea."

Then he wrote something on a paper and read it over, and says:

"There — you see it says 'for a consideration.' That means I have bought it of you and paid you for it. Here's a dollar for you. Now, you sign it."

So I signed it, and left.

Miss Watson's nigger, Jim, had a hair-ball as big as your fist, which had been took out of the fourth stomach of an ox, and he used to do magic with it. He said there was a spirit inside of it, and it knowed everything. So I went to him that night and told him pap was here again, for I found his tracks in the snow. What I wanted to know, was, what he was going to do, and was he going to stay? Jim got out his hairball, and said something over it, and then he held it up and dropped it on the floor. It fell pretty solid, and only rolled about an inch. Jim tried it again, and then another time, and it acted just the same. Jim got down on his knees and put his ear against it and listened. But it warn't no use; he said it wouldn't talk. He said sometimes it wouldn't talk without money. I told him I had an old slick counterfeit quarter that warn't no good because the brass showed through the silver a little, and it wouldn't pass nohow, even if the brass didn't show, because it was so slick it felt greasy, and so that would tell on it every time. (I reckoned I wouldn't say nothing about the dollar I got from the judge.) I said it was pretty bad money, but maybe the hair-ball would take it, because maybe it wouldn't know the difference. Jim smelt it, and bit it, and rubbed it, and said he would manage so the hair-ball would think it was good. He said he would split open a raw Irish potato and stick the quarter in between and keep it there all night, and next morning you couldn't see no brass, and it wouldn't feel greasy no more, and so anybody in town would take it in a minute, let alone a hair-ball. Well, I knowed a potato would do that, before, but I had forgot it.

Jim put the quarter under the hair-ball and got down and listened again. This time he said the hair-ball was all right. He said it would tell my whole fortune if I wanted it to. I says, go on. So the hair-ball talked to Jim, and Jim told it to me. He says:

"Yo' ole father doan' know, yit, what he's a-gwyne to do. Sometimes he spec he'll go 'way, en den agin he spec he'll stay. De bes' way is to res' easy en let de ole man take his own way. Dey's two angels hoverin' roun' 'bout him. One uv 'em is white en shiny, en 'tother one is black. De white one gits him to go right, a little while, den de black one sail in en bust it all up. A body can't tell, yit, which one gwyne to fetch him at de las'. But you is all right. You gwyne to have considable trouble in yo' life, en considable joy. Sometimes you gwyne to git hurt, en sometimes you gwyne to git sick; but every time you's gwyne to git well agin. Dey's two gals flyin' 'bout you in yo' life. One uv 'em's light en 'tother one is dark. One is rich en 'tother is po'. You's gwyne to marry de po' one fust en de rich one by-en-by. You wants to keep 'way fum de water as much as you kin, en don't run no resk, 'kase it's down in de bills dat you's gwyne to git hung."

When I lit my candle and went up to my room that night, there set pap, his own self!

Chapter V

I had shut the door to. Then I turned around, and there he was. I used to be scared of him all the time, he tanned me so much. I reckoned I was scared now, too; but in a minute I see I was mistaken. That is, after the first jolt, as you may say, when my breath sort of hitched —

he being so unexpected; but right away after, I see I warn't scared of
him worth bothering about.

He was most fifty, and he looked it. His hair was long and tangled
and greasy, and hung down, and you could see his eyes shining through
like he was behind vines. It was all black, no gray; so was his long,
mixed-up whiskers. There warn't no color in his face, where his face
showed; it was white; not like another man's white, but a white to make
a body sick, a white to make a body's flesh crawl — a tree-toad white, a
fish-belly white. As for his clothes — just rags, that was all. He had one
ankle resting on 'tother knee; the boot on that foot was busted, and
two of his toes stuck through, and he worked them now and then. His
hat was laying on the floor; an old black slouch with the top caved in,
like a lid.

I stood a-looking at him; he set there a-looking at me, with his chair
tilted back a little. I set the candle down. I noticed the window was up;
so he had clumb in by the shed. He kept a-looking me all over. By-and-
by he says:

"Starchy clothes — very. You think you're a good deal of a big-
bug, *don't* you?"

"Maybe I am, maybe I ain't," I says.

"Don't you give me none o' your lip," says he. "You've put on considerble many frills since I been away. I'll take you down a peg before
I get done with you. You're educated, too, they say; can read and
write. You think you're better'n your father, now, don't you, because
he can't? *I'll* take it out of you. Who told you you might meddle with
such hifalut'n foolishness, hey? — who told you you could?"

"The widow. She told me."

"The widow, hey? — and who told the widow she could put in her
shovel about a thing that ain't none of her business?"

"Nobody never told her."

"Well, I'll learn her how to meddle. And looky here — you drop
that school, you hear? I'll learn people to bring up a boy to put on airs
over his own father and let on to be better'n what *he* is. You lemme
catch you fooling around that school again, you hear? Your mother
couldn't read, and she couldn't write, nuther, before she died. None of
the family couldn't, before *they* died. *I* can't; and here you're a-swelling
yourself up like this. I ain't the man to stand it — you hear? Say —
lemme hear you read."

I took up a book and begun something about General Washington
and the wars. When I'd read about a half a minute, he fetched the book
a whack with his hand and knocked it across the house. He says:

"It's so. You can do it. I had my doubts when you told me. Now looky here; you stop that putting on frills. I won't have it. I'll lay for you, my smarty; and if I catch you about that school I'll tan you good. First you know you'll get religion, too. I never see such a son."

He took up a little blue and yaller picture of some cows and a boy, and says:

"What's this?"

"It's something they give me for learning my lessons good."

He tore it up, and says —

"I'll give you something better — I'll give you a cowhide."

He set there a-mumbling and a-growling a minute, and then he says —

"*Ain't* you a sweet-scented dandy, though? A bed; and bedclothes; and a look'n-glass; and a piece of carpet on the floor — and your own father got to sleep with the hogs in the tanyard. I never see such a son. I bet I'll take some o' these frills out o' you before I'm done with you. Why there ain't no end to your airs — they say you're rich. Hey? — how's that?"

"They lie — that's how."

"Looky here — mind how you talk to me; I'm a-standing about all I can stand, now — so don't gimme no sass. I've been in town two days, and I hain't heard nothing but about you bein' rich. I heard about it away down the river, too. That's why I come. You git me that money to-morrow — I want it."

"I hain't got no money."

"It's a lie. Judge Thatcher's got it. You git it. I want it."

"I hain't got no money, I tell you. You ask Judge Thatcher; he'll tell you the same."

"All right. I'll ask him; and I'll make him pungle,° too, or I'll know the reason why. Say — how much you got in your pocket? I want it."

"I hain't got only a dollar, and I want that to ——"

"It don't make no difference what you want it for — you just shell it out."

He took it and bit it to see if it was good, and then he said he was going down town to get some whisky; said he hadn't had a drink all day. When he had got out on the shed, he put his head in again, and cussed me for putting on frills and trying to be better than him; and when I reckoned he was gone, he come back and put his head in again,

pungle: Pay up.

and told me to mind about that school, because he was going to lay for me and lick me if I didn't drop that.

Next day he was drunk, and he went to Judge Thatcher's and bully-ragged° him and tried to make him give up the money, but he couldn't, and then he swore he'd make the law force him.

The judge and the widow went to law to get the court to take me away from him and let one of them be my guardian; but it was a new judge that had just come, and he didn't know the old man; so he said courts mustn't interfere and separate families if they could help it; said he'd druther not take a child away from its father. So Judge Thatcher and the widow had to quit on the business.

That pleased the old man till he couldn't rest. He said he'd cowhide me till I was black and blue if I didn't raise some money for him. I borrowed three dollars from Judge Thatcher, and pap took it and got drunk and went a-blowing around and cussing and whooping and carrying on; and he kept it up all over town, with a tin pan, till most midnight; then they jailed him, and next day they had him before court, and jailed him again for a week. But he said *he* was satisfied; said he was boss of his son, and he'd make it warm for *him*.

When he got out the new judge said he was agoing to make a man of him. So he took him to his own house, and dressed him up clean and nice, and had him to breakfast and dinner and supper with the family, and was just old pie to him, so to speak. And after supper he talked to him about temperance and such things till the old man cried, and said he'd been a fool, and fooled away his life; but now he was agoing to turn over a new leaf and be a man nobody wouldn't be ashamed of, and he hoped the judge would help him and not look down on him. The judge said he could hug him for them words; so *he* cried, and his wife she cried again; pap said he'd been a man that had always been misunderstood before, and the judge said he believed it. The old man said that what a man wanted that was down, was sympathy; and the judge said it was so; so they cried again. And when it was bedtime, the old man rose up and held out his hand, and says:

"Look at it gentlemen, and ladies all; take ahold of it; shake it. There's a hand that was the hand of a hog; but it ain't so no more; it's the hand of a man that's started in on a new life, and 'll die before he'll go back. You mark them words — don't forget I said them. It's a clean hand now; shake it — don't be afeard."

---

bullyragged: Intimidated by bullying.

So they shook it, one after the other, all around, and cried. The judge's wife she kissed it. Then the old man he signed a pledge — made his mark. The judge said it was the holiest time on record, or something like that. Then they tucked the old man into a beautiful room, which was the spare room, and in the night sometime he got powerful thirsty and clumb out onto the porch-roof and slid down a stanchion and traded his new coat for a jug of forty-rod, and clumb back again and had a good old time; and towards daylight he crawled out again, drunk as a fiddler, and rolled off the porch and broke his left arm in two places and was most froze to death when somebody found him after sun-up. And when they come to look at that spare room, they had to take soundings° before they could navigate it.

The judge he felt kind of sore. He said he reckoned a body could reform the ole man with a shot-gun, maybe, but he didn't know no other way.

Chapter VI

Well, pretty soon the old man was up and around again, and then he went for Judge Thatcher in the courts to make him give up that money, and he went for me, too, for not stopping school. He catched me a couple of times and thrashed me, but I went to school just the same, and dodged him or out-run him most of the time. I didn't want to go to school much, before, but I reckoned I'd go now to spite pap. That law trial was a slow business; appeared like they warn't ever going to get started on it; so every now and then I'd borrow two or three dollars off of the judge for him, to keep from getting a cowhiding. Every time he got money he got drunk; and every time he got drunk he raised Cain around town; and every time he raised Cain he got jailed. He was just suited — this kind of thing was right in his line.

He got to hanging around the widow's too much, and so she told him at last, that if he didn't quit using around there she would make trouble for him. Well, *wasn't* he mad? He said he would show who was Huck Finn's boss. So he watched out for me one day in the spring, and catched me, and took me up the river about three mile, in a skiff, and crossed over to the Illinois shore where it was woody and there warn't no houses but an old log hut in a place where the timber was so thick you couldn't find it if you didn't know where it was.

---

take soundings: Measure the depth.

He kept me with him all the time, and I never got a chance to run off. We lived in that old cabin, and he always locked the door and put the key under his head, nights. He had a gun which he had stole, I reckon, and we fished and hunted, and that was what we lived on. Every little while he locked me in and went down to the store, three miles, to the ferry, and traded fish and game for whisky and fetched it home and got drunk and had a good time, and licked me. The widow she found out where I was, by-and-by, and she sent a man over to try to get hold of me, but pap drove him off with the gun, and it warn't long after that till I was used to being where I was, and liked it, all but the cowhide part.

It was kind of lazy and jolly, laying off comfortable all day, smoking and fishing, and no books nor study. Two months or more run along, and my clothes got to be all rags and dirt, and I didn't see how I'd ever got to like it so well at the widow's, where you had to wash, and eat on a plate, and comb up, and go to bed and get up regular, and be forever bothering over a book and have old Miss Watson pecking at you all the time. I didn't want to go back no more. I had stopped cussing, because the widow didn't like it; but now I took to it again because pap hadn't no objections. It was pretty good times up in the woods there, take it all around.

But by-and-by pap got too handy with his hick'ry, and I couldn't stand it. I was all over welts. He got to going away so much, too, and locking me in. Once he locked me in and was gone three days. It was dreadful lonesome. I judged he had got drowned and I wasn't ever going to get out any more. I was scared. I made up my mind I would fix up some way to leave there. I had tried to get out of that cabin many a time, but I couldn't find no way. There warn't a window to it big enought for a dog to get through. I couldn't get up the chimbly, it was too narrow. The door was thick solid oak slabs. Pap was pretty careful not to leave a knife or anything in the cabin when he was away; I reckon I had hunted the place over as much as a hundred times; well, I was 'most all the time at it, because it was about the only way to put in the time. But this time I found something at last; I found an old rusty wood-saw without any handle; it was laid in between a rafter and the clapboards of the roof. I greased it up and went to work. There was an old horse-blanket nailed against the logs at the far end of the cabin behind the table, to keep the wind from blowing through the chinks and putting the candle out. I got under the table and raised the blanket and went to work to saw a section of the big bottom log out, big enough to let me through. Well, it was a good long job, but I was getting towards the end of it when I heard pap's gun in the woods. I got rid of the signs of my work, and dropped the blanket and hid my saw, and pretty soon pap come in.

Pap warn't in a good humor — so he was his natural self. He said he was down to town, and everything was going wrong. His lawyer said he reckoned he would win his lawsuit and get the money, if they ever got started on the trial; but then there was ways to put it off a long time, and Judge Thatcher knowed how to do it. And he said people allowed there'd be another trial to get me away from him and give me to the widow for my guardian, and they guessed it would win, this time. This shook me up considerable, because I didn't want to go back to the widow's any more and be so cramped up and sivilized, as they called it. Then the old man got to cussing, and cussed everything and everybody he could think of, and then cussed them all over again to make sure he hadn't skipped any, and after that he polished off with a kind of a general cuss all round, including a considerable parcel of people which he didn't know the names of, and so called them what's-his-name, when he got to them, and went right along with his cussing.

He said he would like to see the widow get me. He said he would watch out, and if they tried to come any such game on him he knowed of a place six or seven mile off, to stow me in, where they might hunt till they dropped and they couldn't find me. That made me pretty uneasy again, but only for a minute; I reckoned I wouldn't stay on hand till he got that chance.

The old man made me go to the skiff and fetch the things he had got. There was a fifty-pound sack of corn meal, and a side of bacon, ammunition, and a four-gallon jug of whisky, and an old book and two newspapers for wadding, besides some tow. I toted up a load, and went back and set down on the bow of the skiff to rest. I thought it all over, and I reckoned I would walk off with the gun and some lines, and take to the woods when I run away. I guessed I wouldn't stay in one place, but just tramp right across the country, mostly night times, and hunt and fish to keep alive, and so get so far away that the old man nor the widow couldn't ever find me any more. I judged I would saw out and leave that night if pap got drunk enough, and I reckoned he would. I got so full of it I didn't notice how long I was staying, till the old man hollered and asked me whether I was asleep or drownded.

I got the things all up to the cabin, and then it was about dark. While I was cooking supper the old man took a swig or two and got sort of warmed up, and went to ripping again. He had been drunk over in town, and laid in the gutter all night, and he was a sight to look at.

A body would a thought he was Adam, he was just all mud. Whenever his liquor begun to work, he most always went for the govment. This time he says:

"Call this a govment! why, just look at it and see what it's like. Here's the law a-standing ready to take a man's son away from him — a man's own son, which he has had all the trouble and all the anxiety and all the expense of raising. Yes, just as that man has got that son raised at last, and ready to go to work and begin to do suthin' for *him* and give him a rest, the law up and goes for him. And they call *that* govment! That ain't all, nuther. The law backs that old Judge Thatcher up and helps him to keep me out o' my property. Here's what the law does. The law takes a man worth six thousand dollars and upards, and jams him into an old trap of a cabin like this, and lets him go round in clothes that ain't fitten for a hog. They call that govment! A man can't get his rights in a govment like this. Sometimes I've a mighty notion to just leave the country for good and all. Yes, and I *told* 'em so; I told old Thatcher so to his face. Lots of 'em heard me, and can tell what I said. Says I, for two cents I'd leave the blamed country and never come anear it agin. Them's the very words. I says, look at my hat — if you call it a hat — but the lid raises up and the rest of it goes down till it's below my chin, and then it ain't rightly a hat at all, but more like my head was shoved up through a jint o' stove-pipe. Look at it, says I — such a hat for me to wear — one of the wealthiest men in this town, if I could git my rights.

"Oh, yes, this is a wonderful govment, wonderful. Why, looky here. There was a free nigger there, from Ohio; a mulatter, most as white as a white man. He had the whitest shirt on you ever see, too, and the shiniest hat; and there ain't a man in that town that's got as fine clothes as what he had; and he had a gold watch and chain, and a silver-headed cane — the awfulest old gray-headed nabob in the State. And what do you think? they said he was a p'fessor in a college, and could talk all kinds of languages, and knowed everything. And that ain't the wust. They said he could *vote*, when he was at home. Well, that let me out. Thinks I, what is the country a-coming to? It was 'lection day, and I was just about to go and vote, myself, if I warn't too drunk to get there; but when they told me there was a State in this country where they'd let that nigger vote, I drawed out. I says I'll never vote agin. Them's the very words I said; they all heard me; and the country may rot for all me — I'll never vote agin as long as I live. And to see the cool way of that nigger — why, he wouldn't a give me the road if I hadn't shoved him out o' the way. I says to the people, why ain't this nigger auction and sold? — that's what I want to know. And what reckon they said? Why, they said he couldn't be sold till he'd been in the State six months, and he hadn't been there that long yet. There, now — that's a specimen. They call that a govment that can't sell a free nigger till he's been in the State six months. Here's a govment that calls itself a govment, and lets on to be a govment, and thinks it is a govment, and yet's got to set stock-still for six whole months before it can take ahold of a prowling, thieving, infernal, white-shirted free nigger, and ——"

Pap was agoing on so, he never noticed where his old limber legs was taking him to, so he went head over heels over the tub of salt pork, and barked both shins, and the rest of his speech was all the hottest kind of language — mostly hove at the nigger and the govment, though he give the tub some, too, all along, here and there. He hopped around the cabin considerable, first on one leg and then on the other, holding first one shin and then the other one, and at last he let out with his left foot all of a sudden and fetched the tub a rattling kick. But it warn't good judgment, because that was the boot that had a couple of his toes leaking out of the front end of it; so now he raised a howl that fairly made a body's hair raise, and down he went in the dirt, and rolled there, and hold his toes; and the cussing he done then laid over anything he had ever done previous. He said so his own self, afterwards. He had heard old Sowberry Hagan in his best days, and he said it laid over him, too; but I reckon that was sort of piling it on, maybe.

After supper pap took the jug, and said he had enough whisky there for two drunks and one delirium tremens. That was always his word. I judged he would be blind drunk in about an hour, and then I would steal the key, or saw myself out, one or 'tother. He drank, and drank, and tumbled down on his blankets, by-and-by; but luck didn't run my way. He didn't go sound asleep, but was uneasy. He groaned, and moaned, and thrashed around this way and that, for a long time. At last I got so sleepy I couldn't keep my eyes open, all I could do, and so before I knowed what I was about I was sound asleep, and the candle burning.

I don't know how long I was asleep, but all of a sudden there was an awful scream and I was up. There was pap, looking wild and skipping around every which way and yelling about snakes. He said they was crawling up his legs; and then he would give a jump and scream, and say one had bit him on the cheek — but I couldn't see no snakes.

He started and run round and round the cabin, hollering "take him off! take him off! he's biting me on the neck!" I never see a man look so wild in the eyes. Pretty soon he was all fagged out, and fell down panting; then he rolled over and over, wonderful fast, kicking things every which way, and striking and grabbing at the air with his hands, and screaming, and saying there was devils ahold of him. He wore out, by-and-by, and laid still a while, moaning. Then he laid stiller, and didn't make a sound. I could hear the owls and the wolves, away off in the woods, and it seemed terrible still. He was laying over by the corner. By-and-by he raised up, part way, and listened, with his head to one side. He says very low:

"Tramp — tramp — tramp; that's the dead; tramp — tramp — tramp; they're coming after me; but I won't go — Oh, they're here! don't touch me — don't! hands off — they're cold; let go — Oh, let a poor devil alone!"

Then he went down on all fours and crawled off begging them to let him alone, and he rolled himself up in his blanket and wallowed in under the old pine table, still a-begging; and then he went to crying. I could hear him through the blanket.

By-and-by he rolled out and jumped up on his feet looking wild, and he see me and went for me. He chased me round and round the place, with a clasp-knife, calling me the Angel of Death and saying he would kill me and then I couldn't come for him no more. I begged, and told him I was only Huck, but he laughed *such* a screechy laugh, and roared and cussed, and kept on chasing me up. Once when I turned short and dodged under his arm he made a grab and got me by the jacket between my shoulders, and I thought I was gone; but I slid out of the jacket quick as lightning, and saved myself. Pretty soon he was all tired out, and dropped down with his back against the door, and said he would rest a minute and then kill me. He put his knife under him, and said he would sleep and get strong, and then he would see who was who.

So he dozed off, pretty soon. By-and-by I got the old split-bottom chair° and clumb up, as easy as I could, not to make any noise, and got down the gun. I slipped the ramrod down it to make sure it was loaded, and then I laid it across the turnip barrel, pointing towards pap, and set down behind it to wait for him to stir. And how slow and still the time did drag along.

---

split-bottom chair: A chair with a woven cane seat.

Chapter VII

"Git up! what you 'bout!"

I opened my eyes and looked around, trying to make out where I was. It was after sun-up, and I had been sound asleep. Pap was standing over me, looking sour — and sick, too. He says —

"What you doin' with this gun?"

I judged he didn't know nothing about what he had been doing, so I says:

"Somebody tried to get in, so I was laying for him."

"Why didn't you roust me out?"

"Well I tried to, but I couldn't; I couldn't budge you."

"Well, all right. Don't stand there palavering all day, but out with you and see if there's a fish on the lines for breakfast. I'll be along in a minute."

He unlocked the door and I cleared out, up the river bank. I noticed some pieces of limbs and such things floating down, and a sprinkling of bark; so I knowed the river had begun to rise. I reckoned I would have great times, now, if I was over at the town. The June rise used to be always luck for me; because as soon as that rise begins, here comes cord-wood floating down, and pieces of log rafts — sometimes a dozen logs together; so all you have to do is to catch them and sell them to the wood yards and the sawmill.

I went along up the bank with one eye out for pap and 'tother one out for what the rise might fetch along. Well, all at once, here comes a canoe; just a beauty, too, about thirteen or fourteen foot long, riding high like a duck. I shot head first off of the bank, like a frog, clothes and all on, and struck out for the canoe. I just expected there'd be somebody laying down in it, because people often done that to fool folks, and when a chap had pulled a skiff out most to it they'd raise up and laugh at him. But it warn't so this time. It was a drift-canoe, sure enough, and I clumb in and paddled her ashore. Thinks I, the old man will be glad when he sees this — she's worth ten dollars. But when I got to shore pap wasn't in sight yet, and as I was running her into a little creek like a gully, all hung over with vines and willows, I struck another idea; I judged I'd hide her good, and then, stead of taking to the woods when I run off, I'd go down the river about fifty mile and camp in one place for good, and not have such a rough time tramping on foot.

It was pretty close to the shanty, and I thought I heard the old man coming, all the time; but I got her hid; and then I out and looked around a bunch of willows, and there was the old man down the path apiece just drawing a bead on a bird with his gun. So he hadn't seen anything.

When he got along, I was hard at it taking up a "trot" line. He abused me a little for being so slow, but I told him I fell in the river and that was what made me so long. I knowed he would see I was wet, and then he would be asking questions. We got five cat-fish off of the lines and went home.

While we laid off, after breakfast, to sleep up, both of us being about wore out, I got to thinking that if I could fix up some way to keep pap and the widow from trying to follow me, it would be a certainer thing than trusting to luck to get far enough off before they missed me; you see, all kinds of things might happen. Well, I didn't see no way for a while, but by-and-by pap raised up a minute, to drink another barrel of water, and he says:

"Another time a man comes a-prowling round here, you roust me out, you hear? That man warn't here for no good. I'd a shot him. Next time, you roust me out, you hear?"

Then he dropped down and went to sleep again — but what he had been saying give me the very idea I wanted. I says to myself, I can fix it now so nobody won't think of following me.

About twelve o'clock we turned out and went along up the bank. The river was coming up pretty fast, and lots of drift-wood going by on the rise. By-and-by, along comes part of a log raft — nine logs fast together. We went out with the skiff and towed it ashore. Then we had dinner. Anybody but pap would a waited and seen the day through, so as to catch more stuff; but that warn't pap's style. Nine logs was enough for one time; he must shove right over to town and sell. So he locked me in and took the skiff and started off towing the raft about half-past three. I judged he wouldn't come back that night. I waited till I reckoned he had got a good start, then I out with my saw and went to work on that log again. Before he was 'tother side of the river I was out of the hole; him and his raft was just a speck on the water away off yonder.

I took the sack of corn meal and took it to where the canoe was hid, and shoved the vines and branches apart and put it in; then I done the same with the side of bacon; then the whisky jug; I took all the coffee and sugar there was, and all the ammunition; I took the wadding; I took the bucket and gourd, I took a dipper and a tin cup, and my old saw and two blankets, and the skillet and the coffee-pot. I took fish-lines and matches and other things — everything that was worth a cent.

I cleaned out the place. I wanted an axe, but there wasn't any, only the one out at the wood pile, and I knowed why I was going to leave that. I fetched out the gun, and now I was done.

I had wore the ground a good deal, crawling out of the hole and dragging out so many things. So I fixed that as good as I could from the outside by scattering dust on the place, which covered up the smoothness and the sawdust. Then I fixed the piece of log back into its place, and put two rocks under it and one against it to hold it there, — for it was bent up at that place, and didn't quite touch ground. If you stood four or five foot away and didn't know it was sawed, you wouldn't ever notice it; and besides, this was the back of the cabin and it warn't likely anybody would go fooling around there.

It was all grass clear to the canoe; so I hadn't left a track. I followed around to see. I stood on the bank and looked out over the river. All safe. So I took the gun and went up a piece into the woods and was hunting around for some birds, when I see a wild pig; hogs soon went wild in them bottoms after they had got away from the prairie farms. I shot this fellow and took him into camp.

I took the axe and smashed in the door — I beat it and hacked it considerable, a-doing it. I fetched the pig in and took him back nearly to the table and hacked into his throat with the ax, and laid him down on the ground to bleed — I say ground, because it *was* ground — hard packed, and no boards. Well, next I took an old sack and put a lot of big rocks in it, — all I could drag — and I started it from the pig and dragged it to the door and through the woods down to the river and dumped it in, and down it sunk, out of sight. You could easy see that something had been dragged over the ground. I did wish Tom Sawyer was there, I knowed he would take an interest in this kind of business, and throw in the fancy touches. Nobody could spread himself like Tom Sawyer in such a thing as that.

Well, last I pulled out some of my hair, and bloodied the ax good, and stuck it on the back side, and slung the ax in the corner. Then I took up the pig and held him to my breast with my jacket (so he couldn't drip) till I got a good piece below the house and then dumped him into the river. Now I thought of something else. So I went and got the bag of meal and my old saw out of the canoe and fetched them to the house. I took the bag to where it used to stand, and ripped a hole in the bottom of it with the saw, for there warn't no knives and forks on the place — pap done everything with his clasp-knife, about the cooking. Then I carried the sack about a hundred yards across the grass and through the willows east of the house, to a shallow lake that was five

mile wide and full of rushes — and ducks too, you might say, in the sea-
son. There was a slough or a creek leading out of it on the other side,
that went miles away, I don't know where, but it didn't go to the river.
The meal sifted out and made a little track all the way to the lake. I
dropped pap's whetstone there too, so as to look like it had been done
by accident. Then I tied up the rip in the meal sack with a string, so it
wouldn't leak no more, and took it and my saw to the canoe again.

It was about dark, now; so I dropped the canoe down the river
under some willows that hung over the bank, and waited for the moon
to rise. I made fast to a willow; then I took a bite to eat, and by-and-by
laid down in the canoe to smoke a pipe and lay out a plan. I says to
myself, they'll follow the track of that sackful of rocks to the shore and
then drag the river for me. And they'll follow that meal track to the lake
and go browsing down the creek that leads out of it to find the robbers
that killed me and took the things. They won't ever hunt the river for
anything but my dead carcass. They'll soon get tired of that, and won't
bother no more about me. All right; I can stop anywhere I want to.
Jackson's Island is good enough for me; I know that island pretty well,
and nobody ever comes there. And then I can paddle over to town,
nights, and slink around and pick up things I want. Jackson's Island's
the place.

I was pretty tired, and the first thing I knowed, I was asleep. When I
woke up I didn't know where I was, for a minute. I set up and looked
around, a little scared. Then I remembered. The river looked miles and
miles across. The moon was so bright I could a counted the drift logs
that went a slipping along, black and still, hundred of yards out from
shore. Everything was dead quiet, and it looked late, and *smelt* late. You
know what I mean — I don't know the words to put it in.

I took a good gap and a stretch, and was just going to unhitch and
start, when I heard a sound away over the water. I listened. Pretty soon
I made it out. It was that dull kind of a regular sound that comes from
oars working in rowlocks when it's a still night. I peeped out through
the willow branches, and there it was — a skiff, away across the water. I
couldn't tell how many was in it. It kept a-coming, and when it was
abreast of me I see there warn't but one man in it. Thinks I, maybe it's
pap, though I warn't expecting him. He dropped below me, with the
current, and by-and-by he come a-swinging up shore in the easy water,
and he went by so close I could a reached out the gun and touched
him. Well, it *was* pap, sure enough — and sober, too, by the way he laid
to his oars.

I didn't lose no time. The next minute I was a-spinning down stream soft but quick in the shade of the bank. I made two mile and a half, and then struck out a quarter of a mile or more towards the middle of the river, because pretty soon I would be passing the ferry landing and people might see me and hail me. I got amongst the driftwood and then laid down in the bottom of the canoe and let her float. I laid there and had a good rest and a smoke out of my pipe, looking away into the sky, not a cloud in it. The sky looks ever so deep when you lay down on your back in the moonshine; I never knowed it before. And how far a body can hear on the water such nights! I heard people talking at the ferry landing. I heard what they said, too, every word of it. One man said it was getting towards the long days and the short nights, now. 'Tother one said *this* warn't one of the short ones, he reckoned — and then they laughed, and he said it over again and they laughed again; then they waked up another fellow and told him, and laughed, but he didn't laugh; he ripped out something brisk and said let him alone. The first fellow said he 'lowed to tell it to his old woman — she would think it was pretty good; but he said that warn't nothing to some things he had said in his time. I heard one man say it was nearly three o'clock, and he hoped daylight wouldn't wait more than about a week longer. After that, the talk got further and further away, and I couldn't make out the words any more, but I could hear the mumble; and now and then a laugh, too, but it seemed a long ways off.

I was away below the ferry now. I rose up and there was Jackson's Island, about two mile and a half down stream, heavy-timbered and standing up out of the middle of the river, big and dark and solid, like a steamboat without any lights. There warn't any signs of the bar at the head — it was all under water, now.

It didn't take me long to get there. I shot past the head at a ripping rate, the current was so swift, and then I got into the dead water and landed on the side towards the Illinois shore. I run the canoe into a deep dent in the bank that I knowed about; I had to part the willow branches to get in; and when I made fast nobody could a seen the canoe from the outside.

I went up and set down on a log at the head of the island and looked out on the big river and the black driftwood, and away over to the town, three mile away, where there was three or four lights twinkling. A monstrous big lumber raft was about a mile up stream, coming along down, with a lantern in the middle of it. I watched it come creeping down, and when it was most abreast of where I stood I heard a man say, "Stern oars, there! heave her head to stabboard!" I heard that just as plain as if the man was by my side.

There was a little gray in the sky, now; so I stepped into the woods and laid down for a nap before breakfast.

Chapter VIII

The sun was up so high when I waked, that I judged it was after eight o'clock. I laid there in the grass and the cool shade, thinking about things and feeling rested and ruther comfortable and satisfied. I could see the sun out at one or two holes, but mostly it was big trees all about, and gloomy in there amongst them. There was freckled places on the ground where the light sifted down through the leaves, and the freckled places swapped about a little, showing there was a little breeze up there. A couple of squirrels set on a limb and jabbered at me very friendly.

I was powerful lazy and comfortable — didn't want to get up and cook breakfast. Well, I was dozing off again, when I thinks I hears a deep sound of "boom!" away up the river. I rouses up and rests on my elbow and listens; pretty soon I hears it again. I hopped up and went and looked out at a hole in the leaves, and I see a bunch of smoke laying on the water a long ways up — about abreast the ferry. And there was the ferry-boat full of people, floating along down. I knowed what was the matter, now. "Boom!" I see the white smoke squirt out of the ferry-boat's side. You see, they was firing cannon over the water, trying to make my carcass come to the top.

I was pretty hungry, but it warn't going to do for me to start a fire, because they might see the smoke. So I set there and watched the cannon-smoke and listened to the boom. The river was a mile wide, there, and it always looks pretty on a summer morning — so I was having a good enough time seeing them hunt for my remainders, if I only had a bite to eat. Well, then I happened to think how they always put quicksilver in loaves of bread and float them off because they always go right to the drownded carcass and stop there. So says I, I'll keep a lookout, and if any of them's floating around after me, I'll give them a show. I changed to the Illinois edge of the island to see what luck I could have, and I warn't disappointed. A big double loaf come along, and I most got it, with a long stick, but my foot slipped and she floated out further. Of course I was where the current set in the closest to the shore — I knowed enough for that. But by-and-by along comes another one, and this time I won. I took out the plug and shook out the little dab of quicksilver, and set my teeth in. It was "baker's bread" — what the quality eat — none of your low-down corn-pone.

I got a good place amongst the leaves, and set there on a log, munching the bread and watching the ferry-boat, and very well satisfied. And then something struck me. I says, now I reckon the widow or the parson or somebody prayed that this bread would find me, and here it has gone and done it. So there ain't no doubt but there is something in that thing. That is, there's something in it when a body like the widow or the parson prays, but it don't work for me, and I reckon it don't work for only just the right kind.

I lit a pipe and had a good long smoke and went on watching. The ferry-boat was floating with the current, and I allowed I'd have a chance to see who was aboard when she come along, because she would come in close, where the bread did. When she'd got pretty well along down towards me, I put out my pipe and went to where I fished out the bread, and laid down behind a log on the bank in a little open place. Where the log forked I could peep through.

By-and-by she come along, and she drifted in so close that they could a run out a plank and walked ashore. Most everybody was on the boat. Pap, and Judge Thatcher, and Bessie Thatcher, and Jo Harper, and Tom Sawyer, and his old Aunt Polly, and Sid and Mary, and plenty more. Everybody was talking about the murder, but the captain broke in and says:

"Look sharp, now; the current sets in the closest here, and maybe he's washed ashore and got tangled amongst the brush at the water's edge. I hope so, anyway."

I didn't hope so. They all crowded up and leaned over the rails, nearly in my face, and kept still, watching with all their might. I could see them first-rate, but they couldn't see me. Then the captain sung out:

"Stand away!" and the cannon let off such a blast right before me that it made me deef with the noise and pretty near blind with the smoke, and I judged I was gone. If they'd a had some bullets in, I reckon they'd a got the corpse they was after. Well, I see I warn't hurt, thanks to goodness. The boat floated on and went out of sight around the shoulder of the island. I could hear the booming, now and then, further and further off, and by-and-by after an hour, I didn't hear it no more. The island was three mile long. I judged they had got to the foot, and was giving it up. But they didn't yet a while. They turned around the foot of the island and started up the channel on the Missouri side, under steam, and booming once in a while as they went. I crossed over to that side and watched them. When they got abreast the head of the island they quit shooting and dropped over to the Missouri shore and went home to the town.

I knowed I was all right now. Nobody else would come a-hunting after me. I got my traps out of the canoe and made me a nice camp in the thick woods. I made a kind of a tent out of my blankets to put my things under so the rain couldn't get at them. I catched a cat-fish and haggled him open with my saw, and towards sundown I started my camp fire and had supper. Then I set out a line to catch some fish for breakfast.

When it was dark I set by my camp fire smoking, and feeling pretty satisfied; but by-and-by it got sort of lonesome, and so I went and set on the bank and listened to the currents washing along, and counted the stars and drift-logs and rafts that come down, and then went to bed; there ain't no better way to put in time when you are lonesome; you can't stay so, you soon get over it.

And so for three days and nights. No difference — just the same thing. But the next day I went exploring around down through the island. I was boss of it; it all belonged to me, so to say, and I wanted to know all about it; but mainly I wanted to put in the time. I found plenty strawberries, ripe and prime; and green summer-grapes, and green razberries; and the green blackberries was just beginning to show. They would all come handy by-and-by, I judged.

Well, I went fooling along in the deep woods till I judged I warn't far from the foot of the island. I had my gun along, but I hadn't shot nothing; it was for protection; thought I would kill some game nigh home. About this time I mighty near stepped on a good sized snake, and it went sliding off through the grass and flowers, and I after it, try-ing to get a shot at it. I clipped along, and all of a sudden I bounded right on to the ashes of a camp fire that was still smoking.

My heart jumped up amongst my lungs. I never waited for to look further, but uncocked my gun and went sneaking back on my tip-toes as fast as ever I could. Every now and then I stopped a second, amongst the thick leaves, and listened; but my breath come so hard I couldn't hear nothing else. I slunk along another piece further, then listened again; and so on, and so on; if I see a stump, I took it for a man; if I trod on a stick and broke it, it made me feel like a person had cut one of my breaths in two and I only got half, and the short half, too.

When I got to camp I warn't feeling very brash, there warn't much sand in my craw; but I says, this ain't no time to be fooling around. So I got all my traps into my canoe again so as to have them out of sight, and

I put out the fire and scattered the ashes around to look like an old last year's camp, and then clumb a tree.

I reckon I was up in the tree two hours; but I didn't see nothing, I didn't hear nothing — I only *thought* I heard and seen as much as a thousand things. Well, I couldn't stay up there forever; so at last I got down, but I kept in the thick woods and on the lookout all the time. All I could get to eat was berries and what was left over from breakfast.

By the time it was night I was pretty hungry. So when it was good and dark, I slid out from shore before moonrise and paddled over to the Illinois bank — about a quarter of a mile. I went out in the woods and cooked a supper, and I had about made up my mind I would stay there all night, when I hear a *plunkety-plunk, plunkety-plunk,* and says to myself, horses coming; and next I hear people's voices. I got everything into the canoe as quick as I could, and then went creeping through the woods to see what I could find out. I hadn't got far when I hear a man say:

"We better camp here, if we can find a good place; the horses is about beat out. Let's look around."

I didn't wait, but shoved out and paddled away easy. I tied up in the old place, and reckoned I would sleep in the canoe.

I didn't sleep much. I couldn't, somehow, for thinking. And every time I waked up I thought somebody had me by the neck. So the sleep didn't do me no good. By-and-by I says to myself, I can't live this way; I'm agoing to find out who it is that's here on the island with me; I'll find it out or bust. Well, I felt better, right off.

So I took my paddle and slid out from shore just a step or two, and then let the canoe drop along down amongst the shadows. The moon was shining, and outside of the shadows it made it most as light as day. I poked along well onto an hour, everything still as rocks and sound asleep. Well by this time I was most down to the foot of the island. A little ripply, cool breeze begun to blow, and that was as good as saying the night was about done. I give her a turn with the paddle and brung her nose to shore; then I got my gun and slipped out and into the edge of the woods. I set down there on a log and looked out through the leaves. I see the moon go off watch and the darkness begin to blanket the river. But in a little while I see a pale streak over the tree-tops, and knowed the day was coming. So I took my gun and slipped off towards where I had run across that camp fire, stopping every minute or two to listen. But I hadn't no luck, somehow; I couldn't seem to find the place. But by-and-by, sure enough, I catched a glimpse of fire, away

through the trees. I went for it, cautious and slow. By-and-by I was
close enough to have a look, and there laid a man on the ground. It
most give me the fan-tods.° He had a blanket around his head, and his
head was nearly in the fire. I set there behind a clump of bushes, in
about six foot of him, and kept my eyes on him steady. It was getting
gray daylight, now. Pretty soon he gapped, and stretched himself, and
hove off the blanket, and it was Miss Watson's Jim! I bet I was glad to
see him. I says:

"Hello, Jim!" and skipped out.

He bounced up and stared at me wild. Then he drops down on his
knees, and puts his hands together and says:

"Doan' hurt me — don't! I hain't ever done no harm to a ghos'. I
awluz liked dead people, en done all I could for 'em. You go en git in de
river agin, whah you b'longs, en doan' do nuffn to Ole Jim, 'at 'uz
awluz yo' fren'."

Well, I warn't long making him understand I warn't dead. I was
ever so glad to see Jim. I warn't lonesome, now. I told him I warn't
afraid of *him* telling the people where I was. I talked along, but he only
set there and looked at me; never said nothing. Then I says:

"It's good daylight. Le's get breakfast. Make up your camp fire
good."

"What's de use er makin' up de camp fire to cook strawbries en sich
truck? But you got a gun, hain't you? Den we kin git sumfn better den
strawbries."

"Strawberries and such truck," I says. "Is that what you live on?"

"I couldn' git nuffn else," he says.

"Why, how long you been on the island, Jim?"

"I come heah de night arter you's killed."

"What, all that time?"

"Yes-indeedy."

"And ain't you had nothing but that kind of rubbage to eat?"

"No, sah — nuffn else."

"Well, you must be most starved, ain't you?"

"I reck'n I could eat a hoss. I think I could. How long you ben on
de islan'?"

"Since the night I got killed."

"No! W'y, what has you lived on? But you got a gun. Oh, yes, you
got a gun. Dat's good. Now you kill sumfn en I'll make up de fire."

---

fan-tods: The fidgets or "the creeps."

So we went over to where the canoe was, and while he built a fire in a grassy open place amongst the trees, I fetched meal and bacon and coffee, and coffee-pot and frying-pan, and sugar and tin cups, and the nigger was set back considerable, because he reckoned it was all done with witchcraft. I catched a good big cat-fish, too, and Jim cleaned him with his knife, and fried him.

When breakfast was ready, we lolled on the grass and eat it smoking hot. Jim laid it in with all his might, for he was most about starved. Then when we had got pretty well stuffed, we laid off and lazied.

By-and-by Jim says:

"But looky here, Huck, who wuz it dat 'uz killed in dat shanty, ef it warn't you?"

Then I told him the whole thing, and he said it was smart. He said Tom Sawyer couldn't get up no better plan than what I had. Then I says:

"How do you come to be here, Jim, and how'd you get here?"

He looked pretty uneasy, and didn't say nothing for a minute. Then he says:

"Maybe I better not tell."

"Why, Jim?"

"Well, dey's reasons. But you wouldn' tell on me ef I 'uz to tell you, would you, Huck?"

"Blamed if I would, Jim."

"Well, I b'lieve you, Huck. I — I *run off*."

"Jim!"

"But mind, you said you wouldn't tell — you know you said you wouldn't tell, Huck."

"Well, I did. I said I wouldn't, and I'll stick to it. Honest *injun* I will. People would call me a low down Ablitionist and despise me for keeping mum — but that don't made no difference. I ain't agoing to tell, and I ain't agoing back there anyways. So now, le's know all about it."

"Well, you see, it 'uz dis way. Ole Missus — dat's Miss Watson — she pecks on me all de time, en treats me pooty rough, but she awluz said she wouldn' sell me down to Orleans. But I noticed dey wuz a nigger trader roun' de place considable, lately, en I begin to git oneasy. Well, one night I creeps to de do', pooty late, en de do' warn't quite shet, en I hear ole missus tell de widder she gwyne to sell me down to Orleans, but she didn' want to, but she could git eight hund'd dollars for me, en it 'uz sich a big stack o' money she couldn' resis'. De widder she try to git her to say she wouldn' do it, but I never waited to hear de res'. I lit out mighty quick, I tell you.

"I tuck out en shin down de hill en 'spec to steal a skift 'long de sho' som'ers 'bove de town, but dey wuz people a-stirrin' yit, so I hid in de ole tumble-down cooper shop on de bank to wait for everybody to go 'way. Well, I wuz dah all night. Dey wuz somebody roun' all de time. 'Long 'bout six in de mawnin', skifts begin to go by, en 'bout eight er nine every skift dat went 'long wuz talkin' 'bout how yo' pap come over to de town en say you's killed. Dese las' skifts wuz full o' ladies en genlmen agoin' over for to see de place. Sometimes dey'd pull up at de sho' en take a res' b'fo' dey started acrost, so by de talk I got to know all 'bout de killin'. I 'uz powerful sorry you's killed, Huck, but I ain't no mo', now.

"I laid dah under de shavins all day. I 'uz hungry, but I warn't afeared; bekase I knowed ole missus en de widder wuz goin' to start to de camp-meetn' right arter breakfas' en be gone all day, en dey knows I goes off wid de cattle 'bout daylight, so dey wouldn' 'spec to see me roun' de place, en so dey wouldn' miss me tell arter dark in de evenin'. De yuther servants wouldn' miss me, kase dey'd shin out en take holiday, soon as de ole folks 'uz out'n de way.

"Well, when it come dark I tuck out up de river road, en went 'bout two mile er more to whah dey warn't no houses. I'd made up my mine 'bout what I's agwyne to do. You see ef I kep' on tryin' to git away afoot, de dogs 'ud track me; ef I stole a skift to cross over, dey'd miss dat skift, you see, en dey'd know 'bout whah I'd lan' on de yuther side en whah to pick up my track. So I says, a raff is what I's arter; it doan' *make* no track.

"I see a light a-comin' roun' de p'int, bymeby, so I wade' in en shove' a log ahead o' me, en swum more'n half-way acrost de river, en got in 'mongst de drift-wood, en kep' my head down low, en kinder swum agin de current tell de raff come along. Den I swum to de stern uv it, en tuck aholt. It clouded up en 'uz pooty dark for a little while. So I clumb up en laid down on de planks. De men 'uz all 'way yonder in de middle, whah de lantern wuz. De river wuz arisin' en dey wuz a good current; so I reck'n'd 'at by fo' in de mawnin' I'd be twenty-five mile down de river, en den I'd slip in, jis' b'fo' daylight, en swim asho' en take to de woods on de Illinoi side.

"But I didn' have no luck. When we 'uz mos' down to de head er de islan', a man begin to come aft wid de lantern. I see it warn't no use fer to wait, so I slid overboad, en struck out fer de islan'. Well, I had a notion I could lan' mos' anywhers, but I couldn' — bank too bluff. I 'uz mos' to de foot er de islan' b'fo' I foun' a good place. I went into de woods en jedged I wouldn' fool wid raffs no mo', long as dey move de lantern roun' so. I had my pipe en a plug er dog-leg, en some matches in my cap, en dey warn't wet, so I 'uz all right."

"And so you ain't had no meat nor bread to eat all this time? Why didn't you get mud-turkles?"

"How you gwyne to git'm? You can't slip up on um en grab um; en how's a body gwyne to hit um wid a rock? How could a body do it in de night? en I warn't gwyne to show mysef on de bank in de daytime."

"Well, that's so. You've had to keep in the woods all the time, of course. Did you hear 'em shooting the cannon?"

"Oh, yes. I knowed dey was arter you. I see um go by heah; watched um thoo de bushes."

Some young birds come along, flying a yard or two at a time and lighting. Jim said it was a sign it was going to rain. He said it was a sign when young chickens flew that way, and so he reckoned it was the same way when young birds done it. I was going to catch some of them, but Jim wouldn't let me. He said it was death. He said his father laid mighty sick once, and some of them catched a bird, and his old granny said his father would die, and he did.

And Jim said you musn't count the things you are going to cook for dinner, because that would bring bad luck. The same if you shook the table-cloth after sundown. And he said if a man owned a bee-hive, and that man died, the bees must be told about it before sun-up next morning, or else the bees would all weaken down and quit work and die. Jim said bees wouldn't sting idiots; but I didn't believe that, because I had tried them lots of times myself, and they wouldn't sting me.

I had heard about some of these things before, but not all of them. Jim knowed all kinds of signs. He said he knowed most everything. I said it looked to me like all the signs was about bad luck, and so I asked him if there warn't any good-luck signs. He says:

"Mighty few — an' *dey* ain' no use to a body. What you want to know when good luck's a-comin' for? want to keep it off?" And he said: "Ef you's got hairy arms en a hairy breas', it's a sign dat you's agwyne to be rich. Well, dey's some use in a sign like dat, 'kase it's so fur ahead. You see, maybe you's got to be po' a long time fust, en so you might git discourage' en kill yo'sef 'f you didn' know by de sign dat you gwyne to be rich bymeby."

"Have you got hairy arms and a hairy breast, Jim?"

"What's de use to ax dat question? don' you see I has?"

"Well, are you rich?"

"No, but I ben rich wunst, and gwyne to be rich agin. Wunst I had foteen dollars, but I tuck to specalat'n', en got busted out."

"What did you speculate in, Jim?"

"Well, fust I tackled stock."

"What kind of stock?"

"Why, live stock. Cattle, you know. I put ten dollars in a cow. But I ain' gwyne to resk no mo' money in stock. De cow up 'n' died on my han's."

"So you lost the ten dollars."

"No, I didn' lose it all. I on'y los' 'bout nine of it. I sole de hide en taller for a dollar en ten cents."

"You had five dollars and ten cents left. Did you speculate any more?"

"Yes. You know dat one-laigged nigger dat b'longs to old Misto Bradish? well, he sot up a bank, en say anybody dat put in a dollar would git fo' dollars mo' at de en' er de year. Well, all de niggers went in, but dey didn' have much. I wuz de on'y one dat had much. So I stuck out for mo' dan fo' dollars, en I said 'f I didn' git it I'd start a bank mysef. Well o' course dat nigger want' to keep me out er de business, bekase he say dey warn't business 'nough for two banks, so he say I could put in my five dollars en he pay me thirty-five at de en' er de year.

"So I done it. Den I reck'n'd I'd inves' de thirty-five dollars right off en keep things a-movin'. Dey wuz a nigger name' Bob, dat had ketched a wood-flat, en his marster didn' know it; en I bought it off'n him en told him to take de thirty-five dollars when de en' er de year come; but somebody stole de wood-flat dat night, en nex' day de one-laigged nigger say de bank's busted. So dey didn' none uv us git no money."

"What did you do with the ten cents, Jim?"

"Well, I 'uz gwyne to spen' it, but I had a dream, en de dream tole me to give it to a nigger name' Balum — Balum's Ass dey call him for short, he's one er dem chuckle-heads, you know. But he's lucky, dey say, en I see I warn't lucky. De dream say let Balum inves' de ten cents en he'd make a raise for me. Well, Balum he tuck de money, en when he wuz in church he hear de preacher say dat whoever give to de po' len' to de Lord, en boun' to git his money back a hund'd times. So Balum he tuck en give de ten cents to de po,' en laid low to see what wuz gwyne to come of it."

"Well, what did come of it, Jim?"

"Nuffn' never come of it. I couldn' manage to k'leck dat money no way; en Balum he couldn'. I ain' gwyne to len' no mo' money 'dout I see de security. Boun' to git yo' money back a hund'd times, de preacher says! Ef I could git de ten *cents* back, I'd call it squah, en be glad er de chanst."

"Well, it's all right, anyway, Jim, long as you're going to be rich again some time or other."

"Yes — en I's rich now, come to look at it. I owns mysef, en I's wuth eight hund'd dollars. I wisht I had de money, I wouldn' want no mo'."

Chapter IX

I wanted to go and look at a place right about the middle of the island, that I'd found when I was exploring; so we started, and soon got to it, because the island was only three miles long and a quarter of a mile wide.

This place was a tolerable long steep hill or ridge, about forty foot high. We had a rough time getting to the top, the sides was so steep and the bushes so thick. We tramped and clumb around all over it, and by-and-by found a good big cavern in the rock, most up to the top on the side towards Illinois. The cavern was as big as two or three rooms bunched together, and Jim could stand up straight in it. It was cool in there. Jim was for putting our traps in there, right away, but I said we didn't want to be climbing up and down there all the time.

Jim said if we had the canoe hid in a good place, and had all the traps in the cavern, we could rush there if anybody was to come to the island, and they would never find us without dogs. And besides, he said them little birds had said it was going to rain, and did I want the things to get wet?

So we went back and got the canoe and paddled up abreast the cavern, and lugged all the traps up there. Then we hunted up a place close by to hide the canoe in, amongst the thick willows. We took some fish off of the lines and set them again, and begun to get ready for dinner.

The door of the cavern was big enough to roll a hogshead in, and on one side of the door the floor stuck out a little bit and was flat and a good place to build a fire on. So we built it there and cooked dinner.

We spread the blankets inside for a carpet, and eat our dinner in there. We put all the other things handy at the back of the cavern. Pretty soon it darkened up and begun to thunder and lighten; so the birds was right about it. Directly it begun to rain, and it rained like all fury, too, and I never see the wind blow so. It was one of these regular summer storms. It would get so dark that it looked all blue-black outside, and lovely; and the rain would thrash along by so thick that the trees off a little ways looked dim and spider-webby; and here would come a blast of wind that would bend the trees down and turn up the pale underside of the leaves; and then a perfect ripper of a gust would follow along and set the branches to tossing their arms as if they was just wild; and next, when it was just about the bluest and blackest — *fst!* it was as bright as glory and you'd have a little glimpse of tree-tops a-plunging about, away off yonder in the storm, hundreds of yards further than you could see before; dark as sin again in a second, and now you'd hear the thunder let go with an awful crash and then go rumbling, grumbling, tumbling down the sky towards the under side of the world, like rolling empty barrels down stairs, where it's long stairs and they bounce a good deal, you know.

"Jim, this is nice," I says. "I wouldn't want to be nowhere else but here. Pass me along another hunk of fish and some hot corn-bread."

"Well, you wouldn't a ben here, 'f it hadn't a ben for Jim. You'd a ben down dah in de woods widout any dinner, en gittn' mos' drownded, too, dat you would, honey. Chickens knows when its gwyne to rain, en so do de birds, chile."

The river went on raising and raising for ten or twelve days, till at last it was over the banks. The water was three or four foot deep on the island in the low places and on the Illinois bottom. On that side it was a good many miles wide; but on the Missouri side it was the same old distance across — a half a mile — because the Missouri shore was just a wall of high bluffs.

Daytimes we paddled all over the island in the canoe. It was mighty cool and shady in the deep woods even if the sun was blazing outside. We went winding in and out amongst the trees; and sometimes the vines hung so thick we had to back away and go some other way. Well, on every old broken-down tree, you could see rabbits, and snakes, and such things; and when the island had been overflowed a day or two, they got so tame, on account of being hungry, that you could paddle right up and put your hand on them if you wanted to; but not the snakes and turtles — they would slide off in the water. The ridge our cavern was in, was full of them. We could a had pets enough if we'd wanted them.

One night we catched a little section of a lumber raft — nice pine planks. It was twelve foot wide and about fifteen or sixteen foot long, and the top stood above water six or seven inches, a solid level floor. We could see saw-logs go by in the daylight, sometimes, but we let them go; we didn't show ourselves in daylight.

Another night, when we was up at the head of the island, just before daylight, here comes a frame house down, on the west side. She was a two-story, and tilted over, considerable. We paddled out and got aboard — clumb in at an up-stairs window. But it was too dark to see yet, so we made the canoe fast and set in her to wait for daylight.

The light begun to come before we got to the foot of the island. Then we looked in at the window. We could make out a bed, and a table, and two old chairs, and lots of things around about on the floor; and there was clothes hanging against the wall. There was something laying on the floor in the far corner that looked like a man. So Jim says:

"Hello, you!"

But it didn't budge. So I hollered again, and then Jim says:

"De man ain't asleep — he's dead. You hold still — I'll go en see."

He went and bent down and looked, and says:

"It's a dead man. Yes, indeedy; naked, too. He's ben shot in de back. I reck'n he's ben dead two er three days. Come in, Huck, but doan' look at his face — it's too gashly."

I didn't look at him at all. Jim throwed some old rags over him, but he needn't done it; I didn't want to see him. There was heaps of old greasy cards scattered around over the floor, and old whisky bottles, and a couple of masks made out of black cloth; and all over the walls was the ignorantest kind of words and pictures, made with charcoal. There was two old dirty calico dresses, and a sun-bonnet, and some women's under-clothes, hanging against the wall, and some men's clothing, too. We put the lot into the canoe; it might come good. There was a boy's old speckled straw hat on the floor; I took that too. And there was a bottle that had had milk in it; and it had a rag stopper for a baby to suck. We would a took the bottle, but it was broke. There was a seedy old chest, and an old hair trunk with the hinges broke. They stood open, but there warn't nothing left in them that was any account. The way things was scattered about, we reckoned the people left in a hurry and warn't fixed so as to carry off most of their stuff.

We got an old tin lantern, and a butcher knife without any handle, and a bran-new Barlow knife worth two bits in any store, and a lot of tallow candles, and a tin candlestick, and a gourd, and a tin cup, and a ratty old bed-quilt off the bed, and a reticule with needles and pins and beeswax and buttons and thread and all such truck in it, and a hatchet and some nails, and a fish-line as thick as my little finger, with some monstrous hooks on it, and a roll of buckskin, and a leather dog-collar, and a horse-shoe, and some vials of medicine that didn't have no label on them; and just as we was leaving I found a tolerable good curry-comb, and Jim he found a ratty old fiddle-bow, and a wooden leg. The straps was broke off of it, but barring that, it was a good enough leg, though it was too long for me and not long enough for Jim, and we couldn't find the other one, though we hunted all around.

And so, take it all around, we made a good haul. When we was ready to shove off, we was a quarter of a mile below the island, and it was pretty broad day; so I made Jim lay down in the canoe and cover up with the quilt, because if he set up, people could tell he was a nigger a good ways off. I paddled over to the Illinois shore, and drifted down most a half a mile doing it. I crept up the dead water under the bank, and hadn't no accidents and didn't see nobody. We got home all safe.

Chapter X

After breakfast I wanted to talk about the dead man and guess out how he come to be killed, but Jim didn't want to. He said it would fetch bad luck; and besides, he said, he might come and ha'nt us; he said a man that warn't buried was more likely to go a-ha'nting around than one that was planted and comfortable. That sounded pretty reasonable, so I didn't say no more; but I couldn't keep from studying over it and wishing I knowed who shot the man, and what they done it for.

We rummaged the clothes we'd got, and found eight dollars in silver sewed up in the lining of an old blanket overcoat. Jim said he reckoned the people in that house stole the coat, because if they'd a knowed the money was there they wouldn't a left it. I said I reckoned they killed him, too; but Jim didn't want to talk about that. I says:

"Now you think it's bad luck; but what did you say when I fetched in the snake-skin that I found on the top of the ridge day before yesterday? You said it was the worst bad luck in the world to touch a snake-skin with my hands. Well, here's your bad luck! We've raked in all this truck and eight dollars besides. I wish we could have some bad luck like this every day, Jim."

"Never you mind, honey, never you mind. Don't you git too peart.° It's a-comin'. Mind I tell you, it's a-comin'."

It did come, too. It was a Tuesday that we had that talk. Well, after dinner Friday, we was laying around in the grass at the upper end of the ridge, and got out of tobacco. I went to the cavern to get some, and

peart: In good spirits.

found a rattlesnake in there. I killed him, and curled him up on the foot of Jim's blanket, ever so natural, thinking there'd be some fun when Jim found him there. Well, by night I forgot all about the snake, and when Jim flung himself down on the blanket while I struck a light, the snake's mate was there, and bit him.

He jumped up yelling, and the first thing the light showed was the varmint curled up and ready for another spring. I laid him out in a second with a stick, and Jim grabbed pap's whisky jug and begun to pour it down.

He was barefooted, and the snake bit him right on the heel. That all comes of my being such a fool as to not remember that wherever you leave a dead snake its mate always comes there and curls around it. Jim told me to chop off the snake's head and throw it away, and then skin the body and roast a piece of it. I done it, and he eat it and said it would help cure him. He made me take off the rattles and tie them around his wrist, too. He said that that would help. Then I slid out quiet and throwed the snakes clear away amongst the bushes; for I warn't going to let Jim find out it was all my fault, not if I could help it.

Jim sucked and sucked at the jug, and now and then he got out of his head and pitched around and yelled; but every time he come to himself he went to sucking at the jug again. His foot swelled up pretty big, and so did his leg; but by-and-by the drunk begun to come, and so I judged he was all right; but I'd druther been bit with a snake than pap's whisky.

Jim was laid up for four days and nights. Then the swelling was all gone and he was around again. I made up my mind I wouldn't ever take aholt of a snake-skin again with my hands, now that I see what had come of it. Jim said he reckoned I would believe him next time. And he said that handling a snake-skin was such awful bad luck that maybe we hadn't got to the end of it yet. He said he druther see the new moon over his left shoulder as much as a thousand times than take up a snake-skin in his hand. Well, I was getting to feel that way myself, though I've always reckoned that looking at the new moon over your left shoulder is one of the carelessest and foolishest things a body can do. Old Hank Bunker done it once, and bragged about it; and in less than two years he got drunk and fell off of the shot tower and spread himself out so that he was just a kind of a layer, as you may say; and they slid him edgeways between two barn doors for a coffin, and buried him so, so they say, but I didn't see it. Pap told me. But anyway, it all come of looking at the moon that way, like a fool.

Well, the days went along, and the river went down between its banks again; and about the first thing we done was to bait one of the big hooks with a skinned rabbit and set it and catch a cat-fish that was as big as a man, being six foot two inches long, and weighed over two hundred pounds. We couldn't handle him, of course; he would a flung us into Illinois. We just set there and watched him rip and tear around till he drownded. We found a brass button in his stomach, and a round ball, and lots of rubbage. We split the ball open with the hatchet, and there was a spool in it. Jim said he'd had it there a long time, to coat it over so and make a ball of it. It was as big a fish as was ever catched in the Mississippi, I reckon. Jim said he hadn't ever seen a bigger one. He would a been worth a good deal over at the village. They peddle out such a fish as that by the pound in the market house there; everybody buys some of him; his meat's as white as snow and makes a good fry.

Next morning I said it was getting slow and dull, and I wanted to get a stirring up, some way. I said I reckoned I would slip over the river and find out what was going on. Jim liked that notion; but he said I must go in the dark and look sharp. Then he studied it over and said, couldn't I put on some of them old things and dress up like a girl? That was a good notion, too. So we shortened up one of the calico gowns and I turned up my trowser-legs to my knees and got into it. Jim hitched it behind with the hooks, and it was a fair fit. I put on the sun-bonnet and tied it under my chin, and then for a body to look in and see my face was like looking down a joint of stove-pipe. Jim said nobody would know me, even in the daytime, hardly. I practiced around all day to get the hang of the things, and by-and-by I could do pretty well in them, only Jim said I didn't walk like a girl; and he said I must quit pulling up my gown to get at my britches pocket. I took notice, and done better.

I started up the Illinois shore in the canoe just after dark.

I started across to the town from a little below the ferry landing, and the drift of the current fetched me in at the bottom of the town. I tied up and started along the bank. There was a light burning in a little shanty that hadn't been lived in for a long time, and I wondered who had took up quarters there. I slipped up and peeped in at the window. There was a woman about forty year old in there, knitting by a candle that was on a pine table. I didn't know her face; she was a stranger, for you couldn't start a face in that town that I didn't know. Now this was lucky, because I was weakening; I was getting afraid I had come; people might know my voice and find me out. But if this woman had been in such a little town two days she could tell me all I wanted to know; so I knocked at the door, and made up my mind I wouldn't forget I was a girl.

Chapter XI

"Come in," says the woman, and I did. She says:

"Take a cheer."

I done it. She looked me all over with her little shiny eyes, and says:

"What might your name be?"

"Sarah Williams."

"Where 'bouts do you live? In this neighborhood?"

"No'm. In Hookerville, seven mile below. I've walked all the way and I'm all tired out."

"Hungry, too, I reckon. I'll find you something."

"No'm, I ain't hungry. I was so hungry I had to stop two mile below here at a farm; so I ain't hungry no more. It's what makes me so late. My mother's down sick, and out of money and everything, and I come to tell my uncle Abner Moore. He lives at the upper end of the town, she says. I hain't ever been here before. Do you know him?"

"No; but I don't know everybody yet. I haven't lived here quite two weeks. It's a considerable ways to the upper end of the town. You better stay here all night. Take off your bonnet."

"No," I says, "I'll rest a while, I reckon, and go on. I ain't afeard of the dark."

She said she wouldn't let me go by myself, but her husband would be in by-and-by, maybe in a hour and a half, and she'd send him along with me. Then she got to talking about her husband, and about her relations up the river, and her relations down the river, and about how much better off they used to was, and how they didn't know but they'd made a mistake coming to our town, instead of letting well alone — and so on and so on, till I was afeard *I* had made a mistake coming to her to find out what was going on in the town; but by-and-by she dropped onto pap and the murder, and then I was pretty willing to let her clatter right along. She told about me and Tom Sawyer finding the six thousand dollars (only she got it ten) and all about pap and what a hard lot he was, and what a hard lot I was, and at last she got down to where I was murdered. I says:

"Who done it? We've heard considerable about these goings on, down in Hookerville, but we don't know who 'twas that killed Huck Finn."

"Well, I reckon there's a right smart chance of people *here* that'd like to know who killed him. Some thinks old Finn done it himself."

"No — is that so?"

"Most everybody thought it at first. He'll never know how nigh he come to getting lynched. But before night they changed around and judged it was done by a runaway nigger named Jim."

"Why *he* ——"

I stopped. I reckoned I better keep still. She run on, and never noticed I had put in at all.

"The nigger run off the very night Huck Finn was killed. So there's a reward out for him — three hundred dollars. And there's a reward out for old Finn too — two hundred dollars. You see, he come to town the morning after the murder, and told about it, and was out with 'em on the ferry-boat hunt, and right away after he up and left. Before night they wanted to lynch him, but he was gone, you see. Well, next day they found out the nigger was gone; they found out he hadn't ben seen sence ten o'clock the night the murder was done. So then they put it on him, you see, and while they was full of it, next day back comes old Finn and went boo-hooing to Judge Thatcher to get money to hunt for the nigger all over Illinois with. The judge give him some, and that evening he got drunk and was around till after midnight with a couple of mighty hard looking strangers, and then went off with them. Well, he hain't come back sence, and they ain't looking for him back till this thing blows over a little, for people thinks now that he killed his boy and fixed things so folks would think robbers done it, and then he'd get Huck's money without having to bother a long time with a lawsuit. People do say he warn't any too good to do it. Oh, he's sly, I reckon. If he don't come back for a year, he'll be all right. You can't prove anything on him, you know; everything will be quieted down then, and he'll walk into Huck's money as easy as nothing."

"Yes, I reckon so, 'm. I don't see nothing in the way of it. Has everybody quit thinking the nigger done it?"

"Oh, no, not everybody. A good many thinks he done it. But they'll get the nigger pretty soon, now, and maybe they can scare it out of him."

"Why, are they after him yet?"

"Well, you're innocent, ain't you! Does three hundred dollars lay round every day for people to pick up? Some folks thinks the nigger ain't far from here. I'm one of them — but I hain't talked it around. A few days ago I was talking with an old couple that lives next door in the log shanty, and they happened to say hardly anybody ever goes to that island over yonder that they call Jackson's Island. Don't anybody live there? says I. No, nobody, says they. I didn't say any more, but I done some thinking. I was pretty near certain I'd seen smoke over there, about the head of the island, a day or two before that, so I says to myself, like as not that nigger's hiding over there; anyway, says I, it's worth the trouble to give the place a hunt. I hain't seen any smoke sence, so I reckon maybe he's gone, if it was him; but husband's going over to see — him and another man. He was gone up the river; but he got back to-day and I told him as soon as he got here two hours ago."

I had got so uneasy I couldn't set still. I had to do something with my hands; so I took up a needle off of the table and went to threading it. My hands shook, and I was making a bad job of it. When the woman stopped talking, I looked up, and she was looking at me pretty curious, and smiling a little. I put down the needle and thread and let on to be interested — and I was, too — and says:

"Three hundred dollars is a power of money. I wish my mother could get it. Is your husband going over there to-night?"

"Oh, yes. He went up town with the man I was telling you of, to get a boat and see if they could borrow another gun. They'll go over after midnight."

"Couldn't they see better if they was to wait till daytime?"

"Yes. And couldn't the nigger see better, too? After midnight he'll likely be asleep, and they can slip around through the woods and hunt up his camp fire all the better for the dark, if he's got one."

"I didn't think of that."

The woman kept looking at me pretty curious, and I didn't feel a bit comfortable. Pretty soon she says:

"What did you say your name was, honey?"

"M — Mary Williams."

Somehow it didn't seem to me that I said it was Mary before, so I didn't look up; seemed to me I said it was Sarah; so I felt sort of cornered, and was afeared maybe I was looking it, too. I wished the woman would say something more; the longer she set still, the uneasier I was. But now she says:

"Honey, I thought you said it was Sarah when you first come in?"

"Oh, yes'm, I did. Sarah Mary Williams. Sarah's my first name. Some calls me Sarah, some calls me Mary."

"Oh, that's the way of it?"

"Yes'm."

I was feeling better, then, but I wished I was out of there, anyway. I couldn't look up yet.

Well, the woman fell to talking about how hard times was, and how poor they had to live, and how the rats was as free as if they owned the place, and so forth, and so on, and then I got easy again. She was right about the rats. You'd see one stick his nose out of a hole in the corner every little while. She said she had to have things handy to throw at them when she was alone, or they wouldn't give her no peace. She showed me a bar of lead, twisted up into a knot, and said she was a good shot with it generly, but she'd wrenched her arm a day or two ago, and didn't know whether she could throw true, now. But she watched for a chance, and directly she banged away at a rat, but she missed him wide, and said "Ouch!" it hurt her arm so. Then she told me to try for the next one. I wanted to be getting away before the old man got back, but of course I didn't let on. I got the thing, and the first rat that showed his nose I let drive, and if he'd a stayed where he was he'd a been a tolerable sick rat. She said that that was first-rate, and she reckoned I would hive the next one. She went and got the lump of lead and fetched it back and brought along a hank of yarn, which she wanted me to help her with. I held up my two hands and she put the hank over them and went on talking about her and her husband's matters. But she broke off to say:

"Keep your eye on the rats. You better have the lead in your lap, handy."

So she dropped the lump into my lap, just at that moment, and I clapped my legs together on it and she went on talking. But only about a minute. Then she took off the hank and looked me straight in the face, but very pleasant, and says:

"Come, now — what's your real name?"

"Wh-what, mum?"

"What's your real name? Is it Bill, or Tom, or Bob? — or what is it?"

I reckon I shook like a leaf, and I didn't know hardly what to do. But I says:

"Please to don't poke fun at a poor girl like me, mum. If I'm in the way, here, I'll ——"

"No, you won't. Set down and stay where you are. I ain't going to hurt you, and I ain't going to tell on you, nuther. You just tell me your secret, and trust me. I'll keep it; and what's more, I'll help you. So'll my old man, if you want him to. You see, you're a runaway 'prentice — that's all. It ain't anything. There ain't any harm in it. You've been treated bad, and you made up your mind to cut. Bless you, child, I wouldn't tell on you. Tell me all about it, now — that's a good boy."

So I said it wouldn't be no use to try to play it any longer, and I would just make a clean breast and tell her everything, but she mustn't go back on her promise. Then I told her my father and mother was dead, and the law had bound me out to a mean old farmer in the country thirty mile back from the river, and he treated me so bad I couldn't stand it no longer; he went away to be gone a couple of days, and so I took my chance and stole some of his daughter's old clothes, and cleared out, and I had been three nights coming the thirty miles; I traveled nights, and hid day-times and slept, and the bag of bread and meat I carried from home lasted me all the way and I had a plenty. I said I believed my uncle Abner Moore would take care of me, and so that was why I struck out for this town of Goshen."

"Goshen, child? This ain't Goshen. This is St. Petersburg. Goshen's ten mile further up the river. Who told you this was Goshen?"

"Why, a man I met at day-break this morning, just as I was going to turn into the woods for my regular sleep. He told me when the roads forked I must take the right hand, and five mile would fetch me to Goshen."

"He was drunk I reckon. He told you just exactly wrong."

"Well, he did act like he was drunk, but it ain't no matter now. I got to be moving along. I'll fetch Goshen before day-light."

"Hold on a minute. I'll put you up a snack to eat. You might want it."

So she put me up a snack, and says:

"Say — when a cow's laying down, which end of her gets up first? Answer up prompt, now — don't stop to study over it. Which end gets up first?"

"The hind end, mum."

"Well, then, a horse?"

"The for'rard end, mum."

"Which side of a tree does the most moss grow on?"

"North side."

"If fifteen cows is browsing on a hillside, how many of them eats with their heads pointed the same direction?"

"The whole fifteen, mum."

"Well, I reckon you *have* lived in the country. I thought maybe you was trying to hocus me again. What's your real name, now?"

"George Peters, mum."

"Well, try to remember it, George. Don't forget and tell me it's Elexander before you go, and then get out by saying it's George-Elexander when I catch you. And don't go about women in that old calico. You do a girl tolerable poor, but you might fool men, maybe. Bless you, child, when you set out to thread a needle, don't hold the thread still and fetch the needle up to it; hold the needle still and poke the thread at it — that's the way a woman most always does; but a man always does 'tother way. And when you throw at a rat or any-thing, hitch yourself up a tip-toe, and fetch your hand up over your head as awkard as you can, and miss your rat about six or seven foot. Throw stiff-armed from the shoulder, like there was a pivot there for it to turn on — like a girl; not from the wrist and elbow, with your arm out to one side, like a boy. And mind you, when a girl tries to catch any-thing in her lap, she throws her knees apart; she don't clap them together, the way you did when you catched the lump of lead. Why, I spotted you for a boy when you was threading the needle; and I con-trived the other things just to make certain. Now trot along to your uncle, Sarah Mary Williams George Elexander Peters, and if you get into trouble you send word to Mrs. Judith Loftus, which is me, and I'll do what I can to get you out of it. Keep the river road, all the way, and next time you tramp, take shoes and socks with you. The river road's a rocky one, and your feet 'll be in a condition when you get to Goshen, I reckon."

I went up the bank about fifty yards, and then I doubled on my tracks and slipped back to where my canoe was, a good piece below the house. I jumped in and was off in a hurry. I went up stream far enough to make the head of the island, and then started across. I took off the sun-bonnet, for I didn't want no blinders on, then. When I was about the middle, I hear the clock begin to strike; so I stops and listens; the sound come faint over the water, but clear — eleven. When I struck the head of the island I never waited to blow, though I was most winded, but I shoved right into the timber where my old camp used to be, and started a good fire there on a high-and-dry spot.

Then I jumped in the canoe and dug out for our place a mile and a half below, as hard as I could go. I landed, and slopped through the timber and up the ridge and into the cavern. There Jim laid, sound asleep on the ground. I roused him out and says:

"Git up and hump yourself,° Jim! There ain't a minute to lose. They're after us!"

Jim never asked no questions, he never said a word; but the way he worked for the next half an hour showed about how he was scared. By that time everything we had in the world was on our raft and she was

hump yourself: Hurry up.

ready to be shoved out from the willow cove where she was hid. We put out the camp fire at the cavern the first thing, and didn't show a candle outside after that.

I took the canoe out from shore a little piece and took a look, but if there was a boat around I couldn't see it, for stars and shadows ain't good to see by. Then we got out the raft and slipped along down in the shade, past the foot of the island dead still, never saying a word.

Chapter XII

It must a been close onto one o'clock when we got below the island at last, and the raft did seem to go mighty slow. If a boat was to come along, we was going to take to the canoe and break for the Illinois shore; and it was well a boat didn't come, for we hadn't ever thought to put the gun into the canoe, or a fishing-line or anything to eat. We was in ruther too much of a sweat to think of so many things. It warn't good judgment to put *everything* on the raft.

If the men went to the island, I just expect they found the camp fire I built, and watched it all night for Jim to come. Anyways, they stayed away from us, and if my building the fire never fooled them it warn't no fault of mine. I played it as low-down on them as I could.

When the first streak of day begun to show, we tied up to a tow-head in a big bend on the Illinois side, and hacked off cotton-wood branches with the hatchet and covered up the raft with them so she looked like there had been a cave-in in the bank there. A tow-head is a sand-bar that has cotton-woods on it as thick as harrow-teeth.

We had mountains on the Missouri shore and heavy timber on the Illinois side, and the channel was down the Missouri shore at that place, so we warn't afraid of anybody running across us. We laid there all day and watched the rafts and steamboats spin down the Missouri shore, and up-bound steamboats fight the big river in the middle. I told Jim all about the time I had jabbering with that woman; and Jim said she was a smart one, and if she was to start after us herself *she* wouldn't set down and watch a camp fire — no, sir, she'd fetch a dog. Well, then, I said, why couldn't she tell her husband to fetch a dog? Jim said he bet she did think of it by the time the men was ready to start, and he believed they must a gone up town to get a dog and so they lost all that time, or else we wouldn't be here on a tow-head sixteen or seventeen mile below the village — no, indeedy, we would be in that same old town again. So I said I didn't care what was the reason they didn't get us, as long as they didn't.

When it was beginning to come on dark, we poked our heads out of the cottonwood thicket and looked up, and down, and across; nothing in sight; so Jim took up some of the top planks of the raft and built a snug wigwam to get under in blazing weather and rainy, and to keep the things dry. Jim made a floor for the wigwam, and raised it a foot or more above the level of the raft, so now the blankets and all the traps was out of the reach of steamboat waves. Right in the middle of the wigwam we made a layer of dirt about five or six inches deep with a frame around it for to hold it to its place; this was to build a fire on in sloppy weather or chilly; the wigwam would keep it from being seen. We made an extra steering oar, too, because one of the others might get broke, on a snag or something. We fixed up a short forked stick to hang the old lantern on; because we must always light the lantern whenever we see a steamboat coming down stream, to keep from getting run over; but we wouldn't have to light it for upstream boats unless we see we was in what they call a "crossing"; for the river was pretty high yet, very low banks being still a little under water; so up-bound boats didn't always run the channel, but hunted easy water.

This second night we run between seven and eight hours, with a current that was making over four mile an hour. We catched fish, and talked, and we took a swim now and then to keep off sleepiness. It was kind of solemn, drifting down the big still river, laying on our backs looking up at the stars, and we didn't ever feel like talking loud, and it warn't often that we laughed, only a little kind of a low chuckle. We had mighty good weather, as a general thing, and nothing ever happened to us at all, that night, nor the next, nor the next.

Every night we passed towns, some of them away up on black hill-sides, nothing but just a shiny bed of lights, not a house could you see. The fifth night we passed St. Louis, and it was like the whole world lit up. In St. Petersburg they used to say there was twenty or thirty thousand people in St. Louis, but I never believed it till I see that wonderful spread of lights at two o'clock that still night. There warn't a sound there; everybody was asleep.

Every night, now, I used to slip ashore, towards ten o'clock, at some little village, and buy ten or fifteen cents' worth of meal or bacon or other stuff to eat; and sometimes I lifted a chicken that warn't roosting comfortable, and took him along. Pap always said, take a chicken when you get a chance, because if you don't want him yourself you can easy find somebody that does, and a good deed ain't ever forgot. I never see pap when he didn't want the chicken himself, but that is what he used to say, anyway.

Mornings, before daylight, I slipped into corn fields and borrowed a watermelon, or a mushmelon, or a punkin, or some new corn, or things of that kind. Pap always said it warn't no harm to borrow things, if you was meaning to pay them back, sometime; but the widow said it warn't anything but a soft name for stealing, and no decent body would do it. Jim said he reckoned the widow was partly right and pap was partly right; so the best way would be for us to pick out two or three things from the list and say we wouldn't borrow them any more — then he reckoned it wouldn't be no harm to borrow the others. So we talked it over all one night, drifting along down the river, trying to make up our minds whether to drop the watermelons, or the cantelopes, or the mushmelons, or what. But towards daylight we got it all settled satisfactory, and concluded to drop crabapples and p'simmons. We warn't feeling just right, before that, but it was all comfortable now. I was glad the way it come out, too, because crabapples ain't ever good, and the p'simmons wouldn't be ripe for two or three months yet.

We shot a water-fowl, now and then, that got up too early in the morning or didn't go to bed early enough in the evening. Take it all around, we lived pretty high.

The fifth night below St. Louis we had a big storm after midnight, with a power of thunder and lightning, and the rain poured down in a solid sheet. We stayed in the wigwam and let the raft take care of itself. When the lightning glared out we could see a big straight river ahead, and high rocky bluffs on both sides. By-and-by says I, "Hel-*lo*, Jim, looky yonder!" It was a steamboat that had killed herself on a rock. We was drifting straight down for her. The lightning showed her very distinct. She was leaning over, with part of her upper deck above water, and you could see every little chimbly-guy clean and clear, and a chair by the big bell, with an old slouch hat hanging on the back of it when the flashes come.

Well, it being away in the night, and stormy, and all so mysterious-like, I felt just the way any other boy would a felt when I see that wreck laying there so mournful and lonesome in the middle of the river. I wanted to get aboard of her and slink around a little, and see what there was there. So I says:

"Le's land on her, Jim."

But Jim was dead against it, at first. He says:

"I doan' want to go fool'n 'long er no wrack. We's doin' blame' well, en we better let blame' well alone, as de good book says. Like as not dey's a watchman on dat wrack.'

"Watchman your grandmother," I says; "there ain't nothing to watch but the texas° and the pilot-house; and do you reckon anybody's going to resk his life for a texas and a pilot-house such a night as this, when it's likely to break up and wash off down the river any minute?" Jim couldn't say nothing to that, so he didn't try. "And besides," I says, "we might borrow something worth having, out of the captain's state-room. Seegars, *I* bet you — and cost five cents apiece, solid cash. Steamboat captains is always rich, and get sixty dollars a month, and *they* don't care a cent what a thing costs, you know, long as they want it. Stick a candle in your pocket; I can't rest, Jim, till we give her a rummaging. Do you reckon Tom Sawyer would ever go by this thing? Not for pie, he wouldn't. He'd call it an adventure — that's what he'd call it; and he'd land on that wreck if it was his last act. And wouldn't he throw style into it? — wouldn't he spread himself, nor nothing? Why, you'd think it was Christopher C'lumbus discovering Kingdom-Come. I wish Tom Sawyer *was* here."

Jim he grumbled a little, but give in. He said we mustn't talk any more than we could help, and then talk mighty low. The lightning showed us the wreck again, just in time, and we fetched the starboard derrick, and made fast there.

The deck was high out, here. We went sneaking down the slope of it to labboard,° in the dark, towards the texas, feeling our way slow with our feet, and spreading our hands out to fend off the guys,° for it was so dark we couldn't see no sign of them. Pretty soon we struck the forward end of the skylight, and clumb onto it; and the next step fetched us in front of the captain's door, which was open, and by Jimminy, away down through the texas-hall we see a light! and all in the same second we seem to hear low voices in yonder!

Jim whispered and said he was feeling powerful sick, and told me to come along. I says, all right; and was going to start for the raft; but just then I heard a voice wail out and say:

"Oh, please don't, boys; I swear I won't ever tell!"

Another voice said, pretty loud:

"It's a lie, Jim Turner. You've acted this way before. You always want more'n your share of the truck, and you've always got it, too, because you've swore 't if you didn't you'd tell. But this time you've said

---

texas: The cabin on the uppermost deck of a steamboat, usually used by officers; on Mississippi steamboats, cabins were named after states — the texas was the largest cabin. **labboard:** Larboard, the left side of the ship; also called *port*.   **guys:** Guywires.

it jest one time too many. You're the meanest, treacherousest hound in this country."

By this time Jim was gone for the raft. I was just a-biling with curiosity; and I says to myself, Tom Sawyer wouldn't back out now, and so I won't either; I'm agoing to see what's going on here. So I dropped on my hands and knees, in the little passage, and crept aft in the dark, till there warn't but about one stateroom betwixt me and the cross-hall of the texas. Then, in there I see a man stretched on the floor and tied hand and foot, and two men standing over him, and one of them had a dim lantern in his hand, and the other one had a pistol. This one kept pointing the pistol at the man's head on the floor and saying —

"I'd *like* to! And I orter, too, a mean skunk!"

The man on the floor would shrivel up, and say: "Oh, please don't, Bill — I hain't ever goin' to tell."

And every time he said that, the man with the lantern would laugh, and say:

"'Deed you *ain't!* You never said no truer thing 'n that, you bet you." And once he said: "Hear him beg! and yit if we hadn't got the best of him and tied him, he'd a killed us both. And what *for?* Jist for noth'n. Jist because we stood on our *rights* — that's what for. But I lay you ain't agoin' to threaten nobody any more, Jim Turner. Put *up* that pistol, Bill."

Bill says:

"I don't want to, Jake Packard. I'm for killin' him — and didn't he kill old Hatfield jist the same way — and don't he deserve it?"

"But I don't *want* him killed, and I've got my reasons for it."

"Bless yo' heart for them words, Jake Packard! I'll never forgit you, long's I live!" says the man on the floor, sort of blubbering.

Packard didn't take no notice of that, but hung up his lantern on a nail, and started towards where I was, there in the dark, and motioned Bill to come. I crawfished as fast as I could, about two yards, but the boat slanted so that I couldn't make very good time; so to keep from getting run over and catched I crawled into a stateroom on the upper side. The man come a-pawing along in the dark, and when Packard got to my stateroom, he says:

"Here — come in here."

And in he come, and Bill after him. But before they got in, I was up in the upper berth, cornered, and sorry I come. Then they stood there, with their hands on the ledge of the berth, and talked. I couldn't see them, but I could tell where they was, by the whisky they'd been having. I was glad I didn't drink whisky; but it wouldn't made much difference, anyway, because most of the time they couldn't a treed me because I didn't breathe. I was too scared. And besides, a body *couldn't* breathe, and hear such talk. They talked low and earnest. Bill wanted to kill Turner. He says:

"He's said he'll tell, and he will. If we was to give both our shares to him *now*, it wouldn't make no difference after the row, and the way we've served him. Shore's you're born, he'll turn State's evidence; now you hear *me*. I'm for putting him out of his troubles."

"So'm I," says Packard, very quiet.

"Blame it, I'd sorter begun to think you wasn't. Well, then, that's all right. Les' go and do it."

"Hold on a minute; I hain't had my say yit. You listen to me. Shooting's good, but there's quieter ways if the thing's *got* to be done. But what *I* say, is this; it ain't good sense to go court'n around after a halter, if you can git at what you're up to in some way that's jist as good and at the same time don't bring you into no resks. Ain't that so?"

"You bet it is. But how you goin' to manage it this time?"

"Well, my idea is this: we'll rustle around and gether up whatever pickins we've overlooked in the staterooms, and shove for shore and hide the truck. Then we'll wait. Now I say it ain't agoin' to be more 'n two hours befo' this wrack breaks up and washes off down the river. See? He'll be drownded, and won't have nobody to blame for it but his own self. I reckon that's a considerble sight better'n killin' of him. I'm unfavorable to killin' a man as long as you can git around it; it ain't good sense, it ain't good morals. Ain't I right?"

"Yes — I reck'n you are. But s'pose she *don't* break up and wash off?"

"Well, we can wait the two hours, anyway, and see, can't we?"

"All right, then; come along."

So they started, and I lit out, all in a cold sweat, and scrambled forward. It was dark as pitch there; but I said in a kind of a coarse whisper, "Jim!" and he answered up, right at my elbow, with a sort of a moan, and I says:

"Quick, Jim, it ain't no time for fooling around and moaning; there's a gang of murderers in yonder, and if we don't hunt up their boat and set her drifting down the river so these fellows can't get away from the wreck, there's one of 'em going to be in a bad fix. But if we find their boat we can put *all* of 'em in a bad fix — for the Sheriff 'll get 'em. Quick — hurry! I'll hunt the labboard side, you hunt the stabboard. You start at the raft, and ——"

"Oh, my lordy, lordy! *Raf'*? Dey ain' no raf' no mo', she done broke loose en gone! — 'en here we is!"

Chapter XIII

Well, I catched my breath and most fainted. Shut up on a wreck with such a gang as that! But it warn't no time to be sentimentering. We'd *got* to find that boat, now — had to have it for ourselves. So we went a-quaking and shaking down the stabboard side, and slow work it was, too — seemed a week before we got to the stern. No sign of a boat. Jim said he didn't believe he could go any further — so scared he hadn't hardly any strength left, he said. But I said come on, if we get left on this wreck, we are in a fix, sure. So on we prowled, again. We struck for the stern of the texas, and found it, and then scrabbled along forwards on the skylight, hanging on from shutter to shutter, for the edge of the skylight was in the water. When we got pretty close to the cross-hall door, there was the skiff, sure enough! I could just barely see her. I felt ever so thankful. In another second I would a been aboard of her; but just then the door opened. One of the men stuck his head out, only about a couple of foot from me, and I thought I was gone; but he jerked it in again, and says:

"Heave that blame lantern out o' sight, Bill!"

He flung a bag of something into the boat, and then got in himself, and set down. It was Packard. Then Bill *he* come out and got in. Packard says, in a low voice:

"All ready — shove off!"

I couldn't hardly hang onto the shutters, I was so weak. But Bill says:

"Hold on — 'd you go through him?"

"No. Didn't you?"

"No. So he's got his share o' the cash, yet."

"Well, then, come along — no use to take truck and leave money."

"Say — won't he suspicion what we're up to?"

"Maybe he won't. But we got to have it anyway. Come along."

So they got out and went in.

The door slammed to, because it was on the careened side; and in a half second I was in the boat, and Jim come a tumbling after me. I out with my knife and cut the rope, and away we went!

We didn't touch an oar, and we didn' speak nor whisper, nor hardly even breathe. We went gliding swift along, dead silent, past the tip of the paddle-box, and past the stern; then in a second or two more we was a hundred yards below the wreck, and the darkness soaked her up, every last sign of her, and we was safe, and knowed it.

When we was three or four hundred yards down stream, we see the lantern show like a little spark at the texas door, for a second, and we knowed by that that the rascals had missed their boat, and was beginning to understand that they was in just as much trouble, now, as Jim Turner was.

Then Jim manned the oars, and we took out after our raft. Now was the first time that I begun to worry about the men — I reckon I hadn't had time to before. I begun to think how dreadful it was, even for murderers, to be in such a fix. I says to myself, there ain't no telling but I might come to be a murderer myself, yet, and then how would *I* like it? So says I to Jim:

"The first light we see, we'll land a hundred yards below it or above it, in a place where it's a good hiding-place for you and the skiff, and then I'll go and fix up some kind of a yarn, and get somebody to go for that gang and get them out of their scrape, so they can be hung when their time comes."

But that idea was a failure; for pretty soon it begun to storm again, and this time worse than ever. The rain poured down, and never a light showed; everybody in bed, I reckon. We boomed along down the river, watching for lights and watching for our raft. After a long time the rain let up, but the clouds staid, and the lightning kept whimpering, and by-and-by a flash showed us a black thing ahead, floating, and we made for it.

It was the raft, and mighty glad was we to get aboard of it again. We seen a light, now, away down to the right, on shore. So I said I would go for it. The skiff was half full of plunder which that gang had stole, there on the wreck. We hustled it onto the raft in a pile, and I told Jim to float along down, and show a light when he judged he had gone about two mile, and keep it burning till I come; then I manned my oars and shoved for the light. As I got down towards it, three or four more showed — up on a hillside. It was a village. I closed in above the shore-light, and laid on my oars and floated. As I went by, I see it was a lantern hanging on the jackstaff of a double-hull ferry-boat. I skimmed around for the watchman, a-wondering whereabouts he slept; and by-and-by I found him roosting on the bitts, forward, with his head down between his knees. I give his shoulder two or three little shoves, and begun to cry.

He stirred up, in a kind of a startlish way; but when he see it was only me, he took a good gap and stretch, and then he says:

"Hello, what's up? Don't cry, bub. What's the trouble?"

I says:

"Pap, and mam, and sis, and ——"

Then I broke down. He says:

"Oh, dang it, now, *don't* take on so, we all has to have our troubles and this'n 'll come out all right. What's the matter with 'em?"

"They're — they're — are you the watchman of the boat?"

"Yes," he says, kind of pretty-well-satisfied like. "I'm the captain and the owner, and the mate, and the pilot, and watchman, and head deck-hand; and sometimes I'm the freight and passengers. I ain't as rich as old Jim Hornback, and I can't be so blame' generous and good to Tom, Dick and Harry as what he is, and slam around money the way he does; but I've told him a many a time 't I wouldn't trade places with him; for, says I, a sailor's life's the life for me, and I'm derned if *I'd* live two mile out o' town, where there ain't nothing ever goin' on, not for all his spondulicks° and as much more on top of it. Says I ——"

I broke in and says:

"They're in an awful peck of trouble, and ——"

" *Who* is?"

"Why, pap, and mam, and sis, and Miss Hooker; and if you'd take your ferry-boat and go up there ——"

"Up where? Where are they?"

"On the wreck."

"What wreck?"

"Why, there ain't but one."

"What, you don't mean the *Walter Scott?*"

"Yes."

"Good land! what are they doin' *there*, for gracious sakes?"

"Well, they didn't go there a-purpose."

"I bet they didn't! Why, great goodness, there ain't no chance for 'em if they don't git off mighty quick! Why, how in the nation did they ever git into such a scrape?"

"Easy enough. Miss Hooker was a-visiting, up there to the town ——"

"Yes, Booth's Landing — go on."

"She was a-visiting, there at Booth's Landing, and just in the edge of the evening she started over with her nigger woman in the horse-ferry, to stay all night at her friend's house, Miss What-you-may-call-her, I disremember her name, and they lost their steering-oar, and

spondulicks: Money, cash.

swung around and went a-floating down, stern-first, about two mile, and saddle-baggsed on the wreck, and the ferry man and the nigger woman and the horses was all lost, but Miss Hooker she made a grab and got aboard the wreck. Well, about an hour after dark, we come along down in our trading-scow, and it was so dark we didn't notice the wreck till we was right on it; and so *we* saddle-baggsed; but all of us was saved but Bill Whipple — and oh, he *was* the best cretur! — I most wish't it had been me, I do."

"My George! It's the beatenest thing I ever struck. And *then* what did you all do?"

"Well, we hollered and took on, but it's so wide there, we couldn't make nobody hear. So pap said somebody got to get ashore and get help somehow. I was the only one that could swim, so I made a dash for it, and Miss Hooker she said if I didn't strike help sooner, come here and hunt up her uncle, and he'd fix the thing. I made the land about a mile below, and been fooling along ever since, trying to get people to do something, but they said, 'What, in such a night and such a current? there ain't no sense in it; go for the steam-ferry.' Now if you'll go, and ——"

"By Jackson, I'd *like* to, and blame it I don't know but I will; but who in the dingnation's agoin' to *pay* for it? Do you reckon your pap ——"

"Why *that's* all right. Miss Hooker she told me, *particular,* that her uncle Hornback ——"

"Great guns! is *he* her uncle? Looky here, you break for that light over yonder-way, and turn out west when you git there, and about a quarter of a mile out you'll come to the tavern; tell 'em to dart you out to Jim Hornback's and he'll foot the bill. And don't you fool around any, because he'll want to know the news. Tell him I'll have his niece all safe before he can get to town. Hump yourself, now; I'm agoing up around the corner here, to roust out my engineer."

I struck for the light, but as soon as he turned the corner I went back and got into my skiff and bailed her out and then pulled up shore in the easy water about six hundred yards, and tucked myself in among some woodboats; for I couldn't rest easy till I could see the ferry-boat start. But take it all around, I was feeling ruther comfortable on accounts of taking all this trouble for that gang, for not many would a done it. I wished the widow knowed about it. I judged she would be proud of me for helping these rapscallions, because rapscallions and dead beats is the kind the widow and good people takes the most interest in.

Well, before long, here comes the wreck, dim and dusky, sliding along down! A kind of cold shiver went through me, and then I struck out for her. She was very deep, and I see in a minute there warn't much chance for anybody being alive in her. I pulled all around her and hollered a little, but there wasn't any answer; all dead still. I felt a little bit heavy-hearted about the gang, but not much, for I reckoned if they could stand it, I could.

Then here comes the ferry-boat; so I shoved for the middle of the river on a long down-stream slant; and when I judged I was out of eye-reach, I laid on my oars, and looked back and see her go and smell around the wreck for Miss Hooker's remainders, because the captain would know her uncle Hornback would want them; and then pretty soon the ferry-boat give it up and went for shore, and I laid into my work and went a-booming down the river.

It did seem a powerful long time before Jim's light showed up; and when it did show, it looked like it was a thousand mile off. By the time I got there the sky was beginning to get a little gray in the east; so we struck for an island, and hid the raft, and sunk the skiff, and turned in and slept like dead people.

Chapter XIV

By-and-by, when we got up, we turned over the truck the gang had stole off of the wreck, and found boots, and blankets, and clothes, and all sorts of other things, and a lot of books, and a spyglass, and three boxes of seegars. We hadn't ever been this rich before, in neither of our lives. The seegars was prime. We laid off all the afternoon in the woods talking, and me reading the books, and having a general good time. I told Jim all about what happened inside the wreck, and at the ferry-boat; and I said these kinds of things was adventures; but he said he didn't want no more adventures. He said that when I went in the texas and he crawled back to get on the raft and found her gone, he nearly died; because he judged it was all up with *him*, anyway it could be fixed; for if he didn't get saved he would get drownded; and if he did get saved, whoever saved him would send him back home so as to get the reward, and then Miss Watson would sell him South, sure. Well, he was right; he was most always right; he had an uncommon level head, for a nigger.

I read considerable to Jim about kings, and dukes, and earls, and such, and how gaudy they dressed, and how much style they put on, and called each other your majesty, and your grace, and your lordship, and so on, 'stead of mister; and Jim's eyes bugged out, and he was interested. He says:

"I didn' know dey was so many un um. I hain't hearn 'bout none un um, skasely, but ole King Sollermun, onless you counts dem kings dat's in a pack er k'yards. How much do a king git?"

"Get?" I says; "why, they get a thousand dollars a month if they want it; they can have just as much as they want; everything belongs to them."

"*Ain'* dat gay? En what dey got to do, Huck?"

"*They* don't do nothing! Why how you talk. They just set around."

"No — is dat so?"

"Of course it is. They just set around. Except maybe when there 's a war; then they go to the war. But other times they just lazy around; or go hawking — just hawking and sp — Sh! — d' you hear a noise?"

We skipped out and looked; but it warn't nothing but the flutter of a steamboat's wheel, away down coming around the point; so we come back.

"Yes," says I, "and other times, when things is dull, they fuss with the parlyment; and if everybody don't go just so he whacks their heads off. But mostly they hang round the harem."

"Roun' de which?"

"Harem."

"What's de harem?"

"The place where he keep his wives. Don't you know about the harem? Solomon had one; he had about a million wives."

"Why, yes, dat's so; I — I'd done forgot it. A harem's a bo'd'n-house,° I reck'n. Mos' likely dey has rackety times in de nussery. En I reck'n de wives quarrels considable; en dat 'crease de racket. Yit dey say Sollermun de wises' man dat ever live'. I doan' take no stock in dat. Bekase why: would a wise man want to live in de mids' er sich a blim-blammin' all de time? No — 'deed he wouldn't. A wise man 'ud take en buil' a biler-factry;° en den he could shet *down* de biler-factry when he want to res'."

"Well, but he *was* the wisest man, anyway; because the widow she told me so, her own self."

"I doan k'yer what de widder say, he *warn't* no wise man, nuther. He had some er de dad-fetchedes' ways I ever see. Does you know 'bout dat chile dat he 'uz gwyne to chop in two?"

---

bo'd'n-house: Boarding house.   **biler-factry:** Twain's coinage to mean great noise or pandemonium.

"Yes, the widow told me all about it."

"*Well,* den! Warn' dat de beatenes' notion in de worl'? You jes' take en look at it a minute. Dah's de stump, dah — dat's one er de women; heah's you — dat's de yuther one; I's Sollermun; en dish-yer dollar bill's de chile. Bofe un you claims it. What does I do? Does I shin aroun' mongs' de neighbors en fine out which un you de bill *do* b'long to, en han' it over to de right one, all safe en soun', de way dat anybody dat had any gumption would? No — I take en whack de bill in *two,* en give half un it to you, en de yuther half to de yuther woman. Dat's de way Sollermun was gwyne to do wid de chile. Now I want to ast you: what's de use er dat half a bill? — can't buy noth'n wid it. En what use is a half a chile? I would'n give a dern for a million un um."

"But hang it, Jim, you've clean missed the point — blame it, you've missed it a thousand mile."

"Who? Me? Go 'long. Doan' talk to *me* 'bout yo' pints. I reck'n I knows sense when I sees it; en dey ain' no sense in sich doin's as dat. De 'spute warn't 'bout a half a chile, de 'spute was 'bout a whole chile; en de man dat think he kin settle a 'spute 'bout a whole chile wid a half a chile, doan' know enough to come in out'n de rain. Doan' talk to me 'bout Sollermun, Huck, I knows him by de back."

"But I tell you you don't get the point."

"Blame de pint! I reck'n I knows what I knows. En mine you, de *real* pint is down furder — it's down deeper. It lays in de way Sollermun was raised. You take a man dat's got on'y one er two chillen; is dat man gwyne to be waseful o' chillen? No, he ain't; he can't 'ford it. *He* know how to value 'em. But you take a man dat's got 'bout five million chillen runnin' roun' de house, en it's diffunt. *He* as soon chop a chile in two as a cat. Dey's plenty mo'. A chile er two, mo' er less, warn't no consekens to Sollermun, dad fetch him!"

I never see such a nigger. If he got a notion in his head once, there warn't no getting it out again. He was the most down on Solomon of any nigger I ever see. So I went to talking about other kings, and let Solomon slide. I told about Louis Sixteenth that got his head cut off in France long time ago; and about his little boy the dolphin, that would a been a king, but they took and shut him up in jail, and some say he died there.

"Po' little chap."

"But some says he got out and got away, and come to America."

"Dat's good! But he'll be pooty lonesome — dey ain' no kings here, is dey, Huck?"

"No."

"Den he cain't git no situation. What he gwyne to do?"

"Well, I don't know. Some of them gets on the police, and some of them learns people how to talk French."

"Why, Huck, doan' de French people talk de same way we does?"

"*No*, Jim; you couldn't understand a word they said — not a single word."

"Well, now, I be ding-busted! How do dat come?"

"*I* don't know; but it's so. I got some of their jabber out of a book. Spose a man was to come to you and say *Polly-voo-franzy* — what would you think?"

"I wouldn' think nuff'n; I'd take en bust him over de head. Dat is, if he warn't white. I wouldn't 'low no nigger to call me dat."

"Shucks, it ain't calling you anything. It's only saying do you know how to talk French."

"Well, den, why couldn't he *say* it?"

"Why, he *is* a-saying it. That's a Frenchman's *way* of saying it."

"Well, it's a blame' ridicklous way, en I doan' want to hear no mo' 'bout it. Dey ain' no sense in it."

"Looky here, Jim; does a cat talk like we do?"

"No, a cat don't."

"Well, does a cow?"

"No, a cow don't, nuther."

"Does a cat talk like a cow, or a cow talk like a cat?"

"No, dey don't."

"It's natural and right for 'em to talk different from each other, ain't it?"

"'Course."

"And ain't it natural and right for a cat and a cow to talk different from *us*?"

"Why, mos' sholy it is."

"Well, then, why ain't it natural and right for a *Frenchman* to talk different from us? You answer me that."

"Is a cat a man, Huck?"

"No."

"Well, den, dey ain't no sense in a cat talkin' like a man. Is a cow a man? — er is a cow a cat?"

"No, she ain't either of them."

"Well, den, she ain' got no business to talk like either one er the yuther of 'em. Is a Frenchman a man?"

"Yes."

"*Well*, den! Dad blame it, why doan' he *talk* like a man? You answer me *dat!*"

I see it warn't no use wasting words — you can't learn a nigger to argue. So I quit.

Chapter XV

We judged that three nights more would fetch us to Cairo, at the bottom of Illinois, where the Ohio River comes in, and that was what we was after. We would sell the raft and get on a steamboat and go way up the Ohio amongst the free States, and then be out of trouble.

Well, the second night a fog begun to come on, and we made for a tow-head° to tie to, for it wouldn't do to try to run in fog; but when I paddled ahead in the canoe, with the line, to make fast, there warn't anything but little saplings to tie to. I passed the line around one of them right on the edge of the cut bank, but there was a stiff current, and the raft come booming down so lively she tore it out by the roots and away she went. I see the fog closing down, and it made me so sick and scared I couldn't budge for most a half a minute it seemed to me — and then there warn't no raft in sight; you couldn't see twenty yards. I jumped into the canoe and run back to the stern and grabbed the paddle and set her back a stroke. But she didn't come. I was in such a hurry I hadn't untied her. I got up and tried to untie her, but I was so excited my hands shook so I couldn't hardly do anything with them.

As soon as I got started I took out after the raft, hot and heavy, right down the tow-head. That was all right as far as it went, but the tow-head warn't sixty yards long, and the minute I flew by the foot of it I shot out into the solid white fog, and hadn't no more idea which way I was going than a dead man.

Thinks I, it won't do to paddle; first I know I'll run into the bank or a tow-head or something; I got to set still and float, and yet it's mighty fidgety business to have to hold your hands still at such a time. I whooped and listened. Away down there, somewheres, I hears a small whoop, and up comes my spirits. I went tearing after it, listening sharp to hear it again. The next time it come, I see I warn't heading for it but heading away to the right of it. And the next time, I was heading away to the left of it — and not gaining on it much, either, for I was flying around, this way and that and 'tother, but it was going straight ahead all the time.

---

tow-head: A sandbar with cottonwood trees growing on it.

I did wish the fool would think to beat a tin pan, and beat it all the time, but he never did, and it was the still places between the whoops that was making the trouble for me. Well, I fought along, and directly I hears the whoop *behind* me. I was tangled good, now. That was somebody else's whoop, or else I was turned around.

I throwed the paddle down. I heard the whoop again; it was behind me yet, but in a different place; it kept coming, and kept changing its place, and I kept answering, till by-and-by it was in front of me again and I knowed the current had swung the canoe's head down stream and I was all right, if that was Jim and not some other raftsman hollering. I couldn't tell nothing about voices in a fog, for nothing don't look natural nor sound natural in a fog.

The whooping went on, and in about a minute I come a booming down on a cut bank with smoky ghosts of big trees on it, and the current throwed me off to the left and shot by, amongst a lot of snags that fairly roared, the current was tearing by them so swift.

In another second or two it was solid white and still again. I set perfectly still, then, listening to my heart thump, and I reckon I didn't draw a breath while it thumped a hundred.

I just give up, then: I knowed what the matter was. That cut bank was an island, and Jim had gone down 'tother side of it. It warn't no tow-head, that you could float by in ten minutes. It had the big timber of a regular island; it might be five or six mile long and more than a half a mile wide.

I kept quiet, with my ears cocked, about fifteen minutes, I reckon. I was floating along, of course, four or five mile an hour; but you don't ever think of that. No, you *feel* like you are laying dead still on the water; and if a little glimpse of a snag slips by, you don't think to yourself how fast *you're* going, but you catch your breath and think, my! how that snag's tearing along. If you think it ain't dismal and lonesome out in a fog that way, by yourself, in the night, you try it once — you'll see.

Next, for about a half an hour, I whoops now and then; at last I hears the answer a long ways off, and tries to follow it, but I couldn't do it, and directly I judged I'd got into a nest of tow-heads, for I had little dim glimpses of them on both sides of me, sometimes just a narrow channel between; and some that I couldn't see, I knowed was there, because I'd hear the wash of the current against the old dead brush and trash that hung over the banks. Well, I warn't long losing the whoops, down amongst the tow-heads; and I only tried to chase them a little while, anyway, because it was worse than chasing a Jack-o-lantern. You never knowed a sound dodge around so, and swap places so quick and so much.

I had to claw away from the bank pretty lively, four or five times, to keep from knocking the islands out of the river; and so I judged the raft must be butting into the bank every now and then, or else it would get further ahead and clear out of hearing — it was floating a little faster than what I was.

Well, I seemed to be in the open river again, by-and-by, but I couldn't hear no sign of a whoop nowheres. I reckoned Jim had fetched up on a snag, maybe, and it was all up with him. I was good and tired, so I laid down in the canoe and said I wouldn't bother no more. I didn't want to go to sleep, of course; but I was so sleepy I couldn't help it; so I thought I would take just one little cat-nap.

But I reckon it was more than a cat-nap, for when I waked up the stars was shining bright, the fog was all gone, and I was spinning down a big bend stern first. First I didn't know where I was; I thought I was dreaming; and when things begun to come back to me, they seemed to come up dim out of last week.

It was a monstrous big river here, with the tallest and the thickest kind of timber on both banks; just a solid wall, as well as I could see, by the stars. I looked away down stream, and seen a black speck on the water. I took out after it; but when I got to it it warn't nothing but a couple of saw-logs made fast together. Then I see another speck, and chased that; then another, and this time I was right. It was the raft.

When I got to it Jim was setting there with his head down between his knees, asleep, with his right arm hanging over the steering oar. The other oar was smashed off, and the raft was littered up with leaves and branches and dirt. So she'd had a rough time.

I made fast and laid down under Jim's nose on the raft, and begun to gap,° and stretch my fists out against Jim, and says:

"Hello, Jim, have I been asleep? Why didn't you stir me up?"

"Goodness gracious, is dat you, Huck? En you ain' dead — you ain' drownded — you's back agin? It's too good for true, honey, it's too good for true. Lemme look at you, chile, lemme feel o' you. No, you ain' dead! you's back agin, 'live en soun', jis de same ole Huck — de same ole Huck, thanks to goodness!"

"What's the matter with you, Jim? You been a drinking?"

"Drinkin'? Has I ben a drinkin'? Has I had a chance to be a drinkin'?"

gap: Yawn.

"Well, then, what makes you talk so wild?"

"How does I talk wild?"

"*How?* why, hain't you been talking about my coming back, and all that stuff, as if I'd been gone away?"

"Huck — Huck Finn, you look me in de eye; look me in de eye. *Hain't* you ben gone away?"

"Gone away? Why, what in the nation do you mean? *I* hain't been gone anywheres. Where would I go to?"

"Well, looky here, boss, dey's sumf'n wrong, dey is. Is I *me*, or who *is* I? Is I heah, or whah *is* I? Now dat's what I wants to know?"

"Well, I think you're here, plain enough, but I think you're a tangle-headed old fool, Jim."

"I is, is I? Well you answer me dis. Didn't you tote out de line in de canoe, fer to make fas' to de tow-head?"

"No, I didn't. What tow-head? I hain't seen no tow-head."

"You hain't seen no tow-head? Looky here — didn't de line pull loose en de raf' go a hummin' down de river, en leave you en de canoe behine in de fog?"

"What fog?"

"Why *de* fog. De fog dat's ben aroun' all night. En didn't you whoop, en didn't I whoop, tell we got mix' up in de islands en one un us got los' en 'tother one was jis' as good as los', 'kase he didn' know whah he wuz? En didn't I bust up agin a lot er dem islands en have a turrible time en mos' git drownded? Now ain' dat so, boss — ain't it so? You answer me dat."

"Well, this is too many for me, Jim. I hain't seen no fog, nor no islands, nor no troubles, nor nothing. I been setting here talking with you all night till you went to sleep about ten minutes ago, and I reckon I done the same. You couldn't a got drunk in that time, so of course you've been dreaming."

"Dad fetch it, how is I gwyne to dream all dat in ten minutes?"

"Well, hang it all, you did dream it, because there didn't any of it happen."

"But Huck, it's all jis' as plain to me as ——"

"It don't make no difference how plain it is, there ain't nothing in it. I know, because I've been here all the time."

Jim didn't say nothing for about five minutes, but set there studying over it. Then he says:

"Well, den, I reck'n I did dream it, Huck; but dog my cats ef it ain't de powerfullest dream I ever see. En I hain't ever had no dream b'fo' dat's tired me like dis one."

"Oh, well, that's all right, because a dream does tire a body like everything, sometimes. But this one was a staving° dream — tell me all about it, Jim."

So Jim went to work and told me the whole thing right through, just as it happened, only he painted it up considerable. Then he said he must start in and " 'terpret" it, because it was sent for a warning. He said the first tow-head stood for a man that would try to do us some good, but the current was another man that would get us away from him. The whoops was warnings that would come to us every now and then, and if we didn't try hard to make out to understand them they'd just take us into bad luck, 'stead of keeping us out of it. The lot of tow-heads was troubles we was going to get into with quarrelsome people and all kinds of mean folks, but if we minded our business and didn't talk back and aggravate them, we would pull through and get out of the fog and into the big clear river, which was the free States, and wouldn't have no more trouble.

It had clouded up pretty dark just after I got onto the raft, but it was clearing up again, now.

"Oh, well, that's all interpreted well enough, as far as it goes, Jim," I says; "but what does *these* things stand for?"

It was the leaves and rubbish on the raft, and the smashed oar. You could see them first rate, now.

Jim looked at the trash, and then looked at me, and back at the trash again. He had got the dream fixed so strong in his head that he couldn't seem to shake it loose and get the facts back into its place again, right away. But when he did get the thing straightened around, he looked at me steady, without ever smiling, and says:

"What do dey stan' for? I's gwyne to tell you. When I got all wore out wid work, en wid de callin' for you, en went to sleep, my heart wuz mos' broke bekase you wuz los', en I didn' k'yer no mo' what become er me en de raf'. En when I wake up en fine you back agin', all safe en soun', de tears come en I could a got down on my knees en kiss' yo' foot I's so thankful. En all you wuz thinkin 'bout wuz how you could make a fool uv ole Jim wid a lie. Dat truck dah is *trash;* en trash is what people is dat puts dirt on de head er dey fren's en makes 'em ashamed."

Then he got up slow, and walked to the wigwam, and went in there, without saying anything but that. But that was enough. It made me feel so mean I could almost kissed *his* foot to get him to take it back.

staving: Smashing.

It was fifteen minutes before I could work myself up to go and humble myself to a nigger — but I done it, and I warn't ever sorry for it afterwards, neither. I didn't do him no more mean tricks, and I wouldn't done that one if I'd a knowed it would make him feel that way.

Chapter XVI

We slept most all day, and started out at night, a little ways behind a monstrous long raft that was as long going by as a procession. She had four long sweeps at each end, so we judged she carried as many as thirty men, likely. She had five big wig-wams aboard, wide apart, and an open camp fire in the middle, and a tall flag-pole at each end. There was a power of style about her. It *amounted* to something being a raftsman on such a craft as that.

We went drifting down into a big bend, and the night clouded up and got hot. The river was very wide, and was walled with solid timber on both sides; you couldn't see a break in it hardly ever, or a light. We talked about Cairo, and wondered whether we would know it when we got to it. I said likely we wouldn't, because I had heard say there warn't but about a dozen houses there, and if they didn't happen to have them lit up, how was we going to know we was passing a town? Jim said if the two big rivers joined together there, that would show. But I said maybe we might think we was passing the foot of an island and coming into the same old river again. That disturbed Jim — and me too. So the question was, what to do? I said, paddle ashore the first time a light showed, and tell them pap was behind, coming along with a trading-scow, and was a green hand at the business, and wanted to know how far it was to Cairo. Jim thought it was a good idea, so we took a smoke on it and waited.

There warn't nothing to do, now, but to look out sharp for the town, and not pass it without seeing it. He said he'd be mighty sure to see it, because he'd be a free man the minute he seen it, but if he missed it he'd be in the slave country again and no more show for freedom. Every little while he jumps up and says:

"Dah she is!"

But it warn't. It was Jack-o-lanterns, or lightning-bugs; so he set down again, and went to watching, same as before. Jim said it made him all over trembly and feverish to be so close to freedom. Well, I can tell you it made me all over trembly and feverish, too, to hear him, because I begun to get it through my head that he *was* most free — and who was to blame for it? Why, *me*. I couldn't get that out of my conscience, no how nor no way. It got to troubling me so I couldn't rest; I couldn't stay still in one place. It hadn't ever come home to me before, what this thing was that I was doing. But now it did; and it staid with me, and scorched me more and more. I tried to make out to myself that *I* warn't to blame, because *I* didn't run Jim off from his rightful owner; but it warn't no use, conscience up and says, every time, "But you knowed he was running for his freedom, and you could a paddled ashore and told somebody." That was so — I couldn't get around that, noway. That was where it pinched. Conscience says to me, "What had poor Miss Watson done to you, that you could see her nigger go off right under your eyes and never say one single word? What did that poor old woman do to you, that you could treat her so mean? Why, she tried to learn you your book, she tried to learn you your manners, she tried to be good to you every way she knowed how. *That's* what she done."

I got to feeling so mean and so miserable I most wished I was dead. I fidgeted up and down the raft, abusing myself to myself, and Jim was fidgeting up and down past me. We neither of us could keep still. Every time he danced around and says, "Dah's Cairo!" it went through me like a shot, and I thought if it *was* Cairo I reckoned I would die of miserableness.

Jim talked out loud all the time while I was talking to myself. He was saying how the first thing he would do when he got to a free State he would go to saving up money and never spend a single cent, and when he got enough he would buy his wife, which was owned on a farm close to where Miss Watson lived; and then they would both work to buy the two children, and if their master wouldn't sell them, they'd get an Ab'litionist to go and steal them.

It most froze me to hear such talk. He wouldn't ever dared to talk such talk in his life before. Just see what a difference it made in him the minute he judged he was about free. It was according to the old saying, "give a nigger an inch and he'll take an ell."° Thinks I, this is what comes of my not thinking. Here was this nigger which I had as good as helped to run away, coming right out flat-footed and saying he would steal his children — children that belonged to a man I didn't even know; a man that hadn't ever done me no harm.

I was sorry to hear Jim say that, it was such a lowering of him. My conscience got to stirring me up hotter than ever, until at last I says to

[handwritten margin note: Still think like Society]

---

ell: A unit of length equal to 45 inches.

it, "Let up on me — it ain't too late, yet — I'll paddle ashore at the first light, and tell." I felt easy, and happy, and light as a feather, right off. All my troubles was gone. I went to looking out sharp for a light, and sort of singing to myself. By-and-by one showed. Jim sings out:

"We's safe, Huck, we's safe! Jump up and crack yo' heels, dat's de good ole Cairo at las', I jis knows it!"

I says:

"I'll take the canoe and go see, Jim. It mightn't be, you know."

He jumped and got the canoe ready, and put his old coat in the bottom for me to set on, and give me the paddle; and as I shoved off, he says:

"Pooty soon I'll be a-shout'n for joy, en I'll say, it's all on accounts o' Huck; I's a free man, en I couldn't ever ben free ef it hadn' ben for Huck; Huck done it. Jim won't ever forgit you, Huck; you's de bes' fren' Jim's ever had; en you's de *only* fren' ole Jim's got now."

I was paddling off, all in a sweat to tell on him; but when he says this, it seemed to kind of take the tuck all out of me. I went along slow then, and I warn't right down certain whether I was glad I started or whether I warn't. When I was fifty yards off, Jim says:

"Dah you goes, de ole true Huck; de on'y white genlman dat ever kep' his promise to ole Jim."

Well, I just felt sick. But I says, I *got* to do it — I can't get *out* of it. Right then, along comes a skiff with two men in it, with guns, and they stopped and I stopped. One of them says:

"What's that, yonder?"

"A piece of a raft," I says.

"Do you belong on it?"

"Yes, sir."

"Any men on it?"

"Only one, sir."

"Well, there's five niggers run off to-night, up yonder above the head of the bend. Is your man white or black?"

I didn't answer up prompt. I tried to, but the words wouldn't come. I tried, for a second or two, to brace up and out with it, but I warn't man enough — hadn't the spunk of a rabbit. I see I was weakening; so I just give up trying, and up and says —

"He's white."

"I reckon we'll go and see for ourselves."

"I wish you would," says I, "because it's pap that's there, and maybe you'd help me tow the raft ashore where the light is. He's sick — and so is mam and Mary Ann."

"Oh, the devil! we're in a hurry, boy. But I s'pose we've got to. Come — buckle to your paddle, and let's get along."

I buckled to my paddle and they laid to their oars. When we had made a stroke or two, I says:

"Pap'll be mighty much obleeged to you, I can tell you. Everybody goes away when I want them to help me tow the raft ashore, and I can't do it by myself."

"Well, that's infernal mean. Odd, too. Say, boy, what's the matter with your father?"

"It's the — a — the — well, it ain't anything, much."

They stopped pulling. It warn't but a mighty little ways to the raft, now. One says:

"Boy, that's a lie. What *is* the matter with your pap? Answer up square, now, and it'll be the better for you."

"I will, sir, I will, honest — but don't leave us, please. It's the — the — gentlemen, if you'll only pull ahead, and let me heave you the head-line, you won't have to come a-near the raft — please do."

"Set her back, John, set her back!" says one. They backed water. "Keep away, boy — keep to looard. Confound it, I just expect the wind has blowed it to us. Your pap's got the small-pox, and you know it precious well. Why didn't you come out and say so? Do you want to spread it all over?"

"Well," says I, a-blubbering, "I've told everybody before, and then they just went away and left us."

"Poor devil, there's something in that. We are right down sorry for you, but we — well, hang it, we don't want the small-pox, you see. Look here, I'll tell you what to do. Don't you try to land by yourself, or you'll smash everything to pieces. You float along down about twenty miles and you'll come to a town on the left-hand side of the river. It will be long after sun-up, then, and when you ask for help, you tell them your folks are all down with chills and fever. Don't be a fool again, and let people guess what is the matter. Now we're trying to do you a kindness; so you just put twenty miles between us, that's a good boy. It wouldn't do any good to land yonder where the light is — it's only a wood-yard. Say — I reckon your father's poor, and I'm bound to say he's in pretty hard luck. Here — I'll put a twenty dollar gold piece on this board, and you get it when it floats by. I feel mighty mean to leave you, but my kingdom! it won't do to fool with small-pox, don't you see?"

"Hold on, Parker," says the other man, "here's a twenty to put on the board for me. Good-bye, boy, you do as Mr. Parker told you, and you'll be all right."

"That's so, my boy — good-bye, good-bye. If you see any runaway niggers, you get help and nab them, and you can make some money by it."

"Good-bye, sir," says I, "I won't let no runaway niggers get by me if I can help it."

They went off, and I got aboard the raft, feeling bad and low, because I knowed very well I had done wrong, and I see it warn't no use for me to try to learn to do right; a body that don't get *started* right when he's little, ain't got no show — when the pinch comes there ain't nothing to back him up and keep him to his work, and so he gets beat. Then I thought a minute, and says to myself, hold on — spose you'd a done right and give Jim up; would you felt better than what you do now? No, says I, I'd feel bad — I'd feel just the same way I do now. Well, then, says I, what's the use you learning to do right, when it's troublesome to do right and ain't no trouble to do wrong, and the wages is just the same? I was stuck. I couldn't answer that. So I reckoned I wouldn't bother no more about it, but after this always do whichever come handiest at the time.

I went into the wigwam; Jim warn't there. I looked all around; he warn't anywhere. I says:

"Jim!"

"Here I is, Huck. Is dey out o' sight yit? Don't talk loud."

He was in the river, under the stern oar, with just his nose out. I told him they was out of sight, so he come aboard. He says:

"I was a-listenin' to all de talk, en I slips into de river en was gwyne to shove for sho' if dey come aboard. Den I was gwyne to swim to de raf' agin when dey was gone. But lawsy, how you did fool 'em, Huck! Dat *wuz* de smartes' dodge! I tell you, chile, I 'speck it save' ole Jim — ole Jim ain't gwyne to forget you for dat, honey."

Then we talked about the money. It was a pretty good raise, twenty dollars apiece. Jim said we could take deck passage on a steamboat now, and the money would last us as far as we wanted to go in the free States. He said twenty mile more warn't far for the raft to go, but he wished we was already there.

Towards daybreak we tied up, and Jim was mighty particular about hiding the raft good. Then he worked all day fixing things in bundles, and getting all ready to quit rafting.

That night about ten we hove in sight of the lights of a town away down in a left-hand bend.

I went off in the canoe, to ask about it. Pretty soon I found a man out in the river with a skiff, setting a trot-line. I ranged up and says:

"Mister, is that town Cairo?"

"Cairo? no. You must be a blame' fool."

"What town is it, mister?"

"If you want to know, go and find out. If you stay here botherin'
around me for about a half a minute longer, you'll get something you
won't want."

I paddled to the raft. Jim was awful disappointed, but I said never
mind, Cairo would be the next place, I reckoned.

We passed another town before daylight, and I was going out again;
but it was high ground, so I didn't go. No high ground about Cairo,
Jim said. I had forgot it. We laid up for the day, on a tow-head tolerable
close to the left-hand bank. I begun to suspicion something. So did
Jim. I says:

"Maybe we went by Cairo in the fog that night."

He says:

"Doan' less' talk about it, Huck. Po' niggers can't have no luck. I
awluz 'spected dat rattle-snake skin warn't done wid its work."

"I wish I'd never seen that snake-skin, Jim — I do wish I'd never
laid eyes on it."

"It ain't yo' fault, Huck; you didn' know. Don't you blame yo'self
'bout it."

When it was daylight, here was the clear Ohio water in shore, sure
enough, and outside was the old regular Muddy! So it was all up with
Cairo.

We talked it all over. It wouldn't do to take to the shore; we couldn't
take the raft up the stream, of course. There warn't no way but to wait
for dark, and start back in the canoe and take the chances. So we slept
all day amongst the cotton-wood thicket, so as to be fresh for the work,
and when we went back to the raft about dark the canoe was gone!

We didn't say a word for a good while. There warn't anything to
say. We both knowed well enough it was some more work of the rattlesnake skin; so what was the use to talk about it? It would only look
like we was finding fault, and that would be bound to fetch more bad
luck — and keep on fetching it, too, till we knowed enough to keep
still.

By-and-by we talked about what we better do, and found there
warn't no way but just to go along down with the raft till we got a
chance to buy a canoe to go back in. We warn't going to borrow it
when there warn't anybody around, the way pap would do, for that
might set people after us.

So we shoved out, after dark, on the raft.

Anybody that don't believe yet, that it's foolishness to handle a snake-skin, after all that that snake-skin done for us, will believe it now, if they read on and see what more it done for us.

The place to buy canoes is off of rafts laying up at shore. But we didn't see no rafts laying up; so we went along during three hours and more. Well, the night got gray, and ruther thick, which is the next meanest thing to fog. You can't tell the shape of the river, and you can't see no distance. It got to be very late and still, and then along comes a steamboat up the river. We lit the lantern, and judged she would see it. Up-stream boats didn't generly come close to us; they go out and follow the bars and hunt for easy water under the reefs; but nights like this they bull right up the channel against the whole river.

We could hear her pounding along, but we didn't see her good till she was close. She aimed right for us. Often they do that and try to see how close they can come without touching; sometimes the wheel bites off a sweep, and then the pilot sticks his head out and laughs, and thinks he's mighty smart. Well, here she comes, and we said she was going to try to shave us; but she didn't seem to be sheering off a bit. She was a big one, and she was coming in a hurry, too, looking like a black cloud with rows of glow-worms around it; but all of a sudden she bulged out, big and scary, with a long row of wide-open furnace doors shining like red-hot teeth, and her monstrous bows and guards hanging right over us. There was a yell at us, and a jingling of bells to stop the engines, a pow-wow of cussing, and whistling of steam — and as Jim went overboard on one side and I on the other, she come smashing straight through the raft.

I dived — and I aimed to find the bottom, too, for a thirty-foot wheel had got to go over me, and I wanted it to have plenty of room. I could always stay under water a minute; this time I reckon I staid under water a minute and a half. Then I bounced for the top in a hurry, for I was nearly busting. I popped out to my arm-pits and blowed the water out of my nose, and puffed a bit. Of course there was a booming current; and of course that boat started her engines again ten seconds after she stopped them, for they never cared much for raftsmen; so now she was churning along up the river, out of sight in the thick weather, though I could hear her.

I sung out for Jim about a dozen times, but I didn't get any answer; so I grabbed a plank that touched me while I was "treading water," and struck out for shore, shoving it ahead of me. But I made out to see that the drift of the current was towards the left-hand shore, which meant that I was in a crossing; so I changed off and went that way.

It was one of these long, slanting, two-mile crossings; so I was a good long time in getting over. I made a safe landing, and clum up the bank. I couldn't see but a little ways, but I went poking along over rough ground for a quarter of a mile or more, and then I run across a big old-fashioned double log house before I noticed it. I was going to rush by and get away, but a lot of dogs jumped out and went to howling and barking at me, and I knowed better than to move another peg.

Chapter XVII

In about half a minute somebody spoke out of a window, without putting his head out, and says:

"Be done, boys! Who's there?"

I says:

"It's me."

"Who's me?"

"George Jackson, sir."

"What do you want?"

"I don't want nothing, sir. I only want to go along by, but the dogs won't let me."

"What are you prowling around here this time of night, for — hey?"

"I warn't prowling around, sir; I fell overboard off of the steamboat."

"Oh, you did, did you? Strike a light there, somebody. What did you say your name was?"

"George Jackson, sir. I'm only a boy."

"Look here; if you're telling the truth, you needn't be afraid — nobody 'll hurt you. But don't try to budge; stand right where you are. Rouse out Bob and Tom, some of you, and fetch the guns. George Jackson, is there anybody with you?"

"No, sir, nobody."

I heard the people stirring around in the house, now, and see a light. The man sung out:

"Snatch that light away, Betsy, you old fool — ain't you got any sense? Put it on the floor behind the front door. Bob, if you and Tom are ready, take your places."

"All ready."

"Now, George Jackson, do you know the Shepherdsons?"

"No, sir — I never heard of them."

"Well, that may be so, and it mayn't. Now, all ready. Step forward, George Jackson. And mind, don't you hurry — come mighty slow. If there's anybody with you, let him keep back — if he shows himself he'll be shot. Come along, now. Come slow; push the door open, yourself — just enough to squeeze in, d' you hear?"

I didn't hurry, I couldn't if I'd a wanted to. I took one slow step at a time, and there warn't a sound, only I thought I could hear my heart. The dogs were as still as the humans, but they followed a little behind me. When I got to the three log door-steps, I heard them unlocking and unbarring and unbolting. I put my hand on the door and pushed it a little and a little more, till somebody said, "There, that's enough — put your head in." I done it, but I judged they would take it off.

The candle was on the floor, and there they all was, looking at me, and me at them, for about a quarter of a minute. Three big men with guns pointed at me, which made me wince, I tell you; the oldest, gray and about sixty, the other two thirty or more — all of them fine and handsome — and the sweetest old gray-headed lady, and back of her two young women which I couldn't see right well. The old gentleman says:

"There — I reckon it's all right. Come in."

As soon as I was in, the old gentleman he locked the door and barred it and bolted it, and told the young men to come in with their guns, and they all went in a big parlor that had a new rag carpet on the floor, and got together in a corner that was out of range of the front windows — there warn't none on the side. They held the candle, and took a good look at me, and all said, "Why *he* ain't a Shepherdson — no, there ain't any Shepherdson about him." Then the old man said he hoped I wouldn't mind being searched for arms, because he didn't mean no harm by it — it was only to make sure. So he didn't pry into my pockets, but only felt outside with his hands, and said it was all right. He told me to make myself easy and at home, and tell all about myself; but the old lady says:

"Why bless you, Saul, the poor thing's as wet as he can be; and don't you reckon it may be he's hungry?"

"True for you, Rachel — I forgot."

So the old lady says:

"Betsy" (this was a nigger woman), "you fly around and get him something to eat, as quick as you can, poor thing; and one of you girls go and wake up Buck and tell him — Oh, here he is himself. Buck, take this little stranger and get the wet clothes off from him and dress him up in some of yours that's dry."

Buck looked about as old as me — thirteen or fourteen or along there, though he was a little bigger than me. He hadn't on anything but a shirt, and he was very frowsy-headed. He come in gaping and digging one fist into his eyes, and he was dragging a gun along with the other one. He says:

"Ain't they no Shepherdsons around?"

They said, no, 'twas a false alarm.

"Well," he says, "if they'd a ben some, I reckon I'd a got one."

They all laughed, and Bob says:

"Why, Buck, they might have scalped us all, you've been so slow in coming."

"Well, nobody come after me, and it ain't right. I'm always kep' down; I don't get no show."

"Never mind, Buck, my boy," says the old man, "you'll have show enough, all in good time, don't you fret about that. Go 'long with you now, and do as your mother told you."

When we got up stairs to his room, he got me a coarse shirt and a round-about° and pants of his, and I put them on. While I was at it he asked me what my name was, but before I could tell him, he started to telling me about a blue jay and a young rabbit he had catched in the woods day before yesterday, and he asked me where Moses was when the candle went out. I said I didn't know; I hadn't heard about it before, no way.

"Well, guess," he says.

"How'm I going to guess," says I, "when I never heard tell about it before?"

"But you can guess, can't you? It's just as easy."

"*Which* candle?" I says.

"Why, any candle," he says.

"I don't know where he was," says I; "where was he?"

"Why he was in the *dark!* That's where he was!"

"Well, if you knowed where he was, what did you ask me for?"

"Why, blame it, it's a riddle, don't you see? Say, how long are you going to stay here? You got to stay always. We can just have booming times — they don't have no school now. Do you own a dog? I've got a dog — and he'll go in the river and bring out chips that you throw in. Do you like to comb up, Sundays, and all that kind of foolishness? You bet I don't, but ma she makes me. Confound these old britches, I reckon I'd better put 'em on, but I'd ruther not, it's so warm. Are you all ready? All right — come along, old hoss."

round-about: A close-fitting jacket worn by men and boys of the time.

Cold corn-pone, cold corn-beef, butter and butter-milk — that is what they had for me down there, and there ain't nothing better that ever I've come across yet. Buck and his ma and all of them smoked cob pipes, except the nigger woman, which was gone, and the two young women. They all smoked and talked, and I eat and talked. The young women had quilts around them, and their hair down their backs. They all asked me questions, and I told them how pap and me and all the family was living on a little farm down at the bottom of Arkansaw, and my sister Mary Ann run off and got married and never was heard of no more, and Bill went to hunt them and he warn't heard of no more, and Tom and Mort died, and then there warn't nobody but just me and pap left, and he was just trimmed down to nothing, on account of his troubles; so when he died I took what there was left, because the farm didn't belong to us, and started up the river, deck passage, and fell overboard; and that was how I come to be here. So they said I could have a home there as long as I wanted it. Then it was most daylight, and everybody went to bed, and I went to bed with Buck, and when I waked up in the morning, drat it all, I had forgot what my name was. So I laid there about an hour trying to think, and when Buck waked up, I says:

"Can you spell, Buck?"

"Yes," he says.

"I bet you can't spell my name," says I.

"I bet you what you dare I can," says he.

"All right," says I, "go ahead."

"G-o-r-g-e J-a-x-o-n — there now," he says.

"Well," says I, "you done it, but I didn't think you could. It ain't no slouch of a name to spell — right off without studying."

I set it down, private, because somebody might want *me* to spell it, next, and so I wanted to be handy with it and rattle it off like I was used to it.

It was a mighty nice family, and a mighty nice house, too. I hadn't seen no house out in the country before that was so nice and had so much style. It didn't have an iron latch on the front door, nor a wooden one with a buckskin string, but a brass knob to turn, the same as houses in a town. There warn't no bed in the parlor, not a sign of a bed; but heaps of parlors in towns has beds in them. There was a big fireplace that was bricked on the bottom, and the bricks was kept clean and red by pouring water on them and scrubbing them with another brick; sometimes they washed them over with red water-paint that they call Spanish-brown, same as they do in town. They had big brass dog-irons that could hold up a saw-log. There was a clock on the middle of the mantel-piece, with a picture of a town painted on the bottom half of the glass front, and a round place in the middle of it for the sun, and you could see the pendulum swing behind it. It was beautiful to hear that clock tick; and sometimes when one of these peddlers had been along and scoured her up and got her in good shape, she would start in and strike a hundred and fifty before she got tuckered out. They wouldn't took any money for her.

Well, there was a big outlandish parrot on each side of the clock, made out of something like chalk, and painted up gaudy. By one of the parrots was a cat made of crockery, and a crockery dog by the other; and when you pressed down on them they squeaked, but didn't open their mouths nor look different nor interested. They squeaked through underneath. There was a couple of big wild-turkey-wing fans spread out behind those things. On a table in the middle of the room was a kind of a lovely crockery basket that had apples and oranges and peaches and grapes piled up in it which was much redder and yellower and prettier than real ones is, but they warn't real because you could see where pieces had got chipped off and showed the white chalk or whatever it was, underneath.

This table had a cover made out of beautiful oil-cloth, with a red and blue spread-eagle painted on it, and a painted border all around. It come all the way from Philadelphia, they said. There was some books too, piled up perfectly exact, on each corner of the table. One was a big family Bible, full of pictures. One was "Pilgrim's Progress," about a man that left his family it didn't say why. I read considerable in it now and then. The statements was interesting, but tough. Another was "Friendship's Offering," full of beautiful stuff and poetry; but I didn't read the poetry. Another was Henry Clay's Speeches, and another was Dr. Gunn's Family Medicine, which told you all about what to do if a body was sick or dead. There was a Hymn Book, and a lot of other books. And there was nice split-bottom chairs, and perfectly sound, too — not bagged down in the middle and busted, like an old basket.

They had pictures hung on the walls — mainly Washingtons and Lafayettes, and battles, and Highland Marys, and one called "Signing the Declaration." There was some that they called crayons, which one of the daughters which was dead made her own self when she was only fifteen years old. They was different from any pictures I ever see before; blacker, mostly, than is common. One was a woman in a slim black dress, belted small under the arm-pits, with bulges like a cabbage in the middle of the sleeves, and a large black scoop-shovel bonnet with a black veil, and white slim ankles crossed about with black tape, and very wee black slippers, like a chisel, and she was leaning pensive on a tomb-stone on her right elbow, under a weeping willow, and her other hand hanging down her side holding a white handkerchief and a reticule,° and underneath the picture it said "Shall I Never See Thee More Alas." Another one was a young lady with her hair all combed up straight to the top of her head, and knotted there in front of a comb like a chair-back, and she was crying into a handkerchief and had a dead bird laying on its back in her other hand with its heels up, and underneath the pic-ture it said "I Shall Never Hear Thy Sweet Chirrup More Alas." There was one where a young lady was at a window looking up at the moon, and tears running down her cheeks; and she had an open letter in one hand with black sealing-wax showing on one edge of it, and she was mashing a locket with a chain to it against her mouth, and underneath the picture it said "And Art Thou Gone Yes Thou Art Gone Alas." These was all nice pictures, I reckon, but I didn't somehow seem to take to them, because if ever I was down a little, they always give me the fan-tods. Everybody was sorry she died, because she had laid out a lot more of these pictures to do, and a body could see by what she had done what they had lost. But I reckoned, that with her disposition, she was having a better time in the graveyard. She was at work on what they said was her greatest picture when she took sick, and every day and every night it was her prayer to be allowed to live till she got it done, but she never got the chance. It was a picture of a young woman in a long white gown, standing on the rail of a bridge all ready to jump off, with her hair all down her back, and looking up to the moon, with the tears running down her face, and she had two arms folded across her breast, and two arms stretched out in front, and two more reaching up towards the moon — and the idea was, to see which pair would look best and then scratch out all the other arms; but, as I was saying, she died before she got her mind made up, and now they kept this picture over the head of the bed in her room, and every time her birthday come they hung flowers on it. Other times it was hid with a little curtain. The young woman in the picture had a kind of a nice sweet face, but there was so many arms it made her look too spidery, seemed to me.

This young girl kept a scrap-book when she was alive, and used to paste obituaries and accidents and cases of patient suffering in it out of the *Presbyterian Observer,* and write poetry after them out of her own head. It was very good poetry. This is what she wrote about a boy

---

reticule: A woman's drawstring bag, often used as a carryall.

by the name of Stephen Dowling Bots that fell down a well and was drownded:

ODE TO STEPHEN DOWLING BOTS, DEC'D.

And did young Stephen sicken,
    And did young Stephen die?
And did the sad hearts thicken,
    And did the mourners cry?

No; such was not the fate of
    Young Stephen Dowling Bots;
Though sad hearts round him thickened,
    'Twas not from sickness' shots.

No whopping-cough did rack his frame,
    Nor measles drear, with spots;
Not these impaired the sacred name
    Of Stephen Dowling Bots.

Despised love struck not with woe
    That head of curly knots,
Nor stomach troubles laid him low,
    Young Stephen Dowling Bots.

O no. Then list with tearful eye,
    Whilst I his fate do tell.
His soul did from this cold world fly,
    By falling down a well.

They got him out and emptied him;
    Alas it was too late;
His spirit was gone for to sport aloft
    In the realms of the good and great.

If Emmeline Grangerford could make poetry like that before she was fourteen, there ain't no telling what she could a done by-and-by. Buck said she could rattle off poetry like nothing. She didn't ever have to stop to think. He said she would slap down a line, and if she couldn't find anything to rhyme with it she would just scratch it out and slap down another one, and go ahead. She warn't particular, she could write about anything you choose to give her to write about, just so it was sadful. Every time a man died, or a woman died, or a child died, she would be on hand with her "tribute" before he was cold. She called them tributes. The neighbors said it was the doctor first, then Emmeline, then the undertaker — the undertaker never got in ahead of Emmeline but once, and then she hung fire on a rhyme for the dead person's name, which was Whistler. She warn't ever the same, after that; she never complained, but she kind of pined away and did not live long. Poor thing, many's the time I made myself go up to the little room that used to be hers and get out her poor old scrap-book and read in it when her pictures had been aggravating me and I had soured on her a little. I liked all that family, dead ones and all, and warn't going to let anything come between us. Poor Emmeline made poetry about all the dead people when she was alive, and it didn't seem right that there warn't nobody to make some about her, now she was gone; so I tried to sweat out a verse or two myself, but I couldn't seem to make it go, somehow. They kept Emmeline's room trim and nice and all the things fixed in it just the way she liked to have them when she was alive, and nobody ever slept there. The old lady took care of the room herself, though there was plenty of niggers, and she sewed there a good deal and read her Bible there, mostly.

Well, as I was saying about the parlor, there was beautiful curtains on the windows: white, with pictures painted on them, of castles with vines all down the walls, and cattle coming down to drink. There was a little old piano, too, that had tin pans in it, I reckon, and nothing was ever so lovely as to hear the young ladies sing, "The Last Link is Broken" and play "The Battle of Prague" on it. The walls of all the rooms was plastered, and most had carpets on the floors, and the whole house was whitewashed on the outside.

It was a double house, and the big open place betwixt them was roofed and floored, and sometimes the table was set there in the middle of the day, and it was a cool, comfortable place. Nothing couldn't be better. And warn't the cooking good, and just bushels of it too!

Chapter XVIII

Col. Grangerford was a gentleman, you see. He was a gentleman all over; and so was his family. He was well born, as the saying is, and that's worth as much in a man as it is in a horse, so the Widow Douglas said, and nobody ever denied that she was of the first aristocracy in our town; and pap he always said it, too, though he warn't no more quality than a mudcat, himself. Col. Grangerford was very tall and very slim, and had a darkish-paly complexion, not a sign of red in it anywheres; he was clean-shaved every morning, all over his thin face, and he had the thinnest kind of lips, and the thinnest kind of nostrils, and a high nose, and heavy eyebrows, and the blackest kind of eyes, sunk so deep back that they seemed like they was looking out of caverns at you, as you may say. His forehead was high, and his hair was black and straight, and hung to his shoulders. His hands was long and thin, and every day of his life he put on a clean shirt and a full suit from head to foot made out of linen so white it hurt your eyes to look at it; and on Sundays he wore a blue tail-coat with brass buttons on it. He carried a mahogany cane with a silver head to it. There warn't no frivolishness about him, not a bit, and he warn't ever loud. He was as kind as he could be — you could feel that, you know, and so you had confidence. Sometimes he smiled, and it was good to see; but when he straightened himself up like a liberty-pole, and the lightning begun to flicker out from under his eyebrows you wanted to climb a tree first, and find out what the matter was afterwards. He didn't ever have to tell anybody to mind their manners — everybody was always good mannered where he was. Everybody loved to have him around, too; he was sunshine most always — I mean he made it seem like good weather. When he turned into a cloud-bank it was awful dark for a half a minute and that was enough; there wouldn't nothing go wrong again for a week.

When him and the old lady come down in the morning, all the family got up out of their chairs and give them good-day, and didn't set down again till they had set down. Then Tom and Bob went to the sideboard where the decanters was, and mixed a glass of bitters and handed it to him, and he held it in his hand and waited till Tom's and Bob's was mixed, and then they bowed and said "Our duty to you, sir, and madam;" and *they* bowed the least bit in the world and said thank you, and so they drank, all three, and Bob and Tom poured a spoonful of water on the sugar and the mite of whisky or apple brandy in the bottom of their tumblers, and give it to me and Buck, and we drank to the old people too.

Bob was the oldest, and Tom next. Tall, beautiful men with very broad shoulders and brown faces, and long black hair and black eyes. They dressed in white linen from head to foot, like the old gentleman, and wore broad Panama hats.

Then there was Miss Charlotte, she was twenty-five, and tall and proud and grand, but as good as she could be, when she warn't stirred up; but when she was, she had a look that would make you wilt in your tracks, like her father. She was beautiful.

So was her sister, Miss Sophia, but it was a different kind. She was gentle and sweet, like a dove, and she was only twenty.

Each person had their own nigger to wait on them — Buck, too. My nigger had a monstrous easy time, because I warn't used to having anybody do anything for me, but Buck's was on the jump most of the time.

This was all there was of the family, now; but there used to be more — three sons; they got killed; and Emmeline that died.

The old gentleman owned a lot of farms, and over a hundred niggers. Sometimes a stack of people would come there, horseback, from ten or fifteen mile around, and stay five or six days, and have such junketings round about and on the river, and dances and picnics in the woods, day-times, and balls at the house, nights. These people was mostly kin-folks of the family. The men brought their guns with them. It was a handsome lot of quality, I tell you.

There was another clan of aristocracy around there — five or six families — mostly of the name of Shepherdson. They was as high-toned, and well born, and rich and grand, as the tribe of Grangerfords. The Shepherdsons and the Grangerfords used the same steamboat landing, which was about two mile above our house; so sometimes when I went up there with a lot of our folks I used to see a lot of the Shepherdsons there, on their fine horses.

One day Buck and me was away out in the woods, hunting, and heard a horse coming. We was crossing the road. Buck says:

"Quick! Jump for the woods!"

We done it, and then peeped down the woods through the leaves. Pretty soon a splendid young man come galloping down the road, setting his horse easy and looking like a soldier. He had his gun across his pommel. I had seen him before. It was young Harney Shepherdson. I heard Buck's gun go off at my ear, and Harney's hat tumbled off from his head. He grabbed his gun and rode straight to the place where we was hid. But we didn't wait. We started through the woods on a run. The woods warn't thick, so I looked over my shoulder, to dodge the bullet, and twice I seen Harney cover Buck with his gun; and then he rode away the way he come — to get his hat, I reckon, but I couldn't see. We never stopped running till we got home. The old gentleman's eyes blazed a minute — 'twas pleasure, mainly, I judged — then his face sort of smoothed down, and he says, kind of gentle:

"I don't like that shooting from behind a bush. Why didn't you step into the road, my boy?"

"The Shepherdsons don't, father. They always take advantage."

Miss Charlotte she held her head up like a queen while Buck was telling his tale, and her nostrils spread and her eyes snapped. The two young men looked dark, but never said nothing. Miss Sophia she turned pale, but the color come back when she found the man warn't hurt.

Soon as I could get Buck down by the corn-cribs under the trees by ourselves, I says:

"Did you want to kill him, Buck?"

"Well, I bet I did."

"What did he do to you?"

"Him? He never done nothing to me."

"Well, then, what did you want to kill him for?"

"Why nothing — only it's on account of the feud."

"What's a feud?"

"Why, where was you raised? Don't you know what a feud is?"

"Never heard of it before — tell me about it."

"Well," says Buck, "a feud is this way. A man has a quarrel with another man, and kills him; then that other man's brother kills *him;* then the other brothers, on both sides, goes for one another; then the *cousins* chip in — and by-and-by everybody's killed off, and there ain't no more feud. But it's kind of slow, and takes a long time."

"Has this one been going on long, Buck?"

"Well I should *reckon!* it started thirty year ago, or som'ers along there. There was trouble 'bout something and then a lawsuit to settle it; and the suit went agin one of the men, and so he up and shot the man that won the suit — which he would naturally do, of course. Anybody would."

"What was the trouble about, Buck? — land?"

"I reckon maybe — I don't know."

"Well, who done the shooting? — was it a Grangerford or a Shepherdson?"

"Laws, how do *I* know? it was so long ago."

"Don't anybody know?"

"Oh, yes, pa knows, I reckon, and some of the other old folks; but they don't know, now, what the row was about in the first place."

"Has there been many killed, Buck?"

"Yes — right smart chance of funerals. But they don't always kill. Pa's got a few buck-shot in him; but he don't mind it 'cuz he don't weigh much anyway. Bob's been carved up some with a bowie, and Tom's been hurt once or twice."

"Has anybody been killed this year, Buck?"

"Yes, we got one and they got one. 'Bout three months ago, my cousin Bud, fourteen year old, was riding through the woods, on t'other side of the river, and didn't have no weapon with him, which was blame' foolishness, and in a lonesome place he hears a horse a-coming behind him, and sees old Baldy Shepherdson a-linkin' after him with his gun in his hand and his white hair a-flying in the wind; and 'stead of jumping off and taking to the brush, Bud 'lowed he could outrun him; so they had it, nip and tuck, for five mile or more, the old man a-gaining all the time; so at last Bud seen it warn't any use, so he stopped and faced around so as to have the bullet holes in front, you know, and the old man he rode up and shot him down. But he didn't git much chance to enjoy his luck, for inside of a week our folks laid *him* out."

"I reckon that old man was a coward, Buck."

"I reckon he *warn't* a coward. Not by a blame' sight. There ain't a coward amongst them Shepherdsons — not a one. And there ain't no cowards amongst the Grangerfords, either. Why, that old man kep' up his end in a fight one day, for a half an hour, against three Grangerfords, and come out winner. They was all a-horseback; he lit off of his horse and got behind a little wood-pile, and kep' his horse before him to stop the bullets; but the Grangerfords staid on their horses and capered around the old man, and peppered away at him, and he peppered away at them. Him and his horse both went home pretty leaky and crippled, but the Grangerfords had to be *fetched* home — and one of 'em was dead, and another died the next day. No, sir, if a body's out hunting for cowards, he don't want to fool away any time amongst them Shepherdsons, becuz they don't breed any of that *kind*."

Next Sunday we all went to church, about three mile, everybody a-horseback. The men took their guns along, so did Buck, and kept them between their knees or stood them handy against the wall. The Shepherdsons done the same. It was pretty ornery preaching — all about brotherly love, and such-like tiresomeness; but everybody said it was a good sermon, and they all talked it over going home, and had such a powerful lot to say about faith, and good works, and free grace, and preforeordestination, and I don't know what all, that it did seem to me to be one of the roughest Sundays I had run across yet.

About an hour after dinner everybody was dozing around, some in their chairs and some in their rooms, and it got to be pretty dull. Buck and a dog was stretched out on the grass in the sun, sound asleep. I went up to our room, and judged I would take a nap myself. I found that sweet Miss Sophia standing in her door, which was next to ours, and she took me in her room and shut the door very soft, and asked me if I liked her, and I said I did; and she asked me if I would do something for her and not tell anybody, and I said I would. Then she said she'd forgot her Testament, and left it in the seat at church, between two other books and would I slip out quiet and go there and fetch it to her, and not say nothing to nobody. I said I would. So I slid out and slipped off up the road, and there warn't anybody at the church, except maybe a hog or two, for there warn't any lock on the door, and hogs likes a puncheon floor in summer-time because it's cool. If you notice, most folks don't go to church only when they've got to; but a hog is different.

Says I to myself something's up — it ain't natural for a girl to be in such a sweat about a Testament; so I give it a shake, and out drops a little piece of paper with *"Half-past two"* wrote on it with a pencil. I ransacked it, but couldn't find anything else. I couldn't make anything out of that, so I put the paper in the book again, and when I got home and up stairs, there was Miss Sophia in her door waiting for me. She pulled me in and shut the door; then she looked in the Testament till she found the paper, and as soon as she read it she looked glad; and before a body could think, she grabbed me and give me a squeeze, and said I was the best boy in the world, and not to tell anybody. She was mighty red in the face, for a minute, and her eyes lighted up and it made her powerful pretty. I was a good deal astonished, but when I got my breath I asked her what the paper was about, and she asked me if I had read it, and I said no, and she asked me if I could read writing, and I told her "no, only coarse-hand," and then she said the paper warn't anything but a book-mark to keep her place, and I might go and play now.

I went off down to the river, studying over this thing, and pretty soon I noticed that my nigger was following along behind. When we was out of sight of the house, he looked back and around a second, and then comes a-running, and says:

"Mars Jawge, if you'll come down into de swamp, I'll show you a whole stack o' water-moccasins."

Thinks I, that's mighty curious; he said that yesterday. He oughter know a body don't love water-moccasins enough to go around hunting for them. What is he up to anyway? So I says —

"All right, trot ahead."

I followed a half a mile, then he struck out over the swamp and waded ankle deep as much as another half mile. We come to a little flat piece of land which was dry and very thick with trees and bushes and vines, and he says —

"You shove right in dah, jist a few steps, Mars Jawge, dah's whah dey is. I's seed 'm befo', I don't k'yer to see 'em no mo'."

Then he slopped right along and went away, and pretty soon the trees hid him. I poked into the place a-ways, and come to a little open patch as big as a bedroom, all hung around with vines, and found a man laying there asleep — and by jings it was my old Jim!

I waked him up, and I reckoned it was going to be a grand surprise to him to see me again, but it warn't. He nearly cried, he was so glad, but he warn't surprised. Said he swum along behind me, that night, and heard me yell every time, but dasn't answer, because he didn't want nobody to pick *him* up, and take him into slavery again. Says he —

"I got hurt a little, en couldn't swim fas', so I wuz a considable ways behine you, towards de las'; when you landed I reck'ned I could ketch up wid you on de lan' 'dout havin' to shout at you, but when I see dat house I begin to go slow. I 'uz off too fur to hear what dey say to you — I wuz 'fraid o' de dogs — but when it uz all quiet agin, I knowed you's in de house, so I struck out for de woods to wait for day. Early in de mawnin' some er de niggers come along, gwyne to de fields, en dey tuck me en showed me dis place, whah de dogs can't track me on accounts o' de water, en dey brings me truck to eat every night, en tells me how you's a gitt'n along."

"Why didn't you tell my Jack to fetch me here sooner, Jim?"

"Well, 'twarn't no use to 'sturb you, Huck, tell we could do sumfn — but we's all right, now. I ben a-buyin' pots en pans en vittles, as I got a chanst, en a patchin' up de raf', nights, when ———"

"*What* raft, Jim?"

"Our ole raf '."

"You mean to say our old raft warn't smashed all to flinders?"

"No, she warn't. She was tore up a good deal — one en' of her was — but dey warn't no great harm done, on'y our traps was mos' all los'. Ef we hadn' dive' so deep en swum so fur under water, en de night hadn' ben so dark, en we warn't so sk'yerd, en ben sich punkin-heads, as de sayin' is, we'd a seed de raf'. But it's jis' as well we didn't, 'kase now she's all fixed up agin mos' as good as new, en we's got a new lot o' stuff, too, in de place o' what 'uz los'."

"Why, how did you get hold of the raft again, Jim — did you catch her?"

"How I gwyne to ketch her, en I out in de woods? No, some er de niggers foun' her ketched on a snag, along heah in de ben', en dey hid her in a crick, 'mongst de willows, en dey wuz so much jawin' 'bout which un 'um she b'long to de mos', dat I come to heah 'bout it pooty soon, so I ups en settles de trouble by tellin' 'um she don't b'long to none uv um, but to you en me; en I ast 'm if dey gwyne to grab a young white genlman's propaty, en git a hid'n for it? Den I gin 'm ten cents apiece, en dey 'uz mighty well satisfied, en wisht some mo' raf's 'ud come along en make 'm rich agin. Dey's mighty good to me, dese niggers is, en whatever I wants 'm to do fur me, I doan' have to ast 'm twice, honey. Dat Jack's a good nigger, en pooty smart."

"Yes, he is. He ain't ever told me you was here; told me to come, and he'd show me a lot of water-moccasins. If anything happens, *he* ain't mixed up in it. He can say he never seen us together, and it'll be the truth."

I don't want to talk much about the next day. I reckon I'll cut it pretty short. I waked up about dawn, and was agoing to turn over and go to sleep again, when I noticed how still it was — didn't seem to be anybody stirring. That warn't usual. Next I noticed that Buck was up and gone. Well, I gets up, a-wondering, and goes down stairs — nobody around; everything as still as a mouse. Just the same outside; thinks I, what does it mean? Down by the wood-pile I comes across my Jack, and says:

"What's it all about?"

Says he:

"Don't you know, Mars Jawge?"

"No," says I, "I don't."

"Well, den, Miss Sophia's run off! 'deed she has. She run off in de night, sometime — nobody don't know jis' when — run off to git married to dat young Harney Shepherdson, you know — leastways, so dey 'spec. De fambly foun' it out, 'bout half an hour ago — maybe a little mo' — en' I *tell* you dey warn't no time los'. Sich another hurryin' up guns en hosses *you* never see! De women folks has gone for to stir up de relations, en ole Mars Saul en de boys tuck dey guns en rode up de river road for to try to ketch dat young man en kill him 'fo' he kin git acrost de river wid Miss Sophia. I reck'n dey's gwyne to be mighty rough times."

"Buck went off 'thout waking me up."

"Well I reck'n he *did!* Dey warn't gwyne to mix you up in it. Mars Buck he loaded up his gun en 'lowed he's gwyne to fetch home a Shepherdson or bust. Well, dey'll be plenty un 'm dah, I reck'n, en you bet you he'll fetch one ef he gits a chanst."

I took up the river road as hard as I could put. By-and-by I begin to hear guns a good ways off. When I come in sight of the log store and the wood-pile where the steamboats lands, I worked along under the trees and brush till I got to a good place, and then I clumb up into the forks of a cotton-wood that was out of reach, and watched. There was a wood-rank four foot high, a little ways in front of the tree, and first I was going to hide behind that; but maybe it was luckier I didn't.

There was four or five men cavorting around on their horses in the open place before the log store, cussing and yelling, and trying to get at a couple of young chaps that was behind the wood-rank alongside of the steamboat landing — but they couldn't come it. Every time one of them showed himself on the river side of the wood-pile he got shot at. The two boys was squatting back to back behind the pile, so they could watch both ways.

By-and-by the men stopped cavorting around and yelling. They started riding towards the store; then up gets one of the boys, draws a steady bead over the wood-rank, and drops one of them out of his saddle. All the men jumped off of their horses and grabbed the hurt one and started to carry him to the store; and that minute the two boys started on the run. They got half-way to the tree I was in before the men noticed. Then the men see them, and jumped on their horses and took out after them. They gained on the boys, but it didn't do no good, the boys had too good a start; they got to the wood-pile that was in front of my tree, and slipped in behind it, and so they had the bulge on the men again. One of the boys was Buck, and the other was a slim young chap about nineteen years old.

The men ripped around awhile, and then rode away. As soon as they was out of sight, I sung out to Buck and told him. He didn't know what to make of my voice coming out of the tree, at first. He was awful surprised. He told me to watch out sharp and let him know when the men come in sight again; said they was up to some devilment or other — wouldn't be gone long. I wished I was out of that tree, but I dasn't come down. Buck begun to cry and rip, and 'lowed that him and his cousin Joe (that was the other young chap) would make up for this day, yet. He said his father and his two brothers was killed, and two or three of the enemy. Said the Shepherdsons laid for them, in ambush. Buck said his father and brothers ought to waited for their relations — the Shepherdsons was too strong for them. I asked him what was become of young Harney and Miss Sophia. He said they'd got across the river and was safe. I was glad of that; but the way Buck did take on because he didn't manage to kill Harney that day he shot at him — I hain't ever heard anything like it.

All of a sudden, bang! bang! bang! goes three or four guns — the men had slipped around through the woods and come in from behind without their horses! The boys jumped for the river — both of them hurt — and as they swum down the current the men run along the bank shooting at them and singing out, "Kill them, kill them!" It made me so sick I most fell out of the tree. I ain't agoing to tell *all* that happened — it would make me sick again if I was to do that. I wished I hadn't ever come ashore that night, to see such things. I ain't ever going to get shut of them — lots of times I dream about them.

I staid in the tree till it begun to get dark, afraid to come down. Sometimes I heard guns away off in the woods; and twice I seen little gangs of men gallop past the log store with guns; so I reckoned the trouble was still agoing on. I was mighty down-hearted; so I made up my mind I wouldn't ever go anear that house again, because I reckoned I was to blame, somehow. I judged that that piece of paper meant that Miss Sophia was to meet Harney somewheres at half-past two and run off; and I judged I ought to told her father about that paper and the curious way she acted, and then maybe he would a locked her up and this awful mess wouldn't ever happened.

When I got down out of the tree, I crept along down the river bank a piece, and found the two bodies laying in the edge of the water, and tugged at them till I got them ashore; then I covered up their faces, and got away as quick as I could. I cried a little when I was covering up Buck's face, for he was mighty good to me.

It was just dark, now. I never went near the house, but struck through the woods and made for the swamp. Jim warn't on his island, so I tramped off in a hurry for the crick, and crowded through the willows, red-hot to jump aboard and get out of that awful country — the raft was gone! My souls, but I was scared! I couldn't get my breath for most a minute. Then I raised a yell. A voice not twenty-five foot from me, says —

"Good lan'! is dat you, honey? Doan' make no noise."

It was Jim's voice — nothing ever sounded so good before. I run along the bank a piece and got aboard, and Jim he grabbed me and hugged me, he was so glad to see me. He says —

"Laws bless you, chile, I 'uz right down sho' you's dead agin. Jack's been heah, he say he reck'n you's ben shot, kase you didn' come home no mo'; so I's jes' dis minute a startin' de raf' down towards de mouf er de crick, so's to be all ready for to shove out en leave soon as Jack comes agin en tells me for certain you *is* dead. Lawsy, I's mighty glad to git you back agin, honey."

I says —

"All right — that's mighty good; they won't find me, and they'll think I've been killed, and floated down the river — there's something up there that'll help them to think so — so don't you lose no time, Jim, but just shove off for the big water as fast as ever you can."

I never felt easy till the raft was two mile below there and out in the middle of the Mississippi. Then we hung up our signal lantern, and

judged that we was free and safe once more. I hadn't had a bite to eat
since yesterday; so Jim he got out some corn-dodgers and buttermilk,
and pork and cabbage, and greens — there ain't nothing in the world
so good, when it's cooked right — and whilst I eat my supper we
talked, and had a good time. I was powerful glad to get away from the
feuds, and so was Jim to get away from the swamp. We said there warn't
no home like a raft, after all. Other places do seem so cramped up and
smothery, but a raft don't. You feel mighty free and easy and comfortable on a raft.

Chapter XIX

Two or three days and nights went by; I reckon I might say they
swum by, they slid along so quiet and smooth and lovely. Here is the
way we put in the time. It was a monstrous big river down there —
sometimes a mile and a half wide; we run nights, and laid up and hid
day-times; soon as night was most gone, we stopped navigating and
tied up — nearly always in the dead water under a tow-head; and then
cut young cotton-woods and willows and hid the raft with them. Then
we set out the lines. Next we slid into the river and had a swim, so as
to freshen up and cool off; then we set down on the sandy bottom
where the water was about knee deep, and watched the daylight come.
Not a sound, anywheres — perfectly still — just like the whole world
was asleep, only sometimes the bull-frogs a-cluttering, maybe. The first
thing to see, looking away over the water, was a kind of dull line — that
was the woods on t'other side — you couldn't make nothing else out;
then a pale place in the sky; then more paleness, spreading around; then
the river softened up, away off, and warn't black any more, but gray;
you could see little dark spots drifting along, ever so far away — trading
scows, and such things; and long black streaks — rafts; sometimes you
could hear a sweep screaking; or jumbled up voices, it was so still, and
sounds come so far; and by-and-by you could see a streak on the water
which you know by the look of the streak that there's a snag there in a
swift current which breaks on it and makes that streak look that way;
and you see the mist curl up off of the water, and the east reddens up,
and the river, and you make out a log cabin in the edge of the woods,
away on the bank on t'other side of the river, being a wood-yard, likely,
and piled by them cheats so you can throw a dog through it anywheres;
then the nice breeze springs up, and comes fanning you from over
there, so cool and fresh, and sweet to smell, on account of the woods
and the flowers; but sometimes not that way, because they've left dead

fish laying around, gars, and such, and they do get pretty rank; and next you've got the full day, and everything smiling in the sun, and the song-birds just going it!

A little smoke couldn't be noticed, now, so we would take some fish off of the lines, and cook up a hot breakfast. And afterwards we would watch the lonesomeness of the river, and kind of lazy along, and by-and-by lazy off to sleep. Wake up, by-and-by, and look to see what done it, and maybe see a steamboat, coughing along up stream, so far off towards the other side you couldn't tell nothing about her only whether she was stern-wheel or side-wheel; then for about an hour there wouldn't be nothing to hear nor nothing to see — just solid lone-someness. Next you'd see a raft sliding by, away off yonder, and maybe a galoot on it chopping, because they're most always doing it on a raft; you'd see the ax flash, and come down — you don't hear nothing; you see that ax go up again, and by the time it's above the man's head, then you hear the *k'chunk!* — it had took all that time to come over the water. So we would put in the day, lazying around, listening to the still-ness. Once there was a thick fog, and the rafts and things that went by was beating tin pans so the steamboats wouldn't run over them. A scow or a raft went by so close we could hear them talking and cussing and laughing — heard them plain; but we couldn't see no sign of them; it made you feel crawly, it was like spirits carrying on that way in the air. Jim said he believed it was spirits; but I says:

"No, spirits wouldn't say, 'dern the dern fog.'"

Soon as it was night, out we shoved; when we got her out to about the middle, we let her alone, and let her float wherever the current wanted her to; then we lit the pipes, and dangled our legs in the water and talked about all kinds of things — we was always naked, day and night, whenever the mosquitoes would let us — the new clothes Buck's folks made for me was too good to be comfortable, and besides I didn't go much on clothes, no-how.

Sometimes we'd have that whole river all to ourselves for the long-est time. Yonder was the banks and the islands, across the water; and maybe a spark — which was a candle in a cabin window — and some-times on the water you could see a spark or two — on a raft or a scow, you know; and maybe you could hear a fiddle or a song coming over from one of them crafts. It's lovely to live on a raft. We had the sky, up there, all speckled with stars, and we used to lay on our backs and look up at them, and discuss about whether they was made, or only just hap-pened — Jim he allowed they was made, but I allowed they happened; I judged it would have took too long to *make* so many. Jim said the

moon could a *laid* them; well, that looked kind of reasonable, so I
didn't say nothing against it, because I've seen a frog lay most as many,
so of course it could be done. We used to watch the stars that fell, too,
and see them streak down. Jim allowed they'd got spoiled and was hove
out of the nest.

Once or twice of a night we would see a steamboat slipping along in
the dark, and now and then she would belch a whole world of sparks up
out of her chimbleys, and they would rain down in the river and look
awful pretty; then she would turn a corner and her lights would wink
out and her pow-wow shut off and leave the river still again; and by-
and-by her waves would get to us, a long time after she was gone, and
joggle the raft a bit, and after that you wouldn't hear nothing for you
couldn't tell how long, except maybe frogs or something.

After midnight the people on shore went to bed, and then for two
or three hours the shores was black — no more sparks in the cabin windows. These sparks was our clock — the first one that showed again
meant morning was coming, so we hunted a place to hide and tie up,
right away.

One morning about day-break, I found a canoe and crossed over a
chute to the main shore — it was only two hundred yards — and paddled about a mile up a crick amongst the cypress woods, to see if I
couldn't get some berries. Just as I was passing a place where a kind of a
cow-path crossed the crick, here comes a couple of men tearing up the
path as tight as they could foot it. I thought I was a goner, for whenever
anybody was after anybody I judged it was *me* — or maybe Jim. I was
about to dig out from there in a hurry, but they was pretty close to me
then, and sung out and begged me to save their lives — said they hadn't
been doing nothing, and was being chased for it — said there was men
and dogs a-coming. They wanted to jump right in, but I says —

"Don't you do it. I don't hear the dogs and horses yet; you've got
time to crowd through the brush and get up the crick a little ways; then
you take to the water and wade down to me and get in — that'll throw
the dogs off the scent."

They done it, and soon as they was aboard I lit out for our tow-
head, and in about five or ten minutes we heard the dogs and the men
away off, shouting. We heard them come along towards the crick, but
couldn't see them; they seemed to stop and fool around a while; then,
as we got further and further away all the time, we couldn't hardly hear
them at all; by the time we had left a mile of woods behind us and
struck the river, everything was quiet, and we paddled over to the tow-
head and hid in the cotton-woods and was safe.

They would have been caught but still treat bad

One of these fellows was about seventy, or upwards, and had a bald head and very gray whiskers. He had an old battered-up slouch hat on, and a greasy blue woolen shirt, and ragged old blue jeans britches stuffed into his boot tops, and home-knit galluses° — no, he only had one. He had an old long-tailed blue jeans coat with slick brass buttons, flung over his arm, and both of them had big fat ratty-looking carpet-bags.

The other fellow was about thirty and dressed about as ornery. After breakfast we all laid off and talked, and the first thing that come out was that these chaps didn't know one another.

"What got you into trouble?" says the baldhead to t'other chap.

"Well, I'd been selling an article to take the tartar off the teeth — and it does take it off, too, and generly the enamel along with it — but I staid about one night longer than I ought to, and was just in the act of sliding out when I ran across you on the trail this side of town, and you told me they were coming, and begged me to help you to get off. So I told you I was expecting trouble myself and would scatter out *with* you. That's the whole yarn — what's yourn?"

"Well, I'd ben a-runnin' a little temperance revival thar, 'bout a week, and was the pet of the women-folks, big and little, for I was makin' it mighty warm for the rummies, I *tell* you, and takin' as much as five or six dollars a night — ten cents a head, children and niggers free — and business a growin' all the time; when somehow or another a little report got around, last night, that I had a way of puttin' in my time with a private jug, on the sly. A nigger rousted me out this mornin', and told me the people was getherin' on the quiet, with their dogs and horses, and they'd be along pretty soon and give me 'bout half an hour's start, and then run me down, if they could; and if they got me they'd tar and feather me and ride me on a rail, sure. I didn't wait for no breakfast — I warn't hungry."

"Old man," says the young one, "I reckon we might double-team it together; what do you think?"

"I ain't undisposed. What's your line — mainly?"

"Jour° printer, by trade; do a little in patent medicines; theatre-actor — tragedy, you know; take a turn at mesmerism and phrenology when there's a chance; teach singing-geography school for a change; sling a lecture, sometimes — oh, I do lots of things — most anything that comes handy, so it ain't work. What's your lay?"

galluses: Suspenders.   **jour:** Journeyman.

voluntary give up freedom

"I've done considerble in the doctoring way in my time. Layin' on o' hands is my best holt — for cancer, and paralysis, and sich things; and I k'n tell a fortune pretty good, when I've got somebody along to find out the facts for me. Preachin's my line, too; and workin' camp-meetin's; and missionaryin around."

Nobody never said anything for a while; then the young man hove a sigh and says —

"Alas!"

"What 're you alassin' about?" says the baldhead.

"To think I should have lived to be leading such a life, and be degraded down into such company." And he begun to wipe the corner of his eye with a rag.

"Dern your skin, ain't the company good enough for you?" says the bald-head, pretty pert and uppish.

"Yes, it *is* good enough for me; it's as good as I deserve; for who fetched me so low, when I was so high? *I* did myself. I don't blame *you*, gentlemen — far from it; I don't blame anybody. I deserve it all. Let the cold world do its worst; one thing I know — there's a grave somewhere for me. The world may go on just as its always done, and take everything from me — loved ones, property, everything — but it can't take that. Some day I'll lie down in it and forget it all, and my poor broken heart will be at rest." He went on a-wiping.

"Drot your pore broken heart," says the baldhead; "what are you heaving your pore broken heart at *us* f'r? *We* hain't done nothing."

"No, I know you haven't. I ain't blaming you, gentlemen. I brought myself down — yes, I did it myself. It's right I should suffer — perfectly right — I don't make any moan."

"Brought you down from whar? Whar was you brought down from?"

"Ah, you would not believe me; the world never believes — let it pass — 'tis no matter. The secret of my birth ——"

"The secret of your birth? Do you mean to say ——"

"Gentlemen," says the young man, very solemn, "I will reveal it to you, for I feel I may have confidence in you. By rights I am a duke!"

Jim's eyes bugged out when he heard that; and I reckon mine did, too. Then the baldhead says: "No! you can't mean it?"

"Yes. My great-grandfather, eldest son of the Duke of Bridgewater, fled to this country about the end of the last century, to breathe the pure air of freedom; married here, and died, leaving a son, his own father dying about the same time. The second son of the late duke seized the title and estates — the infant real duke was ignored. I am the lineal descendant of that infant — I am the rightful Duke of Bridge-water; and here am I, forlorn, torn from my high estate, hunted of men, despised by the cold world, ragged, worn, heart-broken, and degraded to the companionship of felons on a raft!"

Jim pitied him ever so much, and so did I. We tried to comfort him, but he said it warn't much use, he couldn't be much comforted; said if we was a mind to acknowledge him, that would do him more good than most anything else; so we said we would, if he would tell us how. He said we ought to bow, when we spoke to him, and say "Your Grace," or "My Lord," or "Your Lordship" — and he wouldn't mind it if we called him plain "Bridgewater," which he said was a title, anyway, and not a name; and one of us ought to wait on him at dinner, and do any little thing for him he wanted done.

Well, that was all easy, so we done it. All through dinner Jim stood around and waited on him, and says, "Will yo' Grace have some o' dis, or some o' dat?" and so on, and a body could see it was mighty pleasing to him.

But the old man got pretty silent, by-and-by — didn't have much to say, and didn't look pretty comfortable over all that petting that was going on around that duke. He seemed to have something on his mind. So, along in the afternoon, he says:

"Looky here, Bilgewater," he says, "I'm nation sorry for you, but you ain't the only person that's had troubles like that."

"No?"

"No, you ain't. You ain't the only person that's ben snaked down wrongfully out'n a high place."

"Alas!"

"No, you ain't the only person that's had a secret of his birth." And by jings, *he* begins to cry.

"Hold! What do you mean?"

"Bilgewater, kin I trust you?" says the old man, still sort of sobbing.

"To the bitter death!" He took the old man by the hand and squeezed it, and says, "The secret of your being: speak!"

"Bilgewater, I am the late Dauphin!"

You bet you Jim and me stared, this time. Then the duke says:

"You are what?"

"Yes, my friend, it is too true — your eyes is lookin' at this very moment on the pore disappeared Dauphin, Looy the Seventeen, son of Looy the Sixteen and Marry Antonette."

"You! At your age! No! You mean you're the late Charlemagne; you must be six or seven hundred years old, at the very least."

"Trouble has done it, Bilgewater, trouble has done it; trouble has brung these gray hairs and this premature balditude. Yes, gentlemen, you see before you, in blue jeans and misery, the wanderin', exiled, trampled-on and sufferin' rightful King of France."

Well, he cried and took on so, that me and Jim didn't know hardly what to do, we was so sorry — and so glad and proud we'd got him with us, too. So we set in, like we done before with the duke, and tried to comfort *him*. But he said it warn't no use, nothing but to be dead and done with it all could do him any good; though he said it often made him feel easier and better for a while if people treated him according to his rights, and got down on one knee to speak to him, and always called him "Your Majesty," and waited on him first at meals, and didn't set down in his presence till he asked them. So Jim and me set to majestying him, and doing this and that and t'other for him, and standing up till he told us we might set down. This done him heaps of good, and so he got cheerful and comfortable. But the duke kind of soured on him, and didn't look a bit satisfied with the way things was going; still, the king acted real friendly towards him, and said the duke's great-grandfather and all the other Dukes of Bilgewater was a good deal thought of by *his* father and was allowed to come to the palace considerable; but the duke staid huffy a good while, till by-and-by the king says:

"Like as not we got to be together a blamed long time, on this h-yer raft, Bilgewater, and so what's the use o' your bein' sour? It'll only make things oncomfortable. It ain't my fault I warn't born a duke, it ain't your fault you warn't born a king — so what's the use to worry? Make the best o' things the way you find 'em, says I — that's my motto. This ain't no bad thing that we've struck here — plenty grub and an easy life — come, give us your hand, Duke, and less all be friends."

The duke done it, and Jim and me was pretty glad to see it. It took away all the uncomfortableness, and we felt mighty good over it, because it would a been a miserable business to have any unfriendliness on the raft; for what you want, above all things, on a raft, is for everybody to be satisfied, and feel right and kind towards the others.

It didn't take me long to make up my mind that these liars warn't no kings nor dukes, at all, but just low-down humbugs and frauds. But I never said nothing, never let on; kept it to myself; it's the best way; then you don't have no quarrels, and don't get into no trouble. If they wanted us to call them kings and dukes, I hadn't no objections, 'long as it would keep peace in the family; and it warn't no use to tell Jim, so I didn't tell him. If I never learnt nothing else out of pap, I learnt that the best way to get along with his kind of people is to let them have their own way.

Chapter XX

They asked us considerable many questions; wanted to know what we covered up the raft that way for, and laid by in the day-time instead of running — was Jim a runaway nigger? Says I —

"Goodness sakes, would a runaway nigger run *south?*"

No, they allowed he wouldn't. I had to account for things some way, so I says:

"My folks was living in Pike County, in Missouri, where I was born, and they all died off but me and pa and my brother Ike. Pa, he 'lowed he'd break up and go down and live with Uncle Ben, who's got a little one-horse place on the river, forty-four mile below Orleans. Pa was pretty poor, and had some debts; so when he'd squared up there warn't nothing left but sixteen dollars and our nigger, Jim. That warn't enough to take us fourteen hundred mile, deck passage nor no other way. Well, when the river rose, pa had a streak of luck one day; he ketched this piece of a raft; so we reckoned we'd go down to Orleans on it. Pa's luck didn't hold out; a steamboat run over the forrard corner of the raft, one night, and we all went overboard and dove under the wheel; Jim and me come up, all right, but pa was drunk, and Ike was only four years old, so they never come up no more. Well, for the next day or two we had considerable trouble, because people was always coming out in skiffs and trying to take Jim away from me, saying they believed he was a runaway nigger. We don't run day-times no more, now; nights they don't bother us."

The duke says —

"Leave me alone to cipher out a way so we can run in the day-time if we want to. I'll think the thing over — I'll invent a plan that'll fix it. We'll let it alone for to-day, because of course we don't want to go by that town yonder in daylight — it mightn't be healthy."

Towards night it begun to darken up and look like rain; the heat lightning was squirting around, low down in the sky, and the leaves was beginning to shiver — it was going to be pretty ugly, it was easy to see that. So the duke and the king went to overhauling our wigwam, to see what the beds was like. My bed was a straw tick — better than Jim's, which was a corn-shuck tick; there's always cobs around about in a shuck tick, and they poke into you and hurt; and when you roll over, the dry shucks sound like you was rolling over in a pile of dead leaves; it makes such a rustling that you wake up. Well, the duke allowed he would take my bed; but the king allowed he wouldn't. He says —

"I should a reckoned the difference in rank would a sejested to you that a corn-shuck bed warn't just fitten for me to sleep on. Your Grace'll take the shuck bed yourself."

Jim and me was in a sweat again, for a minute, being afraid there was going to be some more trouble amongst them; so we was pretty glad when the duke says —

" 'Tis my fate to be always ground into the mire under the iron heel of oppression. Misfortune has broken my once haughty spirit; I yield, I submit; 'tis my fate. I am alone in the world — let me suffer; I can bear it."

We got away as soon as it was good and dark. The king told us to stand well out towards the middle of the river, and not show a light till we got a long ways below the town. We come in sight of the little bunch of lights by-and-by — that was the town, you know — and slid by, about a half a mile out, all right. When we was three-quarters of a mile below, we hoisted up our signal lantern; and about ten o'clock it come on to rain and blow and thunder and lighten like everything; so the king told us to both stay on watch till the weather got better; then him and the duke crawled into the wigwam and turned in for the night. It was my watch below, till twelve, but I wouldn't a turned in, anyway, if I'd had a bed; because a body don't see such a storm as that every day in the week, not by a long sight. My souls, how the wind did scream along! And every second or two there'd come a glare that lit up the white-caps for a half a mile around, and you'd see the islands looking dusty through the rain, and the trees thrashing around in the wind; then comes a *h-wack!* — bum! bum! bumble-umble-um-bum-bum-bum-bum — and the thunder would go rumbling and grumbling away, and quit — and then *rip* comes another flash and another sockdolager.° The waves most washed me off the raft, sometimes, but I hadn't any clothes on, and didn't mind. We didn't have no trouble about snags; the lightning was glaring and flittering around so constant that we could see them plenty soon enough to throw her head this way or that and miss them.

I had the middle watch, you know, but I was pretty sleepy by that time, so Jim he said he would stand the first half of it for me; he was always mighty good, that way, Jim was. I crawled into the wigwam, but the king and the duke had their legs sprawled around so there warn't

sockdolager: A very heavy blow from the storm.

no show for me; so I laid outside — I didn't mind the rain, because it was warm, and the waves warn't running so high, now. About two they come up again, though, and Jim was going to call me, but he changed his mind because he reckoned they warn't high enough yet to do any harm; but he was mistaken about that, for pretty soon all of a sudden along comes a regular ripper, and washed me overboard. It most killed Jim a-laughing. He was the easiest nigger to laugh that ever was, anyway.

I took the watch, and Jim he laid down and snored away; and by-and-by the storm let up for good and all; and the first cabin-light that showed, I rousted him out and we slid the raft into hiding-quarters for the day.

The king got out an old ratty deck of cards, after breakfast, and him and the duke played seven-up a while, five cents a game. Then they got tired of it, and allowed they would "lay out a campaign," as they called it. The duke went down into his carpet-bag and fetched up a lot of little printed bills, and read them out loud. One bill said "The celebrated Dr. Armand de Montalban of Paris," would "lecture on the Science of Phrenology" at such and such a place, on the blank day of blank, at ten cents admission, and "furnish charts of character at twenty-five cents apiece." The duke said that was *him*. In another bill he was the "world renowned Shaksperean tragedian, Garrick the Younger, of Drury Lane, London." In other bills he had a lot of other names and done other wonderful things, like finding water and gold with a "divining rod," "dissipating witch-spells," and so on. By-and-by he says —

"But the histrionic muse is the darling. Have you ever trod the boards, Royalty?"

"No," says the king.

"You shall, then, before you're three days older, Fallen Grandeur," says the duke. "The first good town we come to, we'll hire a hall and do the sword-fight in Richard III. and the balcony scene in Romeo and Juliet. How does that strike you?"

"I'm in, up to the hub, for anything that will pay, Bilgewater, but you see I don't know nothing about play-actn', and hain't ever seen much of it. I was too small when pap used to have 'em at the palace. Do you reckon you can learn me?"

"Easy!"

"All right. I'm jist a-freezn' for something fresh, anyway. Less commence, right away."

So the duke he told him all about who Romeo was, and who Juliet was, and said he was used to being Romeo, so the king could be Juliet.

"But if Juliet's such a young gal, Duke, my peeled head and my white whiskers is goin' to look oncommon odd on her, maybe."

"No, don't you worry — these country jakes won't ever think of that. Besides, you know, you'll be in costume, and that makes all the difference in the world; Juliet's in a balcony, enjoying the moonlight before she goes to bed, and she's got on her night-gown and her ruffled night-cap. Here are the costumes for the parts."

He got out two or three curtain-calico suits, which he said was meedyevil armor for Richard III. and t'other chap, and a long white cotton night-shirt and a ruffled night-cap to match. The king was satisfied; so the duke got out his book and read the parts over in the most splendid spread-eagle way, prancing around and acting at the same time, to show how it had got to be done; then he give the book to the king and told him to get his part by heart.

There was a little one-horse town about three mile down the bend, and after dinner the duke said he had ciphered out his idea about how to run in daylight without it being dangersome for Jim; so he allowed he would go down to the town and fix that thing. The king allowed he would go too, and see if he couldn't strike something. We was out of coffee, so Jim said I better go along with them in the canoe and get some.

When we got there, there warn't nobody stirring; streets empty, and perfectly dead and still, like Sunday. We found a sick nigger sunning himself in a back yard, and he said everybody that warn't too young or too sick or too old, was gone to camp-meeting, about two mile back in the woods. The king got the directions, and allowed he'd go and work that camp-meeting for all it was worth, and I might go, too.

The duke said what he was after was a printing office. We found it; a little bit of a concern, up over a carpenter shop — carpenters and printers all gone to the meeting, and no doors locked. It was a dirty, littered-up place, and had ink marks, and handbills with pictures of horses and runaway niggers on them, all over the walls. The duke shed his coat and said he was all right, now. So me and the king lit out for the camp-meeting.

We got there in about a half an hour, fairly dripping, for it was a most awful hot day. There was as much as a thousand people there, from twenty mile around. The woods was full of teams and wagons, hitched everywheres, feeding out of the wagon troughs and stomping to keep off the flies. There was sheds made out of poles and roofed over with branches, where they had lemonade and gingerbread to sell, and piles of watermelons and green corn and such-like truck.

The preaching was going on under the same kinds of sheds, only they was bigger and held crowds of people. The benches was made out of outside slabs of logs, with holes bored in the round side to drive sticks into for legs. They didn't have no backs. The preachers had high platforms to stand on, at one end of the sheds. The women had on sun-bonnets: and some had linsey-woolsey frocks, some gingham ones, and a few of the young ones had on calico. Some of the young men was barefooted, and some of the children didn't have on any clothes but just a tow-linen shirt. Some of the old women was knitting, and some of the young folks was courting on the sly.

The first shed we come to, the preacher was lining out a hymn.° He lined out two lines, everybody sung it, and it was kind of grand to hear it, there was so many of them and they done it in such a rousing way; then he lined out two more for them to sing — and so on. The people woke up more and more, and sung louder and louder; and towards the end, some begun to groan, and some begun to shout. Then the preacher begun to preach; and begun in earnest, too; and went weaving first to one side of the platform and then the other, and then a leaning down over the front of it, with his arms and his body going all the time, and shouting his words out with all his might; and every now and then he would hold up his Bible and spread it open, and kind of pass it around this way and that, shouting, "It's the brazen serpent in the wilderness! Look upon it and live!" And people would shout out, "Glory! — A-a-*men!*" And so he went on, and the people groaning and crying and saying amen:

"Oh, come to the mourners' bench! come, black with sin! (*amen!*) come, sick and sore! (*amen!*) come, lame and halt, and blind! (*amen!*) come, pore and needy, sunk in shame! (*a-a-men!*) come all that's worn, and soiled, and suffering! — come with a broken spirit! come with a contrite heart! come in your rags and sin and dirt! the waters that cleanse is free, the door of heaven stands open — oh, enter in and be at rest!" (*a-a-men! glory, glory hallelujah!*)

And so on. You couldn't make out what the preacher said, any more, on account of the shouting and crying. Folks got up, everywheres in the crowd, and worked their way, just by main strength, to the mourners' bench, with the tears running down their faces; and when all the mourners had got up there to the front benches in a crowd, they sung, and shouted, and flung themselves down on the straw, just crazy and wild.

---

lining out a hymn: The preacher is singing out individual lines for his congregation to follow, since hymnals were most likely scarce and illiteracy not uncommon.

Well, the first I knowed, the king got agoing; and you could hear him over everybody; and next he went a-charging up on to the platform and the preacher he begged him to speak to the people, and he done it. He told them he was a pirate — been a pirate for thirty years, out in the Indian Ocean, and his crew was thinned out considerable, last spring, in a fight, and he was home now, to take out some fresh men, and thanks to goodness he'd been robbed last night, and put ashore off of a steamboat without a cent, and he was glad of it, it was the blessedest thing that ever happened to him, because he was a changed man now, and happy for the first time in his life; and poor as he was, he was going to start right off and work his way back to the Indian Ocean and put in the rest of his life trying to turn the pirates into the true path; for he could do it better than anybody else, being acquainted with all the pirate crews in that ocean; and though it would take him a long time to get there, without money, he would get there anyway, and every time he convinced a pirate he would say to him, "Don't you thank me, don't you give me no credit, it all belongs to them dear people in Pokeville camp-meeting, natural brothers and benefactors of the race — and that dear preacher there, the truest friend a pirate ever had!"

And then he busted into tears, and so did everybody. Then somebody sings out, "Take up a collection for him, take up a collection!" Well, a half a dozen made a jump to do it, but somebody sings out, "Let *him* pass the hat around!" Then everybody said it, the preacher too.

So the king went all through the crowd with his hat, swabbing his eyes, and blessing the people and praising them and thanking them for being so good to the poor pirates away off there; and every little while the prettiest kind of girls, with the tears running down their cheeks, would up and ask him would he let them kiss him, for to remember him by; and he always done it; and some of them he hugged and kissed as many as five or six times — and he was invited to stay a week; and everybody wanted him to live in their houses, and said they'd think it was an honor; but he said as this was the last day of the camp-meeting he couldn't do no good, and besides he was in a sweat to get to the Indian Ocean right off and go to work on the pirates.

When we got back to the raft and he come to count up, he found he had collected eighty-seven dollars and seventy-five cents. And then he had fetched away a three-gallon jug of whisky, too, that he found under a wagon when we was starting home through the woods. The king said, take it all around, it laid over any day he'd ever put in the missionarying line. He said it warn't no use talking, heathens don't amount to shucks, alongside of pirates, to work a camp-meeting with.

The duke was thinking *he'd* been doing pretty well, till the king come to show up, but after that he didn't think so so much. He had set up and printed off two little jobs for farmers, in that printing office — horse bills — and took the money, four dollars. And he had got in ten dollars worth of advertisements for the paper, which he said he would put in for four dollars if they would pay in advance — so they done it. The price of the paper was two dollars a year, but he took in three sub-scriptions for half a dollar apiece on condition of them paying him in advance; they were going to pay in cord-wood and onions, as usual, but he said he had just bought the concern and knocked down the price as low as he could afford it, and was going to run it for cash. He set up a little piece of poetry, which he made, himself, out of his own head — three verses — kind of sweet and saddish — the name of it was, "Yes, crush, cold world, this breaking heart" — and he left that all set up and ready to print in the paper and didn't charge nothing for it. Well, he took in nine dollars and a half, and said he'd done a pretty square day's work for it.

Then he showed us another little job he'd printed and hadn't charged for, because it was for us. It had a picture of a runaway nigger, with a bundle on a stick, over his shoulder, and "$200 reward" under it. The reading was all about Jim, and just described him to a dot. It said he run away from St. Jacques' plantation, forty mile below New Orleans, last winter, and likely went north, and whoever would catch him and send him back, he could have the reward and expenses.

"Now," says the duke, "after to-night we can run in the daytime if we want to. Whenever we see anybody coming, we can tie Jim hand and foot with a rope, and lay him in the wigwam and show this handbill and say we captured him up the river, and were too poor to travel on a steamboat, so we got this little raft on credit from our friends and are going down to get the reward. Handcuffs and chains would look still better on Jim, but it wouldn't go well with the story of us being so poor. Too much like jewelry. Ropes are the correct thing — we must preserve the unities, as we say on the boards."

We all said the duke was pretty smart, and there couldn't be no trouble about running daytimes. We judged we could make miles enough that night to get out of the reach of the pow-wow we reckoned the duke's work in the printing office was going to make in that little town — then we could boom right along, if we wanted to.

We laid low and kept still, and never shoved out till nearly ten o'clock; then we slid by, pretty wide away from the town, and didn't hoist our lantern till we was clear out of sight of it.

When Jim called me to take the watch at four in the morning, he
says —

"Huck, does you reck'n we gwyne to run acrost any mo' kings on
dis trip?"

"No," I says, "I reckon not."

"Well," says he, "dat's all right, den. I doan' mine one er two kings,
but dat's enough. Dis one's powerful drunk, en de duke ain' much
better."

I found Jim had been trying to get him to talk French, so he could
hear what it was like; but he said he had been in this country so long,
and had so much trouble, he'd forgot it.

Chapter XXI

It was after sun-up, now, but we went right on, and didn't tie up.
The king and the duke turned out, by-and-by, looking pretty rusty; but
after they'd jumped overboard and took a swim, it chippered them up
a good deal. After breakfast the king he took a seat on a corner of the
raft, and pulled off his boots and rolled up his britches, and let his legs
dangle in the water, so as to be comfortable, and lit his pipe, and went
to getting his Romeo and Juliet by heart. When he had got it pretty
good, him and the duke begun to practice it together. The duke had to
learn him over and over again, how to say every speech; and he made
him sigh, and put his hand on his heart, and after while he said he done
it pretty well; "only," he says, "you mustn't bellow out *Romeo!* that
way, like a bull — you must say it soft, and sick, and languishy, so —
R—o—o—meo! that is the idea; for Juliet's a dear sweet mere child of a
girl, you know, and she don't bray like a jackass."

Well, next they got out a couple of long swords that the duke made
out of oak laths, and begun to practice the sword-fight — the duke
called himself Richard III.; and the way they laid on, and pranced
around the raft was grand to see. But by-and-by the king tripped and
fell overboard, and after that they took a rest, and had a talk about all
kinds of adventures they'd had in other times along the river.

After dinner, the duke says:

"Well, Capet, we'll want to make this a first-class show, you know,
so I guess we'll add a little more to it. We want a little something to
answer encores with, anyway."

"What's onkores, Bilgewater?"

The duke told him, and then says:

"I'll answer by doing the Highland fling or the sailor's hornpipe;

and you — well, let me see — oh, I've got it — you can do Hamlet's soliloquy."

"Hamlet's which?"

"Hamlet's soliloquy, you know; the most celebrated thing in Shakespeare. Ah, it's sublime, sublime! Always fetches the house. I haven't got it in the book — I've only got one volume — but I reckon I can piece it out from memory. I'll just walk up and down a minute, and see if I can call it back from recollection's vaults."

So he went to marching up and down, thinking, and frowning horrible every now and then; then he would hoist up his eyebrows; next he would squeeze his hand on his forehead and stagger back and kind of moan; next he would sigh, and next he'd let on to drop a tear. It was beautiful to see him. By-and-by he got it. He told us to give attention. Then he strikes a most noble attitude, with one leg shoved forwards, and his arms stretched away up, and his head tilted back, looking up at the sky; and then he begins to rip and rave and grit his teeth; and after that, all through his speech he howled, and spread around, and swelled up his chest, and just knocked the spots out of any acting ever *I* see before. This is the speech — I learned it, easy enough, while he was learning it to the king:

> To be, or not to be; that is the bare bodkin
> That makes calamity of so long life;
> For who would fardels bear, till Birnam Wood do come to
> Dunsinane,
> But that the fear of something after death
> Murders the innocent sleep,
> Great nature's second course,
> And makes us rather sling the arrows of outrageous fortune
> Than fly to others that we know not of.
> There's the respect must give us pause:
> Wake Duncan with thy knocking! I would thou couldst;
> For who would bear the whips and scorns of time,
> The oppressor's wrong, the proud man's contumely,
> The law's delay, and the quietus which his pangs might take,
> In the dead waste and middle of the night, when churchyards
> yawn
> In customary suits of solemn black,
> But that the undiscovered country from whose bourne no
> traveler returns,
> Breathes forth contagion on the world,
> And thus the native hue of resolution, like the poor cat i' the
> adage,

Is sicklied o'er with care.
And all the clouds that lowered o'er our housetops,
With this regard their currents turn awry,
And lose the name of action.
'Tis a consummation devoutly to be wished. But soft you, the
  fair Ophelia:
Ope not thy ponderous and marble jaws,
But get thee to a nunnery — go!

Well, the old man he liked that speech, and he mighty soon got it so
he could do it first rate. It seemed like he was just born for it; and when
he had his hand in and was excited, it was perfectly lovely the way he
would rip and tear and rair up behind when he was getting it off.

The first chance we got, the duke he had some show bills printed;
and after that, for two or three days as we floated along, the raft was
a most uncommon lively place, for there warn't nothing but sword-
fighting and rehearsing — as the duke called it — going on all the time.
One morning, when we was pretty well down the State of Arkansaw, we
come in sight of a little one-horse town in a big bend; so we tied up
about three-quarters of a mile above it, in the mouth of a crick which
was shut in like a tunnel by the cypress trees, and all of us but Jim took
the canoe and went down there to see if there was any chance in that
place for our show.

We struck it mighty lucky; there was going to be a circus there that
afternoon, and the country people was already beginning to come in, in
all kinds of old shackly wagons, and on horses. The circus would leave
before night, so our show would have a pretty good chance. The duke
he hired the court house, and we went around and stuck up our bills.
They read like this:

Shaksperean Revival!!!
Wonderful Attraction!
For One Night Only!
The world renowned tragedians,
David Garrick the younger, of Drury Lane Theatre, London,
and
Edmund Kean the elder, of the Royal Haymarket Theatre, White-
chapel, Pudding Lane, Piccadilly, London, and the
Royal Continental Theatres, in their sublime
Shaksperean Spectacle entitled
The Balcony Scene
in
Romeo and Juliet!!!

Romeo . . . . Mr. Garrick.
Juliet. Mr. Kean.
Assisted by the whole strength of the company!
New costumes, new scenery, new appointments!
Also:
The thrilling, masterly, and blood-curdling
Broad-sword conflict
In Richard III. !!!
Richard III . . . . Mr. Garrick.
Richmond. . . . . Mr. Kean.
also:
(by special request,)
Hamlet's Immortal Soliloquy!!
By the Illustrious Kean!
Done by him 300 consecutive nights in Paris!
For One Night Only,
On account of imperative European engagements!
Admission 25 cents; children and servants, 10 cents.

Then we went loafing around the town. The stores and houses was most all old shackly dried-up frame concerns that hadn't ever been painted; they was set up three or four foot above ground on stilts, so as to be out of reach of the water when the river was overflowed. The houses had little gardens around them, but they didn't seem to raise hardly anything in them but jimpson weeds, and sunflowers, and ash-piles, and old curled-up boots and shoes, and pieces of bottles, and rags, and played-out tin-ware. The fences was made of different kinds of boards, nailed on at different times; and they leaned every which-way, and had gates that didn't generly have but one hinge — a leather one. Some of the fences had been whitewashed, some time or another, but the duke said it was in Clumbus's time, like enough. There was generly hogs in the garden, and people driving them out.

All the stores was along one street. They had white-domestic awnings in front, and the country people hitched their horses to the awning-posts. There was empty dry-goods boxes under the awnings, and loafers roosting on them all day long, whittling them with their Barlow knives; and chawing tobacco, and gaping and yawning and stretching — a mighty ornery lot. They generly had on yellow straw hats most as wide as an umbrella, but didn't wear no coats nor waist-coats; they called one another Bill, and Buck, and Hank, and Joe, and Andy, and talked lazy and drawly, and used considerable many cuss-words. There was as many as one loafer leaning up against every awning-post, and he most always had his hands in his britches pockets, except when he fetched them out to lend a chaw of tobacco or scratch. What a body was hearing amongst them, all the time was —

"Gimme a chaw 'v tobacker, Hank."

"Cain't — I hain't got but one chaw left. Ask Bill."

Maybe Bill he gives him a chaw; maybe he lies and says he ain't got none. Some of them kinds of loafers never has a cent in the world, nor a chaw of tobacco of their own. They get all their chawing by borrowing — they say to a fellow, "I wisht you'd len' me a chaw, Jack, I jist this minute give Ben Thompson the last chaw I had" — which is a lie, pretty much every time; it don't fool nobody but a stranger; but Jack ain't no stranger, so he says —

"*You* give him a chaw, did you? so did your sister's cat's grand-mother. You pay me back the chaws you've awready borry'd off'n me, Lafe Buckner, then I'll loan you one or two ton of it, and won't charge you no back intrust, nuther."

"Well, I *did* pay you back some of it wunst."

"Yes, you did — 'bout six chaws. You borry'd store tobacker and paid back nigger-head."

Store tobacco is flat black plug, but these fellows mostly chaws the natural leaf twisted. When they borrow a chaw, they don't generly cut it off with a knife, but they set the plug in between their teeth, and gnaw with their teeth and tug at the plug with their hands till they get it in two — then sometimes the one that owns the tobacco looks mournful at it when it's handed back, and says, sarcastic —

"Here, gimme the *chaw*, and you take the *plug*."

All the streets and lanes was just mud, they warn't nothing else *but* mud — mud as black as tar, and nigh about a foot deep in some places; and two or three inches deep in *all* the places. The hogs loafed and grunted around, everywheres. You'd see a muddy sow and a litter of pigs come lazying along the street and whollop herself right down in the way, where folks had to walk around her, and she'd stretch out, and shut her eyes, and wave her ears, whilst the pigs was milking her, and look as happy as if she was on salary. And pretty soon you'd hear a loafer sing out, "Hi! *so* boy! sick him, Tige!" and away the sow would go, squealing most horrible, with a dog or two swinging to each ear, and three or four dozen more a-coming; and then you would see all the loafers get up and watch the thing out of sight, and laugh at the fun and look grateful for the noise. Then they'd settle back again till there was a dog-fight. There couldn't anything wake them up all over, and make them happy all over, like a dog-fight — unless it might be putting turpentine on a stray dog and setting fire to him, or tying a tin pan to his tail and see him run himself to death.

On the river front some of the houses was sticking out over the bank, and they was bowed and bent, and about ready to tumble in. The people had moved out of them. The bank was caved away under one corner of some others, and that corner was hanging over. People lived in them yet, but it was dangersome, because sometimes a strip of land as wide as a house caves in at a time. Sometimes a belt of land a quarter of a mile deep will start in and cave along and cave along till it all caves into the river in one summer. Such a town as that has to be always moving back, and back, and back, because the river's always gnawing at it.

The nearer it got to noon that day, the thicker and thicker was the wagons and horses in the streets, and more coming all the time. Families fetched their dinners with them, from the country, and eat them in the wagons. There was considerable whiskey drinking going on, and I seen three fights. By-and-by somebody sings out —

"Here comes old Boggs! — in from the country for his little old monthly drunk — here he comes, boys!"

All the loafers looked glad — I reckoned they was used to having fun out of Boggs. One of them says —

"Wonder who he's a gwyne to chaw up this time. If he'd a chawed up all the men he's ben a gwyne to chaw up in the last twenty year, he'd have considerble ruputation, now."

Another one says, "I wisht old Boggs 'd threaten me, 'cuz then I'd know I warn't gwyne to die for a thousan' year."

Boggs comes a-tearing along on his horse, whooping and yelling like an Injun, and singing out —

"Cler the track, thar. I'm on the waw-path, and the price uv coffins is a gwyne to raise."

He was drunk, and weaving about in his saddle; he was over fifty year old, and had a very red face. Everybody yelled at him, and laughed at him, and sassed him, and he sassed back, and said he'd attend to them and lay them out in their regular turns, but he couldn't wait now, because he'd come to town to kill old Colonel Sherburn, and his motto was, "meat first, and spoon vittles to top off on."

He see me, and rode up and says —

"Whar'd you come f'm, boy? You prepared to die?"

Then he rode on. I was scared; but a man says —

"He don't mean nothing; he's always a carryin' on like that, when he's drunk. He's the best-naturedest old fool in Arkansaw — never hurt nobody, drunk nor sober."

Boggs rode up before the biggest store in town and bent his head
down so he could see under the curtain of the awning, and yells —

"Come out here, Sherburn! Come out and meet the man you've
swindled. You're the houn' I'm after, and I'm a gwyne to have you, too!"

And so he went on, calling Sherburn everything he could lay his
tongue to, and the whole street packed with people listening and laughing and going on. By-and-by a proud-looking man about fifty-five —
and he was a heap the best dressed man in that town, too — steps out
of the store, and the crowd drops back on each side to let him come.
He says to Boggs, mighty ca'm and slow — he says:

"I'm tired of this; but I'll endure it till one o'clock. Till one o'clock,
mind — no longer. If you open your mouth against me only once, after
that time, you can't travel so far but I will find you."

Then he turns and goes in. The crowd looked mighty sober;
nobody stirred, and there warn't no more laughing. Boggs rode off
blackguarding Sherburn as loud as he could yell, all down the street;
and pretty soon back he comes and stops before the store, still keeping
it up. Some men crowded around him and tried to get him to shut up,
but he wouldn't; they told him it would be one o'clock in about fifteen minutes, and so he *must* go home — he must go right away. But it
didn't do no good. He cussed away, with all his might, and throwed his
hat down in the mud and rode over it, and pretty soon away he went
a-raging down the street again, with his gray hair a-flying. Everybody
that could get a chance at him tried their best to coax him off of his
horse so they could lock him up and get him sober; but it warn't no
use — up the street he would tear again, and give Sherburn another
cussing. By-and-by somebody says —

"Go for his daughter! — quick, go for his daughter; sometimes
he'll listen to her. If anybody can persuade him, she can."

So somebody started on a run. I walked down street a ways, and
stopped. In about five or ten minutes, here comes Boggs again — but
not on his horse. He was a-reeling across the street towards me, bareheaded, with a friend on both sides of him aholt of his arms and hurrying him along. He was quiet, and looked uneasy; and he warn't
hanging back any, but was doing some of the hurrying himself. Somebody sings out —

"Boggs!"

I looked over there to see who said it, and it was that Colonel Sherburn. He was standing perfectly still, in the street, and had a pistol
raised in his right hand — not aiming it, but holding it out with the
barrel tilted up towards the sky. The same second I see a young girl

coming on the run, and two men with her. Boggs and the men turned round, to see who called him, and when they see the pistol the men jumped to one side, and the pistol barrel come down slow and steady to a level — both barrels cocked. Boggs throws up both of his hands, and says, "O Lord, don't shoot!" Bang! goes the first shot, and he staggers back clawing at the air — bang! goes the second one, and he tumbles backwards onto the ground, heavy and solid, with his arms spread out. That young girl screamed out, and comes rushing, and down she throws herself on her father, crying, and saying, "Oh, he's killed him, he's killed him!" The crowd closed up around them, and shouldered and jammed one another, with their necks stretched, trying to see, and people on the inside trying to shove them back, and shouting, "Back, back! give him air, give him air!"

Colonel Sherburn he tossed his pistol onto the ground, and turned around on his heels and walked off.

They took Boggs to a little drug store, the crowd pressing around, just the same, and the whole town following, and I rushed and got a good place at the window, where I was close to him and could see in. They laid him on the floor, and put one large Bible under his head, and opened another one and spread it on his breast — but they tore open his shirt first, and I seen where one of the bullets went in. He made about a dozen long gasps, his breast lifting the Bible up when he drawed in his breath, and letting it down again when he breathed it out — and after that he laid still; he was dead. Then they pulled his daughter away from him, screaming and crying, and took her off. She was about sixteen, and very sweet and gentle-looking, but awful pale and scared.

Well, pretty soon the whole town was there, squirming and scrouging and pushing and shoving to get at the window and have a look, but people that had the places wouldn't give them up, and folks behind them was saying all the time, "Say, now, you've looked enough, you fellows; 'taint right and 'taint fair, for you to stay thar all the time, and never give nobody a chance; other folks has their rights as well as you."

There was considerable jawing back, so I slid out, thinking maybe there was going to be trouble. The streets was full, and everybody was excited. Everybody that seen the shooting was telling how it happened, and there was a big crowd packed around each one of these fellows, stretching their necks and listening. One long lanky man, with long hair and a big white fur stove-pipe hat on the back of his head, and a crooked-handled cane, marked out the places on the ground where Boggs stood, and where Sherburn stood, and the people following him around from one place to t'other and watching everything he done, and bobbing their heads to show they understood, and stooping a little and resting their hands on their thighs to watch him mark the places on the ground with his cane; and then he stood up straight and stiff where Sherburn had stood, frowning and having his hat-brim down over his eyes, and sung out, "Boggs!" and then fetched his cane down slow to a level, and says "Bang!" staggered backwards, says "Bang!" again, and fell down flat on his back. The people that had seen the thing said he done it perfect; said it was just exactly the way it all happened. Then as much as a dozen people got out their bottles and treated him.

Well, by-and-by somebody said Sherburn ought to be lynched. In about a minute everybody was saying it; so away they went, mad and yelling, and snatching down every clothes-line they come to, to do the hanging with.

Chapter XXII

They swarmed up the street towards Sherburn's house, a-whooping and yelling and raging like Injuns, and everything had to clear the way or get run over and tromped to mush, and it was awful to see. Children was heeling it ahead of the mob, screaming and trying to get out of the way; and every window along the road was full of women's heads, and there was nigger boys in every tree, and bucks and wenches looking over every fence; and as soon as the mob would get nearly to them they would break and skaddle back out of reach. Lots of the women and girls was crying and taking on, scared most to death.

They swarmed up in front of Sherburn's palings as thick as they could jam together, and you couldn't hear yourself think for the noise. It was a little twenty-foot yard. Some sung out "Tear down the fence! tear down the fence!" Then there was a racket of ripping and tearing and smashing, and down she goes, and the front wall of the crowd begins to roll in like a wave.

Just then Sherburn steps out on to the roof of his little front porch, with a double-barrel gun in his hand, and takes his stand, perfectly ca'm and deliberate, not saying a word. The racket stopped, and the wave sucked back.

Sherburn never said a word — just stood there, looking down. The stillness was awful creepy and uncomfortable. Sherburn run his eye slow along the crowd; and wherever it struck, the people tried a little to outgaze him, but they couldn't; they dropped their eyes and looked sneaky. Then pretty soon Sherburn sort of laughed; not the pleasant kind, but the kind that makes you feel like when you are eating bread that's got sand in it.

Then he says, slow and scornful:

"The idea of *you* lynching anybody! It's amusing. The idea of you thinking you had pluck enough to lynch a *man!* Because you're brave enough to tar and feather poor friendless cast-out women that come along here, did that make you think you had grit enough to lay your hands on a *man?* Why, a *man's* safe in the hands of ten thousand of your kind — as long as it's day-time and you're not behind him.

"Do I know you? I know you clear through. I was born and raised in the South, and I've lived in the North; so I know the average all around. The average man's a coward. In the North he lets anybody walk over him that wants to, and goes home and prays for a humble spirit to bear it. In the South one man, all by himself, has stopped a stage full of men, in the day-time, and robbed the lot. Your newspapers call you a brave people so much that you think you *are* braver than any other people — whereas you're just *as* brave, and no braver. Why don't your juries hang murderers? Because they're afraid the man's friends will shoot them in the back, in the dark — and it's just what they *would* do.

"So they always acquit; and then a *man* goes in the night, with a hundred masked cowards at his back, and lynches the rascal. Your mistake is, that you didn't bring a man with you; that's one mistake, and the other is that you didn't come in the dark, and fetch your masks. You brought *part* of a man — Buck Harkness, there — and if you hadn't had him to start you, you'd a taken it out in blowing.

"You didn't want to come. The average man don't like trouble and danger. *You* don't like trouble and danger. But if only *half* a man — like Buck Harkness, there — shouts 'Lynch him, lynch him!' you're afraid to back down — afraid you'll be found out to be what you are — *cowards* — and so you raise a yell, and hang yourselves onto that half-a-man's coat tail, and come raging up here, swearing what big things you're going to do. The pitifulest thing out is a mob; that's what an army is — a mob; they don't fight with courage that's born in them, but with courage that's borrowed from their mass, and from their officers. But a mob without any *man* at the head of it, is *beneath* pitifulness. Now the thing for *you* to do, is to droop your tails and go home and crawl in a hole. If any real lynching's going to be done, it will be done in the dark, Southern fashion; and when they come they'll bring their masks, and fetch a *man* along. Now *leave* — and take your half-a-man with you" — tossing his gun up across his left arm and cocking it, when he says this.

The crowd washed back sudden, and then broke all apart and went
tearing off every which way, and Buck Harkness he heeled it after them,
looking tolerable cheap. I could a staid, if I'd a wanted to, but I didn't
want to.

I went to the circus, and loafed around the back side till the watchman went by, and then dived in under the tent. I had my twenty-dollar
gold piece and some other money, but I reckoned I better save it,
because there ain't no telling how soon you are going to need it, away
from home and amongst strangers, that way. You can't be too careful. I
ain't opposed to spending money on circuses, when there ain't no other
way, but there ain't no use in *wasting* it on them.

It was a real bully circus. It was the splendidest sight that ever was,
when they all come riding in, two and two, a gentleman and lady, side
by side, the men just in their drawers and under-shirts, and no shoes
nor stirrups, and resting their hands on their thighs, easy and comfortable — there must a' been twenty of them — and every lady with a
lovely complexion, and perfectly beautiful, and looking just like a gang
of real sure-enough queens, and dressed in clothes that cost millions of
dollars, and just littered with diamonds. It was a powerful fine sight; I
never see anything so lovely. And then one by one they got up and
stood, and went a-weaving around the ring so gentle and wavy and
graceful, the men looking ever so tall and airy and straight, with their
heads bobbing and skimming along, away up there under the tent-roof,
and every lady's rose-leafy dress flapping soft and silky around her hips,
and she looking like the most loveliest parasol.

And then faster and faster they went, all of them dancing, first one
foot stuck out in the air and then the other, the horses leaning more
and more, and the ring-master going round and round the centre-pole,
cracking his whip and shouting "hi! — hi!" and the clown cracking
jokes behind him; and by-and-by all hands dropped the reins, and every
lady put her knuckles on her hips and every gentleman folded his arms,
and then how the horses did lean over and hump themselves! And so,
one after the other they all skipped off into the ring, and made the
sweetest bow I ever see, and then scampered out, and everybody
clapped their hands and went just about wild.

Well, all through the circus they done the most astonishing things;
and all the time that clown carried on so it most killed the people. The
ring-master couldn't ever say a word to him but he was back at him
quick as a wink with the funniest things a body ever said; and how he
ever *could* think of so many of them, and so sudden and so pat, was
what I couldn't noway understand. Why, I couldn't a thought of them

in a year. And by-and-by a drunk man tried to get into the ring — said he wanted to ride; said he could ride as well as anybody that ever was. They argued and tried to keep him out, but he wouldn't listen, and the whole show come to a standstill. Then the people begun to holler at him and make fun of him, and that made him mad, and he begun to rip and tear; so that stirred up the people, and a lot of men begun to pile down off of the benches and swarm towards the ring, saying, "Knock him down! throw him out!" and one or two women begun to scream. So, then, the ring-master he made a little speech, and said he hoped there wouldn't be no disturbance, and if the man would promise he wouldn't make no more trouble, he would let him ride, if he thought he could stay on the horse. So everybody laughed and said all right, and the man got on. The minute he was on, the horse begun to rip and tear and jump and cavort around, with two circus men hanging onto his bridle trying to hold him, and the drunk man hanging onto his neck, and his heels flying in the air every jump, and the whole crowd of people standing up shouting and laughing till the tears rolled down. And at last, sure enough, all the circus men could do, the horse broke loose, and away he went like the very nation, round and round the ring, with that sot laying down on him and hanging to his neck, with first one leg hanging most to the ground on one side, and then t'other one on t'other side, and the people just crazy. It warn't funny to me, though; I was all of a tremble to see his danger. But pretty soon he struggled up astraddle and grabbed the bridle, a-reeling this way and that; and the next minute he sprung up and dropped the bridle and stood! and the horse agoing like a house afire too. He just stood up there, a-sailing around as easy and comfortable as if he warn't ever drunk in his life — and then he begun to pull off his clothes and sling them. He shed them so thick they kind of clogged up the air, and altogether he shed seventeen suits. And then, there he was, slim and handsome, and dressed the gaudiest and prettiest you ever saw, and he lit into that horse with his whip and made him fairly hum — and finally skipped off, and made his bow and danced off to the dressing-room, and everybody just a-howling with pleasure and astonishment.

Then the ring-master he see how he had been fooled, and he *was* the sickest ring-master you ever see, I reckon. Why, it was one of his own men! He had got up that joke all out of his own head, and never let on to nobody. Well, I felt sheepish enough, to be took in so, but I wouldn't a been in that ring-master's place, not for a thousand dollars. I don't know; there may be bullier circuses than what that one was, but I never struck them yet. Anyways it was plenty good enough for *me;* and wherever I run across it, it can have all of *my* custom,° every time.

Well, that night we had *our* show; but there warn't only about twelve people there; just enough to pay expenses. And they laughed all the time, and that made the duke mad; and everybody left, anyway, before the show was over, but one boy which was asleep. So the duke said these Arkansaw lunkheads couldn't come up to Shakspeare; what they wanted was low comedy — and may be something ruther worse than low comedy, he reckoned. He said he could size their style. So next morning he got some big sheets of wrapping-paper and some black paint, and drawed off some handbills and stuck them up all over the village. The bills said:

AT THE COURT HOUSE!
FOR 3 NIGHTS ONLY!
The World-Renowned Tragedians
DAVID GARRICK THE YOUNGER!
AND
EDMUND KEAN THE ELDER!
*Of the London and Continental
Theatres,*
In their Thrilling Tragedy of
THE KING'S CAMELOPARD
OR
THE ROYAL NONESUCH!!!
Admission 50 *cents.*

Then at the bottom was the biggest line of all — which said:

LADIES AND CHILDREN NOT ADMITTED.

"There," says he, "if that line don't fetch them, I don't know Arkansaw!"

Chapter XXIII

Well, all day him and the king was hard at it, rigging up a stage, and a curtain, and a row of candles for footlights; and that night the house was jam full of men in no time. When the place couldn't hold no more, the duke he quit tending door and went around the back way and come onto the stage and stood up before the curtain, and made a little speech, and praised up this tragedy, and said it was the most thrillingest

custom: Business.

one that ever was; and so he went on a-bragging about the tragedy and about Edmund Kean the Elder, which was to play the main principal part in it; and at last when he'd got everybody's expectations up high enough, he rolled up the curtain, and the next minute the king come a-prancing out on all fours, naked; and he was painted all over, ring-streaked-and-striped, all sorts of colors, as splendid as a rainbow. And — but never mind the rest of his outfit, it was just wild, but it was awful funny. The people most killed themselves laughing; and when the king got done capering, and capered off behind the scenes, they roared and clapped and stormed and haw-hawed till he come back and done it over again; and after that, they made him do it another time. Well, it would a made a cow laugh to see the shines that old idiot cut.

Then the duke he lets the curtain down, and bows to the people, and says the great tragedy will be performed only two nights more, on accounts of pressing London engagements, where the seats is all sold aready for it in Drury Lane; and then he makes them another bow, and says if he has succeeded in pleasing them and instructing them, he will be deeply obleeged if they will mention it to their friends and get them to come and see it.

Twenty people sings out:

"What, is it over? Is that *all?*"

The duke says yes. Then there was a fine time. Everybody sings out "sold," and rose up mad, and was agoing for that stage and them trage-dians. But a big fine-looking man jumps up on a bench, and shouts:

"Hold on! Just a word, gentlemen." They stopped to listen. "We are sold — mighty badly sold. But we don't want to be the laughing-stock of this whole town, I reckon, and never hear the last of this thing as long as we live. *No.* What we want, is to go out of here quiet, and talk this show up, and sell the *rest* of the town! Then we'll all be in the same boat. Ain't that sensible?" ("You bet it is! — the jedge is right!" every-body sings out.) "All right, then — not a word about any sell. Go along home, and advise everybody to come and see the tragedy."

Next day you couldn't hear nothing around that town but how splendid that show was. House was jammed again, that night, and we sold this crowd the same way. When me and the king and the duke got home to the raft, we all had a supper; and by-and-by, about midnight, they made Jim and me back her out and float her down the middle of the river and fetch her in and hide her about two mile below town.

The third night the house was crammed again — and they warn't new-comers, this time, but people that was at the show the other two nights. I stood by the duke at the door, and I see that every man that went in had his pockets bulging, or something muffled up under his coat — and I see it warn't no perfumery neither, not by a long sight. I smelt sickly eggs by the barrel, and rotten cabbages, and such things; and if I know the signs of a dead cat being around, and I bet I do, there was sixty-four of them went in. I shoved in there for a minute, but it was too various for me, I couldn't stand it. Well, when the place couldn't hold no more people, the duke he give a fellow a quarter and told him to tend door for him a minute, and then he started around for the stage door, I after him; but the minute we turned the corner and was in the dark, he says:

"Walk fast, now, till you get away from the houses, and then shin for the raft like the dickens was after you!"

I done it, and he done the same. We struck the raft at the same time, and in less than two seconds we was gliding down stream, all dark and still, and edging towards the middle of the river, nobody saying a word. I reckoned the poor king was in for a gaudy time of it with the audience; but nothing of the sort; pretty soon he crawls out from under the wigwam, and says:

"Well, how'd the old thing pan out this time, Duke?"

He hadn't been up town at all.

We never showed a light till we was about ten mile below that village. Then we lit up and had a supper, and the king and the duke fairly laughed their bones loose over the way they'd served them people. The duke says:

"Greenhorns, flatheads! *I* knew the first house would keep mum and let the rest of the town get roped in; and I knew they'd lay for us the third night, and consider it was *their* turn now. Well, it *is* their turn, and I'd give something to know how much they'd take for it. I *would* just like to know how they're putting in their opportunity. They can turn it into a picnic, if they want to — they brought plenty provisions."

Them rapscallions took in four hundred and sixty-five dollars in that three nights. I never see money hauled in by the wagon-load like that, before.

By-and-by, when they was asleep and snoring, Jim says:

"Don't it 'sprise you, de way dem kings carries on, Huck?"

"No," I says, "it don't."

"Why don't it, Huck?"

"Well, it don't, because it's in the breed. I reckon they're all alike."

"But, Huck, dese kings o' ourn is regular rapscallions; dat's jist what dey is; dey's reglar rapscallions."

"Well, that's what I'm a-saying; all kings is mostly rapscallions, as fur as I can make out."

"Is dat so?"

"You read about them once — you'll see. Look at Henry the Eight; this'n 's a Sunday-School Superintendent to *him*. And look at Charles Second, and Louis Fourteen, and Louis Fifteen, and James Second, and Edward Second, and Richard Third, and forty more; besides all them Saxon heptarchies that used to rip around so in old times and raise Cain. My, you ought to seen old Henry the Eight when he was in bloom. He *was* a blossom. He used to marry a new wife every day, and chop off her head next morning. And he would do it just as indifferent as if he was ordering up eggs. 'Fetch up Nell Gwynn,' he says. They fetch her up. Next morning, 'Chop off her head!' And they chop it off. 'Fetch up Jane Shore,' he says; and up she comes. Next morning 'Chop off her head' — and they chop it off. 'Ring up Fair Rosamun.' Fair Rosamun answers the bell. Next morning, 'Chop off her head.' And he made every one of them tell him a tale every night; and he kept that up till he had hogged a thousand and one tales that way, and then he put them all in a book, and called it Domesday Book — which was a good name and stated the case. You don't know kings, Jim, but I know them; and this old rip of ourn is one of the cleanest I've struck in history. Well, Henry he takes a notion he wants to get up some trouble with this country. How does he go at it — give notice? — give the country a show? No. All of a sudden he heaves all the tea in Boston Harbor overboard, and whacks out a declaration of independence, and dares them to come on. That was *his* style — he never give anybody a chance. He had suspicions of his father, the Duke of Wellington. Well, what did he do? — ask him to show up? No — drownded him in a butt of mamsey,° like a cat. Spose people left money laying around where he was — what did he do? He collared it. Spose he contracted to do a thing; and you paid him, and didn't set down there and see that he done it — what did he do? He always done the other thing. Spose he opened his mouth — what then? If he didn't shut it up powerful quick, he'd lose a lie, every time. That's the kind of a bug Henry was; and if we'd a had him along 'stead of our kings, he'd a fooled that town a heap worse than ourn done. I don't say that ourn is lambs, because they ain't, when you come right down to the cold facts; but they ain't nothing to *that* old ram, anyway. All I say is, kings is kings, and you got to make allowances.

butt of mamsey: A barrel of sweet, strong wine.

Take them all around, they're a mighty ornery lot. It's the way they're raised."

"But dis one do *smell* so like de nation, Huck."

"Well, they all do, Jim. *We* can't help the way a king smells; history don't tell no way."

"Now de duke, he's a tolerble likely man, in some ways."

"Yes, a duke's different. But not very different. This one's a middling hard lot, for a duke. When he's drunk, there ain't no near-sighted man could tell him from a king."

"Well, anyways, I doan' hanker for no mo' un um, Huck. Dese is all I kin stan'."

"It's the way I feel, too, Jim. But we've got them on our hands, and we got to remember what they are, and make allowances. Sometimes I wish we could hear of a country that's out of kings."

What was the use to tell Jim these warn't real kings and dukes? It wouldn't a done no good; and besides, it was just as I said; you couldn't tell them from the real kind.

I went to sleep, and Jim didn't call me when it was my turn. He often done that. When I waked up, just at day-break, he was setting there with his head down betwixt his knees, moaning and mourning to himself. I didn't take notice, nor let on. I knowed what it was about. He was thinking about his wife and his children, away up yonder, and he was low and homesick; because he hadn't ever been away from home before in his life; and I do believe he cared just as much for his people as white folks does for their'n. It don't seem natural, but I reckon it's so. He was often moaning and mourning that way, nights, when he judged I was asleep, and saying, "Po' little 'Lizabeth! po' little Johnny! its mighty hard; I spec' I ain't ever gwyne to see you no mo', no mo'!" He was a mighty good nigger, Jim was.

But this time I somehow got to talking to him about his wife and young ones; and by-and-by he says:

"What makes me feel so bad dis time, 'uz bekase I hear sumpn over yonder on de bank like a whack, er a slam, while ago, en it mine me er de time I treat my little 'Lizabeth so ornery. She warn't on'y 'bout fo' year ole, en she tuck de sk'yarlet-fever, en had a powful rough spell; but she got well, en one day she was a-stannin' aroun', en I says to her, I says:

" 'Shet de do'.'

"She never done it; jis' stood dah, kiner smilin' up at me. It make me mad; en I says agin, mighty loud, I says:

" 'Doan' you hear me? — shet de do'!'

"She jis' stood de same way, kiner smilin' up. I was a-bilin'! I says:
" 'I lay I *make* you mine!'

"En wid dat I fetch' her a slap side de head dat sont her a-sprawlin'. Den I went into de yuther room, en 'uz gone 'bout ten minutes; en when I come back, dah was dat do' a-stannin' open *yit*, en dat chile stannin' mos' right in it, a-lookin' down and mournin', en de tears runnin' down. My, but I *wuz* mad, I was agwyne for de chile, but jis' den — it was a do' dat open innerds — jis' den, 'long come de wind en slam it to, behine de chile, ker-*blam!* — en my lan', de chile never move'! My breff mos' hop outer me; en I feel so — so — I doan' know *how* I feel. I crope out, all a-tremblin', en crope aroun' en open de do' easy en slow, en poke my head in behine de child, sof' en still, en all uv a sudden, I says *pow!* jis' as loud as I could yell. *She never budge!* Oh, Huck, I bust out a-cryin' en grab her up in my arms, en say, 'Oh, de po' little thing! de Lord God Amighty fogive po' ole Jim, kaze he never gwyne to fogive hisself as long's he live!' Oh, she was plumb deef en dumb, Huck, plumb deef en dumb — en I'd ben a-treat'n her so!' "

Chapter XXIV

Next day, towards night, we laid up under a little willow tow-head out in the middle, where there was a village on each side of the river, and the duke and the king begun to lay out a plan for working them towns. Jim he spoke to the duke, and said he hoped it wouldn't take but a few hours, because it got mighty heavy and tiresome to him when he had to lay all day in the wigwam tied with the rope. You see, when we left him all alone we had to tie him, because if anybody happened on him all by himself and not tied, it wouldn't look much like he was a runaway nigger, you know. So the duke said it *was* kind of hard to have to lay roped all day, and he'd cipher out some way to get around it.

He was uncommon bright, the duke was, and he soon struck it. He dressed Jim up in King Lear's outfit — it was a long curtain-calico gown, and a white horse-hair wig and whiskers; and then he took his theatre-paint and painted Jim's face and hands and ears and neck all over a dead dull solid blue, like a man that's been drownded nine days. Blamed if he warn't the horriblest looking outrage I ever see. Then the duke took and wrote out a sign on a shingle so —

Sick Arab — but harmless when not out of his head.

And he nailed that shingle to a lath, and stood the lath up four or five foot in front of the wigwam. Jim was satisfied. He said it was a sight better than laying tied a couple of years every day and trembling all over every time there was a sound. The duke told him to make himself free and easy, and if anybody ever come meddling around, he must hop out of the wigwam, and carry on a little, and fetch a howl or two like a wild beast, and he reckoned they would light out and leave him alone. Which was sound enough judgment; but you take the average man, and he wouldn't wait for him to howl. Why, he didn't only look like he was dead, he looked considerable more than that.

These rapscallions wanted to try the Nonesuch again, because there was so much money in it, but they judged it wouldn't be safe, because maybe the news might a worked along down by this time. They couldn't hit no project that suited, exactly; so at last the duke said he reckoned he'd lay off and work his brains an hour or two and see if he couldn't put up something on the Arkansaw village; and the king he allowed he would drop over to t'other village, without any plan, but just trust in Providence to lead him the profitable way — meaning the devil, I reckon. We had all bought store clothes where we stopped last; and now the king put his'n on, and he told me to put mine on. I done it, of course. The king's duds was all black, and he did look real swell and starchy. I never knowed how clothes could change a body before. Why, before, he looked like the orneriest old rip that ever was; but now, when he'd take off his new white beaver and make a bow and do a smile, he looked that grand and good and pious that you'd say he had walked right out of the ark, and maybe was old Leviticus himself. Jim cleaned up the canoe, and I got my paddle ready. There was a big steamboat laying at the shore away up under the point, about three mile above town — been there a couple of hours, taking on freight. Says the king:

"Seein' how I'm dressed, I reckon maybe I better arrive down from St. Louis or Cincinnati, or some other big place. Go for the steamboat, Huckleberry; we'll come down to the village on her."

I didn't have to be ordered twice, to go and take a steamboat ride. I fetched the shore a half a mile above the village, and then went scooting along the bluff bank in the easy water. Pretty soon we come to a nice innocent-looking young country jake setting on a log swabbing the sweat off of his face, for it was powerful warm weather; and he had a couple of big carpet-bags by him.

"Run her nose in shore," says the king. I done it. "Wher' you bound for, young man?"

"For the steamboat; going to Orleans."

"Git aboard," says the king. "Hold on a minute, my servant 'll he'p you with them bags. Jump out and he'p the gentleman, Adolphus" — meaning me, I see.

I done so, and then we all three started on again. The young chap was mighty thankful; said it was tough work toting his baggage such weather. He asked the king where he was going, and the king told him he'd come down the river and landed at the other village this morning, and now he was going up a few mile to see an old friend on a farm up there. The young fellow says:

"When I first see you, I says to myself, 'It's Mr. Wilks, sure, and he come mighty near getting here in time.' But then I says again, 'No, I reckon it ain't him, or else he wouldn't be paddling up the river.' You *ain't* him, are you?"

"No, my name's Blodgett — Elexander Blodgett — *Reverend* Elexander Blodgett, I spose I must say, as I'm one o' the Lord's poor servants. But still I'm jist as able to be sorry for Mr. Wilks for not arriving in time, all the same, if he's missed anything by it — which I hope he hasn't."

"Well, he don't miss any property by it, because he'll get that all right; but he's missed seeing his brother Peter die — which he mayn't mind, nobody can tell as to that — but his brother would a give anything in this world to see *him* before he died; never talked about nothing else all these three weeks; hadn't seen him since they was boys together — and hadn't ever seen his brother William at all — that's the deef and dumb one — William ain't more than thirty or thirty-five. Peter and George was the only ones that come out here; George was the married brother; him and his wife both died last year. Harvey and William's the only ones that's left now; and, as I was saying, they haven't got here in time."

"Did anybody send 'em word?"

"Oh, yes; a month or two ago, when Peter was first took; because Peter said then that he sorter felt like he warn't going to get well this time. You see, he was pretty old, and George's g'yirls was too young to be much company for him, except Mary Jane the red-headed one; and so he was kinder lonesome after George and his wife died, and didn't seem to care much to live. He most desperately wanted to see Harvey — and William too, for that matter — because he was one of them kind that can't bear to make a will. He left a letter behind for Harvey, and said he'd told in it where his money was hid, and how he wanted the rest of the property divided up so George's g'yirls would be all right — for George didn't leave nothing. And that letter was all they could get him to put a pen to."

"Why do you reckon Harvey don't come? Wher' does he live?"

"Oh, he lives in England — Sheffield — preaches there — hasn't ever been in this country. He hasn't had any too much time — and besides he mightn't a got the letter at all, you know."

"Too bad, too bad he couldn't a lived to see his brothers, poor soul. You going to Orleans, you say?"

"Yes, but that ain't only a part of it. I'm going in a ship, next Wednesday, for Ryo Janeero, where my uncle lives."

"It's a pretty long journey. But it'll be lovely; I wisht I was agoing. Is Mary Jane the oldest? How old is the others?"

"Mary Jane's nineteen, Susan's fifteen, and Joanna's about fourteen — that's the one that gives herself to good works and has a hare-lip."

"Poor things! to be left alone in the cold world so."

"Well, they could be worse off. Old Peter had friends, and they ain't going to let them come to no harm. There's Hobson, the Babtis' preacher; and Deacon Lot Hovey, and Ben Rucker, and Abner Shackleford, and Levi Bell, the lawyer; and Dr. Robinson, and their wives, and the widow Bartley, and — well, there's a lot of them; but these are the ones that Peter was thickest with, and used to write about sometimes, when he wrote home; so Harvey 'll know where to look for friends when he gets here."

Well, the old man he went on asking questions till he just fairly emptied that young fellow. Blamed if he didn't inquire about everybody and everything in that blessed town, and all about all the Wilkses; and about Peter's business — which was a tanner; and about George's — which was a carpenter; and about Harvey's — which was a dissentering minister; and so on, and so on. Then he says:

"What did you want to walk all the way up to the steamboat for?"

"Because she's a big Orleans boat, and I was afeard she mightn't stop there. When they're deep they won't stop for a hail. A Cincinnati boat will, but this is a St. Louis one."

"Was Peter Wilks well off?"

"Oh, yes, pretty well off. He had houses and land, and it's reckoned he left three or four thousand in cash hid up som'ers."

"When did you say he died?"

"I didn't say, but it was last night."

"Funeral to-morrow, likely?"

"Yes, 'bout the middle of the day."

"Well, it's all terrible sad; but we've all got to go, one time or another. So what we want to do is to be prepared; then we're all right."

"Yes, sir, it's the best way. Ma used to always say that."

When we struck the boat, she was about done loading, and pretty soon she got off. The king never said nothing about going aboard, so I lost my ride, after all. When the boat was gone, the king made me paddle up another mile to a lonesome place, and then he got ashore, and says:

"Now hustle back, right off, and fetch the duke up here, and the new carpet-bags. And if he's gone over to t'other side, go over there and git him. And tell him to git himself up regardless. Shove along, now."

I see what *he* was up to; but I never said nothing, of course. When I got back with the duke, we hid the canoe and then they set down on a log, and the king told him everything, just like the young fellow had said it — every last word of it. And all the time he was a doing it, he tried to talk like an Englishman; and he done it pretty well too, for a slouch. I can't imitate him, and so I ain't agoing to try to; but he really done it pretty good. Then he says:

"How are you on the deef and dumb, Bilgewater?"

The duke said, leave him alone for that; said he had played a deef and dumb person on the histrionic boards. So then they waited for a steamboat.

About the middle of the afternoon a couple of little boats come along, but they didn't come from high enough up the river; but at last there was a big one, and they hailed her. She sent out her yawl, and we went aboard, and she was from Cincinnati; and when they found we only wanted to go four or five mile, they was booming mad, and give us a cussing, and said they wouldn't land us. But the king was ca'm. He says:

"If gentlemen kin afford to pay a dollar a mile apiece, to be took on and put off in a yawl, a steamboat kin afford to carry 'em, can't it?"

So they softened down and said it was all right; and when we got to the village, they yawled us ashore. About two dozen men flocked down, when they see the yawl a coming; and when the king says —

"Kin any of you gentlemen tell me wher' Mr. Peter Wilks lives?" they give a glance at one another, and nodded their heads, as much as to say, "What d' I tell you?" Then one of them says, kind of soft and gentle:

"I'm sorry, sir, but the best we can do is to tell you where he *did* live yesterday evening."

Sudden as winking, the ornery old cretur went all to smash, and fell up against the man, and put his chin on his shoulder, and cried down his back, and says:

"Alas, alas, our poor brother — gone, and we never got to see him; oh, it's too, *too* hard!"

Then he turns around, blubbering, and makes a lot of idiotic signs to the duke on his hands, and blamed if *he* didn't drop a carpet-bag and bust out a-crying. If they warn't the beatenest lot, them two frauds, that ever I struck.

Well, the men gethered around, and sympathized with them, and said all sorts of kind things to them, and carried their carpet-bags up the hill for them, and let them lean on them and cry, and told the king all about his brother's last moments, and the king he told it all over again on his hands to the duke, and both of them took on about that dead tanner like they'd lost the twelve disciples. Well, if ever I struck any-thing like it, I'm a nigger. It was enough to make a body ashamed of the human race.

Chapter XXV

The news was all over town in two minutes, and you could see the people tearing down on the run, from every which way, some of them putting on their coats as they come. Pretty soon we was in the middle of a crowd, and the noise of the tramping was like a soldier-march. The windows and door-yards was full; and every minute somebody would say, over a fence:

"Is it *them?*"

And somebody trotting along with the gang would answer back and say,

"You bet it is."

When we got to the house, the street in front of it was packed, and the three girls was standing in the door. Mary Jane *was* red-headed, but that don't make no difference, she was most awful beautiful, and her face and her eyes was all lit up like glory, she was so glad her uncles was come. The king he spread his arms, and Mary Jane she jumped for them, and the hare-lip jumped for the duke, and there they *had* it! Everybody most, leastways women, cried for joy to see them meet again at last and have such good times.

Then the king he hunched the duke, private — I see him do it — and then he looked around and see the coffin, over in the corner on two chairs; so then, him and the duke, with a hand across each other's shoulder, and t'other hand to their eyes, walked slow and solemn over there, everybody dropping back to give them room, and all the talk and noise stopping, people saying "Sh!" and all the men taking their hats off and drooping their heads, so you could a heard a pin fall. And when they got there, they bent over and looked in the coffin, and took one sight, and then they bust out a crying so you could a heard them to Orleans, most; and then they put their arms around each other's necks, and hung their chins over each other's shoulders; and then for three minutes, or maybe four, I never see two men leak the way they done. And mind you, everybody was doing the same; and the place was that damp I never see anything like it. Then one of them got on one side of the coffin, and t'other on t'other side, and they kneeled down and rested their foreheads on the coffin, and let on to pray all to theirselves. Well, when it come to that, it worked the crowd like you never see anything like it, and so everybody broke down and went to sobbing right out loud — the poor girls, too; and every woman, nearly, went up to the girls, without saying a word, and kissed them, solemn, on the forehead, and then put their hand on their head, and looked up towards the sky, with the tears running down, and then busted out and went off sobbing and swabbing, and give the next woman a show. I never see anything so disgusting.

Well, by-and-by the king he gets up and comes forward a little, and works himself up and slobbers out a speech, all full of tears and flapdoodle about its being a sore trial for him and his poor brother to lose the diseased, and to miss seeing diseased alive, after the long journey of four thousand mile, but its a trial that's sweetened and sanctified to us by this dear sympathy and these holy tears, and so he thanks them out of his heart and out of his brother's heart, because out of their mouths they can't, words being too weak and cold, and all that kind of rot and slush, till it was just sickening; and then he blubbers out a pious goody-goody Amen, and turns himself loose and goes to crying fit to bust.

And the minute the words was out of his mouth somebody over in the crowd struck up the doxolojer,° and everybody joined in with all their might, and it just warmed you up and made you feel as good as church letting out. Music *is* a good thing; and after all that soul-butter and hog-wash, I never see it freshen up things so, and sound so honest and bully.

---

doxolojer: Doxology, a hymn in praise of God.

Then the king begins to work his jaw again, and says how him and his nieces would be glad if a few of the main principal friends of the family would take supper here with them this evening, and help set up with the ashes of the diseased; and says if his poor brother laying yonder could speak, he knows who he would name, for they was names that was very dear to him, and mentioned often in his letters; and so he will name the same, to-wit, as follows, vizz: — Rev. Mr. Hobson, and Deacon Lot Hovey, and Mr. Ben Rucker, and Abner Shackleford, and Levi Bell, and Dr. Robinson, and their wives, and the widow Bartley.

Rev. Hobson and Dr. Robinson was down to the end of the town, a-hunting together; that is, I mean the doctor was shipping a sick man to t'other world, and the preacher was pinting him right. Lawyer Bell was away up to Louisville on some business. But the rest was on hand, and so they all come and shook hands with the king and thanked him and talked to him; and then they shook hands with the duke, and didn't say nothing but just kept a-smiling and bobbing their heads like a passel of sapheads whilst he made all sorts of signs with his hands and said "Goo-goo — goo-goo-goo," all the time, like a baby that can't talk.

So the king he blatted along, and managed to inquire about pretty much everybody and dog in town, by his name, and mentioned all sorts of little things that happened one time or another in the town, or to George's family, or to Peter; and he always let on that Peter wrote him the things, but that was a lie, he got every blessed one of them out of that young flathead that we canoed up to the steamboat.

Then Mary Jane she fetched the letter her father left behind, and the king he read it out loud and cried over it. It give the dwelling-house and three thousand dollars, gold, to the girls; and it give the tanyard (which was doing a good business), along with some other houses and land (worth about seven thousand), and three thousand dollars in gold to Harvey and William, and told where the six thousand cash was hid, down cellar. So these two frauds said they'd go and fetch it up, and have everything square and above-board; and told me to come with a candle. We shut the cellar door behind us, and when they found the bag they spilt it out on the floor, and it was a lovely sight, all them yaller-boys.° My, the way the king's eyes did shine! He slaps the duke on the shoulder, and says:

"Oh, *this* ain't bully, nor noth'n! Oh, no, I reckon not! Why, Biljy, it beats the Nonesuch, *don't* it!"

yaller-boys: Gold coins.

The duke allowed it did. They pawed the yaller-boys, and sifted them through their fingers and let them jingle down on the floor; and the king says:

"It ain't no use talkin'; bein' brothers to a rich dead man, and representatives of furrin heirs that's got left, is the line for you and me, Bilge. Thish-yer comes of trust'n to Providence. It's the best way, in the long run. I've tried 'em all, and ther' ain't no better way."

Most everybody would a been satisfied with the pile, and took it on trust; but no, they must count it. So they counts it, and it comes out four hundred and fifteen dollars short. Says the king:

"Dern him, I wonder what he done with that four hundred and fifteen dollars?"

They worried over that a while, and ransacked all around for it. Then the duke says:

"Well, he was a pretty sick man, and likely he made a mistake — I reckon that's the way of it. The best way's to let it go, and keep still about it. We can spare it."

"Oh, shucks, yes, we can *spare* it. I don't k'yer noth'n 'bout that — it's the *count* I'm thinkin' about. We want to be awful square and open and above-board, here, you know. We want to lug this h-yer money up stairs and count it before everybody — then ther' ain't noth'n suspicious. But when the dead man says ther's six thous'n dollars, you know, we don't want to ——"

"Hold on," says the duke. "Less make up the deffisit" — and he begun to haul out yaller-boys out of his pocket.

"It's a most amaz'n' good idea, duke — you *have* got a rattlin' clever head on you," says the king. "Blest if the old Nonesuch ain't a heppin' us out agin" — and *he* begun to haul out yaller-jackets and stack them up.

It most busted them, but they made up the six thousand clean and clear.

"Say," says the duke, "I got another idea. Let's go up stairs and count this money, and then take and *give it to the girls.*"

"Good land, duke, lemme hug you! It's the most dazzling idea 'at ever a man struck. You have cert'nly got the most astonishin' head I ever see. Oh, this is the boss dodge, ther' ain't no mistake 'bout it. Let 'em fetch along their suspicions now, if they want to — this'll lay 'em out."

When we got up stairs, everybody gethered around the table, and the king he counted it and stacked it up, three hundred dollars in a pile — twenty elegant little piles. Everybody looked hungry at it, and licked their chops. Then they raked it into the bag again, and I see the king begin to swell himself up for another speech. He says:

"Friends all, my poor brother that lays yonder, has done generous by them that's left behind in the vale of sorrers. He has done generous by these-yer poor little lambs that he loved and sheltered, and that's left fatherless and motherless. Yes, and we that knowed him, knows that he would a done *more* generous by 'em if he hadn't ben afeard o' woundin' his dear William and me. Now, *wouldn't* he? Ther' ain't no question 'bout it, in *my* mind. Well, then — what kind o' brothers would it be, that 'd stand in his way at sech a time? And what kind o' uncles would it be that 'd rob — yes, *rob* — sech poor sweet lambs as these 'at he loved so, at sech a time? If I know William — and I *think* I do — he — well, I'll jest ask him." He turns around and begins to make a lot of signs to the duke with his hands; and the duke he looks at him stupid and leather-headed a while, then all of a sudden he seems to catch his meaning, and jumps for the king, goo-gooing with all his might for joy, and hugs him about fifteen times before he lets up. Then the king says, "I knowed it; I reckon *that* 'll convince anybody the way *he* feels about it. Here, Mary Jane, Susan, Joanner, take the money — take it *all*. It's the gift of him that lays yonder, cold but joyful."

Mary Jane she went for him, Susan and the hare-lip went for the duke, and then such another hugging and kissing I never see yet. And everybody crowded up with the tears in their eyes, and most shook the hands off of them frauds, saying all the time:

"You *dear* good souls! — how *lovely*! — how *could* you!"

Well, then, pretty soon all hands got to talking about the diseased again, and how good he was, and what a loss he was, and all that; and before long a big iron-jawed man worked himself in there from outside, and stood a listening and looking, and not saying anything; and nobody saying anything to him either, because the king was talking and they was all busy listening. The king was saying — in the middle of something he'd started in on —

"— they bein' partickler friends o' the diseased. That's why they're invited here this evenin'; but to-morrow we want *all* to come — everybody; for he respected everybody, he liked everybody, and so it's fitten that his funeral orgies sh'd be public."

And so he went a-mooning on and on, liking to hear himself talk, and every little while he fetched in his funeral orgies again, till the duke he couldn't stand it no more; so he writes on a little scrap of paper, "*obsequies*, you old fool," and folds it up and goes to goo-gooing and reaching it over people's heads to him. The king he reads it, and puts it in his pocket, and says:

"Poor William, afflicted as he is, his *heart's* aluz right. Asks me to invite everybody to come to the funeral — wants me to make 'em all welcome. But he needn't a worried — it was jest what I was at."

Then he weaves along agin, perfectly ca'm, and goes to dropping in his funeral orgies again every now and then, just like he done before. And when he done it the third time, he says:

"I say orgies, not because it's the common term, because it ain't — obsequies bein' the common term — but because orgies is the right term. Obsequies ain't used in England no more, now — it's gone out. We say orgies now, in England. Orgies is better, because it means the thing you're after, more exact. It's a word that's made up out'n the Greek *orgo*, outside, open, abroad; and the Hebrew *jeesum*, to plant, cover up; hence *inter*. So, you see, funeral orgies is an open er public funeral."

He was the *worst* I ever struck. Well, the iron-jawed man he laughed right in his face. Everybody was shocked. Everybody says, "Why *doctor!*" and Abner Shackleford says:

"Why, Robinson, hain't you heard the news? This is Harvey Wilks."

The king he smiled eager, and shoved out his flapper, and says:

"*Is* it my poor brother's dear good friend and physician? I ———"

"Keep your hands off of me!" says the doctor. "*You* talk like an Englishman — *don't* you? It's the worse imitation I ever heard. *You* Peter Wilks's brother. You're a fraud, that's what you are!"

Well, how they all took on! They crowded around the doctor, and tried to quiet him down, and tried to explain to him, and tell him how Harvey'd showed in forty ways that he *was* Harvey, and knowed everybody by name, and the names of the very dogs, and begged and *begged* him not to hurt Harvey's feelings and the poor girls' feelings, and all that; but it warn't no use, he stormed right along, and said any man that pretended to be an Englishman and couldn't imitate the lingo no better than what he did, was a fraud and a liar. The poor girls was hanging to the king and crying; and all of a sudden the doctor ups and turns on *them*. He says:

"I was your father's friend, and I'm your friend; and I warn you *as* a friend, and an honest one, that wants to protect you and keep you out of harm and trouble, to turn your backs on that scoundrel, and have nothing to do with him, the ignorant tramp, with his idiotic Greek and Hebrew as he calls it. He is the thinnest kind of an impostor — has come here with a lot of empty names and facts which he has picked up

somewheres, and you take them for *proofs,* and are helped to fool yourselves by these foolish friends here, who ought to know better. Mary
Jane Wilks, you know me for your friend, and for your unselfish friend,
too. Now listen to me; turn this pitiful rascal out — I *beg* you to do it.
Will you?"

Mary Jane straightened herself up, and my, but she was handsome!
She says:

"*Here* is my answer." She hove up the bag of money and put it in
the king's hands, and says, "Take this six thousand dollars, and invest it
for me and my sisters any way you want to, and don't give us no receipt
for it."

Then she put her arm around the king on one side, and Susan and
the hare-lip done the same on the other. Everybody clapped their hands
and stomped on the floor like a perfect storm, whilst the king held up
his head and smiled proud. The doctor says:

"All right, I wash *my* hands of the matter. But I warn you all that a
time's coming when you're going to feel sick whenever you think of
this day" — and away he went.

"All right, doctor," says the king, kinder mocking him, "we'll try
and get 'em to send for you" — which made them all laugh, and they
said it was a prime good hit.

Chapter XXVI

Well when they was all gone, the king he asks Mary Jane how they
was off for spare rooms, and she said she had one spare room, which
would do for Uncle William, and she'd give her own room to Uncle
Harvey, which was a little bigger, and she would turn into the room
with her sisters and sleep on a cot; and up garret was a little cubby, with
a pallet in it. The king said the cubby would do for his valley — meaning me.

So Mary Jane took us up, and she showed them their rooms, which
was plain but nice. She said she'd have her frocks and a lot of other traps
took out of her room if they was in Uncle Harvey's way, but he said
they warn't. The frocks was hung along the wall, and before them was a
curtain made out of calico that hung down to the floor. There was an
old hair trunk in one corner, and a guitar box in another, and all sorts of
little knickknacks and jimcracks around, like girls brisken up a room
with. The king said it was all the more homely and more pleasanter for
these fixings, and so don't disturb them. The duke's room was pretty
small, but plenty good enough, and so was my cubby.

That night they had a big supper, and all them men and women was there, and I stood behind the king and the duke's chairs and waited on them, and the niggers waited on the rest. Mary Jane she set at the head of the table, with Susan along side of her, and said how bad the biscuits was, and how mean the preserves was, and how ornery and tough the fried chickens was — and all that kind of rot, the way women always do for to force out compliments; and the people all knowed everything was tip-top, and said so — said "How *do* you get biscuits to brown so nice?" and "Where, for the land's sake *did* you get these amaz'n pickles?" and all that kind of humbug talky-talk, just the way people always does at a supper, you know.

And when it was all done, me and the hare-lip had supper in the kitchen off of the leavings, whilst the others was helping the niggers clean up the things. The hare-lip she got to pumping me about England, and blest if I didn't think the ice was getting mighty thin, sometimes. She says:

"Did you ever see the king?"

"Who? William Fourth? Well, I bet I have — he goes to our church." I knowed he was dead years ago, but I never let on. So when I says he goes to our church, she says:

"What — regular?"

"Yes — regular. His pew's right over opposite ourn — on 'tother side the pulpit."

"I thought he lived in London?"

"Well, he does. Where *would* he live?"

"But I thought *you* lived in Sheffield?"

I see I was up a stump. I had to let on to get choked with a chicken bone, so as to get time to think how to get down again. Then I says:

"I mean he goes to our church regular when he's in Sheffield. That's only in the summer-time, when he comes there to take the sea baths."

"Why, how you talk — Sheffield ain't on the sea."

"Well, who said it was?"

"Why, you did."

"I *didn't*, nuther."

"You did!"

"I didn't."

"You did."

"I never said nothing of the kind."

"Well, what *did* you say, then?"

"Said he come to take the sea *baths* — that's what I said."

"Well, then! how's he going to take the sea baths if it ain't on the sea?"

"Looky here," I says; "did you ever see any Congress water?"

"Yes."

"Well, did you have to go to Congress to get it?"

"Why, no."

"Well, neither does William Fourth have to go to the sea to get a sea bath."

"How does he get it, then?"

"Gets it the way people down here gets Congress-water — in barrels. There in the palace at Sheffield they've got furnaces, and he wants his water hot. They can't bile that amount of water away off there at the sea. They haven't got no conveniences for it."

"Oh, I see, now. You might a said that in the first place and saved time."

When she said that, I see I was out of the woods again, and so I was comfortable and glad. Next, she says:

"Do you go to church, too?"

"Yes — regular."

"Where do you set?"

"Why, in our pew."

"*Whose* pew?"

"Why, *ourn* — your Uncle Harvey's."

"His'n? What does *he* want with a pew?"

"Wants it to set in. What did you *reckon* he wanted with it?"

"Why, I thought he'd be in the pulpit."

Rot him, I forgot he was a preacher. I see I was up a stump again, so I played another chicken bone and got another think. Then I says:

"Blame it, do you suppose there ain't but one preacher to a church?"

"Why, what do they want with more?"

"What! — to preach before a king? I never see such a girl as you. They don't have no less than seventeen."

"Seventeen! My land! Why, I wouldn't set out such a string as that, not if I *never* got to glory. It must take 'em a week."

"Shucks, they don't *all* of 'em preach the same day — only *one* of 'em."

"Well, then, what does the rest of 'em do?"

"Oh, nothing much. Loll around, pass the plate — and one thing or another. But mainly they don't do nothing."

"Well, then, what are they *for*?"

"Why, they're for *style*. Don't you know nothing?"

"Well, I don't *want* to know no such foolishness as that. How is servants treated in England? Do they treat 'em better 'n we treat our niggers?"

"*No!* A servant ain't nobody there. They treat them worse than dogs."

"Don't they give 'em holidays, the way we do, Christmas and New Year's week, and Fourth of July?"

"Oh, just listen! A body could tell *you* hain't ever been to England, by that. Why, Hare-l — why, Joanna, they never see a holiday from year's end to year's end; never go to the circus, nor theatre, nor nigger shows, nor nowheres."

"Nor church?"

"Nor church."

"But *you* always went to church."

Well, I was gone up again. I forgot I was the old man's servant. But next minute I whirled in on a kind of an explanation how a valley was different from a common servant, and *had* to go to church whether he wanted to or not, and set with the family, on account of it's being the law. But I didn't do it pretty good, and when I got done I see she warn't satisfied. She says:

"Honest injun, now, hain't you been telling me a lot of lies?"

"Honest injun," says I.

"None of it at all?"

"None of it at all. Not a lie in it," says I.

"Lay your hand on this book and say it."

I see it warn't nothing but a dictionary, so I laid my hand on it and said it. So then she looked a little better satisfied, and says:

"Well, then, I'll believe some of it; but I hope to gracious if I'll believe the rest."

"What is it you won't believe, Joe?" says Mary Jane, stepping in with Susan behind her. "It ain't right nor kind for you to talk so to him, and him a stranger and so far from his people. How would you like to be treated so?"

"That's always your way, Maim — always sailing in to help somebody before they're hurt. I hain't done nothing to him. He's told some stretchers, I reckon; and I said I wouldn't swallow it all; and that's every bit and grain I *did* say. I reckon he can stand a little thing like that, can't he?"

"I don't care whether 'twas little or whether 'twas big, he's here in our house and a stranger, and it wasn't good of you to say it. If you was in his place, it would make you feel ashamed; and so you oughtn't to say a thing to another person that will make *them* feel ashamed."

"Why, Maim, he said —— "

"It don't make no difference what he *said* — that ain't the thing. The thing is for you to treat him *kind*, and not be saying things to make him remember he ain't in his own country and amongst his own folks."

I says to myself, *this* is a girl that I'm letting that old reptile rob her of her money!

Then Susan *she* waltzed in; and if you'll believe me, she did give Hare-lip hark from the tomb!

Says I to myself, And this is *another* one that I'm letting him rob her of her money!

Then Mary Jane she took another inning, and went in sweet and lovely again — which was her way — but when she got done there warn't hardly anything left o' poor Hare-lip. So she hollered.

"All right, then," says the other girls, "you just ask his pardon."

She done it, too. And she done it beautiful. She done it so beautiful it was good to hear; and I wished I could tell her a thousand lies, so she could do it again.

I says to myself, this is *another* one that I'm letting him rob her of her money. And when she got through, they all jest laid theirselves out to make me feel at home and know I was amongst friends. I felt so ornery and low down and mean, that I says to myself, My mind's made up; I'll hive that money for them or bust.

So then I lit out — for bed, I said, meaning some time or another. When I got by myself, I went to thinking the thing over. I says to myself, shall I go to that doctor, private, and blow on these frauds? No — that won't do. He might tell who told him; then the king and the duke would make it warm for me. Shall I go, private, and tell Mary Jane? No — I dasn't do it. Her face would give them a hint, sure; they've got the money, and they'd slide right out and get away with it. If she was to fetch in help, I'd get mixed up in the business, before it was done with, I judge. No, there ain't no good way but one. I got to steal that money, somehow; and I got to steal it some way that they won't suspicion that I done it. They've got a good thing, here; and they ain't agoing to leave till they've played this family and this town for all they're worth, so I'll find a chance time enough. I'll steal it, and hide it; and by-and-by, when I'm away down the river, I'll write a letter and tell Mary Jane where it's hid. But I better hive it to-night, if I can, because the doctor maybe hasn't let up as much as he lets on he has; he might scare them out of here, yet.

So, thinks I, I'll go and search them rooms. Up stairs the hall was dark, but I found the duke's room, and started to paw around it with my hands; but I recollected it wouldn't be much like the king to let anybody else take care of that money but his own self; so then I went to his room and begun to paw around there. But I see I couldn't do nothing without a candle, and I dasn't light one, of course. So I judged I'd got to do the other thing — lay for them, and eavesdrop. About that time, I hears their footsteps coming, and was going to skip under the bed; I reached for it, but it wasn't where I thought it would be; but I touched the curtain that hid Mary Jane's frocks, so I jumped in behind that and snuggled in amongst the gowns, and stood there perfectly still.

They come in and shut the door; and the first thing the duke done was to get down and look under the bed. Then I was glad I hadn't found the bed when I wanted it. And yet, you know, it's kind of natural to hide under the bed when you are up to anything private. They sets down, then, and the king says:

"Well, what is it? and cut it middlin' short, because it's better for us to be down there a whoopin'-up the mournin', than up here givin' 'em a chance to talk us over."

"Well, this is it, Capet. I ain't easy; I ain't comfortable. That doctor lays on my mind. I wanted to know your plans. I've got a notion, and I think it's a sound one."

"What is it, duke?"

"That we better glide out of this, before three in the morning, and clip it down the river with what we've got. Specially, seeing we got it so easy — *given* back to us, flung at our heads, as you may say, when of course we allowed to have to steal it back. I'm for knocking off and lighting out."

That made me feel pretty bad. About an hour or two ago, it would a been a little different, but now it made me feel bad and disappointed. The king rips out and says:

"What! And not sell out the rest o' the property? March off like a passel o' fools and leave eight or nine thous'n' dollars' worth o' property layin' around jest sufferin' to be scooped in? — and all good salable stuff, too."

The duke he grumbled; said the bag of gold was enough, and he didn't want to go no deeper — didn't want to rob a lot of orphans of *everything* they had.

"Why, how you talk!" says the king. "We shan't rob 'em of nothing at all but jest this money. The people that *buys* the property is the suff'rers; because as soon's it's found out 'at we didn't own it — which

won't be long after we've slid — the sale won't be valid, and it'll all go
back to the estate. These-yer orphans 'll git their house back agin, and
that's enough for *them;* they're young and spry, and k'n easy earn a
livin.' *They* ain't agoing to suffer. Why, jest think — there's thous'n's
and thous'n's that ain't nigh so well off. Bless you, *they* ain't got noth'n
to complain of."

Well, the king he talked him blind; so at last he give in, and said all
right, but said he believed it was blame foolishness to stay, and that doctor hanging over them. But the king says:

"Cuss the doctor! What do we k'yer for *him?* Hain't we got all the
fools in town on our side? and ain't that a big enough majority in any
town?"

So they got ready to go down stairs again. The duke says:

"I don't think we put that money in a good place."

That cheered me up. I'd begun to think I warn't going to get a hint
of no kind to help me. The king says:

"Why?"

"Because Mary Jane 'll be in mourning from this out; and first you
know the nigger that does up the rooms will get an order to box these
duds up and put 'em away; and do you reckon a nigger can run across
money and not borrow some of it?"

"Your head's level, agin, duke," says the king; and he come a fumbling under the curtain two or three foot from where I was. I stuck
tight to the wall, and kept mighty still, though quivery; and I wondered
what them fellows would say to me if they catched me; and I tried to
think what I'd better do if they did catch me. But the king he got the
bag before I could think more than about a half a thought, and he
never suspicioned I was around. They took and shoved the bag through
a rip in the straw tick that was under the feather bed, and crammed it
in a foot or two amongst the straw and said it was all right, now,
because a nigger only makes up the feather bed, and don't turn over the
straw tick only about twice a year, and so it warn't in no danger of getting stole, now.

But I knowed better. I had it out of there before they was half-way
down stairs. I groped along up to my cubby, and hid it there till I could
get a chance to do better. I judged I better hide it outside of the house
somewheres, because if they missed it they would give the house a good
ransacking. I knowed that very well. Then I turned in, with my clothes
all on; but I couldn't a gone to sleep, if I'd a wanted to, I was in such a
sweat to get through with the business. By-and-by I heard the king and
the duke come up; so I rolled off of my pallet and laid with my chin at

the top of my ladder and waited to see if anything was going to happen. But nothing did.

So I held on till all the late sounds had quit and the early ones hadn't begun, yet; and then I slipped down the ladder.

Chapter XXVII

I crept to their doors and listened; they was snoring, so I tip-toed along, and got down stairs all right. There warn't a sound any-wheres. I peeped through a crack of the dining-room door, and see the men that was watching the corpse all sound asleep on their chairs. The door was open into the parlor, where the corpse was laying, and there was a candle in both rooms. I passed along, and the parlor door was open; but I see there warn't nobody in there but the remainders of Peter; so I shoved on by; but the front door was locked, and the key wasn't there. Just then I heard somebody coming down the stairs, back behind me. I run in the parlor, and took a swift look around, and the only place I see to hide the bag was in the coffin. The lid was shoved along about a foot, showing the dead man's face down in there, with a wet cloth over it, and his shroud on. I tucked the money-bag in under the lid, just down beyond where his hands was crossed, which made me creep, they was so cold, and then I run back across the room and in behind the door.

The person coming was Mary Jane. She went to the coffin, very soft, and kneeled down and looked in; then she put up her handkerchief and I see she begun to cry, though I couldn't hear her, and her back was to me. I slid out, and as I passed the dining-room I thought I'd make sure them watchers hadn't seen me; so I looked through the crack and everything was all right. They hadn't stirred.

I slipped up to bed, feeling ruther blue, on accounts of the thing playing out that way after I had took so much trouble and run so much resk about it. Says I, if it could stay where it is, all right; because when we get down the river a hundred mile or two, I could write back to Mary Jane, and she could dig him up again and get it; but that ain't the thing that's going to happen; the thing that's going to happen is, the money 'll be found when they come to screw on the lid. Then the king 'll get it again, and it 'll be a long day before he gives anybody another chance to smouch it from him. Of course I *wanted* to slide down and get it out of there, but I dasn't try it. Every minute it was getting ear-lier, now, and pretty soon some of them watchers would begin to stir, and I might get catched — catched with six thousand dollars in my hands that nobody hadn't hired me to take care of. I don't wish to be mixed up in no such business as that, I says to myself.

When I got down stairs in the morning, the parlor was shut up, and the watchers was gone. There warn't nobody around but the family and the widow Bartley and our tribe. I watched their faces to see if anything had been happening, but I couldn't tell.

Towards the middle of the day the undertaker come, with his man, and they set the coffin in the middle of the room on a couple of chairs, and then set all our chairs in rows, and borrowed more from the neighbors till the hall and the parlor and the dining-room was full. I see the coffin lid was the way it was before, but I dasn't go to look in under it, with folks around.

Then the people begun to flock in, and the beats° and the girls took seats in the front row at the head of the coffin, and for a half an hour the people filed around slow, in single rank, and looked down at the dead man's face a minute, and some dropped in a tear, and it was all very still and solemn, only the girls and the beats holding handkerchiefs to their eyes and keeping their heads bent, and sobbing a little. There warn't no other sound but the scraping of the feet on the floor, and blowing noses — because people always blows them more at a funeral than they do at other places except church.

When the place was packed full, the undertaker he slid around in his black gloves with his softy soothering ways, putting on the last touches, and getting people and things all ship-shape and comfortable, and making no more sound than a cat. He never spoke; he moved people around, he squeezed in late ones, he opened up passage-ways, and done it all with nods, and signs with his hands. Then he took his place over against the wall. He was the softest, glidingest, stealthiest man I ever see; and there warn't no more smile to him than there is to a ham.

They had borrowed a melodeum° — a sick one; and when everything was ready, a young woman set down and worked it, and it was pretty skreeky and colicky, and everybody joined in and sung, and Peter was the only one that had a good thing, according to my notion. Then the Reverend Hobson opened up, slow and solemn, and begun to talk; and straight off the most outrageous row busted out in the cellar a body ever heard; it was only one dog, but he made a most powerful racket, and he kept it up, right along; the parson he had to stand there, over the coffin, and wait — you couldn't hear yourself think. It was right down

---

beats: Deadbeats (the king and the duke).   **melodeum:** A melodion, or small reed organ.

awkward, and nobody didn't seem to know what to do. But pretty soon they see that long-legged undertaker make a sign to the preacher as much as to say, "Don't you worry — just depend on me." Then he stooped down and begun to glide along the wall, just his shoulders showing over the people's heads. So he glided along, and the pow-wow and racket getting more and more outrageous all the time; and at last, when he had gone around two sides of the room, he disappears down cellar. Then, in about two seconds we heard a whack, and the dog he finished up with a most amazing howl or two, and then everything was dead still, and the parson begun his solemn talk where he left off. In a minute or two here comes this undertaker's back and shoulders gliding along the wall again; and so he glided, and glided, around three sides of the room, and then rose up, and shaded his mouth with his hands, and stretched his neck out towards the preacher, over the people's heads, and says, in a kind of a coarse whisper, *"He had a rat!"* Then he drooped down and glided along the wall again to his place. You could see it was a great satisfaction to the people, because naturally they wanted to know. A little thing like that don't cost nothing, and it's just the little things that makes a man to be looked up to and liked. There warn't no more popular man in town than what that undertaker was.

Well, the funeral sermon was very good, but pison long and tiresome; and then the king he shoved in and got off some of his usual rubbage, and at last the job was through, and the undertaker begun to sneak up on the coffin with his screw-driver. I was in a sweat then, and watched him pretty keen. But he never meddled at all; just slid the lid along, as soft as mush, and screwed it down tight and fast. So there I was! I didn't know whether the money was in there, or not. So, says I, spose somebody has hogged that bag on the sly? — now how do *I* know whether to write to Mary Jane or not? 'Spose she dug him up and didn't find nothing — what would she think of me? Blame, it, I says, I might get hunted up and jailed; I'd better lay low and keep dark, and not write at all; the thing's awful mixed, now; trying to better it, I've worsened it a hundred times, and I wish to goodness I'd just let it alone, dad fetch the whole business!

They buried him, and we come back home, and I went to watching faces again — I couldn't help it, and I couldn't rest easy. But nothing come of it; the faces didn't tell me nothing.

The king he visited around, in the evening, and sweetened every body up, and made himself ever so friendly; and he give out the idea that his congregation over in England would be in a sweat about him, so he must hurry and settle up the estate right away, and leave for home. He was very sorry he was so pushed, and so was everybody; they wished he could stay longer, but they said they could see it couldn't be done. And he said of course him and William would take the girls home with them; and that pleased everybody too, because then the girls would be well fixed, and amongst their own relations; and it pleased the girls, too — tickled them so they clean forgot they ever had a trouble in the world; and told him to sell out as quick as he wanted to, they would be ready. Them poor things was that glad and happy it made my heart ache to see them getting fooled and lied to so, but I didn't see no safe way for me to chip in and change the general tune.

Well, blamed if the king didn't bill the house and the niggers and all the property for auction straight off — sale two days after the funeral; but anybody could buy private beforehand if they wanted to.

So the next day after the funeral, along about noontime, the girls' joy got the first jolt; a couple of nigger traders come along, and the king sold them the niggers reasonable, for three-day drafts as they called it, and away they went, the two sons up the river to Memphis, and their mother down the river to Orleans. I thought them poor girls and them niggers would break their hearts for grief; they cried around each other, and took on so it most made me down sick to see it. The girls said they hadn't ever dreamed of seeing the family separated or sold away from the town. I can't ever get it out of my memory, the sight of them poor miserable girls and niggers hanging around each other's necks and crying; and I reckon I couldn't a stood it all but would a had to bust out and tell on our gang if I hadn't knowed the sale warn't no account and the niggers would be back home in a week or two.

The thing made a big stir in the town, too, and a good many come out flat-footed and said it was scandalous to separate the mother and the children that way. It injured the frauds some; but the old fool he bulled right along, spite of all the duke could say or do, and I tell you the duke was powerful uneasy.

Next day was auction day. About broad-day in the morning, the king and the duke come up in the garret and woke me up, and I see by their look that there was trouble. The king says:

"Was you in my room night before last?"

"No, your majesty" — which was the way I always called him when nobody but our gang warn't around.

"Was you in there yisterday er last night?"

"No, your majesty."

"Honor bright, now — no lies."

"Honor bright, your majesty, I'm telling you the truth. I hain't been anear your room since Miss Mary Jane took you and the duke and showed it to you."

The duke says:

"Have you seen anybody else go in there?"

"No, your grace, not as I remember, I believe."

"Stop and think."

I studied a while, and see my chance, then I says:

"Well, I see the niggers go in there several times."

Both of them give a little jump; and looked like they hadn't ever expected it, and then like they *had*. Then the duke says:

"What, *all* of them?"

"No — leastways not all at once. That is, I don't think I ever see them all come *out* at once but just one time."

"Hello — when was that?"

"It was the day we had the funeral. In the morning. It warn't early, because I overslept. I was just starting down the ladder, and I see them."

"Well, go on, *go* on — what did they do? How'd they act?"

"They didn't do nothing. And they didn't act anyway, much, as fur as I see. They tip-toed away; so I seen, easy enough, that they'd shoved in there to do up your majesty's room, or something, sposing you was up; and found you *warn't* up, and so they was hoping to slide out of the way of trouble without waking you up, if they hadn't already waked you up."

"Great guns, *this* is a go!" says the king; and both of them looked pretty sick, and tolerable silly. They stood there a thinking and scratching their heads, a minute, and then the duke he bust into a kind of a little raspy chuckle, and says:

"It does beat all, how neat the niggers played their hand. They let on to be *sorry* they was going out of this region! and I believed they *was* sorry. And so did you, and so did everybody. Don't ever tell *me* any more that a nigger ain't got any histrionic talent. Why, the way they played that thing, it would fool *anybody*. In my opinion there's a fortune in 'em. If I had capital and a theatre, I wouldn't want a better lay out than that — and here we've gone and sold 'em for a song. Yes, and ain't privileged to sing the song, yet. Say, where *is* that song? — that draft."

"In the bank for to be collected. Where *would* it be?"

"Well, *that's* all right then, thank goodness."

Says I, kind of timid-like:

"Is something gone wrong?"

The king whirls on me and rips out:

"None o' your business! You keep your head shet, and mind y'r own affairs — if you got any. Long as you're in this town, don't you forgit *that*, you hear?" Then he says to the duke, "We got to jest swaller it, and say noth'n: mum's the word for *us*."

As they was starting down the ladder, the duke he chuckles again, and says:

"Quick sales *and* small profits! It's a good business — yes."

The king snarls around on him and says,

"I was trying to do for the best, in sellin' 'm out so quick. If the profits has turned out to be none, lackin' considable, and none to carry, is it my fault any more'n it's yourn?"

"Well, *they'd* be in this house yet, and we *wouldn't* if I could a got my advice listened to."

The king sassed back, as much as was safe for him, and then swapped around and lit into *me* again. He give me down the banks for not coming and *telling* him I see the niggers come out of his room acting that way — said any fool would a *knowed* something was up. And then waltzed in and cussed *himself* a while; and said it all come of him not laying late and taking his natural rest that morning, and he'd be blamed if he'd ever do it again. So they went off a jawing; and I felt dreadful glad I'd worked it all off onto the niggers and yet hadn't done the niggers no harm by it.

Chapter XXVIII

By-and-by it was getting-up time; so I come down the ladder and started for down stairs, but as I come to the girls' room, the door was open, and I see Mary Jane setting by her old hair trunk, which was open and she'd been packing things in it — getting ready to go to England. But she had stopped now, with a folded gown in her lap, and had her face in her hands, crying. I felt awful bad to see it; of course anybody would. I went in there, and says:

"Miss Mary Jane, you can't abear to see people in trouble, and *I* can't — most always. Tell me about it."

So she done it. And it was the niggers — I just expected it. She said the beautiful trip to England was most about spoiled for her; she didn't know *how* she was ever going to be happy there, knowing the mother and the children warn't ever going to see each other no more — and then busted out bitterer than ever, and flung up her hands, and says

"Oh, dear, dear, to think they ain't *ever* going to see each other any more!"

"But they *will* — and inside of two weeks — and I *know* it!" says I.

Laws it was out before I could think! — and before I could budge, she throws her arms around my neck, and told me to say it *again*, say it *again*, say it *again!*

I see I had spoke too sudden, and said too much, and was in a close place. I asked her to let me think a minute; and she set there, very impatient and excited, and handsome, but looking kind of happy and eased-up, like a person that's had a tooth pulled out. So I went to studying it out. I says to myself, I reckon a body that ups and tells the truth when he is in a tight place, is taking considerable many resks, though I ain't had no experience, and can't say for certain; but it looks so to me, anyway; and yet here's a case where I'm blest if it don't look to me like the truth is better, and actuly *safer,* than a lie. I must lay it by in my mind, and think it over some time or other, it's so kind of strange and unregular. I never see nothing like it. Well, I says to myself at last, I'm agoing to chance it; I'll up and tell the truth this time, though it does seem most like setting down on a kag of powder and touching it off just to see where you'll go to. Then I says:

"Miss Mary Jane, is there any place out of town a little ways, where you could go and stay three or four days?"

"Yes — Mr. Lothrop's. Why?"

"Never mind why, yet. If I'll tell you how I know the niggers will see each other again — inside of two weeks — here in this house — and *prove* how I know it — will you go to Mr. Lothrop's and stay four days?"

"Four days!" she says; "I'll stay a year!"

"All right," I says, "I don't want nothing more out of *you* than just your word — I druther have it than another man's kiss-the-Bible." She smiled, and reddened up very sweet, and I says, "If you don't mind it, I'll shut the door — and bolt it."

Then I come back and set down again, and says:

"Don't you holler. Just set still, and take it like a man. I got to tell the truth, and you want to brace up, Miss Mary, because it's a bad kind, and going to be hard to take, but there ain't no help for it. These uncles of yourn ain't no uncles at all — they're a couple of frauds — regular dead-beats. There, now we're over the worst of it — you can stand the rest middling easy."

It jolted her up like everything, of course; but I was over the shoal
water now, so I went right along, her eyes a blazing higher and higher
all the time, and told her every blame thing, from where we first struck
that young fool going up to the steamboat, clear through to where she
flung herself onto the king's breast at the front door and he kissed her
sixteen or seventeen times — and then up she jumps, with her face afire
like sunset, and says:

"The brute! Come — don't waste a minute — not a *second* — we'll
have them tarred and feathered, and flung in the river!"

Says I:

"Cert'nly. But do you mean, *before* you go to Mr. Lothrop's, or ——"

"Oh," she says, "what am I *thinking* about!" she says, and set right
down again. "Don't mind what I said — please don't — you *won't*,
now, *will* you?" Laying her silky hand on mine in that kind of a way that
I said I would die first. "I never thought, I was so stirred up," she says;
"now go on, and I won't do so any more. You tell me what to do, and
whatever you say, I'll do it."

"Well," I says, "it's a rough gang, them two frauds, and I'm fixed so
I got to travel with them a while longer, whether I want to or not — I
druther not tell you why — and if you was to blow on them this town
would get me out of their claws, and *I'*d be all right, but there'd be
another person that you don't know about who'd be in big trouble.
Well, we got to save *him*, hain't we? Of course. Well, then, we won't
blow on them."

Saying them words put a good idea in my head. I see how maybe I
could get me and Jim rid of the frauds; get them jailed here, and then
leave. But I didn't want to run the raft in day-time, without anybody
aboard to answer questions but me; so I didn't want the plan to begin
working till pretty late to-night. I says:

"Miss Mary Jane, I'll tell you what we'll do — and you won't have
to stay at Mr. Lothrop's so long, nuther. How fur is it?"

"A little short of four miles — right out in the country, back
here."

"Well, that'll answer. Now you go along out there, and lay low till
nine or half-past, to-night, and then get them to fetch you home
again — tell them you've thought of something. If you get here before
eleven, put a candle in this window, and if I don't turn up, wait *till*
eleven, and *then* if I don't turn up it means I'm gone, and out of the
way, and safe. Then you come out and spread the news around, and get
these beats jailed."

"Good," she says, "I'll do it."

"And if it just happens so that I don't get away, but get took up along with them, you must up and say I told you the whole thing beforehand, and you must stand by me all you can."

"Stand by you, indeed I will. They sha'n't touch a hair of your head!" she says, and I see her nostrils spread and her eyes snap when she said it, too.

"If I get away, I sha'n't be here," I says, "to prove these rapscallions ain't your uncles, and I couldn't do it if I *was* here. I could swear they was beats and bummers, that's all; though that's worth something. Well, there's others can do that better than what I can — and they're people that ain't going to be doubted as quick as I'd be. I'll tell you how to find them. Gimme a pencil and a piece of paper. There — '*Royal Nonesuch, Bricksville.*' Put it away, and don't lose it. When the court wants to find out something about these two, let them send up to Bricksville and say they've got the men that played the Royal Nonesuch, and ask for some witnesses — why, you'll have that entire town down here before you can hardly wink, Miss Mary. And they'll come a-biling, too."

I judged we had got everything fixed about right, now. So I says:

"Just let the auction go right along, and don't worry. Nobody don't have to pay for the things they buy till a whole day after the auction, on accounts of the short notice, and they ain't going out of this till they get that money — and the way we've fixed it the sale ain't going to count, and they ain't going to *get* no money. It's just like the way it was with the niggers — it warn't no sale, and the niggers will be back before long. Why, they can't collect the money for the *niggers,* yet — they're in the worst kind of a fix, Miss Mary."

"Well," she says, "I'll run down to breakfast now, and then I'll start straight for Mr. Lothrop's."

" 'Deed, *that* ain't the ticket, Miss Mary Jane," I says, "by no manner of means; go *before* breakfast."

"Why?"

"What did you reckon I wanted you to go at all for, Miss Mary?"

"Well, I never thought — and come to think, I don't know. What was it?"

"Why, it's because you ain't one of these leather-face people. I don't want no better book than what your face is. A body can set down and read it off like coarse print. Do you reckon you can go and face your uncles, when they come to kiss you good-morning, and never ——"

"There, there, don't! Yes, I'll go before breakfast — I'll be glad to. And leave my sisters with them?"

"Yes — never mind about them. They've got to stand it yet a while. They might suspicion something if all of you was to go. I don't want you to see them, nor your sisters, nor nobody in this town — if a neighbor was to ask how is your uncles this morning, your face would tell something. No, you go right along, Miss Mary Jane, and I'll fix it with all of them. I'll tell Miss Susan to give your love to your uncles and say you've went away for a few hours for to get a little rest and change, or to see a friend, and you'll be back to-night or early in the morning."

"Gone to see a friend is all right, but I won't have my love given to them."

"Well, then, it sha'n't be." It was well enough to tell _her_ so — no harm in it. It was only a little thing to do, and no trouble; and it's the little things that smoothes people's roads the most, down here below; it would make Mary Jane comfortable, and it wouldn't cost nothing. Then I says: "There's one more thing — that bag of money."

"Well, they've got that; and it makes me feel pretty silly to think _how_ they got it."

"No, you're out, there. They hain't got it."

"Why, who's got it?"

"I wish I knowed, but I don't. I _had_ it, because I stole it from them: and I stole it to give to you; and I know where I hid it, but I'm afraid it ain't there no more. I'm awful sorry, Miss Mary Jane, I'm just as sorry as I can be; but I done the best I could; I did, honest. I come nigh getting caught, and I had to shove it into the first place I come to, and run — and it warn't a good place."

"Oh, stop blaming yourself — it's too bad to do it, and I won't allow it — you couldn't help it; it wasn't your fault. Where did you hide it?"

I didn't want to set her to thinking about her troubles again; and I couldn't seem to get my mouth to tell her what would make her see that corpse laying in the coffin with that bag of money on his stomach. So for a minute I didn't say nothing — then I says:

"I'd rather not _tell_ you where I put it, Miss Mary Jane, if you don't mind letting me off; but I'll write it for you on a piece of paper, and you can read it along the road to Mr. Lothrop's, if you want to. Do you reckon that'll do?"

"Oh, yes."

So I wrote: "I put it in the coffin. It was in there when you was crying there, away in the night. I was behind the door, and I was mighty sorry for you, Miss Mary Jane."

It made my eyes water a little, to remember her crying there all by herself in the night, and them devils laying there right under her own roof, shaming her and robbing her; and when I folded it up and give it to her, I see the water come into her eyes, too; and she shook me by the hand, hard, and says:

"*Good*-bye — I'm going to do everything just as you've told me; and if I don't ever see you again, I sha'n't ever forget you, and I'll think of you a many and a many a time, and I'll *pray* for you, too!" — and she was gone.

Pray for me! I reckoned if she knowed me she'd take a job that was more nearer her size. But I bet she done it, just the same — she was just that kind. She had the grit to pray for Judus if she took the notion — there warn't no back-down to her, I judge. You may say what you want to, but in my opinion she had more sand in her than any girl I ever see; in my opinion she was just full of sand. It sounds like flattery, but it ain't no flattery. And when it comes to beauty — and goodness too — she lays over them all. I hain't ever seen her since that time that I see her go out of that door; no, I hain't ever seen her since, but I reckon I've thought of her a many and a many a million times, and of her saying she would pray for me; and if ever I'd a thought it would do any good for me to pray for *her,* blamed if I wouldn't a done it or bust.

Well, Mary Jane she lit out the back way, I reckon; because nobody see her go. When I struck Susan and the hare-lip, I says:

"What's the name of them people over on t'other side of the river that you-all goes to see sometimes?"

They says:

"There's several; but it's the Proctors, mainly."

"That's the name," I says; "I most forgot it. Well, Miss Mary Jane she told me to tell you she's gone over there in a dreadful hurry — one of them's sick."

"Which one?"

"I don't know; leastways I kinder forget; but I think it's ———"

"Sakes alive, I hope it ain't *Hanner?*"

"I'm sorry to say it," I says, "but Hanner's the very one."

"My goodness — and she so well only last week! Is she took bad?"

"It ain't no name for it. They set up with her all night, Miss Mary Jane said, and they don't think she'll last many hours."

"Only think of that, now! What's the matter with her!"

I couldn't think of anything reasonable, right off that way, so I says:

"Mumps."

"Mumps your granny! They don't set up with people that's got the mumps."

"They don't, don't they? You better bet they do with *these* mumps. These mumps is different. It's a new kind, Miss Mary Jane said."

"How's it a new kind?"

"Because it's mixed up with other things."

"What other things?"

"Well, measles, and whooping-cough, and erysiplas, and consumption, and yaller janders, and brain fever, and I don't know what all."

"My land! And they call it the *mumps?*"

"That's what Miss Mary Jane said."

"Well, what in the nation do they call it the *mumps* for?"

"Why, because it *is* the mumps. That's what it starts with."

"Well, ther' ain't no sense in it. A body might stump his toe, and take pison, and fall down the well, and break his neck, and bust his brains out, and somebody come along and ask what killed him, and some numskull up and say, 'Why, he stumped his *toe.'* Would ther' be any sense in that? *No.* And ther' ain't no sense in *this*, nuther. Is it ketching?"

"Is it *ketching?* Why, how you talk. Is a *harrow* catching? — in the dark? If you don't hitch onto one tooth, you're bound to on another, ain't you? And you can't get away with that tooth without fetching the whole harrow along, can you? Well, these kind of mumps is a kind of a harrow, as you may say — and it ain't no slouch of a harrow, nuther, you come to get it hitched on good."

"Well, it's awful, *I* think," says the hare-lip. "I'll go to Uncle Harvey and ——"

"Oh, yes," I says, "I *would*. Of *course* I would. I wouldn't lose no time."

"Well, why wouldn't you?"

"Just look at it a minute, and maybe you can see. Hain't your uncles obleeged to get along home to England as fast as they can? And do you reckon they'd be mean enough to go off and leave you to go all that journey by yourselves? *You* know they'll wait for you. So fur, so good. Your uncle Harvey's a preacher, ain't he? Very well, then; is a *preacher* going to deceive a steamboat clerk? is he going to deceive a *ship clerk?* — so as to get them to let Miss Mary Jane go aboard? Now *you* know he ain't. What *will* he do, then? Why, he'll say, 'It's a great pity, but my church matters has got to get along the best way they can; for my niece has been exposed to the dreadful pluribus-unum mumps, and so it's my bounden duty to set down here and wait the three months it takes to show on her if she's got it.' But never mind, if you think it's best to tell your uncle Harvey ——"

"Shucks, and stay fooling around here when we could all be having good times in England whilst we was waiting to find out whether Mary Jane's got it or not? Why, you talk like a muggins."

"Well, anyway, maybe you better tell some of the neighbors."

"Listen at that, now. You do beat all, for natural stupidness. Can't you *see* that *they'd* go and tell? Ther' ain't no way but just to not tell anybody at *all.*"

"Well, maybe you're right — yes, I judge you *are* right."

"But I reckon we ought to tell Uncle Harvey she's gone out a while, anyway, so he wont be uneasy about her?"

"Yes, Miss Mary Jane she wanted you to do that. She says, 'Tell them to give Uncle Harvey and William my love and a kiss, and say I've run over the river to see Mr. — Mr. — what *is* the name of that rich family your uncle Peter used to think so much of? — I mean the one that ——"

"Why, you must mean the Apthorps, ain't it?"

"Of course; bother them kind of names, a body can't ever seem to remember them, half the time, somehow. Yes, she said, say she has run over for to ask the Apthorps to be sure and come to the auction and buy this house, because she allowed her uncle Peter would ruther they had it than anybody else; and she's going to stick to them till they say they'll come, and then, if she ain't too tired, she's coming home; and if she is, she'll be home in the morning anyway. She said, don't say nothing about the Proctors, but only about the Apthorps — which'll be perfectly true, because she *is* going there to speak about their buying the house; I know it, because she told me so, herself."

"All right," they said, and cleared out to lay for their uncles, and give them the love and the kisses, and tell them the message.

Everything was all right now. The girls wouldn't say nothing because they wanted to go to England; and the king and the duke would ruther Mary Jane was off working for the auction than around in reach of Doctor Robinson. I felt very good; I judged I had done it pretty neat — I reckoned Tom Sawyer couldn't a done it no neater himself. Of course he would a throwed more style into it, but I can't do that very handy, not being brung up to it.

Well, they held the auction in the public square, along towards the end of the afternoon, and it strung along, and strung along, and the old man he was on hand and looking his level piousest, up there longside of the auctioneer, and chipping in a little Scripture, now and then, or a little goody-goody saying, of some kind, and the duke he was around goo-gooing for sympathy all he knowed how, and just spreading himself generly.

But by-and-by the thing dragged through, and everything was sold. Everything but a little old trifling lot in the graveyard. So they'd got to work *that* off — I never see such a girafft as the king was for wanting to swallow *everything*. Well, whilst they was at it, a steamboat landed, and in about two minutes up comes a crowd a whooping and yelling and laughing and carrying on, and singing out:

"*Here's* your opposition line! here's your two sets o' heirs to old Peter Wilks — and you pays your money and you takes your choice!"

Chapter XXIX

They was fetching a very nice looking old gentleman along, and a nice looking younger one, with his right arm in a sling. And my souls, how the people yelled, and laughed, and kept it up. But I didn't see no joke about it, and I judged it would strain the duke and the king some to see any. I reckoned they'd turn pale. But no, nary a pale did *they* turn. The duke he never let on he suspicioned what was up, but just went a goo-gooing around, happy and satisfied, like a jug that's googling out buttermilk; and as for the king, he just gazed and gazed down sorrowful on them newcomers like it give him the stomach-ache in his very heart to think there could be such frauds and rascals in the world. Oh, he done it admirable. Lots of the principal people gethered around the king, to let him see they was on his side. That old gentleman that had just come looked all puzzled to death. Pretty soon he begun to speak, and I see, straight off, he pronounced *like* an Englishman, not the king's way, though the king's *was* pretty good, for an imitation. I can't give the old gent's words, nor I can't imitate him; but he turned around to the crowd, and says, about like this:

"This is a surprise to me which I wasn't looking for; and I'll acknowledge, candid and frank, I ain't very well fixed to meet it and answer it; for my brother and me has had misfortunes, he's broke his arm, and our baggage got put off at a town above here, last night in the night by a mistake. I am Peter Wilks's brother Harvey, and this is his brother William, which can't hear nor speak — and can't even make signs to amount to much, now 't he's only got one hand to work them with. We are who we say we are; and in a day or two, when I get the baggage, I can prove it. But, up till then, I won't say nothing more, but go to the hotel and wait."

So him and the new dummy started off; and the king he laughs, and blethers out:

"Broke his arm — *very* likely *ain't* it? — and very convenient, too, for a fraud that's got to make signs, and hain't learnt how. Lost their baggage! That's *mighty* good! — and mighty ingenious — under the *circumstances!*"

So he laughed again; and so did everybody else, except three or four, or maybe half a dozen. One of these was that doctor; another one was a sharp looking gentleman, with a carpet-bag of the old-fashioned kind made out of carpet-stuff, that had just come off of the steamboat and was talking to him in a low voice, and glancing towards the king now and then and nodding their heads — it was Levi Bell, the lawyer that was gone up to Louisville; and another one was a big rough husky that come along and listened to all the old gentleman said, and was listening to the king now. And when the king got done, this husky up and says:

"Say, looky here; if you are Harvey Wilks, when'd you come to this town?"

"The day before the funeral, friend," says the king.

"But what time o' day?"

"In the evenin' — 'bout an hour er two before sundown."

"*How'd* you come?"

"I come down on the *Susan Powell,* from Cincinnati."

"Well, then, how'd you come to be up at the Pint in the *mornin'* — in a canoe?"

"I warn't up at the Pint in the mornin'."

"It's a lie."

Several of them jumped for him and begged him not to talk that way to an old man and a preacher.

"Preacher be hanged, he's a fraud and a liar. He was up at the Pint that mornin'. I live up there, don't I? Well, I was up there, and he was up there. I *see* him there. He come in a canoe, along with Tim Collins and a boy."

The doctor he up and says:

"Would you know the boy again if you was to see him, Hines?"

"I reckon I would, but I don't know. Why, yonder he is, now. I know him perfectly easy."

It was me he pointed at. The doctor says:

"Neighbors, I don't know whether the new couple is frauds or not; but if *these* two ain't frauds, I am an idiot, that's all. I think it's our duty to see that they don't get away from here till we've looked into this thing. Come along, Hines; come along, the rest of you. We'll take these fellows to the tavern and affront them with t'other couple, and I reckon we'll find out *something* before we get through."

It was nuts for the crowd, though maybe not for the king's friends; so we all started. It was about sundown. The doctor he led me along by the hand, and was plenty kind enough, but he never let *go* my hand.

We all got in a big room in the hotel, and lit up some candles, and fetched in the new couple. First, the doctor says:

"I don't wish to be too hard on these two men, but *I* think they're frauds, and they may have complices that we don't know nothing about. If they have, won't the complices get away with that bag of gold Peter Wilks left? It ain't unlikely. If these men ain't frauds, they won't object to sending for that money and letting us keep it till they prove they're all right — ain't that so?"

Everybody agreed to that. So I judged they had our gang in a pretty tight place, right at the outstart. But the king he only looked sorrowful, and says:

"Gentlemen, I wish the money was there, for I ain't got no disposition to throw anything in the way of a fair, open, out-and-out investigation o' this misable business; but alas, the money ain't there; you k'n send and see, if you want to."

"Where is it, then?"

"Well, when my niece give it to me to keep for her, I took and hid it inside o' the straw tick o' my bed, not wishin' to bank it for the few days we'd be here, and considerin' the bed a safe place, we not bein' used to niggers, and suppos'n' 'em honest, like servants in England. The niggers stole it the very next mornin' after I had went down stairs; and when I sold 'em, I hadn't missed the money yit, so they got clean away with it. My servant here k'n tell you 'bout it gentlemen."

The doctor and several said "Shucks!" and I see nobody didn't altogether believe him. One man asked me if I see the niggers steal it. I said no, but I see them sneaking out of the room and hustling away, and I never thought nothing, only I reckoned they was afraid they had waked up my master and was trying to get away before he made trouble with them. That was all they asked me. Then the doctor whirls on me and says:

"Are *you* English too?"

I says yes; and him and some others laughed, and said, "Stuff!"

Well, then they sailed in on the general investigation, and there we had it, up and down, hour in, hour out, and nobody never said a word about supper, nor ever seemed to think about it — and so they kept it up, and kept it up; and it *was* the worst mixed-up thing you ever see. They made the king tell his yarn, and they made the old gentleman tell his'n; and anybody but a lot of prejudiced chuckleheads would a *seen* that the old gentleman was spinning truth and t'other one lies. And by-and-by they had me up to tell what I knowed. The king he give me a left-handed look out of the corner of his eye, and so I knowed enough to talk on the right side. I begun to tell about Sheffield, and how we lived there, and all about the English Wilkses, and so on; but I didn't get pretty fur till the doctor begun to laugh; and Levi Bell, the lawyer, says:

"Set down, my boy, I wouldn't strain myself, if I was you. I reckon you ain't used to lying, it don't seem to come handy; what you want is practice. You do it pretty awkward."

I didn't care nothing for the compliment, but I was glad to be let off, anyway.

The doctor he started to say something, and turns and says:

"If you'd been in town at first, Levi Bell ———"

The king broke in and reached out his hand, and says:

"Why, is this my poor dead brother's old friend that he's wrote so often about?"

The lawyer and him shook hands, and the lawyer smiled and looked pleased, and they talked right along a while, and then got to one side and talked low; and at last the lawyer speaks up and says:

"That'll fix it. I'll take the order and send it, along with your brother's, and then they'll know it's all right."

So they got some paper and a pen, and the king he set down and twisted his head to one side, and chawed his tongue, and scrawled off something; and then they give the pen to the duke — and then for the first time, the duke looked sick. But he took the pen and wrote. So then the lawyer turns to the new old gentleman and says:

"You and your brother please write a line or two and sign your names."

The old gentleman wrote, but nobody couldn't read it. The lawyer looked powerful astonished, and says:

"Well, it beats *me*" — and snaked a lot of old letters out of his pocket, and examined them, and then examined the old man's writing, and then *them* again; and then says: "These old letters is from Harvey Wilks; and here's *these* two's handwritings, and anybody can see *they* didn't write them" (the king and the duke looked sold and foolish, I tell you, to see how the lawyer had took them in), "and here's *this* old gentleman's handwriting, and anybody can tell, easy enough, *he* didn't write them — fact is, the scratches he makes ain't properly *writing,* at all. Now here's some letters from ———"

The new old gentleman says:

"If you please, let me explain. Nobody can read my hand but my brother there — so he copies for me. It's *his* hand you've got there, not mine."

"*Well!*" says the lawyer, "this *is* a state of things. I've got some of William's letters too; so if you'll get him to write a line or so we can com ———"

"He *can't* write with his left hand," says the old gentleman. "If he could use his right hand, you would see that he wrote his own letters and mine too. Look at both, please — they're by the same hand."

The lawyer done it, and says:

"I believe it's so — and if it ain't so, there's a heap stronger resemblance than I'd noticed before, anyway. Well, well, well! I thought we was right on the track of a slution, but it's gone to grass, partly. But anyway, *one* thing is proved — *these* two ain't either of 'em Wilkses" — and he wagged his head towards the king and the duke.

Well, what do you think? — that muleheaded old fool wouldn't give in *then!* Indeed he wouldn't. Said it warn't no fair test. Said his brother William was the cussedest joker in the world, and hadn't *tried* to write — *he* see William was going to play one of his jokes the minute he put the pen to paper. And so he warmed up and went warbling and warbling right along, till he was actuly beginning to believe what he was saying, *himself* — but pretty soon the new old gentleman broke in, and says:

"I've thought of something. Is there anybody here that helped to lay out my br — helped to lay out the late Peter Wilks for burying?"

"Yes," says somebody, "me and Ab Turner done it. We're both here."

Then the old man turns towards the king, and says:

"Peraps this gentleman can tell me what was tatooed on his breast?"

Blamed if the king didn't have to brace up mighty quick, or he'd a squshed down like a bluff bank that the river has cut under, it took him so sudden — and mind you, it was a thing that was calculated to make most *anybody* sqush to get fetched such a solid one as that without any notice — because how was *he* going to know what was tatooed on the man? He whitened a little; he couldn't help it; and it was mighty still in there, and everybody bending a little forwards and gazing at him. Says I to myself, *Now* he'll throw up the sponge — there ain't no more use. Well, did he? A body can't hardly believe it, but he didn't. I reckon he

thought he'd keep the thing up till he tired them people out, so they'd
thin out, and him and the duke could break loose and get away. Anyway, he set there, and pretty soon he begun to smile, and says:

"Mf! It's a *very* tough question, *ain't* it! *Yes,* sir, I k'n tell you
what's tatooed on his breast. It's jest a small, thin, blue arrow — that's
what it is; and if you don't look clost, you can't see it. *Now* what do you
say — hey?"

Well, *I* never see anything like that old blister for clean out-and-out
cheek.

The new old gentleman turns brisk towards Ab Turner and his
pard, and his eye lights up like he judged he'd got the king *this* time,
and says:

"There — you've heard what he said! Was there any such mark on
Peter Wilks's breast?"

Both of them spoke up and says:

"We didn't see no such mark."

"Good!" says the old gentleman. "Now, what you *did* see on his
breast was a small dim P, and a B (which is an initial he dropped when
he was young), and a W, with dashes between them, so: P—B—W" —
and he marked them that way on a piece of paper. "Come — ain't that
what you saw?"

Both of them spoke up again, and says:

"No, we *didn't*. We never seen any marks at all."

Well, everybody *was* in a state of mind, now; and they sings out:

"The whole *bilin'* of 'm 's frauds! Le's duck 'em! le's drown 'em!
le's ride 'em on a rail!" and everybody was whooping at once, and there
was a rattling pow-wow. But the lawyer he jumps on the table and yells,
and says:

"Gentlemen — gentle*men!* Hear me just a word — just a *single*
word — if you PLEASE! There's one way yet — let's go and dig up the
corpse and look."

That took them.

"Hooray!" they all shouted, and was starting right off; but the
lawyer and the doctor sung out:

"Hold on, hold on! Collar all these four men and the boy, and fetch
them along, too!"

"We'll do it!" they all shouted: "and if we don't find them marks
we'll lynch the whole gang!"

I *was* scared, now, I tell you. But there warn't no getting away, you
know. They gripped us all, and marched us right along, straight for the
graveyard, which was a mile and a half down the river, and the whole

town at our heels, for we made noise enough, and it was only nine in the evening.

As we went by our house I wished I hadn't sent Mary Jane out of town; because now if I could tip her the wink, she'd light out and save me, and blow on our dead-beats.

Well, we swarmed along down the river road, just carrying on like wild-cats; and to make it more scary, the sky was darking up, and the lightning beginning to wink and flitter, and the wind to shiver amongst the leaves. This was the most awful trouble and most dangersome I ever was in; and I was kinder stunned; everything was going so different from what I had allowed for; stead of being fixed so I could take my own time, if I wanted to, and see all the fun, and have Mary Jane at my back to save me and set me free when the close-fit come, here was nothing in the world betwixt me and sudden death but just them tatoomarks. If they didn't find them —

I couldn't bear to think about it; and yet, somehow, I couldn't think about nothing else. It got darker and darker, and it was a beautiful time to give the crowd the slip; but that big husky had me by the wrist — Hines — and a body might as well try to give Goliar the slip. He dragged me right along, he was so excited; and I had to run to keep up.

When they got there they swarmed into the graveyard and washed over it like an overflow. And when they got to the grave, they found they had about a hundred times as many shovels as they wanted, but nobody hadn't thought to fetch a lantern. But they sailed into digging, anyway, by the flicker of the lightning, and sent a man to the nearest house a half a mile off, to borrow one.

So they dug and dug, like everything; and it got awful dark, and the rain started, and the wind swished and swushed along, and the lightning come brisker and brisker, and the thunder boomed; but them people never took no notice of it, they was so full of this business; and one minute you could see everything and every face in that big crowd, and the shovelfuls of dirt sailing up out of the grave, and the next second the dark wiped it all out, and you couldn't see nothing at all.

At last they got out the coffin, and begun to unscrew the lid, and then such another crowding, and shouldering, and shoving as there was, to scrouge in and get a sight, you never see; and in the dark, that way, it was awful. Hines he hurt my wrist dreadful, pulling and tugging so, and I reckon he clean forgot I was in the world, he was so excited and panting.

All of a sudden the lightning let go a perfect sluice of white glare, and somebody sings out:

"By the living jingo, here's the bag of gold on his breast!"

Hines let out a whoop, like everybody else, and dropped my wrist and give a big surge to bust his way in and get a look, and the way I lit out and shinned for the road in the dark, there ain't nobody can tell.

I had the road all to myself, and I fairly flew — leastways I had it all to myself except the solid dark, and the now-and-then glares, and the buzzing of the rain, and the thrashing of the wind, and the splitting of the thunder; and sure as you are born I did clip it along!

When I struck the town, I see there warn't nobody out in the storm, so I never hunted for no back streets, but humped it straight through the main one; and when I begun to get towards our house I aimed my eye and set it. No light there; the house all dark — which made me feel sorry and disappointed, I didn't know why. But at last, just as I was sailing by, *flash* comes the light in Mary Jane's window! and my heart swelled up sudden, like to bust; and the same second the house and all was behind me in the dark, and wasn't ever going to be before me no more in this world. She *was* the best girl I ever see, and had the most sand.

The minute I was far enough above the town to see I could make the tow-head, I begun to look sharp for a boat to borrow; and the first time the lightning showed me one that wasn't chained, I snatched it and shoved. It was a canoe, and warn't fastened with nothing but a rope. The tow-head was a rattling big distance off, away out there in the middle of the river, but I didn't lose no time; and when I struck the raft at last, I was so fagged I would a just laid down to blow and gasp if I could afforded it. But I didn't. As I sprung aboard I sung out:

"Out with you Jim, and set her loose! Glory be to goodness, we're shut of them!"

Jim lit out, and was a coming for me with both arms spread, he was so full of joy; but when I glimpsed him in the lightning, my heart shot up in my mouth, and I went overboard backwards; for I forgot he was old King Lear and a drownded A-rab all in one, and it most scared the livers and lights out of me. But Jim fished me out, and was going to hug me and bless me, and so on, he was so glad I was back and we was shut of the king and the duke, but I says:

"Not now — have it for breakfast, have it for breakfast! Cut loose and let her slide!"

So, in two seconds, away we went, a sliding down the river, and it *did* seem so good to be free again and all by ourselves on the big river and nobody to bother us. I had to skip around a bit, and jump up and crack my heels a few times, I couldn't help it; but about the third crack, I noticed a sound that I knowed mighty well — and held my breath and listened and waited — and sure enough, when the next flash busted out over the water, here they come! — and just a laying to their oars and making their skiff hum! It was the king and the duke.

So I wilted right down onto the planks, then, and give up; and it was all I could do to keep from crying.

Chapter XXX

When they got aboard, the king went for me, and shook me by the collar, and says:

"Tryin' to give us the slip, was ye, you pup! Tired of our company — hey?"

I says:

"No, your majesty, we warn't — *please* don't, your majesty!"

"Quick, then, and tell us what *was* your idea, or I'll shake the insides out o' you!"

"Honest, I'll tell you everything, just as it happened, your majesty. The man that had aholt of me was very good to me, and kept saying he had a boy about as big as me that died last year, and he was sorry to see a boy in such a dangerous fix; and when they was all took by surprise by finding the gold, and made a rush for the coffin, he lets go of me and whispers, 'Heel it, now, or they'll hang ye, sure!' and I lit out. It didn't seem no good for *me* to stay — *I* couldn't do nothing, and I didn't want to be hung if I could get away. So I never stopped running till I found the canoe; and when I got here I told Jim to hurry, or they'd catch me and hang me yet, and said I was afeard you and the duke wasn't alive, now, and I was awful sorry, and so was Jim, and was awful glad when we see you coming, you may ask Jim if I didn't."

Jim said it was so; and the king told him to shut up, and said, "Oh, yes, it's *mighty* likely!" and shook me up again, and said he reckoned he'd drownd me. But the duke says:

"Leggo the boy, you old idiot! Would *you* a done any different? Did you inquire around for *him*, when you got loose? *I* don't remember it."

So the king let go of me, and begun to cuss that town and everybody in it. But the duke says:

"You better a blame sight give *yourself* a good cussing, for you're the one that's entitled to it most. You hain't done a thing, from the start, that had any sense in it, except coming out so cool and cheeky with that imaginary blue-arrow mark. That *was* bright — it was right down bully; and it was the thing that saved us. For if it hadn't been for that, they'd a jailed us till them Englishmen's baggage come — and then — the penitentiary, you bet! But that trick took 'em to the grave-yard, and the gold done us a still bigger kindness; for if the excited fools hadn't let go all holts and made that rush to get a look, we'd aslept in our cravats to-night — cravats warranted to *wear*, too — longer than *we'd* need 'em."

They was still a minute — thinking — then the king says, kind of absent-minded like:

"Mf! And we reckoned the *niggers* stole it!"

That made me squirm!

"Yes," says the duke, kinder slow, and deliberate, and sarcastic, "*We* did."

After about a half a minute, the king drawls out:

"Leastways — *I* did."

The duke says, the same way:

"On the contrary — *I* did."

The king kind of ruffles up, and says:

"Looky here, Bilgewater, what'r you referrin' to?"

The duke says, pretty brisk:

"When it comes to that, maybe you'll let me ask, what was *you* re-ferring to?"

"Shucks!" says the king, very sarcastic; "but *I* don't know — maybe you was asleep, and didn't know what you was about."

The duke bristles right up, now, and says:

"Oh, let *up* on this cussed nonsense — do you take me for a blame' fool? Don't you reckon *I* know who hid that money in that coffin?"

"*Yes*, sir! I know you *do* know — because you done it yourself!"

"It's a lie!" — and the duke went for him. The king sings out:

"Take y'r hands off! — leggo my throat! — I take it all back!"

The duke says:

"Well, you just own up, first, that you *did* hide that money there, intending to give me the slip one of these days, and come back and dig it up, and have it all to yourself."

"Wait jest a minute, duke — answer me this one question, honest and fair; if you didn't put the money there, say it, and I'll b'lieve you, and take back everything I said."

"You old scoundrel, I didn't, and you know I didn't. There, now!"

"Well, then, I b'lieve you. But answer me only jest this one more — now *don't* git mad; didn't you have it in your *mind* to hook the money and hide it?"

The duke never said nothing for a little bit; then he says:

"Well — I don't care if I *did*, I didn't *do* it, anyway. But you not only had it in mind to do it, but you *done* it."

"I wisht I may never die if I done it, duke, and that's honest. I won't say I warn't *goin'* to do it, because I *was;* but you — I mean somebody — got in ahead o' me."

"It's a lie! You done it, and you got to *say* you done it, or ——"

The king begun to gurgle, and then he gasps out:

"'Nough! — *I own up!*"

I was very glad to hear him say that, it made me feel much more easier than what I was feeling before. So the duke took his hands off, and says:

"If you ever deny it again, I'll drown you. It's *well* for you to set there and blubber like a baby — it's fitten for you, after the way you've acted. I never see such an old ostrich for wanting to gobble everything — and I a trusting you all the time, like you was my own father. You ought to been ashamed of yourself to stand by and hear it saddled onto a lot of poor niggers and you never say a word for 'em. It makes me feel ridiculous to think I was soft enough to *believe* that rubbage. Cuss you, I can see, now, why you was so anxious to make up the deffe-sit — you wanted to get what money I'd got out of the Nonesuch and one thing or another, and scoop it *all!*"

The king says, timid, and still a snuffling:

"Why, duke, it was you that said make up the deffersit, it warn't me."

"Dry up! I don't want to hear no more *out* of you!" says the duke. "And *now* you see what you *got* by it. They've got all their own money back, and all of *ourn* but a shekel or two, *besides.* G'long to bed — and don't you deffersit *me* no more deffersits, long 's *you* live!"

So the king sneaked into the wigwam, and took to his bottle for comfort; and before long the duke tackled *his* bottle; and so in about a half an hour they was as thick as thieves again, and the tighter they got, the lovinger they got; and went off a snoring in each other's arms. They both got powerful mellow, but I noticed the king didn't get mellow enough to forget to remember to not deny about hiding the money-bag again. That made me feel easy and satisfied. Of course when they got to snoring, we had a long gabble, and I told Jim everything.

Chapter XXXI

We dasn't stop again at any town, for days and days; kept right along down the river. We was down south in the warm weather, now, and a mighty long ways from home. We begun to come to trees with Spanish moss on them, hanging down from the limbs like long gray beards. It was the first I ever see it growing, and it made the woods look solemn and dismal. So now the frauds reckoned they was out of danger, and they begun to work the villages again.

First they done a lecture on temperance; but they didn't make enough for them both to get drunk on. Then in another village they started a dancing school; but they didn't know no more how to dance than a kangaroo does; so the first prance they made, the general public jumped in and pranced them out of town. Another time they tried a go at yellocution; but they didn't yellocute long till the audience got up and give them a solid good cussing and made them skip out. They tackled missionarying, and mesmerizering, and doctoring, and telling fortunes, and a little of everything; but they couldn't seem to have no luck. So at last they got just about dead broke, and laid around the raft, as she floated along, thinking, and thinking, and never saying nothing, by the half a day at a time, and dreadful blue and desperate.

And at last they took a change, and begun to lay their heads together in the wigwam and talk low and confidential two or three hours at a time. Jim and me got uneasy. We didn't like the look of it. We judged they was studying up some kind of worse deviltry than ever. We turned it over and over, and at last we made up our minds they was going to break into somebody's house or store, or was going into the counterfeit-money business, or something. So then we was pretty scared, and made up an agreement that we wouldn't have nothing in the world to do with such actions, and if we ever got the least show we would give them the cold shake, and clear out and leave them behind. Well, early one morning we hid the raft in a good safe place about two mile below a little bit of a shabby village, named Pikesville, and the king he went ashore, and told us all to stay hid whilst he went up to town and smelt around to see if anybody had got any wind of the Royal Nonesuch there yet. ("House to rob, you *mean*," says I to myself; "and when you get through robbing it you'll come back here and wonder what's become of me and Jim and the raft — and you'll have to take it out in wondering.") And he said if he warn't back by midday, the duke and me would know it was all right, and we was to come along.

So we staid where we was. The duke he fretted and sweated around, and was in a mighty sour way. He scolded us for everything, and we couldn't seem to do nothing right; he found fault with every little thing. Something was a-brewing, sure. I was good and glad when mid-day come and no king; we could have a change, anyway — and maybe a chance for *the* change, on top of it. So me and the duke went up to the village, and hunted around there for the king, and by-and-by we found him in the back room of a little low doggery, very tight, and a lot of loafers bullyragging him for sport, and he a cussing and threatening with all his might, and so tight he couldn't walk, and couldn't do noth-ing to them. The duke he begun to abuse him for an old fool, and the king begun to sass back; and the minute they was fairly at it, I lit out, and shook the reefs out of my hind legs, and spun down the river road like a deer — for I see our chance; and I made up my mind that it would be a long day before they ever see me and Jim again. I got down there all out of breath but loaded up with joy, and sung out —

"Set her loose, Jim, we're all right, now!"

But there warn't no answer, and nobody come out of the wig-wam. Jim was gone! I set up a shout — and then another — and then another one; and run this way and that in the woods, whooping and screeching; but it warn't no use — old Jim was gone. Then I set down and cried; I couldn't help it. But I couldn't set still long. Pretty soon I went out on the road, trying to think what I better do, and I run across a boy walking, and asked him if he'd seen a strange nigger, dressed so and so, and he says:

"Yes."

"Whereabouts?" says I.

"Down to Silas Phelps's place, two mile below here. He's a runaway nigger, and they've got him. Was you looking for him?"

"You bet I ain't! I run across him in the woods about an hour or two ago, and he said if I hollered he'd cut my livers out — and told me to lay down and stay where I was; and I done it. Been there ever since; afeard to come out."

"Well," he says, "you needn't be afeard no more, becuz they've got him. He run off f'm down South, som'ers."

"It's a good job they got him."

"Well, I *reckon!* There's two hunderd dollars reward on him. It's like picking up money out'n the road."

"Yes, it is — and *I* could a had it if I'd been big enough; I see him *first.* Who nailed him?"

"It was an old fellow — a stranger — and he sold out his chance in him for forty dollars, becuz he's got to go up the river and can't wait. Think o' that, now! You bet I'd wait, if it was seven year."

"That's me, every time," says I. "But maybe his chance ain't worth no more than that, if he'll sell it so cheap. Maybe there's something ain't straight about it."

"But it is, though — straight as a string. I see the handbill myself. It tells all about him, to a dot — paints him like a picture, and tells the plantation he's frum, below Newr*leans*. No-sirree-*bob*, they ain't no trouble 'bout *that* speculation, you bet you. Say, gimme a chaw tobacker, won't ye?"

I didn't have none, so he left. I went to the raft, and set down in the wigwam to think. But I couldn't come to nothing. I thought till I wore my head sore, but I couldn't see no way out of the trouble. After all this long journey, and after all we'd done for them scoundrels, here was it all come to nothing, everything all busted up and ruined, because they could have the heart to serve Jim such a trick as that, and make him a slave again all his life, and amongst strangers, too, for forty dirty dollars.

Once I said to myself it would be a thousand times better for Jim to be a slave at home where his family was, as long as he'd *got* to be a slave, and so I'd better write a letter to Tom Sawyer and tell him to tell Miss Watson where he was. But I soon give up that notion, for two things: she'd be mad and disgusted at his rascality and ungratefulness for leaving her, and so she'd sell him straight down the river again; and if she didn't, everybody naturally despises an ungrateful nigger, and they'd make Jim feel it all the time, and so he'd feel ornery and disgraced, And then think of *me!* It would get all around, that Huck Finn helped a nigger to get his freedom; and if I was to ever see anybody from that town again, I'd be ready to get down and lick his boots for shame. That's just the way: a person does a low-down thing, and then he don't want to take no consequences of it. Thinks as long as he can hide it, it ain't no disgrace. That was my fix exactly. The more I studied about this, the more my conscience went to grinding me, and the more wicked and low-down and ornery I got to feeling. And at last, when it hit me all of a sudden that here was the plain hand of Providence slapping me in the face and letting me know my wickedness was being watched all the time from up there in heaven, whilst I was stealing a poor old woman's nigger that hadn't ever done me no harm, and now was showing me there's One that's always on the lookout, and ain't agoing to allow no such miserable doings to go only just so fur and no further, I most dropped in my tracks I was so scared. Well, I tried the best I could to kinder soften it up somehow for myself, by saying I was brung up wicked, and so I warn't so much to blame; but something inside of me kept saying, "There was the Sunday school, you could a gone to it; and if you'd a done it they'd a learnt you, there, that people that acts as I'd been acting about that nigger goes to everlasting fire."

It made me shiver. And I about made up my mind to pray; and see if I couldn't try to quit being the kind of a boy I was, and be better. So I kneeled down. But the words wouldn't come. Why wouldn't they? It warn't no use to try and hide it from Him. Nor from *me,* neither. I knowed very well why they wouldn't come. It was because my heart warn't right; it was because I warn't square; it was because I was playing double. I was letting *on* to give up sin, but away inside of me I was holding on to the biggest one of all. I was trying to make my mouth *say* I would do the right thing and the clean thing, and go and write to that nigger's owner and tell where he was; but deep down in me I knowed it was a lie — and He knowed it. You can't pray a lie — I found that out.

So I was full of trouble, full as I could be; and didn't know what to do. At last I had an idea; and I says, I'll go and write the letter — and *then* see if I can pray. Why, it was astonishing, the way I felt as light as a feather, right straight off, and my troubles all gone. So I got a piece of paper and a pencil, all glad and excited, and set down and wrote:

> Miss Watson your runaway nigger Jim is down here two mile
> below Pikesville and Mr. Phelps has got him and he will give him
> up for the reward if you send.   HUCK FINN.

I felt good and all washed clean of sin for the first time I had ever felt so in my life, and I knowed I could pray now. But I didn't do it straight off, but laid the paper down and set there thinking — thinking how good it was all this happened so, and how near I come to being lost and going to hell. And went on thinking. And got to thinking over our trip down the river; and I see Jim before me, all the time, in the day, and in the night-time, sometimes moonlight, sometimes storms, and we a floating along, talking, and singing, and laughing. But somehow I couldn't seem to strike no places to harden me against him, but only the other kind. I'd see him standing my watch on top of his'n, stead of calling me, so I could go on sleeping; and see him how glad he was when I come back out of the fog; and when I come to him again in the swamp, up there where the feud was; and such-like times; and would always call me honey, and pet me, and do everything he could think of for me, and how good he always was; and at last I struck the time I saved him by telling the men we had small-pox aboard, and he was so grateful, and said I was the best friend old Jim ever had in the world, and the *only* one he's got now; and then I happened to look around, and see that paper.

It was a close place. I took it up, and held it in my hand. I was a trembling, because I'd got to decide, forever, betwixt two things, and I knowed it. I studied a minute, sort of holding my breath, and then says to myself:

"All right, then, I'll *go* to hell" — and tore it up.

It was awful thoughts, and awful words, but they was said. And I let them stay said; and never thought no more about reforming. I shoved the whole thing out of my head; and said I would take up wickedness again, which was in my line, being brung up to it, and the other warn't. And for a starter, I would go to work and steal Jim out of slavery again; and if I could think up anything worse, I would do that, too; because as long as I was in, and in for good, I might as well go the whole hog.

Then I set to thinking over how to get at it, and turned over considerable many ways in my mind; and at last fixed up a plan that suited me. So then I took the bearings of a woody island that was down the river a piece, and as soon as it was fairly dark I crept out with my raft and went for it, and hid it there, and then turned in. I slept the night through, and got up before it was light, and had my breakfast, and put on my store clothes, and tied up some others and one thing or another in a bundle, and took the canoe and cleared for shore. I landed below where I judged was Phelps's place, and hid my bundle in the woods, and then filled up the canoe with water, and loaded rocks into her and sunk her where I could find her again when I wanted her, about a quarter of a mile below a little steam sawmill that was on the bank.

Then I struck up the road, and when I passed the mill I see a sign on it, "Phelps's Sawmill," and when I come to the farm-houses, two or three hundred yards further along, I kept my eyes peeled, but didn't see nobody around, though it was good daylight, now. But I didn't mind, because I didn't want to see nobody just yet — I only wanted to get the lay of the land. According to my plan, I was going to turn up there from the village, not from below. So I just took a look, and shoved along, straight for town. Well, the very first man I see, when I got there, was the duke. He was sticking up a bill for the Royal Nonesuch — three-night performance — like that other time. *They* had the cheek, them frauds! I was right on him, before I could shirk. He looked astonished, and says:

"Hel-*lo*! Where'd *you* come from?" Then he says, kind of glad and eager, "Where's the raft? — got her in a good place?"

I says:

"Why, that's just what I was agoing to ask your grace."

Then he didn't look so joyful — and says:

"What was your idea for asking *me?*" he says.

"Well," I says, "when I see the king in that doggery yesterday, I says to myself, we can't get him home for hours, till he's soberer; so I went a loafing around town to put in the time, and wait. A man up and offered me ten cents to help him pull a skiff over the river and back to fetch a sheep, and so I went along; but when we was dragging him to the boat, and the man left me aholt of the rope and went behind him to shove him along, he was too strong for me, and jerked loose and run, and we after him. We didn't have no dog, and so we had to chase him all over the country till we tired him out. We never got him till dark, then we fetched him over, and I started down for the raft. When I got there and see it was gone, I says to myself, 'they've got into trouble and had to leave; and they've took my nigger, which is the only nigger I've got in the world, and now I'm in a strange country, and ain't got no property no more, nor nothing, and no way to make my living;' so I set down and cried. I slept in the woods all night. But what *did* become of the raft then? — and Jim, poor Jim!"

"Blamed if *I* know — that is, what's become of the raft. That old fool had made a trade and got forty dollars, and when we found him in the doggery the loafers had matched half dollars with him and got every cent but what he'd spent for whisky; and when I got him home late last night and found the raft gone, we said, 'That little rascal has stole our raft and shook us, and run off down the river.'"

"I wouldn't shake my *nigger*, would I? — the only nigger I had in the world, and the only property."

"We never thought of that. Fact is, I reckon we'd come to consider him *our* nigger; yes, we did consider him so — goodness knows we had trouble enough for him. So when we see the raft was gone, and we flat broke, there warn't anything for it but to try the Royal Nonesuch another shake. And I've pegged along ever since, dry as a powder-horn. Where's that ten cents? Give it here."

I had considerable money, so I give him ten cents, but begged him to spend it for something to eat, and give me some, because it was all the money I had, and I hadn't had nothing to eat since yesterday. He never said nothing. The next minute he whirls on me and says:

"Do you reckon that nigger would blow on us? We'd skin him if he done that!"

"How can he blow? Hain't he run off?"

"No! That old fool sold him, and never divided with me, and the money's gone."

"*Sold* him?" I says, and begun to cry; "why, he was *my* nigger, and that was my money. Where is he? — I want my nigger."

"Well, you can't *get* your nigger, that's all — so dry up your blubbering. Looky here — do you think *you'd* venture to blow on us? Blamed if I think I'd trust you. Why, if you *was* to blow on us ——"

He stopped, but I never see the duke look so ugly out of his eyes before. I went on a-whimpering, and says:

"I don't want to blow on nobody; and I ain't got no time to blow, nohow. I got to turn out and find my nigger."

He looked kinder bothered, and stood there with his bills fluttering on his arm, thinking, and wrinkling up his forehead. At last he says:

"I'll tell you something. We got to be here three days. If you'll promise you won't blow, and won't let the nigger blow, I'll tell you where to find him."

So I promised, and he says:

"A farmer by the name of Silas Ph ——" and then he stopped. You see he started to tell me the truth; but when he stopped, that way, and begun to study and think again, I reckoned he was changing his mind. And so he was. He wouldn't trust me; he wanted to make sure of having me out of the way the whole three days. So pretty soon he says: "The man that bought him is named Abram Foster — Abram G. Foster — and he lives forty mile back here in the country, on the road to Lafayette."

"All right," I says, "I can walk it in three days. And I'll start this very afternoon."

"No, you won't, you'll start *now;* and don't you lose any time about it, neither, nor do any gabbling by the way. Just keep a tight tongue in your head and move right along, and then you won't get into trouble with *us,* d'ye hear?"

That was the order I wanted, and that was the one I played for. I wanted to be left free to work my plans.

"So clear out," he says; "and you can tell Mr. Foster whatever you want to. Maybe you can get him to believe that Jim *is* your nigger — some idiots don't require documents — leastways I've heard there's such down South here. And when you tell him the handbill and the reward's bogus, maybe he'll believe you when you explain to him what the idea was for getting 'em out. Go 'long, now, and tell him anything you want to; but mind you don't work your jaw any *between* here and there."

So I left, and struck for the back country. I didn't look around, but I kinder felt like he was watching me. But I knowed I could tire him out at that. I went straight out in the country as much as a mile, before I stopped; then I doubled back through the woods towards Phelps's. I reckoned I better start in on my plan straight off, without fooling around, because I wanted to stop Jim's mouth till these fellows could get away. I didn't want no trouble with their kind. I'd seen all I wanted to of them, and wanted to get entirely shut of them.

Chapter XXXII

When I got there it was all still and Sundaylike, and hot and sunshiny — the hands was gone to the fields; and there was them kind of faint dronings of bugs and flies in the air that makes it seem so lonesome and like everybody's dead and gone; and if a breeze fans along and quivers the leaves, it makes you feel mournful, because you feel like it's spirits whispering — spirits that's been dead ever so many years — and you always think they're talking about *you*. As a general thing it makes a body wish *he* was dead, too, and done with it all.

Phelps's was one of these little one-horse cotton plantations; and they all look alike. A rail fence round a two-acre yard; a stile, made out of logs sawed off and up-ended, in steps, like barrels of a different length, to climb over the fence with, and for the women to stand on when they are going to jump onto a horse; some sickly grass-patches in the big yard, but mostly it was bare and smooth, like an old hat with the nap rubbed off; big double log house for the white folks — hewed logs, with the chinks stopped up with mud or mortar, and these mud-stripes been whitewashed some time or another; round-log kitchen, with a big broad, open but roofed passage joining it to the house; log smokehouse back of the kitchen; three little log nigger-cabins in a row t'other side the smoke-house; one little hut all by itself away down against the back fence, and some out-buildings down a piece the other side; ashhopper, and big kettle to bile soap in, by the little hut; bench by the kitchen door, with bucket of water and a gourd; hound asleep there, in the sun; more hounds asleep, round about; about three shade-trees away off in a corner; some currant bushes and gooseberry bushes in one place by the fence; outside of the fence a garden and a water-melon patch; then the cotton fields begins; and after the fields, the woods.

I went around and clumb over the back stile by the ash-hopper, and started for the kitchen. When I got a little ways, I heard the dim hum of a spinning-wheel wailing along up and sinking along down again; and then I knowed for certain I wished I was dead — for that *is* the lone-somest sound in the whole world.

I went right along, not fixing up any particular plan, but just trust-ing to Providence to put the right words in my mouth when the time come; for I'd noticed that Providence always did put the right words in my mouth, if I left it alone.

When I got half-way, first one hound and then another got up and went for me, and of course I stopped and faced them, and kept still. And such another pow-wow as they made! In a quarter of a minute I was a kind of a hub of a wheel, as you may say — spokes made out of dogs — circle of fifteen of them packed together around me, with their necks and noses stretched up towards me, a barking and howling; and more a coming; you could see them sailing over fences and around cor-ners from everywheres.

A nigger woman come tearing out of the kitchen with a rolling-pin in her hand, singing out, "Begone! *you* Tige! you Spot! begone, sah!" and she fetched first one and then another of them a clip and sent him howling, and then the rest followed; and the next second, half of them come back, wagging their tails around me and making friends with me. There ain't no harm in a hound, nohow.

And behind the woman comes a little nigger girl and two little nig-ger boys, without anything on but tow-linen shirts, and they hung onto their mother's gown, and peeped out from behind her at me, bashful, the way they always do. And here comes the white woman running from the house, about forty-five or fifty year old, bareheaded, and her spinning-stick in her hand; and behind her comes her little white chil-dren, acting the same way the little niggers was doing. She was smiling all over so she could hardly stand — and says:

"It's *you*, at last! — *ain't* it?"

I out with a "Yes'm," before I thought.

She grabbed me and hugged me tight; and then gripped me by both hands and shook and shook; and the tears come in her eyes, and run down over; and she couldn't seem to hug and shake enough, and kept saying, "You don't look as much like your mother as I reckoned you would, but law sakes, I don't care for that, I'm *so* glad to see you! Dear, dear, it does seem like I could eat you up! Children, it's your cousin Tom! — tell him howdy."

But they ducked their heads, and put their fingers in their mouths, and hid behind her. So she run on:

"Lize, hurry up and get him a hot breakfast, right away — or did you get your breakfast on the boat?"

I said I had got it on the boat. So then she started for the house, leading me by the hand, and the children tagging after. When we got there, she set me down in a split-bottomed chair, and set herself down on a little low stool in front of me, holding both of my hands, and says:

"Now I can have a *good* look at you: and laws-a-me, I've been hungry for it a many and a many a time, all these long years, and it's come at last! We been expecting you a couple of days and more. What's kep' you? — boat get aground?"

"Yes'm — she ——"

"Don't say yes'm — say Aunt Sally. Where'd she get aground?"

I didn't rightly know what to say, because I didn't know whether the boat would be coming up the river or down. But I go a good deal on instinct; and my instinct said she would be coming up — from down towards Orleans. That didn't help me much, though; for I didn't know the names of bars down that way. I see I'd got to invent a bar, or forget the name of the one we got aground on — or — Now I struck an idea, and fetched it out:

"It warn't the grounding — that didn't keep us back but a little. We blowed out a cylinder-head."

"Good gracious! anybody hurt?"

"No'm. Killed a nigger."

"Well, it's lucky; because sometimes people do get hurt. Two years ago last Christmas, your uncle Silas was coming up from Newrleans on the old *Lally Rook,* and she blowed out a cylinder-head and crippled a man. And I think he died afterwards. He was a Babtist. Your uncle Silas knowed a family in Baton Rouge that knowed his people very well. Yes, I remember, now he *did* die. Mortification set in, and they had to amputate him. But it didn't save him. Yes, it was mortification — that was it. He turned blue all over, and died in the hope of a glorious resurrection. They say he was a sight to look at. Your uncle's been up to the town every day to fetch you. And he's gone again, not more'n an hour ago; he'll be back any minute, now. You must a met him on the road, didn't you? — oldish man, with a ——"

"No, I didn't see nobody, Aunt Sally. The boat landed just at daylight, and I left my baggage on the wharf-boat and went looking around the town and out a piece in the country, to put in the time and not get here too soon; and so I come down the back way."

"Who'd you give the baggage to?"

"Nobody."

"Why, child, it'll be stole!"

"Not where *I* hid it I reckon it won't," I says.

"How'd you get your breakfast so early on the boat?"

It was kinder thin ice, but I says:

"The captain see me standing around, and told me I better have something to eat before I went ashore; so he took me in the texas to the officers' lunch, and give me all I wanted."

I was getting so uneasy I couldn't listen good. I had my mind on the children all the time; I wanted to get them out to one side, and pump them a little, and find out who I was. But I couldn't get no show, Mrs. Phelps kept it up and run on so. Pretty soon she made the cold chills streak all down my back, because she says:

"But here we're a running on this way, and you hain't told me a word about Sis, nor any of them. Now I'll rest my works a little, and you start up yourn; just tell me *everything* — tell me all about 'm all — every one of 'm; and how they are, and what they're doing, and what they told you to tell me; and every last thing you can think of."

Well, I see I was up a stump — and up it good. Providence had stood by me this fur, all right, but I was hard and tight aground, now. I see it warn't a bit of use to try to go ahead — I'd *got* to throw up my hand. So I says to myself, here's another place where I got to resk the truth. I opened my mouth to begin; but she grabbed me and hustled me in behind the bed, and says:

"Here he comes! stick your head down lower — there, that'll do; you can't be seen, now. Don't you let on you're here. I'll play a joke on him. Childern, don't you say a word."

I see I was in a fix, now. But it warn't no use to worry; there warn't nothing to do but just hold still, and try and be ready to stand from under when the lightning struck.

I had just one little glimpse of the old gentleman when he come in, then the bed hid him. Mrs. Phelps she jumps for him and says:

"Has he come?"

"No," says her husband.

"Good-*ness* gracious!" she says, "what in the world *can* have become of him?"

"I can't imagine," says the old gentleman; "and I must say, it makes me dreadful uneasy."

"Uneasy!" she says, "I'm ready to go distracted! He *must* a come; and you've missed him along the road. I *know* it's so — something *tells* me so."

"Why Sally, I *couldn't* miss him along the road — *you* know that."

"But oh, dear, dear, what *will* Sis say! He must a come! You must a missed him. He ——"

"Oh, don't distress me any more'n I'm already distressed. I don't know what in the world to make of it. I'm at my wit's end, and I don't mind acknowledging 't I'm right down scared. But there's no hope that he's come; for he *couldn't* come and me miss him. Sally, it's terrible — just terrible — something's happened to the boat, sure!"

"Why, Silas! Look yonder! — up the road! — ain't that somebody coming?"

He sprung to the window at the head of the bed, and that give Mrs. Phelps the chance she wanted. She stooped down quick, at the foot of the bed, and give me a pull, and out I come; and when he turned back from the window, there she stood, a-beaming and a-smiling like a house afire, and I standing pretty meek and sweaty alongside. The old gentleman stared, and says:

"Why, who's that?"

"Who do you reckon 't is?"

"I haint no idea. Who *is* it?"

"It's *Tom Sawyer!*"

By jings, I most slumped though the floor. But there warn't no time to swap knives; the old man grabbed me by the hand and shook, and kept on shaking; and all the time, how the woman did dance around and laugh and cry; and then how they both did fire off questions about Sid, and Mary, and the rest of the tribe.

But if they was joyful, it warn't nothing to what I was; for it was like being born again, I was so glad to find out who I was. Well, they froze to me for two hours; and at last when my chin was so tired it couldn't hardly go, any more, I had told them more about my family — I mean the Sawyer family — than ever happened to any six Sawyer families. And I explained all about how we blowed out a cylinder-head at the mouth of White River and it took us three days to fix it. Which was all right, and worked first rate; because *they* didn't know but what it would take three days to fix it. If I'd a called it a bolt-head it would a done just as well.

Now I was feeling pretty comfortable all down one side, and pretty uncomfortable all up the other. Being Tom Sawyer was easy and comfortable; and it stayed easy and comfortable till by-and-by I hear a steamboat coughing along down the river — then I says to myself, spose Tom Sawyer come down on that boat? — and spose he steps in here, any minute, and sings out my name before I can throw him a wink to keep quiet? Well, I couldn't *have* it that way — it wouldn't do at all. I must go up the road and waylay him. So I told the folks I reckoned I would go up to the town and fetch down my baggage. The old gentleman was for going along with me, but I said no, I could drive the horse myself, and I druther he wouldn't take no trouble about me.

Chapter XXXIII

So I started for town, in the wagon, and when I was half-way I see a wagon coming, and sure enough it was Tom Sawyer, and I stopped and waited till he come along. I says "Hold on!" and it stopped alongside, and his mouth opened up like a trunk, and staid so; and he swallowed two or three times like a person that's got a dry throat, and then says:

"I hain't ever done you no harm. You know that. So then, what you want to come back and ha'nt *me* for?"

I says:

"I hain't come back — I hain't been *gone*."

When he heard my voice, it righted him up some, but he warn't quite satisfied yet. He says:

"Don't you play nothing on me, because I wouldn't on you. Honest injun, now, you ain't a ghost?"

"Honest injun, I ain't," I says.

"Well — I — I — well, that ought to settle it, of course; but I can't somehow seem to understand it, no way. Looky here, warn't you ever murdered *at all?*"

"No. I warn't ever murdered at all — I played it on them. You come in here and feel of me if you don't believe me."

So he done it; and it satisfied him; and he was that glad to see me again, he didn't know what to do. And he wanted to know all about it right off; because it was a grand adventure, and mysterious, and so it hit him where he lived. But I said, leave it alone till by-and-by; and told his driver to wait, and we drove off a little piece, and I told him the kind of a fix I was in, and what did he reckon we better do? He said, let him alone a minute, and don't disturb him. So he thought and thought, and pretty soon he says:

"It's all right, I've got it. Take my trunk in your wagon, and let on it's your'n; and you turn back and fool along slow, so as to get to the house about the time you ought to; and I'll go towards town a piece, and take a fresh start, and get there a quarter or a half an hour after you; and you needn't let on to know me, at first."

I says:

"All right; but wait a minute. There's one more thing — a thing that *nobody* don't know but me. And that is, there's a nigger here that I'm a trying to steal out of slavery — and his name is *Jim* — old Miss Watson's Jim."

He says:

"What! Why Jim is ——"

He stopped and went to studying. I says:

"*I* know what you'll say. You'll say it's dirty low-down business; but what if it is? — *I*'m low down; and I'm agoing to steal him, and I want you to keep mum and not let on. Will you?"

His eye lit up, and he says:

"I'll *help* you steal him!"

Well, I let go all holts then, like I was shot. It was the most astonishing speech I ever heard — and I'm bound to say Tom Sawyer fell, considerable, in my estimation. Only I couldn't believe it. Tom Sawyer a *nigger stealer!*

"Oh, shucks," I says, "you're joking."

"I ain't joking, either."

"Well, then," I says, "joking or no joking, if you hear anything said about a runaway nigger, don't forget to remember that *you* don't know nothing about him, and *I* don't know nothing about him."

Then we took the trunk and put it in my wagon, and he drove off his way, and I drove mine. But of course I forgot all about driving slow, on accounts of being glad and full of thinking; so I got home a heap too quick for that length of a trip. The old gentleman was at the door, and he says:

"Why, this is wonderful. Who ever would a thought it was in that mare to do it. I wish we'd a timed her. And she hain't sweated a hair — not a hair. It's wonderful. Why, I wouldn't take a hunderd dollars for that horse now; I wouldn't, honest; and yet I'd a sold her for fifteen before, and thought 'twas all she was worth."

That's all he said. He was the innocentest, best old soul I ever see. But it warn't surprising; because he warn't only just a farmer, he was a preacher, too, and had a little one-horse log church down back of the plantation, which he built it himself at his own expense, for a church and school-house, and never charged nothing for his preaching, and it was worth it, too. There was plenty other farmer-preachers like that, and done the same way, down South.

In about half an hour Tom's wagon drove up to the front stile, and Aunt Sally she see it through the window because it was only about fifty yards, and says:

"Why, there's somebody come! I wonder who 'tis? Why, I do believe it's a stranger. Jimmy" (that's one of the children), "run and tell Lize to put on another plate for dinner."

Everybody made a rush for the front door, because, of course, a stranger don't come *every* year, and so he lays over the yaller fever, for interest,° when he does come. Tom was over the stile and starting for the house; the wagon was spinning up the road for the village, and we was all bunched in the front door. Tom had his store clothes on, and an audience — and that was always nuts for Tom Sawyer. In them circumstances it warn't no trouble to him to throw in an amount of style that was suitable. He warn't a boy to meeky along up that yard like a sheep; no, he come ca'm and important, like the ram. When he got afront of us, he lifts his hat ever so gracious and dainty, like it was the lid of a box that had butterflies asleep in it and he didn't want to disturb them, and says:

"Mr. Archibald Nichols, I presume?"

"No, my boy," says the old gentleman, "I'm sorry to say 't your driver has deceived you; Nichols's place is down a matter of three mile more. Come in, come in."

Tom he took a look back over his shoulder, and says, "Too late — he's out of sight."

"Yes, he's gone, my son, and you must come in and eat your dinner with us; and then we'll hitch up and take you down to Nichols's."

"Oh, I *can't* make you so much trouble; I couldn't think of it. I'll walk — I don't mind the distance."

"But we won't *let* you walk — it wouldn't be Southern hospitality to do it. Come right in."

"Oh, *do*," says Aunt Sally; "it ain't a bit of trouble to us, not a bit in the world. You *must* stay. It's a long, dusty three mile, and we *can't* let you walk. And besides, I've already told 'em to put on another plate, when I see you coming; so you mustn't disappoint us. Come right in, and make yourself at home."

So Tom he thanked them very hearty and handsome, and let himself be persuaded, and come in; and when he was in, he said he was a stranger from Hicksville, Ohio, and his name was William Thompson — and he made another bow.

Well, he run on, and on, and on, making up stuff about Hicksville and everybody in it he could invent, and I getting a little nervous, and

---

lays over . . . ., for interest: Is more interesting than even a serious illness.

wondering how this was going to help me out of my scrape; and at last, still talking along, he reached over and kissed Aunt Sally right on the mouth, and then settled back again in his chair, comfortable, and was going on talking; but she jumped up and wiped it off with the back of her hand, and says:

"You owdacious puppy!"

He looked kind of hurt, and says:

"I'm surprised at you, m'am."

"You're s'rp — Why, what do you reckon *I* am? I've a good notion to take and — say, what do you mean by kissing me?"

He looked kind of humble, and says:

"I didn't mean nothing, m'am. I didn't mean no harm. I — I — thought you'd like it."

"Why, you born fool!" She took up the spinning-stick, and it looked like it was all she could do to keep from giving him a crack with it. "What made you think I'd like it?"

"Well, I don't know. Only, they — they — told me you would."

"*They* told you I would. Whoever told you 's *another* lunatic. I never heard the beat of it. Who's *they?*"

"Why — everybody. They all said so, m'am."

It was all she could do to hold in; and her eyes snapped, and her fingers worked like she wanted to scratch him; and she says:

"Who's 'everybody?' Out with their names — or ther'll be an idiot short."

He got up and looked distressed, and fumbled his hat, and says:

"I'm sorry, and I warn't expecting it. They told me to. They all told me to. They all said kiss her; and said she'll like it. They all said it — every one of them. But I'm sorry, m'am, and I won't do it no more — I won't, honest."

"You won't, won't you? Well, I sh'd *reckon* you won't!"

"No'm, I'm honest about it; I won't ever do it again. Till you ask me."

"Till I *ask* you! Well, I never see the beat of it in my born days! I lay you'll be the Methusalem-numskull of creation before ever *I* ask you — or the likes of you."

"Well," he says, "it does surprise me so. I can't make it out, somehow. They said you would, and I thought you would. But —" He stopped and looked around slow, like he wished he could run across a friendly eye, somewhere's; and fetched up on the old gentleman's, and says, "Didn't *you* think she'd like me to kiss her, sir?"

"Why, no, I — I — well, no, I b'lieve I didn't."

Then he looks on around, the same way, to me — and says:

"Tom, didn't *you* think Aunt Sally 'd open out her arms and say, 'Sid Sawyer ——' "

"My land!" she says, breaking in and jumping for him, "you impudent young rascal, to fool a body so —" and was going to hug him, but he fended her off, and says:

"No, not till you've asked me, first."

So she didn't lose no time, but asked him; and hugged him and kissed him, over and over again, and then turned him over to the old man, and he took what was left. And after they got a little quiet again, she says:

"Why, dear me, I never see such a surprise. We warn't looking for *you*, at all, but only Tom. Sis never wrote to me about anybody coming but him."

"It's because it warn't *intended* for any of us to come but Tom," he says; "but I begged and begged, and at the last minute she let me come, too; so, coming down the river, me and Tom thought it would be a first-rate surprise for him to come here to the house first, and for me to by-and-by tag along and drop in and let on to be a stranger. But it was a mistake, Aunt Sally. This ain't no healthy place for a stranger to come."

"No — not impudent whelps, Sid. You ought to had your jaws boxed; I hain't been so put out since I don't know when. But I don't care, I don't mind the terms — I'd be willing to stand a thousand such jokes to have you here. Well, to think of that performance! I don't deny it, I was most putrified with astonishment when you give me that smack."

We had dinner out in that broad open passage betwixt the house and the kitchen; and there was things enough on that table for seven families — and all hot, too; none of your flabby tough meat that's laid in a cupboard in a damp cellar all night and tastes like a hunk of old cold cannibal in the morning. Uncle Silas he asked a pretty long blessing over it, but it was worth it; and it didn't cool it a bit, neither, the way I've seen them kind of interruptions do, lots of times.

There was a considerable good deal of talk, all the afternoon, and me and Tom was on the lookout all the time, but it warn't no use, they didn't happen to say nothing about any runaway nigger, and we was afraid to try to work up to it. But at supper, at night, one of the little boys says:

"Pa, mayn't Tom and Sid and me go to the show?"

"No," says the old man, "I reckon there ain't going to be any; and you couldn't go if there was; because the runaway nigger told Burton and me all about that scandalous show, and Burton said he would tell the people; so I reckon they've drove the owdacious loafers out of town before this time."

So there it was! — but I couldn't help it. Tom and me was to sleep in the same room and bed; so, being tired, we bid good-night and went up to bed, right after supper, and clumb out of the window and down the lightning-rod, and shoved for the town; for I didn't believe anybody was going to give the king and the duke a hint, and so, if I didn't hurry up and give them one they'd get into trouble sure.

On the road Tom he told me all about how it was reckoned I was murdered, and how pap disappeared, pretty soon, and didn't come back no more, and what a stir there was when Jim run away; and I told Tom all about our Royal Nonesuch rapscallions, and as much of the raft-voyage as I had time to; and as we struck into the town and up through the middle of it — it was as much as half-after eight, then — here comes a raging rush of people, with torches, and an awful whooping and yelling, and banging tin pans and blowing horns; and we jumped to one side to let them go by; and as they went by, I see they had the king and the duke astraddle of a rail — that is, I knowed it *was* the king and the duke, though they was all over tar and feathers, and didn't look like nothing in the world that was human — just looked like a couple of monstrous big soldier-plumes. Well, it made me sick to see it; and I was sorry for them poor pitiful rascals, it seemed like I couldn't ever feel any hardness against them any more in the world. It was a dreadful thing to see. Human beings *can* be awful cruel to one another.

We see we was too late — couldn't do no good. We asked some stragglers about it, and they said everybody went to the show looking very innocent; and laid low and kept dark till the poor old king was in the middle of his cavortings on the stage; then somebody give a signal, and the house rose up and went for them.

So we poked along back home, and I warn't feeling so brash as I was before, but kind of ornery, and humble, and to blame, somehow — though I hadn't done nothing. But that's always the way; it don't make no difference whether you do right or wrong, a person's conscience ain't got no sense, and just goes for him *anyway*. If I had a yaller dog that didn't know no more than a person's conscience does, I would pison him. It takes up more room than all the rest of a person's insides, and yet ain't no good, nohow. Tom Sawyer he says the same.

Chapter XXXIV

We stopped talking, and got to thinking.

By-and-by Tom says:

"Looky here, Huck, what fools we are, to not think of it before! I bet I know where Jim is."

"No! Where?"

"In that hut down by the ash-hopper. Why, looky here. When we was at dinner, didn't you see a nigger man go in there with some vittles?"

"Yes."

"What did you think the vittles was for?"

"For a dog."

"So'd I. Well, it wasn't for a dog."

"Why?"

"Because part of it was watermelon."

"So it was — I noticed it. Well, it does beat all, that I never thought about a dog not eating watermelon. It shows how a body can see and don't see at the same time."

"Well, the nigger unlocked the padlock when he went in, and he locked it again when he come out. He fetched uncle a key, about the time we got up from table — same key, I bet. Watermelon shows man, lock shows prisoner; and it ain't likely there's two prisoners on such a little plantation, and where the people's all so kind and good. Jim's the prisoner. All right — I'm glad we found it out detective fashion; I wouldn't give shucks for any other way. Now you work your mind and study out a plan to steal Jim, and I will study out one, too; and we'll take the one we like the best."

What a head for just a boy to have! If I had Tom Sawyer's head, I wouldn't trade it off to be a duke, nor mate of a steamboat, nor clown in a circus, nor nothing I can think of. I went to thinking out a plan, but only just to be doing something; I knowed very well where the right plan was going to come from. Pretty soon, Tom says:

"Ready?"

"Yes," I says.

"All right — bring it out."

"My plan is this," I says. "We can easy find out if it's Jim in there. Then get up my canoe to-morrow night, and fetch my raft over from the island. Then the first dark night that comes, steal the key out of the old man's britches, after he goes to bed, and shove off down the river on the raft, with Jim, hiding day-times and running nights, the way me and Jim used to do before. Wouldn't that plan work?"

"*Work?* Why cert'nly, it would work, like rats a fighting. But it's too blame' simple; there ain't nothing *to* it. What's the good of a plan that ain't no more trouble than that? It's as mild as goose-milk. Why, Huck, it wouldn't make no more talk than breaking into a soap factory."

I never said nothing, because I warn't expecting nothing different; but I knowed mighty well that whenever he got *his* plan ready it wouldn't have none of them objections to it.

And it didn't. He told me what it was, and I see in a minute it was worth fifteen of mine, for style, and would make Jim just as free a man as mine would, and maybe get us all killed besides. So I was satisfied, and said we would waltz in on it. I needn't tell what it was, here, because I knowed it wouldn't stay the way it was. I knowed he would be changing it around, every which way, as we went along, and heaving in new bullinesses wherever he got a chance. And that is what he done.

Well, one thing was dead sure; and that was, that Tom Sawyer was in earnest and was actuly going to help steal that nigger out of slavery. That was the thing that was too many for me. Here was a boy that was respectable, and well brung up; and had a character to lose; and folks at home that had characters; and he was bright and not leather-headed; and knowing and not ignorant; and not mean, but kind; and yet here he was, without any more pride, or rightness, or feeling, than to stoop to this business, and make himself a shame, and his family a shame, before everybody. I *couldn't* understand it, no way at all. It was outrageous, and I knowed I ought to just up and tell him so; and so be his true friend, and let him quit the thing right where he was, and save himself. And I *did* start to tell him; but he shut me up, and says:

"Don't you reckon I know what I'm about? Don't I generly know what I'm about?"

"Yes."

"Didn't I *say* I was going to help steal the nigger?"

"Yes."

"*Well* then."

That's all he said, and that's all I said. It warn't no use to say any more; because when he said he'd do a thing, he always done it. But *I* couldn't make out how he was willing to go into this thing; so I just let it go, and never bothered no more about it. If he was bound to have it so, *I* couldn't help it.

When we got home, the house was all dark and still; so we went on down to the hut by the ash hopper, for to examine it. We went through the yard, so as to see what the hounds would do. They knowed us, and didn't make no more noise than country dogs is always doing when anything comes by in the night. When we got to the cabin, we took a look at the front and the two sides; and on the side I warn't acquainted with — which was the north side — we found a square window-hole, up tolerable high, with just one stout board nailed across it. I says:

"Here's the ticket. This hole's big enough for Jim to get through, if we wrench off the board."

Tom says:

"It's as simple as tit-tat-toe, three-in-a-row, and as easy as playing hooky. I should *hope* we can find a way that's a little more complicated than *that*, Huck Finn."

"Well then," I says, "how'll it do to saw him out, the way I done before I was murdered, that time?"

"That's more *like*," he says. "It's real mysterious, and troublesome, and good," he says; "but I bet we can find a way that's twice as long. There ain't no hurry; le's keep on looking around."

Betwixt the hut and the fence, on the back side, was a lean-to, that joined the hut at the eaves, and was made out of plank. It was as long as the hut, but narrow — only about six foot wide. The door to it was at the south end, and was padlocked. Tom he went to the soap kettle, and searched around and fetched back the iron thing they lift the lid with; so he took it and prized out one of the staples. The chain fell down, and we opened the door and went in, and shut it, and struck a match, and see the shed was only built against the cabin and hadn't no connection with it; and there warn't no floor to the shed, nor nothing in it but some old rusty played-out hoes, and spades, and picks, and a crippled plow. The match went out, and so did we, and shoved in the staple again, and the door was locked as good as ever. Tom was joyful. He says:

"Now we're all right. We'll *dig* him out. It'll take about a week!"

Then we started for the house, and I went in the back door — you only have to pull a buckskin latch-string, they don't fasten the doors — but that warn't romantical enough for Tom Sawyer: no way would do him but he must climb up the lightning-rod. But after he got up half-way about three times, and missed fire and fell every time, and the last time most busted his brains out, he thought he'd got to give it up; but after he was rested, he allowed he would give her one more turn for luck, and this time he made the trip.

In the morning we was up at break of day, and down to the nigger cabins to pet the dogs and make friends with the nigger that fed Jim —

if it *was* Jim that was being fed. The niggers was just getting through breakfast and starting for the fields; and Jim's nigger was piling up a tin pan with bread and meat and things; and whilst the others was leaving, the key come from the house.

This nigger had a good-natured, chuckle-headed face, and his wool was all tied up in little bunches with thread. That was to keep witches off. He said the witches was pestering him awful, these nights, and making him see all kinds of strange things, and hear all kinds of strange words and noises, and he didn't believe he was ever witched so long, before, in his life. He got so worked up, and got to running on so about his troubles, he forgot all about what he'd been agoing to do. So Tom says:

"What's the vittles for? Going to feed the dogs?"

The nigger kind of smiled around graduly over his face, like when you heave a brickbat in a mud puddle, and he says:

"Yes, Mars Sid, *a* dog. Cur'us dog, too. Does you want to go en look at 'im?"

"Yes."

I hunched Tom, and whispers:

"You going, right here in the day-break? *That* warn't the plan."

"No, it warn't — but it's the plan *now*."

So, drat him, we went along, but I didn't like it much. When we got in, we couldn't hardly see anything, it was so dark; but Jim was there, sure enough, and could see us; and he sings out:

"Why, *Huck!* En good *lan'!* ain' dat Misto Tom?"

I just knowed how it would be; I just expected it. *I* didn't know nothing to do; and if I had, I couldn't a done it; because that nigger busted in and says:

"Why, de gracious sakes! do he know you genlmen?"

We could see pretty well, now. Tom he looked at the nigger, steady and kind of wondering, and says:

"Does *who* know us?"

"Why, dish-yer runaway nigger."

"I don't reckon he does; but what put that into your head?"

"What *put* it dar? Didn' he jis' dis minute sing out like he knowed you?"

Tom says, in a puzzled-up kind of way:

"Well, that's mighty curious. *Who* sung out? *When* did he sing out? *What* did he sing out?" And turns to me, perfectly c'am, and says, "Did *you* hear anybody sing out?"

Of course there warn't nothing to be said but the one thing; so I says:

"No; *I* ain't heard nobody say nothing."

Then he turns to Jim, and looks him over like he never see him before; and says:

"Did you sing out?"

"No, sah," says Jim; "*I* hain't said nothing, sah."

"Not a word?"

"No, sah, I hain't said a word."

"Did you ever see us before?"

"No, sah; not as *I* knows on."

So Tom turns to the nigger, which was looking wild and distressed, and says, kind of severe:

"What do you reckon's the matter with you, anyway? What made you think somebody sung out?"

"Oh, it's de dad-blame' witches, sah, en I wisht I was dead, I do. Dey's awluz at it, sah, en dey do mos' kill me, dey sk'yers me so. Please to don't tell nobody 'bout it sah, er ole Mars Silas he'll scole me; 'kase he say dey *ain't* no witches. I jis' wish to goodness he was heah now — *den* what would he say! I jis' bet he couldn' fine no way to git aroun' it *dis* time. But it's awluz jis' so; people dat's *sot*,° stays sot; dey won't look into nothn' en fine it out f'r deyselves, en when *you* fine it out en tell um 'bout it, dey doan' b'lieve you."

Tom give him a dime, and said we wouldn't tell nobody; and told him to buy some more thread to tie up his wool with; and then looks at Jim, and says:

"I wonder if Uncle Silas is going to hang this nigger. If I was to catch a nigger that was ungrateful enough to run away, *I* wouldn't give him up, I'd hang him." And whilst the nigger stepped to the door to look at the dime and bite it to see if it was good, he whispers to Jim, and says:

"Don't ever let on to know us. And if you hear any digging going on nights, it's us: we're going to set you free."

Jim only had time to grab us by the hand and squeeze it, then the nigger come back, and we said we'd come again some time if the nigger wanted us to; and he said he would, more particular if it was dark, because the witches went for him mostly in the dark, and it was good to have folks around then.

sot: Set.

Chapter XXXV

It would be most an hour, yet, till breakfast, so we left, and struck down into the woods; because Tom said we got to have *some* light to see how to dig by, and a lantern makes too much, and might get us into trouble; what we must have was a lot of them rotten chunks that's called fox-fire and just makes a soft kind of a glow when you lay them in a dark place. We fetched an armful and hid it in the weeds, and set down to rest, and Tom says, kind of dissatisfied:

"Blame it, this whole thing is just as easy and awkard as it can be. And so it makes it so rotten difficult to get up a difficult plan. There ain't no watchman to be drugged — now there *ought* to be a watchman. There ain't even a dog to give a sleeping-mixture to. And there's Jim chained by one leg, with a ten-foot chain, to the leg of his bed: why, all you got to do is to lift up the bedstead and slip off the chain. And Uncle Silas he trusts everybody; sends the key to the punkin-headed nigger, and don't send nobody to watch the nigger. Jim could a got out of that window hole before this, only there wouldn't be no use trying to travel with a ten-foot chain on his leg. Why, drat it, Huck, it's the stupidest arrangement I ever see. You got to invent *all* the difficulties. Well, we can't help it, we got to do the best we can with the materials we've got. Anyhow, there's one thing — there's more honor in getting him out through a lot of difficulties and dangers, where there warn't one of them furnished to you by the people who it was their duty to furnish them, and you had to contrive them all out of your own head. Now look at just that one thing of the lantern. When you come down to the cold facts, we simply got to *let on* that a lantern's resky. Why, we could work with a torchlight procession if we wanted to, *I* believe. Now, whilst I think of it, we got to hunt up something to make a saw out of, the first chance we get."

"What do we want of a saw?"

"What do we *want* of it? Hain't we got to saw the leg of Jim's bed off, so as to get the chain loose?"

"Why, you just said a body could lift up the bedstead and slip the chain off."

"Well, if that ain't just like you, Huck Finn. You *can* get up the infant-schooliest ways of going at a thing. Why, hain't you ever read any books at all? — Baron Trenck, nor Casanova, nor Benvenuto Chelleeny, nor Henri IV., nor none of them heroes? Whoever heard of getting a prisoner loose in such an old-maidy way as that? No; the way all the best authorities does, is to saw the bed-leg in two, and leave it just so, and swallow the sawdust, so it can't be found, and put some dirt and grease around the sawed place so the very keenest seneskal° can't see no sign of it's being sawed, and thinks the bed-leg is perfectly sound. Then, the night you're ready, fetch the leg a kick, down she goes; slip off your chain, and there you are. Nothing to do but hitch your rope-ladder to the battlements, shin down it, break your leg in the moat — because a rope-ladder is nineteen foot too short, you know — and there's your horses and your trusty vassles, and they scoop you up and fling you across a saddle and away you go, to your native Langudoc, or Navarre, or wherever it is. It's gaudy, Huck. I wish there was a moat to this cabin. If we get time, the night of the escape, we'll dig one."

I says:

"What do we want of a moat, when we're going to snake him out from under the cabin?"

But he never heard me. He had forgot me and everything else. He had his chin in his hand, thinking. Pretty soon, he sighs, and shakes his head; then sighs again, and says:

"No, it wouldn't do — there ain't necessity enough for it."

"For what?" I says.

"Why, to saw Jim's leg off," he says.

"Good land!" I says, "why, there ain't *no* necessity for it. And what would you want to saw his leg off for, anyway?"

"Well, some of the best authorities has done it. They couldn't get the chain off, so they just cut their hand off, and shoved. And a leg would be better still. But we got to let that go. There ain't necessity enough in this case; and besides, Jim's a nigger and wouldn't understand the reasons for it, and how it's the custom in Europe; so we'll let it go. But there's one thing — he can have a rope-ladder; we can tear up our sheets and make him a rope-ladder easy enough. And we can send it to him in a pie; it's mostly done that way. And I've et worse pies."

"Why, Tom Sawyer, how you talk," I says; "Jim ain't got no use for a rope-ladder."

"He *has* got use for it. How *you* talk, you better say; you don't know nothing about it. He's *got* to have a rope ladder; they all do."

"What in the nation can he *do* with it?"

"*Do* with it? He can hide it in his bed, can't he? That's what they all do; and *he's* got to, too. Huck, you don't ever seem to want to do any-

---

seneskal: Seneschal, an agent or steward in charge of a lord's estate in feudal times.

thing that's regular; you want to be starting something fresh all the
time. Spose he *don't* do nothing with it? ain't it there in his bed, for a
clew, after he's gone? and don't you reckon they'll want clews? Of
course they will. And you wouldn't leave them any? That would be a
pretty howdy-do, *wouldn't* it! I never heard of such a thing."

"Well," I says, "if it's in the regulations, and he's got to have it, all
right, let him have it; because I don't wish to go back on no regulations; but there's one thing, Tom Sawyer — if we go to tearing up our
sheets to make Jim a rope-ladder, we're going to get into trouble with
Aunt Sally, just as sure as you're born. Now, the way I look at it, a
hickry-bark ladder don't cost nothing, and don't waste nothing, and is
just as good to load up a pie with, and hide in a straw tick, as any rag
ladder you can start; and as for Jim, he ain't had no experience, and so
he don't care what kind of a ——"

"Oh, shucks, Huck Finn, if I was as ignorant as you, I'd keep still —
that's what *I'd* do. Who ever heard of a state prisoner escaping by a
hickry-bark ladder? Why, it's perfectly ridiculous."

"Well, all right, Tom, fix it your own way; but if you'll take my
advice, you'll let me borrow a sheet off of the clothes-line."

He said that would do. And that give him another idea, and he says:

"Borrow a shirt, too."

"What do we want of a shirt, Tom?"

"Want it for Jim to keep a journal on."

"Journal your granny — *Jim* can't write."

"Spose he *can't* write — he can make marks on the shirt, can't he, if
we make him a pen out of an old pewter spoon or a piece of an old iron
barrel-hoop?"

"Why, Tom, we can pull a feather out of a goose and make him a
better one; and quicker, too."

"*Prisoners* don't have geese running around the donjon-keep to
pull pens out of, you muggins. They *always* make their pens out of
the hardest, toughest, troublesomest piece of old brass candlestick or
something like that they can get their hands on; and it takes them weeks
and weeks, and months and months to file it out, too, because they've
got to do it by rubbing it on the wall. *They* wouldn't use a goose-quill if
they had it. It ain't regular."

"Well, then, what'll we make him the ink out of?"

"Many makes it out of iron-rust and tears; but that's the common
sort and women; the best authorities uses their own blood. Jim can do
that; and when he wants to send any little common ordinary mysterious
message to let the world know where he's captivated, he can write it on

the bottom of a tin plate with a fork and throw it out of the window. The Iron Mask always done that, and it's a blame' good way, too."

"Jim ain't got no tin plates. They feed him in a pan."

"That ain't anything; we can get him some."

"Can't nobody *read* his plates."

"That ain't got nothing to *do* with it, Huck Finn. All *he's* got to do is to write on the plate and throw it out. You don't *have* to be able to read it. Why, half the time you can't read anything a prisoner writes on a tin plate, or anywhere else."

"Well, then, what's the sense in wasting the plates?"

"Why, blame it all, it ain't the *prisoner's* plates."

"But it's *somebody's* plates, ain't it?"

"Well, spos'n it is? What does the *prisoner* care whose ——"

He broke off there, because we heard the breakfast-horn blowing. So we cleared out for the house.

Along during that morning I borrowed a sheet and a white shirt off of the clothes-line; and I found an old sack and put them in it, and we went down and got the fox-fire, and put that in too. I called it borrowing, because that was what pap always called it; but Tom said it warn't borrowing, it was stealing. He said we was representing prisoners; and prisoners don't care how they get a thing so they get it, and nobody don't blame them for it, either. It ain't no crime in a prisoner to steal the thing he needs to get away with, Tom said; it's his right; and so, as long as we was representing a prisoner, we had a perfect right to steal anything on this place we had the least use for, to get ourselves out of prison with. He said if we warn't prisoners it would be a very different thing, and nobody but a mean ornery person would steal when he warn't a prisoner. So we allowed we would steal everything there was that come handy. And yet he made a mighty fuss, one day, after that, when I stole a watermelon out of the nigger patch and eat it; and he made me go and give the niggers a dime, without telling them what it was for. Tom said that what he meant was, we could steal anything we *needed*. Well, I says, I needed the watermelon. But he said I didn't need it to get out of prison with, there's where the difference was. He said if I'd a wanted it to hide a knife in, and smuggle it to Jim to kill the seneskal with, it would a been all right. So I let it go at that, though I couldn't see no advantage in my representing a prisoner, if I got to set down and chaw over a lot of gold-leaf distinctions like that, every time I see a chance to hog a watermelon.

Well, as I was saying, we waited that morning till everybody was settled down to business, and nobody in sight around the yard; then Tom he carried the sack into the lean-to whilst I stood off a piece to keep watch. By-and-by he come out, and we went and set down on the wood-pile, to talk. He says:

"Everything's all right, now, except tools; and that's easy fixed."

"Tools?" I says.

"Yes."

"Tools for what?"

"Why, to dig with. We ain't agoing to *gnaw* him out, are we?"

"Ain't them old crippled picks and things in there good enough to dig a nigger out with?" I says.

He turns on me looking pitying enough to make a body cry, and says:

"Huck Finn, did you *ever* hear of a prisoner having picks and shovels, and all the modern conveniences in his wardrobe to dig himself out with? Now I want to ask you — if you got any reasonableness in you at all — what kind of a show would *that* give him to be a hero? Why, they might as well lend him the key, and done with it. Picks and shovels — why they wouldn't furnish 'em to a king."

"Well, then," I says, "if we don't want the picks and shovels, what do we want?"

"A couple of case-knives."°

"To dig the foundations out from under that cabin with?"

"Yes."

"Confound it, it's foolish, Tom."

"It don't make no difference how foolish it is, it's the *right* way — and it's the regular way. And there ain't no *other* way, that ever *I* heard of, and I've read all the books that gives any information about these things. They always dig out with a case-knife — and not through dirt, mind you; generly it's through solid rock. And it takes them weeks and weeks and weeks, and for ever and ever. Why, look at one of them prisoners in the bottom dungeon of the Castle Deef, in the harbor of Marseilles, that dug himself out that way; how long was *he* at it, you reckon?"

"I don't know."

"Well, guess."

"I don't know. A month and a half?"

"*Thirty-seven year* — and he come out in China. *That's* the kind. I wish the bottom of *this* fortress was solid rock."

case-knives: Table knives.

"*Jim* don't know nobody in China."

"What's *that* got to do with it? Neither did that other fellow. But you're always a-wandering off on a side issue. Why can't you stick to the main point?"

"All right — *I* don't care where he comes out, so he *comes* out; and Jim don't, either, I reckon. But there's one thing, anyway — Jim's too old to be dug out with a case-knife. He won't last."

"Yes he will *last*, too. You don't reckon it's going to take thirty-seven years to dig out through a *dirt* foundation, do you?"

"How long will it take, Tom?"

"Well, we can't resk being as long as we ought to, because it mayn't take very long for Uncle Silas to hear from down there by New Orleans. He'll hear Jim ain't from there. Then his next move will be to advertise Jim, or something like that. So we can't resk being as long digging him out as we ought to. By rights I reckon we ought to be a couple of years; but we can't. Things being so uncertain, what I recommend is this: that we really dig right in, as quick as we can; and after that, we can *let on*, to ourselves, that we was at it thirty-seven years. Then we can snatch him out and rush him away the first time there's an alarm. Yes, I reckon that'll be the best way."

"Now, there's *sense* in that," I says. "Letting on don't cost nothing; letting on ain't no trouble; and if it's any object, I don't mind letting on we was at it a hundred and fifty year. It wouldn't strain me none, after I got my hand in. So I'll mosey along now, and smouch a couple of case-knives."

"Smouch three," he says; "we want one to make a saw out of."

"Tom, if it ain't unregular and irreligious to sejest it," I says, "there's an old rusty saw-blade around yonder sticking under the weatherboarding behind the smoke-house."

He looked kind of weary and discouraged-like, and says:

"It ain't no use to try to learn you nothing, Huck. Run along and smouch the knives — three of them." So I done it.

Chapter XXXVI

As soon as we reckoned everybody was asleep, that night, we went down the lightning-rod, and shut ourselves up in the lean-to, and got out our pile of fox-fire, and went to work. We cleared everything out of the way, about four or five foot along the middle of the bottom log. Tom said he was right behind Jim's bed now, and we'd dig in under it, and when we got through there couldn't nobody in the cabin ever know there was any hole there, because Jim's counterpin° hung down most to the ground, and you'd have to raise it up and look under to see the hole. So we dug and dug, with the case-knives, till most midnight; and then we was dog-tired, and our hands was blistered, and yet you couldn't see we'd done anything, hardly. At last I says:

"This ain't no thirty-seven year job, this is a thirty-eight year job, Tom Sawyer."

He never said nothing. But he sighed, and pretty soon he stopped digging, and then for a good little while I knowed he was thinking. Then he says:

"It ain't no use, Huck, it ain't agoing to work. If we was prisoners it would, because then we'd have as many years as we wanted, and no hurry; and we wouldn't get but a few minutes to dig, every day, while they was changing watches, and so our hands wouldn't get blistered, and we could keep it up right along, year in and year out, and do it right, and the way it ought to be done. But *we* can't fool along, we got to rush; we ain't got no time to spare. If we was to put in another night this way, we'd have to knock off for a week to let our hands get well — couldn't touch a case-knife with them sooner."

"Well, then, what we going to do, Tom?"

"I'll tell you. It ain't right, and it ain't moral, and I wouldn't like it to get out — but there ain't only just the one way; we got to dig him out with the picks, and *let on* it's case-knives."

"*Now* you're *talking!*" I says; "your head gets leveler and leveler all the time, Tom Sawyer," I says. "Picks is the thing, moral or no moral; and as for me, I don't care shucks for the morality of it, no-how. When I start in to steal a nigger, or a watermelon, or a Sunday-school book, I ain't no ways particular how it's done so it's done. What I want is my nigger; or what I want is my watermelon; or what I want is my Sunday-school book; and if a pick's the handiest thing, that's the thing I'm agoing to dig that nigger or that watermelon or that Sunday-school book out with; and I don't give a dead rat what the authorities thinks about it nuther."

"Well," he says, "there's excuse for picks and letting-on in a case like this; if it warn't so, I wouldn't approve of it, nor I wouldn't stand by and see the rules broke — because right is right, and wrong is wrong, and a body ain't got no business doing wrong when he ain't ignorant and knows better. It might answer for *you* to dig Jim out with a pick,

---

counterpin: Counterpane, bedcover.

without any letting-on, because you don't know no better; but it wouldn't for me, because I do know better. Gimme a case-knife."

He had his own by him, but I handed him mine. He flung it down, and says:

"Gimme a *case-knife*."

I didn't know just what to do — but then I thought. I scratched around amongst the old tools, and got a pick-ax and give it to him, and he took it and went to work, and never said a word.

He was always just that particular. Full of principle.

So then I got a shovel, and then we picked and shoveled, turn about, and made the fur fly. We stuck to it about a half an hour, which was as long as we could stand up; but we had a good deal of a hole to show for it. When I got up stairs, I looked out at the window and see Tom doing his level best with the lightning-rod, but he couldn't come it, his hands was so sore. At last he says:

"It ain't no use, it can't be done. What you reckon I better do? Can't you think up no way?"

"Yes," I says, "but I reckon it ain't regular. Come up the stairs, and let on it's a lightning-rod."

So he done it.

Next day Tom stole a pewter spoon and a brass candlestick in the house, for to make some pens for Jim out of, and six tallow candles; and I hung around the nigger cabins, and laid for a chance, and stole three tin plates. Tom said it wasn't enough; but I said nobody wouldn't ever see the plates that Jim throwed out, because they'd fall in the dog-fennel and jimpson weeds under the window-hole — then we could tote them back and he could use them over again. So Tom was satisfied. Then he says:

"Now, the thing to study out is, how to get the things to Jim."

"Take them in through the hole," I says, "when we get it done."

He only just looked scornful, and said something about nobody ever heard of such an idiotic idea, and then he went to studying. By-and-by he said he had ciphered out two or three ways, but there warn't no need to decide on any of them yet. Said we'd got to post Jim first.

That night we went down the lightning-rod a little after ten, and took one of the candles along, and listened under the window-hole, and heard Jim snoring; so we pitched it in, and it didn't wake him. Then we whirled in with the pick and shovel, and in about two hours and a half the job was done. We crept in under Jim's bed and into the cabin, and pawed around and found the candle and lit it, and stood over Jim a while, and found him looking hearty and healthy, and then

we woke him up gentle and gradual. He was so glad to see us he most
cried; and called us honey, and all the pet names he could think of;
and was for having us hunt up a cold chisel to cut the chain off of his
leg with, right away, and clearing out without losing any time. But
Tom he showed him how unregular it would be, and set down and told
him all about our plans, and how we could alter them in a minute any
time there was an alarm; and not to be the least afraid, because we
would see he got away, *sure*. So Jim he said it was all right, and we set
there and talked over old times a while, and then Tom asked a lot
of questions, and when Jim told him Uncle Silas come in every day or
two to pray with him, and Aunt Sally come in to see if he was comfortable and had plenty to eat, and both of them was kind as they could be,
Tom says:

"*Now* I know how to fix it. We'll send you some things by them."

I said, "Don't do nothing of the kind; it's one of the most jackass
ideas I ever struck;" but he never paid no attention to me; went right
on. It was his way when he'd got his plans set.

So he told Jim how we'd have to smuggle in the rope-ladder pie,
and other large things, by Nat, the nigger that fed him, and he must be
on the lookout, and not be surprised, and not let Nat see him open
them; and we would put small things in uncle's coat pockets and he
must steal them out; and we would tie things to aunt's apron strings or
put them in her apron pocket, if we got a chance; and told him what
they would be and what they was for. And told him how to keep a journal on the shirt with his blood, and all that. He told him everything.
Jim he couldn't see no sense in the most of it, but he allowed we was
white folks and knowed better than him; so he was satisfied, and said he
would do it all just as Tom said.

Jim had plenty corn-cob pipes and tobacco; so we had a right down
good sociable time; then we crawled out through the hole, and so
home to bed, with hands that looked like they'd been chawed. Tom was
in high spirits. He said it was the best fun he ever had in his life, and the
most intellectural; and said if he only could see his way to it we would
keep it up all the rest of our lives and leave Jim to our children to get
out; for he believed Jim would come to like it better and better the
more he got used to it. He said that in that way it could be strung out
to as much as eighty year, and would be the best time on record. And
he said it would make us all celebrated that had a hand in it.

In the morning we went out to the wood-pile and chopped up the
brass candlestick into handy sizes, and Tom put them and the pewter
spoon in his pocket. Then we went to the nigger cabins, and while I got

Nat's notice off, Tom shoved a piece of candlestick into the middle of a corn-pone that was in Jim's pan, and we went along with Nat to see how it would work, and it just worked noble; when Jim bit into it it most mashed all his teeth out; and there warn't ever anything could a worked better. Tom said so himself. Jim he never let on but what it was only just a piece of rock or something like that that's always getting into bread, you know; but after that he never bit into nothing but what he jabbed his fork into it in three or four places, first.

And whilst we was a standing there in the dimmish light, here comes a couple of the hounds bulging in, from under Jim's bed; and they kept on piling in till there was eleven of them, and there warn't hardly room in there to get your breath. By jings, we forgot to fasten that lean-to door. The nigger Nat he only just hollered "witches!" once, and keeled over onto the floor amongst the dogs, and begun to groan like he was dying. Tom jerked the door open and flung out a slab of Jim's meat, and the dogs went for it, and in two seconds he was out himself and back again and shut the door, and I knowed he'd fixed the other door too. Then he went to work on the nigger, coaxing him and petting him, and asking him if he'd been imagining he saw something again. He raised up, and blinked his eyes around, and says:

"Mars Sid, you'll say I's a fool, but if I didn't b'lieve I see most a million dogs, er devils, er some'n, I wisht I may die right heah in dese tracks. I did, mos' sholy. Mars Sid, I *felt* um — I *felt* um, sah; dey was all over me. Dad fetch it, I jis' wisht I could git my han's on one er dem witches jis' wunst — on'y jis' wunst — it's all I'd ast. But mos'ly I wisht dey'd lemme 'lone, I does."

Tom says:

"Well, I tell you what *I* think. What makes them come here just at this runaway nigger's breakfast-time? It's because they're hungry; that's the reason. You make them a witch pie; that's the thing for *you* to do."

"But my lan', Mars Sid, how's *I* gwyne to make 'm a witch pie? I doan' know how to make it. I hain't ever hearn er sich a thing b'fo.'"

"Well, then, I'll have to make it myself."

"Will you do it, honey? — will you? I'll wusshup de groun' und' yo' foot, I will!"

"All right, I'll do it, seeing it's you, and you've been good to us and showed us the runaway nigger. But you got to be mighty careful. When we come around, you turn your back; and then whatever we've put in the pan, don't you let on you see it at all. And don't you look, when Jim unloads the pan — something might happen, I don't know what. And above all, don't you *handle* the witch-things."

"*Hannel* 'm Mars Sid? What *is* you talkin' 'bout? I wouldn' lay de weight er my finger on um, not f'r ten hund'd thous'n' billion dollars, I wouldn't."

Chapter XXXVII

That was all fixed. So then we went away and went to the rubbage-pile in the back yard where they keep the old boots, and rags, and pieces of bottles, and wore-out tin things, and all such truck, and scratched around and found an old tin washpan and stopped up the holes as well as we could, to bake the pie in, and took it down cellar and stole it full of flour, and started for breakfast and found a couple of shingle-nails that Tom said would be handy for a prisoner to scrabble his name and sorrows on the dungeon walls with, and dropped one of them in Aunt Sally's apron pocket which was hang-ing on a chair, and t'other we stuck in the band of Uncle Silas's hat, which was on the bureau, because we heard the children say their pa and ma was going to the runaway nigger's house this morning, and then went to breakfast, and Tom dropped the pewter spoon in Uncle Silas's coat pocket, and Aunt Sally wasn't come yet, so he had to wait a little while.

And when she come she was hot, and red, and cross, and couldn't hardly wait for the blessing; and then she went to sluicing out coffee with one hand and cracking the handiest child's head with her thimble with the other, and says:

"I've hunted high, and I've hunted low, and it does beat all, what *has* become of your other shirt."

My heart fell down amongst my lungs and livers and things, and a hard piece of corn-crust started down my throat after it and got met on the road with a cough and was shot across the table and took one of the children in the eye and curled him up like a fishing-worm, and let a cry out of him the size of a war-whoop, and Tom he turned kinder blue around the gills, and it all amounted to a considerable state of things for about a quarter of a minute or as much as that, and I would a sold out for half price if there was a bidder. But after that we was all right again — it was the sudden surprise of it that knocked us so kind of cold. Uncle Silas he says:

"It's most uncommon curious, I can't understand it. I know per-fectly well I took it *off,* because ——"

"Because you hain't got but one *on.* Just *listen* at the man! *I* know you took it off, and know it by a better way than your wool-gethering memory, too, because it was on the clo'es-line yesterday — I see it there myself. But it's gone — that's the long and the short of it, and you'll just have to change to a red flann'l one till I can get time to make a new one. And it'll be the third I've made in two years; it just keeps a body on the jump to keep you in shirts; and whatever you do manage to *do* with 'm all, is more'n *I* can make out. A body'd think you *would* learn to take some sort of care of 'em, at your time of life."

"I know it, Sally, and I do try all I can. But it oughtn't to be altogether my fault, because you know I don't see them nor have nothing to do with them except when they're on me; and I don't believe I've ever lost one of them *off* of me."

"Well, it ain't *your* fault if you haven't, Silas — you'd a done it if you could, I reckon. And the shirt ain't all that's gone, nuther. Ther's a spoon gone; and *that* ain't all. There was ten, and now ther's only nine. The calf got the shirt I reckon, but the calf never took the spoon, *that's* certain."

"Why, what else is gone, Sally?"

"Ther's six *candles* gone — that's what. The rats could a got the candles, and I reckon they did; I wonder they don't walk off with the whole place, the way you're always going to stop their holes and don't do it; and if they warn't fools they'd sleep in your hair, Silas — *you'd* never find it out; but you can't lay the *spoon* on the rats, and that I *know.*"

"Well, Sally, I'm in fault, and I acknowledge it; I've been remiss; but I won't let to-morrow go by without stopping up them holes."

"Oh, I wouldn't hurry, next year'll do. Matilda Angelina Araminta *Phelps!*"

Whack comes the thimble, and the child snatches her claws out of the sugar-bowl without fooling around any. Just then, the nigger woman steps onto the passage, and says:

"Missus, dey's a sheet gone."

"A *sheet* gone! Well, for the land's sake!"

"I'll stop up them holes *to-day,*" says Uncle Silas, looking sorrowful.

"Oh, *do* shet up! — spose the rats took the *sheet? Where's* it gone, Lize?"

"Clah to goodness I hain't no notion, Miss Sally. She wuz on de clo's-line yistiddy, but she done gone; she ain' dah no mo,' now."

"I reckon the world *is* coming to an end. I *never* see the beat of it, in all my born days. A shirt, and a sheet, and a spoon, and six can ——"

"Missus," comes a young yaller wench, "dey's a brass cannelstick miss'n."

"Cler out from here, you hussy, er I'll take a skillet to ye!"

Well, she was just a biling. I begun to lay for a chance; I reckoned I would sneak out and go for the woods till the weather moderated. She kept a raging right along, running her insurrection all by herself, and everybody else mighty meek and quiet; and at last Uncle Silas, looking kind of foolish, fishes up that spoon out of his pocket. She stopped, with her mouth open and her hands up; and as for me, I wished I was in Jeruslem or somewheres. But not long; because she says:

"It's *just* as I expected. So you had it in your pocket all the time; and like as not you've got the other things there, too. How'd it get there?"

"I reely don't know, Sally," he says, kind of apologizing, "or you know I would tell. I was a-studying over my text in Acts Seventeen, before breakfast, and I reckon I put it in there, not noticing, meaning to put my Testament in, and it must be so, because my Testament ain't in, but I'll go and see, and if the Testament is where I had it, I'll know I didn't put it in, and that will show that I laid the Testament down and took up the spoon, and ——"

"Oh, for the land's sake! Give a body a rest! Go 'long now, the whole kit and biling of ye; and don't come nigh me again till I've got back my peace of mind."

I'd a heard her, if she'd a said it to herself, let alone speaking it out; and I'd a got up and obeyed her, if I'd a been dead. As we was passing through the setting-room, the old man he took up his hat, and the shingle-nail fell out on the floor, and he just merely picked it up and laid it on the mantel-shelf, and never said nothing, and went out. Tom see him do it, and remembered about the spoon, and says:

"Well, it ain't no use to send things by *him* no more, he ain't reliable." Then he says: "But he done us a good turn with the spoon, anyway, without knowing it, and so we'll go and do him one without *him* knowing it — stop up his rat-holes."

There was a noble good lot of them, down cellar, and it took us a whole hour, but we done the job tight and good, and ship-shape. Then we heard steps on the stairs, and blowed out our light, and hid; and here comes the old man, with a candle in one hand and a bundle of stuff in t'other, looking as absent-minded as year before last. He went a mooning around, first to one rat-hole and then another, till he'd been to them all. Then he stood about five minutes, picking tallow-drip off of his candle and thinking. Then he turns off slow and dreamy towards the stairs, saying:

"Well, for the life of me I can't remember when I done it. I could show her now that I warn't to blame on account of the rats. But never mind — let it go. I reckon it wouldn't do no good."

And so he went on a mumbling up stairs, and then we left. He was a mighty nice old man. And always is.

Tom was a good deal bothered about what to do for a spoon, but he said we'd got to have it; so he took a think. When he had ciphered it out, he told me how we was to do; then we went and waited around the spoon-basket till we see Aunt Sally coming, and then Tom went to counting the spoons and laying them out to one side, and I slid one of them up my sleeve, and Tom says:

"Why, Aunt Sally, there ain't but nine spoons, *yet.*"

She says:

"Go 'long to your play, and don't bother me. I know better, I counted 'm myself."

"Well, I've counted them twice, Aunty, and *I* can't make but nine."

She looked out of all patience, but of course she come to count — anybody would.

"I declare to gracious ther' *ain't* but nine!" she says. "Why, what in the world — plague *take* the things, I'll count 'm again."

So I slipped back the one I had, and when she got done counting, she says:

"Hang the troublesome rubbage, ther's *ten,* now!" and she looked huffy and bothered both. But Tom says:

"Why, Aunty, *I* don't think there's ten."

"You numskull, didn't you see me *count* 'm?"

"I know, but ——"

"Well, I'll count 'm *again.*"

So I smouched one, and they come out nine same as the other time. Well, she *was* in a tearing way — just a trembling all over, she was so mad. But she counted and counted, till she got that addled she'd start to count-in the *basket* for a spoon, sometimes; and so, three times they come out right, and three times they come out wrong. Then she grabbed up the basket and slammed it across the house and knocked the cat galley-west; and she said cle'r out and let her have some peace, and if we come bothering around her again betwixt that and dinner, she'd skin us. So we had the odd spoon; and dropped it in her apron pocket whilst she was a giving us our sailing-orders, and Jim got it all right, along with her shingle-nail, before noon. We was very well satis-fied with this business, and Tom allowed it was worth twice the trouble it took, because he said *now* she couldn't ever count them spoons twice alike again to save her life; and wouldn't believe she'd counted them right, if she *did;* and said that after she'd about counted her head off, for the next three days, he judged she'd give it up and offer to kill anybody that wanted her to ever count them any more.

So we put the sheet back on the line, that night, and stole one out of her closet; and kept on putting it back and stealing it again, for a couple of days, till she didn't know how many sheets she had, any more, and said she didn't *care,* and warn't agoing to bullyrag the rest of her soul out about it, and wouldn't count them again not to save her life, she druther die first.

So we was all right now, as to the shirt and the sheet and the spoon and the candles, by the help of the calf and the rats and the mixed-up counting; and as to the candlestick, it warn't no consequence, it would blow over by-and-by.

But that pie was a job; we had no end of trouble with that pie. We fixed it up away down in the woods, and cooked it there; and we got it done at last, and very satisfactory, too; but not all in one day; and we had to use up three washpans full of flour, before we got through, and we got burnt pretty much all over, in places, and eyes put out with the smoke; because, you see, we didn't want nothing but a crust, and we couldn't prop it up right, and she would always cave in. But of course we thought of the right way at last; which was to cook the ladder, too, in the pie. So then we laid in with Jim, the second night, and tore up the sheet all in little strings, and twisted them together, and long before daylight we had a lovely rope, that you could a hung a person with. We let on it took nine months to make it.

And in the forenoon we took it down to the woods, but it wouldn't go in the pie. Being made of a whole sheet, that way, there was rope enough for forty pies, if we'd a wanted them, and plenty left over for soup, or sausage, or anything you choose. We could a had a whole dinner.

But we didn't need it. All we needed was just enough for the pie, and so we throwed the rest away. We didn't cook none of the pies in the washpan, afraid the solder would melt; but Uncle Silas he had a noble brass warming-pan which he thought considerable of, because it belonged to one of his ancestors with a long wooden handle that come over from England with William the Conqueror in the *Mayflower* or one of them early ships and was hid away up garret with a lot of other old pots and things that was valuable, not on account of being any account because they warn't, but on account of them being relicts, you know, and we snaked her out, private, and took her down there, but she failed on the first pies, because we didn't know how, but she come up smiling on the last one. We took and lined her with dough, and set her in the coals, and loaded her up with rag-rope, and put on a dough roof, and shut down the lid, and put hot embers on top, and stood off five foot, with the long handle, cool and comfortable, and in fifteen minutes she turned out a pie that was a satisfaction to look at. But the person that et it would want to fetch a couple of kags of toothpicks along, for if that rope-ladder wouldn't cramp him down to business, I don't know nothing what I'm talking about, and lay him in enough stomach-ache to last him till next time, too.

Nat didn't look, when we put the witch-pie in Jim's pan; and we put the three tin plates in the bottom of the pan under the vittles; and so Jim got everything all right, and as soon as he was by himself he busted into the pie and hid the rope-ladder inside of his straw tick, and scratched some marks on a tin plate and throwed it out of the window-hole.

Chapter XXXVIII

Making them pens was a distressid-tough job, and so was the saw; and Jim allowed the inscription was going to be the toughest of all. That's the one which the prisoner has to scrabble on the wall. But we had to have it; Tom said we'd *got* to; there warn't no case of a state prisoner not scrabbling his inscription to leave behind, and his coat of arms.

"Look at Lady Jane Grey," he says; "look at Gilford Dudley; look at old Northumberland! Why, Huck, spose it *is* considerble trouble? — what you going to do? — how you going to get around it? Jim's *got* to do his inscription and coat of arms. They all do."

Jim says:

"Why, Mars Tom, I hain't got no coat o' arms; I hain't got nuffn but dish-yer ole shirt, en you knows I got to keep de journal on dat."

"Oh, you don't understand, Jim; a coat of arms is very different."

"Well," I says, "Jim's right, anyway, when he says he hain't got no coat of arms, because he hain't."

"I reckon *I* knowed that," Tom says, "but you bet he'll have one before he goes out of this — because he's going out *right,* and there ain't going to be no flaws in his record."

So whilst me and Jim filed away at the pens on a brickbat apiece, Jim a making his'n out of the brass and I making mine out of the spoon, Tom set to work to think out the coat of arms. By-and-by he said he'd struck so many good ones he didn't hardly know which to take, but there was one which he reckoned he'd decide on. He says:

"On the scutcheon° we'll have a bend *or*° in the dexter base,° a saltire *murrey* in the fess,° with a dog, couchant,° for common charge, and under his foot a chain embattled,° for slavery, with a chevron *vert*° in a chief engrailed, and three invected lines on a field *azure,*° with the nombril points rampant° on a dancette° indented; crest, a runaway nigger, *sable,*° with his bundle over his shoulder on a bar sinister:° and a couple of gules° for supporters, which is you and me; motto, *Maggiore fretta, minore atto.*° Got it out of a book — means, the more haste, the less speed."

"Geewhillikins," I says, "but what does the rest of it mean?"

"We ain't got no time to bother over that," he says, "we got to dig in like all git-out."

"Well, anyway," I says, "what's *some* of it? What's a fess?"

"A fess — a fess is — *you* don't need to know what a fess is. I'll show him how to make it when he gets to it."

"Shucks, Tom," I says, "I think you might tell a person. What's a bar sinister?"

"Oh, *I* don't know. But he's got to have it. All the nobility does."

That was just his way. If it didn't suit him to explain a thing to you, he wouldn't do it. You might pump at him a week, it wouldn't make no difference.

He'd got all that coat of arms business fixed, so now he started in to finish up the rest of that part of the work, which was to plan out a mournful inscription — said Jim got to have one, like they all done. He made up a lot, and wrote them out on a paper, and read them off, so:

1. *Here a captive heart busted.*
2. *Here a poor prisoner, forsook by the world and friends, fretted out his sorrowful life.*
3. *Here a lonely heart broke, and a worn spirit went to its rest, after thirty-seven years of solitary captivity.*

---

scutcheon: Escutcheon, the surface or background for the rest of the arms.   **bend *or*:** A horizontal band in gold.   **dexter base:** Technically *dexter baston*, an area extending across the shield.   **saltire *murrey* in the fess:** A diagonal cross, colored mulberry, on its side within a horizontal band.   **dog, couchant:** A dog, lying down with its head erect.   **chain embattled:** A chain across the shield.   **chevron *vert*:** Green band in the shape of an upside down V.   **azure:** Clear blue.   **nombril points rampant:** Points between the base of the shield and the horizontal band in the middle, here pointing upward.   **dancette:** A zizag band.   **sable:** Black.   **bar sinister:** A band running from bottom left to top right.   **gules:** Tom gets even more carried away here; *gules* just means "red."   *Maggiore fretta, minore atto:* Italian for "The more pace, the less speed."

4. *Here, homeless and friendless, after thirty-seven years of bitter captivity, perished a noble stranger, natural son of Louis XIV.*

Tom's voice trembled, whilst he was reading them, and he most broke down. When he got done, he couldn't no way make up his mind which one for Jim to scrabble onto the wall, they was all so good; but at last he allowed he would let him scrabble them all on. Jim said it would take him a year to scrabble such a lot of truck onto the logs with a nail, and he didn't know how to make letters, besides; but Tom said he would block them out for him, and then he wouldn't have nothing to do but just follow the lines. Then pretty soon he says:

"Come to think, the logs ain't agoing to do; they don't have log walls in a dungeon: we got to dig the inscriptions into a rock. We'll fetch a rock."

Jim said the rock was worse than the logs; he said it would take him such a pison long time to dig them into a rock, he wouldn't ever get out. But Tom said he would let me help him do it. Then he took a look to see how me and Jim was getting along with the pens. It was most pesky tedious hard work and slow, and didn't give my hands no show to get well of the sores, and we didn't seem to make no headway, hardly. So Tom says:

"I know how to fix it. We got to have a rock for the coat of arms and mournful inscriptions, and we can kill two birds with that same rock. There's a gaudy big grindstone down at the mill, and we'll smouch it, and carve the things on it, and file out the pens and the saw on it, too."

It warn't no slouch of an idea; and it warn't no slouch of a grindstone nuther; but we allowed we'd tackle it. It warn't quite midnight, yet, so we cleared out for the mill, leaving Jim at work. We smouched the grindstone, and set out to roll her home, but it was a most nation tough job. Sometimes, do what we could, we couldn't keep her from falling over, and she come mighty near mashing us, every time. Tom said she was going to get one of us, sure, before we got through. We got her half way; and then we was plumb played out, and most drownded with sweat. We see it warn't no use, we got to go and fetch Jim. So he raised up his bed and slid the chain off of the bed-leg, and wrapt it round and round his neck, and we crawled out through our hole and down there, and Jim and me laid into that grindstone and walked her along like nothing; and Tom superintended. He could out-superintend any boy I ever see. He knowed how to do everything.

Our hole was pretty big, but it warn't big enough to get the grindstone through; but Jim he took the pick and soon made it big enough.

Then Tom marked out them things on it with the nail, and set Jim to work on them, with the nail for a chisel and an iron bolt from the rubbage in the lean-to for a hammer, and told him to work till the rest of his candle quit on him, and then he could go to bed, and hide the grindstone under his straw tick and sleep on it. Then we helped him fix his chain back on the bed-leg, and was ready for bed ourselves. But Tom thought of something, and says:

"You got any spiders in here, Jim?"

"No, sah, thanks to goodness I hain't, Mars Tom."

"All right, we'll get you some."

"But bless you, honey, I doan' *want* none. I's afeard un um. I jis' 's soon have rattlesnakes aroun'."

Tom thought a minute or two, and says:

"It's a good idea. And I reckon it's been done. It *must* a been done; it stands to reason. Yes, it's a prime good idea. Where could you keep it?"

"Keep what, Mars Tom?"

"Why, a rattlesnake."

"De goodness gracious alive, Mars Tom! Why, if dey was a rattlesnake to come in heah, I'd take en bust right out thoo dat log wall, I would, wid my head."

"Why, Jim, you wouldn't be afraid of it, after a little. You could tame it."

"*Tame* it!"

"Yes — easy enough. Every animal is grateful for kindness and petting, and they wouldn't *think* of hurting a person that pets them. Any book will tell you that. You try — that's all I ask; just try for two or three days. Why, you can get him so, in a little while, that he'll love you; and sleep with you; and won't stay away from you a minute; and will let you wrap him round your neck and put his head in your mouth."

"*Please*, Mars Tom — *doan'* talk so! I can't *stan'* it! He'd let me shove his head in my mouf — fer a favor, hain't it? I lay he'd wait a pow'ful long time 'fo' I *ast* him. En mo' en dat, I doan' *want* him to sleep wid me."

"Jim, don't act so foolish. A prisoner's *got* to have some kind of a dumb pet, and if a rattlesnake hain't ever been tried, why, there's more glory to be gained in your being the first to ever try it than any other way you could ever think of to save your life."

"Why, Mars Tom, I doan' *want* no sich glory. Snake take 'n bite Jim's chin off, den *whah* is de glory? No, sah, I doan' want no sich doin's."

"Blame it, can't you *try?* I only *want* you to try — you needn't keep it up if it don't work."

"But de trouble all *done,* ef de snake bite me while I's a tryin' him. Mars Tom, I's willin' to tackle mos' anything 'at ain't onreasonable, but ef you en Huck fetches a rattlesnake in heah for me to tame, I's gwyne to *leave,* dat's *shore.*"

"Well, then, let it go, let it go, if you're so bullheaded about it. We can get you some garter-snakes and you can tie some buttons on their tails, and let on they're rattlesnakes, and I reckon that'll have to do."

"I k'n stan' *dem,* Mars Tom, but blame' 'f I couldn' get along widout um, I tell you dat. I never knowed b'fo', 'twas so much bother and trouble to be a prisoner."

"Well, it *always* is, when it's done right. You got any rats around here?"

"No, sah, I hain't seed none."

"Well, we'll get you some rats."

"Why, Mars Tom, I doan' *want* no rats. Dey's de dad-blamedest creturs to sturb a body, en rustle roun' over 'im, en bite his feet, when he's tryin' to sleep, I ever see. No, sah, gimme g'yarter-snakes, 'f I's got to have 'm, but doan' gimme no rats, I ain' got no use f'r um, skasely."

"But Jim, you *got* to have 'em — they all do. So don't make no more fuss about it. Prisoners ain't ever without rats. There ain't no instance of it. And they train them, and pet them, and learn them tricks, and they get to be as sociable as flies. But you got to play music to them. You got anything to play music on?"

"I ain' got nuffn but a coase comb° en a piece o' paper, en a juice-harp;° but I reck'n dey wouldn' take no stock in a juice-harp."

"Yes they would. *They* don't care what kind of music 'tis. A jews-harp's plenty good enough for a rat. All animals like music — in a prison they dote on it. Specially, painful music; and you can't get no other kind out of a jews-harp. It always interests them; they come out to see what's the matter with you. Yes, you're all right; you're fixed very well. You want to set on your bed, nights, before you go to sleep, and early in the mornings, and play your jews-harp; play The Last Link is Broken — that's the thing that'll scoop a rat, quicker'n anything else: and when you've played about two minutes, you'll see all the rats, and the snakes, and spiders, and things begin to feel worried about you, and come. And they'll just fairly swarm over you, and have a noble good time."

coase comb: Coarse comb.   juice-harp: Jew's harp.

"Yes, *dey* will, I reck'n, Mars Tom, but what kine er time is *Jim* havin'? Blest if I kin see de pint. But I'll do it ef I got to. I reck'n I better keep de animals satisfied, en not have no trouble in de house."

Tom waited to think over, and see if there wasn't nothing else; and pretty soon he says:

"Oh — there's one thing I forgot. Could you raise a flower here, do you reckon?"

"I doan' know but maybe I could, Mars Tom; but it's tolable dark in heah, en I ain' got no use f'r no flower, nohow, en she'd be a pow'ful sight o' trouble."

"Well, you try it, anyway. Some other prisoners has done it."

"One er dem big cat-tail-lookin' mullen-stalks° would grow in heah, Mars Tom, I reck'n, but she wouldn' be wuth half de trouble she'd coss."

"Don't you believe it. We'll fetch you a little one, and you plant it in the corner, over there, and raise it. And don't call it mullen, call it Pitchiola° — that's its right name, when it's in a prison. And you want to water it with your tears."

"Why, I got plenty spring water, Mars Tom."

"You don't *want* spring water; you want to water it with your tears. It's the way they always do."

"Why, Mars Tom, I lay I kin raise one er dem mullen-stalks twyste wid spring water whiles another man's a *start'n* one wid tears."

"That ain't the idea. You *got* to do it with tears."

"She'll die on my han's, Mars Tom, she sholy will; kase I doan' skasely ever cry."

So Tom was stumped. But he studied it over, and then said Jim would have to worry along the best he could with an onion. He promised he would go to the nigger cabins and drop one, private, in Jim's coffee-pot, in the morning. Jim said he would "jis' 's soon have tobacker in his coffee;" and found so much fault with it, and with the work and bother of raising the mullen, and jews-harping the rats, and petting and flattering up the snakes and spiders and things, on top of all the other work he had to do on pens, and inscriptions, and journals, and things, which made it more trouble and worry and responsibility to be a prisoner than anything he ever undertook, that Tom most lost all patience with him; and said he was just loadened down with more

---

mullen-stalks: A plant of the foxglove family that has large leaves and yellow flowers.
Pitchiola: In one of Tom's French sources, *Picciola*, the prisoner calls the plant growing in his cell *le picciola* (the stalk).

gaudier chances than a prisoner ever had in the world to make a name for himself, and yet he didn't know enough to appreciate them, and they was just about wasted on him. So Jim he was sorry, and said he wouldn't behave so no more, and then me and Tom shoved for bed.

Chapter XXXIX

In the morning we went up to the village and bought a wire rat trap and fetched it down, and unstopped the best rat hole, and in about an hour we had fifteen of the bulliest kind of ones; and then we took it and put it in a safe place under Aunt Sally's bed. But while we was gone for spiders, little Thomas Franklin Benjamin Jefferson Elexander Phelps found it there, and opened the door of it to see if the rats would come out, and they did; and Aunt Sally she come in, and when we got back she was a standing on top of the bed raising Cain, and the rats was doing what they could to keep off the dull times for her. So she took and dusted us both with the hickry, and we was as much as two hours catching another fifteen or sixteen, drat that meddlesome cub, and they warn't the likeliest, nuther, because the first haul was the pick of the flock. I never see a likelier lot of rats than what that first haul was.

We got a splendid stock of sorted spiders, and bugs, and frogs, and caterpillars, and one thing or another; and we like-to got a hornet's nest, but we didn't. The family was at home. We didn't give it right up, but staid with them as long as we could; because we allowed we'd tire them out or they'd got to tire us out, and they done it. Then we got allycumpain° and rubbed on the places, and was pretty near all right again, but couldn't set down convenient. And so we went for the snakes, and grabbed a couple of dozen garters and house-snakes, and put them in a bag, and put it in our room, and by that time it was supper time, and a rattling good honest day's work; and hungry? — oh, no, I reckon not! And there warn't a blessed snake up there, when we went back — we didn't half tie the sack, and they worked out, somehow, and left. But it didn't matter much, because they was still on the premises somewheres. So we judged we could get some of them again. No, there warn't no real scarcity of snakes about the house for a considerble spell. You'd see them dripping from the rafters and places, every now and then; and they generly landed in your plate, or down the back of your neck, and most of the time where you didn't want them.

allycumpain: Elecampane, a medicinal herb.

Well, they was handsome, and striped, and there warn't no harm in a million of them: but that never made no difference to Aunt Sally, she despised snakes, be the breed what they might, and she couldn't stand them no way you could fix it; and every time one of them flopped down on her, it didn't make no difference what she was doing, she would just lay that work down and light out. I never see such a woman. And you could hear her whoop to Jericho. You couldn't get her to take aholt of one of them with the tongs. And if she turned over and found one in bed, she would scramble out and lift a howl that you would think the house was afire. She disturbed the old man so, that he said he could most wish there hadn't ever been no snakes created. Why, after every last snake had been gone clear out of the house for as much as a week, Aunt Sally warn't over it yet; she warn't near over it; when she was set-ting thinking about something, you could touch her on the back of her neck with a feather and she would jump right out of her stockings. It was very curious. But Tom said all women was just so. He said they was made that way; for some reason or other.

We got a licking every time one of our snakes come in her way; and she allowed these lickings warn't nothing to what she would do if we ever loaded up the place again with them. I didn't mind the lickings, because they didn't amount to nothing; but I minded the trouble we had, to lay in another lot. But we got them laid in, and all the other things; and you never see a cabin as blithesome as Jim's was when they'd all swarm out for music and go for him. Jim didn't like the spi-ders, and the spiders didn't like Jim; and so they'd lay for him and make it mighty warm for him. And he said that between the rats, and the snakes, and the grindstone, there warn't no room in bed for him, skasely; and when there was, a body couldn't sleep, it was so lively, and it was always lively, he said, because *they* never all slept at one time, but took turn about, so when the snakes was asleep the rats was on deck, and when the rats turned in the snakes come on watch, so he always had one gang under him, in his way, and t'other gang having a circus over him, and if he got up to hunt a new place, the spiders would take a chance at him as he crossed over. He said if he ever got out, this time, he wouldn't ever be a prisoner again, not for a salary.

Well, by the end of three weeks, everything was in pretty good shape. The shirt was sent in early, in a pie, and every time a rat bit Jim he would get up and write a little in his journal whilst the ink was fresh; the pens was made, the inscriptions and so on was all carved on the grindstone; the bed-leg was sawed in two, and we had et up the saw-dust, and it give us a most amazing stomach-ache. We reckoned we was all going to die, but didn't. It was the most undigestible sawdust I ever see; and Tom said the same. But as I was saying, we'd got all the work done, now, at last; and we was all pretty much fagged out, too, but mainly Jim. The old man had wrote a couple of times to the plantation below Orleans to come and get their runaway nigger, but hadn't got no answer, because there warn't no such plantation; so he allowed he would advertise Jim in the St. Louis and New Orleans papers; and when he mentioned the St. Louis ones, it give me the cold shivers, and I see we hadn't no time to lose. So Tom said, now for the nonnamous letters.

"What's them?" I says.

"Warnings to the people that something is up. Sometimes it's done one way, sometimes another. But there's always somebody spying around, that gives notice to the governor of the castle. When Louis XVI. was going to light out of the Tooleries, a servant girl done it. It's a very good way, and so is the nonnamous letters. We'll use them both. And it's usual for the prisoner's mother to change clothes with him, and she stays in, and he slides out in her clothes. We'll do that too."

"But looky here, Tom, what do we want to *warn* anybody for, that something's up? Let them find it out for themselves — it's their lookout."

"Yes, I know; but you can't depend on them. It's the way they've acted from the very start — left us to do *everything*. They're so confiding and mullet-headed they don't take notice of nothing at all. So if we don't *give* them notice, there won't be nobody nor nothing to interfere with us, and so after all our hard work and trouble this escape 'll go off perfectly flat: won't amount to nothing — won't be nothing *to* it."

"Well, as for me, Tom, that's the way I'd like."

"Shucks," he says, and looked disgusted. So I says:

"But I ain't going to make no complaint. Anyway that suits you suits me. What you going to do about the servant-girl?"

"You'll be her. You slide in, in the middle of the night, and hook that yaller girl's frock."

"Why, Tom, that'll make trouble next morning; because of course she prob'ly hain't got any but that one."

"I know; but you don't want it but fifteen minutes, to carry the nonnamous letter and shove it under the front door."

"All right, then, I'll do it; but I could carry it just as handy in my own togs."

"You wouldn't look like a servant-girl *then*, would you?"

"No, but there won't be nobody to see what I look like, *anyway*."

"That ain't got nothing to do with it. The thing for us to do, is just to do our *duty*, and not worry about whether anybody *sees* us do it or not. Hain't you got no principle at all?"

"All right, I ain't saying nothing; I'm the servant-girl. Who's Jim's mother?"

"I'm his mother. I'll hook a gown from Aunt Sally."

"Well, then, you'll have to stay in the cabin when me and Jim leaves."

"Not much. I'll stuff Jim's clothes full of straw and lay it on his bed to represent his mother in disguise, and Jim 'll take Aunt Sally's gown off of me and wear it, and we'll all evade together. When a prisoner of style escapes, it's called an evasion. It's always called so when a king escapes, f'rinstance. And the same with a king's son; it don't make no difference whether he's a natural one or an unnatural one."

So Tom he wrote the nonnamous letter, and I smouched the yaller wench's frock, that night, and put it on, and shoved it under the front door, the way Tom told me to. It said:

Beware. Trouble is brewing. Keep a sharp lookout. UNKNOWN FRIEND.

Next night we stuck a picture which Tom drawed in blood, of a skull and crossbones, on the front door; and next night another one of a coffin, on the back door. I never see a family in such a sweat. They couldn't a been worse scared if the place had a been full of ghosts laying for them behind everything and under the beds and shivering through the air. If a door banged, Aunt Sally she jumped, and said "ouch!" if anything fell, she jumped and said "ouch!" if you happened to touch her, when she warn't noticing, she done the same; she couldn't face noway and be satisfied, because she allowed there was something behind her every time — so she was always a whirling around, sudden, and saying "ouch," and before she'd get two-thirds around, she'd whirl back again, and say it again; and she was afraid to go to bed, but she dasn't set up. So the thing was working very well, Tom said; he said he never see a thing work more satisfactory. He said it showed it was done right.

So he said, now for the grand bulge! So the very next morning at the streak of dawn we got another letter ready, and was wondering what we better do with it, because we heard them say at supper they was going to have a nigger on watch at both doors all night. Tom he went down the lightning-rod to spy around; and the nigger at the back door was asleep, and he stuck it in the back of his neck and come back. This letter said:

Don't betray me, I wish to be your friend. There is a desprate gang of cutthroats from over in the Ingean Territory going to steal your runaway nigger to-night, and they have been trying to scare you so as you will stay in the house and not bother them. I am one of the gang, but have got religgion and wish to quit it and lead a honest life again, and will betray the helish design. They will sneak down from northards, along the fence, at midnight exact, with a false key, and go in the nigger's cabin to get him. I am to be off a piece and blow a tin horn if I see any danger; but stead of that, I will BA *like a sheep soon as they get in and not blow at all; then whilst they are getting his chains loose, you slip there and lock them in, and can kill them at your leasure. Don't do anything but just the way I am telling you, if you do they will suspicion something and raise whoopjamboreehoo. I do not wish any reward but to know I have done the right thing.*

UNKNOWN FRIEND

Chapter XL

We was feeling pretty good, after breakfast, and took my canoe and went over the river a fishing, with a lunch, and had a good time, and took a look at the raft and found her all right, and got home late to supper, and found them in such a sweat and worry they didn't know which end they was standing on, and made us go right off to bed the minute we was done supper, and wouldn't tell us what the trouble was, and never let on a word about the new letter, but didn't need to, because we knowed as much about it as anybody did, and as soon as we was half up stairs and her back was turned, we slid for the cellar cubboard and loaded up a good lunch and took it up to our room and went to bed, and got up about half-past eleven, and Tom put on Aunt Sally's dress that he stole and was going to start with the lunch, but says:

"Where's the butter?"

"I laid out a hunk of it," I says, "on a piece of a corn-pone."

"Well, you *left* it laid out, then — it ain't here."

"We can get along without it," I says.

"We can get along *with* it, too," he says; "just you slide down cellar and fetch it. And then mosey right down the lightning-rod and come along. I'll go and stuff the straw into Jim's clothes to represent his mother in disguise, and be ready to *ba* like a sheep and shove soon as you get there."

So out he went, and down cellar went I. The hunk of butter, big as a person's fist, was where I had left it, so I took up the slab of corn-pone with it on, and blowed out my light, and started up stairs, very stealthy, and got up to the main floor all right, but here comes Aunt Sally with a candle, and I clapped the truck in my hat, and clapped my hat on my head, and the next second she see me; and she says:

"You been down cellar?"

"Yes'm."

"What you been doing down there?"

"Noth'n."

"*Noth'n!*"

"No'm."

"Well, then, what possessed you to go down there, this time of night?"

"I don't know'm."

"You don't *know*? Don't answer me that way, Tom, I want to know what you been *doing* down there?"

"I hain't been doing a single thing, Aunt Sally, I hope to gracious if I have."

I reckoned she'd let me go, now, and as a generl thing she would; but I spose there was so many strange things going on she was just in a sweat about every little thing that warn't yard-stick straight; so she says, very decided:

"You just march into that setting-room and stay there till I come. You been up to something you no business to, and I lay I'll find out what it is before *I'm* done with you."

So she went away as I opened the door and walked into the setting-room. My, but there was a crowd there! Fifteen farmers, and every one of them had a gun. I was most powerful sick, and slunk to a chair and set down. They was setting around, some of them talking a little, in a low voice, and all of them fidgety and uneasy, but trying to look like they warn't; but I knowed they was, because they was always taking off their hats, and putting them on, and scratching their heads, and changing their seats, and fumbling with their buttons. I warn't easy myself, but I didn't take my hat off, all the same.

I did wish Aunt Sally would come, and get done with me, and lick me, if she wanted to, and let me get away and tell Tom how we'd overdone this thing, and what a thundering hornet's nest we'd got ourselves into, so we could stop fooling around, straight off, and clear out with Jim before these rips got out of patience and come for us.

At last she come, and begun to ask me questions, but I *couldn't* answer them straight, I didn't know which end of me was up; because these men was in such a fidget now, that some was wanting to start right *now* and lay for them desperadoes, and saying it warn't but a few minutes to midnight; and others was trying to get them to hold on and wait for the sheep-signal; and here was aunty pegging away at the questions, and me a shaking all over and ready to sink down in my tracks I was that scared; and the place getting hotter and hotter, and the butter beginning to melt and run down my neck and behind my ears; and pretty soon, when one of them says, "*I'm* for going and getting in the cabin *first,* and right *now,* and catching them when they come," I most dropped; and a streak of butter come a trickling down my forehead, and Aunt Sally she see it, and turns white as a sheet, and says:

"For the land's sake what *is* the matter with the child! — he's got the brain fever as shore as you're born, and they're oozing out!"

And everybody runs to see, and she snatches off my hat, and out comes the bread, and what was left of the butter, and she grabbed me, and hugged me, and says:

"Oh, what a turn you did give me! and how glad and grateful I am it ain't no worse; for luck's against us, and it never rains but it pours, and when I see that truck I thought we'd lost you, for I knowed by the color and all, it was just like your brains would be if — Dear, dear, whyd'nt you *tell* me that was what you'd been down there for, *I* wouldn't a cared. Now cler out to bed, and don't lemme see no more of you till morning!"

I was up stairs in a second, and down the lightning-rod in another one, and shinning through the dark for the lean-to. I couldn't hardly get my words out, I was so anxious; but I told Tom as quick as I could, we must jump for it, now, and not a minute to lose — the house full of men, yonder, with guns!

His eyes just blazed; and he says:

"No! — is that so? *Ain't* it bully! Why, Huck, if it was to do over again, I bet I could fetch two hundred! If we could put it off till ——"

"Hurry! *hurry!*" I says. "Where's Jim?"

"Right at your elbow; if you reach out your arm you can touch him. He's dressed, and everything's ready. Now we'll slide out and give the sheep-signal."

But then we heard the tramp of men, coming to the door, and heard them begin to fumble with the padlock; and heard a man say:

"I *told* you we'd be too soon; they haven't come — the door is locked. Here, I'll lock some of you into the cabin and you lay for 'em in the dark and kill 'em when they come; and the rest scatter around a piece, and listen if you can hear 'em coming."

So in they come, but couldn't see us in the dark, and most trod on us whilst we was hustling to get under the bed. But we got under all

right, and out through the hole, swift but soft — Jim first, me next, and
Tom last, which was according to Tom's orders. Now we was in the
lean-to, and heard trampings close by outside. So we crept to the door,
and Tom stopped us there and put his eye to the crack, but couldn't
make out nothing, it was so dark; and whispered and said he would listen for the steps to get further, and when he nudged us Jim must glide
out first, and him last. So he set his ear to the crack and listened, and listened, and listened, and the steps a scraping around, out there, all the
time; and at last he nudged us, and we slid out, and stooped down, not
breathing, and not making the least noise, and slipped stealthy towards
the fence, in Injun file, and got to it, all right, and me and Jim over it;
but Tom's britches catched fast on a splinter on the top rail, and then
he hear the steps coming, so he had to pull loose, which snapped the
splinter and made a noise; and as he dropped in our tracks and started,
somebody sings out:

"Who's that? Answer, or I'll shoot!"

But we didn't answer; we just unfurled our heels and shoved. Then
there was a rush, and a *bang, bang, bang!* and the bullets fairly whizzed
around us! We heard them sing out:

"Here they are! They've broke for the river! after 'em, boys! And
turn loose the dogs!"

So here they come, full tilt. We could hear them, because they wore
boots, and yelled, but we didn't wear no boots, and didn't yell. We was
in the path to the mill; and when they got pretty close onto us, we
dodged into the bush and let them go by, and then dropped in behind
them. They'd had all the dogs shut up, so they wouldn't scare off the
robbers; but by this time somebody had let them loose, and here they
come, making pow-wow enough for a million; but they was our dogs;
so we stopped in our tracks till they catched up; and when they see
it warn't nobody but us, and no excitement to offer them, they only
just said howdy, and tore right ahead towards the shouting and clatter-
ing; and then we up steam again and whizzed along after them till we
was nearly to the mill, and then struck up through the bush to where
my canoe was tied, and hopped in and pulled for dear life towards the
middle of the river, but didn't make no more noise than we was obleeged
to. Then we struck out, easy and comfortable, for the island where my
raft was; and we could hear them yelling and barking at each other all
up and down the bank, till we was so far away the sounds got dim and
died out. And when we stepped onto the raft, I says:

"*Now*, old Jim, you're a free man *again*, and I bet you won't ever be
a slave no more."

"En a mighty good job it wuz, too, Huck. It 'uz planned beautiful, en it 'uz *done* beautiful; en dey ain't *nobody* kin git up a plan dat's mo' mixed-up en splendid den what dat one wuz."

We was all as glad as we could be, but Tom was the gladdest of all, because he had a bullet in the calf of his leg.

When me and Jim heard that, we didn't feel so brash as what we did before. It was hurting him considerble, and bleeding; so we laid him in the wigwam and tore up one of the duke's shirts for to bandage him, but he says:

"Gimme the rags, I can do it myself. Don't stop, now; don't fool around here, and the evasion booming along so handsome; man the sweeps, and set her loose! Boys, we done it elegant! — 'deed we did. I wish *we'd* a had the handling of Louis XVI., there wouldn't a been no 'Son of Saint Louis, ascend to heaven!' wrote down in *his* biography: no, sir, we'd a whooped him over the *border* — that's what we'd a done with *him* — and done it just as slick as nothing at all, too. Man the sweeps — man the sweeps!"

But me and Jim was consulting — and thinking. And after we'd thought a minute, I says:

"Say it, Jim."

So he says:

"Well, den, dis is de way it look to me, Huck. Ef it wuz *him* dat 'uz bein' sot free, en one er de boys wuz to git shot, would he say, 'Go on en save me, nemmine 'bout a doctor f'r to save dis one? Is dat like Mars Tom Sawyer? Would he say dat? You *bet* he wouldn't! *Well*, den, is *Jim* gwyne to say it? No, sah — I doan' budge a step out'n dis place, 'dout a *doctor*; not if it's forty year!"

I knowed he was white inside, and I reckoned he'd say what he did say — so it was all right, now, and I told Tom I was agoing for a doctor. He raised considerble row about it, but me and Jim stuck to it and wouldn't budge; so he was for crawling out and setting the raft loose himself; but we wouldn't let him. Then he give us a piece of his mind — but it didn't do no good.

So when he see me getting the canoe ready, he says:

"Well, then, if you're bound to go, I'll tell you the way to do, when you get to the village. Shut the door, and blindfold the doctor tight and fast, and make him swear to be silent as the grave, and put a purse full of gold in his hand, and then take and lead him all around the back alleys and everywheres, in the dark, and then fetch him here in the canoe, in a roundabout way amongst the islands, and search him and take his chalk away from him, and don't give it back to him till you get him back to the village, or else he will chalk this raft so he can find it again. It's the way they all do."

So I said I would, and left, and Jim was to hide in the woods when he see the doctor coming, till he was gone again.

Chapter XLI

The doctor was an old man; a very nice, kind-looking old man, when I got him up. I told him me and my brother was over on Spanish Island hunting, yesterday afternoon, and camped on a piece of a raft we found, and about midnight he must a kicked his gun in his dreams, for it went off and shot him in the leg, and we wanted him to go over there and fix it and not say nothing about it, nor let anybody know, because we wanted to come home this evening, and surprise the folks.

"Who is your folks?" he says.

"The Phelpses, down yonder."

"Oh," he says. And after a minute, he says: "How'd you say he got shot?"

"He had a dream," I says, "and it shot him."

"Singular dream," he says.

So he lit up his lantern, and got his saddle-bags, and we started. But when he see the canoe, he didn't like the look of her — said she was big enough for one, but didn't look pretty safe for two. I says:

"Oh, you needn't be afeard, sir, she carried the three of us, easy enough."

"What three?"

"Why, me and Sid, and — and — and *the guns;* that's what I mean."

"Oh," he says.

But he put his foot on the gunnel, and rocked her; and shook his head, and said he reckoned he'd look around for a bigger one. But they was all locked and chained; so he took my canoe, and said for me to wait till he come back, or I could hunt around further, or maybe I better go down home and get them ready for the surprise, if I wanted to. But I said I didn't; so I told him just how to find the raft, and then he started.

I struck an idea, pretty soon. I says to myself, spos'n he can't fix that leg just in three shakes of a sheep's tail, as the saying is? spos'n it takes him three or four days? What are we going to do? — lay around there till he lets the cat out of the bag? No, sir, I know what *I'll* do. I'll wait, and when he comes back, if he says he's got to go any more, I'll get down there, too, if I swim; and we'll take and tie him, and keep him, and shove out down the river; and when Tom's done with him, we'll give him what it's worth, or all we got, and then let him get shore.

So then I crept into a lumber pile to get some sleep; and next time I waked up the sun was away up over my head! I shot out and went for the doctor's house, but they told me he'd gone away in the night, some time or other, and warn't back yet. Well, thinks I, that looks powerful bad for Tom, and I'll dig out for the island, right off. So away I shoved, and turned the corner, and nearly rammed my head into Uncle Silas's stomach! He says:

"Why, *Tom!* Where you been, all this time, you rascal?"

"*I* hain't been nowheres," I says, "only just hunting for the run-away nigger — me and Sid."

"Why, where ever did you go?" he says. "Your aunt's been mighty uneasy."

"She needn't," I says, "because we was all right. We followed the men and the dogs, but they out-run us, and we lost them; but we thought we heard them on the water, so we got a canoe and took out after them, and crossed over but couldn't find nothing of them; so we cruised along up-shore till we got kind of tired and beat out; and tied up the canoe and went to sleep, and never waked up till about an hour ago, then we paddled over here to hear the news, and Sid's at the post-office to see what he can hear, and I'm a branching out to get something to eat for us, and then we're going home."

So then we went to the post-office to get "Sid"; but just as I suspicioned, he warn't there; so the old man he got a letter out of the office, and we waited a while longer but Sid didn't come; so the old man said come along, let Sid foot it home, or canoe-it, when he got done fooling around — but we would ride. I couldn't get him to let me stay and wait for Sid; and he said there warn't no use in it, and I must come along, and let Aunt Sally see we was all right.

When we got home, Aunt Sally was that glad to see me she laughed and cried both, and hugged me, and give me one of them lickings of hern that don't amount to shucks, and said she'd serve Sid the same when he come.

And the place was plumb full of farmers and farmers' wives, to dinner; and such another clack a body never heard. Old Mrs. Hotchkiss was the worst; her tongue was agoing all the time. She says:

"Well, Sister Phelps, I've ransacked that-air cabin over an' I b'lieve the nigger was crazy. I says so to Sister Damrell — didn't I, Sister Damrell? — s'I, he's crazy, s'I — them's the very words I said. You all hearn me: he's crazy, s'I; everything shows it, s'I. Look at that-air grindstone, s'I; want to tell *me*'t any cretur 'ts in his right mind 's agoin' to scrabble all them crazy things onto a grindstone, s'I? Here sich 'n' sich a person busted his heart; 'n' here so 'n' so pegged along for thirty-seven year, 'n' all that — natcherl son o' Louis somebody, 'n' sich everlast'n rubbage. He's plumb crazy, s'I; it's what I says in the fust place, it's what I says in the middle, 'n' it's what I says last 'n' all the time — the nigger's crazy — crazy 's Nebokoodneezer, s'I."

"An' look at that-air ladder made out'n rags, Sister Hotchkiss," says old Mrs. Damrell, "what in the name o' goodness *could* he ever want of ——"

"The very words I was a-sayin' no longer ago th'n this minute to Sister Utterback, 'n' she'll tell you so herself. Sh-she, look at that-air rag ladder, sh-she; 'n' s'I, yes, *look* at it, s'I — what *could* he a wanted of it, s'I. Sh-she, Sister Hotchkiss, sh-she ——"

"But how in the nation'd they ever *git* that grindstone *in* there, *anyway*? 'n' who dug that-air *hole*? 'n' who ——"

"My very *words*, Brer Penrod! I was a-sayin' — pass that-air sasser o' m'lasses, won't ye? — I was a-sayin' to Sister Dunlap, jist this minute, how *did* they git that grindstone in there, s'I. Without *help*, mind you — 'thout *help*! *Thar's* wher' 'tis. Don't tell *me*, s'I; there *wuz* help, s'I; 'n' ther' wuz a *plenty* help, too, s'I; ther's ben a *dozen* a-helpin' that nigger, 'n' I lay I'd skin every last nigger on this place, but *I'd* find out who done it, s'I; 'n' moreover, s'I ——"

"A *dozen* says you! — *forty* couldn't a done everything that's been done. Look at them case-knife saws and things, how tedious they've been made; look at that bed-leg sawed off with 'm, a week's work for six men; look at that nigger made out'n straw on the bed; and look at ——"

"You may *well* say it, Brer Hightower! It's jist as I was a-sayin' to Brer Phelps, his own self. S'e, what do *you* think of it, Sister Hotchkiss, s'e? think o' what, Brer Phelps, s'I? think o' that bed-leg sawed off that a way, s'e? *think* of it, s'I? I lay it never sawed *itself* off, s'I — somebody *sawed* it, s'I; that's my opinion, take it or leave it, it mayn't be no 'count, s'I, but sich as 't is, it's my opinion, s'I, 'n' if anybody k'n start a better one, s'I, let him *do* it, s'I, that's all. I says to Sister Dunlap, s'I ——"

"Why, dog my cats, they must a ben a house-full o' niggers in there every night for four weeks, to a done all that work, Sister Phelps. Look at that shirt — every last inch of it kivered over with secret African writ'n done with blood! Must a ben a raft uv 'm at it right along, all the time, amost. Why, I'd give two dollars to have it read to me; 'n' as for the niggers that wrote it, I 'low I'd take 'n' lash 'm t'll ——"

"People to *help* him, Brother Marples! Well, I reckon you'd *think* so, if you'd a been in this house for a while back. Why, they've stole everything they could lay their hands on — and we a watching, all the time, mind you. They stole that shirt right off o' the line! and as for that sheet they made the rag ladder out of ther' ain't no telling how many times they *didn't* steal that; and flour, and candles, and candlesticks, and spoons, and the old warming-pan, and most a thousand things that I disremember, now, and my new calico dress; and me, and Silas, and my Sid and Tom on the constant watch day *and* night, as I was a telling you, and not a one of us could catch hide nor hair, nor sight nor sound of them; and here at the last minute, lo and behold you, they slides right in under our noses, and fools us, and not only fools *us* but the Injun Territory robbers too, and actuly gets *away* with that nigger, safe and sound, and that with sixteen men and twenty-two dogs right on their very heels at that very time! I tell you, it just bangs anything I ever *heard* of. Why, *sperits* couldn't a done better, and been no smarter. And I reckon they must a *been* sperits — because, *you* know our dogs, and ther' ain't no better; well, them dogs never even got on the *track* of 'm, once! You explain *that* to me, if you can! — *any* of you!"

"Well, it does beat ——"

"Laws alive, I never ——"

"So help me, I wouldn't a be ——"

"*House* thieves as well as ——"

"Goodnessgraciousssakes, I'd a ben afeard to *live* in sich a ——"

" 'Fraid to *live*! — why, I was that scared I dasn't hardly go to bed, or get up, or lay down, or *set* down, Sister Ridgeway. Why, they'd steal the very — why, goodness sakes, you can guess what kind of a fluster *I* was in by the time midnight come, last night. I hope to gracious if I warn't afraid they'd steal some o' the family! I was just to that pass, I didn't have no reasoning faculties no more. It looks foolish enough, *now*, in the day-time; but I says to myself, there's my two poor boys asleep, 'way up stairs in that lonesome room, and I declare to goodness I was that uneasy 't I crep' up there and locked 'em in! I *did*. And anybody would. Because, you know, when you get scared, that way, and it keeps running on, and getting worse and worse, all the time, and your wits gets to addling, and you get to doing all sorts o' wild things, and by-and-by you think to yourself, spos'n *I* was a boy, and was away up there, and the door ain't locked, and you ——" She stopped, looking kind of wondering, and then she turned her head around slow, and when her eye lit on me — I got up and took a walk.

Says I to myself, I can explain better how we come to not be in that room this morning if I go out to one side and study over it a little. So I done it. But I dasn't go fur, or she'd a sent for me. And when it was late in the day, the people all went, and then I come in and told her the noise and shooting waked up me and "Sid," and the door was locked, and we wanted to see the fun, so we went down the lightning-rod, and both of us got hurt a little, and we didn't never want to try *that* no more. And then I went on and told her all what I told Uncle Silas before; and then she said she'd forgive us, and maybe it was all right enough anyway, and about what a body might expect of boys, for all boys was a pretty harum-scarum lot, as fur as she could see; and so, as long as no harm hadn't come of it, she judged she better put in her time being grateful we was alive and well and she had us still, stead of fretting over what was past and done. So then she kissed me, and patted me on the head, and dropped into a kind of a brown study; and pretty soon jumps up, and says:

"Why, lawsamercy, it's most night, and Sid not come yet! What *has* become of that boy?"

I see my chance; so I skips up and says:

"I'll run right up to town and get him," I says.

"No you won't," she says. "You'll stay right wher' you are; *one's* enough to be lost at a time. If he ain't here to supper, your uncle 'll go."

Well, he warn't there to supper; so right after supper uncle went.

He come back about ten, a little bit uneasy; hadn't run across Tom's track. Aunt Sally was a good *deal* uneasy; but Uncle Silas he said there warn't no occasion to be — boys will be boys, he said, and you'll see this one turn up in the morning, all sound and right. So she had to be satisfied. But she said she'd set up for him a while, anyway, and keep a light burning, so he could see it.

And then when I went up to bed she come up with me and fetched her candle, and tucked me in, and mothered me so good I felt mean, and like I couldn't look her in the face; and she set down on the bed and talked with me a long time, and said what a splendid boy Sid was, and didn't seem to want to ever stop talking about him; and kept asking me every now and then, if I reckoned he could a got lost, or hurt, or maybe drownded, and might be laying at this minute, somewheres, suffering or dead, and she not by him to help him, and so the tears would drip down, silent, and I would tell her that Sid was all right, and would be home in the morning, sure; and she would squeeze my hand, or maybe kiss me, and tell me to say it again, and keep on saying it, because it done her good, and she was in so much trouble. And when she was going away, she looked down in my eyes, so steady and gentle, and says:

"The door ain't going to be locked, Tom; and there's the window and the rod; but you'll be good, *won't* you? And you won't go? For *my* sake."

Laws knows I *wanted* to go, bad enough, to see about Tom, and was all intending to go; but after that, I wouldn't a went, not for kingdoms.

But she was on my mind, and Tom was on my mind; so I slept very restless. And twice I went down the rod, away in the night, and slipped around front, and see her setting there by her candle in the window with her eyes towards the road and the tears in them; and I wished I could do something for her, but I couldn't, only to swear that I wouldn't never do nothing to grieve her any more. And the third time, I waked up at dawn, and slid down, and she was there yet, and her candle was most out, and her old gray head was resting on her hand, and she was asleep.

Chapter XLII

The old man was up town again, before breakfast, but couldn't get no track of Tom; and both of them set at the table, thinking, and not saying nothing, and looking mournful, and their coffee getting cold, and not eating anything. And by-and-by the old man says:

"Did I give you the letter?"

"What letter?"

"The one I got yesterday out of the post-office."

"No, you didn't give me no letter."

"Well, I must a forgot it."

So he rummaged his pockets, and then went off somewheres where he had laid it down, and fetched it, and give it to her. She says:

"Why, it's from St. Petersburg — it's from Sis."

I allowed another walk would do me good; but I couldn't stir. But before she could break it open, she dropped it and run — for she see something. And so did I. It was Tom Sawyer on a mattress; and that old doctor; and Jim, in *her* calico dress, with his hands tied behind him; and a lot of people. I hid the letter behind the first thing that come handy, and rushed. She flung herself at Tom, crying, and says:

"Oh, he's dead, he's dead, I know he's dead!"

And Tom he turned his head a little, and muttered something or other, which showed he warn't in his right mind; then she flung up her hands, and says:

"He's alive, thank God! And that's enough!" and she snatched a kiss of him, and flew for the house to get the bed ready, and scattering orders right and left at the niggers and everybody else, as fast as her tongue could go, every jump of the way.

I followed the men to see what they was going to do with Jim; and the old doctor and Uncle Silas followed after Tom into the house. The men was very huffy, and some of them wanted to hang Jim, for an example to all the other niggers around there, so they wouldn't be trying to run away, like Jim done, and making such a raft of trouble, and keeping a whole family scared most to death for days and nights. But the others said, don't do it, it wouldn't answer at all, he ain't our nigger, and his owner would turn up and make us pay for him, sure. So that cooled them down a little, because the people that's always the most anxious for to hang a nigger that hain't done just right, is always the very ones that ain't the most anxious to pay for him when they've got their satisfaction out of him.

They cussed Jim considerble, though, and give him a cuff or two, side the head, once in a while, but Jim never said nothing, and he never let on to know me, and they took him to the same cabin, and put his own clothes on him, and chained him again, and not to no bed-leg, this time, but to a big staple drove into the bottom log, and chained his hands, too, and both legs, and said he warn't to have nothing but bread and water to eat, after this, till his owner come or he was sold at auction, because he didn't come in a certain length of time, and filled up our hole, and said a couple of farmers with guns must stand watch around about the cabin every night, and a bull-dog tied to the door in the day-time; and about this time they was through with the job and was tapering off with a kind of generl good-bye cussing, and then the old doctor comes and takes a look, and says:

"Don't be no rougher on him than you're obleeged to, because he ain't a bad nigger. When I got to where I found the boy, I see I couldn't cut the bullet out without some help, and he warn't in no condition for me to leave, to go and get help; and he got a little worse and a little worse, and after a long time he went out of his head, and wouldn't let me come anigh him, any more, and said if I chalked his raft he'd kill me, and no end of wild foolishness like that, and I see I couldn't do anything at all with him; so I says, I got to have *help*, somehow; and the minute I says it, out crawls this nigger from somewheres, and says he'll help, and he done it, too, and done it very well. Of course I judged he must be a runaway nigger, and there I *was!* and there I had to stick, right straight along all the rest of the day, and all night. It was a fix, I tell you! I had a couple of patients with the chills, and of course I'd of liked to run up to town and see them, but I dasn't, because the nigger might get away, and then I'd be to blame; and yet never a skiff come close enough for me to hail. So there I had to stick, plumb till daylight this morning; and I never see a nigger that was a better nuss or faithfuller, and yet he was resking his freedom to do it, and was all tired out, too, and I see plain enough he'd been worked main hard, lately. I liked the nigger for that; I tell you, gentlemen, a nigger like that is worth a thousand dollars — and kind treatment, too. I had everything I needed, and the boy was doing as well there as he would a done at home — better, maybe, because it was so quiet; but there I *was,* with both of 'm on my hands; and there I had to stick, till about dawn this morning; then some men in a skiff come by, and as good luck would have it, the nigger was setting by the pallet with his head propped on his knees, sound asleep; so I motioned them in, quiet, and they slipped up on him and grabbed him and tied him before he knowed what he was about, and we never had no trouble. And the boy being in a kind of a flighty sleep, too, we muffled the oars and hitched the raft on, and towed her over very nice and quiet, and the nigger never made the least row nor said a word, from the start. He ain't no bad nigger, gentlemen; that's what I think about him."

Somebody says:

"Well, it sounds very good, doctor, I'm obleeged to say."

Then the others softened up a little, too, and I was mighty thankful to that old doctor for doing Jim that good turn; and I was glad it was according to my judgment of him, too; because I thought he had a good heart in him and was a good man, the first time I see him. Then they all agreed that Jim had acted very well, and was deserving to have some notice took of it, and reward. So every one of them promised, right out and hearty, that they wouldn't cuss him no more.

Then they come out and locked him up. I hoped they was going to say he could have one or two of the chains took off, because they was rotten heavy, or could have meat and greens with his bread and water, but they didn't think of it, and I reckoned it warn't best for me to mix in, but I judged I'd get the doctor's yarn to Aunt Sally, somehow or other, as soon as I'd got through the breakers that was laying just ahead of me. Explanations, I mean, of how I forgot to mention about Sid being shot, when I was telling how him and me put in that dratted night paddling around hunting the runaway nigger.

But I had plenty time. Aunt Sally she stuck to the sick-room all day and all night; and every time I see Uncle Silas mooning around, I dodged him.

Next morning I heard Tom was a good deal better, and they said Aunt Sally was gone to get a nap. So I slips to the sick-room, and if I found him awake I reckoned we could put up a yarn for the family that would wash. But he was sleeping, and sleeping very peaceful, too; and pale, not fire-faced the way he was when he come. So I set down and laid for him to wake. In about a half an hour, Aunt Sally comes gliding in, and there I was, up a stump again! She motioned me to be still, and set down by me, and begun to whisper, and said we could all be joyful now, because all the symptoms was first rate, and he'd been sleeping like that for ever so long, and looking better and peacefuller all the time, and ten to one he'd wake up in his right mind.

So we set there watching, and by-and-by he stirs a bit, and opened his eyes very natural, and takes a look, and says:

"Hello, why I'm at *home!* How's that? Where's the raft?"

"It's all right," I says.

"And *Jim?*"

"The same," I says, but couldn't say it pretty brash. But he never noticed, but says:

"Good! Splendid! *Now* we're all right and safe! Did you tell Aunty?"

I was going to say yes; but she chipped in and says:

"About what, Sid?"

"Why, about the way the whole thing was done."

"What whole thing?"

"Why, *the* whole thing. There ain't but one; how we set the runaway nigger free — me and Tom."

"Good land! Set the run — What *is* the child talking about! Dear, dear, out of his head again!"

" *No,* I ain't out of my HEAD; I know all what I'm talking about. We *did* set him free — me and Tom. We laid out to do it, and we *done* it. And we done it elegant, too." He'd got a start, and she never checked him up, just set and stared and stared, and let him clip along, and I see it warn't no use for *me* to put in. "Why, Aunty, it cost us a power of work — weeks of it — hours and hours, every night, whilst you was all asleep. And we had to steal candles, and the sheet, and the shirt, and your dress, and spoons, and tin plates, and case-knives, and the warming-pan, and the grindstone, and flour, and just no end of things, and you can't think what work it was to make the saws, and pens, and inscriptions, and one thing or another, and you can't think *half* the fun it was. And we had to make up the pictures of coffins and things, and nonnamous letters from the robbers, and get up and down the lightning-rod, and dig the hole into the cabin, and make the rope-ladder and send it in cooked up in a pie, and send in spoons and things to work with, in your apron pocket" ——

"Mercy sakes!"

—— "and load up the cabin with rats and snakes and so on, for company for Jim; and then you kept Tom here so long with the butter in his hat that you come near spiling the whole business, because the men come before we was out of the cabin, and we had to rush, and they heard us and let drive at us, and I got my share, and we dodged out of the path and let them go by, and when the dogs come they warn't interested in us, but went for the most noise, and we got our canoe, and made for the raft, and was all safe, and Jim was a free man, and we done it all by ourselves, and *wasn't* it bully, Aunty!"

"Well, I never heard the likes of it in all my born days! So it was *you*, you little rapscallions, that's been making all this trouble, and turned everybody's wits clean inside out and scared us all most to death. I've as good a notion as ever I had in my life, to take it out o' you this very minute. To think, here I've been, night after night, a — *you* just get well once, you young scamp, and I lay I'll tan the Old Harry° out o' both o' ye!"

But Tom, he *was* so proud and joyful, he just *couldn't* hold in, and his tongue just *went* it — she a-chipping in, and spitting fire all along, and both of them going it at once, like a cat-convention; and she says:

"*Well*, you get all the enjoyment you can out of it *now*, for mind I tell you if I catch you meddling with him again ——"

"Meddling with *who*?" Tom says, dropping his smile and looking surprised.

"With *who*? Why, the runaway nigger, of course. Who'd you reckon?"

Tom looks at me very grave, and says:

"Tom, didn't you just tell me he was all right? Hasn't he got away?"

"*Him*?" says Aunt Sally; "the runaway nigger? 'Deed he hasn't. They've got him back, safe and sound, and he's in that cabin again, on bread and water, and loaded down with chains, till he's claimed or sold!"

Old Harry: The devil.

Tom rose square up in bed, with his eye hot, and his nostrils opening and shutting like gills, and sings out to me:

"They hain't no *right* to shut him up! *Shove!* — and don't you lose
a minute. Turn him loose! he ain't no slave; he's as free as any cretur
that walks this earth!"

"What *does* the child mean?"

"I mean every word I *say*, Aunt Sally, and if somebody don't go, *I'll*
go. I've knowed him all his life, and so has Tom, there. Old Miss Watson died two months ago, and she was ashamed she ever was going to
sell him down the river, and *said* so; and she set him free in her will."

"Then what on earth did *you* want to set him free for, seeing he was
already free?"

"Well, that *is* a question, I must say; and *just* like women! Why, I
wanted the *adventure* of it; and I'd a waded neck-deep in blood to —
goodness alive, AUNT POLLY!"

If she warn't standing right there, just inside the door, looking as
sweet and contented as an angel half-full of pie, I wish I may never!

Aunt Sally jumped for her, and most hugged the head off of her,
and cried over her, and I found a good enough place for me under the
bed, for it was getting pretty sultry for *us,* seemed to me. And I peeped
out, and in a little while Tom's Aunt Polly shook herself loose and
stood there looking across at Tom over her spectacles — kind of grinding him into the earth, you know. And then she says:

"Yes, you *better* turn y'r head away — I would if I was you, Tom."

"Oh, deary me!" says Aunt Sally; "*is* he changed so? Why, that ain't
Tom it's Sid; Tom's — Tom's — why, where is Tom? He was here a
minute ago."

"You mean where's Huck *Finn* — that's what you mean! I reckon I
hain't raised such a scamp as my Tom all these years, not to know him
when I *see* him. That *would* be a pretty howdy-do. Come out from
under that bed, Huck Finn."

So I done it. But not feeling brash.

Aunt Sally she was one of the mixed-upest looking persons I ever
see; except one, and that was Uncle Silas, when he come in, and they
told it all to him. It kind of made him drunk, as you may say, and he
didn't know nothing at all the rest of the day, and preached a prayer-
meeting sermon that night that give him a rattling ruputation, because
the oldest man in the world couldn't a understood it. So Tom's Aunt
Polly, she told all about who I was, and what; and I had to up and tell
how I was in such a tight place that when Mrs. Phelps took me for Tom

Sawyer — she chipped in and says, "Oh, go on and call me Aunt Sally,
I'm used to it, now, and 'tain't no need to change" — that when Aunt
Sally took me for Tom Sawyer, I had to stand it — there warn't no
other way, and I knowed he wouldn't mind, because it would be nuts
for him, being a mystery, and he'd make an adventure out of it and be
perfectly satisfied. And so it turned out, and he let on to be Sid, and
made things as soft as he could for me.

And his Aunt Polly she said Tom was right about old Miss Watson
setting Jim free in her will; and so, sure enough, Tom Sawyer had gone
and took all that trouble and bother to set a free nigger free! and I
couldn't ever understand, before, until that minute and that talk, how
he *could* help a body set a nigger free, with his bringing-up.

Well, Aunt Polly she said that when Aunt Sally wrote to her that
Tom and *Sid* had come, all right and safe, she says to herself:

"Look at that, now! I might have expected it, letting him go off
that way without anybody to watch him. So now I got to go and trapse
all the way down the river, eleven hundred mile, and find out what that
creetur's up to, *this* time; as long as I couldn't seem to get any answer
out of you about it."

"Why, I never heard nothing from you," says Aunt Sally.

"Well, I wonder! Why, I wrote to you twice, to ask you what you
could mean by Sid being here."

"Well, I never got 'em, Sis."

Aunt Polly, she turns around slow and severe, and says:

"You, Tom!"

"Well — *what?*" he says, kind of pettish.

"Don't you what *me*, you impudent thing — hand out them letters."

"What letters?"

"*Them* letters. I be bound, if I have to take aholt of you I'll ——"

"They're in the trunk. There, now. And they're just the same as
they was when I got them out of the office. I hain't looked into them, I
hain't touched them. But I knowed they'd make trouble, and I thought
if you warn't in no hurry, I'd ——"

"Well, you *do* need skinning, there ain't no mistake about it. And I
wrote another one to tell you I was coming; and I spose he ——"

"No, it come yesterday; I hain't read it yet, but *it's* all right, I've got
that one."

I wanted to offer to bet two dollars she hadn't, but I reckoned
maybe it was just as safe to not to. So I never said nothing.

Chapter the Last

The first time I catched Tom, private, I asked him what was his idea, time of the evasion? — what it was he'd planned to do if the evasion worked all right and he managed to set a nigger free that was already free before? And he said, what he had planned in his head, from the start, if we got Jim out all safe, was for us to run him down the river, on the raft, and have adventures plumb to the mouth of the river, and then tell him about his being free, and take him back up home on a steamboat, in style, and pay him for his lost time, and write word ahead and get out all the niggers around, and have them waltz him into town with a torchlight procession and a brass band, and then he would be a hero, and so would we. But I reckened it was about as well the way it was.

We had Jim out of the chains in no time, and when Aunt Polly and Uncle Silas and Aunt Sally found out how good he helped the doctor nurse Tom, they made a heap of fuss over him, and fixed him up prime, and give him all he wanted to eat, and a good time, and nothing to do. And we had him up to the sick-room; and had a high talk; and Tom give Jim forty dollars for being prisoner for us so patient, and doing it up so good, and Jim was pleased most to death, and busted out, and says:

"*Dah*, now, Huck, what I tell you? — what I tell you up dah on Jackson islan'? I *tole* you I got a hairy breas', en what's de sign un it; en I *tole* you I ben rich wunst, en gwineter to be rich *agin;* en it's come true; en heah she *is! Dah*, now! doan' talk to *me* — signs is *signs*, mine I tell you; en I knowed jis' 's well 'at I 'uz gwineter be rich agin as I's a stannin' heah dis minute!"

And then Tom he talked along, and talked along, and says, le's all three slide out of here, one of these nights, and get an outfit, and go for howling adventures amongst the Injuns, over in the Territory, for a couple of weeks or two; and I says, all right, that suits me, but I aint got no money for to buy the outfit, and I reckon I couldn't get none from home, because it's likely pap's been back before now, and got it all away from Judge Thatcher and drunk it up.

"No he hain't," Tom says; "it's all there, yet — six thousand dollars and more; and your pap hain't ever been back since. Hadn't when I come away, anyhow."

Jim says, kind of solemn:

"He ain't a comin' back no mo', Huck."

I says:

"Why, Jim?"

"Nemmine why, Huck — but he ain't comin' back no mo'."

But I kept at him; so at last he says:

"Doan' you 'member de house dat was float'n down de river, en dey wuz a man in dah, kivered up, en I went in en unkivered him and didn' let you come in? Well, den, you k'n git yo' money when you wants it; kase dat wuz him."

Tom's most well, now, and got his bullet around his neck on a watch-guard for a watch, and is always seeing what time it is, and so there ain't nothing more to write about, and I am rotten glad of it, because if I'd a knowed what a trouble it was to make a book I wouldn't a tackled it and ain't agoing to no more. But I reckon I got to light out for the Territory ahead of the rest, because Aunt Sally she's going to adopt me and sivilize me and I can't stand it. I been there before.

THE END. YOURS TRULY, HUCK FINN.

A Portfolio of Illustrations
from the 1885 Edition

Our selection of seventeen of Edward Windsor Kemble's illustrations from the first edition of *Huckleberry Finn* is designed to highlight specific features of this edition. The frontispiece is the pictorial source for most readers' image of Huck. The three drawings of Huck dressed as a girl illustrate a scene Myra Jehlen discusses in her essay "Reading Gender in *Adventures of Huckleberry Finn*." The drawing of the king cavorting in the Royal Nonesuch and one of Huck and Jim sleeping side by side are relevant to questions of sexuality addressed in Leslie Fiedler's "Come Back to the Raft Ag'in, Huck Honey!" and Christopher Looby's " 'Innocent Homosexuality': The Fiedler Thesis in Retrospect." The final illustration, in which a smiling Huck tips his cap to his audience, and the frontispiece serve as pictorial bookends for Huck's narrative.

The drawings of Jim are worthy of further comment because they add visual evidence to record for considerations of Twain's treatment of race. Kemble was a popular illustrator of the late nineteenth century whose illustrations of works by such writers as George Washington Cable, Richard Malcolm Johnson, and Thomas Nelson Page established him, in his own words, as "a delineator of the South, the Negro being my specialty." Twain had a hand in commissioning Kemble and personally authorizing his drawings. One scholar, Earl F. Briden, after studying Kemble's illustrations and Twain's comments on them, concludes that

Twain, in employing Kemble, "might be said to have sold Jim down the river himself" (405). In Briden's view, Kemble depicts Jim as a comic stereotype who appears variously "as an image of wholesouled astonishment, or delight, or earnestness, or humility" (395), reinforcing racist images that Kemble would later exaggerate and cash in on in his own unequivocally racist books. Although Twain expressed some disappointment with Kemble's first efforts for *Huckleberry Finn,* he never complained about the illustrator's depictions of Jim. By approving Kemble's illustrations, Briden maintains, Twain approved a pictorial narrative that runs counter to what he takes to be a verbal narrative of Huck's growing realizations about Jim's individual humanity. As you'll see, not everyone agrees with Briden's view of the verbal narrative, and not everyone would agree with his view of the illustrations. But his view complicates the debate about race by opening up the issue of whether — and how well — Twain's attitudes about race can be inferred from Kemble's drawings of Jim.

FOR FURTHER READING

Briden, Earl F. "Kemble's 'Specialty' and the Pictorial Countertext of *Huckleberry Finn.*" *Mark Twain Journal* 26.2 (1988): 2–14.

Wonham, Henry B. "'I Want a Real Coon': Mark Twain and Late-Nineteenth-Century Ethnic Caricature." *American Literature* 72.1 (2000): 117–52.

Figure 1. Huckleberry Finn (frontispiece)

Figure 2. Jim (ch. 2)

Figure 3. Jim Listening (ch. 4)

Figure 4. Jim and the Ghost (ch. 8)

Figure 5. Jim Sees a Dead Man (ch. 9)

Figure 6. "A Fair Fit" (ch. 10)

Figure 7. "Come In" (ch. 11)

Figure 8. "Hump Yourself!" (ch. 11)

Figure 9. "O My Lordy, Lordy!" (ch. 12)

Figure 10. We Turned in and Slept (ch. 13)

Figure 11. Asleep on the Raft (ch. 15)

Figure 12. Tragedy (ch. 23)

Figure 13. Harmless (ch. 24)

Figure 14. The Breakfast Horn (ch. 35)

Figure 15. Jim's Coat of Arms (ch. 38)

Figure 16. Jim Advises a Doctor (ch. 40)

Figure 17. Yours Truly, Huck Finn (ch. 43, "Chapter the Last")

PART TWO

A Case Study in Critical Controversy

The Controversy over the Ending: Did Mark Twain Sell Jim down the River?

Did Mark Twain botch his masterpiece in its final chapters, or is this section in keeping with the earlier part of the book? Until the late 1960s, the aspect of *Huckleberry Finn* that occasioned the most heated debate was the final eleven chapters, involving Jim's imprisonment in the hut at the Phelps farm and Tom Sawyer's fanciful schemes for "freeing" him even though Tom knows that Jim has already been freed by Miss Watson's will. Many readers have felt that these chapters constitute an anticlimactic letdown, even a betrayal, in which Twain lapses into trivial slapstick comedy and thus loses sight of the heroic moral theme he has developed up to this point — Jim's struggle for freedom from slavery. Since the 1960s, debates on the novel have shifted to the question of Twain's treatment of race. Yet because views of Twain's treatment of race often hinge on judgments of the ending, critics are no closer to reaching a consensus than they ever were. In fact, the status of the ending remains a topic of unresolved controversy today, and some adaptations of the novel solve the problem of the ending by rewriting it. A recent film version eliminates Tom Sawyer's return and has Jim escape from a lynch mob.

In 1935 Ernest Hemingway set the tone that many critiques of the ending would take when he stated that "all modern American literature comes from" *Huckleberry Finn,* while warning that "if you read [the novel] you must stop where the Nigger Jim is stolen from the boys. [*sic*].[1] This is the real end. The rest is cheating" (22). Hemingway was echoing the critic Bernard De Voto, who in 1932 had judged the final chapters to fall "far below the accomplishment of what had gone before. Mark was once more betrayed. . . . Nothing in his mind or training enabled him to understand that this extemporized burlesque was a defacement of his purer work" (312).

Two distinguished critics, Lionel Trilling and T. S. Eliot, briefly responded to criticisms of the ending in introductions written for editions of *Huckleberry Finn*. In his introduction to the 1948 Rinehart edition (excerpted on pp. 283–84 in this volume), Trilling argues that though "Tom Sawyer's elaborate, too elaborate, game of Jim's escape" certainly constitutes an artistic "falling-off" from what has gone before, this way of ending the book has "a certain formal aptness" (p. 284). According to Trilling, Twain uses the device of Tom Sawyer's return so that Huck may quite appropriately move away from center stage and over to the wings where he is more comfortable. Throughout the novel, Huck has been a self-effacing antihero, one who does not fit into the conventional social roles; consequently, it is only proper, in Trilling's view, for Huck to give way at the end to the more self-assertive and social Tom Sawyer.

Two years later, in his introduction to the Chanticleer edition, T. S. Eliot argues along similar lines to counter the charge "that the escapades invented by Tom, in the attempted 'rescue' of Jim, are only a tedious development of themes with which we were already too familiar. . . ." In the excerpt included here (pp. 285–89), Eliot replies that "it is right that the mood of the end of the book should bring us back to that of the beginning" (p. 288), evidently suggesting that Tom's dominance over Huck in the concluding chapters reestablishes their relations at the beginning of the book where Huck is enthralled by Tom's "style." It is right, then, for Huck to "disappear" at the end of the book, according to Eliot, "and his disappearance can only be accomplished by bringing forward another performer to obscure the disappearance in a cloud of whimsicalities" (p. 288).

As this summary suggests, both critics and defenders of the ending were at this stage primarily concerned with the problem of Huck's displacement by Tom and his "game of Jim's escape." So far, neither critics nor defenders had asked how Twain's choice of ending affected the

---

[1]As Jonathan Arac notes in his essay in the next section, the text of the novel does not contain the phrase "Nigger Jim."

racial theme of the book. This was the question at the center of Leo Marx's 1953 essay, "Mr. Eliot, Mr. Trilling, and *Huckleberry Finn*" (reprinted on pp. 289–304), which still comprises the most comprehensive statement of the case against the ending.

Marx responds not only to Trilling and Eliot, but to the post–World War II trend that he sees represented in their essays to substitute "considerations of technique for considerations of truth" and to evade "complex questions of political morality" (p. 304). Thus the quarrel he provokes with Eliot and Trilling foreshadows the conflict between aesthetic and political readings of literature that has erupted in our own time in the debates over multiculturalism and political correctness.

Marx's central contentions can be summarized as follows:

1. In having Miss Watson free Jim in her will, Twain sins against the laws of realism — real Southern slaveowners were not characteristically prone to such changes of heart. Furthermore, in ascribing benevolence to Miss Watson, Twain abandons the powerful critique of respectable society that has given the novel its meaning and direction.

2. The burlesque comedy perpetrated by Tom Sawyer, in which the imprisoned Jim is made an object of slapstick humor, is also disastrously "out of keeping" with the heroic struggle for freedom that has been the dominant action up to that point: "[T]he most serious motive in the novel, Jim's yearning for freedom, is made the object of nonsense" (p. 294).

3. In letting Tom Sawyer's escapades take over the action of the final chapters, Twain undermines the meaning of Huck's moral maturation. When Huck falls back under Tom's sway again and becomes an instrument of Tom's juvenile fascination with "adventure," serious art is replaced by clowning and gameplaying. We are asked to believe that the boy who courageously committed himself to Jim's liberation "is now capable of making Jim's capture the occasion of a game" (p. 295).

4. Perhaps most troubling of all, "the maze of farcical invention" that takes over the action at this point humiliates Jim himself and deprives him of the dignity of the freedom fighter into which he had developed. By having Jim largely tolerate Tom's absurd pranks, Twain robs Jim of his humanity and turns him into "a flat stereotype: the submissive stage-Negro" (p. 295–96).

Marx contends that the failure of the ending is a symptom of a personal "failure of nerve" in Samuel Clemens himself (p. 288). Here Marx echoes a view that had been developed by earlier Twain critics (most notably Van Wyck Brooks in *The Ordeal of Mark Twain* [1920]), that Clemens the man never resolved a split in his personality between rebellion and genteel respectability, and that this split resulted in a contradiction in the writings of Mark Twain the author, who aspired to be a true rebel like Huck but could never bring himself to go farther than the safe, conventional rebellion of Tom.

In other words, then, one line of argument has it that Twain had incompatible desires: he wished both to subvert "the genteel tradition" of the respectable Christian society of his day and to be successful and admired by this same respectable genteel society. Unable to decide whether he wished to be Huck Finn or Tom Sawyer, Twain, according to this argument, drew back from the moments of sharpest social and moral criticism in his works and lapsed into unthreatening comedy and clowning. Here presumably is why Twain seemingly drops the devastating critique of the moral hypocrisy of respectable America that is implicit in Huck's rebellious rejection of his "conscience" and his determination to "go to hell," and why he turns the final chapters of his novel over to the safer rebelliousness of Tom, which does not finally challenge the respectable world at all. Here, according to this view, is why Twain contrives it that Jim has already been freed by Miss Watson, so that Tom's schemes to free him only pretend to transgress the law and the social code.

This line of argument has been persuasive to many, but Marx has not had the last word by any means. The three other essays in this section are very aware of Marx's line of argument and of the continuing controversy, but each of them approaches the ending from a different direction. Toni Morrison considers the controversy as part of a larger case that canonical American literature, including texts that seem only marginally concerned with race, have a significant "Africanist presence" and that coming to terms with this presence "is central to any understanding of [American] literature" (p. 305). For Morrison, coming to terms with Jim's presence in *Huckleberry Finn* means recognizing that the ending works effectively, even if it does so in spite of itself. Because the novel links Huck's maturation to Jim's presence, "there is no way, given the confines of the novel, for Huck to mature into a moral human being *in America* without Jim" (p. 309, Morrison's emphasis). This insight allows us to shift our attention from Jim himself to what "Twain, Huck, and especially Tom need from him" (p. 310), and what they need during the ending is his subservience. Consequently, while Morrison agrees that the way Huck and Tom treat Jim during the evasion is painful to read, she sees a value in that pain: "the book may indeed be 'great' because in its structure, in the hell it puts its readers through at the end, the frontal debate it forces, it simulates and describes the parasitical nature of white freedom" (p. 310).

Stacey Margolis's approach is to read the ending, and the novel as a whole, in the context of debates in nineteenth-century American legal theory about the relation among intentions, actions, consequences, and accountability. She notes that the courts initially tried to limit accountability for the consequences of actions by linking accountability to negligence: one was accountable only if one was negligent. But the doctrine of negligence "implied that persons (even corporate persons) have at all times an obligation to act with caution," and that implication in turn meant negligence would be judged against "a general standard of care" (p. 321). The recognition of this general standard paved the way for the position that consequences of actions were more important than the intentions behind them. Margolis contends that Twain uses the novel to argue for this position, and, from this perspective, the ending is very effective. The gap between Huck's good intentions toward Jim and his actual behavior toward him is not a flaw in the novel but an important means by which Twain shows that consequences matter more than intentions. Furthermore, Margolis suggests, Twain is concerned less with the actions of any one individual and more with the larger system that supports the racist actions of virtually all the white characters — Huck (during the final chapters), Tom, the King and the Duke, the Phelps family and their neighbors, Miss Watson. In this way, Margolis can agree with Marx — and with Jonathan Arac and Jane Smiley, whose essays are included in the next section — that Huck's and Tom's actions during the Phelps farm episode have serious negative consequences for Jim, even as she contends that this recognition contributes to rather than detracts from Twain's accomplishment of his purpose. Margolis extends this argument through her keen-eyed reading of the significance, in both legal and literary terms, of the "forty dollars" that Tom pays to Jim for enduring Tom's efforts to set him free.

Sacvan Bercovitch's approach is to reconsider the nature of Twain's "deadpan" humor, a reconsideration that leads him to argue that we have underestimated both the way it works and the force it wields. More specifically, we have not recognized the extent to which Twain's humor is "directed against his readership, then and later, even unto our own time — against, that is, the conscience-driven forms of liberal interpretation" (p. 351). We have underestimated Twain because we have not properly understood his use of deadpan humor, a mode that depends on being funny in three different ways: (1) being amusing, as in children's humor or the tall tale; (2) being deceptive, as in satiric humor and confidence games; and (3) being sinister or chilling, as when we say ominously that there's "something funny" about a person or situation. Twain's particular use of deadpan humor is both innovative and challenging because it initially conceals the third way of being funny. It is only upon reflection that we realize that there's something "funny about the fact that we've found [his story] funny" (p. 335) — and that "something" is the sinister element, what Bercovitch calls the "nub" or the "snapper." Thus, we may not realize that Huck's behavior during the final chapters is actually consistent with his earlier behavior, that Twain's snapper involves trapping us into thinking that Huck has changed when in fact he never escapes the racism he holds at the beginning of the action, and that is, in Bercovitch's view, so clearly displayed in Huck's exchange with Aunt Sally. Bercovitch puts it this way: *"Huck doesn't develop so that we can be conned into believing that he does"* (p. 348, Bercovitch's emphasis). If we join previous liberal critics, then, in seeing Huck as a great spokesperson for equality, we miss the point that Twain is satirizing their liberalism and self-congratulation. Bercovitch argues that Twain held a skeptical, even contemptuous, view of *all* races: "All that I need to know is that a man is a human being; that is enough for me; he can't be any worse." Consequently, "[f]ar from being a moral and aesthetic collapse, as critics have lamented, the novel's third and last section is perfectly in keeping with Twain's design" (p. 347) — the design to have us ultimately recognize the sinister element of his deadpan style. If Bercovitch is right, in other words, the ending is a brilliant part of a far darker novel than we have yet recognized.

WORK CITED

Brooks, Van Wyck. *The Ordeal of Mark Twain.* New York: AMS, 1977 [1920].

De Voto, Bernard. *Mark Twain's America.* Cambridge: Houghton, 1932.

Hemingway, Ernest. *The Green Hills of Africa.* New York: Scribner's, 1935.

FURTHER READING IN THE CONTROVERSY

Cox, James M. *Mark Twain: The Fate of Humor.* Princeton: Princeton UP, 1966.

Hill, Richard. "Overreaching: Critical Agenda and the Ending of *Adventures of Huckleberry Finn.*" *Texas Studies in Language and Literature* 33.4 (Winter 1991): 492–513.

Holland, Laurence B. "A 'Raft of Trouble': Word and Deed in *Huckleberry Finn.*" *American Realism: New Essays.* Ed. Eric J. Sundquist. Baltimore: Johns Hopkins UP, 1982. 66–81.

Kaufmann, David. "Satiric Deceit in the Ending of *Adventures of Huckleberry Finn.*" *Studies in the Novel* 19 (1987): 66–78.

Oehlschlaeger, Fritz. "'Gwyne to Git Hung': The Conclusion of *Huckleberry Finn.*" *One Hundred Years of "Huckleberry Finn": The Boy, His Book, and American Culture.* Ed. Robert Sattelmeyer and J. Donald Crowley. Columbia: U of Missouri P, 1985. 117–27.

Quirk, Tom. "Learning a Nigger to Argue: Quitting *Huckleberry Finn.*" *Coming to Grips with Huckleberry Finn.* Columbia: U of Missouri P, 1993. 63–82.

Reichert, John. *Making Sense of Literature.* Chicago: U of Chicago P, 1977. 191–203.

Rowe, Joyce A. "Mark Twain's Great Evasion: *Adventures of Huckleberry Finn.*" *Equivocal Endings in Classic American Novels.* New York: Cambridge UP, 1988. 46–74.

LIONEL TRILLING

A Certain Formal Aptness

Lionel Trilling (1905–1975) received his M.A. (1926) and Ph.D. (1938) at Columbia University, where, after short stints at the University of Wisconsin and Hunter College, he taught from 1931 until his death. Trilling's talents were impressive. In addition to criticism, he wrote fiction, including a widely read novel, *The Middle of the Journey* (1947), and a frequently anthologized short story, "Of This Time, of That Place" (1943). Unlike most of his contemporaries (and ours), Trilling was less interested in different schools and principles of interpretation than he was with assessing literature's moral and cultural significance, and for the last twenty-five years of his life he was a highly influential commentator on American literature and culture. His critical books include *Matthew Arnold* (1939), *E. M. Forster* (1943), *The Liberal Imagination* (1950), *Beyond Culture: Essays on Literature and Learning* (1965), *Sincerity and Authenticity* (1972), *Mind in the Modern World* (1972), and two books on Sigmund Freud: *Freud and the Crisis of Our Culture* (1955) and *The Life and Work of Sigmund Freud* (1962). This selection is excerpted from his introduction to the 1948 Rinehart edition of *Huckleberry Finn*.

. . . In form and style *Huckleberry Finn* is an almost perfect work. Only one mistake has ever been charged against it, that it concludes with Tom Sawyer's elaborate, too elaborate, game of Jim's escape. Certainly this episode is too long — in the original draft it was much longer — and certainly it is a falling-off, as almost anything would have to be, from the incidents of the river. Yet it has a certain formal aptness — like, say, that of the Turkish initiation which brings Molière's *Le Bourgeois Gentilhomme* to its close. It is a rather mechanical development of an idea, and yet some device is needed to permit Huck to return to his anonymity, to give up the role of hero, to fall into the background which he prefers, for he is modest in all things and could not well endure the attention and glamour which attend a hero at a book's end. For this purpose nothing could serve better than the mind of Tom Sawyer with its literary furnishings, its conscious romantic desire for experience and the hero's part, and its ingenious schematization of life to achieve that aim.

The form of the book is based on the simplest of all novel-forms, the so-called picaresque novel, or novel of the road, which strings its incidents on the line of the hero's travels. But, as Pascal says, "rivers are roads that move," and the movement of the road in its own mysterious life transmutes the primitive simplicity of the form: The road itself is the greatest character in this novel of the road, and the hero's departures from the river and his returns to it compose a subtle and significant pattern. The linear simplicity of the picaresque novel is further modified by the story's having a clear dramatic organization: It has a beginning, a middle and an end, and a mounting suspense of interest. . . .

T. S. ELIOT

The Boy and the River:
Without Beginning or End

Thomas Stearns Eliot (1888–1965) is one of the most influential figures of twentieth-century English and American literature; he is best known for his achievements in poetry, but he was an important playwright, editor, and literary critic as well. Eliot was born in St. Louis and educated in the East, receiving his B.A. (1909) from Harvard and fulfilling all the requirements for a Ph.D. in philosophy except for the final oral examination — which he never came back from Europe to take. A member of the disillusioned expatriate generation of American writers, Eliot, in his poetry and his criticism, helped to define the literary movement known as Modernism, which sought to find appropriate forms for the expression of feeling and the affirmation of meaning in the fragmented, dissociated, post–World War I West. His most important poems are *The Waste Land* (1922) and *Four Quartets* (1943). His most important critical essays are "Tradition and the Individual Talent" (1920), "Hamlet and His Problems" (1920), and "The Metaphysical Poets" (1921); in these essays, Eliot argued for an anti-Romantic poetry, one that placed less emphasis on the poet's individual expression of feeling and more on the poet's impersonal ability to evoke emotion through poetic imagery — as Eliot suggests Mark Twain did in the image of the Mississippi River. His most important plays are *Murder in the Cathedral* (1935) and *The Cocktail Party* (1950). The 1980s musical *Cats* is based not on any of his plays but on his playful book of poetry *Old Possum's Book of Practical Cats* (1939). As an editor of the quarterly journal *The Criterion* (1922–39) and for Faber and Faber Publishers (from the 1920s until his death), he had additional influence on the modern literary scene. In 1948, he was awarded the Nobel Prize for Literature.

. . . *The Adventures of Huckleberry Finn* is the only one of Mark Twain's various books which can be called a masterpiece. I do not suggest that it is his only book of permanent interest; but it is the only one in which his genius is completely realized, and the only one which creates its own category. There are pages in *Tom Sawyer* and in *Life on the Mississippi* which are, within their limits, as good as anything with which one can compare them in *Huckleberry Finn*; and in other books there are drolleries just as good of their kind. But when we find one book by a prolific author which is very much superior to all the rest, we look for the peculiar accident or concourse of accidents which made that book possible. In the writing of *Huckleberry Finn* Mark Twain had two elements which, when treated with his sensibility and his experience, formed a great book: these two are the Boy and the River. . . .

It is Huck who gives the book style. The River gives the book its form. But for the River, the book might be only a sequence of adventures with a happy ending. . . .

It is the River that controls the voyage of Huck and Jim; that will not let them land at Cairo, where Jim could have reached freedom; it is the River that separates them and deposits Huck for a time in the Grangerford household; the River that re-unites them, and then compels upon them the unwelcome company of the King and the Duke. Recurrently we are reminded of its presence and its power.

> When I woke up I didn't know where I was, for a minute. I set up and looked around, a little scared. Then I remembered. The river looked miles and miles across. The moon was so bright I could a counted the drift logs that went a slipping along, black and still, hundreds of yards out from shore. Everything was dead quiet, and it looked late, and *smelt* late. You know what I mean — I don't know the words to put it in. (p. 58)

> It was kind of solemn, drifting down the big still river, laying on our backs looking up at the stars, and we didn't ever feel like talking loud, and it warn't often that we laughed, only a little kind of a low chuckle. We had mighty good weather, as a general thing, and nothing ever happened to us at all, that night, nor the next, nor the next.
>
> Every night we passed towns, some of them away up on black hillsides, nothing but just a shiny bed of lights, not a house could you see. The fifth night we passed St. Louis, and it was like the whole world lit up. In St. Petersburg they used to say there was twenty or thirty thousand people in St. Louis, but I never believed it till I see that wonderful spread of lights at two o'clock that still night. There warn't a sound there; everybody was asleep. (p. 82)

We come to understand the River by seeing it through the eyes of the Boy; but the Boy is also the spirit of the River. *Huckleberry Finn,* like other great works of imagination, can give to every reader whatever he is capable of taking from it. On the most superficial level of observation, Huck is convincing as a boy. On the same level, the picture of social life on the shores of the Mississippi a hundred years ago is, I feel sure, accurate. On any level, Mark Twain makes you see the River, as it is and was and always will be, more clearly than the author of any other description of a river known to me. But you do not merely see the River, you do not merely become acquainted with it through the senses: you experience the River. Mark Twain, in his later years of success and fame, referred to his early life as a steamboat pilot as the happiest he had known. With all allowance for the illusions of age, we can agree that those years were the years in which he was most fully alive. Certainly, but for his having practiced that calling, earned his living by that profession, he would never have gained the understanding which his genius for expression communicates in this book. In the pilot's daily struggle with the River, in the satisfaction of activity, in the constant attention to the River's unpredictable vagaries, his consciousness was fully occupied, and he absorbed knowledge of which, as an artist, he later made use. There are, perhaps, only two ways in which a writer can acquire the understanding of environment which he can later turn to account: by having spent his childhood in that environment — that is, living in it at a period of life in which one experiences much more than one is aware of; and by having had to struggle for a livelihood in that environment — a livelihood bearing no direct relation to any intention of writing about it, of *using* it as literary material. Most of Joseph Conrad's understanding came to him in the latter way. Mark Twain knew the Mississippi in both ways: He had spent his childhood on its banks, and he had earned his living matching his wits against its currents.

Thus the River makes the book a great book. As with Conrad, we are continually reminded of the power and terror of Nature, and the isolation and feebleness of Man. Conrad remains always the European observer of the tropics, the white man's eye contemplating the Congo and its black gods. But Mark Twain is a native, and the River God is his God. It is as a native that he accepts the River God, and it is the subjection of Man that gives to Man his dignity. For without some kind of God, Man is not even very interesting.

Readers sometimes deplore the fact that the story descends to the level of *Tom Sawyer* from the moment that Tom himself re-appears.

Such readers protest that the escapades invented by Tom, in the attempted "rescue" of Jim, are only a tedious development of themes with which we were already too familiar — even while admitting that the escapades themselves are very amusing, and some of the incidental observations memorable.[1] But it is right that the mood of the end of the book should bring us back to that of the beginning. Or, if this was not the right ending for the book, what ending would have been right?

In *Huckleberry Finn* Mark Twain wrote a much greater book than he could have known he was writing. Perhaps all great works of art mean much more than the author could have been aware of meaning: Certainly, *Huckleberry Finn* is one book of Mark Twain's which, as a whole, has this unconsciousness. So what seems to be the rightness, of reverting at the end of the book to the mood of *Tom Sawyer,* was perhaps unconscious art. For Huckleberry Finn, neither a tragic nor a happy ending would be suitable. No worldly success or social satisfaction, no domestic consummation would be worthy of him; a tragic end also would reduce him to the level of those whom we pity. Huck Finn must come from nowhere and be bound for nowhere. His is not the independence of the typical or symbolic American Pioneer, but the independence of the vagabond. His existence questions the values of America as much as the values of Europe; he is as much an affront to the "pioneer spirit" as he is to "business enterprise"; he is in a state of nature as detached as the state of the saint. In a busy world, he represents the loafer; in an acquisitive and competitive world, he insists on living from hand to mouth. He could not be exhibited in any amorous encounters or engagements, in any of the juvenile affections which are appropriate to Tom Sawyer. He belongs neither to the Sunday School nor to the Reformatory. He has no beginning and no end. Hence, he can only disappear; and his disappearance can only be accomplished by bringing forward another performer to obscure the disappearance in a cloud of whimsicalities.

Like Huckleberry Finn, the River itself has no beginning or end. In its beginning, it is not yet the River; in its end, it is no longer the River. What we call its headwaters is only a selection from among the innumerable sources which flow together to compose it. At what point in its course does the Mississippi become what the Mississippi *means*? It is both one and many; it is the Mississippi of this book only after its union with the Big Muddy — the Missouri; it derives some of its character from the Ohio, the Tennessee, and other confluents. And at the end it

[1]E.g., "*Jim* don't know nobody in China" (p. 225).

merely disappears among its deltas: It is no longer there, but i
where it was, hundreds of miles to the North. The River cannot ιoιerate
any design, to a story which is its story, that might interfere with its
dominance. Things must merely happen, here and there, to the people
who live along its shores or who commit themselves to its current. And
it is as impossible for Huck as for the River to have a beginning or
end — a *career.* So the book has the right, the only possible concluding
sentence. I do not think that any book ever written ends more certainly
with the right words:

> But I reckon I got to light out for the Territory ahead of the rest,
> because Aunt Sally she's going to adopt me and sivilize me, and I
> can't stand it. I been there before. (p. 263)

LEO MARX

Mr. Eliot, Mr. Trilling, and *Huckleberry Finn*

Leo Marx (b. 1919) is professor emeritus of American cultural
history in the Program in Science, Technology, and Society at
the Massachusetts Institute of Technology. After receiving
his B.S. (1941) and Ph.D. (1950) from Harvard University, he
began his teaching career at the University of Minnesota–Twin
Cities (1949–58). In 1958, Marx moved to Amherst College,
where he remained until 1976, when he accepted a position
at MIT. With the publication of *The Machine in the Garden*
(1964), Marx established himself as one of the leading critics
of American literature and culture. His other books include *The
Pilot and the Passenger: Essays on Literature, Technology, and
Culture in the United States* (1987), *The Railroad in American
Art* (ed., 1987), *Does Technology Drive History?: The Dilemma
of Technological Determinism* (ed., 1994), and *Progress: Fact or
Illusion* (ed., 1996). In 2002, in recognition of Marx's lifetime
contributions to the history of technology, the Society for the
History of Technology awarded him the Leonardo da Vinci
Award. This essay was first published in 1953 in *The American
Scholar.*

In the losing battle that the plot fights with the characters, it often takes a cowardly revenge. Nearly all novels are feeble at the end. This is because the plot requires to be wound up. Why is this necessary? Why is there not a convention which allows a novelist to stop as soon as he feels muddled or bored? Alas, he has to round things off, and usually the characters go dead while he is at work, and our final impression of them is thorough deadness.

–E. M. Forster

The Adventures of Huckleberry Finn has not always occupied its present high place in the canon of American literature. When it was first published in 1885, the book disturbed and offended many reviewers, particularly spokesmen for the genteel tradition.[1] In fact, a fairly accurate inventory of the narrow standards of such critics might be made simply by listing epithets they applied to Clemens's novel. They called it vulgar, rough, inelegant, irreverent, coarse, semi-obscene, trashy, and vicious.[2] So much for them. Today (we like to think) we know the true worth of the book. Everyone agrees that Huckleberry Finn is a masterpiece: It is probably the one book in our literature about which highbrows and lowbrows can agree. Our most serious critics praise it. Nevertheless, a close look at what two of the best among them have recently written will likewise reveal, I believe, serious weaknesses in current criticism. Today the problem of evaluating the book is as much obscured by unqualified praise as it once was by parochial hostility.

I have in mind essays by Lionel Trilling and T. S. Eliot.[3] Both praise the book, but in praising it both feel obligated to say something in justification of what so many readers have felt to be its great flaw: the dis-

---

[1] I use the term "genteel tradition" as George Santayana characterized it in his famous address "The Genteel Tradition in American Philosophy," first delivered in 1911 and published the following year in his Winds of Doctrine. Santayana described the genteel tradition as an "old mentality" inherited from Europe. It consists of the various dilutions of Christian theology and morality, as in transcendentalism — a fastidious and stale philosophy of life no longer relevant to the thought and activities of the United States. "America," he said, "is a young country with an old mentality." (Later references to Santayana also refer to this essay.)

[2] For an account of the first reviews, see A. L. Vogelback, "The Publication and Reception of Huckleberry Finn in America," American Literature 11 (November 1939), pp. 160–272.

[3] Mr. Eliot's essay is the introduction to the edition of Huckleberry Finn published by Chanticleer Press, New York, 1950. Mr. Trilling's is in the introduction to an edition of the novel published by Rinehart, New York, 1948, and later reprinted in his The Liberal Imagination, Viking, New York, 1950.

appointing "ending," the episode which begins when Huck arrives at the Phelps place and Tom Sawyer reappears. There are good reasons why Mr. Trilling and Mr. Eliot should feel the need to face this issue. From the point of view of scope alone, more is involved than the mere "ending"; the episode comprises almost one-fifth of the text. The problem, in any case, is unavoidable. I have discussed *Huckleberry Finn* in courses with hundreds of college students, and I have found only a handful who did not confess their dissatisfaction with the extravagant mock rescue of Nigger Jim and the denouement itself. The same question always comes up: "What went wrong with Twain's novel?" Even Bernard De Voto, whose whole-hearted commitment to Clemens's genius is well known, has said of the ending that "in the whole reach of the English novel there is no more abrupt or more chilling descent."[4] Mr. Trilling and Mr. Eliot do not agree. They both attempt, and on similar grounds, to explain and defend the conclusion.

Of the two, Mr. Trilling makes the more moderate claim for Clemens's novel. He does admit that there is a "falling-off" at the end; nevertheless he supports the episode as having "a certain formal aptness." Mr. Eliot's approval is without serious qualification. He allows no objections, asserts that "it is right that the mood of the end of the book should bring us back to the beginning." I mean later to discuss their views in some detail, but here it is only necessary to note that both critics see the problem as one of form. And so it is. Like many questions of form in literature, however, this one is not finally separable from a question of "content," of value, or, if you will, of moral insight. To bring *Huckleberry Finn* to a satisfactory close, Clemens had to do more than find a neat device for ending a story. His problem, though it may never have occurred to him, was to invent an action capable of placing in focus the meaning of the journey down the Mississippi.

I believe that the ending of *Huckleberry Finn* makes so many readers uneasy because they rightly sense that it jeopardizes the significance of the entire novel. To take seriously what happens at the Phelps farm is to take lightly the entire downstream journey. What is the meaning of the journey? With this question all discussion of *Huckleberry Finn* must begin. It is true that the voyage down the river has many aspects of a boy's idyl. We owe much of its hold upon our imagination to the enchanting image of the raft's unhurried drift with the current. The leisure, the absence of constraint, the beauty of the river — all these

---

[4] *Mark Twain at Work* (Cambridge, 1942), p. 92.

things delight us. "It's lovely to live on a raft." And the multitudinous life of the great valley we see through Huck's eyes has a fascination of its own. Then, of course, there is humor — laughter so spontaneous, so free of the bitterness present almost everywhere in American humor that readers often forget how grim a spectacle of human existence Huck contemplates. Humor in this novel flows from a bright joy of life as remote from our world as living on a raft.

Yet along with the idyllic and the epical and the funny in *Huckleberry Finn,* there is a coil of meaning which does for the disparate elements of the novel what a spring does for a watch. The meaning is not in the least obscure. It is made explicit again and again. The very words with which Clemens launches Huck and Jim upon their voyage indicate that theirs is not a boy's lark but a quest for freedom. From the electrifying moment when Huck comes back to Jackson's Island and rouses Jim with the news that a search party is on the way, we are meant to believe that Huck is enlisted in the cause of freedom. "Git up and hump yourself, Jim!" he cries. "There ain't a minute to lose. They're after us!" What particularly counts here is the *us.* No one is after Huck; no one but Jim knows he is alive. In that small word Clemens compresses the exhilarating power of Huck's instinctive humanity. His unpremeditated identification with Jim's flight from slavery is an unforgettable moment in American experience, and it may be said at once that any culmination of the journey which detracts from the urgency and dignity with which it begins will necessarily be unsatisfactory. Huck realizes this himself, and says so when, much later, he comes back to the raft after discovering that the Duke and the King have sold Jim:

> After all this long journey . . . here was it all come to nothing, everything all busted up and ruined, because they could have the heart to serve Jim such a trick as that, and make him a slave again all his life, and amongst strangers, too, for forty dirty dollars. (p. 199)

Huck knows that the journey will have been a failure unless it takes Jim to freedom. It is true that we do discover, in the end, that Jim is free, but we also find out that the journey was not the means by which he finally reached freedom.

The most obvious thing wrong with the ending, then, is the flimsy contrivance by which Clemens frees Jim. In the end we not only discover that Jim has been a free man for two months, but that his freedom has been granted by old Miss Watson. If this were only a mechanical device for terminating the action, it might not call for much comment. But it is more than that: It is a significant clue to the import of the last ten chapters. Remember who Miss Watson is. She is the Widow's sister whom Huck introduces in the first pages of the novel. It is she who keeps "pecking" at Huck, who tries to teach him to spell and to pray and to keep his feet off the furniture. She is an ardent proselytizer for piety and good manners, and her greed provides the occasion for the journey in the first place. She is Jim's owner, and he decides to flee only when he realizes that she is about to break her word (she can't resist a slave trader's offer of eight hundred dollars) and sell him down the river away from his family.

Miss Watson, in short, is the Enemy. If we except a predilection for physical violence, she exhibits all the outstanding traits of the valley society. She pronounces the polite lies of civilization that suffocate Huck's spirit. The freedom which Jim seeks, and which Huck and Jim temporarily enjoy aboard the raft, is accordingly freedom *from* everything for which Miss Watson stands. Indeed, the very intensity of the novel derives from the discordance between the aspirations of the fugitives and the respectable code for which she is a spokesman. Therefore, her regeneration, of which the deathbed freeing of Jim is the unconvincing sign, hints a resolution of the novel's essential conflict. Perhaps because this device most transparently reveals that shift in point of view which he could not avoid, and which is less easily discerned elsewhere in the concluding chapters, Clemens plays it down. He makes little attempt to account for Miss Watson's change of heart, a change particularly surprising in view of Jim's brazen escape. Had Clemens given this episode dramatic emphasis appropriate to its function, Miss Watson's bestowal of freedom upon Jim would have proclaimed what the rest of the ending actually accomplishes — a vindication of persons and attitudes Huck and Jim had symbolically repudiated when they set forth downstream.

It may be said, and with some justice, that a reading of the ending as a virtual reversal of meanings implicit in the rest of the novel misses the point — that I have taken the final episode too seriously. I agree that Clemens certainly did not intend us to read it so solemnly. The ending, one might contend, is simply a burlesque upon Tom's taste for literary romance. Surely the tone of the episode is familiar to readers of Mark Twain. The preposterous monkey business attendant upon Jim's "rescue," the careless improvisation, the nonchalant disregard for commonsense plausibility — all these things should not surprise readers of Twain or any low comedy in the tradition of "Western humor."

However, the trouble is, first, that the ending hardly comes off as burlesque: it is *too* fanciful, *too* extravagant; and it is tedious. For example,
to provide a "gaudy" atmosphere for the escape, Huck and Tom catch a
couple of dozen snakes. Then the snakes escape.

> No, there warn't no real scarcity of snakes about the house for a
> considerble spell. You'd see them dripping from the rafters and
> places, every now and then; and they generly landed in your plate,
> or down the back of your neck. . . . (p. 241)

Even if this were good burlesque, which it is not, what is it doing here?
It is out of keeping; the slapstick tone jars with the underlying seriousness of the voyage.

   Huckleberry Finn is a masterpiece because it brings Western humor
to perfection and yet transcends the narrow limits of its conventions.
But the ending does not. During the final extravaganza we are forced to
put aside many of the mature emotions evoked earlier by the vivid rendering of Jim's fear of capture, the tenderness of Huck's and Jim's
regard for each other, and Huck's excruciating moments of wavering
between honesty and respectability. None of these emotions are called
forth by the anticlimactic final sequence. I do not mean to suggest that
the inclusion of low comedy per se is a flaw in *Huckleberry Finn*. One
does not object to the shenanigans of the rogues; there is ample prece-
dent for the place of extravagant humor even in the works of high seriousness. But here the case differs from most which come to mind: The
major characters themselves are forced to play low comedy roles. Moreover, the most serious motive in the novel, Jim's yearning for freedom,
is made the object of nonsense. The conclusion, in short, is farce, but
the rest of the novel is not.

   That Clemens reverts in the end to the conventional manner of
Western low comedy is most evident in what happens to the principals.
Huck and Jim become comic characters; that is a much more serious
ground for dissatisfaction than the unexplained regeneration of Miss
Watson. Remember that Huck has grown in stature throughout the
journey. By the time he arrives at the Phelps place, he is not the boy
who had been playing robbers with Tom's gang in St. Petersburg the
summer before. All he has seen and felt since he parted from Tom has
deepened his knowledge of human nature and of himself. Clemens
makes a point of Huck's development in two scenes which occur just
before he meets Tom again. The first describes Huck's final capitulation
to his own sense of right and wrong: "All right, then, I'll *go* to hell."

This is the climactic moment in the ripening of his self-knowledge. Shortly afterward, when he comes upon a mob riding the Duke and the King out of town on a rail, we are given his most memorable insight into the nature of man. Although these rogues had subjected Huck to every indignity, what he sees provokes this celebrated comment:

> Well, it made me sick to see it; and I was sorry for them poor pitiful rascals, it seemed like I couldn't ever feel any hardness against them any more in the world. It was a dreadful thing to see. Human beings *can* be awful cruel to one another. (p. 214)

The sign of Huck's maturity here is neither the compassion nor the skepticism, for both had been marks of his personality from the first. Rather, the special quality of these reflections is the extraordinary combination of the two, a mature blending of his instinctive suspicion of human motives with his capacity for pity.

But at this point Tom reappears. Soon Huck has fallen almost completely under his sway once more, and we are asked to believe that the boy who felt pity for the rogues is now capable of making Jim's capture the occasion for a game. He becomes Tom's helpless accomplice, submissive and gullible. No wonder that Clemens has Huck remark, when Huck first realizes Aunt Sally has mistaken him for Tom, that "it was like being born again." Exactly. In the end, Huck regresses to the subordinate role in which he had first appeared in *The Adventures of Tom Sawyer*. Most of those traits which made him so appealing a hero now disappear. He had never, for example, found pain or misfortune amusing. At the circus, when a clown disguised as a drunk took a precarious ride on a prancing horse, the crowd loved the excitement and danger: "It warn't funny to me, though," said Huck. But now, in the end, he submits in awe to Tom's notion of what is amusing. To satisfy Tom's hunger for adventure he makes himself a party to sport which aggravates Jim's misery.

It should be added at once that Jim doesn't mind too much. The fact is that he has undergone a similar transformation. On the raft he was an individual, man enough to denounce Huck when Huck made him the victim of a practical joke. In the closing episode, however, we lose sight of Jim in the maze of farcical invention. He ceases to be a man. He allows Huck and "Mars Tom" to fill his hut with rats and snakes, "and every time a rat bit Jim he would get up and write a line in his journal whilst the ink was fresh." This creature who bleeds ink and feels no pain is something less than human. He has been made over in the image of a flat stereotype: the submissive stage-Negro. These antics divest Jim, as well as Huck, of much of his dignity and individuality.[5]

What I have been saying is that the flimsy devices of plot, the discordant farcical tone, and the disintegration of the major characters all betray the failure of the ending. These are not aspects merely of form in a technical sense, but of meaning. For that matter, I would maintain that this book has little or no formal unity independent of the joint purpose of Huck and Jim. What components of the novel, we may ask, provide the continuity which links one adventure with another? The most important is the unifying consciousness of Huck, the narrator, and the fact that we follow the same principals through the entire string of adventures. Events, moreover, occur in a temporal sequence. Then there is the river; after each adventure Huck and Jim return to the raft and the river. Both Mr. Trilling and Mr. Eliot speak eloquently of the river as a source of unity, and they refer to the river as a god. Mr. Trilling says that Huck is "the servant of the river-god." Mr. Eliot puts it this way: "The River gives the book its form. But for the River, the book might be only a sequence of adventures with a happy ending." This seems to me an extravagant view of the function of the neutral agency of the river. Clemens had a knowledgeable respect for the Mississippi, and, without sanctifying it, was able to provide excellent reasons for Huck's and Jim's intense relation with it. It is a source of food and beauty and terror and serenity of mind. But above all, it provides motion; it is the means by which Huck and Jim move away from a menacing civilization. They return to the river to continue their journey. The river cannot, does not, supply purpose. That purpose is a facet of their consciousness, and without the motive of escape from society, *Huckleberry Finn* would indeed "be only a sequence of adventures." Mr. Eliot's remark indicates how lightly he takes the quest for freedom. His somewhat fanciful exaggeration of the river's role is of a piece with his neglect of the theme at the novel's center.

That theme is heightened by the juxtaposition of sharp images of contrasting social orders: the microcosmic community Huck and Jim establish aboard the raft and the actual society which exists along the Mississippi's banks. The two are separated by the river, the road to freedom upon which Huck and Jim must travel. Huck tells us what the

---

[5]For these observations on the transformation of Jim in the closing episodes, I am indebted to the excellent unpublished essay by Mr. Chadwick Hansen on the subject of Clemens and Western humor.

river means to them when, after the Wilks episode, he and Jim once again shove their raft into the current: "It *did* seem so good to be free again and all by ourselves on the big river, and nobody to bother us." The river is indifferent. But its sphere is relatively uncontaminated by the civilization they flee, and so the river allows Huck and Jim some measure of freedom at once, the moment they set foot on Jackson's Island or the raft. Only on the island and the raft do they have a chance to practice that idea of brotherhood to which they are devoted. "Other places do seem so cramped and smothery," Huck explains, "but a raft don't. You feel mighty free and easy and comfortable on a raft." The main thing is freedom.

On the raft the escaped slave and the white boy try to practice their code: "What you want, above all things, on a raft, is for everybody to be satisfied, and feel right and kind towards the others." This human credo constitutes the paramount affirmation of *The Adventures of Huckleberry Finn,* and it obliquely aims a devastating criticism at the existing social order. It is a creed which Huck and Jim bring to the river. It neither emanates from nature nor is it addressed to nature. Therefore I do not see that it means much to talk about the river as a god in this novel. The river's connection with this high aspiration for man is that it provides a means of escape, a place where the code can be tested. The truly profound meanings of the novel are generated by the impingement of the actual world of slavery, feuds, lynching, murder, and a spurious Christian morality upon the ideal of the raft. The result is a tension which somehow demands release in the novel's ending.

But Clemens was unable to effect this release and at the same time control the central theme. The unhappy truth about the ending of *Huckleberry Finn* is that the author, having revealed the tawdry nature of the culture of the great valley, yielded to its essential complacency. The general tenor of the closing scenes, to which the token regeneration of Miss Watson is merely one superficial clue, amounts to just that. In fact, this entire reading of *Huckleberry Finn* merely confirms the brilliant insight of George Santayana, who many years ago spoke of American humorists, of whom he considered Mark Twain an outstanding representative, as having only "half escaped" the genteel tradition. Santayana meant that men like Clemens were able to "point to what contradicts it in the facts; but not in order to abandon the genteel tradition, for they have nothing solid to put in its place." This seems to me the real key to the failure of *Huckleberry Finn.* Clemens had presented the contrast between the two social orders but could not, or would not, accept the tragic fact that the one he had rejected was an image of solid reality and the other an ecstatic dream. Instead he gives us the cozy reunion with Aunt Polly in a scene fairly bursting with approbation of the entire family, the Phelpses included.

Like Miss Watson, the Phelpses are almost perfect specimens of the dominant culture. They are kind to their friends and relatives; they have no taste for violence; they are people capable of devoting themselves to their spectacular dinners while they keep Jim locked in the little hut down by the ash hopper, with its lone window boarded up. (Of course Aunt Sally visits Jim to see if he is "comfortable," and Uncle Silas comes in "to pray with him.") These people, with their comfortable Sunday-dinner conviviality and the runaway slave padlocked nearby, are reminiscent of those solid German citizens we have heard about in our time who tried to maintain a similarly *gemütlich* way of life within virtual earshot of Buchenwald. I do not mean to imply that Clemens was unaware of the shabby morality of such people. After the abortive escape of Jim, when Tom asks about him, Aunt Sally replies: "Him? . . . the runaway nigger? . . . They've got him back, safe and sound, and he's in the cabin again, on bread and water, and loaded down with chains, till he's claimed or sold!" Clemens understood people like the Phelpses, but nevertheless he was forced to rely upon them to provide his happy ending. The satisfactory outcome of Jim's quest for freedom must be attributed to the benevolence of the very people whose inhumanity first made it necessary.

But to return to the contention of Mr. Trilling and Mr. Eliot that the ending is more or less satisfactory after all. As I have said, Mr. Trilling approves of the "formal aptness" of the conclusion. He says that "some device is needed to permit Huck to return to his anonymity, to give up the role of hero," and that therefore "nothing could serve better than the mind of Tom Sawyer with its literary furnishings, its conscious romantic desire for experience and the hero's part, and its ingenious schematization of life. . . ." Though more detailed, this is essentially akin to Mr. Eliot's blunt assertion that "it is right that the mood at the end of the book should bring us back to that of the beginning." I submit that it is wrong for the end of the book to bring us back to that mood. The mood of the beginning of *Huckleberry Finn* is the mood of Huck's attempt to accommodate himself to the ways of St. Petersburg. It is the mood of the end of *The Adventures of Tom Sawyer,* when the boys had been acclaimed heroes, and when Huck was accepted as a candidate for respectability. That is the state in which we find him at the beginning of *Huckleberry Finn.* But Huck cannot stand the new way of life, and his mood gradually shifts to the mood of rebellion which dominated the novel until he meets Tom again. At first, in the second chapter, we see him still eager to be accepted by the nice boys of the town. Tom leads the gang in re-enacting adventures he has culled from books, but gradually Huck's pragmatic turn of mind gets him in trouble. He has little tolerance for Tom's brand of make-believe. He irritates Tom. Tom calls him a "numbskull," and finally Huck throws up the whole business:

> So then I judged that all that stuff was only just one of Tom Sawyer's lies. I reckoned he believed in the A-rabs and the elephants, but as for me I think different. It had all the marks of a Sunday school. (pp. 42–43)

With this statement, which ends the third chapter, Huck parts company with Tom. The fact is that Huck has rejected Tom's romanticizing of experience; moreover, he has rejected it as part of the larger pattern of society's make-believe, typified by Sunday school. But if he cannot accept Tom's harmless fantasies about the A-rabs, how are we to believe that a year later Huck is capable of awe-struck submission to the far more extravagant fantasies with which Tom invests the mock rescue of Jim?

After Huck's escape from his "pap," the drift of the action, like that of the Mississippi's current, is *away* from St. Petersburg. Huck leaves Tom and the A-rabs behind, along with the Widow, Miss Watson, and all the pseudoreligious ritual in which nice boys must partake. The return, in the end, to the mood of the beginning therefore means defeat — Huck's defeat; to return to that mood *joyously* is to portray defeat in the guise of victory.

Mr. Eliot and Mr. Trilling deny this. The overriding consideration for them is form — form which seems largely to mean symmetry of structure. It is fitting, Mr. Eliot maintains, that the book should come full circle and bring Huck once more under Tom's sway. Why? Because it begins that way. But it seems to me that such structural unity is *imposed* upon the novel, and therefore is meretricious. It is a jerry-built structure, achieved only by sacrifice of characters and theme. Here the controlling principle of form apparently is unity, but unfortunately a unity much too superficially conceived. Structure, after all, is only one element — indeed, one of the more mechanical elements — of unity. A unified work must surely manifest coherence of meaning and clear development of theme, yet the ending of *Huckleberry Finn* blurs both.

The eagerness of Mr. Eliot and Mr. Trilling to justify the ending is symptomatic of that absolutist impulse of our critics to find reasons, once a work has been admitted to the highest canon of literary reputability, for admiring every bit of it.

What is perhaps most striking about these judgments of Mr. Eliot's and Mr. Trilling's is that they are so patently out of harmony with the basic standards of both critics. For one thing, both men hold far more complex ideas of the nature of literary unity than their comments upon *Huckleberry Finn* would suggest. For another, both critics are essentially moralists, yet here we find them turning away from a moral issue in order to praise a dubious structural unity. Their efforts to explain away the flaw in Clemens's novel suffer from a certain narrowness surprising to anyone who knows their work. These facts suggest that we may be in the presence of a tendency in contemporary criticism which the critics themselves do not fully recognize.

Is there an explanation? How does it happen that two of our most respected critics should seem to treat so lightly the glaring lapse of moral imagination in *Huckleberry Finn*? Perhaps — and I stress the conjectural nature of what I am saying — perhaps the kind of moral issue raised by *Huckleberry Finn* is not the kind of moral issue to which today's criticism readily addresses itself. Today our critics, no less than our novelists and poets, are most sensitively attuned to moral problems which arise in the sphere of individual behavior. They are deeply aware of sin, of individual infractions of our culture's Christian ethic. But my impression is that they are, possibly because of the strength of the reaction against the mechanical sociological criticism of the thirties, less sensitive to questions of what might be called social or political morality.

By social or political morality I refer to the values implicit in a social system, values which may be quite distinct from the personal morality of any given individual within the society. Now *The Adventures of Huckleberry Finn*, like all novels, deals with the behavior of individuals. But one mark of Clemens's greatness is his deft presentation of the disparity between what people do when they behave as individuals and what they do when forced into roles imposed upon them by society. Take, for example, Aunt Sally and Uncle Silas Phelps, who consider themselves Christians, who are by impulse generous and humane, but who happen also to be staunch upholders of certain degrading and inhuman social institutions. When they are confronted with an escaped slave, the imperatives of social morality outweigh all pious professions.

The conflict between what people think they stand for and what social pressure forces them to do is central to the novel. It is present to the mind of Huck and, indeed, accounts for his most serious inner conflicts. He knows how he feels about Jim, but he also knows what he is expected to do about Jim. This division within his mind corresponds to the division of the novel's moral terrain into the areas represented by the raft on the one hand and society on the other. His victory over his "yaller dog" conscience therefore assumes heroic size: It is a victory over the prevailing morality. But the last fifth of the novel has the effect of diminishing that importance and uniqueness of Huck's victory. We are asked to assume that somehow freedom can be achieved in spite of the crippling power of what I have called the social morality. Consequently the less importance we attach to that force as it operates in the novel, the more acceptable the ending becomes.

Moreover, the idea of freedom, which Mr. Eliot and Mr. Trilling seem to slight, takes on its full significance only when we acknowledge the power which society exerts over the minds of men in the world of *Huckleberry Finn*. For freedom in this book specifically means freedom from society and its imperatives. This is not the traditional Christian conception of freedom. Huck and Jim seek freedom not from a burden of individual guilt and sin, but from social constraint. That is to say, evil in *Huckleberry Finn* is the product of civilization, and if this is indicative of Clemens's rather too simple view of human nature, nevertheless the fact is that Huck, when he can divest himself of the taint of social conditioning (as in the incantatory account of sunrise on the river), is entirely free of anxiety and guilt. The only guilt he actually knows arises from infractions of a social code. (The guilt he feels after playing the prank on Jim stems from his betrayal of the law of the raft.) Huck's and Jim's creed is secular. Its object is harmony among men, and so Huck is not much concerned with his own salvation. He repeatedly renounces prayer in favor of pragmatic solutions to his problems. In other words, the central insights of the novel belong to the tradition of the Enlightenment. The meaning of the quest itself is hardly reconcilable with that conception of human nature embodied in the myth of original sin. In view of the current fashion of reaffirming man's innate depravity, it is perhaps not surprising to find the virtues of *Huckleberry Finn* attributed not to its meaning but to its form.

But "if this was not the right ending for the book," Mr. Eliot asks, "what ending would have been right?" Although this question places the critic in an awkward position (he is not always equipped to rewrite what he criticizes), there are some things which may justifiably be said about the "right" ending of *Huckleberry Finn*. It may be legitimate, even if presumptuous, to indicate certain conditions which a hypothetical ending would have to satisfy if it were to be congruent with the rest of the novel. If the conclusion is not to be something merely tacked on to close the action, then its broad outline must be immanent in the body of the work.

It is surely reasonable to ask that the conclusion provide a plausible outcome to the quest. Yet freedom, in the ecstatic sense that Huck and Jim knew it aboard the raft, was hardly to be had in the Mississippi Valley in the 1840s, or, for that matter, in any other known human society. A satisfactory ending would inevitably cause the reader some frustration. That Clemens felt such disappointment to be inevitable is borne out by an examination of the novel's clear, if unconscious, symbolic pattern. Consider, for instance, the inferences to be drawn from the book's geography. The river, to whose current Huck and Jim entrust themselves, actually carries them to the heart of slave territory. Once the raft passes Cairo, the quest is virtually doomed. Until the steamboat smashes the raft, we are kept in a state of anxiety about Jim's escape. (It may be significant that at this point Clemens found himself unable to continue work on the manuscript, and put it aside for several years.) Beyond Cairo, Clemens allows the intensity of that anxiety to diminish, and it is probably no accident that the fainter it becomes, the more he falls back upon the devices of low comedy. Huck and Jim make no serious effort to turn north, and there are times (during the Wilks episode) when Clemens allows Huck to forget all about Jim. It is as if the author, anticipating the dilemma he had finally to face, instinctively dissipated the power of his major theme.

Consider, too, the circumscribed nature of the raft as a means of moving toward freedom. The raft lacks power and maneuverability. It can only move easily with the current — southward into slave country. Nor can it evade the mechanized power of the steamboat. These impotencies of the raft correspond to the innocent helplessness of its occupants. Unresisted, the rogues invade and take over the raft. Though it is the symbolic locus of the novel's central affirmations, the raft provides an uncertain and indeed precarious mode of traveling toward freedom. This seems another confirmation of Santayana's perception. To say that Clemens only half escaped the genteel tradition is not to say that he failed to note any of the creed's inadequacies, but rather that he had "nothing solid" to put in its place. The raft patently was not capable of carrying the burden of hope Clemens placed upon it.[6] (Whether this is to be attributed to the nature of his vision or to the actual state of American society in the nineteenth century is another interesting question.) In any case, the geography of the novel, the raft's powerlessness, the goodness and vulnerability of Huck and Jim, all prefigure a conclusion quite different in tone from that which Clemens gave us. These facts constitute what Hart Crane might have called the novel's "logic of metaphor," and this logic — probably inadvertent — actually takes us to the underlying meaning of *The Adventures of Huckleberry Finn*. Through the symbols we reach a truth which the ending obscures: The quest cannot succeed.

Fortunately, Clemens broke through to this truth in the novel's last sentences:

> But I reckon I got to light out for the territory ahead of the rest, because Aunt Sally she's going to adopt me and sivilize me, and I can't stand it. I been there before. (p. 263)

Mr. Eliot properly praises this as "the only possible concluding sentence." But one sentence can hardly be advanced, as Mr. Eliot advances this one, to support the rightness of ten chapters. Moreover, if this sentence is right, then the rest of the conclusion is wrong, for its meaning clashes with that of the final burlesque. Huck's decision to go west ahead of the inescapable advance of civilization is a confession of defeat. It means that the raft is to be abandoned. On the other hand, the jubilation of the family reunion and the proclaiming of Jim's freedom create a quite different mood. The tone, except for these last words, is one of unclouded success. I believe this is the source of the almost universal dissatisfaction with the conclusion. One can hardly forget that a bloody civil war did not resolve the issue.

Should Clemens have made Huck a tragic hero? Both Mr. Eliot and Mr. Trilling argue that that would have been a mistake, and they are very probably correct. But between the ending as we have it and tragedy in

---

[6]Gladys Bellamy (*Mark Twain as a Literary Artist,* Norman, Oklahoma, 1950, p. 221) has noted the insubstantial, dreamlike quality of the image of the raft. Clemens thus discusses travel by a raft in *A Tramp Abroad:* "The motion of the raft is . . . gentle, and gliding, and smooth, and noiseless; it calms down all feverish activities, it soothes to sleep all nervous . . . impatience; under its restful influence all the troubles and vexations and sorrows that harass the mind vanish away, and existence becomes a dream . . . a deep and tranquil ecstasy."

the fullest sense, there was vast room for invention. Clemens might have contrived an action which left Jim's fate as much in doubt as Huck's. Such an ending would have allowed us to assume that the principals were defeated but alive, and the quest unsuccessful but not abandoned. This, after all, would have been consonant with the symbols, the characters, and the theme as Clemens had created them — and with history.

Clemens did not acknowledge the truth his novel contained. He had taken hold of a situation in which a partial defeat was inevitable, but he was unable to — or unaware of the need to — give imaginative substance to that fact. If an illusion of success was indispensable, where was it to come from? Obviously, Huck and Jim could not succeed by their own efforts. At this point Clemens, having only half escaped the genteel tradition, one of whose preeminent characteristics was an optimism undaunted by disheartening truth, returned to it. *Why* he did so is another story, having to do with his parents and his boyhood, with his own personality and his wife's, and especially with the character of his audience. But whatever the explanation, the fainthearted ending of *The Adventures of Huckleberry Finn* remains an important datum in the record of American thought and imagination. It has been noted before, both by critics and nonprofessional readers. It should not be forgotten now.

To minimize the seriousness of what must be accounted a major flaw in so great a work is, in a sense, to repeat Clemens's failure of nerve. This is a disservice to criticism. Today we particularly need a criticism alert to lapses of moral vision. A measured appraisal of the failures and successes of our writers, past and present, can show us a great deal about literature and about ourselves. That is the critic's function. But he cannot perform that function if he substitutes considerations of technique for considerations of truth. Not only will such methods lead to errors of literary judgment, but beyond that, they may well encourage comparable evasions in other areas. It seems not unlikely, for instance, that the current preoccupation with matters of form is bound up with a tendency, by no means confined to literary quarters, to shy away from painful answers to complex questions of political morality. The conclusion to *The Adventures of Huckleberry Finn* shielded both Clemens and his audience from such an answer. But we ought not to be as tender-minded. For Huck Finn's besetting problem, the disparity between his best impulses and the behavior the community attempted to impose upon him, is as surely ours as it was Twain's.

TONI MORRISON

Jim's Africanist Presence in *Huckleberry Finn*

Toni Morrison (b. 1931) received the 1993 Nobel Prize for Literature and is currently the Robert F. Goheen Professor of Humanities at Princeton University. Born in Lorain, Ohio, Morrison attended Howard University and received her M.A. (1955) in English from Cornell University. After teaching at Texas Southern University and then at Howard University, Morrison worked during the 1960s as an editor for the publishing company Random House. She is the author of numerous novels, including *The Bluest Eye* (1970), *Sula* (1974), *Tar Baby* (1981), *Jazz* (1991), and *Paradise* (1998). Morrison's third novel, *Song of Solomon* (1977), won the National Book Critics Circle Award, and her fifth novel, *Beloved* (1987), won the Pulitzer Prize. Morrison has coedited a collection of essays on the Senate hearings regarding Clarence Thomas's appointment as a Supreme Court justice, *Race-ing Justice, Engendering Power.* In 1990 she delivered the Massey Lectures in the History of American Civilization at Princeton, out of which developed a book on race in American literature, *Playing in the Dark: Whiteness and the Literary Imagination* (1991), from which the following excerpt is taken.

. . . There seems to be a more or less tacit agreement among literary scholars that, because American literature has been clearly the preserve of white male views, genius, and power, those views, genius, and power are without relationship to and removed from the overwhelming presence of black people in the United States. This agreement is made about a population that preceded every American writer of renown and was, I have come to believe, one of the most furtively radical impinging forces on the country's literature. The contemplation of this black presence is central to any understanding of our national literature and should not be permitted to hover at the margins of the literary imagination.

These speculations have led me to wonder whether the major and championed characteristics of our national literature — individualism, masculinity, social engagement versus historical isolation; acute and ambiguous moral problematics; the thematics of innocence coupled with an obsession with figurations of death and hell — are not in fact responses to a dark, abiding, signing Africanist presence. It has occurred to me that the very manner by which American literature distinguishes itself as a coherent entity exists because of this unsettled and unsettling population. Just as the formation of the nation necessitated coded language and purposeful restriction to deal with the racial disingenuousness and moral frailty at its heart, so too did the literature, whose founding characteristics extend into the twentieth century, reproduce the necessity for codes and restriction. Through significant and underscored omissions, startling contradictions, heavily nuanced conflicts, through the way writers peopled their work with the signs and bodies of this presence — one can see that a real or fabricated Africanist presence was crucial to their sense of Americanness. And it shows. . . .

Let me propose some topics that need critical investigation.

First, the Africanist character as surrogate and enabler. In what ways does the imaginative encounter with Africanism enable white writers to think about themselves? What are the dynamics of Africanism's self-reflexive properties? Note, for instance, the way Africanism is used to conduct a dialogue concerning American space in *The Narrative of Arthur Gordon Pym*. Through the use of Africanism, Poe meditates on place as a means of containing the fear of borderlessness and trespass, but also as a means of releasing and exploring the desire for a limitless empty frontier. Consider the ways that Africanism in other American writers (Mark Twain, Melville, Hawthorne) serves as a vehicle for regulating love and the imagination as defenses against the psychic costs of guilt and despair. Africanism is the vehicle by which the American self knows itself as not enslaved, but free; not repulsive, but desirable; not helpless, but licensed and powerful; not history-less, but historical; not damned, but innocent; not a blind accident of evolution, but a progressive fulfillment of destiny.

A second topic in need of critical attention is the way an Africanist idiom is used to establish difference or, in a later period, to signal modernity. We need to explicate the ways in which specific themes, fears, forms of consciousness, and class relationships are embedded in the use of Africanist idiom: how the dialogue of black characters is construed as an alien, estranging dialect made deliberately unintelligible by spellings contrived to disfamiliarize it; how Africanist language practices are employed to evoke the tension between speech and speechlessness; how it is used to establish a cognitive world split between speech and text, to reinforce class distinctions and otherness as well as to assert privilege and power; how it serves as a marker and vehicle for illegal sexuality, fear of madness, expulsion, self-loathing. Finally, we should look at how a black idiom and the sensibilities it has come to imply are appropriated for the associative value they lend to modernism — to being hip, sophisticated, ultra-urbane.

Third, we need studies of the technical ways in which an Africanist character is used to limn out and enforce the invention and implications of whiteness. We need studies that analyze the strategic use of black characters to define the goals and enhance the qualities of white characters. Such studies will reveal the process of establishing others in order to know them, to display knowledge of the other so as to ease and to order external and internal chaos. Such studies will reveal the process by which it is made possible to explore and penetrate one's own body in the guise of the sexuality, vulnerability, and anarchy of the other — and to control projections of anarchy with the disciplinary apparatus of punishment and largess.

Fourth, we need to analyze the manipulation of the Africanist narrative (that is, the story of a black person, the experience of being bound and/or rejected) as a means of meditation — both safe and risky — on one's own humanity. Such analyses will reveal how the representation and appropriation of that narrative provides opportunities to contemplate limitation, suffering, rebellion, and to speculate on fate and destiny. They will analyze how that narrative is used for discourse on ethics, social and universal codes of behavior, and assertions about and definitions of civilization and reason. Criticism of this type will show how that narrative is used in the construction of a history and a context for whites by positing history-lessness and context-lessness for blacks.

These topics surface endlessly when one begins to look carefully, without restraining, protective agenda beforehand. They seem to me to render the nation's literature a much more complex and rewarding body of knowledge.

Two examples may clarify: one a major American novel that is both a source and a critique of romance as a genre; the other the fulfillment of the promise I made earlier to return to those mute white images of Poe's.

If we supplement our reading of *Huckleberry Finn*, expand it — release it from its clutch of sentimental nostrums about lighting out to the territory, river gods, and the fundamental innocence of Americanness — to incorporate its contestatory, combative critique of antebellum America, it seems to be another, fuller novel. It becomes a more beautifully complicated work that sheds much light on some of the problems it has accumulated through traditional readings too shy to linger over the implications of the Africanist presence at its center. We understand that, at a certain level, the critique of class and race is there, although disguised or enhanced by humor and naiveté. Because of the combination of humor, adventure, and the viewpoint of the naif, Mark Twain's readers are free to dismiss the critique, the contestatory qualities, of the novel and focus on its celebration of savvy innocence, at the same time voicing polite embarrassment over the symptomatic racial attitude it enforces. Early criticism (that is, the reappraisals in the 1950s that led to the reification of *Huckleberry Finn* as a great novel) missed or dismissed the social quarrel in that work because it appears to assimilate the ideological assumptions of its society and culture; because it is narrated in the voice and controlled by the gaze of a child-without-status — someone outside, marginal, and already "othered" by the middle-class society he loathes and seems never to envy; and because the novel masks itself in the comic, parodic, and exaggerated tall-tale format.

On this young but street-smart innocent, Huck, who is virginally uncorrupted by bourgeois yearnings, fury, and helplessness, Mark Twain inscribes a critique of slavery and the pretensions of the would-be middle class, a resistance to the loss of Eden and the difficulty of becoming a social individual. The agency, however, for Huck's struggle is the nigger Jim, and it is absolutely necessary (for reasons I tried to illuminate earlier) that the term *nigger* be inextricable from Huck's deliberations about who and what he himself is — or, more precisely, is not. The major controversies about the greatness or near greatness of *Huckleberry Finn* as an American (or even "world") novel exist as controversies because they forgo a close examination of the interdependence of slavery and freedom, of Huck's growth and Jim's serviceability within it, and even of Mark Twain's inability to continue, to explore the journey into free territory.

The critical controversy has focused on the collapse of the so-called fatal ending of the novel. It has been suggested that the ending is brilliant finesse that returns Tom Sawyer to the center stage where he should be. Or it is a brilliant play on the dangers and limitations of romance. Or it is a sad and confused ending to the book of an author who, after a long blocked period, lost narrative direction; who changed the serious adult focus back to a child's story out of disgust. Or the ending is a valuable learning experience for Jim and Huck for which we and they should be grateful. What is not stressed is that there is no way, given the confines of the novel, for Huck to mature into a moral human being *in America* without Jim. To let Jim go free, to let him enter the mouth of the Ohio River and pass into free territory, would be to abandon the whole premise of the book. Neither Huck nor Mark Twain can tolerate, in imaginative terms, Jim freed. That would blast the predilection from its mooring.

Thus the fatal ending becomes the elaborate deferment of a necessary and necessarily unfree Africanist character's escape, because freedom has no meaning to Huck or to the text without the specter of enslavement, the anodyne to individualism; the yardstick of absolute power over the life of another; the signed, marked, informing, and mutating presence of a black slave.

The novel addresses at every point in its structural edifice, and lingers over in every fissure, the slave's body and personality: the way it speaks, what passion legal or illicit it is prey to, what pain it can endure, what limits, if any, there are to its suffering, what possibilities there are for forgiveness, compassion, love. Two things strike us in this novel: the apparently limitless store of love and compassion the black man has for his white friend and white masters; and his assumption that the whites are indeed what they say they are, superior and adult. This representation of Jim as the visible other can be read as the yearning of whites for forgiveness and love, but the yearning is made possible only when it is understood that Jim has recognized his inferiority (not as slave, but as black) and despises it. Jim permits his persecutors to torment him, humiliate him, and responds to the torment and humiliation with boundless love. The humiliation that Huck and Tom subject Jim to is baroque, endless, foolish, mind-softening — and it comes *after* we have experienced Jim as an adult, a caring father and a sensitive man. If Jim had been a white ex-convict befriended by Huck, the ending could not have been imagined or written: because it would not have been possible for two children to play so painfully with the life of a white man (regardless of his class, education, or fugitiveness) once he had been revealed to us as a moral adult. Jim's slave status makes play and deferment possible but it also dramatizes, in style and mode of narration, the connection between slavery and the achievement (in actual and imaginary terms) of freedom. Jim seems unassertive, loving, irrational, passionate, dependent, inarticulate (except for the "talks" he and Huck have, long sweet talks we are not privy to — but what did you talk about, Huck?). It is not what Jim seems that warrants inquiry, but what

Mark Twain, Huck, and especially Tom need from him that should solicit our attention. In that sense the book may indeed be "great" because in its structure, in the hell it puts its reader through at the end, the frontal debate it forces, it simulates and describes the parasitical nature of white freedom. . . .

STACEY MARGOLIS

Huckleberry Finn; Or, Consequences

Stacey Margolis (b. 1966) is assistant professor of English at the University of Utah. She received her B.A. (1988) from Northwestern University before earning her M.A. (1990) and her Ph.D. (1997) from the University of Chicago. The author of articles on Edith Wharton and on tales of addiction, Margolis is currently completing a book titled *The Public Life of Privacy in Nineteenth-Century American Literature.* The following essay was first published in the March 2001 issue of *PMLA.*

> "You are very kind; but there must be some mistake. I have not killed anything."
> "Your house did, anyway," replied the little old woman, with a laugh; "and that is the same thing."
> –L. Frank Baum, *The Wonderful Wizard of Oz* (1900)

That two forceful polemics against the continued investment in *Adventures of Huckleberry Finn* as an American classic were recently published for two very different audiences — Jane Smiley's "Say It Ain't So, Huck: Second Thoughts on Mark Twain's 'Masterpiece'" in *Harper's Magazine* and Jonathan Arac's Huckleberry Finn *as Idol and Target: The Functions of Criticism in Our Time* as part of the Wisconsin Project on American Writers series — suggests that nothing has become as much an American classic as the continuing controversy itself. What is different and worth noting about these two works, however, is their attempt to do something new, to shift the focus of critique away

I would like to thank Andrew Franta, Kevin Gilmartin, and Cathy Jurca for their invaluable contributions to this project.

from the novel to the social consequences of its canonization. Rather than ask if *Huckleberry Finn* is a good or bad book, they ask if it has good or bad effects. To claim, then (as a number of Smiley's respondents in *Harper's* did about her essay), that these two works misread the novel or refuse to attend to its historical context is to miss the point.[1] Smiley and Arac have far less interest in interpreting the novel than in addressing the way it has been used and the "cultural work" it continues to perform (Arac 21; p. 440 in this volume); they are making claims not so much about what *Huckleberry Finn* means as about what it does.

Thus, despite the fact that Arac confesses early on that he believes "*Huckleberry Finn* is a wonderful book" (16; p. 435 in this volume), his goal is to assess the consequences of excessive admiration, to "explore how Twain's book came to be endowed with the values of Americanness and anti-racism, and with what effects" (vii). Predictably, these effects are shown to be devastating. In Arac's view, the novel's prominent and seemingly unshakable position as a "quintessentially American book" (vii) has led to "white" complacency about racism ("[n]orthern liberal smugness" [65]), the legitimation of racial epithets, and the delegitimation of African American experience. For Arac and Smiley, the novel's pernicious influence is demonstrated most clearly in the way that a series of well-known critics have made Huck's change of heart about Jim (Huck's decision in chapter 31 to "go to hell") serve as a model of social responsibility. What mid-twentieth-century critics admired as a form of redemption, Arac and Smiley see as a distasteful form of liberal bad faith: the problem, in Smiley's terms, is the sense that if "Huck *feels* positive toward Jim, and *loves* him, and *thinks* of him as a man, then that's enough. He doesn't actually have to act in accordance with his feelings" (63; p. 460 in this volume).[2] It is this investment in

---

[1]The responses in *Harper's* were uniformly hostile to Smiley. Although they raised different objections, most were troubled by her insistence on using contemporary standards of political correctness to criticize Twain. One example: "It's too bad Smiley couldn't judge Twain for the book he wrote rather than for his failure to meet her 1990s political agenda" (Pendleton 7).

[2]Both polemics can be understood as extensions of Leo Marx's influential 1953 essay contending that American idolatry of *Huckleberry Finn* had gone so far that it had blinded readers to the novel's serious flaws. Against Lionel Trilling's and T. S. Eliot's well-known celebrations of *Huckleberry Finn*, Marx argued that the "burlesque" Phelps farm sequence destroyed the novel by undermining its moral seriousness. For recent attacks on the ending that follow Marx's logic, see Carton; Jehlen. For recent defenses of the ending, see Hill; Morrison. (The essays by Trilling, Eliot, Jehlen, Marx, and Morrison are all in this edition. Eds.)

good intentions (both in the novel and in celebrations of the novel) that, more than anything else, bothers Arac and Smiley. After all, what could be more politically suspect than to applaud moral courage that can never be translated into social change?

One could argue that the reading of chapter 31 to which Arac and Smiley object — the reading of Huck's decision as moral triumph — has never been as influential, at least in literary circles, as they seem to believe. Critics have been claiming since the 1960s that the futility of Huck's decision to free Jim, as well as the entire evasion sequence at the Phelps farm, must be read as a satire of white complacency and of the perils of legal freedom for blacks in late-nineteenth-century America. This reading is developed brilliantly by Laurence Holland in by far the best, if least cited, essay on the novel. In "A 'Raft of Trouble,'" Holland argues that the novel undercuts the importance of Huck's change of heart: the necessity and the futility of his decision to free an already free Jim satirize the fact that in the post-Reconstruction era (and, Holland suggests, even "in more recent decades" [75]) black Americans were systematically denied civil and economic rights and thus, in a real sense, still needed to be freed.[3] In much the same way, Russell Reising has weighed in against those critics who relegate the racial violence of *Huckleberry Finn* to a past that is "diffused [. . .] with a nostalgic gloss" as a way of avoiding the presentness of Twain's nightmare America (159).

The interest of Smiley's and Arac's polemics is that they effectively invalidate all such defenses of the novel. At issue in these arguments is not what Twain intended or even what the novel really means (if these things are different) but how it has been and continues to be experienced by readers. Arac, for example, argues that to defend *Huckleberry Finn*'s treatment of Jim or its use of racial epithets by pointing to the novel's irony is to dismiss the legitimate concerns of African Americans who experience the book not as a satire of racial injustice but as a form of racial insult. "If civil rights means anything," he asks, "shouldn't it

---

[3]When Holland's essay appeared in *Glyph* in 1979, James Cox had already made a version of this argument about the ending (although Cox sees the ending as an indictment of the complacent liberal reader). This tendency to read the novel in the light of post-Reconstruction politics has only gained steam in recent years, during which the imperative to historicize has been taken to mean addressing the moment in which the novel was written. One of the latest of these essays is by Christine Macleod, who interestingly extends Holland's claims without ever citing his essay. See also the essays collected in *Satire or Evasion? Black Perspectives on* Huckleberry Finn (Leonard, Tenney, and Davis), especially by Nilon; Barksdale; and Smith.

mean that African Americans ought to have a real voice in public definitions of what counts as a model of enlightened race relations?" (9). While Arac's and Smiley's claims about *Huckleberry Finn* paradoxically seem aimed at rescuing black readers from the "racist" effects of arguments by black intellectuals like Ralph Ellison and Toni Morrison (who have eloquently defended the novel), the more general problems Arac and Smiley have with any appeal to the novel's real meaning is that its meaning has been overshadowed by its powerful cultural effects. Indeed, Arac's project is a kind of postdeconstructive attempt to treat *Huckleberry Finn* not as itself a chain of uncontrollable iterations but as an object that fosters a chain of prescribed responses (that the novel is quintessentially American, that it is antiracist, that black readers who hate it must be wrong), so that "what counts is not the attitudes that the book supposedly teaches, but rather the opportunity the book provides for the incessant reiteration, the ritual repetition, of practical behavior" (11).

To divorce Twain from the effects of his novel — indeed, to absolve him of any blame for those effects — is, for Arac and Smiley, to demonstrate a commitment to effect over intention that they claim most Americans refuse to countenance.[4] The problem with liberal readers of Twain is that they insist on reducing everything — including racism — to sentiment. "White Americans," Smiley argues, "always think racism is a feeling, and they reject it or they embrace it. To most Americans it seems more honorable and nicer to reject it, so they do, but they almost invariably fail to understand that how they *feel* means very little to black Americans, who understand racism as a way of structuring American culture, American politics, and the American economy" (63; p. 460 in this volume). For Arac, it is defenders of the novel who make this mistake, acting "as if racism were only a matter of specific intention to harm, of attitude rather than habitual practice and social structure" (13).

To make this case against white Americans or the liberal reader is to advance certain claims about what it means to be responsible for racism and, more generally, about the connections among what we do, what we intend, and what happens to us or to the people around us. It is, in

---

[4]This impulse both to berate and to absolve Twain is shared by Arac and Smiley themselves. Arac claims, "I am not holding Twain solely responsible for such use of his book" (23). Smiley claims, "These are only authors, after all, and once a book is published the author can't be held accountable for its role in the culture. For that we have to blame the citizens themselves, or their teachers, or *their* teachers, the arbiters of critical taste" (66; p. 464 in this volume).

fact, to make the claim that we can be held responsible not only for what we mean (or what we mean to do) but also for the unintended effects of what we do. On this account, our actions can count as racist even if we "don't know it" and even if we have no "specific intention to harm" (Arac 13). It is in making this claim, I think, that Arac and Smiley are most interesting, most convincing, and, ironically enough, most indebted to *Huckleberry Finn*. For in their belief in responsibility for effects rather than for intentions, they are clearly the inheritors of a nineteenth-century cultural shift in notions of accountability that involved not only the rise of a new legal paradigm (the law of negligence) but also the social satire of a novel like *Huckleberry Finn*.

Far from being irrelevant to questions of institutionalized racism, Twain's novel is centrally concerned with the production of effects and the assignment of responsibility for them. *Huckleberry Finn* participates in this cultural shift in the conception of responsibility by articulating a form of moral action on which individual intention — whether good or bad — finally has no bearing. In this essay I argue that Twain's interest in exploring the ways in which a wide variety of unknowing people could be held responsible for Jim's fate and be made to compensate him for his injuries must be read as an attempt to imagine what it would mean to extend the logic of negligence to the national level. In this commitment to examining unintentional harms, Twain not only makes his strongest case against postbellum racism but also proves himself the intellectual forerunner of social critics like Arac and Smiley. For, from this perspective, *Huckleberry Finn* is an attempt to imagine accountability even in the absence of malice.

"HOW A BODY CAN SEE AND DON'T SEE AT THE SAME TIME"

Whether they like it or hate it, critics of *Huckleberry Finn* have always seen the real drama of the novel in Huck's internal conflict, the contest (as Twain once put it) between his conscience and his heart, so that the suspense for the reader lies in the uncertainty of Huck's decision rather than in the uncertainty of his actions. This sense that Huck's decision — whether read straight or as satire — is at the center of *Huckleberry Finn* is the one thing that supporters and detractors of the novel have always had in common. Thus, the novel's most famous detractor, Leo Marx, claiming that Huck's "victory over his 'yaller dog' conscience" in chapter 31 ultimately "assumes heroic size" (p. 301), sounds a great deal like the novel's most famous supporter, Lionel Trilling, who claims that Huck "becomes an heroic character when, on the urging of affection, [he] discards the moral code he has always taken for granted and resolves to help Jim in his escape from slavery" (111–12).

This sense that what counts in chapter 31 is Huck's conscience hardly seems surprising since it is intention rather than action that gets the final word. Announcing his decision to destroy the letter he has written Miss Watson disclosing Jim's whereabouts, Huck says, "It was awful thoughts, and awful words, but they was said. And I let them stay said; and never thought no more about reforming" (p. 201). While it is clear what it would mean to let a letter stay written (by not ripping it up), it is not as easy to picture what it would mean to let words, once uttered, "stay said." But one might make the case for the priority of intention in this novel by asserting that the permanence of these words consists in the purity of the intention that produced them, in Huck's determined refusal to change his mind. The novel dramatizes this commitment to consciousness over action most explicitly in the way that it nearly undoes the action of this key scene: Huck demonstrates his loyalty to Jim by ripping up the letter. The fact that this decision is emblematized by a letter written and then destroyed — an action done and then undone — seems even in its formal structure to privilege the coherence of intentions over the vagaries of actions.

It is the futility of Huck's commitment to Jim — a futility made visible in the destroyed letter — that has always angered the novel's detractors. The direct result of Huck's decision, after all, is not a serious attempt to free Jim but a game invented by Tom Sawyer. Yet if Miss Watson's decision to set Jim free makes the final rescue attempt a mere game, it is a game only to Tom, who knows the truth from the moment he arrives at the Phelps farm. For Huck, the stakes of freeing Jim are just as high, and the consequences just as real, when Tom takes control of the rescue as they were when Huck agonized over sending the letter to Miss Watson. Only after the rescue fails does Huck discover what he and Tom have, in fact, been doing all along: not rescuing Jim but only pretending to: "and so, sure enough, Tom Sawyer had gone and took all that trouble and bother to set a free nigger free! and I couldn't ever understand, before, until that minute and that talk how he *could* help a body set a nigger free, with his bringing-up" (p. 261). That Huck describes the evasion as Tom's action rather than his own is an issue to which I return below. For now, it is important to note that what Miss Watson's will reveals is not that Huck has failed in his commitment to liberate Jim but the more surprising fact that Huck could neither have succeeded nor have failed to free him. Already free in the eyes of the law, Jim, it seems, can never be freer than he is.

What is most striking about this revision of the rescue is that it illustrates a paradigm for the novel's representation of action. Indeed, all the central actions of the novel depend on this kind of gap in knowledge: characters repeatedly come to know what they really did (or what their actions really mean) only after the fact, only retrospectively. Thus, Jim discovers that he has not been running away from enslavement but has, as Tom announces, been simply running (p. 260). Thus, Huck discovers that he has not been escaping from his father since, as Jim informs him, by the time they leave Jackson's Island his father is dead (pp. 262–63). The novel at once highlights intention (by focusing completely on the development of Huck's consciousness) and works to make intentions irrelevant to understanding certain kinds of action. No matter how deeply Huck is invested in his good intentions toward Jim or how powerful his decision to save Jim seems to the reader, this recasting of the rescue by Miss Watson's will already moves us well beyond an intentional model of action.

From a point of view that places the reader beyond intention, Huck's role in the evasion must be understood less as a heroic individual gesture than as an act essentially defined by other people. The game Huck finds he is playing must be understood less as something he *shares* with Tom than as something *created* by Tom. In the end, Tom's revelation neither enforces Huck's decision (as pure intention) nor invalidates it (as completely futile) but insists on the conflict between what Huck thinks he is doing and what he is told he has done. In thus recasting Huck's role in the rescue, *Huckleberry Finn* undertakes a project much more radical than imagining a self that can inhabit a variety of roles (after all, disguises and mistaken identities have always been central to the novel). Instead, the novel imagines what it would mean for someone to perform an action that can be narrated intelligibly only from outside the self, what it would mean, in other words, for Tom to understand what Huck is doing better than Huck can understand it himself. "It shows," as Huck puts it, "how a body can see and don't see at the same time" (p. 215).

This retrospective account of action is so central to *Huckleberry Finn* that it ultimately comes to undermine the authority exercised by Huck's self-presentation. The novel thematizes this powerlessness over narration in its meticulous tracking of textual effects, in its exploration of how texts come to define and even transform what characters can do.

That is, the novel is concerned less with the ways that texts represent actions than with the ways that texts can determine what counts as someone's action. Miss Watson's will casts a shadow over the entire plot, redefining what everyone has been doing to Jim, just as Tom's adventure stories prescript the fake rescue. In the evasion sequence, tales prompt adventures not so much by providing Tom and Huck with an intention as by standing in for intention, by becoming intention's substitute. Far from exercises in improvisation, Tom's games are the products of textual blueprints: "Why blame it all, we've *got* to do it. Don't I tell you it's in the books? Do you want to go to doing different from what's in the books, and get things all muddled up?" (p. 38).

If Tom's perfect commitment to enforcing the rules of the romance is satirized, however, the power he accords texts is never questioned. Beyond the innovative use of dialect, what seems to mark *Huckleberry Finn* as the first recognizably modern American novel — what might explain the kinship a modernist like Hemingway felt for Twain's project — is the way it experiments with the production of textual effects. Through steady adherence to the illusion of presentness, the novel works to enforce a kind of readerly retrospection, so that just as Tom and Jim withhold important pieces of information until the end of the "adventure," Huck withholds their revelations from the reader. Presentness is an illusion here because Huck, who claims to be narrating his tale after the fact, tells it as if experiencing it for the first time. As Holland points out, *Huckleberry Finn* presents itself as a historical novel, but it is narrated as if it were happening in the "here and now" (73). What he does not remark on is that this illusion enables *Huckleberry Finn* to enact its retrospection formally, forcing readers into the same kind of recognition that Huck and Jim experience in the world of the novel. It is only after the fact that readers understand the descriptions they have been reading: of a game rather than a rescue, of a free man rather than a slave, of an orphan rather than a runaway. This withholding of information, finally, makes it impossible for one ever to read the same story again by making it impossible for one to be the same reader the second time around. If one reads the novel the first time as Huck, one must read it the second time as Tom.

Such shifting positions and tenses might explain how a novel that purports to focus on the South of "forty to fifty years" before the time of its publication can be understood as a novel essentially about the post-Reconstruction era. Certainly, if the novel's setting has always suggested a kind of nostalgia — for boyhood, for the antebellum South, for the small town — the fact that Twain detaches Huck and Jim from a familiar context and sets them literally afloat already begins to suggest a concern with the chaos of postwar America. There could hardly be a better image of modernization than the move from the familiarity of the village to the anonymity of the city. And this interest in the relation between strangers connects the novel most explicitly with the politics of the post-Reconstruction era not because it raises questions about individual disorientation in a rapidly industrializing America but because it raises broader questions about accountability in a changing public sphere.

If all the actors in the evasion sequence misunderstand what they have done to Jim — Huck imagines that he is freeing a slave, the Phelpses and their neighbors imagine that by catching Jim they are quelling a slave revolt, Tom imagines that Jim's freedom can be turned into a game, and even Miss Watson imagines that signing her will is enough to make Jim free — how are they answerable for the harms they cause him? What, in the end, are these willing and unwilling participants in the evasion responsible for? These questions are at the center of *Huckleberry Finn*, and the novel attempts to answer them by reframing actions not merely in a wider context but also in terms of their consequences. If *Huckleberry Finn* is a novel about intention, it might best be read as a novel about the limits of intention, even at the moments when interiority rather than action is presented as the privileged form of self-relation. It is, finally, a novel in which your effects on other people rather than your feelings about them define what you have done and, more important, what you can be held accountable for.

"NOBODY TO BLAME"

The problem with most critiques of *Huckleberry Finn* is that they assume Twain was invoking an intentional model of morality (thus the frequent allusions to Huck's decision to act, for better or worse, against the mores of the community and in accordance with his "heart"), when he was exploring a model of moral action in which any particular state of mind or change of attitude is finally irrelevant. This model did not originate with Twain or emerge full-fledged in nineteenth-century America. In fact, it resembles what Bernard Williams, examining classical texts, calls the "whole person response" to harm (61). By this Williams means an understanding that the existence of a harm requires us to trace causation and to hold someone accountable, even if the harm was caused unintentionally. The relevant question about a harm, in other words, is not "whether the agent intended the outcome" but rather "what exactly his action may be said to have caused" (63). Thus, in the *Odyssey*, Telemachus, having left open the door to the storeroom by accident, is nonetheless to blame — for this and for the fact that the suitors could subsequently get at the weapons. To hold persons responsible in this way, to insist that they are accountable for their accidents and mistakes, is to make certain assumptions about what constitutes individuality. It is, according to Williams, to concede that committing an action "unintentionally does not, in itself, dissociate that action from yourself" and thus to know "that in the story of one's life there is an authority exercised by what one has done, and not merely by what one has intentionally done." "Telemachus can be held responsible for things he did unintentionally, and so, of course, can we" (54, 69, 54).

As Williams points out, nowhere is this model of responsibility for unintended effects more powerfully expressed than in the law of torts. Virtually nonexistent in antebellum America, torts became one of the most important elements of common law in the late nineteenth century, when industrialization, urbanization, and improved systems of transportation forced masses of people into close proximity and thus gave rise to an increasing number of accidental injuries. What made such accidents unprecedented (aside from their numbers) was that they at once demanded some form of reparation for suffering and raised serious questions about accountability, including questions about who should be held responsible for accidental harms and who should bear the cost of them. With the dramatic rise of such harms, what had been an insignificant branch of the law dealing with torts became an increasingly important remedy precisely because it did not make intention the ground of liability.[5]

In *The Common Law* (1881), which advanced one of the first and most influential theories of tort in America, Oliver Wendell Holmes, Jr., made explicit this model of responsibility for effects. He claimed, "It may be said that, generally speaking, a man meddles with [tangible objects] at his own risk" (153) — that the owner of an object might be understood as responsible for harms caused by that object.[6] Antebellum American courts were basically committed to this model of strict liability, under which actors are held responsible for the harms caused by their actions no matter how blameless their conduct. By midcentury, however, legal scholars were concerned about the economic effects of

[5]My discussion of tort law and the novel is indebted to Ferguson.
[6]For another important contemporary treatise on torts, see Cooley. For legal histories of the period, see Friedman; Horwitz.

such a system; strict liability threatened American industry (which would have to pay for the damage it caused) by promising a radical redistribution of wealth. Holmes, reacting to the ever-increasing demand for compensation, dismissed calls for a system of strict liability, denying that the state's role was to "make itself a mutual insurance company against accidents, and distribute the burden of its citizens' mishaps among all its members" (96). In fact, the story that legal historians generally tell about tort in the nineteenth century is the story of its limitation, of the way that the promise of compensation was routinely undermined in the American courts.

More than anything else, the courts' growing insistence that there be a standard of negligence significantly limited liability. If under a system of strict liability persons are liable for every harm they cause, under a system of negligence they are liable for a harm they cause only if they are at fault. According to Holmes, who was instrumental in establishing negligence as the general principle of liability in tort, persons are at fault when they act carelessly, when they cause a harm that anyone could have foreseen and avoided. "Unless my act," Holmes says, "is of a nature to threaten others, unless under the circumstances a prudent man would have foreseen the possibility of harm, it is no more justifiable to make me indemnify my neighbor against the consequences, than to make me do the same thing if I had fallen upon him in a fit, or to compel me to insure him against lightning" (96). Thus, the key distinction in a determination of guilt "is not between results which are and those which are not the consequences of the defendant's acts" but rather "between consequences which [the defendant] was bound as a reasonable man to contemplate, and those which he was not." For example, "[h]ard spurring is just so much more likely to lead to harm than merely riding a horse in the street [. . .] that the defendant would be bound to look out for the consequences of the one," although he would not be held responsible "for those resulting merely from the other; because the possibility of being run away with when riding quietly, though familiar, is comparatively slight" (93–94). By proclaiming the harmful consequences of some actions to be predictable and by making agents pay only for their mistakes, American law drew formal boundaries around how much agents would have to pay for the harms they accidentally caused.

As *The Gilded Age* (Twain and Warner; 1873) makes clear, by the 1870s Twain was concerned about the consequences of such limitations on liability. This novel is, at least in part, a condemnation of the American courts for their failure to protect people from the damaging side effects of economic progress. Twain and his coauthor, Charles

Dudley Warner, devote an entire chapter to an account of a deadly steamboat accident and its aftermath. While the painstaking depiction of this accident seems, at least initially, out of place in a novel satirizing Washington, the account of the explosion reveals a great deal about the general mechanisms of guilt and blame in the age of industry. If the captains and crews of the two ships were clearly responsible for the race that led to the accident — the head engineer of the *Amaranth* calls his second engineer a "murderer" for refusing to heed his warnings about stress on the engines — the "jury of inquest" on the case refuses to find anyone liable for the accident: "after due deliberation and inquiry they returned the inevitable American verdict which has been too familiar to our ears all the days of our lives — NOBODY TO BLAME" (52).

On the one hand, then, *The Gilded Age* registers the way in which the courts limited liability, favoring industry over the persons it injured. On the other, this scene, in its sense of justified outrage over the verdict, also dramatizes the important ways in which common-sense expectations about liability had been transformed. While it is true that legal devices like negligence limited liability and thus eased the burden placed on industry, the logic of negligence worked out by Holmes and other scholars actually succeeded (often despite their intentions) in articulating new forms of individual and corporate obligation. Making carelessness the ground of responsibility implied that persons (even corporate persons) have at all times an obligation to act with caution. Formerly understood only as the failure to live up to a specific duty — the failure to fulfill a contract, say, or to perform a public office adequately — negligence began to be defined as the failure to meet a general standard of care. With the rise of negligence, not only were professionals like doctors bound by particular duties but everyone was imagined to be bound by an obligation to others, an obligation not to cause harm. Negligence, designed to limit liability, ended up producing a much more expansive form of obligation owed to "all the world" (Holmes's phrase, qtd. in White 19).

The system of negligence installed by theorists like Holmes created a range of impersonal obligations. If one had a duty to "all the world," this duty had nothing to do with how one felt about one's fellows.[7] The law, that is, did not require people to love their neighbors. Thus, while Holmes was adamant in his support of the fault principle's limitation of liability, arguing that "undertaking to redistribute losses" for injuries

---

[7]For an opposing view, see Goodman.

resulting from blameless action would not only hinder progress but also undermine any "sense of justice" (96), he nevertheless insisted that individuals were always acting under a general obligation to the public. If the move to a system of negligence meant that the law often failed to provide adequate compensation for the harms occasioned by industrialization, it nonetheless extended the reach of social obligation and thus transformed what it meant to act in public.

Huckleberry Finn invokes the rise of negligence in fantasizing solutions to the post-Reconstruction racial crisis. Unlike earlier and later stories by Twain involving the adventures of Tom, Huck, and Jim, however, *Huckleberry Finn* contains no courtroom scene, no overt intrusion of the law into the world of the novel.[8] Instead, Twain derives from the system of negligence that had become central to American common law a general model of responsibility for the consequences of action. The model he invokes is impersonal and universally applicable. It is impersonal because it measures conduct not against the agent's intentions but against a general standard. As H. L. A. Hart argues, negligence "is not the name of 'a state of mind'" but the name of an action, a failure "to comply with a standard of conduct with which any ordinary reasonable man *could* and *would* have complied" (147). In negligence cases, the courts did not ask whether actors had in fact predicted the harm that would follow from their actions; the courts measured the actions against a general standard of behavior. The model is universally applicable because it is not subject to individual consent. The law of negligence, as Holmes claimed, is grounded in "some general view of the conduct which everyone may fairly expect and demand from every other, whether that other has agreed to it or not" (77).[9]

---

[8]Twain continues this pattern in later stories like "Tom Sawyer Abroad," "Huck Finn and Tom Sawyer among the Indians," and "Tom Sawyer's Conspiracy" (the last two were unfinished), in which Huck and Tom endanger Jim so that they might have adventures rescuing him. It seems worth noting, however, that in the years following *Huckleberry Finn* (esp. after the *Plessy* decision, when almost all hope for racial justice evaporated), Twain does not address the problem of responsibility for harm in the same terms. The relevant legal context had changed. In "Tom Sawyer's Conspiracy," for example, Jim is falsely accused of murder and threatened with execution; he is thus no longer a victim in need of legal remedy but a victim of the criminal law.

[9]Wai Chee Dimock has suggested that this sense of universal liability must be understood as an extension of contractual relations. Yet to imagine that one could calculate responsibilities as one calculates the benefits of entering a contract is to miss what is most important about the form of responsibility created by negligence: it is nonnegotiable. One cannot, generally speaking, contract out of liability. See Dimock's "Economy." For an account of the late-nineteenth-century American novel in relation to contract, see Thomas.

In the broadest terms, what Twain recognizes in negligence as a way of judging behavior is its potential to solve the problem of post-bellum civil rights, a problem he conceives as structural rather than personal. If Jim's precarious position in the text — free in name but not in fact — represents the precarious political and economic situation of African Americans after Reconstruction, this position cannot be transformed by the power of sentiment, because it is held in place by people who have the best of intentions. By the end of the novel, Huck's love for and commitment to freeing Jim become paradoxically essential to the game of humiliating him. I do not mean to claim that *Huckleberry Finn* simply replaces an intentional model of responsibility with one that disregards intention — it would be wrong to argue that Twain merely ironizes Huck's love for Jim. Rather, I am suggesting that the form of impersonal responsibility explored in the novel supplements an intentional model (just as negligence supplements criminal law); it is a way of imagining remedies for different kinds of harms. Twain, in other words, raises questions of sentiment in *Huckleberry Finn* to suggest that sentimental conversions go only so far to remedy wrongs that can be traced to no one agent.

Indeed, in *Huckleberry Finn,* intention is consistently overshadowed by the problem it attempts to address, the problem of racial discrimination that is embedded in (to echo Smiley) American cultural, economic, and political systems. From this perspective, it makes more sense to see each character's ignorance of the true meaning of his actions less as a moral failing than as a generalization about the unpredictable effects of individual action. Critics have been too quick to blame Tom for Jim's suffering, not acknowledging how the formal structure of the novel links Tom to much larger networks of action that include not only Huck but also Miss Watson and the widow Douglas, the Phelpses and their neighbors, the slave catchers, and the King and the Duke. The narrative's enforced retrospection reveals that we have effects in the world that go beyond our intentions but for which we are nonetheless accountable. In drawing on a model of responsibility derived from the law of negligence, *Huckleberry Finn* enacts a fantasy of national responsibility for the bottoming out of black civil rights in postbellum America.

"FORTY ACRES AND A MULE"

The relation of the novel to the law has, in much recent criticism, been seen primarily in terms of opposition. Where the law is rigid, critics say, the novel is flexible; where the law is impersonal, the novel is committed to the human character; where the law fails in its mission to act justly, the novel provides a comforting form of "poetic justice" (see Nussbaum; Dimock, *Residues*). Yet this vision of literature as law's supplement has perplexing implications. To claim that novels humanize the law is to suggest that novels in and of themselves are somehow more human than the law and thus inherently better at determining what is just. Moreover, it is to suggest that the legal concept of justice must be understood as "a formal universal," which "necessarily does violence to what it abstracts" (Dimock, *Residues* 9). This apparent conflict between the formal and the quotidian, the abstract and the particular, prompts Martha Nussbaum, in her analysis of actual legal cases, to attribute all judicial attention paid to "history and social context" and all judicial expressions of empathy to "the literary" rather than the legal "imagination" (115). The novel, according to Nussbaum, not only describes but also creates sympathy by addressing "an implicit reader who shares with the characters certain hopes, fears, and general human concerns, and who for that reason is able to form bonds of identification and sympathy with them" (7).

Such defenses of the novel against the deadening abstractions of the law require us to concede that the novel, as a form, is always and inevitably devoted to the sanctity of individual experience and thus committed to the production of "bonds of identification and sympathy." But just as there is no reason to imagine that legal reasoning excludes the personal and the particular (after all, legal cases depend on individual stories of harm or damage), there is no reason to imagine that novels are limited to producing an experiential model of personhood. *Huckleberry Finn* attempts to move away from a model of responsibility that requires such bonds and changes of heart by disarticulating the meaning of individual and collective action from questions of sympathy or intention. This disarticulation emerges most strikingly in the novel's investment in producing actions that can only be understood retrospectively. But it also emerges in Huck's failure ever to recognize his own role in the evasion — in his sense that it was Tom alone who "had gone and took all that trouble and bother to set a free nigger free!" (p. 261). When it comes to describing the harm done to Jim and to assigning responsibility for it, the novel implies that Huck's experience — what he recognizes or fails to recognize about himself — is irrelevant. In the end, *Huckleberry Finn* is concerned less with the harms that individuals do to one another than with the harms done by systems. The novel ultimately envisions a form of collective or corporate responsibility for systematic harm that has nothing to do with individual experience. To imagine that a novel, especially a novel about race, divorces collectivity from experience goes against a great deal of recent work that sees collectivity almost exclusively in terms of its effects on individual experience and individual identity. The collective, in other words, has been understood to extend the limits of experience, making it possible for individuals to imagine that they could, as part of a collective, remember things that they never experienced. Thus American Jews are enjoined to remember the Holocaust.[10] Such work often literalizes the metaphor of the social body by claiming that membership in an ethnic group gives one access to certain memories that then serve as the sign of one's ethnicity. From this point of view, collective memory and collective guilt look like two sides of the same coin: one is imagined to inherit guilt for ancestral crimes in the same way that one inherits a cultural past. But *Huckleberry Finn* refuses to make collective responsibility contingent on guilt or on ghostly notions of inheritance. Instead, it attempts to extend the logic of corporate responsibility — responsibility not simply for harms you have caused but also for harms committed in your name — to the nation.

What it would mean to hold an entire nation accountable for harm is articulated most compellingly in the novel's final scene of compensation — the much discussed moment in which Tom hands Jim forty dollars for playing the part of prisoner "so patient, and doing it up so good" (p. 262). Almost all critics of *Huckleberry Finn* — proponents and detractors alike — are united in their condemnation of Tom's attempt to settle the score. Critics as diverse as Holland and Arac have suggested that this forty-dollar payment is, at best, condescending and have seen in Tom only the manifestation of postwar racism. Not only is this payment a paltry sum in comparison with Tom and Huck's wealth, the argument goes, but it is hardly enough to give Jim a fair chance to support himself or to buy his family out of slavery. That the number forty is something of an obsession in this text suggests, however, that it represents more than a pittance. Twain seems to insist on the symbolic weight of the payment by referring to the number with astonishing frequency in the evasion sequence. The Duke, lying to Huck, tells him that Jim is being held "forty mile back here in the country, on the road

---

[10]There is a vast archive that sees the Jewish relation to the Holocaust in terms of memory. Some of the most interesting recent examples are Hansen; Hartman; and Young. For a critique of this position, see Michaels.

326 THE CONTROVERSY OVER THE ENDING

to Lafayette" (p. 203). Huck and Tom, plotting to sneak a ladder into Jim's cabin in a pie, claim that they had "rope enough for forty pies" (p. 234). When Tom is injured, Jim agrees to stay with him: "No sah — I doan' budge a step out'n dis place, 'dout a *doctor;* not ef it's forty year!" (p. 249). And the neighbors surveying the damage after the evasion imagine that the slaves have been plotting: "A *dozen* says you! — *forty* couldn't a done everything that's been done" (p. 252).

This interest in the number gives Tom's payment an iconic quality; the payment appears as the culmination of a complicated circuit through the text, as a sum repeatedly given to and withheld from Jim. He first receives the money, indirectly, from the two slave catchers who offer Huck forty dollars after they refuse to help tow his raft to safety. The money then resurfaces with the King and Duke (who sell Jim for forty dollars) and reverts back to Jim when Tom pays him for his patience at the end. Both payments to Jim, it is worth noting, serve as damages for harm, even if the donor misunderstands the harm he has caused. If Tom's final gesture counts, then, it counts as an attempt to imagine what real compensation for a series of harms would look like. By linking these characters — Huck, the slave traders, the King and the Duke, the Phelpses and their neighbors — through their relation to Tom's largely symbolic payment, Twain ties the scene of compensation that ends his antebellum tale to the post-Reconstruction era of failed national promises.

Set against both the rise of negligence and the fall of the Freedmen's Bureau, Tom's offer begins to look like the antithesis of buying Jim off for a pittance and thus maintaining the fiction that he is property. It looks instead like formal, legal recognition of his personhood, of the obligation to compensate him for his injuries. Surely forty is meant to recall the promise of forty acres and a mule, which were to make the freedmen equal as well as free.[11] From this perspective, Tom's payment looks less like further injury to Jim — a refusal to see him as a man — than like a form of compensation much broader in its effects because it makes him representative of a group. In the post-Reconstruction era, Tom's payment would have recalled not only the promise of the Freedmen's Bureau to support freed slaves through the redistribution of

---

[11]Richard Gollin and Rita Gollin link Tom's claim that it would take thirty-seven years to free Jim to Lincoln's suggestion during the war that the slaves be freed by the year 1900 (thirty-seven years later). Their argument that this number ties Twain's text to the history it seems to be evading remains relevant to the current debate over the novel and to my account.

confiscated or abandoned lands but also, and more forcefully, the government's total failure to fulfill its obligation. It was, at the time, the nation's most famous broken promise.[12]

This investment in collective forms of compensation also helps explain why Huck virtually disappears from the last third of the novel: Twain attempts to dissolve him, finally, not simply into Tom (whose name he takes) but also into the collective that Tom (always the mouthpiece for the authorities) has come to represent. Since Tom is the source of this collective voice, his final gesture, far from a dismissal of the economic problems faced by the freedmen, symbolically enacts the compensation that the nation withheld.[13] And if, as I have been arguing, the force of the novel is to disarticulate accountability from intention, to make it possible to imagine guilt even in the absence of malice, then Tom's gesture is collective not because it stems from a shared experience of hatred reformed but because it offers Jim compensation for a series of systematic harms. To end the novel by recalling the promise of forty acres and a mule is thus to suggest a very different way of defining collective accountability. Instead of imagining a spiritual connection among disparate individuals, it imagines "some general view of the conduct which every one may fairly expect and demand from every other, whether that other has agreed to it or not" (Holmes 77). Like the law of negligence, which created (even as it tried to limit) new forms of corporate responsibility, Twain's novel imagines extending this version of the collective — the corralling of actions for which no individual is to blame — to the nation.

From this perspective, *Huckleberry Finn* represents Twain's way of rewriting history or, more accurately, of fantasizing a new racial history of postwar America. What remains puzzling is that his biography suggests a much more ambivalent position on and within post-Reconstruction racism than this reading of the ending might seem to allow. Assessing the political and economic situation of African Americans in 1885, Twain remarked, "We have ground the manhood out of them. The shame is ours, not theirs, and we should pay for it" (qtd. in Fishkin, "Racial Attitudes" 613). This "brutally succinct comment on racism," according to Shelley Fisher Fishkin, "is a rare nonironic statement of the personal anguish he felt regarding the destructive legacy of

---

[12]To say that the nation's offer of forty acres and a mule functioned as a promise suggests that it was a kind of contract. But not all promises are contracts. In this case, there was not even the pretense that the freedmen and the government were equal partners.

[13]For a history of the Freedmen's Bureau, see Foner.

slavery" (613). Of course, as Fishkin has pointed out, Twain had a habit of contradicting himself. "What would it take," she asks, "to acknowledge the complexity and diversity of this man?" (*Lighting Out* 127). One thing it might take is a clear-sighted sense of Twain's equivocations on the subject of race: he was both a critic of political discrimination and a fan of minstrel shows and "darky jokes" (Pettit 127), a defender of both George Washington Cable and Joel Chandler Harris.[14] *Huckleberry Finn* is full of these kinds of puzzles: why, for instance, does Jim reprimand Huck for his selfishness early in the novel and then silently bear his humiliations at the end? Tom Quirk, grappling with this problem, asks us to separate "Mark Twain, the imaginative artist" from "Samuel Clemens, U.S. citizen" (74–75) and thus attempts to rescue Twain from his own opinions. Smiley and Arac ask us to absolve the man by blaming the book.

The reading of the ending advanced in this essay depends on a recognition of Twain's commitment to black civil rights. But it would be a mistake, I think, simply to add *Huckleberry Finn* to the list of evidence in his favor. For the interest of the novel lies in its attempt to think about the problem of American racism in structural rather than personal terms and thus to shift the focus (not permanently but, perhaps, strategically) from belief to practice, from intentions to effects. The fantasy enacted by the novel demands that the ascription of responsibility be seen as a formal rather than a moral question and that the world accordingly begin to see the problem of the freedmen as political rather than moral. What Twain recognizes is the poverty of treating racial justice as a question of sentiment (requiring a "change of heart") instead of as a question of structure (requiring new political policies). Unlike Cable, who frames his answer to the problem of postwar black civil rights in terms of "equity," so that people might begin to judge on the basis of "the eternal principles of justice" (74), Twain frames his answer in the context of negligence, so that the individual's blindness and petty prejudice might be replaced by a system that overrides the accidents of personal opinion. Ultimately, the logic of Twain's novel — which fantasizes a political solution to Jim's troubles — works to override the deficiencies of its representations, in which Jim is often made a fool.

Since I have set aside until now the difference this reading makes to the issue of the novel's canonization, let me return briefly to the ques-

---

[14]For an interesting account of Twain's use of ethnic caricature, see Wonham.

tion of readership with which I began. It would be tempting to argue that, given *Huckleberry Finn*'s critique of Jim Crow America and its fantasy of racial justice, those who have argued so strenuously against its continued presence in the canon and curriculum are wrong and must stop. Indeed, if my reading is persuasive, it counters Arac's and Smiley's arguments against the novel not only because it sees an interest in social effects where they see only liberal bad faith but also because it has the potential to change the way readers experience the novel. But taking the project of *Huckleberry Finn* seriously means taking effects seriously, and that must include bad as well as good effects that the novel has had on readers. To insist that effects, whether bad or good, are irrelevant or based on misreading is, as the novel itself illustrates, to misread the way in which objects and actions can produce profound social consequences that cannot be explained in terms of intentions. *Huckleberry Finn* is about both the difficulty and the necessity of valuing effects over intentions. Thus, one of Twain's implications is that no reading of the novel can put an end to the debate it has engendered. Taking effects on readers seriously means acknowledging that responses to the novel can be neither dictated nor replaced by a reading of the novel; even more important, it suggests that *Huckleberry Finn* provides the grounds for its own reassessment. Seen in this light, both proponents and detractors get the novel wrong. That Arac and Smiley have finally pointed us to the social effects of Twain's project should not, despite their best intentions, be understood as entailing its dismissal. Their use of *Huckleberry Finn* to oppose the politics of good intentions must count as a sign that we are beginning to get the novel right.

WORKS CITED

Arac, Jonathan. *"Huckleberry Finn" as Idol and Target: The Functions of Criticism in Our Time*. Madison: U of Wisconsin P, 1997.

Barksdale, Richard K. "History, Slavery, and Thematic Irony." Leonard, Tenney, and Davis 49–55.

Cable, George Washington. "The Freedman's Case in Equity." *The Negro Question*. Ed. Arlin Turner. New York: Anchor-Doubleday, 1958. 54–82.

Carton, Evan. "Speech Acts and Social Action: Mark Twain and the Politics of Literary Performance." Robinson 153–74.

Cooley, Thomas M. *A Treatise on the Law of Torts; or, The Wrongs Which Arise Independent of Contract*. Chicago, 1880.

Cox, James. *Mark Twain: The Fate of Humor.* Princeton: Princeton UP, 1966.

Dimock, Wai Chee. "The Economy of Pain: Capitalism, Humanitarianism, and the Realistic Novel." *New Essays on* The Rise of Silas Lapham. Ed. Donald Pease. New York: Cambridge UP, 1991. 67–90.

——. *Residues of Justice: Literature, Law, Philosophy.* Berkeley: U of California P, 1996.

Ellison, Ralph. "Twentieth-Century Fiction and the Black Mask of Humanity." *Shadow and Act.* New York: Random, 1964, 22–44.

Ferguson, Frances. "*Justine;* or, The Law of the Road." *Aesthetics and Ideology.* Ed. George Levine. New Brunswick: Rutgers UP, 1994. 106–23.

Fishkin, Shelley Fisher. *Lighting Out for the Territory: Reflections on Mark Twain and American Culture.* New York: Oxford UP, 1997.

——. "Racial Attitudes." *The Mark Twain Encyclopedia.* Ed. J. R. LeMaster and James D. Wilson. New York: Garland, 1993. 609–15.

Foner, Eric. *Reconstruction: America's Unfinished Revolution, 1863–1877.* New York: Harper, 1988.

Friedman, Lawrence M. *A History of American Law.* New York: Simon, 1973.

Gollin, Richard, and Rita Gollin. "*Huckleberry Finn* and the Time of the Evasion." *Modern Language Studies* 9.2 (1979): 5–15.

Goodman, Nan. "A Clear Showing: The Problem of Fault in James Fenimore Cooper's *The Pioneers.*" *Arizona Quarterly* 49 (1993): 1–22.

Hansen, Miriam Bratu. "*Schindler's List* Is Not *Shoah:* Second Commandment, Popular Modernism, and Public Memory." *Spielberg's Holocaust: Critical Perspectives on* Schindler's List. Ed. Yosefa Loshitzky. Bloomington: Indiana UP, 1997. 77–103.

Hart, H. L. A. *Punishment and Responsibility.* New York: Oxford UP, 1968.

Hartman, Geoffrey, ed. *Holocaust Remembrance: The Shapes of Memory.* Cambridge: Blackwell, 1994.

Hill, Richard. "Overreaching: Critical Agenda and the Ending of *Huckleberry Finn.*" *Texas Studies in Literature and Language* 33 (1991): 492–513.

Holland, Laurence. "A 'Raft of Trouble': Word and Deed in *Huckleberry Finn.*" *American Realism: New Essays.* Ed. Eric Sundquist. Baltimore: Johns Hopkins UP, 1982. 66–81.

Holmes, Oliver Wendell, Jr. *The Common Law.* New York: Dover, 1991.

Horwitz, Morton. *The Transformation of American Law, 1780–1860.* Cambridge: Harvard UP, 1977.

Jehlen, Myra. "Banned in Concord: *Adventures of Huckleberry Finn* and Classic American Literature." Robinson 93–115.

Leonard, James S., Thomas A. Tenney, and Thadious M. Davis, eds. *Satire or Evasion? Black Perspectives on "Huckleberry Finn."* Durham: Duke UP, 1992.

Macleod, Christine. "Telling the Truth in a Tight Place: *Huckleberry Finn* and the Reconstruction Era." *Southern Quarterly* 34 (1995): 5–15.

Marx, Leo. "Mr. Eliot, Mr. Trilling, and *Huckleberry Finn.*" Adventures of Huckleberry Finn: *A Case Study in Critical Controversy.* Ed. Gerald Graff and James Phelan. Boston: Bedford, 2004. 273–88.

Michaels, Walter Benn. " 'You Who Never Was There': Slavery and the New Historicism, Deconstruction and the Holocaust." *Narrative* 4.1 (1996): 1–16.

Morrison, Toni. Introduction. Twain, *Adventures* xxxi–xli.

Nilon, Charles H. "The Ending of *Huckleberry Finn:* 'Freeing the Free Negro.' " Leonard, Tenney, and Davis 62–76.

Nussbaum, Martha. *Poetic Justice: The Literary Imagination and Public Life.* Boston: Beacon, 1995.

Pendleton, James D. Letter. *Harper's Magazine* Apr. 1996: 6–7.

Pettit, Arthur G. *Mark Twain and the South.* Lexington: UP of Kentucky, 1974.

Quirk, Tom. *Coming to Grips with* Huckleberry Finn: *Essays on a Book, a Boy, and a Man.* Columbia: U of Missouri P. 1993.

Reising, Russell. *The Unusable Past: Theory and the Study of American Literature.* New York: Methuen, 1986.

Robinson, Forrest G., ed. *The Cambridge Companion to Mark Twain.* New York: Cambridge UP, 1995.

Smiley, Jane. "Say It Ain't So, Huck: Second Thoughts on Mark Twain's 'Masterpiece.' " *Harper's Magazine* Jan. 1996: 61–67.

Smith, David L. "Huck, Jim, and American Racial Discourse." Leonard, Tenney, and Davis 103–20.

Thomas, Brook. *American Literary Realism and the Failed Promise of Contract.* Berkeley: U of California P, 1997.

Trilling, Lionel. *"Huckleberry Finn." The Liberal Imagination.* New York: Viking, 1950. 104–17.

Twain, Mark. *Adventures of Huckleberry Finn.* Ed. Shelley Fisher Fishkin. New York: Oxford UP, 1996.

———. "Huck Finn and Tom Sawyer among the Indians." *"Huck Finn and Tom Sawyer among the Indians" and Other Unfinished Stories.* Berkeley: U of California P, 1989. 33–81.

———. "Tom Sawyer Abroad." *"Tom Sawyer Abroad," "Tom Sawyer, Detective," and Other Stories.* New York: Harper, 1904. 7–136.

———. "Tom Sawyer's Conspiracy." *"Huck Finn and Tom Sawyer among the Indians" and Other Unfinished Stories.* Berkeley: U of California P, 1989. 134–213.

Twain, Mark, and Charles Dudley Warner. *The Gilded Age: A Tale of Today.* New York: Oxford UP, 1996 [1873].

White, G. Edward. *Tort Law in America: An Intellectual History.* New York: Oxford UP, 1980.

Williams, Bernard. *Shame and Necessity.* Berkeley: U of California P, 1993.

Wonham, Henry B. "'I Want a Real Coon': Mark Twain and Late-Nineteenth-Century Ethnic Caricature." *American Literature* 72.1 (2000): 117–52.

Young, James E. *The Texture of Memory: Holocaust Memorials and Meaning.* New Haven: Yale UP, 1993.

SACVAN BERCOVITCH

FROM Deadpan Huck

Sacvan Bercovitch (b. 1933) is professor emeritus of English at Harvard University, where he served as Powell M. Cabot Research Professor. He earned his B.A. (1961) from Sir George William College and received both his M.A. (1963) and his Ph.D. (1965) from Claremont Graduate University. Bercovitch began his teaching career in 1966, spending two years each at Brandeis University and the University of California, San Diego before moving to Columbia University in 1970. In 1983, Bercovitch accepted a position at Harvard, where he has remained since. He is the author of *The American Puritan Imagination* (1974), *The Puritan Origins of the American Self* (1975), *The American Jeremiad* (1978), *The Office of The Scarlet Letter* (1991), and *The Rites of Assent* (1993). Bercovitch is also the editor of *Reconstructing American Literary History* (1986) and of *Ideology and Classic American Literature* (with Myra Jehlen, 1986), and is general editor of the *Cambridge History of American Literature* (1994–). "Deadpan Huck," the essay excerpted here, first appeared in the *Kenyon Review.*

Tall tale, con game, deadpan: in all three cases, the humor that Twain inherited reflects the particular conditions of the southwestern frontier. These are well known but worth rehearsing, since they help explain the distinctive connections *within the deadpan mode* between the tall tale and the con game. Consider first Henry Wonham's description of the turbulent context of the tall tale:

Tall [Tale] Humor is American not because it is incongruous — all humor is that — but because it articulates incongruities that are embedded in the American experience. A country founded, settled, and closely observed by men and women with extraordinary expectations, both exalted and depraved, could not help but appreciate the distance that separated the ideal from the real, the "language of culture" from the "language of sweat," the democratic dream from the social and economic reality of the early American republic.[1]

The social group, then, which the tall tale expresses and celebrates, is characterized by instability, defined by extreme alternations between exaltation and despair. Its rampant incongruities, its raw discrepancies between real and ideal, make it a con-man's paradise. Recently, Hilton Obenzinger has amplified Wonham's description in a way that extends this link between con man and tall tale and clarifies the relation of both to the deadpan mode. Following Wonham, he points out that the

"gap" between culture and sweat found in frontier experiences — which characteristically included Indian wars, slave-dealing, *herrenvolk* white racial solidarity, endemic violence, economic instability, fluidity, humbuggery, and speculative fantasy — cultivated a vernacular humor of extremes, along with pleasure in horror and depravity. . . .
    Tall [tale] humor was a form of initiation and survival in response to radical physical and social uncertainties on the edge of

[1]Henry B. Wonham, *Mark Twain and the Art of the Tall Tale* (Oxford: Oxford UP, 1993) 20–21.

settler-colonial expansion. This humor thrived at the borderland of displacement, migration, and violence, finding much of its pleasure in dethroning the condescension of gentility at the thickly settled Eastern core, while at the same time reproducing the radical incongruities and discrepancies at the root of all American experience.[2]

These are the social and psychological uncertainties of a new capitalist nation in the process of emergence. It makes for a world of physical turbulence and shifting identities where one way of being funny slides naturally into another.

A handy way to see the different kinds of fun involved in this process is through what (according to the *OED* and the *American Heritage Dictionary*) are the three basic meanings of the word: (1) *Funny* as in "just plain fun" — the childlike humor we designate as "kidding around," a humor commensurate with the traditional tall tale, "designed to amuse." (2) *Funny* in its antiquated meaning of "befool," as in "tricky or deceitful" — a satiric form of humor that plays upon social norms, and thus relates closely to the confidence game. (3) *Funny* as in "strangely or suspiciously odd, curious," the chilling sense of some sinister hidden meaning, as when we say there's "something funny" about that con man; he might be a killer. This sinister humor, which characterizes a certain form of deadpan, and which is latent in all deadpan modes, tends towards "horror and depravity." In our post-frontier times (the era of *Beavis and Butt-Head* and *Pulp Fiction*) it's the pleasure we take in sick jokes and the absurd.

Usually humorists specialize in one way or another of being funny — let us call them cheerful, satirical, and sinister. But as we've seen, these modes slip readily into one another; and American deadpan reaches its highest pitch, the finest turn of its "high and delicate art," when the joke reverberates with all three layers of fun, from (laughingly) "that's *funny*" to (suspiciously) "*that's* funny."

Mark Twain's humor is deadpan at its best, and *Huckleberry Finn* is his funniest book, in all three senses of the term. Accordingly, in what follows I use the terms tall tale, con man, and deadpan reciprocally, fluidly, on the grounds that Twain's deadpan — the third, sinister, "odd or curious" sense of funny — incorporates (without submerging, indeed while deliberately drawing out) the other two forms of humor.

[2]Hilton Manfred Obenzinger, *American Palestine: Melville, Twain, and the Holy Land Mania* (Princeton: Princeton UP, 1999) 166.

His method involves a drastic turnabout in deadpan effect. In order to enlist the tall tale and con game in the service of deadpan, Twain actually reverses conventional techniques. That is to say, the novel *overturns the very tradition of deadpan that it builds upon*. As a rule, that tradition belongs to the narrator. Huck has often been said to speak deadpan-style; but the funny thing is, he is *not* a humorist, not even when he's putting someone on (as he does Aunt Sally when he pretends to be Tom Sawyer). In fact, he rarely has fun; he's usually "in a sweat"[3]; and on the rare occasion when he does try to kid around (as when he tells Jim they were *not* separated in the fog) the joke turns back on itself to humiliate him. Huck's voice may be described as pseudo-deadpan; it *sounds* comic, but actually it's troubled, earnest. The real deadpan artist is Mark Twain of course, and what's remarkable, what makes for the inversion I just spoke of, is that this con man is not straight-faced (as Huck is), but smiling. To recall Twain's distinction between the English comic story and the American humorous story, the author is wearing the Mask of Comedy. He hides his humor, we might say, behind a comic facade. The humor, a vehicle of deceit, is directed against the audience. The tale itself, however, is constantly entertaining, often amusing, sometimes hilarious; apparently the storyteller is having a wonderful time, laughing through it all — and actually so are we.

So here's the odd or curious setup of *Huckleberry Finn*: the deadpan artist is Mark Twain, wearing the Comic Mask, doing his best to conceal the fact that he suspects that there's anything grave, let alone sinister, about his story, and he succeeds famously. Then, as we laugh, or after we've laughed, we may realize, if we're alert, that there's something we've overlooked. We haven't seen what's funny about the fact that we've found it funny. This artist has gulled us. He has diverted our attention away from the real point, and we have to go back over his story in order to recognize its nub.

The nature of re-cognition in this sense (understanding something all over again, doing a double take) may be simply illustrated. Consider a culture like the late nineteenth-century Southwest, which was both racist and egalitarian. The minstrel show was a genre born out of precisely that contradiction. So imagine a deadpan minstrel act that goes like this. The audience hears a funny story about a stereotype "darkie"

---

[3]Mark Twain, *Adventures of Huckleberry Finn*, eds. Walter Blair and Victor Fischer (Berkeley: U of California P, 1988) 2; see also 7, 77, 84, 125, 141, 167, 174, 233, 234, 334.

and they smile and laugh along. The nub of course is that *they* are being laughed at; they've been taken in and made the butt of a joke. Once they see that, if they do, they understand what's truly funny about the story, and they're free to laugh at themselves for having laughed in the first place. That freedom may be compared to the shock of the funny bone. It's a complex sensation, engaging all three meanings of funny, not unlike the odd tingling vibration you feel when you're hit on the funny bone. A light touch might mean no more than a bit of healthy fun — say, the wake-up call of the tall tale (the joke reminds you of your egalitarian principles). A sharp touch might be unnerving — a satire directed against the system at large (you recognize that this self-proclaimed egalitarian society is fundamentally racist). A direct and vicious cut would be painful, a sensation of violence, as in the sinister sense of "funny" (you realize that egalitarianism itself is a joke and that you're a sucker for having believed in it).

Twain's humor, to repeat, spans all three forms. *Huckleberry Finn* is the apotheosis of American deadpan, a masterfully coordinated synthesis of all three layers of the meaning of *funny*, with the emphasis on the sinister. It is worth remarking that the novel is unique in this regard. Twain achieved this feat only once. His earlier works are rarely sinister, not even when they're brimful of violence, as in *Roughing It* (1872), or for that matter *Tom Sawyer* (1876). His later works are rarely funny, not even when they're brimful of jokes, as in *Puddn'head Wilson* (1892) or the tales of terror collected posthumously as *The Great Dark*. *Adventures of Huckleberry Finn* is Twain's great synthetic work, incorporating every stage of his development as "America's Humorist," from the unalloyed cheer of "The Celebrated Jumping Frog of Calaveras County" through the fierce satire of *The Gilded Age* to the David Lynch- (or Robert Crum-)like world of "The Man Who Corrupted Hadleyburg." Twain's mode of coordination in *Huckleberry Finn,* the dialectic behind his fantastic synthesis, is a drastic reversal of effect: the deadpan artist with the Comic Mask. And the procession of nubs or snappers he delivers constitutes the most severe shocks in our literature to the American funny bone.

The first shock is that the novel is funny at all. The slave hunt serves as both metaphor and metonymy for the world it portrays: *Huckleberry Finn* describes a slave hunt undertaken literally, collectively, by a society which is itself enslaved — a culture in bondage to all the Seven Deadly Sins (in addition to the sin of chattel slavery), and accordingly characterized by violence, mean-spiritedness, ignorance, and deceit. A fair example is Pikesville, a shanty town somewhere along the river:

All the streets and lanes was just mud; they warnt nothing else *but* mud — mud as black as tar and nigh about a foot deep in some places, and two or three inches deep in *all* the places. The hogs loafed and grunted around, everywheres. You'd see a muddy sow and a litter of pigs come lazying along the street and whollop herself right down in the way, where folks had to walk around her, and she'd stretch out, and shut her eyes, and wave her ears, whilst the pigs was milking her, and look as happy as if she was on salary. And pretty soon you'd hear a loafer sing out, "Hi! *so* boy! sick him, Tige!" and away the sow would go, squealing most horrible, with a dog or two swinging to each ear, and three or four dozen more a-coming; and then you would see all the loafers get up and watch the thing out of sight, and laugh at the fun and look grateful for the noise. Then they'd settle back again till there was a dog-fight. There couldn't anything wake them up all over, and make them happy all over, like a dog-fight — unless it might be putting turpentine on a stray dog and setting fire to him, or tying a tin pan to his tail and see him run himself to death. (pp. 142–43 in this volume).

Readers of the novel remember Pikesville not for that bit of "fun" (though that's the town's main source of laughter), but for the Shakespearean soliloquy delivered there by the Duke and the King:

To be or not to be; that is the bare bodkin
That makes calamity of so long life . . .
'Tis a consummation devoutly to be wished. (pp. 139–40)

That's what we laugh at, as we should. Consider, however, that image of a sow on the run, "squealing most horrible," of a dog running himself to death. And now think of the nub concealed within the Shakespearean parody: the Duke and King are debased men, the townspeople are debased, and debasement in both cases is a metonym for the slave trade. The stray dog is Jim on the run, or it's Huck *hounded* by civilization. The animal kingdom is paraded before us as in a deadpan Eden: pigs, dogs, and people mingling contentedly in mud, and the joke lies in the calamity we humans make of "so long life." Clearly, this is the world of what scholars have termed the Late Dark Twain: the world of *The Damned Human Race, The Great Dark,* and the satanic *Letters from the Earth,* where man, the lowest of all animals, is "first and last and all the time . . . a sarcasm"[4] — a world of Calvinism without God. . . .

[4]Mark Twain, *Letters from the Earth,* in *Collected Tales, Sketches, Speeches, and Essays, 1891–1910,* ed. Louis J. Budd (New York: Library of America, 1994) 884.

To that end, I turn to my third and main example. The passage comes when Huck lands at the Phelps Plantation, where he meets Sally Phelps, who mistakes him for her nephew Tom Sawyer. Huck reflexively goes along with his new identity, but gets confused in explaining what now turns out to be his late arrival: Tom had been expected by steamboat some time before. Huck at first explains that the boat had been grounded; then can't think of *which* grounding — but, (resourceful liar that he is),

> I struck an idea, and fetched it out:
> "It warn't the grounding — that didn't keep us back but a little. We blowed out a cylinder-head."
> "Good gracious! anybody hurt?"
> "No'm. Killed a nigger."
> "Well, it's lucky; because sometimes people do get hurt. Two years ago last Christmas, your uncle Silas was coming up from Newrleans on the old Lally Rook, and she blowed out a cylinder-head and crippled a man. And I think he died, afterwards. He was a Babtist." (p. 206)

Again, we're at a structural crux of the narrative. The arrival at the Phelps Plantation unites all three sections of the novel (Hannibal, the river journey, and the Phelps episode), and it connects all three layers of Trickster fun (cheerful, satirical, and sinister). It also demonstrates Twain's hermeneutic imperative — we *must* interpret this scene (its humor leaves us no alternative) — while offering a model example of what's funny about our habits of interpretation. I take the joke to lie in the infamous one-liner "No'm. Killed a nigger." Actually it's a one-liner divided into two parts: "No'm [full stop]. Killed a nigger." We are then diverted from its nub by Aunt Sally's story of the Lally Rook. To recall Twain's instruction: when the joke comes, "the listener must be alert, for . . . the teller will divert attention from the nub by dropping it in a carefully casual or indifferent way, with the pretense that he does not know it is a nub." The "Babtist" is a decoy; it allows the story to bubble gently along. In fact, to keep it bubbling, just in case the reader doesn't laugh straight off, Twain extends Aunt Sally's ruminations: "Yes, I remember now, he *did* die. Mortification set in and they had to amputate him. But it didn't save him. Yes, it was mortification — that was it. He turned blue all over, and died in the hope of a glorious resurrection. They say he was a sight to look at." A very funny sight, but its nub is encoded in Huck's two-part throwaway line: "No'm. Killed a nigger." In what follows I mean to decode Twain's deadpan by outlin-

ing eight points about Huck's response to which we should be alert, if
we're courageous enough to want to get the joke. First, the episode is a model instance of the way Twain combines
the tall tale and con game through the sinister aspect of deadpan.
Huck's response is a comic-fiction exaggeration, defining the values of
a certain social group, which then serves as a successful con job, con-
firming Huck as Tom. And *as such* it stands as one of the most vicious
jokes in the entire literature of prejudice. Huck's "No'm" reflects back
through the narrative, in ways that undermine virtually all of the novel's
"good characters," such as the kindly frontierswoman, Judith Loftus,
who cuts short Huck's visit to join the "nigger hunt." And it serves as a
fit prelude to the long Phelps episode, where Aunt Sally and Uncle Silas
are portrayed as warmly hospitable people, the salt of the earth, even as
the search for Jim reaches its climax and the "no one" joke is fully
enacted, most dramatically, perhaps, when a group of men decide to
lynch Jim for all the trouble he has caused — a "*raft* of trouble," is the
way Twain humorously has one of them phrase it (p. 256, my italics) —
but relent when they realize that, as unclaimed property, Jim is worth
more alive than dead.

Second, Huck's use of "nigger" is profoundly racist. We can't argue
(as too many critics have) that it's just slang — a poor, ignorant boy's
way of saying African American. What Huck *means* is far worse than
what a bigot means by "wop" or "wasp." Huck is saying that a "nigger" is a *no one*, a nonhuman. It's worth noting in this respect that in
1900 the first professor of American literature at Harvard, Barrett Wendell, focused on this passage in his standardized *Literary History of
America*. Huck's "No'm. Killed a nigger," he writes, is a serious statement of relative merit, not only accurate but prescient of what right-
minded people believe: not only "an admirably compact expression of
[the] temper" of the antebellum South, but "more consonant with
New-England temper to-day than it was seventy years ago. Modern
ethnology seems to recognise [*sic*] a pretty marked distinction between
human beings in the Stone Age and human beings as developed into
the civilization of the nineteenth century."[5] Wendell's case is extreme,

[5]Barrett Wendell, *A Literary History of America* (New York: Charles Scribner's Sons,
1900) 342. Wendell later calls *Huckleberry Finn* a "masterpiece" (477). I am uncomfort-
ably aware of my own position in the descent of Harvard professors of American literature, all of whom have contributed significantly to the consecration of Huck Finn as the
quintessential American. The line runs from Wendell through Perry Miller and his students, such as Henry Nash Smith and Leo Marx; and in all its variations, from Wendell's
praise of Huck's racism to Marx's denunciation of what he considered to be Twain's

an *open* white supremacist, but he was giving an academic stamp to attitudes that were pervasive in Twain's America, North and South. His interpretation suggests the full scope of the joke (from the ebullient Pan in deadpan to his sinister incarnation as *dead*pan) in Huck's response to the straight-man query, "anybody hurt?"

Third, Huck's response is gratuitous, totally unnecessary. That's the joke in the *forced* pause at the center of the line. Huck could just as well have stopped at "No'm." And be it noted that that kind of gratuitous remark, in all its racist implications, is typical of Huck. The *casual* N-word is fundamental to his vocabulary. As critics over the past three decades have pointed out, the word "nigger" occurs on virtually every page of the novel, and it's worth emphasizing that it took three generations of readers *before them* to take offense. The first debates about *Huckleberry Finn* centered on issues of class, not race. The complaints had to do with Huck's delinquency, bad habits, and poor grammar. The N-word went largely unnoticed until the 1960s, and I believe that the not-noticing was basic to Twain's deadpan. Part of the joke is that the word was woven into the very fabric of Twain's self-proclaimed democratic culture, at once a vicious slur and a ubiquitous, unexamined byword ("catch a nigger by the toe"), ubiquitous because unexamined and unexamined because ubiquitous. Once again, Huck's response is entirely appropriate, to him and his readership alike.

It's also appropriate to the plot of the novel. That's the fourth point to make about Huck's remark. His joke concerns a dead person, or rather a dead nonperson, and death is a main narrative thread — death in the deadpan mode, gilded over by humor, as in the early passages concerning Tom's gang:

> . . . Tom got out a sheet of paper that he had wrote the oath on, and read it. It swore every boy to stick to the band, and never tell

betrayal of Huck's cause of freedom. My own iconoclasm in this respect is not consciously prompted by an anxiety of influence, but I should note that I first elaborated my views in my first class on *Huckleberry Finn* at Harvard in 1983. My sense then was that my (indignantly received) interpretation was prompted by my relative innocence — my lack of acculturation — as an immigrant in the United States of Huckdom. In retrospect, I feel that my interpretation also registered an era in academia marked by a suspicion of all rhetorics of nationalism and a globalist deconstruction of traditional forms of Americanism. Ironically, this was also the beginnings of what may be called the Americanization of the world; and I venture to predict (since the process of Americanization has long since come to incorporate literary studies as well) that the mythic-liberal-heroic Huck will prevail, in one form or another — not just in the U.S.A., but, in due time, and with due training, globally.

any of the secrets; and if anybody done anything to any boy in the band, whichever boy was ordered to kill that person and his family must do it. . . . And if anybody that belonged to the band told the secrets, he must have his throat cut, and then have his carcass burnt up and the ashes scattered all around, and his name blotted off the list with blood. . . .

Everybody said it was a real beautiful oath . . .

Some thought it would be good to kill the *families* of boys that told the secrets. Tom said it was a good idea, so he took a pencil and wrote it in. Then Ben Rogers says:

"Here's Huck Finn, he hain't got no family; what you going to do 'bout him?"

"Well, hain't he got a father?" says Tom Sawyer.

"Yes, he's got a father, but you can't never find him these days . . . hain't been seen in these parts for a year or more."

They talked it over, and they was going to rule me out, because they said every boy must have a family or somebody to kill, or else it wouldn't be fair and square. . . . Well nobody could think of anything to do — everybody was stumped, and set still. I was most ready to cry; but all at once I thought of a way, and so I offered them Miss Watson — they could kill her. Everybody said:

"Oh, she'll do. That's all right. Huck can come in." (p. 37)

This is funny, although not to Huck (he's "most ready to cry"). It's Tom who's having fun, along with us.

But Twain has a different point in mind. And (as in the case of Huck's N-word, in response to Aunt Sally) the point is obvious once we're on to his method. Death and violence are writ large throughout the novel, in virtually every scene and episode. The blood bond that Tom invents is a mirror reflection of the world of *Huckleberry Finn*. It foreshadows the death hoax that Huck thinks up when he leaves for the river ("I pulled out some of my hair, and bloodied the ax good" and made a track so that they'd look "to find the robbers that killed me" [pp. 57, 58]); and the horrific scene earlier, when his blind-drunk father chases him around the shack with a "clasp-knife" (laughing with "*such* a screechy laugh"), cursing and roaring that Huck is the Angel of Death, and that he will now kill him once and for all (p. 54). These sorts of fantasies and facts *are* the adventures of Huck. They come to life in the Boggs murder, in scenes of lynching and tar and feathering, in the Grangerford-Shepherdson clan massacre, even (and in a way most tellingly) in the wreck of the *Walter Scott* when Huck steals the robbers' skiff, acting as he imagines Tom Sawyer would have —

thereby, presumably, leaving the robbers to drown. According to Twain scholars, there are thirty-three corpses in *Huckleberry Finn,* and that does not include either those probably drowned robbers or the ghastly corpse in the section Twain omitted, surely one of the most vivid and morbid he ever wrote, describing Pap's dead body. One early review (and in this single respect a uniquely discerning one) complained that Huck's adventures were simply one "bloodcurdling" adventure after another;[6] and indeed it's not too much to say that dead bodies, real and imagined, are the anatomical links of his story. It's appropriate that G.G., the deadpan link between Twain and Huck, reader and narrative, should be a Chief of Artillery — appropriate, too, that his Notice should warn that anyone seeking a plot would be shot. Getting killed is a key to the novel's plot line.

The fifth point to make about Huck's "joke" concerns the cause of death. On the river he travels, explosions are a common experience. Aunt Sally confirms this in the case of the poor Baptist, and we can find many other examples in the novel (steamboats grounded, blown up, cutting rafts in two). The point is: this river is sinister. Critics have tended to sentimentalize it — T. S. Eliot called it the "River God that gives to Man his dignity" — and to be sure such sentiments are invited by its deadpan author. But if we pay attention Twain makes it all too plain that this "great brown god" is a deadly con man. "Kill, kill, kill," Satan reports in *Letters from the Earth,* Nature "is murder all along the line," and *Huckleberry Finn* might have been his proof-text.[7] The river is the source of storms and water snakes, it calls up the fog that keeps Huck and Jim from reaching Cairo; it is "dangersome" to those on it and those who live near it. One example of many:

> the houses was sticking out over the bank, and they was bowed and bent, and about ready to tumble in. . . . People lived in them yet, but it was dangersome, because sometimes a strip of land as wide as a house caves in at a time. Sometimes a belt of land a

[6][Robert Bridges], "Mark Twain's Blood-Curdling Humor," *Life,* v (26 Feb. 1885): 119.

[7]T. S. Eliot, "Introduction" to *Adventures of Huckleberry Finn,* in *Adventures of Huckleberry Finn: A Case Study in Critical Controversy,* eds. Gerald Graff and James Phelan [Boston and New York: Bedford Books, 1995] 288; Lionel Trilling, "Introduction" to *Adventures of Huckleberry Finn,* in *Huck Finn and His Critics,* eds. Richard Letis, William E. Morris, and Robert F. McDonnell (New York: Macmillan, 1962) 328 (quoting T. S. Eliot); Mark Twain, *Letters from the Earth,* in *Collected Tales . . . 1890–1910,* ed. Budd 882.

quarter of a mile deep will start in and cave along till it all caves
into the river in one summer . . . the river's always gnawing at
it. (p. 143)

This river affords Huck and Jim some wonderful moments together; and to underscore these, critics like to quote Huck's description
of life on the raft: "what you want . . . is for everybody to be satisfied,
and [to] feel right and kind towards the others" (p. 130). But they have
failed to take stock of Huck's far more typical *melancholy* on the raft
and his overriding sense of loneliness: "there wouldn't be nothing to
hear nor nothing to see," he comments about the river, "— just solid
lonesomeness" (p. 125). They have failed, too, to add that Huck's
desire to please "everybody" registers Jim as a "nobody" once again:
that's how Huck *rationalizes* allowing the King and Duke to have their
way ("it warn't no use to tell Jim" [p. 130]). And perhaps most important, critics have never yet to my knowledge noted that for most of the
river journey (almost two-thirds of it) life on the raft is controlled and
directed by those "rapscallions" (p. 152), as Huck charitably calls them.
There are about three pages devoted to the happy idyll of Huck and Jim
on the river, most of them at the start of chapter 19. Albert Bigelow
Paine rightly commented long ago that "[t]his is the Huck we want,
and this is the Huck we usually have, and [have] . . . been thankful for";
although in the standard edition these three pages — on the basis of
which critics have repeatedly asserted (as a claim "not worth arguing")
that "life on the raft is idyllic, and *Huckleberry Finn* is a pastoral fiction
that looks back nostalgically to an earlier and simpler America" — these
three pages occupy less than one percent of the book.[8] And in what
might well be viewed as a deadpan joke on Twain's part, they *directly*
precede the Duke and King's invasion of the raft. Huck and Jim may be
in flight on the Mississippi, but the Mississippi is the natural habitat of
the Duke and King, just as it is naturally the cause of mud slides. *This*
river is emphatically not an emblem of Nature's Nation; it belongs to
the world of Hobbes, not Emerson. Nothing is more natural about
Huck, nothing more clearly shows how *close* he is to the river, how well
he knows it, than does his spontaneous invention of the exploding
cylinder that (only) "Killed a nigger."

[8]Albert Bigelow Paine, *Mark Twain: A Biography* (New York: Harper and Brothers,
1912) II, 795; Richard Chase, *The American Novel and Its Traditions* (New York:
Doubleday, 1957) 148.

Not that Huck needs the river to prompt his invention; he always thinks in terms of death and disaster. That's the sixth point to note about his casual response. It alerts us to the fact that he's a death-haunted young boy. I'm referring now to the way he thinks and imagines rather than to what he experiences. Twain provides two clues to Huck's inner world: the lies Huck tells and the images he conjures up when he's alone — in other words, the reality that Huck himself makes up, for others and for himself. In both cases, it's the reality of the grotesque. Huck talks not so much "gravely" (deadpan-style) as grave-ly. The stories he invents for strangers are a series of horror tales: families dead, dying, or diseased. And he thinks grave-ly too — except that in his solitary musings the dead return as ghosts. Consider his arrival at the Phelpses' plantation:

> When I got there it was all still and Sundaylike, and hot and sunshiny — the hands was gone to the fields; and there was them kind of faint dronings of bugs and flies in the air that makes it seem so lonesome and like everybody's dead and gone; and if a breeze fans along and quivers the leaves, it makes you feel mournful, because you feel like it's spirits whispering — spirits that's been dead ever so many years — and you always think they're talking about *you*. As a general thing, it makes a body wish *he* was dead, too, and done with it all. (p. 204)

Or consider Huck's first long meditation, sitting alone in his room at Miss Watson's:

> I set down in a chair by the window and tried to think of something cheerful, but it warn't no use. I felt so lonesome I most wished I was dead. The stars were shining and the leaves rustled in the woods ever so mournful; and I heard an owl, away off, who-whooing about somebody that was dead, and a whippowill and a dog crying about someone that was going to die; and the wind was trying to whisper something to me and I couldn't make out what it was, and so it made the cold shivers run over me. Then away out in the woods I heard that kind of sound that a ghost makes when it wants to tell about something that's on its mind and can't make itself understood, and so can't rest easy in its grave, and has to go about that way every night grieving. (p. 34)

What's funny about these descriptions is that actually, to all appearances, it's a lovely Sunday morning, a starry summer night. There's no reason for Huck to think this way, except that that's the way he thinks.

But of course he's not alone when he invents the cylinder explosion; on the contrary, he's trying hard to please someone else. He's being led on by Aunt Sally, who prods him about the grounding. He knows what she'd like to hear, and he knows she'll think a "nigger" is "no one," just as he knows she'd like him to be Tom. And naturally he complies. That's the seventh point to note about his response. Huck *wants* to conform. More precisely, he's a conformist who can't make it. Huck would like to please everyone, including Miss Watson. He would even like to live with Pap, if Pap would let him live; he tries as best he can to "satisfy" the Duke and King; he tells us he'd gladly join the Grangerfords (at the expense of abandoning Jim); and he'd love to be Tom Sawyer — but he can't. Huck Finn is Woody Allen's Zelig in reverse: a deadpan artist's Zelig. Zelig may not want to be a Chinese chef or a Nazi, but he can't help becoming just like whomever he's with. Huck's dilemma is just the opposite: he can't help being different. Certainly we sympathize with his difference, we applaud it, but the nub remains. Huck's desire to fit in is underscored by his inability to do so. That's because he so totally believes in society, He *believes* in racism, class hierarchy, Southern aristocracy, Sunday school religion. Why else would he be so disappointed, towards the end of his adventures, in Tom's plan to "steal" Jim? "Well, one thing was dead sure," he says, crestfallen, after trying to persuade Tom otherwise,

one thing was dead sure; and that was, that Tom Sawyer was in earnest, and was actly going to help steal that nigger out of slavery. That was the thing that was too many for me. Here was a boy that was respectable, and well brung up; and had a character to lose; and folks at home that had characters; and he was bright and not leather headed; and knowing, and not ignorant; and not mean, but kind; and yet here he was, without any more pride, or rightness, or feeling, than to stoop to this business, and make himself a shame, and his family a shame, before everybody. I couldn't understand it no way at all. It was outrageous. . . . (p. 216)

If this were a children's book called *Tom Sawyer,* we could read this passage ironically, as a salutary bit of social satire. The white-trash boy is at once denouncing (when he shouldn't) and looking up to (when he needn't) the respectable head-of-the-gang. But *Adventures of Huckleberry Finn* is something else altogether. It's a complex, sophisticated narrative about a black-white relationship. To recall Twain's phrase, it's a work "of high and delicate art . . . [as] only an artist can tell it" — one in which an African American takes on extraordinary human force.

Jim, we learn, is the noblest person in Huck's life; virtually the novel's hero, if we could get beyond the minstrel-show humor to which (in one of the most vicious cuts of Twain's deadpan) Jim himself is subject; the father we feel Huck deserves and never had; and by any measure the novel's most sympathetic adult figure. Can it be funny that Huck thinks like *this* after his long experience with Jim on the river? After all he has seen of Jim — having acknowledged, however reluctantly, Jim's goodness, intelligence, and caring; having felt so ashamed of his behavior towards Jim, on one singular occasion, that he actually apologizes for it (though "it was fifteen minutes before I could work myself up to go and humble myself to a nigger" [p. 100]) — after all this can Huck believe that it would be "leather headed" for Tom "stoop to this business"?

In order to explain this nub we need to rehearse its context. The last narrative section, occupying almost a third of the novel, has become a familiar critical crux. Twain scholars have debated its merits ever since Hemingway advised readers to skip it altogether. Evidently Tom's tricks at the Phelpses' did amuse the Reconstructionist audience of the time, and in the decades following (the world of Barrett Wendell, of the minstrel show, and of D. W. Griffith's epic celebration of the Ku Klux Klan, *The Birth of a Nation,* filmed in the decade after Twain wrote "The United States of Lyncherdom"): Jim shackled in a wood-shack (into which Tom and Huck "smuggle" rats, spiders, and snakes), rolling a grindstone uphill with a chain "wrapt . . . round and round his neck," writing messages "with his blood," biting into a corn pone with a candlestick hidden in it. "It most mashed all his teeth out," Huck reports, and then explains, straight-faced: "Jim he couldn't see no sense in the most of it, but he allowed we was white folks and knowed better than him; so he was satisfied" (pp. 237, 229, 228). Tom's higher knowledge comes from the romances of Alexander Dumas (whose African ancestry, if Twain knew of it, would add another dimension to the satire); he names his scheme the Great Evasion; and the joke, it turns out, is that Jim has already been freed. If we carry the logic of the joke to its absurd end, we could say Jim was *lucky* he didn't get to Cairo and the North, since he would then never have known that he was a free man.

To their credit, critics over the past half century have roundly denounced the hoax and all it implies. We can now safely say that it's a grand sarcasm on Twain's part directed against Tom Sawyer. The usual critical term here has been irony. But in the ironic situation, classically defined (from Sophocles through Jane Austen), the readers know, or gradually learn, what's actually going on; they are the author's accomplice. In the deadpan situation, they are the author's victims. That's precisely the case in the Great Evasion. The irony of the Good Bad Boy, whose mischief-by-the-book we see through and scorn, deflects us from the snapper. It's as though our eagerness to interpret Tom as reader (applying the rules of Dumas's *Count of Monte Cristo* to Jim in bondage) preempts a view of ourselves as readers of Huck's complicity. For what's really funny about Tom's hoax is that the Bad Bad Boy, *our* Huck, goes along. Fundamentally, he's no different at the end from the racist, death-haunted, would-be conformist he was before he set out on his adventures. That's what makes it appropriate for him to respond to Aunt Sally as he does, in spite of all he has learned about Jim. Or rather, *because* of all he has *not* learned, for (as his gratuitous "Killed a nigger" should shock us into re-cognizing) Huck never develops. Far from being a moral and aesthetic collapse, as critics have lamented, the novel's third and last section is perfectly in keeping with Twain's design — although for reasons antithetical to those usually proffered by his apologists. Huck's final adventures are substantively no different from all his others, as far as he himself is concerned, just as his attitude towards Tom Sawyer remains constant throughout, and just as his subservience here to Tom resembles his subservience to the Duke and King on the raft. Huck speaks and thinks and feels at the Phelpses' pretty much as he does at Miss Watson's or at the Grangerfords'. The great middle part of the novel, the so-called journey to freedom, is the deadpan center piece of a triptych — Tom Sawyer's gang, a precarious raft on a treacherous river, and a wood-shack prison at the Phelps plantation — whose three panels are variations on a nub.

Now, there's a technical reason for this: *Adventures of Huckleberry Finn* is Huck's personal retrospective, specifically intended to set the record straight. He wants to retrieve the true story, he tells us, from Mr. Mark Twain's stretchers. If he had realized what we'd like him to have realized, he would have written an entirely different book. He would have felt different not only about Jim but about Tom and all others, including himself at that time. The boy who might have emerged from his adventures chastened and humbled, as critics have told us he did, would never have said, not even early in his river journey, that "you can't learn a nigger to argue," or later, after one of his particularly horrific experiences, "Well, if I ever struck anything like it, I'm a nigger" (p. 160); he would have felt obliged to explain why he abandoned Jim to live with the Grangerfords (and he would at least have modified the values which he tells us here and elsewhere he learned from his father about the importance of social class); he would have expressed regret for not having confided to Jim what he knew about the Duke and King — or to put this another way, he would have applied to this situation something of what he learned at the Wilkeses, where he *does* report that the Duke and King are frauds, and feels better for it ("I'm blest if it don't look to me like the truth is better, and actually *safer*, than a lie" [p. 152]) — and surely he would not have expected Jim, this grown man eager to free his wife and children, to join him and Tom in the territory. That is to say, if Huck Finn had really grown morally, Twain the deadpan artist could not gull us into thinking that he does. There would be no snapper to the story. Humorously speaking, his tale would be un-American.

Huck doesn't develop so that we can be conned into believing he does: this eighth aspect of the snapper reminds us that what we believe in ultimately is Huck's integrity. He has the same poignant purity from start to finish. He's *always* the lovable boy with the "sound heart"; from the outset his innate decency is set in contrast to society's "deformed conscience." And to draw out this con game, it's precisely that admirable aspect of him, the potential we discern *within* Huck's innocence, which invites us to interpret his narrative. That much-discussed, much-celebrated innocence — that *echt*-American innocence which links United States popular culture, high culture, and global politics — lies at the very heart of the con game. For Huck is emphatically not innocent of the world around him. Quite the contrary: he has been thoroughly socialized into it, as his reply to Aunt Sally demonstrates. He is not innocent, for example, of the abolitionist cause, which he roundly denounces. Nor is he innocent of the values of the Southern class system, as he demonstrates by his awestruck admiration for the pseudo-sentimental, phony-aristocratic, meretricious life at the Grangerfords. Nor of course is he innocent (or critical) of how those he respects will judge him. What will the people of Hannibal "think of *me*!," he trembles, when it gets "around that Huck Finn helped a nigger to get to his freedom[?] . . . if I was to ever see anybody from that town again, I'd be ready to get down and lick his boots for shame" (p. 199). We may say, however, that Huck is innocent insofar as innocence means ineducability. Huck is innocent of alternatives to the way things are. Therefore (to repeat) he doesn't develop, and *therefore* we do it for him. We know him better than he knows himself. Indeed, we know him as he *cannot* know himself, since his naïveté, his forever-*un*realized potential, *is* what we know about him, and what we cherish.

The con game this involves posits two contrary responses on our part: first, our superiority to Huck; and second, our identification with him. The deadpan link in this opposition lies in Twain's directive for interpretation. I said earlier that the deadpan Notice *goads* us into seeking moral, motive, and plot. I would now add that the snapper is then meant to guide us into a *certain* mode of interpretation — one that *compels* us to miss the nub, so as to keep the humor bubbling gently along. Just how this works is well illustrated by the scene that critics have rendered the *locus classicus* of Huck's moral progress. It is perhaps the most frequently cited passage in the novel, along with the river passage at the start of chapter 19, and always with the same heartening interpretation. Huck learns that the Duke and King have disclosed Jim's whereabouts, and he decides that rather than see Jim sold to "strangers," he should return him to Miss Watson, "his true and proper owner." Then he succumbs, conscience-stricken, to memories of how he himself helped this "runaway nigger" so that now "people would [rightly] call me a low down Abolitionist" (p. 65; cf. p. 118):

> I tried the best I could to kinder soften it up somehow for myself, by saying I was brung up wicked, and so I warn't so much to blame; but something inside of me kept saying, "There was the Sunday school, you could a gone to it; and if you'd a done it they'd a learnt you there that people that acts as I'd been acting about that nigger goes to everlasting fire."
>
> It made me shiver. And I about made up my mind to pray; and see if I couldn't try to quit being the kind of a boy I was, and be better. So I kneeled down. But the words wouldn't come. . . . You can't pray a lie — I found that out. . . . At last I had an idea; and I says, I'll go and write the letter — and *then* see if I can pray. . . . So I got a piece of paper and a pencil, all glad and excited, and set down and wrote:
>
>> Miss Watson, your runaway Nigger Jim is down here two mile below Pikesville and Mr. Phelps has got him and he will give him up for the reward if you send. Huck Finn.
>
> I felt good and all washed clean of sin for the first time I had ever felt so in my life, and I knowed I could pray now. But I didn't do it straight off, but laid the paper down and set there thinking . . . [and went on thinking] and then I happened to look around and see that paper.
>
> It was a close place: I took it up, and held it in my hand. I was a trembling. . . . I studied a minute, . . . and then says to myself:
>
> "All right then, I'll *go* to hell" — and tore it up.
>
> It was awful thoughts and awful words, but they was said. And I let them stay said and never thought no more about reforming . . . (pp. 200–01)

What's funny about this scene is [it's]: (1) cheerful — it's a mock-conversion that turns into a Devil's Pact; (2) satirical — it's a sweeping indictment of the ravages of Southern Evangelical Calvinism; and (3) odd, curious, and sinister — it's a mockery of our relation to the text. For in order to get the joke we *have* to interpret, and yet we feel sure that our interpretation is voluntary. This comes straight out of the American con-man's interpretation-by-consent bag of tricks. The meaning we find seems purely subjective, a meaning from the heart, and yet it's entirely predictable, a meaning directed step by step by Twain's deadpan. For notice that we are led to interpret in a perfectly consistent — a suspiciously consistent — pattern of inversions. Huck says "conscience" meaning the Right Thing to Do, and we think "source of evil"; he says "wicked" and we think "kind"; Huck laments that he was "brung up wrong" and we're glad that he has held fast to his virtues; he tells us he shivered with fear and we think he's brave and independent; he says, trembling, "I'll go to hell" and we think "he's saved!"

Is this a tall tale on Twain's part, or a con game? In either case his deadpan point is that our pattern of inversion is an act of protection. Whether or not we're aware of it, we're reaching between the lines to save Huck from everyone around him, from Tom and Miss Watson and the Grangerfords and the Phelpses. And our act of protection is in turn a claim to ownership. It makes Huck *ours*. The opening gang-oath is worth recalling in this regard. The question that Tom raises about family hostages opens into a much larger question: to whom does Huck belong? The narrative plays out a series of options — Pap, Miss Watson, Tom's gang, Jim, the river, the Territory — until it becomes obvious that Huck belongs *only to us*. We adopt him; we take him into our hearts; we interpret him in our likeness; we rewrite his text, figuratively (and sometimes literally, as in the novels of John Seelye and Richard Slotkin or in the many filmic adaptations of the novel, direct and indirect, from children's movies to *Shawshank Redemption*); we appropriate Huck as the child-in-us. The interpretive plot, then — that is, the process of interpretation carefully elicited from us, with all the sly diversions of deadpan art — leads inexorably from inversion to protection to adoption to, triumphantly, appropriation.

Let me name the snappers. First, there's the issue of style. Huck Finn is a great writer; his grammar and spelling are faulty, but that simply accentuates the beauty of his expression, which is extraordinarily simple, spontaneous, and vivid. And yet we have to protect him all the time from his own text. We have to explain away his words, to redefine the emotions he records, to reverse the convictions he sets out. Huck is a master of the literal statement; he writes with unfailing lucidity and directness; he's the prime example, as Hemingway declared, of the American plain style. And yet we have to save Huck at every turn from his own plain meanings. (Think of what fun it would be to read Hemingway this way!) We have no choice, as it were, but to recast "shiver," when Huck says "it made me shiver," into *something* positive, to deny the import *for Huck* (the stated effect) of his decision to choose hell, to white out his numerous N-words. Once we've done all that, we can laugh along *with* Huck, *our* Huck, the uncorrupted child in us who (we're certain) does *not* believe, would never *really* think, that a nigger is a no one. To paraphrase Jim: we're sophisticated folks, and so we know better, and can smile contentedly, and be satisfied.

Still, we should be very uneasy by this point about the process we're engaged in. Our act of appropriation ends with the child-in-us — who is *us*? As Huck tells the story we come to feel that his conscience is the object of Twain's exposé. It's conscience that makes Huck a racist, conscience that keeps leading him astray, and we interpret his conscience, properly, as an indictment of the values of the antebellum Southwest. But there was no need in 1885 to indict slave society. Primarily Twain's deadpan is directed against his readership, then and later, even unto our own time — against, that is, the conscience-driven forms of liberal interpretation. To a certain extent, his project here reflects the frontier sources of tall-tale humor that I quoted at the start of this essay: the storyteller's "pleasure in dethroning the condescension of gentility at the thickly settled Eastern core, while at the same time reproducing the radical discrepancies and incongruities at the root of all American experience," Eastern-intellectual as well as roughneck-Southwest. What better, and more cutting, way to accomplish these ends than to get the Eastern gentility to identify condescendingly with this con-man's outcast-redneck hero?

And it's precisely in this sense, I submit, that a distinct liberal theme permeates the discourse about the novel, a critical main current that runs through virtually all sides of the argument (provided that the critic does not dogmatically, *foolishly*, condemn the book for being racist). To judge from a century of Twain experts, Huck is "self-reliant," "an Adamic innocent," "exemplifying the . . . strong and wholesome [individual that] . . . springs from . . . the great common stock," exemplifying too the heroics of "the private man . . . [for whom] the highest form of freedom [resides in] . . . each man's and each woman's consciousness of what is right," and thereby, in its absolute "liberation," "ultimately transcend[ing] even anarchy as confinement" — in sum, an "independent spirit," "the affirmation of adventure," "enterprise," and "movement," the soul of "toleran[ce], and common sense." More than that: Huck and Jim on the raft have been taken as an emblem of the ideal society. In contrast to the settlements, they represent the "spiritual values" of "individualism compatible with community" — not just the proof of "Twain's commitment to black civil rights" (and his appeal to "compensate" the blacks on "the national level" for "injuries" done them during the slavery era), but his summons to the "cause of freedom" in general. Huck and Jim together forecast "a redeeming hope for the future health of society"; they stand for the very "pinnacle of human community"; they provide "a utopian pattern of all human relationships." Critics have reiterated these "great redemptive fact[s] about the book" over and again, with what can only be called reflexive adoration. As Jonathan Arac observes, "it is as if 'we' uttered in self-congratulation: 'Americans have spiritually solved any problems involved in blacks and whites living together as free human beings and we had already done so by the 1880s'."[9] I would add that, beyond smugness, what this attests to is the process of interpretation as self-acculturation — a striking example of what I called the literary enter-

[9]Richard P. Adams, "Unity and Coherence in *Huckleberry Finn*," and Carmen Bellamy Gladys, "Roads to Freedom," in *Twentieth Century Interpretations of Huckleberry Finn,* ed. Claude M. Simpson (Englewood Cliffs: Prentice Hall, 1968) 18, 22; Harold Beaver, *Huckleberry Finn* (London: Allen and Unwin, 1987) 196; Lawrence Howe, *Mark Twain and the Novel: The Double-Cross of Authority* (Cambridge: Cambridge UP, 1998) 116; Bruce Michelson, *Mark Twain on the Loose: A Comic Writer and the American Self* (Amherst: U of Massachusetts P, 1995) 138; Paul Taylor, "Huck Finn: The Education of a Young Capitalist," Robert Shulman, "Fathers, Brothers, and the 'Diseased': The Family, Individualism, and American Society in *Huck Finn*," Stanley Brodwin, "Mark Twain in the Pulpit: The Theological Comedy of *Huckleberry Finn*," Roy Harvey Pearce, "'Yours Truly, Huck Finn'," and James M. Cox, "A Hard Book to Read," in *One Hundred Years,* eds. Sattelmeyer and Crowley, 317, 337, 353, 385, 401; Leo Marx, "Mr. Eliot, Mr. Trilling, and Huckleberry Finn," in *Huckleberry Finn: A Case Study,* eds. Graff and Phelan, 293; Bernard De Voto, "Mark Twain's America," and Vernon L. Parrington, "The Real Mark Twain," in *Huck Finn and His Critics,* eds. Lettis, Morris, and McDonnell, 306, 308, 315; Stacey Margolis, "Huckleberry Finn; or, Consequences," PMLA (2001) 331, 340; Jocelyn Chadwick-Joshua, *The Jim Dilemma: Reading Race in Huckleberry Finn* (Jackson: UP of Mississippi, 1998) 7; David E. E. Sloan, *Mark Twain as a Literary Comedian* (Baton Rouge: Louisiana State UP, 1979) 144; Arac, *Huckleberry Finn as Idol and Target,* 8. See also the essays collected in James S. Leonard, Thomas A. Tenney, and Thadious M. Davis, eds. *Satire or Evasion? Black Perspectives on Huckleberry Finn* (Durham: Duke UP, 1992).

prise of socialization, in compliance with the charge bequeathed to "teachers of American literature" (society's "special custodians"), to inculcate the values of "enterprise, individualism, self-reliance, and the demand for freedom."

More interesting still, this process of interpretation reveals just how socialization works. The abstractions I've just rehearsed are admittedly *"American* ideals" but they are applied as universals, as though Huck represented not just what America but what all humanity ought to be. Thus a particular cultural vision — individualism, initiative, enterprise, and above all personal freedom (*"What Huckleberry Finn* is about is the process . . . of setting a man free") — becomes a sweeping moral imperative. And as moral imperative it is then reinstated, restored as it were from heaven to earth, from utopian "alternative world" to actual geographical space, as a definition of the quintessential American. As Norman Podhoretz, editor of the conservative journal *Commentary,* has written: "Sooner or later, all discussions of *Huckleberry Finn* turn into discussions of America." Or in the words of the late Irving Howe, writing in his left-wing journal *Dissent:* "Huck is not only the most American boy in our own literature, he is also the character with whom most American readers have most deeply identified." Or once again, according to the centrist Americanist scholar Eric Sundquist, *Huckleberry Finn* is "an autobiographical journey into the past" that tells the great "story of a nation." Harold Bloom accurately summarizes the tone of his collection of "best critical essays" on the novel when he remarks that the "book tells a story which most Americans need to believe is a true representation of the way things were, are, and yet might be."[10]

That "need to believe," is the core of the "American humor" of *Huckleberry Finn.* It may be true that in its magnificent colloquialism the novel marks "America's literary declaration of independence . . . a model of how one breaks free from the colonizers culture." But as a deadpan declaration the model it presents is, mockingly, the illusion of independence. It reveals our imprisonment *within* what Lewis Hyde, in his sweeping overview of the Trickster figure, calls the "joints" of culture. For Hyde, this concept involves a heroic view of the possibilities of interpretation. He pictures the Trickster's cultural work in physiologi-

---

[10]Laurence B. Holland, "A 'Raft of Trouble': Word and Deed in *Huckleberry Finn,*" in *American Realism: New Essays,* ed. Eric J. Sundquist (Baltimore: Johns Hopkins UP) 66; Arac, *"Huckleberry Finn" as Idol and Target,* 8, 3 (quoting Podhoretz, Howe, and Sundquist); Harold Bloom, Introduction to *Mark Twain's Adventures of Huckleberry Finn,* ed. Harold Bloom (New York: Chelsea House, 1986) 1.

cal terms, as an assault upon the vulnerable parts of the social body, most tellingly its *"flexible* or *movable"* joints, where variant spheres of society (home, school, church, job) intersect.[11] At these anatomical weak points, he writes, Tricksters come most vividly to life, unsettling the system, transgressing boundaries, exposing conflicts and contradictions — thus freeing us, he contends, as sympathetic interpreters of their subversion, from social constraints. If so, Mark Twain is a kind of laughing anti-trickster. It's not just that he's mocking the tricksters in the novel: Tom, the Duke and King, Huck himself. It's that he's mocking our would-be capacities for Trickster criticism. What's funny about our interpretation of the novel — both of the narrative and of its autobiographical hero — is that what begins as our independent assessment, and often our oppositional perspective, leads us happily, of our own free will, into the institutions of *our* colonizing culture.

Thus it was all but inevitable that in our multicultural era, Huck should be discovered to be (in addition to everything else that's positively American) multicultural. This is not the place to discuss Huck's blackness — or for that matter the possibility of his ethnic Irish-Americanness — but it's pertinent here as elsewhere to recall Twain's warning that interpretation may be a trap of culture. He speaks abundantly of the nature of that trap in his later writings — in letters to friends, for example, reprimanding them for presuming that "there is still dignity in man," whereas the plain fact is that "Man is . . . an April-fool joke played by a malicious Creator with nothing better to waste his time upon"; and in essays protesting that he has "no race prejudices . . . [nor] color prejudices, nor creed prejudices . . . I can stand any society. All that I need to know is that a man is a human being; that is enough for me; he can't be any worse"; and in journals documenting how "history, in all climes, all ages, and all circumstances, furnishes oceans and continents of proof that of all creatures that were made he [man] is the most detestable . . . below the rats, the grubs, the trichinae. . . . There are certain sweet-smelling, sugar-coated lies current in the world. . . . One of these . . . is that there is heroism in human life: that he is not mainly made up of malice and treachery; that he is sometimes not a coward; that there is something about him that ought to be perpetuated." In his posthumously published novel, *The Mysterious Stranger,* Twain exposes the nub itself — lays bare the mechanism of the trap of

---

[11]Shelley Fisher Fishkin, *Lighting Out for the Territory: Reflections on Mark Twain and American Culture* (New York and Oxford: Oxford UP, 1997) 184–85; Lewis Hyde, *Trickster Makes This World* (New York: Farrar, Straus and Giroux, 1998) 256.

hope. Here his stand-in deadpan artist, Satan, pairs up with a poor-white, innocent, sound-hearted little boy, a boy not unlike Huck — befriends him and conjures up for him a variety of alluring spectacles and promises, only to reveal, at the end, the absurdity of each one of them. "You perceive *now*," Satan declares, that it "is all a Dream, a grotesque and foolish dream." And then the boy's epiphany: "He vanished, and left me appalled: for I knew, and realized, that all that he had said was true."[12]

That's the humorous point of *Huckleberry Finn*, if we're alert. The novel's underlying moral and motive, its deadpan plot, is that this grand flight to freedom — black and white together, the individual regenerated by nature — was all a dream. Not a grotesque dream, to be sure, but a foolish one because it is a dream that befools. Recall the image of the novel with which critical tradition has left us. The plot is a river story, the style is a flow of humor, and our interpretation is a raft that promises protection (from conscience, from civilization, from all the slings and arrows of outrageous adulthood). Now consider the facts. The river keeps returning us again and again and yet again to the settlements, the raft proves to be a con-man haven, and on this "raft of trouble," on this river that betrays and kills, we're left with two mock-symbolic figures. One is Huck Finn, bond-slave to society, mostly scared to death, speaking a language we don't trust, and (as Pap puts it, in a drunken flash of insight) an Angel of Death. The other is Jim, the fugitive black who need never have run off, and who leads Huck into what Jim himself, early in the novel, calls the Black Angel's hell's-pact. So the nub is: the Angel of Death and the Black Angel, on a deadpan raft-to-freedom, drifting deeper and deeper into slave territory. It makes for a savagely funny obituary to the American dream.

[12]Mark Twain, letter to William Dean Howells, quoted in Warwick Waddlington, *The Confidence Game in American Literature* (Princeton: Princeton UP, 1975) 284; "Concerning the Jews" in *Collected Tales . . . 1890–1910,* ed. Budd, 359, 854–55; "The Character of Man," in *Collected Tales . . . 1852–1890,* ed. Budd, 854–55; *No. 44, The Mysterious Stranger,* ed. William M. Gibson (Berkeley: U of California P) 187.

The Controversy over Race:
Does *Huckleberry Finn* Combat
or Reinforce Racist Attitudes?

Readers of *Huckleberry Finn* have had the greatest and sharpest disputes about Twain's treatment of race. On the one hand, many readers argue that the novel is the ultimate expression of the American democratic spirit, a book that seriously criticizes slavery and racism and celebrates Huck's recognition of Jim's individuality and worth. On the other hand, many readers argue that the novel is so fundamentally and unforgivably racist that promoting it as a masterpiece of American literature actually perpetuates the country's racism. Can these two groups be reading the same book? In a sense, the controversy over race picks up where the controversy over the ending leaves off. As the selections on the ending make clear, much of the debate concerns Huck's — and Twain's — treatment of Jim during "the evasion." But from the perspective of those who find the book racist, the problems with Twain's treatment of Jim are there right from the beginning. Those who want to defend Twain must, therefore, also consider his characterization of Jim from beginning to end. As the selections in this section show, both defenders and attackers of the book have been able to fashion strong arguments. The arguments on both sides make appeals to biography, to history, to ethics, to irony, to characterization, and to the differences among readers of different ages and races. In all cases, the arguments show the intersection of interpretations and evaluations, and in all cases, the arguments assume that literary representations have the potential to influence readers' attitudes, feelings, thoughts, and behavior.

Julius Lester, in his essay "Morality and *Adventures of Huckleberry Finn*" (pp. 362–70 in this volume) offers one of the strongest indictments of *Huckleberry Finn* to be found anywhere. He contends that the book is ethically dangerous, and he develops this contention in several ways. First, Twain does not "take slavery, and therefore black people, seriously" and thus depicts a childlike Jim, who also "lacks self-respect, dignity, and a sense of self separate from the one whites want him to have" (pp. 365, 367). It is then not surprising that Twain allows Jim to become a "plaything" for Tom and Huck in the evasion. Second, Twain's book lacks credibility, especially emotional credibility, as seen in such matters as Jim's convenient ignorance about alternatives to heading south on the Mississippi, his lack of anxiety about their direction, and Miss Watson's deathbed grant of freedom to the slave suspected of killing Huck. Third, the book holds out for admiration what is in reality a white male adolescent fantasy about the pleasure of escaping responsibility. In sum, for Lester, the novel "is a dismal portrait of the white male psyche" (p. 370).

Justin Kaplan, in an overview of the various troubles that *Huckleberry Finn* has encountered between 1884 and 1984, offers a sharp contrast to Lester, both in the content and the attitude of his argument. In *Born to Trouble: One Hundred Years of "Huckleberry Finn"* (pp. 371–81), Kaplan sees the book as inculcating an admirable set of ethical values, especially in its representation of Huck's decision to go to hell. Consequently, Kaplan finds it a "bitter irony" that Twain's "savage indictment of a society that accepted slavery as a way of life" has come under attack for its treatment of race (p. 378). Kaplan defends the book, first, on the grounds of historical realism and, second, on the grounds of its use of irony.

> It seems unlikely that anyone, of any color, who had actually read *Huckleberry Finn,* instead of merely reading or hearing about it, and who had allowed himself or herself even the barest minimum of intelligent response to its underlying spirit and intention, could accuse it of being "racist" because some of its characters use offensive racial epithets. These characters belong to their place and time, which is the Mississippi Valley thirty years before Emancipation. (p. 378)

On Kaplan's reading, Jim is "unquestionably the best person in the book" (p. 379), and Twain "may have been the least 'racist' of all the major writers of his time, Herman Melville excepted" (p. 379). For Kaplan, simply recognizing Twain's irony will take care of such apparently problematic passages as the oft-cited exchange between Huck and Aunt Sally after Huck's tale of a steamboat explosion: "'Anybody hurt?' 'No'm. Killed a nigger.' 'Well, it's lucky; because sometimes people do get hurt.'" Kaplan declares that "one has to be deliberately dense to miss the point Mark Twain is making here and to construe such passages as evidences of his 'racism'" (p. 379).

Peaches Henry's "Struggle for Tolerance: Race and Censorship in *Huckleberry Finn*" (pp. 382–405) provides a general overview of the controversy over race and develops a position between Lester's and Kaplan's, one that finds the book exhibiting an "equivocal attitude toward blacks" (p. 404). As we noted in "Why Study Critical Controversies?," Henry's helpful history of the efforts to remove the novel from required reading lists in secondary schools insightfully explores the relations between academic and nonacademic discourse about the novel. In developing her own position through the examination of Twain's use of the racial epithet *nigger*, his characterization of Jim, and the ending, Henry consistently calls attention to the differences between readers of different races and abilities. With regard to Twain's use of the word *nigger*, she points out that, in general, whites have a much easier time doing what Kaplan does — seeing the use of this word as part of Twain's irony — and indeed, Kaplan's disdainful attitude helps "illustrate the incapacity of nonblacks to comprehend the enormous emotional freight attached to the hate-word 'nigger' for each black person" (p. 388).

From this perspective, Huck's interchange with Aunt Sally cannot be so easily read as satiric, since it is not entirely clear that Huck is in on the satire — or that Twain intends it. (See also Sacvan Bercovitch's extensive treatment of Huck's comment to Aunt Sally on pp. 338–45.) Henry regards Twain's characterization of Jim as similarly problematic, since, as African American readers readily recognize, it clearly conforms to stereotypes out of the black minstrel tradition and only sometimes transcends those stereotypes. Furthermore, although some academic critics offer sophisticated analyses to defend Twain's characterization of Jim, Henry cautions that most readers, especially at the secondary school level, are not capable of employing such sophisticated reading strategies. The ending is the most problematic element of the novel because Twain violates the expectations developed by the growing friendship between Huck and Jim and "seems to turn on his characters and his audience" (p. 395). Despite her reservations — indeed, because of them — Henry concludes that the book should continue to be taught and discussed.

> The insolubility of the race question . . . functions as a model of the fundamental racial ambiguity of the American mind-set. Active engagement with Twain's novel provides one method for students to confront their own deepest racial feelings and insecurities. (pp. 404–05)

Gerry Brenner's "More than a Reader's Response: A Letter to 'De Ole True Huck,'" (pp. 405–22) is also very much concerned with the relations between race and voice, as Brenner imagines how Jim, liberated from Huck's perspective, would retell Huck's story. In giving Jim this voice, Brenner is clearly criticizing Twain's subordination of Jim to Huck, especially the way that subordination leads to Jim's characterization as simple and childlike. In Brenner's account of the hidden story in Twain's text, Jim becomes a much more sophisticated character, one whose understanding of the novel's events easily outstrips Huck's, and Huck becomes a much less attractive character, one who is proud, jealous, and determined not to let any slave look better than he does. In his response to this essay, James Phelan suggests that Brenner's effort to uncover the hidden story is only partly successful. Phelan's "On the Nature and Status of Covert Texts" (pp. 423–34) includes a general discussion about the relation between overt and covert stories. It also examines the extent to which Brenner's "exposure" of the hidden story is a creative refashioning of Twain's story and the extent to which it is a persuasive critique of that story. Phelan's more specific argument is that Brenner succeeds in calling attention to the novel's suppression and subordination of Jim's voice but does not succeed in uncovering the real Huck.

Jonathan Arac approaches the problem of race in *Huckleberry Finn* primarily through an analysis of the idolatry accompanying its status as the quintessential "Great American Novel." In the excerpt from *"Huckleberry Finn" as Idol and Target* included here (pp. 435–56), Arac contends that this idolatry leads critics such as Kaplan to dismiss without proper consideration the objections of African American students and their parents who find the novel's 213 uses of the word *nigger* offensive. Consequently, this idolatry "lends authority to the continued honorable circulation of this terribly offensive term of racial antagonism" (p. 442). Furthermore, this idolatry combines with Twain's frequent use of the term to lead countless commentators on the novel to refer to Jim as "Nigger Jim," even though Twain never designates him that way. In these ways, Arac argues, the idolatry of the novel has resulted in its now "being read and publicly used in support of complacency" (p. 449) toward institutional racism rather than as working against that racism. Arac takes on the objection that Twain's use of the term is often ironic by pointing out that the alleged irony is not perceived by all of its readers, and that a thorough application of the strategy of ironic reading would undercut the force of Huck's famous decision to go to hell. After all, Huck says early in the novel that if Miss Watson were going to the "good place" after death, he'd rather go to the "bad place." Why not just see Huck's decision in chapter 31 as consistent with this earlier, less heroic thinking? Similarly, since the novel uses irony to undercut many conventional ideas and attitudes, especially those underlying slavery, why not see Huck's decision as another attitude that Twain wants to undercut?

Arac neither endorses nor refutes these ironic readings, but instead uses them to point to another consequence of the idolatry with which the novel is regarded: the assumption that it has a fully coherent structure. Arac disagrees with this assumption, and his alternative view of the book's structure also helps explain the motive behind the idolatry. Arac contends that *Huckleberry Finn* seeks moments of the sublime, moments when the reader feels transported by the reading experience. In these moments, such as the depiction of Huck's decision to go to hell, author, character, and reader are joined in "interlinked identifications," and consequently, readers feel "highly protective" of the author and character (p. 454). In the case of Twain's novel, this process is further heightened by linking author, character, and reader with the idea of the "quintessentially American" experience. Arac's purpose is to disrupt what he regards as this excessive identification so that we may acknowledge the novel's flaws as well as its virtues.

For Jane Smiley, the novel is without virtues, one that does not even deserve to be considered serious literature let alone the Great American Novel. In "Say It Ain't So, Huck" (pp. 456–66), Smiley sees the problem as twofold: (1) Twain represents Huck's good feelings for Jim as sufficient evidence of Huck's moral worth, not as something that should lead to specific actions to help Jim achieve his freedom; and (2) Jim is always an adjunct character: "Jim is never autonomous, never has a vote, always finds his purposes subordinate to Huck's, and, like every good sidekick, he never minds" (pp. 459–60). (Smiley would no doubt be a more sympathetic respondent to Brenner than Phelan is.) Smiley goes on to compare *Huckleberry Finn* to Harriet Beecher

Stowe's *Uncle Tom's Cabin,* a novel that she finds far superior because it contains "the power of brilliant analysis married to great wisdom of feeling" (p. 462), a novel that recognizes the economic system that supported slavery and the tragic consequences of that system for individual lives. Consequently, Smiley contends that *Uncle Tom's Cabin* deserves the central place in the American literary tradition now accorded to *Huckleberry Finn.*

Seymour Chwast does not idolize the novel in a way that Arac would object to, but in "Selling *Huck Finn* Down the River" (pp. 466–70), he counters Smiley's argument by raising three significant points that he believes she neglects. The first point involves the different historical circumstances in which Stowe and Twain were writing and the consequences of those differences for their purposes. Because Stowe was writing *Uncle Tom's Cabin* in 1850–51, a time when slavery was "a clear and present evil" (p. 467), she sought to arouse her readership in support of abolition. Because Twain began writing *Huckleberry Finn* in 1876, after slavery had been abolished in the United States, he did not write a similar call to action but instead sought "to meld a tenderly remembered boyhood with a profoundly troubled adult recognition" that the society in which that boyhood occurred included "a league of swindlers, drunks, hypocrites, lunkheads, bounty hunters and trigger-happy psychopaths" (p. 467). To praise Stowe for her clarity and to denigrate Twain for his different purpose is, in Chwast's view, "to sell stylistic innovation, humor and imaginative literature down the river" (p. 467). The second point that Chwast believes Smiley neglects involves the troubling aspects of Stowe's representation of race, particularly her characterization based on stereotypes and the consequences of her belief that "blacks were genetically unadaptable both to the climate and the advanced society of the United States" (p. 468). These consequences are evident in the various destructive ends her black characters meet, ends that are quite different from that of Jim, who may still achieve his goal of being reunited with his family. The third point involves *Huckleberry Finn*'s enduring power for generations of readers, including those who have objected to it in the past and object to it today. This power to move and to provoke readers throughout its history means that "we're now as bonded to this nettlesome work as Brer Rabbit was to Tar-Baby" (p. 469).

In sum, the selections here collectively demonstrate the wide-ranging nature of the controversy over race and indicate that it is far from settled. Furthermore, in approaching the controversy through so many avenues — through history, through close textual analysis, through reader response, through a consideration of the novel's cultural status — the selections also suggest directions that new contributors to the debate may want to pursue. Whether you want to attack or champion the book or to mediate between the attackers and champions, these selections can provide both a helpful context for your thoughts and some specific openings for your participation in the debate.

FURTHER READING IN THE CONTROVERSY

Booth, Wayne C. "Doctrinal Questions in Jane Austen, D. H. Lawrence, and Mark Twain." *The Company We Keep: An Ethics of Fiction*. Berkeley: U of California P, 1988. 457–78.

Ellison, Ralph. "Twentieth-Century Fiction and the Black Mask of Humanity." *Shadow and Act*. New York: Random, 1964. 24–44.

Fishkin, Shelley Fisher. *Was Huck Black? Mark Twain and African American Voices*. New York: Oxford UP, 1993.

Leonard, James S., Thomas A. Tenney, and Thadious M. Davis. *Satire or Evasion? Black Perspectives on "Huckleberry Finn."* Durham, NC: Duke UP, 1992.

Mailloux, Steven. "Reading *Huckleberry Finn:* The Rhetoric of Performed Ideology." *New Essays on 'Adventures of Huckleberry Finn.'* Ed. Louis J. Budd. New York: Cambridge UP, 1985. 107–33.

Smith, David L. "Humor, Sentimentality, and Twain's Black Characters." *Constructing Mark Twain: New Directions in Scholarship*. Eds. Laura Skandera-Trombley and Michael Kiskis. Columbia: U of Missouri P, 2001. 151–68.

JULIUS LESTER

Morality and *Adventures of Huckleberry Finn*

Julius Lester (b. 1939) is professor of Judaic and Far Eastern studies at the University of Massachusetts, Amherst, where he has taught since 1971. Born in St. Louis and raised in the South, Lester received his B.A. from Fisk University in 1960. A creative writer who draws on African American folktales in his fiction and his poetry, Lester has published thirty-four books —

some for adults, some for children — since 1968. His children's book *To Be a Slave* (1969) was nominated for the Newbery Award, and his *Long Journey Home: Stories from Black History* (1971) was a finalist for a National Book Award. His recent books include *Ackamarackus: Julius Lester's Sumptuously Silly Fantastically Funny Fables* (2001) and *When Dad Killed Mom* (2001), a novel. In addition to his literary and critical prowess, Lester possesses the skills of a professional musician and a photographer. This essay first appeared in the *Mark Twain Journal* in 1984.

I don't think I'd ever read *Adventures of Huckleberry Finn*. Could that be? Every American child reads it, and a child who read as much as I did must have.

As carefully as I search the ocean floor of memory, however, I find no barnacle-encrusted remnant of Huckleberry Finn. I may have read *Tom Sawyer,* but maybe I didn't. Huckleberry Finn and Tom Sawyer are embedded in the American collective memory like George Washington (about whom I know I have never read). Tom and Huck are part of our American selves, a mythologem we imbibe with our mother's milk.

I do have an emotional memory of going to Hannibal, Missouri, with my parents when I was eight or nine, and visiting the two-story white frame house where Mark Twain lived as a boy — where Huck and Tom lived as boys. In the American collective memory, Twain, Huck, and Tom merge into a paradigm of boyhood which shines as poignantly as a beacon, beckoning, always beckoning to us from some paradise lost, albeit no paradise we (or they) ever had.

I remember that house, and I remember the white picket fence around it. Maybe it was my father who told me the story about Tom Sawyer painting the fence (if it was Tom Sawyer who did), and maybe he told me about Huckleberry Finn, too. But it occurs to me only now to wonder if my father ever read Twain's books — my father born in Mississippi when slavery still cast a cold shadow at brightest and hottest noon. And if he did not read Twain, is there any Lester who did? Probably not, and it doesn't matter. In the character of Huckleberry Finn, Twain evoked something poignant and real in the American psyche, and now, having read the novel, I see that it is something dangerously, fatally seductive.

In the summer of 1973 I drove across country from New York City, where I was living, and returned to Hannibal to visit that two-story white house for the first time since childhood. It was midafternoon when I drove into Hannibal, planning to stay in a motel that night and spend the next morning leisurely going through the Twain boyhood home. As I walked toward the motel desk, there was a noticeable hush among the people in the lobby, and I perceived a tightening of many razor-thin, white lips. I was not surprised, therefore, when the motel clerk said there were no vacancies. The same scenario was repeated at a second and third motel. It was the kind of situation black people know all about and white people say is merely our imaginations, our hypersensitivity, our seeing discrimination where none exists. All I know is that no motel in town could find a room for me and that as I got into the car and drove away from Hannibal, another childhood memory returned. It was my father's voice reminding me that "Hannibal is rough on Negroes."

That's the kind of thing that can happen to a black person when the American collective memory subsumes black reality, when you remember Huck shining brightly and forget to keep an eye on what (or who) may be lurking in the shadows.

I am grateful that among the many indignities inflicted on me in childhood, I escaped *Huckleberry Finn*. As a black parent, however, I sympathize with those who want the book banned, or at least removed from required reading lists in schools. While I am opposed to book banning, I know that my children's education will be enhanced by not reading *Huckleberry Finn*. It is, in John Gardner's phrase, a "well-meant, noble sounding error" that "devalue[s] the world."[1]

That may sound harsh and moralistic, but I cannot separate literature, no matter how well written, from morality. By morality I do not mean bourgeois mores, which seek to govern the behavior of others in order to create (or coerce) that conformity thought necessary for social cohesion. The truly moral is far broader, far more difficult, and less certain of itself than bourgeois morality, because it is not concerned with the "what" of behavior but with the spirit we bring to our living, and, by implication, to literature. Gardner put it this way: "We recognize true art by its careful, thoroughly honest research for and analysis of values. It is not didactic because, instead of teaching by authority and force, it explores, open-mindedly, to learn what it should teach. It clarifies and confirms. . . . [M]oral art tests values and rouses trustworthy feelings about the better and the worse in human action."[2]

[1]John Gardner, *On Moral Fiction* (New York: Basic Books, 1978) 8.
[2]Gardner 19.

It is in this sense, then, that morality can and should be one of the criteria for assessing literature. It must be if a book is to "serve as the axe for the frozen sea within us," as Kafka wrote. *Adventures of Huckleberry Finn* is not the axe; it is the frozen sea, immoral in its major premises, one of which demeans blacks and insults history.

Twain makes an odious parallel between Huck's being "enslaved" by a drunken father who keeps him locked in a cabin and Jim's legal enslavement. Regardless of how awful and wrong it is for a boy to be held physically captive by his father, there is a profound difference between that and slavery. By making them into a parallelism, Twain applies a veneer to slavery which obscures the fact that, by definition, slavery was a horror. Such a parallelism also allowed Twain's contemporaries to comfortably evade responsibility and remorse for the horror they had made.

A boy held captive by a drunken father is not in the same category of human experience as a man enslaved. Twain willfully refused to understand what it meant to be legally owned by another human being and to have that legal ownership supported by the full power of local, state, and federal government enforcement. Twain did not take slavery, and therefore black people, seriously.

Even allowing for the fact that the novel is written from the limited first-person point of view of a fourteen-year-old boy (and at fourteen it is not possible to take anything seriously except oneself), the author must be held responsible for choosing to write from that particular point of view. If the novel had been written before emancipation, Huck's dilemma and conflicting feelings over Jim's escape would have been moving. But in 1884 slavery was legally over. Huck's almost Hamlet-like interior monologues on the rights and wrongs of helping Jim escape are not proof of liberalism or compassion, but evidence of an inability to relinquish whiteness as a badge of superiority. "I knowed he was white inside," is Huck's final assessment of Jim (p. 249 in this volume).

Jim does not exist with an integrity of his own. He is a childlike person who, in attitude and character, is more like one of the boys in Tom Sawyer's gang than a grown man with a wife and children, an important fact we do not learn until much later. But to Twain, slavery was not an emotional reality to be explored extensively or with love.

The novel plays with black reality from the moment Jim runs away and does not immediately seek his freedom. It defies logic that Jim did not know Illinois was a free state. Yet Twain wants us not only to believe he didn't, but to accept as credible that a runaway slave would drift *south* down the Mississippi River, the only route to freedom he knew being at Cairo, Illinois, where the Ohio River meets the Mississippi. If Jim knew that the Ohio met the Mississippi at Cairo, how could he not have known of the closer proximity of freedom to the east in Illinois or north in Iowa? If the reader must suspend intelligence to accept this, intelligence has to be dispensed with altogether to believe that Jim, having unknowingly passed the confluence of the Ohio and Mississippi Rivers, would continue down the river and go deeper and deeper into the heart of slave country. A century of white readers have accepted this as credible, a grim reminder of the abysmal feelings of superiority with which whites are burdened.

The least we expect of a novel is that it be credible — if not wholly in fact, then in emotion; for it is emotions that are the true subject matter of fiction. As Jim floats down the river farther and farther into slave country, without anxiety about his fate and without making the least effort to reverse matters, we leave the realm of factual and emotional credibility and enter the all-too-familiar one of white fantasy in which blacks have all the humanity of Cabbage Patch dolls.

The novel's climax comes when Jim is sold and Tom and Huck concoct a ridiculous scheme to free him. During the course of the rescue, Tom Sawyer is shot. Huck sends the doctor, who cannot administer to Tom alone. Jim comes out of hiding and aids the doctor, knowing he will be recaptured. The doctor recounts the story this way:

> so I says, I got to have *help,* somehow; and the minute I says it, out crawls this nigger from somewheres, and says he'll help, and he done it, too, and done it very well. Of course I judged he must be a runaway nigger, and there I *was!* and there I had to stick, right straight along, all the rest of the day, and all night. . . . *I never see a nigger that was a better nuss or faithfuller* [emphasis added], and yet he was resking his freedom to do it, and was all tired out, too, and I see plain enough he'd been worked main hard, lately. I liked the nigger for that; I tell you, gentlemen, a nigger like that is worth a thousand dollars — and kind treatment, too. . . . there I *was,* . . . and there I had to stick, till about dawn this morning; then some men in a skiff come by, and as good luck would have it, the nigger was setting by the pallet with his head propped on his knees, sound asleep; so I motioned them in, quiet, and they slipped up on him and grabbed him and tied him before he knowed what he was about, and we never had no trouble. . . . the nigger never made the least row nor said a word, from the

start. He ain't no bad nigger, gentlemen; that's what I think about him. (pp. 256–57)

This depiction of a black "hero" is familiar by now since it has been repeated in countless novels and films. It is a picture of the only kind of black that whites have ever truly liked — faithful, tending sick whites, not speaking, not causing trouble, and totally passive. He is the archetypal "good nigger," who lacks self-respect, dignity, and a sense of self separate from the one whites want him to have. A century of white readers have accepted this characterization because it permits their own "humanity" to shine with more luster.

The depth of Twain's contempt for blacks is not revealed fully until Tom Sawyer clears up something that has confused Huck. When Huck first proposed freeing Jim, he was surprised that Tom agreed so readily. The reason Tom did so is because he knew all the while that Miss Watson had freed Jim when she died two months before.

Once again credibility is slain. Early in the novel Jim's disappearance from the town coincided with Huck's. Huck, having manufactured "evidence" of his "murder" to cover his escape, learned that the townspeople believed that Jim had killed him. Yet we are now to believe that an old white lady would free a black slave suspected of murdering a white child. White people may want to believe such fairy tales about themselves, but blacks know better.

But this is not the nadir of Twain's contempt, because when Aunt Sally asks Tom why he wanted to free Jim, knowing he was already free, Tom replies: "Well that *is* a question, I must say; and *just* like women! Why, I wanted the *adventure* of it" (p. 260). Now Huck understands why Tom was so eager to help Jim "escape."

Tom goes on to explain that his plan was "for us to run him down the river, on the raft, and have adventures plumb to the mouth of the river." Then he and Huck would tell Jim he was free and take him "back up home on a steamboat, in style, and pay him for his lost time." They would tell everyone they were coming and "get out all the niggers around, and have them waltz him into town with a torchlight procession and a brass band, and then he would be a hero, and so would we" (p. 262).

There is no honor here; there is no feeling for or sense of what Gardner calls that which "is necessary to humanness." Jim is a plaything, an excuse for "the *adventure* of it," to be used as it suits the fancies of the white folk, whether that fancy be a journey on a raft down the river or a torchlight parade. What Jim clearly is not is a human being, and this is emphasized by the fact that Miss Watson's will frees Jim but makes no mention of his wife and children.

Twain doesn't care about the lives the slaves actually lived. Because he doesn't care, he devalues the world.

> Every hero's proper function is to provide a noble image for men to be inspired by and guided by in their own actions; that is, the hero's business is to reveal what the gods require and love. . . . [T]he hero's function . . . is to set the standard in action . . . the business of the poet (or "memory" . . .) is to celebrate the work of the hero, pass the image on, keep the heroic model of behavior fresh, generation on generation.[3]

Criticizing *Adventures of Huckleberry Finn* because of Twain's portrayal of blacks is almost too easy, and, some would add sotto voce, to be expected from a black writer. But a black writer accepts such arrogant dismissals before he or she sits down to write. We could not write otherwise.

But let me not be cynical. Let me allow for the possibility that what I have written may be accepted as having more than a measure of truth. Yet doesn't *Huckleberry Finn* still deserve to be acknowledged as an American classic, eminently deserving of being read?

The Council on Interracial Books for Children, while highly critical of the book, maintains "that much can be learned from this book — not only about the craft of writing and other issues commonly raised when the work is taught, but also about racism. . . . Unless *Huck Finn*'s racist *and* antiracist messages are considered, the book can have racist results."[4] While it is flattering that the council goes on to recommend one of my books, *To Be a Slave,* as supplementary reading to correct Twain's portrayal of slavery, racism is not the most insidious and damaging of the book's flaws. In its very essence the book offends that morality which would give "a noble image . . . to be inspired and guided by." If it is the hero's task "to reveal what the gods require and love," what do we learn from *Adventures of Huckleberry Finn*?

The novel's major premise is established in the first chapter: "The widow Douglas, she took me for her son, and allowed she would sivilize me; but it was rough living in the house all the time, considering how

---

[3]Gardner 29.

[4]"On Huck, Criticism, and Censorship," editorial, *Interracial Books for Children Bulletin* 15.1–2 (1984): 3.

dismal regular and decent the widow was in all her ways; so when I couldn't stand it no longer, I lit out. I got into my old rags, and my sugar-hogshead again, and was free and satisfied" (p. 32). Civilization is equated with education, regularity, decency, and being "cramped up," and the representatives of civilization are women. Freedom is old clothes and doing what one wants to do. "[A]ll I wanted was a change, I warn't particular" (p. 33).

The fact that the novel is regarded as a classic tells us much about the psyche of the white American male, because the novel is a powerful evocation of the *puer,* the eternal boy for whom growth, maturity, and responsibility are enemies. There is no more powerful evocation in American literature of the eternal adolescent than *Adventures of Huckleberry Finn.* It is a fantasy adolescence, however. Not only is it free of the usual adolescent problems caused by awakening sexuality, but also Huck has a verbal adroitness and cleverness beyond the capability of an actual fourteen-year-old. In the person of Huck, the novel exalts verbal cleverness, lying, and miseducation. The novel presents, with admiration, a model we (men) would and could be if not for the pernicious influence of civilization and women.

In its lyrical descriptions of the river and life on the raft, the novel creates an almost primordial yearning for a life of freedom from responsibility:

> It was kind of solemn, drifting down the big still river, laying on our backs looking up at the stars, and we didn't ever feel like talking loud, and it warn't often that we laughed, only a little kind of low chuckle. We had mighty good weather, as a general thing, and nothing ever happened to us at all. (p. 82)

> Sometimes we'd have that whole river all to ourselves for the longest time. Yonder was the banks and the islands, across the water; and maybe a spark — which was a candle in a cabin window — and sometimes on the water you could see a spark or two — on a raft or a scow, you know; and maybe you could hear a fiddle or a song coming over from one of them crafts. It's lovely to live on a raft. We had the sky, up there, all speckled with stars, and we used to lay on our backs and look up at them, and discuss about whether they was made, or only just happened. (p. 125)

It is in passages such as these that the book is most seductive in its quiet singing of the "natural" life over the life of "sivilization," which is another form of slavery for Huck. It is here also that the novel fails most profoundly as moral literature.

Twain's notion of freedom is the simplistic one of freedom from restraint and responsibility. It is an adolescent vision of life, an exercise in nostalgia for the paradise that never was. Nowhere is this adolescent vision more clearly expressed than in the often-quoted and much-admired closing sentences of the book: "But I reckon I got to light out for the Territory ahead of the rest, because Aunt Sally she's going to adopt me and sivilize me, and I can't stand it. I been there before."

That's just the problem, Huck. You haven't "been there before." Then again, neither have too many other white American males, and that's the problem, too. They persist in clinging to the teat of adolescence long after only blood oozes from the nipples. They persist in believing that freedom from restraint and responsibility represents paradise. The eternal paradox is that this is a mockery of freedom, a void. We express the deepest caring for this world and ourselves only by taking responsibility for ourselves and whatever portion of this world we make ours.

Twain's failure is that he does not care until it hurts, and because he doesn't, his contempt for humanity is disguised as satire, as humor. No matter how charming and appealing Huck is, Twain holds him in contempt. And here we come to the other paradox, the critical one that white Americans have so assiduously resisted: It is not possible to regard blacks with contempt without having first so regarded themselves.

To be moral. It takes an enormous effort of will to be moral, and that's another paradox. Only to the extent that we make the effort to be moral do we grow away from adolescent notions of freedom and begin to see that the true nature of freedom does not lie in "striking out for the territory ahead" but resides where it always has — in the territory within.

Only there does one begin to live with oneself with that seriousness from which genuine humor and satire are born. Twain could not explore the shadowy realms of slavery and freedom with integrity because he did not risk becoming a person. Only by doing so could he have achieved real compassion. Then Jim would have been a man and Huck would have been a boy, and we, the readers, would have learned a little more about the territory ahead which is always within.

Adventures of Huckleberry Finn is a dismal portrait of the white male psyche. Can I really expect white males to recognize that? Yet they must. All of us suffer the consequences as long as they do not.

JUSTIN KAPLAN

Born to Trouble:
One Hundred Years
of *Huckleberry Finn*

From 1992 to 1995, Justin Kaplan (b. 1925) shared the Jenks Chair of Contemporary Letters at the College of the Holy Cross with his wife, Anne F. Bernays, but he has spent the greater part of his career outside academia. After earning his B.A. at Harvard in 1945, Kaplan did freelance writing in New York for about eight years. He then took a job as editor at Simon and Schuster publishers for another five, and from 1959 to 1992 he worked as a full-time professional writer. His books include *Mr. Clemens and Mark Twain* (1966), *Lincoln Steffens: A Biography* (1974), *Mark Twain and His World* (1974), *Walt Whitman: A Life* (1980), and *Back Then: Two Lives in 1950s New York* (2002), a nonfiction work coauthored with Bernays. He has also edited the Library of America edition *Walt Whitman: Collected Poetry and Collected Prose* (1982) and has served as the general editor for the sixteenth and seventeenth editions of *Bartlett's Familiar Quotations* (1992, 2002). Kaplan received the National Book Award and the Pulitzer Prize for *Mr. Clemens and Mark Twain* and the American Book Award for Biography for *Walt Whitman*. "Born to Trouble," a lecture sponsored by the Florida Center for the Book, was presented at the Broward County Library in Fort Lauderdale, Florida, on September 11, 1984. Kaplan's lecture was later published by the Library of Congress. The original did not include any bibliographic citations. In this reprint, page references have been added to the quotations from *Huckleberry Finn*.

"I am tearing along on a new book," Mark Twain told friends in the summer of 1876. "It is Huck Finn's Autobiography. I like it only tolerably well, as far as I have got, and may possibly pigeonhole or burn the MS when it is done." He wrote about one-third of the book then, coming to a full stop at the point in the story where Huck and Jim, an outcast boy and a fugitive slave, pass Cairo, Illinois, in the night. They had planned to sell their raft there, get on a steamboat, and go up the Ohio River to the Free States. Instead, confused by a heavy fog, they continue down the Mississippi into the heart of the slave-holding South. They have no plausible reason for going where they do except, perhaps, for Mark Twain's own familiarity with the region. As Huck himself asks, Why would a runaway slave "run *south?*" (p. 131 in this volume).

The serious, perhaps insoluble plot problem Mark Twain created for himself compelled him to put the manuscript aside for several years. He worked on it again in 1879 or 1880 and got stuck a second time. In 1884, eight years after he started *Huckleberry Finn,* he told his English publisher, "I've just finished writing a book, and modesty compels me to say it's a rattling good one, too." But whether he solved his plot problem even then remains doubtful.

In the final chapters Tom Sawyer shows up at the Phelps plantation in northern Louisiana, helps steal Jim out of slavery, and then tells us that Jim has been a free man all along. This ending, which makes up roughly a quarter of the entire book, has become the center of a continuing critical debate. Ernest Hemingway said that "All modern American literature comes from one book by Mark Twain called *Huckleberry Finn* . . . the best book we've had," but even Hemingway thought that readers ought to stop eleven chapters short of the end. "The rest," he said, "is just cheating." T. S. Eliot and Lionel Trilling were able to live with Mark Twain's ending. Others think he ought to have been shot for it. Professor John Seelye has written his own version, *The True Adventures of Huckleberry Finn* (1970), in order to satisfy the critics. "And now that they've got *their* book," Seelye says, "maybe they'll leave the other one alone."

Mark Twain's long and painful process of creation gives a peculiar force to Huck's concluding words — "[T]here ain't nothing more to write about, and I am rotten glad of it, because if I'd a knowed what trouble it was to make a book I wouldn't a tackled it" (p. 263).

The trouble, however, did not end with the writing. *Century* magazine, which published excerpts in advance of book publication, insisted on deleting references to nakedness, dead cats, and the like. To bring out *Huckleberry Finn* Mark Twain set up his own publishing house and, by entering business on a large scale, prepared the way for his bankruptcy ten years later. As author-publisher, he displayed the extremest genteel severity in reviewing the illustrations by E. W. Kemble. He faulted some of them for being "forbidding" or "repulsive." One, which showed a "lecherous old rascal" kissing a girl at the camp meeting in chapter 20, had to go altogether: "Let's not make any pictures of the camp meeting. The subject won't bear illustrating. It is a disgusting thing." But despite Mark Twain's vigilance, an engraver at the printing plant in New York — his identity was never discovered — added a mischievous last-minute detail, a slight bulge at the fly, that drastically altered the meaning of an otherwise inoffensive picture of Uncle Silas with Aunt Sally. The offending plate was cut out by hand and replaced in the 30,000-copy first printing, but the resulting delay meant that the book missed the 1884 Christmas trade and went on sale in the United States about two months after it did in England and Canada. At stake, a spokesman for the publishing house declared, was the author's reputation for "decency and morality," a reputation that was soon to be put to more severe tests. Meanwhile, Mark Twain launched an unavailing lawsuit against a firm of booksellers, described by him as "thieves and swindlers," who were offering *Huckleberry Finn* at a reduced price. And finally, just when "I am not able to see anything that can save Huck Finn from being another defeat," the trustees of the Concord (Massachusetts) Public Library expelled the book from their shelves as "trash and suitable only for the slums." Their reasoning, summarized as follows by a Boston newspaper, proved to be somewhat — but far from totally — representative of official opinion elsewhere in the country:

> It deals with a series of adventures of a very low grade of morality; it is couched in the language of a rough dialect, and all through its pages there is a systematic use of bad grammar and an employment of rough, coarse, inelegant expressions. It is also very irreverent. To sum up, the book is flippant and irreverent in its style. It deals with a series of experiences that are certainly not elevating. The whole book is of a class that is more profitable for the slums than it is for respectable people, and it is trash of the veriest sort.

"That will sell 25,000 copies for us sure," Mark Twain said, calculating the beneficial effects of excommunication. "For instance, it will deter other libraries from buying the book and you are doubtless aware that one book in a public library prevents the sale of a sure ten and a possible hundred of its mates. And secondly it will cause the purchasers of the book to read it, out of curiosity, instead of merely intending to do so after the usual way of the world and library committees; and then they will discover, to my great advantage and their own indignant disappointment, that there is nothing objectionable in the book, after all."

Huckleberry Finn may have been the first book to become a bestseller because it was banned in Massachusetts, but the banning of an American book of indisputable literary quality was far from being the

last instance of its sort. One has only to think of the troubled history of
Stephen Crane's *Maggie* and of Theodore Dreiser's *Sister Carrie* and
An American Tragedy. Today, books by J. D. Salinger, Bernard Mala-
mud, and Kurt Vonnegut are targets for the vigilance committees,
along with *The American Heritage Dictionary.* No longer merely random, local, or idiosyncratic, book banning today is political, organized,
and therefore more menacing than ever.

"Those idiots in Concord are not a court of last resort," Mark
Twain said, "and I am not disturbed by their moral gymnastics." Still,
he remained hurt and puzzled by the reception of his masterpiece, a
favorite child who had brought disgrace upon his father. As novelist,
humorist, and satirist he most often stood in opposition to the genteel
tradition, but as private citizen, family man, and prominent house-
holder of Hartford, Connecticut, he courted acceptance and respectability; he would have been ashamed to be classed with his older
contemporary, the reprobate poet, Walt Whitman of Camden, New
Jersey. But just four years earlier another work that today represents
America and American culture to the entire world, Whitman's *Leaves of
Grass,* had also been banned. The Boston district attorney, egged on by
some of the same people who later ostracized *Huckleberry Finn,*
warned Whitman's publishers there that *Leaves of Grass,* dismissed by
one early reviewer as "a mass of stupid filth," fell "within the provisions
of the Public Statutes respecting obscene literature." He suggested to
them "the propriety of withdrawing the same from circulation and sup-
pressing the editions thereof." The publishers in Boston retreated.
Whitman, who after a quarter of a century in the doghouse had almost
become resigned to this sort of thing, took his book to another firm,
this time in Philadelphia. As a consequence of having been banned in
Boston, *Leaves of Grass* even enjoyed a mild flurry of sales.

In the aftermath of the Concord expulsion of *Huckleberry Finn*
Mark Twain was more certain than ever that there was no such thing as
a unitary audience in America. Perhaps only seeking to make the best of
a bad situation, he declared that he had always written for "the mighty
mass of the uncultivated," for "the Belly and the Members" instead of
"for the Head." "Indeed I have been misjudged from the very first," he
told Andrew Lang, an English critic who regarded *Huck* as "nothing
less than a masterpiece," the "great American novel." "I have never
tried in even one single instance to help cultivate the cultivated classes. I
was not equipped for it, either by native gifts or training. And I never
had any ambition in that direction, but always hunted for bigger
game — the masses."

By now a fixture among the classics of world literature, *Huckleberry Finn* clearly has reached "the masses." They have read it in English, Chinese, Japanese, Russian, Hebrew, and practically every other tongue spoken on the globe. A 1960 estimate put the cumulative sales of the book at ten million copies, but that was some time ago. (The current total might be closer to fifteen million.) This country alone has about forty editions in print, including the splendid omnibus volume in the Library of America series. But at the same time, as the ongoing critical debate suggests, *Huckleberry Finn* has also become the property of the lettered classes, who have turned it into a sort of fresh-water *Moby Dick*.

H. L. Mencken recalled that his discovery of *Huckleberry Finn* in 1889, when he was only nine years old and the book only four, was "probably the most stupendous event of my whole life. . . . If I undertook to tell you the effect it had upon me my talk would sound frantic, and even delirious." For Mencken, Mark Twain was "the true father of our national literature, the first genuinely American artist of the blood royal." In *Huckleberry Finn,* said T. S. Eliot, Mark Twain reveals himself to be one of those rare writers "who have brought their language up to date," and "who have discovered a new way of writing, valid not only for themselves, but for others." In some way his book has shaped the style and vision of virtually every American writer, including Sherwood Anderson, Dreiser, Faulkner, Fitzgerald, Salinger, and Bellow, in addition to Hemingway. By elevating Huck's vernacular speech to the level of literature, Mark Twain advanced a cultural as well as a literary revolution.

Huckleberry Finn is a relatively rare example, in a divided culture, of a work of high literary art that is cherished by both the "cultivated" and the "uncultivated classes," as Mark Twain distinguished them — by the "Head" as well as "the Belly and the Members." Even so, this novel has never been out of hot water with official or self-appointed guardians of public taste and morality, especially where the young and impressionable are involved. "When a library expels a book of mine," Mark Twain said, "and leaves an unexpurgated Bible around where unprotected youth and age can get hold of it, the deep unconscious irony of it delights me and doesn't anger me."

During the twenty-five years of life remaining to him after the publication of *Huckleberry Finn,* he had many such occasions to enjoy the "deep unconscious irony" of actual or threatened expulsion — from the library of the New York State Reformatory, the Denver Public Library, the Omaha Public Library, the Brooklyn Public Library. The reasons variously given were that the book was "immoral and sacrilegious," put "wrong ideas in youngsters' heads," and set "a bad example." A writer in *Library Journal* for July 1907 reported that each year *Huck* was banned somewhere in the United States (the title of his article was, "The Children's Librarian versus *Huckleberry Finn*"). In 1931 Harper and Brothers published an expurgated edition for elementary and junior high school students. The editors claimed that their bobtailed version would "let Huck . . . step down from his place on the library shelf and enter the classroom," thereby providing "wholesome happiness for boys and girls," and stimulating "even the most apathetic and difficult pupils." In 1957 the New York City Board of Education removed *Huck* from its list of approved texts. In 1976 a comparable action was taken in the high schools of the state of Illinois.

What is it in this universally admired book that offends so many people? Why is Huck always in hot water? Why must he always put "civilization" behind him and light out for the Territory? Many early readers found Mark Twain's great novel objectionable because it violated genteel standards of social and literary decorum. Instead of refined language, an exemplary hero, and an elevating moral they encountered a narrative written in the idiom of a shiftless, unlettered boy from the lowest class of Southern white society. This should not have come as a complete surprise to them. Huck had been introduced nearly ten years earlier, in *The Adventures of Tom Sawyer*, as a "juvenile pariah . . . cordially hated and dreaded by all the mothers of the town, because he was idle, and lawless, and vulgar and bad. . . . He slept on door-steps in fine weather and in empty hogsheads in wet." But now this outcast, son of the town drunkard, instead of being one of Tom Sawyer's many playmates, was the sole hero-narrator of a book that ridiculed the work ethic, polite manners, the Bible, prayer, and pious sentiments in general, characterized as "tears and flapdoodle," "soul-butter and hogwash" (p. 161). In addition to the camp meeting, Huck's story included an obscene stage performance, "The Royal Nonesuch," described by the duke as "ruther worse than low comedy" and featuring a naked man cavorting on all fours (p. 150).

Offensive as they seemed at the time, these violations of decorum only screened a deeper level of threat and affront. *Huckleberry Finn*, Lionel Trilling said, is "a subversive book." No one who responds to its hero's internal struggles over right and wrong, freedom and slavery, humanity and racism, will ever again be certain that what appear to be "clear dictates of moral reason are not merely the engrained customary beliefs" of a particular place and time. The questions that Huck and Jim pose go to the very heart of the social contract and our faith in public opinion as a guide to conduct.

Twenty years after he finished *Huckleberry Finn* Mark Twain described its central and constitutive irony: "A sound heart and a deformed conscience come into collision and conscience suffers defeat." Huck's "deformed conscience" is the internalized voice of public opinion, of a conventional wisdom that found nothing wrong in the institution of slavery and held as mortal sin any attempt to subvert it. Conscience, as Mark Twain remembered from his boyhood in a slaveholding society, "can be trained to approve any wild thing you want it to approve if you begin its education early and stick to it." Huck knows that Tom Sawyer, "with his bringing-up," would never be able to set a slave free. But Huck eventually recognizes slavery for the "wild thing" it was. He follows the dictates of his sound heart and commits a sin as well as a crime by helping Jim to run away from his legal owner. "All right, then, I'll *go* to hell," Huck says. "It was awful thoughts and awful words, but they was said. And I let them stay said; and never thought no more about reforming" (p. 201). Like Thoreau and Captain John Brown, Huck rejects what he considers to be an unjust and immoral law. He also rejects the craving for social approval that, according to Mark Twain, motivates the behavior of most of us. He is happy to remain a pariah. His story satirizes a number of beliefs sacred to Americans, consensual wisdom, for example, and the primacy of the average man. "Do I know you?" Colonel Sherburn says when he faces down the lynch mob. "I know you clear through. I was born and raised in the South, and I've lived in the North; so I know the average all around. The average man's a coward" (p. 147). "Hain't we got all the fools in town on our side?" asks the king. "[A]nd ain't that a big enough majority, in any town?" (p. 172).

Guided by sound hearts rather than deformed consciences, Huck and Jim pass through agonies of remorse that are their own particular hells. Jim rebukes Huck: "[T]rash is what people is dat puts dirt on de head er dey fren's en makes 'em ashamed." "I didn't do him no more mean tricks," says Huck, "and I wouldn't done that one if I'd a knowed it would make him feel that way" (pp. 99, 100). Jim remembers committing an inadvertent act of cruelty to his own daughter: "[D]e Lord God Amighty fogive po' ole Jim, kaze he never gwyne to fogive hisself as long's he live!" (p. 155). Seeking only self-approval, not the approval of others, the white pariah boy and the black runaway slave, "a community of saints," achieve a state of near-perfect intimacy and equality on their raft, a fragile island of freedom between two shores of society. "[W]hat you want, above all things, on a raft," Huck says, "is for everybody to be satisfied, and feel right and kind towards the others" (p. 130). Perhaps another of the affronts that Mark Twain's novel offered and continues to offer is that his two outcasts are a silent reproach to dry-land society. They are simply too good for us, too truthful, too loyal, too passionate, and, in a profounder sense than the one we feel easy with, too moral.

Banning is one way of dealing with this profound affront. Another way is denial. Americans of Mark Twain's time and somewhat after tended to cherish him as a nostalgic recorder of boyhood high-jinks, a genial, harmless entertainer. As soon as the smiles faded from their faces they trivialized his genius and irony, his dark vision of humanity, and his moral passion. We see the same process of lollypopping and willful expropriation of cultural resources in IBM's current advertising campaign for their Personal Computer: It converts Charlie Chaplin, victim of the machine and of Modern Times, into his ideological antithesis, a smiling, even simpering, totem of postindustrial society.

There is one especially bitter irony in the career of *Huckleberry Finn*. This novel, a savage indictment of a society that accepted slavery as a way of life, nevertheless has come under attack in our time for its alleged "racism." In 1957, for example, the NAACP condemned the book as "racially offensive." Such charges have supported exclusionary actions taken in many other states. In 1982 an administrator at the Mark Twain Intermediate School in Fairfax County, Virginia, called it "the most grotesque example of racism I've ever seen in my life." In 1984 school officials in Waukegan, Illinois, removed *Huckleberry Finn* from the required reading list after an alderman, according to the Associated Press, "objected to the book's use of the word 'nigger.'" It seems unlikely that anyone, of any color, who had actually read *Huckleberry Finn*, instead of merely reading or hearing about it, and who had allowed himself or herself even the barest minimum of intelligent response to its underlying spirit and intention, could accuse it of being "racist" because some of its characters use offensive racial epithets. These characters belong to their place and time, which is the Mississippi Valley thirty years before Emancipation.

As a historical portrait of slaveholding society, Mark Twain's novel is probably more faithful as well as less stereotypical than Harriet Beecher Stowe's beloved *Uncle Tom's Cabin*. And it is worth recalling that Mrs. Stowe, like most of her fellow abolitionists, believed that there was no place for free blacks in American society — they advocated colonization and repatriation to Africa. Mark Twain, "the most de-southernized of southerners," according to his friend William Dean Howells, believed that it was henceforward the duty of white people to make amends for the crime of slavery. He may have been the least "racist" of all the major writers of his time, Herman Melville excepted. *Huckleberry Finn* is a matchless satire on racism, bigotry, and property rights in human beings.

Jim considers hiring an Abolitionist to steal his two children from their owner. "It most froze me to hear such talk," says Huck. Here was Jim, whom "I had as good as helped run away, coming right out flat-footed and saying he would steal his children — children that belonged to a man I didn't even know; a man that hadn't ever done me no harm" (p. 101). Here is Aunt Sally's response to a steamboat explosion as described by Huck: "'Good gracious! anybody hurt?' 'No'm. Killed a nigger.' 'Well, it's lucky; because sometimes people do get hurt'" (p. 206). One has to be deliberately dense to miss the point Mark Twain is making here and to construe such passages as evidences of his "racism." Jim, unquestionably the best person in the book, reflects the author's affection, humanity, and moral passion. "I couldn't seem to strike no places to harden me against him, but only the other kind," Huck says. "I'd see him standing my watch on top of his'n, stead of calling me, so I could go on sleeping; and see him how glad he was when I come back out of the fog; and when I come to him again in the swamp, up there where the feud was; and such-like times; and would always call me honey, and pet me, and do everything he could think of for me, and how good he always was" (p. 200).

Mark Twain "told the truth, mainly," Huck says in the opening of the novel. "There was things which he stretched, but mainly he told the truth" (p. 32). ("Truth is the most valuable thing we have," says the author himself, speaking in another voice. "Let us economize it.") Huck confronts a corrupt adult world through a series of day-to-day yarns, stretchers, and downright lies, but he himself is ultimately and unflinchingly truthful. "You can't pray a lie," he says. "I found that out" (p. 200). Much of this great book's power to offend as well as endure derives from a commitment to truth-telling and to a frequently brutal, painful realism. Huck and Jim live on their raft because they are on the run from a nightmare society driven by bigotry, violence, exploitation, greed, ignorance, and a sort of pandemic depravity. The most conspicuous white inhabitants of the Mississippi Valley are swindlers, drunkards, hypocrites, lunkheads, fools, rapscallions, deadbeats, bounty hunters, and trigger-happy psychopaths.

At first Huck appears almost to be matter-of-fact about the horrors he meets up with. "[P]ap got too handy with his hick'ry, and I couldn't stand it," he tells us. "I was all over welts. . . . Once he locked me in and was gone three days" (p. 50). Pap drinks himself into an attack of delirium tremens, confuses Huck with the Angel of Death, and tries to kill him with a clasp-knife. When Pap collapses in a stupor, Huck waits out the night behind a loaded rifle pointed at his father. Having considered the possibility of patricide, the boy instead simulates his own murder and escapes. Soon after, Pap is killed in a brawl. (See chs. 6–7.)

By the time Huck finds himself a witness to the feud between the Shepherdsons and Grangerfords, he is no longer even remotely matter-of-fact. This is his account of the feud's bloody climax:

> All of a sudden, bang! bang! bang! goes three or four guns — the men had slipped around through the woods and come in from behind without their horses! The boys jumped for the river — both of them hurt — and as they swum down the current the men run along the bank shooting at them and singing out, "Kill them, kill them!" It made me so sick I most fell out of the tree. I ain't agoing to tell *all* that happened — it would make me sick again if I was to do that. I wished I hadn't ever come ashore that night, to see such things. I ain't ever going to get shut of them — lots of times I dream about them. (pp. 122–23)

He can't wait to "get out of that awful country" (p. 123).

In the course of his long journey along the shores of "that awful country," Huck sees other murders. One of them is committed in broad daylight on the main street of a river town where the loafers generally entertain themselves with milder spectacles. "There couldn't anything wake them up all over, and make them happy all over, like a dog-fight," Huck says, "unless it might be putting turpentine on a stray dog and setting fire to him, or tying a tin pan to his tail and see him run himself to death" (pp. 142–43). The same village loafers form the lynch mob that swarms up the street toward Colonel Sherburn's house "a-whooping and yelling and raging like Injuns" (p. 146). Much later Huck sees the king and duke, tarred and feathered, being ridden out of another town. There is nothing comic about this punishment. "I see they had the king and the duke astraddle of a rail — that is, I knowed it *was* the king and the duke, though they was all over tar and feathers, and didn't look like nothing in the world that was human — just looked like a couple of monstrous big soldier-plumes. Well, it made me sick to see it" (p. 214). Like the heroes of many more recent American novels Huck is often sickened by what he sees. "It was enough to make a body ashamed of the human race," he says. "I never see anything so disgusting" (pp. 160, 161).

When Mark Twain followed his two heroes South into pain, disgust, and danger, he did more than create a plot problem. Symbolically he enacted and predicted the dilemma of the humorist, a punishing profession in several senses. The human race, says Mark Twain's Satan, has only "one really effective weapon — laughter. Power, money, persuasion, supplication, persecution — these can lift a colossal humbug — push it a little — weaken it a little, century by century — but only laughter can blow it to rags and atoms at a blast. Against the assault of laughter nothing can stand." But, as Satan concludes, this is a weapon that requires of its user "sense and courage," for humor when pressed to its extreme goes beyond the pleasure principle. "Weapon," "blast," "assault" — these are some of Mark Twain's ways of nailing down the essential action of humor. He also compares the action of humor to the "delicious" surprise of the dentist's drill striking the raw nerve. One of the funniest things about humor is that people don't take it seriously enough. If they did they might discover that, at heart, great humorists are not merry as crickets, but quite the contrary. Enduring humor is not kindly, not harmless. It has the power to inflict pain, even commit mayhem, and unless it exercises this power is not likely to endure.

Mark Twain's vocation, as he announced when he was thirty years old, was "to excite the *laughter* of God's creatures." But he discovered this to be a difficult and dangerous undertaking. "Humor must not professedly teach and it must not professedly preach," he said, "but it must do both if it would live forever" (by "forever" he means thirty years or more). From the day he chose his vocation to the day he died he felt compelled to defend humor, to free the noun "humorist" from the adjective "mere" and the synonym "clown." To do this he ventured into ever darker, ever more complex and punishing modes. One theorist of humor, Henri Bergson, says that laughter depends upon "a momentary anaesthesia of the heart" and therefore "has no greater foe than emotion." *Huckleberry Finn,* however, not only inflicts pain but challenges us to feel and laugh at the same time. Perhaps Mark Twain asks too much of us. Perhaps it is in the very nature of humor as he defined it that, like Huck, its outcast hero, Mark Twain's century-old masterpiece was born to trouble.

PEACHES HENRY

The Struggle for Tolerance: Race and Censorship in *Huckleberry Finn*

Peaches Henry (b. 1960) is assistant professor of women's studies at the University of Wyoming. She received her B.A. (1983)
at the University of Texas, Austin, and her M.A. (1988) and
Ph.D. (1997) from Columbia University, where she wrote her
dissertation entitled "Reference and Truth in Autobiography."
Henry has also taught at the University of Notre Dame and
Texas A&M University. The essay reprinted here originally
appeared in *Satire or Evasion? Black Perspectives on "Huckleberry Finn"* (1992), edited by James S. Leonard, Thomas A.
Tenney, and Thadious M. Davis.

In the long controversy that has been *Huckleberry Finn*'s history,
the novel has been criticized, censored, and banned for an array of perceived failings, including obscenity, atheism, bad grammar, coarse manners, low moral tone, and antisouthernism. Every bit as diverse as the
reasons for attacking the novel, *Huck Finn*'s detractors encompass parents, critics, authors, religious fundamentalists, right-wing politicians,
and even librarians.[1]

Ironically, Lionel Trilling, by marking *Huck Finn* as "one of the
world's great books and one of the central documents of American culture,"[2] and T. S. Eliot, by declaring it "a masterpiece,"[3] struck the
novel certainly its most fateful and possibly its most fatal blow. Trilling's
and Eliot's resounding endorsements provided Huck with the academic respectability and clout that assured his admission into America's

[1] Justin Kaplan, *Born to Trouble: One Hundred Years of "Huckleberry Finn,"* Center
for the Book Viewpoint Series, no. 13 (Washington, D.C.: Library of Congress, 1985)
10–11. (See pp. 371–81 in this volume.)

[2] Lionel Trilling, Introduction to *Adventures of Huckleberry Finn* (New York: Rinehart, 1948) v–xviii; reprinted in Norton Critical Edition of *Adventures of Huckleberry
Finn*, eds. Sculley Bradley et al., 2nd ed. (New York: Norton, 1977) 318. (See excerpt on
pp. 283–84 in this volume.)

[3] T. S. Eliot, Introduction to *Adventures of Huckleberry Finn* (London: Cresset,
1950) vii–xvi; reprinted in Norton Critical Edition of *Adventures of Huckleberry Finn*,
ed. Sculley Bradley et al., 2nd ed. (New York: Norton, 1977) 328. (See excerpt on
pp. 285–89 in this volume.)

classrooms. Huck's entrenchment in the English curricula of junior and senior high schools coincided with *Brown vs. Topeka Board of Education,* the Supreme Court case that ended public school segregation, legally if not actually, in 1954. Desegregation and the civil rights movement deposited Huck in the midst of American literature classes which were no longer composed of white children only, but now were dotted with black youngsters as well. In the faces of these children of the revolution, Huck met the group that was to become his most persistent and formidable foe. For while the objections of the Gilded Age, of fundamentalist religious factions, and of unreconstructed southerners had seemed laughable and transitory, the indignation of black students and their parents at the portrayal of blacks in *Huck Finn* was not at all comical and has not been short-lived.

The presence of black students in the classrooms of white America, the attendant tensions of a country attempting to come to terms with its racial tragedies, and the new empowerment of blacks to protest led to *Huck Finn*'s greatest struggle with censorship and banning. Black protesters, offended by the repetitions of "nigger" in the mouths of white and black characters, Twain's minstrel-like portrayal of the escaped slave Jim and of black characters in general, and the negative traits assigned to blacks, objected to the use of *Huck Finn* in English courses. Though blacks may have previously complained about the racially offensive tone of the novel, it was not until September 1957 that the *New York Times* reported the first case that brought about official reaction and obtained public attention for the conflict. The New York City Board of Education had removed *Huck Finn* from the approved textbook lists of elementary and junior high schools. The book was no longer available for classroom use at the elementary and junior high school levels, but could be taught in high school and purchased for school libraries. Though the Board of Education acknowledged no outside pressure to ban the use of *Huck Finn,* a representative of one publisher said that school officials had cited "some passages derogatory to Negroes" as the reason for its contract not being renewed. The NAACP, denying that it had placed any organized pressure on the board to remove *Huck Finn,* nonetheless expressed displeasure with the presence of "racial slurs" and "belittling racial designations" in many of Twain's works.[4] Whether or not the source of dissatisfaction

[4]Leonard Buder, "'Huck Finn' Barred as Textbook by City," *New York Times* 12 Sept. 1957: 1.

could be identified, disapproval of *Huck Finn*'s racial implications existed and had made itself felt.

The discontent with the racial attitudes of *Huck Finn* that began in 1957 has surfaced periodically over the past thirty years. In 1963 the Philadelphia Board of Education, after removing *Huck Finn*, replaced it with an adapted version which "tone[d] down the violence, simplifie[d] the Southern dialect, and delete[d] all derogatory references to Negroes."[5] A civil rights leader in Pasco, Washington, attacked Twain's use of "nigger" in 1967;[6] two years later Miami-Dade Junior College (Miami, Florida) excised the text from its required reading list after Negro students complained that it "embarrassed them."[7] Around 1976, striking a bargain with parents of black students who demanded the removal of *Huck Finn* from the curriculum, the administration of New Trier High School in Winnetka, Illinois, agreed to withdraw the novel from required courses and confined Huck to the environs of elective courses and the school library. This compromise did not end Huck's problems in that north-shore Chicago upper-middle-class community, however, for as recently as March 1988 black parents "discovered" Huck in American Studies, an elective course team-taught by an English teacher and an American history teacher, and once again approached school administrators about banning the book.[8]

The most outspoken opponent to *Huck Finn* has been John Wallace, a former administrator at the Mark Twain Intermediate School (Fairfax County, Virginia), who in 1982, while serving on the school's Human Relations Committee, spearheaded a campaign to have Huck stricken from school curricula. A decision by the school's principal to yield to the Human Relations Committee's recommendations was later overridden by the superintendent of schools. Repeatedly scoring the book as "racist trash," Wallace has raised the issue in other school districts throughout his twenty-eight-year tenure in public education. Since the Fairfax County incident, he has appeared on ABC's "Nightline" and CNN's "Freeman Reports" and has traveled the country championing the cause of black children who he says are embarrassed

[5]"Schools in Philadelphia Edit 'Huckleberry Finn,'" *New York Times* 17 Apr. 1963: 44.

[6]"'Huckleberry Finn' Scored for References to 'Nigger,'" *New York Times* 22 Mar. 1967: 43.

[7]"'Huck Finn' Not Required," *New York Times* 15 Jan. 1969: 44.

[8]Telephone interviews with Lois Fisher, New Trier High School librarian, and Eric Lair, New Trier School District assistant superintendent, 24 Mar. 1988. As of 20 April 1988, New Trier's current controversy over *Huckleberry Finn* had yet to be resolved.

and humiliated by the legitimization of "nigger" in public schools. Devoted to the eradication of *Huck Finn* from the schools, he has "authored" an adapted version of Twain's story.[9] Wallace, aggressively if not eloquently, enunciates many of the deleterious effects that parents and those who support them feel the teaching of *Huck Finn* in junior high and senior high schools has on their children.[10]

The fact that people from Texas to Iowa to Illinois to Pennsylvania to Florida to Virginia to New York City concur with Wallace's assessment of *Huck Finn* demands the attention of the academic community. To condemn concerns about the novel as the misguided rantings of "know nothings and noise makers"[11] is no longer valid or profitable; nor can the invocation of Huck's immunity under the protectorate of "classic" suffice. Such academic platitudes no longer intimidate, nor can they satisfy, parents who have walked the halls of the university and have shed their awe of academe. If the academic establishment remains unmoved by black readers' dismay, the news that *Huck Finn* ranks ninth on the list of thirty books most frequently challenged[12] should serve as testimony that the book's "racial problem" is one of more consequence than the ancillary position to which scholars have relegated it.[13] Certainly, given *Huck Finn*'s high position in the canon of American literature, its failure to take on mythic proportions for, or even to be a pleasant read for, a segment of secondary school students merits academic scrutiny.

The debate surrounding the racial implications of *Huck Finn* and its appropriateness for the secondary school classroom gives rise to myriad considerations. The actual matter and intent of the text are a source of contention. The presence of the word "nigger," the treatment of Jim

[9]John Wallace, *The Adventures of Huckleberry Finn Adapted* (Chicago: Wallace, 1984).

[10]See Wallace's essay, "The Case against *Huck Finn*," in *Satire or Evasion? Black Perspectives on "Huckleberry Finn,"* eds. James S. Leonard, Thomas A. Tenney, and Thadious M. Davis (Durham, NC: Duke UP, 1992) 16–24. Hereafter cited as *Satire or Evasion*.

[11]Christopher Hitchens, "American Notes," (London) *Times Literary Supplement* 9 Mar. 1985: 258.

[12]Nicholas J. Karolides and Lee Burress, eds., *Celebrating Censored Books* (Racine: Wisconsin Council of Teachers of English, 1985) 6. This information is based on six national surveys of censorship pressures on the American public schools between 1965 and 1982.

[13]Most scholars express opinions on whether or not to ban *Huckleberry Finn* in a paragraph or two of an article that deals mainly with another topic. Shelley Fisher Fishkin has given the issues much more attention. In addition to authenticating a letter written by Mark Twain that indicates his nonracist views (see n. 60), Fishkin has debated the issue with John Wallace on "Freeman Reports" (CNN, 14 March 1985).

and blacks in general, the somewhat difficult satiric mode, and the ambiguity of theme give pause to even the most flexible reader. Moreover, as numerous critics have pointed out, neither junior high nor high school students are necessarily flexible or subtle readers. The very profundity of the text renders the process of teaching it problematic and places special emphasis on teacher ability and attitude. Student cognitive and social maturity also takes on special significance in the face of such a complicated and subtle text.

The nature of the complexities of *Huck Finn* places the dynamics of the struggle for its inclusion in or exclusion from public school curricula in two arenas. On the one hand, the conflict manifests itself as a contest between lay readers and so-called scholarly experts, particularly as it concerns the text. Public school administrators and teachers, on the other hand, field criticisms that have to do with the context into which the novel is introduced. In neither case, however, do opponents appear to *hear* each other. Too often, concerned parents are dismissed by academia as "neurotics"[14] who have fallen prey to personal racial insecurities or have failed to grasp Twain's underlying truth. In their turn, censors regard academics as inhabitants of ivory towers who pontificate on the virtue of *Huck Finn* without recognizing its potential for harm. School officials and parents clash over the school's right to intellectual freedom and the parents' right to protect their children from perceived racism.

Critics vilify Twain most often and most vehemently for his aggressive use of the pejorative term "nigger." Detractors, refusing to accept the good intentions of a text that places the insulting epithet so often in the mouths of characters, black and white, argue that no amount of intended irony or satire can erase the humiliation experienced by black children. Reading *Huck Finn* aloud adds deliberate insult to insensitive injury, complain some. In a letter to the *New York Times,* Allan B. Ballard recalls his reaction to having *Huck Finn* read aloud "in a predominantly white junior high school in Philadelphia some thirty years ago."

> I can still recall the anger I felt as my white classmates read aloud the word "nigger." In fact, as I write this letter I am getting angry all over again. I wanted to sink into my seat. Some of the whites snickered, others giggled. I can recall nothing of the literary merits of this work that you term "the greatest of all American novels." I only recall the sense of relief I felt when I would flip ahead

[14]Hitchens 258.

a few pages and see that the word "nigger" would not be read that hour.[15]

Moreover, the presentation of the novel as an "American classic" serves as an official endorsement of a term uttered by the most prejudiced racial bigots to an age group eager to experiment with any language of shock value. One reporter has likened the teaching of the novel to eighth-grade kids to "pulling the pin of a hand grenade and tossing it into the all-too-common American classroom."[16]

Some who have followed *Huck Finn*'s racial problems express dismay that some blacks misunderstand the ironic function Twain assigned "nigger" or that other blacks, in spite of their comprehension of the irony, will allow themselves and their progeny to be defeated by a mere pejorative. Leslie Fiedler would have parents "prize Twain's dangerous and equivocal novel not in spite of its use of that wicked epithet, but for the way in which it manages to ironize it; enabling us finally — without denying our horror or our guilt — to laugh therapeutically at the 'peculiar institution' of slavery."[17] If Wallace has taken it upon himself to speak for the opponents of *Huck Finn*, Nat Hentoff, libertarian journalist for the *Village Voice,* has taken equal duty as spokesperson for the novel's champions. Hentoff believes that confronting Huck will give students "the capacity to see past words like 'nigger' . . . into what the writer is actually *saying.*" He wonders, "What's going to happen to a kid when he gets into the world if he's going to let a word paralyze him so he can't think?"[18] Citing an incident in Warrington, Pennsylvania, where a black eighth-grader was allegedly verbally and physically harassed by white students after reading *Huck Finn* in class, Hentoff declares the situation ripe for the educational plucking by any "reasonably awake teacher." He enthuses:

> What a way to get Huck and Jim, on the one hand, and all those white racists they meet, on the other hand, off the pages of the book and into that very classroom. Talk about a book coming alive!
>
> Look at that Huck Finn. Reared in racism, like all the white kids in his town. And then, on the river, on the raft with Jim,

[15]Allan B. Ballard, letter, *New York Times* 9 May 1982.

[16]"Finishing the Civil War: *Huck Finn* in Racist America," *Young Spartacus* (Summer 1982): 12.

[17]Leslie Fiedler, "*Huckleberry Finn:* The Book We Love to Hate," *Proteus* 1.2 (Fall 1984): 6.

[18]Nat Hentoff, "Huck Finn and the Shortchanging of Black Kids," *Village Voice* 18 May 1982.

shucking off that blind ignorance because this runaway slave is the most honest, perceptive, fair-minded man this white boy has ever known. What a book for the children, all the children, in Warrington, Pennsylvania, in 1982![19]

Hentoff laments the fact that teachers missed such a teachable moment and mockingly reports the compromise agreed upon by parents and school officials, declaring it a "victory for niceness." Justin Kaplan flatly denies that "anyone, of any color, who had actually read *Huckleberry Finn,* instead of merely reading or hearing about it, and who had allowed himself or herself even the barest minimum of intelligent response to its underlying spirit and intention, could accuse it of being 'racist' because some of its characters use offensive racial epithets."[20] Hentoff's mocking tone and reductive language, Kaplan's disdainful and condescending attitude, and Fiedler's erroneous supposition that "nigger" can be objectified so as to allow a black person "to laugh therapeutically" at slavery illustrate the incapacity of nonblacks to comprehend the enormous emotional freight attached to the hate-word "nigger" for each black person. Nigger is "fightin' words and everyone in this country, black and white, knows it."[21] In his autobiography, Langston Hughes offers a cogent explanation of the signification of "nigger" to blacks:

> The word *nigger* to colored people of high and low degree is like a red rag to a bull. Used rightly or wrongly, ironically or seriously, of necessity for the sake of realism, or impishly for the sake of comedy, it doesn't matter. Negroes do not like it in any book or play whatsoever, be the book or play ever so sympathetic in its treatment of the basic problems of the race. Even though the book or play is written by a Negro, they still do not like it.
>
> The word *nigger,* you see, sums up for us who are colored all the bitter years of insult and struggle in America.[22]

Nonblacks know implicitly that to utter "nigger" in the presence of a Negro is to throw down a gauntlet that will be taken up with a vengeance.

---

[19]Hentoff.

[20]Kaplan 18. (See p. 378.)

[21]"Finishing the Civil War" 12.

[22]Langston Hughes, *The Big Sea* (New York: Thunder's Mouth P, 1940) 268–69. At this point in his autobiography, Hughes discusses the furor caused by Carl Van Vechten's novel *Nigger Heaven,* published in 1926.

To dismiss the word's recurrence in the work as an accurate rendition of nineteenth-century American linguistic conventions denies what every black person knows: Far more than a synonym for slave, "nigger" signifies a concept. It conjures centuries of specifically black degradation and humiliation during which the family was disintegrated, education was denied, manhood was trapped within a forced perpetual puerilism, and womanhood was destroyed by concubinage. If one grants that Twain substituted "nigger" for "slave," the implications of the word do not improve; "nigger" denotes the black man as a commodity, as chattel.[23]

In addition to serving as a reminder of the "peculiar institution," "nigger" encapsulates the decades of oppression that followed emancipation. "It means not only racist terror and lynch mobs but that victims 'deserve it.'"[24] Outside Central High in Little Rock in 1954 it was emblazoned across placards; and across the South throughout the 1950s and into the 1960s it was screamed by angry mobs. Currently, it is the chief taunt of the Ku Klux Klan and other white supremacist groups. In short, "nigger" has the odious distinction of signifying all "the shame, the frustration, the rage, the fear" that have been so much a part of the history of race relations in the United States, and blacks still consider it "'dirtier' than any of the once-taboo four-syllable Anglo-Saxon monosyllabics."[25] So to impute blacks' abhorrence of "nigger" to hypersensitivity compounds injustice with callousness and signals a refusal to acknowledge that the connotations of "that word" generate a cultural discomfort that blacks share with no other racial group.

To counteract the Pavlovian response that "nigger" triggers for many black readers, some scholars have striven to reveal the positive function the word serves in the novel by exposing the discrepancy between the dehumanizing effect of the word and the real humanity of Jim.[26] Fiedler cites the passage in which Huck lies to Aunt Sally about a steamboat explosion that hurt no one but "killed a nigger," and Aunt Sally callously responds, "Well, it's lucky, because sometimes people do get hurt" (p. 206); he notes that the passage brims with humor at the expense of Aunt Sally and the convention to which she conforms. But

---

[23]See David L. Smith's essay, "Huck, Jim, and American Racial Discourse," in *Satire or Evasion* 103–20.

[24]"Finishing the Civil War" 12.

[25]Fiedler 5.

[26]Again, see Smith's essay.

Fiedler is also of the opinion that Huck does not get the joke — does not recognize the humor of the fact that he and Aunt Sally by "dehumanizing the Negro diminish their own humanity."[27] It seems to Huck's foes (and to me) that if Huck does not get the joke, then there is no joke, and he becomes as culpable as Aunt Sally.

However, Fiedler's focus on this dialogue is to the point, because racial objectors isolate it as one of the most visible and detrimental slurs of the novel. The highlighting of this passage summons contrasting perspectives on it. Kaplan argues that "[o]ne has to be deliberately dense to miss the point Mark Twain is making here and to construe such passages as evidences of his 'racism.'"[28] Detractors, drawing the obvious inference from the dialogue, arrive at a conclusion different from Kaplan's, and their response cannot simply be disregarded as that of the unsophisticated reader. In order to believe in Twain's satirical intention, one has to believe in Huck's good faith toward Jim. That is to say, one has to believe that, rather than reflecting his own adherence to such conventions, Huck simply weaves a tale that marks him as a "right-thinking" youngster.

The faith in Huck that Twain's defenders display grows out of the manner in which he acquits himself at his celebrated "crisis of conscience," less than twenty-four hours prior to his encounter with Aunt Sally. There is no denying the rightness of Huck's decision to risk his soul for Jim. But there is no tangible reason to assume that the regard Huck acquires for Jim during his odyssey down the river is generalized to encompass all blacks. Further, Huck's choice to "go to hell" has little to do with any respect he has gained for Jim as a human being with an inalienable right to be owned by no one. Rather, his personal affection for the slave governs his overthrow of societal mores. It must be remembered that Huck does not adjudge slavery to be wrong; he selectively disregards a system that he ultimately believes is right. So when he discourses with Aunt Sally, he is expressing views he still holds. His emancipatory attitudes extend no further than his love for Jim. It seems valid to argue that were he given the option of freeing other slaves, Huck would not necessarily choose manumission.

Twain's apparent "perpetuation of racial stereotypes" through his portrayal of Jim and other blacks in *Huck Finn* bears relation to his use of "nigger" and has fostered vociferous criticism from anti–*Huck Finn* forces. Like the concept "nigger," Twain's depiction of blacks, par-

---

[27]Fiedler 6; see also Smith's discussion of this passage.
[28]Kaplan 19. (See p. 279.)

ticularly Jim, represents the tendency of the dominant white culture to saddle blacks with traits that deny their humanity and mark them as inferior. Critics disparage scenes that depict blacks as childish, inherently less intelligent than whites, superstitious beyond reason and common sense, and grossly ignorant of standard English. Further, they charge that in order to entertain his white audience, Twain relied upon the stock conventions of "black minstrelsy," which "drew upon European traditions of using the mask of blackness to mock individuals or social forces."[29] Given the seemingly negative stereotypical portraits of blacks, parents concerned that children, black and white, be exposed to positive models of blacks are convinced that *Huck Finn* is inappropriate for secondary classrooms.

Critics express their greatest displeasure with Twain's presentation of Jim, the runaway slave viewed by most as second only to Huck in importance to the novel's thematic structure. Although he is the catalyst that spurs Huck along his odyssey of conscience, Jim commences the novel (and to some degree remains) as the stereotypical, superstitious "darky" that Twain's white audience would have expected and in which they would have delighted.

In his essay "Change the Joke and Slip the Yoke," Ralph Ellison examines the play Twain gives the minstrel figure. Though Twain does strike Jim in the mold of the minstrel tradition, Ellison believes that we observe "Jim's dignity and human capacity" emerge from "behind this stereotype mask." Yet by virtue of his minstrel mask, Jim's role as an adult is undercut, and he often appears more childlike than Huck. Though Ellison writes that "it is not at all odd that this black-faced figure of white fun [the minstrel darky] is for Negroes a symbol of everything they rejected in the white man's thinking about race, in themselves and in their own group," his final analysis seems to be that Jim's humanity transcends the limits of the minstrel tradition.[30]

Taking a more critical stance than Ellison, Fredrick Woodard and Donnarae MacCann, in "*Huckleberry Finn* and the Traditions of Blackface Minstrelsy," examine specific incidents throughout the novel in the light of the minstrel tradition. Denying that Jim is used to poke fun at

[29]Fredrick Woodard and Donnarae MacCann, "*Huckleberry Finn* and the Traditions of Blackface Minstrelsy," *Interracial Books for Children Bulletin* 15.1–2 (1984): 4–13; reprinted in *The Black American in Books for Children: Readings in Racism*, eds. Donnarae MacCann and Gloria Woodard, 2nd ed. (Metuchen, N.J.: Scarecrow, 1985) 75–103.

[30]Ralph Ellison, "Change the Joke and Slip the Yoke," *Partisan Review* 25 (Spring 1958): 212–22; reprinted in Ellison's *Shadow and Act* (New York: Random, 1964) 45–59.

whites, as some scholars suggest, Woodard and MacCann cite the appeal that the "ridiculous or paternalistic portrayals of Black Americans" held for "the white theatre-going audience," Twain's own delight in minstrel shows, and his "willingness to shape his message to his audience."[31] Noting that the stereotypical blackface portrayals were thought to be realistic by Twain and many of his white contemporaries, the pair highlight various incidents in *Huck Finn* that they think illustrate their contention that Jim plays the minstrel role to Huck's straight man. For instance, Huck's and Jim's debate about French (ch. 14) bears a striking resemblance to the minstrel-show dialogue that Twain deemed "happy and accurate imitation[s] of the *usual and familiar negro quarrel*."[32] Though Jim's logic is superior to Huck's, argue Woodard and MacCann, the scene plays like a minstrel-show act because "Jim has the information-base of a child."[33]

Huck Finn advocates, tending to agree with Ellison's judgment that Jim's fullness of character reveals itself, offer readings of Jim that depart sharply from the Woodard and MacCann assessment. Some view Twain's depiction of Jim early in the novel as the necessary backdrop against which Huck's gradual awareness of Jim's humanity is revealed. These early renditions of Jim serve more to lay bare Huck's initial attitudes toward race and racial relations than they do to characterize Jim, positively or negatively. As the two fugitives ride down the Mississippi deeper and deeper into slave territory, the power of Jim's personality erodes the prejudices Huck's culture (educational, political, social, and legal) has instilled. Such readings of passages that appear to emphasize Jim's superstitions, gullibility, or foolishness allow Twain to escape the charge of racism and be seen as championing blacks by exposing the falseness of stereotypes. This view of Twain's motivation is evident in letters written to the *New York Times* in protest of the New York City Board of Education's decision to ban the book in 1957:

> Of all the characters in Mark Twain's works there probably wasn't any of whom he was fonder than the one that went down the river with Huck Finn. It is true that this character is introduced as "Miss Watson's big nigger, named Jim." That was the Missouri vernacular of the day. But from there on to the end of the story

[31]Woodard and MacCann 76–77.

[32]Mark Twain, quoted in Woodard and MacCann 76 (emphasis added).

[33]Woodard and MacCann 79. See also the Woodard and MacCann essay "Minstrel Shackles and Nineteenth-Century 'Liberality' in *Huckleberry Finn*," in *Satire or Evasion* 141–53.

Miss Watson's Jim is a warm human being, lovable and admirable.[34]

Now, *Huckleberry Finn* . . . is a great document in the progress of human tolerance and understanding. Huck begins by regarding Jim, the fugitive slave, very much as the juvenile delinquents of Little Rock regard the Negro today. Gradually, however, he discovers that Jim, despite the efforts of society to brutalize him, is a noble human being who deserves his protection, friendship, and respect. This theme of growing love is made clear throughout the book.[35]

In another vein, some defenders of Twain's racial sensitivities assign Jim's initial portrayal a more significant role than mere backdrop. The rubric of "performed ideology" frames Steven Mailloux's interpretation of Jim as he appears in the early "philosophical debates" with Huck.[36] Mailloux explains how a "literary text can take up the ideological rhetoric of its historical moment . . . and place it on a fictional stage." As "ideological drama," the literary text — *Huckleberry Finn* in this case — invites readers to become spectators and actors at a rhetorical performance. In fact, the success of the ideological drama depends upon the reader's participation: "The humor and often the ideological point of the novel's many staged arguments . . . rely upon the reader's ability to recognize patterns of false argumentation." Within the framework of rhetorical performances, then, Jim's minstrel scenes serve "as ideological critique[s] of white supremacy." In each case, however, the dominance of Jim's humanity over the racial discourse of white supremacy hinges upon the reader's recognition of the discrepancy between the two ideologies.[37]

[34]"Huck Finn's Friend Jim," editorial, *New York Times* 13 Sept. 1957: 22.

[35]Hoxie N. Fairchild, letter, *New York Times* 14 Sept. 1957: 18.

[36]Steven Mailloux, "Reading *Huckleberry Finn:* The Rhetoric of Performed Ideology," *New Essays on "Huckleberry Finn,"* ed. Louis J. Budd (Cambridge, Eng.: Cambridge UP, 1985) 107–33. For a defense of the early Jim as an example of Twain's strategy to "elaborate [racial stereotypes] in order to undermine them," see David Smith's essay.

[37]Mailloux's discussion of "rhetorical performances" in *Huckleberry Finn* bears kinship to M. M. Bakhtin's discussion of the function of heteroglossia in the comic novel. In "Discourse on the Novel," Bakhtin identifies two features that characterize "the incorporation of heteroglossia and its stylistic utilization" in the comic novel. First, the comic novel incorporates a "multiplicity of 'languages' and verbal-ideological systems," and for the most part these languages are not posited in particular characters, but they can be. Second, "the incorporated languages and socio-ideological belief systems . . . are unmasked and destroyed as something false, hypocritical, greedy, limited, narrowly rationalistic, inadequate to reality." *Huckleberry Finn* seems to me to embody much of what Bakhtin says regarding heteroglossia in the comic novel. The multiplicity of languages is

The interpretive job that Mailloux does on the "French question" in chapter 14 exonerates the passage of any racial negativity. Huck's disdainful comment that "you can't learn a nigger to argue" renders the debate little more than a literary version of a minstrel dialogue unless readers recognize the superior rhetorician:

> Of course, readers reject the racist slur as a rationalization. They know Huck gives up because he has lost the argument: It is precisely because Jim *has* learned to argue by imitating Huck that he reduces his teacher to silence. Far from demonstrating Jim's inferior knowledge, the debate dramatizes his argumentative superiority, and in doing so makes a serious ideological point through a rhetoric of humor.[38]

The vigorous critical acumen with which Mailloux approaches the role played by Jim is illustrative of the interpretative tacks taken by academics. Most view Twain's depiction of Jim as an ironic attempt to transcend the very prejudices that dissidents accuse him of perpetuating.

Though there has been copious criticism of the Jim who shuffles his way across the pages of *Huckleberry Finn*'s opening chapters, the Jim who darkens the closing chapters of the novel elicits even more (and more universally agreed-upon) disapprobation. Most see the closing sequence, which begins at Huck's encounter with Aunt Sally, as a reversal of any moral intention that the preceding chapters imply. The significance that Twain's audience has attached to the journey down the river — Jim's pursuit of freedom and Huck's gradual recognition of the slave's humanness — is rendered meaningless by the entrance of Tom Sawyer and his machinations to "free" Jim.

The particular offensiveness to blacks of the closing sequence of *Huckleberry Finn* results in part from expectations that Twain has built up during the raft ride down the river. As the two runaways drift down

---

clearly recognizable in the lower-class vernacular of Huck and Pap, the exaggerated slave dialect of Jim, the southern genteel tradition, the romantic diction of Scott and Dumas as it has been gleaned by Tom and filtered through Huck, and several other dialects. Twain himself acknowledges the painstaking attention he paid to language in the novel. Clearly, through his play with the "posited author" Huck, Twain's motive is to unmask and destroy various socio-ideological belief systems that are represented by language. So what Mailloux refers to as rhetorical performance Bakhtin identifies as the heteroglossia struggle. Thus Jim's successful appropriation of Huck's argumentative strategy dismantles the hegemony of white supremacy discourse present in Huck's language. M. M. Bakhtin, "Discourse in the Novel," trans. Michael Holquist and Caryl Emerson, in *The Dialogic Imagination: Four Essays,* ed. Michael Holquist (Austin: U of Texas P, 1981) 310–15.

[38]Mailloux 117.

the Mississippi, Huck (along with the reader) watches Jim emerge as a man whose sense of dignity and self-respect dwarf the minstrel mask. No one can deny the manly indignation evinced by Jim when Huck attempts to convince him that he has only dreamed their separation during the night of the heavy fog. Huck himself is so struck by Jim's passion that he humbles himself "to a nigger" and "warn't ever sorry for it afterwards" (p. 100).

From this point, the multidimensionality of Jim's personality erodes Huck's socialized attitudes about blacks. During the night, thinking that Huck is asleep, Jim vents the adult frustrations he does not expect Huck to understand or alleviate; he laments having to abandon his wife and two children: "Po' little Lizabeth! Po' little Johnny! it's mighty hard; I spec' I ain't ever gwyne to see you no mo', no mo'" (p. 154). Berating himself for having struck his four-year-old daughter, Elizabeth, in punishment for what he thought was blatant disobedience, Jim tells Huck of his remorse after discovering that the toddler had gone deaf without his knowledge. Through such poignant moments Huck learns, to his surprise, that Jim "cared just as much for his people as white folks does for their'n. It don't seem natural, but I reckon it's so" (p. 154).

Finally, in the welcome absence of Pap, Jim becomes a surrogate father to Huck, allowing the boy to sleep when he should stand watch on the raft, giving him the affection his natural father did not, and making sure that the raft is stocked and hidden. Thus Twain allows Jim to blossom into a mature, complex human being whom Huck admires and respects. The fullness of character with which Twain imbues Jim compels Huck to "decide, forever, betwixt two things." The reader applauds Huck's acceptance of damnation for helping Jim and affixes all expectations for the rest of the novel to this climactic moment.

Having thus tantalized readers with the prospect of harmonious relations between white and black, Twain seems to turn on his characters and his audience. Leo Marx, who mounted the best-known attack on the novel's ending in his essay "Mr. Eliot, Mr. Trilling, and *Huckleberry Finn*," describes it as a glaring lapse "of moral vision" resulting from Twain's inability to "acknowledge the truth his novel contained."[39] Readers' discomfort with the "evasion" sequence results from discrepancies between the Jim and Huck who grow in stature on the

---

[39]Leo Marx, "Mr. Eliot, Mr. Trilling, and *Huckleberry Finn*," *American Scholar* 22.4 (1953): 423–40; reprinted in Norton Critical Edition of *Adventures of Huckleberry Finn*, eds. Sculley Bradley et al., 2nd ed. (New York: Norton, 1977) 349. (See pp. 289–304 in this volume.)

raft and the impostors who submit to Tom. Fritz Oehschlaeger's "'Gwyne to Git Hung': The Conclusion of *Huckleberry Finn*" expresses the frustrations that many experience regarding the evasion:

> The . . . shift in tone from one of high seriousness to one of low burlesque is so abrupt as to be almost chilling. Clemens has simply made the issues too serious for us to accept a return to the boyhood world of the novel's opening. We are asked to forget Huck's process of moral education, his growing awareness of Jim's value as a human being. Similarly, we are asked to forget Jim's nobility, revealed to us repeatedly in the escape down the river. Instead, Jim becomes again the stereotyped, minstrel-show "nigger" of the novel's first section, a figure to be manipulated, tricked, and ridiculed by the boys. Perhaps even less acceptable is Clemens's apparent decision to allow Miss Watson a partial redemption through her death-bed freeing of Jim. At the end Jim is free and considers himself rich, and Huck is left to pursue further adventures in the Territory. [Yet] . . . something in us longs for quite a different outcome, one that would allow Jim to retain his heroic stature and force Huck to live up to the decision that accompanies his tearing up of the letter to Miss Watson.[40]

By this view, Twain's apparent abandonment of Huck's reformation and Jim's quest for freedom constitutes an absolute betrayal. Consequently, any redemptive racial attitudes that Twain has displayed earlier are nullified; his final portrait of Jim appears sinister and malicious.

Scholars have attempted to read the evasion sequence in ways that would make it palatable by placing it in sync with the preceding chapters. In just such an attempt to render the last ten chapters less irksome, James M. Cox attacks the very thing that has led readers to deplore that last one-fourth — that is, the moral sentiment against which we measure Tom's actions. Our moral sentiment, explains Cox,[41] leads us to

[40]Fritz Oehschlaeger, "'Gwyne to Git Hung': The Conclusion of *Huckleberry Finn*," in *One Hundred Years of "Huckleberry Finn": The Boy, His Book and American Culture,* eds. Robert Sattelmeyer and J. Donald Crowley (Columbia: U of Missouri P, 1985) 117.

[41]James M. Cox, *Mark Twain: The Fate of Humor* (Princeton, N.J.: Princeton UP, 1966); reprinted as "[The Uncomfortable Ending of *Huckleberry Finn*]," in the Norton Critical Edition of *Adventures of Huckleberry Finn,* eds. Sculley Bradley et al., 2nd ed. (New York: Norton, 1977) 350–59. Though he ignores Jim and his aspiration for freedom in *Mark Twain: The Fate of Humor,* in a more recent, related article, "A Hard Book to Take," Cox returns to the evasion sequence and treats Jim's freedom in particular and the concept of freedom in general. He contends that Twain had recognized "the national lie [myth] of freedom" and that the closing movement of *Huckleberry Finn* dramatizes

misconstrue Twain's intent and to declare the ending a failure. Twain does not, as most believe, lose courage and fail to carry through with his indictment of the racial attitudes of the Old South. On the contrary, the closing sequence returns the novel and Huck to Twain's true central meaning.

For thirty-one chapters Twain wages an attack upon conscience — not upon the southern conscience, as we want to believe, but upon any conscience. According to Cox, "the deep wish which *Huckleberry Finn* embodies" is "the wish for freedom from any conscience." Huck flees conscience at every turn, making choices based on what is most comfortable. It is this adherence to the pleasure principle that defines Huck's identity and governs his actions toward Jim, not a racial enlightenment, as we would hope. The moment at which Huck forsakes the pleasure principle and of which we most approve marks the point at which his identity and Twain's central focus, according to Cox, are in the most jeopardy: "In the very act of choosing to go to hell he has surrendered to the notion of a *principle* of right and wrong. He has forsaken the world of pleasure to make a moral choice. Precisely here is where Huck is about to negate himself — where, with an act of positive virtue, he actually commits himself to play the role of Tom Sawyer which he *has* to assume in the closing section of the book."[42] Insofar as the concluding section brings Huck back into line with Twain's determination to subvert conscience, it remains consistent with the preceding chapters. Given this, to declare Twain's ending a failure is to deny his actual thematic intent and to increase our discomfort with the concluding segments.

Cox's argument demonstrates the ingenious lengths to which scholars go to feel comfortable with the final chapters of *Huck Finn*. But the inadequacy of such academic ingenuities in meeting this and other challenges to the novel becomes clear when one considers that the issue remains "hot" enough to make it available for debate on prime-time television.[43] What scholars must realize is that no amount of interpretive acrobatics can mediate the actual *matter* of the closing sequence. Regardless of Twain's motivation or intent, Jim does deflate and climb

---

Twain's realization that Jim is not and never will be truly free. Further, no one, black or white, is or will be free, elaborates Cox, "despite the fictions of history and the Thirteenth Amendment." See "A Hard Book to Take," in *One Hundred Years of "Huckleberry Finn": The Boy, His Book and American Culture*, eds. Robert Sattelmeyer and J. Donald Crowley (Columbia: U of Missouri P, 1985) 386–403.

[42]Cox, *Mark Twain* 356.

[43]"*Huckleberry Finn:* Literature or Racist Trash?" ABC "Nightline," 4 Feb. 1985.

back into the minstrel costume. His self-respect and manly pursuit of freedom bow subserviently before the childish pranks of an adolescent white boy.

Considering the perplexity of the evasion brings us back full circle to *Huckleberry Finn*'s suitability for public schools. Given the powerlessness of highly discerning readers to resolve the novel in a way that unambiguously redeems Jim or Huck, how can students be expected to fare better with the novel's conclusion? Parents question the advisability of teaching to junior and senior high school students a text which requires such sophisticated interpretation in order for its moral statements to come clear. The teaching of such a text presumes a level of intellectual maturity not yet realized by secondary school students, particularly eighth- and ninth-grade students who are in the inchoate stages of literary studies. Parents fear that the more obvious negative aspects of Jim's depiction may overshadow the more subtle uses to which they are put. Critics such as Mailloux point to the reader as the component necessary to obviate the racism inherent in, for example, the interchange between Aunt Sally and Huck.[44] But if an eighth- or ninth-grader proves incapable of completing the process begun by Twain, then the ideological point is lost. This likely possibility causes parents to be hesitant about approving *Huck Finn* for the classroom.

Huck Finn apologists view the objection to the novel on the ground of students' cognitive immaturity as an underestimation of youngsters' abilities. In the third of his four-part series on the censorship of *Huck Finn*,[45] Hentoff boasts that the ability of children in 1982 to fathom Twain's subtleties is at least comparable to that of children who read the novel a century ago. "At ten, or twelve, or fourteen, even with only the beginning ring of meaning," writes Hentoff, "any child who can read will not miss the doltishness and sheer meanness and great foolishness of most whites in the book, particularly in their attitudes toward blacks."[46] He continues, "Nor will the child miss the courage and invincible decency of the white boy and the black man on the river." While Hentoff's confidence in the American schoolchild is commendable, his enthusiasm reveals a naiveté about junior high school students' critical insight. As Cox's and Mailloux's articles show, the points of the novel are anything but "as big as barn doors." There-

---

[44]Mailloux 117.
[45]Hentoff.
[46]Hentoff.

fore, the cognitive maturity of students and the grade-level placement of the novel are of grave importance.

That *Huckleberry Finn* brims with satire and irony is a truism of academic discourse. But a study conducted in 1983 to examine "the effects of reading *Huckleberry Finn* on the racial attitudes of ninth-grade students" corroborates the contention that junior high school students lack the critical perception to successfully negotiate the satire present in the novel. According to the committee that directed the study, the collected data indicated "that the elements of satire which are crucial to an understanding of the novel go largely unobserved by students."[47] That approximately one-third of the group (those students who studied the novel as an instructional unit) regarded *Huckleberry Finn* as merely an adventure story "after several weeks of serious study" left the committee convinced "that many students are not yet ready to understand the novel on its more complex levels." Therefore, although not advising expulsion of the novel, the panel recommended its removal from the ninth-grade curriculum and placement in the eleventh- or twelfth-grade syllabus:

> This recommendation is made, not because the use of *Huckleberry Finn* promotes or furthers negative stereotyping — the preponderance of our data suggests that, if anything, it lessens such stereotyping — but because some of the literary objectives given as justification for the use of the book seem not to have been achieved. Given the degree and instances of irony and satire in the book, the difficult dialects and general reading level of the book, and the tendency of many students to read the book at the level of an adventure story, the committee believes, the novel requires more literary sophistication than can reasonably be expected from an average ninth-grade student.[48]

Though the Penn State study does not support parents' calls for total removal of *Adventures of Huckleberry Finn* from the curriculum, it does validate their reservations about the presence of the work at the junior high level. Possibly a sufficiently mature audience is present in the eleventh- and twelfth-grade classes of America, but it seems not to be available in the eighth, ninth, or even tenth grades.

[47] *The Effects of Reading "Huckleberry Finn" on the Racial Attitudes of Ninth-Grade Students,* a cooperative study of the State College Area School District and the Forum on Black Affairs of Pennsylvania State University (State College, PA, 1983) 22.

[48] *The Effects of Reading "Huckleberry Finn"* 22.

The volatile combination of satire, irony, and questions of race underscores an additional important facet of the controversy: teacher ability and attitude. The position of the classroom teacher in the conflict over *Huckleberry Finn* is delicate: Students not only look to teachers as intellectual mentors, but turn to them for emotional and social guidance as well. So in addition to ensuring that students traverse the scholarly territory that the curriculum requires, teachers must guarantee that students complete the journey with their emotional beings intact.

The tenuous status of race relations in the United States complicates the undertaking of such an instructional unit. Cox, despite his affection for the novel and his libertarian views, admits that were he "teaching an American literature course in Bedford-Stuyvesant or Watts or North Philadelphia," he might choose Twain texts other than *Adventures of Huckleberry Finn.*[49] A situation as emotionally charged as the introduction of the word "nigger" into class discussion requires a sensitivity and perspicacity that parents are unconvinced a majority of teachers possess. Those who want the "classic" expelled dread the occurrence of incidents such as the one described by Hentoff on ABC's "Nightline."[50] According to Hentoff, a teacher in Texas commenced her initial class discussion of the novel with the question "What is a nigger?" In response, the white students in the class looked around the room at the black kids. In addition to this type of ineptness, the lack of commitment to human equality on the part of some teachers looms large in the minds of would-be censors. The "inherent threat" of *Huckleberry Finn* is that in the hands of an unfit, uncommitted teacher it can become a tool of oppression and harmful indoctrination.

Assuming the inverse to be equally possible, a competent, racially accepting educator could transform the potential threat into a challenge. *Huckleberry Finn* presents the secondary teacher with a vehicle to effect powerful, positive interracial exchange among students. Though I have not taught *Huckleberry Finn* in a secondary school, I have taught Harper Lee's *To Kill a Mockingbird,* which is "tainted" with the pejorative "nigger" as well as "nigger-lover," and which is also under fire from censors. Like *Huck Finn, To Kill a Mockingbird* treats a highly emotional racial episode. Different from Twain's novel, however, is the clear-cut use of "nigger-lover" and "nigger" by characters who intend the terms to be derogatory (except where Atticus Finch, a liberal lawyer, forbids his children to use them — an important exception). Set in a

---

[49]Cox, *Mark Twain* 388.
[50]"*Huckleberry Finn:* Literature or Racist Trash?"

small, bigoted Alabama town during the Great Depression, the Pulitzer Prize–winning novel is narrated by Atticus's daughter, Scout, a precocious tomboy. Scout, along with her older brother Jem and playmate Dill, observes the horrors of racial prejudice as they are played out in the trial of a black man, Tom Robinson, wrongfully accused of rape by a white woman.

Over a four-year period in Austin, Texas, I introduced the novel to approximately five hundred public school ninth-graders. Each time I taught the four-week unit on *To Kill a Mockingbird,* the most difficult day of instruction involved the introduction of "nigger" (actually "nigger-lover") into class discussion. My rationale for forcing the word into active class discourse proceeded from my belief that students (black and white) could only face sensitive issues of race after they had achieved a certain emotional distance from the rhetoric of race. I thought (and became convinced over the years) that open confrontation in the controlled setting of the classroom could achieve that emotional distance.

Early in the novel, when another child calls Atticus, who has agreed to defend Robinson, a "nigger-lover," Scout picks a fight with him. When Atticus learns of the fray, Scout asks if he *is* a "nigger-lover." Beautifully undercutting the malice of the phrase, Atticus responds, "Of course, I am. I try to love everybody." A discussion of this episode would constitute my first endeavor to ease my students into open dialogue about "the word" and its derivatives.

My opening query to each class — Why does Scout get into a fight at school? — was invariably answered with a paroxysm of silence. As the reality of racial discomfort and mistrust cast its shadow over the classroom, the tension would become almost palpable. Unable to utter the taboo word "nigger," students would be paralyzed, the whites by their social awareness of the moral injunction against it and the blacks by their heightened sensitivity to it. Slowly, torturously, the wall of silence would begin to crumble before students' timid attempts to approach the topic with euphemism. Finally, after some tense moments, one courageous adolescent would utter the word. As the class released an almost audible sigh of relief, the students and I would embark upon a lively and risk-taking exchange about race and its attendant complexities. The interracial understanding fostered by this careful, enlightened study of *To Kill a Mockingbird* can, I think, be achieved with a similar approach to *Huckleberry Finn.*

It must be understood, on the other hand, that the presence of incompetent, insensitive, or (sometimes unwittingly, sometimes purposefully) bigoted instructors in the public schools is no illusion. Black parents who entrust their children's well-being to such people run the risk of having their offspring traumatized and humiliated; white parents risk having their children inculcated with attitudes that run contrary to a belief in human rights and equality. The possibility of lowering black students' self-esteem and undermining their pride in their heritage is a substantial argument against sanctioning the novel's use, and the likelihood that *Huckleberry Finn* could encourage racial prejudice on the part of white students is a matter of comparable concern.

Though these qualms are legitimate and are partly supported by the Penn State study, other studies charged with the task of determining whether *Huckleberry Finn* causes, furthers, or ameliorates poor self-concept, racial shame, or negative racial stereotyping indicate that the novel's influence on a majority of students is positive. A 1972 study that measured the influence the novel had on the racial attitudes of black and white ninth-grade boys yielded only positive results.[51] Herbert Frankel, director of the study, concluded that significant changes in perceptions of blacks occurred for black *and* white students, and all shifts were of a positive nature. The data indicated that black adolescents' self-concepts were enhanced. Further, "black students tended to identify more strongly and more positively with other members of their race" as a result of having studied *Huckleberry Finn*. For white students, reading the novel "*reduce[d]* hostile or unfavorable feelings toward members of another race and *increase[d]* favorable feelings toward members of another race" (emphasis added). Students who read the novel under a teacher's guidance showed "significantly greater positive change" than those students who read the novel on their own.[52] The Penn State study upholds this last conclusion, judging the novel "suitable for serious literary study by high school students":

> Our data indicate that students who read the novel as part of an instructional unit demonstrated both a deeper sensitivity to the moral and psychological issues central to the novel (a number of which deal with issues of race) and a more positive attitude on matters calling for racial understanding and acceptance. These students were also able to interpret the novel with greater literary sophistication than those students who read the novel without instruction. Additionally, these students were significantly more

[51]Herbert Lewis Frankel, "The Effects of Reading *The Adventures of Huckleberry Finn* on the Racial Attitudes of Selected Ninth-Grade Boys," diss., Temple U, May 1972, 203–04.

[52]Frankel 203–04.

accepting of contacts with Blacks than were the other students involved in the study.[53]

Based on these studies completed eleven years apart (1972 and 1983), it appears that in the right circumstances *Huckleberry Finn* can be taught without perpetuating negative racial attitudes in white students or undermining racial pride in black students.

Still, in the final analysis the concerns voiced by parents and other would-be censors of *Adventures of Huckleberry Finn* are not wholly invalid. One has only to run a mental scan across the nation's news headlines to glean a portrait of the present state of American race relations. Such a glimpse betrays the ambivalence present in the status of blacks and their relations with whites. In "Breaking the Silence," a powerful statement on the plight of the "black underclass," Pete Hamill delineates the duality of the American black experience. Admitting the dismal reality of continued racist behavior, Hamill cites "the antibusing violence in liberal Boston, the Bernhard Goetz and Howard Beach cases[54] in liberal New York, [and] a resurgent Klan in some places."[55] Then, turning to inroads forged toward equality, he mentions that "for the first time in American history, there is a substantial and expanding black middle class, . . . [a] leading contender for the Democratic nomination for President is a black man,"[56] and mayors of eight major American cities are black. Hamill's article points to a fundamental fissure in the American psyche when it comes to race. Further, these details suggest that the teaching of Twain's novel may not be the innocent pedagogical endeavor that we wish it to be.

When we move from the context into which we want to deposit *Huckleberry Finn* and consider the nature of the text and its creator, the matter becomes even more entangled. Though devotees love to praise *Huckleberry Finn* as "a savage indictment of a society that accepted

---

[53] *The Effects of Reading "Huckleberry Finn"* 21.

[54] **the Bernhard Goetz and Howard Beach cases:** Two high-profile, racial incidents. In the first, Goetz, a white man, was on trial for the December 1984 subway shooting of four black youths who he claimed were trying to rob him; they claimed they had only asked him for money. The police received many calls in support of Goetz, including offers to pay for his defense. In the 1986 Howard Beach case, three black men, seeking help after their car stalled, were chased by a white mob through the streets of this predominantly white, middle-class neighborhood in Queens. All three men were severely beaten, and one, Michael Griffith, was struck and killed by a car as he sought to elude the mob. [Editors' note]

[55] Pete Hamill, "Breaking the Silence," *Esquire* 109.3 (1988): 92–93.

[56] **leading contender . . . is a black man:** Referring to civil rights activist Jesse Jackson, who made an unsuccessful bid for the 1988 nomination. [Editors' note]

slavery as a way of life"[57] or "the deadliest satire . . . ever written on . . . the inequality of [the] races,"[58] the truth is that neither the novel nor its author has escaped ambivalence about racial matters. First, the ambiguities of the novel are multiple. The characterization of Jim is a string of inconsistencies. At one point he is the superstitious darky; at another he is the indulgent surrogate father. On the one hand, his desire for freedom is unconquerable; on the other, he submits it to the ridiculous antics of a child. Further, while Jim flees from slavery and plots to steal his family out of bondage, most other slaves in the novel embody the romantic contentment with the "peculiar institution" that slaveholders tried to convince abolitionists all slaves felt.

Twain's equivocal attitude toward blacks extends beyond his fiction into his lifelong struggle with "the Negro question." In his autobiography Twain describes the complaisance with which he accepted slavery while growing up. Leaving slaveholding Missouri seems to have had little effect on his racial outlook, because in 1853 he wrote home to his mother from New York, "I reckon I had better black my face, for in these Eastern States niggers are considerably better than white people." He served briefly as a Confederate soldier before heading west and never seemed to be morally discomfited by his defense of slavery.[59] Set over and against these unflattering details are Twain's advocacies for equality. In 1985 a letter proving that Twain had provided financial assistance to a black student at the Yale University Law School in 1885 was discovered and authenticated by Shelley Fisher Fishkin. In the letter Twain writes, "We [whites] have ground the manhood out of them, & the shame is ours, not theirs, & we should pay for it."[60] He is also known to have teamed with Booker T. Washington in championing several black causes.[61]

The factor of racial uncertainty on the part of Twain, its manifestation in his best-loved piece, and its existence in American society should not be a barrier to *Huckleberry Finn*'s admittance to the classroom. Instead, this should make it the pith of the American literature curriculum. The insolubility of the race question as regards *Huckleberry Finn*

[57]Kaplan 18. (See p. 378.)

[58]"Huck Finn's Friend Jim" 22.

[59]See Bernard Bell's essay, "Twain's 'Nigger' Jim: The Tragic Face behind the Minstrel Mask," in *Satire or Evasion* 124–40.

[60]Wil Haygood, "Twain Letter Revives Old Question: Detractors Say They Still Think 'Huck Finn' Has Racist Taint," *Boston Globe* 15 Mar. 1985: 3.

[61]Jacqueline James Goodwin, "Booker T. Washington and Twain as a Team," letter, *New York Times* 24 Apr. 1985: A22.

functions as a model of the fundamental racial ambiguity of the American mind-set. Active engagement with Twain's novel provides one method for students to confront their own deepest racial feelings and insecurities. Though the problems of racial perspective present in *Huckleberry Finn* may never be satisfactorily explained for censors or scholars, the consideration of them may have a practical, positive bearing on the manner in which America approaches race in the coming century.

GERRY BRENNER

More than a Reader's Response: A Letter to "De Ole True Huck"

Gerry Brenner (b. 1937) is professor emeritus of English at the University of Montana. He received his B.A. (1961), M.A. (1962), and Ph.D. (1965) from the University of Washington. After teaching at the University of Idaho (1965–67) and Boise State University (1967–68), Brenner moved to Montana in 1968 and has been there since. He has published work on American and British writers across the historical spectrum, but his books have primarily focused on the writings of Ernest Hemingway: *Concealments in Hemingway's Works* (1983), *Ernest Hemingway* (1986 rev. ed., coauthored with Earl Rovit, author of the first edition), *The Old Man and the Sea: The Story of a Common Man* (1991), and *A Comprehensive Companion to Hemingway's A Moveable Feast: Annotation to Interpretation* (2000). Brenner's most recent book is *Performative Criticism: Experiments in Reader Response* (2004), and it includes the piece reprinted here, which was originally published in 1990 in *The Journal of Narrative Technique*.

. . . Dear Mister Finn,

It was my ability to read, you'll believe, that led to a conversation one April evening a decade ago, a conversation I wrote down soon after. But it's been my inability to stop grieving over pappy's recent death that has goaded me to locate you — no easy matter — and send you what I had written. I won't bother you with the details of how pappy, after returning with Mister Sawyer and Missus Polly from

Louisiana, worked and saved his money, in time buying mammy's, 'Lizabeth's, and my freedom. Or the details of our move north into a rundown shanty on Chicago's south side, the jobs we found there, or 'Lizabeth's — and now pappy's — death. (Nor will you want me to tell you, I imagine, how, after several months, I found your most recent address.) I'll skip directly to our customary walks every Sunday, to the enjoyment we took in our little bit of finery, to our pleasure in the break from our weekday routines, to our great relief in being far from St. Petersburg. For it was on one of those Sunday walks that we were passing by a bookseller's on Davenport Street. I found my eye snagged by a title in the window: *Adventures of Huckleberry Finn.* I halted the family and read them what I saw. Naturally pappy found it mighty curious to see the name of his former raft-companion on the hard boards of a book cover.

We scrimped for the next three weeks, took on extra jobs and saved up enough to buy a copy of your book. When I got home with it pappy thumbed it over, looking at all the illustrations. Then he declared that every night we would hear some of it, that I would read it aloud. For the next three-and-a-half weeks I read, to a very attentive audience, as you can well imagine, sir. After every stint of reading, mammy and I would ask pappy if things *really* happened as you said they did. But every night he'd only raise his hand, smile, and say, "We gwyneter hyear out Huck honey's 'hole tale. Dis book b'long to him." For the first week I'd get angry with him for not answering our question, but I finally resigned myself to his refusal. I couldn't help but notice, though, that during several episodes he'd chuckle, or a serious look would cloud up his face, or he'd cock an eyebrow, push out his lips, and scratch his wool. And twice — when you wrote about the *Sir Walter Scott* riverboat and watching the sunrise on the river — he got up and paced back and forth, telling me, "Keep readin', chile. Keep readin', please." All through the episodes at the Phelps' farm he concentrated so intently that his corncob pipe would go out early and wouldn't get lit again until I ended the reading session.

When I finally finished reading your book, pappy rocked back in his chair and sucked on his pipe a few times, mammy and I waiting patiently. Then, in almost a whisper, he said, "Well, well. De ole true Huck. De ole true Huck." Then he began to chuckle. Then to laugh. And laugh. And every once in a while, like he was coming up for air, he'd say again, "De ole true Huck. Yes-indeedy, de ole true Huck."

Mammy and I, flies after honey, asked him to explain what he meant. At last his laugh wore itself out.

"Duz bof' o' you goggle-eyed puhsuns 'spect me to dump de 'hole load o' ole Huck's story t'night? I's gwyne let it sit fo' a day so's I kin unpack it right, wun carpetbag at a time. 'Sides, it's too late to go on 'bout dis story now. Good lan', I reck'n it's time we wuz all in bed er in de mawnin' we hain't gwyneter be wuth mo' dan," he cocked an eyebrow, "mo' dan a hairball widout money." He chuckled at his allusion, you can be sure, Mister Finn.

The next day was dreadful long before he returned from the docks. Mammy and I rushed him through dinner, got him seated comfortably in his rocker, fired up his corncob, and began nagging him to tell us about your book.

"Well, den. Heah's what I fines. Fo' thin's, I think. Mebbe mo', mebbe less, 'pendin' how you counts 'em en 'pendin' wedder I kin keep 'em sep'rate, like de cream f'om de milk. Fer wun thin', ole Huck honey's done sum mispropriatin'. En he's tol' sum o' dem 'stretchers,' as he calls 'em. En dey's *considable* buttuh spread on dat meanness o' his. But," and here he began to laugh again so that mammy and I could hardly make out what he was saying, "but all durin' dem adventures, 'spesh'ly durin' dat time we wuz at dem Phelps, I never knowed fo' sure if Huck knowed how much I wuz 'lettin' on,' as Misto Tom called it. Dog my cats ef'n I didn' pull de wool over Huck honey's eyes."

"Now jis' you wait wun doggone minute, James Alexander Hawkins!" said mammy. "You jis' stop all o' dat laffin', you hyear! Jis' you slo' down en 'splain to Johnny en me what you talkin' 'bout. Usin' dat big word, 'miss-propri-what?' 'Taint kind to be laffin' 'bout smufn widout us gettin' a chance to share in de laff. En stop dat f'roshus rockin' b'fo you tip yo'sef out onter de flo'. Commence to tell *us* de joke. Johnny chile, you fetch yo' pappy some o' dat good 'backy. Misto Finn's right 'bout one thin' fo' sure, James Hawkins: You mus' be de easiest nigger to laff dat ever wuz!"

Your "mispropriations," as pappy called them? By that he said he meant that you made it appear that you understood or did things with no help from him. He had me thumb back and find that place where you're telling about how the sun came up on the river. I found it easily, because I'd dogeared that page. I thought that some mighty fine writing, for it took me back to some mornings on the big river when I was still a slave. Pappy had me read it again. Then he asked me if I noticed anything curious about it. I told him that I saw nothing at all curious about it.

"Chile, you means to tell me dey's nuffn strange in dat?"

I read it to myself, looked up at him and shook my head.

"Johnny chile, is dat all fack?"

"No, pappy. Course not. Mister Finn described what he saw. Its poetry-like, not fact."

"Chile, is dey nuffn mo'? Duz Huck honey tell you sumfn dat he don't know fo' sure?"

"Like what, pappy," I asked, exasperated with his niggling.

"Chile, read dem words 'bout de log pile dat Huck honey writes 'bout."

So I read: "'. . . and you make out a log cabin in the edge of the woods, away on the bank on t'other side of the river, being a wood-yard, likely, and piled by them cheats so you can throw a dog through it anywhere; then the . . .'"

"Stop dah. *Now* what you see, chile?"

I just shook my head.

"James Hawkins! You leave dat boy 'lone. Stop yo' pickin' on him."

"Mammy, Johnny's de wun what's sposed to know how t' read. Well, it warn't no use fer to learn him how to read ef'n at sixteen he doan' unnerstan' what he's readin', wuz it? Now, den, Johnny chile, how could Huck honey know dat dat log pile wuz stacked by cheats 'stead of jis' a sloppy stacker? Hain't dat kinder a funny noshun fo' him to draw? Well, jis' you guess who it wuz dat pointed out dat stack full o' holes? But *I* tol' him I reck'n'd it wuz stacked by a cheat *er* a sloppy stacker *er* a lazy hired hand. Kinder curious to me dat Huck would draw on'y de wust noshun. En so, Johnny chile, dat's what I means by Huck's mispropriatin'. He takes de credit fo' pretendin' as if *he* wuz de wun what saw dat leaky log pile."

And who, Mister Finn, came up with the idea that you should make up a story to get someone to scurry out to that wreck, the *Sir Walter Scott*? Pappy says that *you* were all for forgetting about those robbers, especially when that storm came along after you and he made off with their boat. But, chuckling all the while he told it, he remembered that once the two of you caught up with your raft, he suggested that you shove off to shore and get someone to rescue those robbers. He laughed at the recollection of the way your jaw dropped, claiming that you were amazed at his suggestion, that you didn't want to have anything to do with them, that they reminded you too much of your pap — that they could sink with the wreck, for all you cared. Pappy said he got his dander up then. He scolded you and told you it was no way to treat other folks, even if they were only no-account robbers. Of course, what you actually did, once you shoved off for shore, pappy had no way of knowing. He said, though, that he enjoyed my reading the

story you told the ferryboat watchman, said that it was mighty entertaining. Whether it was true or not, he had no way of knowing. For all
he knew, you just rowed to shore, skulked for an hour or so, figured out
what you'd tell him and came back. At least you were pretty mum, he
said, when you and he saw the *Scott* floating down the river.

"Soun's like you 'ccusin' Misto Finn o' tellin' a stretcher, James
Hawkins. I tho't you wuz jis' gwyne tell 'bout his miss-propri — drat
dat word! But you jis done clumb f'om dem thin's to stretchers, I
b'lieve. Wun at a time, ef'n you please."

"But sumtimes, like de shingles on de roof, woman, dey ove'lap.
Besides," he continued, "ef'n dat wuz a stretcher, den it wiz *small
taters* to what Huck could do wif a full head of steam up."

He couldn't get over how you concocted — back at the beginning
of your story — that tall tale of him being ridden by witches all over the
world. He said that he'd only been letting on that he was snoring after
he stretched out beneath that tree, between you and Mister Sawyer. He
figured it was you two up to pranks. After all, sitting in the kitchen
door, he had heard the phoney meowing, and heard you scrambling
out your window. So when you stumbled over the root, he went out,
then faked his snoring to see what you two would do. He was still
awake when Mister Sawyer crawled back, slipped the hat off his head
and hung it on the limb above him.

But according to pappy, he explained to the other slaves that a spirit
had caught him napping. By hanging his hat from a limb, the spirit had
given him a sign. The sign warned him not to nap while white folks
were still awake, for they were not above finding fun in dumping dirt
on slaves.

"How dat ole Huck could stretch sumfn mos' all o' de time," pappy
said, grinning wide and chuckling at the difference between your version and what actually happened.

"Well, pappy. How *did* you get that five-center piece that you still
wear around your neck if it wasn't the money that Mister Sawyer left for
the candles?"

Mammy got up and, with a wrinkly smile playing over her face, left
the room, puzzling me.

Pappy chuckled at her exit. "Chile, doan' you know a luv token
when you sees wun? Why yo' mammy wuz holdin' dis in de pink of her
han' de fust day dat ever I saw her. She en Harbison's Minnie wuz in
Misto' Harper's shackly brick sto' nex' to de Temp'rance Tavern on
Meadow Lane. En dey wuz buyin' a piece o' linsey-woolsey fo' her missus wid dat five-center piece. My but she looked fine in her milk-white

apr'n, calico print en red bandanner — looked like a new pin. En when she lef' de sto', I ax Misto Harper ef'n he'd swap dat five-center fo' wun in my pockit. He reck'n'd dey wuz no reason not to, en when I giv' him mine, he flipped his onto de flo'. I ignored de insult — mo' *trash* from de white folks — tuck it to de blacksmith, en had him work a hole in it so's I could wear it roun' my neck on a string. It's been heah ever since, a rememberer o' de fust gal I ever set eyes on what made my heart go flippity flop."

By this time mammy was back in the room, hands on her hips, her face a-scowling. "James Hawkins, jis' you stop carryin' on like dat. En stop flashin' yo' big brown eyes and yo' love-makin' grin on me b'fo' dat boy. Dat's not decent, en you knows it. Tell us mo' 'bout Misto Finn's stretchers."

"Yes, pappy. Why would Mister Finn want to brew up a stretcher about your so-called witch ride around the world? What good would that do him?"

"Well, mebbe it let Huck honey — when he sat hissef down t' write 'bout us — 'ticipate the journey we wuz gwyne be goin' on. Kinder makes my ride a po' rag-doll version 'o his own adventure, doan' it? Like thowin' a stick into bog water en sendin' a dog arter it — to see ef dey eny snakes in it b'fo' you foot acrost it yo'sef. En I spoze my cock-eyed witch trip would make his tale pow'ful real-like by 'parison, wouldn' you say? En I spoze too dat dis wuz Huck's way, mos' o' de time. He awluz liked to show *me* to be de fool, a saphead, as he liked to call mos' folks."

"But pappy, you sure were a fool lots of times. It was downright embarrassing to read that part where you told Mister Finn — now where's that place? Yes, here it is — "'I ben rich wunst, and gwyne to be rich agin.'" Why, pappy, that whole page, about you investing in a cow, in a bank, in a wood-flat that someone stole, and in Balum — why all of that makes you sound ridiculous, like all you had *inside* your head was the same thing you had on *top* of it — wool."

While I was rattling on, I suddenly realized that pappy's grinning meant one thing; *he* wasn't embarrassed by that page. I laughed out loud too.

"What you two chuckle-heads laughin' 'bout? Dat investin' stuff embarrass me. 'Splain to me, right dis minute, de joke!"

So I explained to her that pappy was only pretending to be a fool, that he was stringing Mister Finn along, inviting him to think poorly of pappy.

"But why you wan' do a thin' like dat to a young chile, James Hawkins?"

Pappy got out of his rocker, went over to mammy, lifted her hands from her mending, and explained. He told her he could feel that something was ruffling you when he finished telling you about his own escape. It dawned on him that you'd puffed yourself up pretty full, telling him about your own scheme of escape. But after he told you about his, you seemed to have lost some air. All he could figure was that you were nettled to discover that he appeared at least as smart as you. And when you made mock of his going without meat and bread or even mud-turkles, then he was sure he'd figured right. But your taunting, he owned, made him forget himself. He got sassy about catching mud-turkles and began boasting about knowing all the signs that would bring bad luck. When he noticed your lower lip stiffening, he realized he was seeing another sign. It meant he'd overstepped himself and that he'd best play dumb for a while. So that was why, he told mammy, he fell in with you and carried on in such a foolish way about his investments.

Returning to his rocker and refilling his corncob, pappy told us that during those first few days with you he kept forgetting that for all of your reputation as a worthless near-orphan you were still a proud white boy who wasn't about to treat him as an equal. He chuckled as he lit his bowl, asked me to find that scene where you and he are snug in the cave on Jackson's Island during that storm, asked me to read what he said after you declared that the cave was nice and that you wouldn't want to be anywhere else but there.

"'Well, you wouldn't a ben here,'" I read, "''f it hadn't a ben for Jim. You'd a ben down dah in de woods widout any dinner, en gittn' mos' drownded, too, dat you would, honey. Chickens knows when its gwyne to rain, en so do de birds, chile.'"

"Well, go on, chile," commanded mammy. "What duz dat Huck say den — arter yo' pappy's sass?"

"He says nothing, mammy — leastwise nothing back to pappy. He just goes on to tell about the river rising."

"See? Dat wuz my mistake. I didn't jedge right. I reck'n I was pooty chuckle-headed not to see dat even Huck didn' like to have folks — 'spesh'ly no slave — sassin' en makin' him feel dat he was beholden to 'em. His silence en dat stiff lip — dey bof warnded me dat he jis' might save up en fetch me a heapin' platter o' comeuppance when it wus *his* servin' time."

"Pappy, that must explain why Mister Finn put that dead rattlesnake in your blanket. That and your refusal to talk about the dead man that you found in that floating house — his pap."

Pappy told me I was "splittin' kindlin' fine," that he learned from that snake-bite episode that you were far from just a prank-playing boy. Shaking his head as if to wish it weren't so, he believed that you had a mean streak clear through, that you resented anyone who got an upper hand, and that you were mighty sneaky about bringing that person down, even though you did a swell job of concealing your meanness and sneakiness in the way you wrote your story.

"Arter dat rattle-snake bit me en I got better, I axed Huck honey how he figured dat snake got on my bed-roll. But I jis' got sum hemmin' en hawwin' f'om him. So I made up my mine 'bout what I's gwyne to do. En dat wuz to test Huck honey a few mo' times to fine out jis' what he wuz made out o'."

"Test him? How'd you do that pappy? I don't remember any tests."

"Well, chile, you need mo' lessons in 'terpretin' signs, it seems. 'Member you dat chapter dat Huck ends by saying ' "you can't learn a nigger to argue?" ' Well all o' dat arguin' 'bout Sollerman's wisdom en de ways de French folks talk — what wuz dat but testin'? I could see dat I had to fine out ef'n I could talk open to dat boy, ef'n he'd 'cept me as his ekal or ef'n he'd try to get back at me fo' doin' so. En you 'member what comes arter dat arguin'?"

"Wasn't it that episode where you and Mister Finn get separated in the fog? But that was — let me check to be sure — yes," I said, finding the place, "yes, that was two nights after that argument."

"Well, I be ding-busted ef'n it wuz! 'Cordin' to *Huck* it wuz two nights later. But 'cordin' to my rek'lekshun it wuz dat very night. He wuz still smould'rin' 'bout my 'sputin' wid him over Sollerman en my bestin' him in de 'spute 'bout de way de French talks. So he tuck it inter his haid to play dat low-down trick on me, lettin' on dat him en me hadn't ben sep'rated at all by de fog."

"How you 'splain, den, all o' dat glad talk, 'bout how happy you wuz to see him on de raf, en sich stuff? Wuz you genuwine 'bout dat?"

"Sholy I wuz, mammy. Arter all, I knowed dat fer all o' his swagger he wuz still nuffn mo' dan a lost young boy, didn' I? En I couldn't help but feel fo' him de way I'd feel ef'n he wuz our own Johnny, could I? Why you think I got inter dat Sollerman 'spute? Jis' fo' de sake o' arguin'? Lan' sakes, but it wuz to try to teach dat boy dat he wuz wuth sumfn to me en to hissef, dat I'd never do to him what dat Sollerman wuz willin' to do to a chile."

"So wuz dat de las' o' yo' testin's?"

"Dey wuz wun mo'. When we wuz gettin' close to Cairo I could tell dat Huck wuz havin' trubbil wid his conshuns 'bout helpin' free a slave. His face wuz clabberin' up like milk sowerin'. So I jedged I'd best deal out sum kyards en see how he'd play 'em. I began to dance 'bout, like he writes, sayin' 'Dah's Cairo,' ever time I seed a gob o' lights on de sho'. En den I rattled on 'bout how arter I got free I'd save money en buy mammy's en my chillens' freedom. 'Deed, I dropped de bucket en let it sink clear down to de bottom o' de well: I 'clared dat ef'n I had to do it, I'd get sum o' dem Ab'lishunists to help steal my chillens out o' bondage.

"Well, it wuzn't hard to see dat *dat* kine o' talk put a slab o' ice on ole Huck, dat I couldn' trust him to act out o' goodheartedness fo' me. So b'fo' he set off fo' sho' in dat canoe to fine out ef'n dem lights wuz Cairo, I did sum mighty thick buttuh-spreadin' o' my own. I carried on like I wuz de mos' 'preciatin' puhsun in de 'hole world, 'clared dat I wuz beholden to Huck, dat he wuz de bes' fren' I ever had, dat he wuz de ole true Huck, de on'y white genlman dat ever kep' his promise to me. I said dem words what's in de book. But I said dem b'kase I knowed dat de on'y hope I had fer gettin' a pail o' merciful feelin's out o' him wuz to shower him wid an outpourin' o' sugared grat'tood."

"Buttuh-spreadin, is it? Wuz de buttuh you spread like dat dat you 'ccusin' dat Huck o'? B'kase ef'n it is, den you gots a wide streak o' meanness in you, too. Hain't dat so?"

Pappy pulled his pipe from between his teeth and looked at mammy with surprise — no, it was disappointment.

Mammy stared back at him. Then suddenly she broke into a laugh. "Nemmine, James Hawkins," she said. "I lay I kin joke you, cain't I? As ef'n I doan' know de diff'rence 'tween bein' mean to folks fo' de sake o' feelin' better dan dem, feelin' bigger dan dey is — like yo' Huck — en bein' mean kase it necess'ry fo' gettin' out o'bondage. But lemme take you back to dat sep'rashun in de fog. Ef'n dat Huck spreads buttuh to make his meanness easy to swaller, den I doan' see eny on dat fog episode. He shows de kine o' lick-spittle feller he is dah, doan' he?"

Pappy told her she was right, that you wrote about that episode the way it truly happened. But he guessed that you wrote about it to use it as a decoy, figured that by owning up to the cruelty of that prank you probably hoped to put readers off the scent. If you could make them believe you felt bad about your treatment of him *there,* he told her, then they'd most likely think you'd learned your lesson and surely wouldn't treat him so shabbily again.

How he rattled on *then,* piling up a heap of tell-tale signs of your cruelty, like they were crackers from a full barrel. Those two men who were hunting for five runaway slaves? Why did you tell them your pap was sick with smallpox on the raft, he asked mammy and me? To save his skin? Maybe, he allowed. But he was sure he heard some low chuckling on your way back to the raft, and it made him wonder if you had suckered those men more to sharpen your skills in gulling others and to add two more sapheads to your belt, like, he said, "dem Injuns do wid dose skyalps."

And when you learned that you'd floated past Cairo and decided to canoe back upstream? Did you both sleep all day, resting up for the work of paddling upstream, he asked us? Were you both genuinely surprised when you found the canoe gone from the raft? Was that some more work of the rattle-snake skin? Indeed it was, answered pappy. It was the work of the rattler he was travelling with, anyway. He believed that to return to the Ohio and steamboat north would end the pleasure trip you were bent on having, would rob you of the lackadaisical floats you were lapping up. Always a light sleeper, he claimed that he woke to the mid-day rustle of those cottonwood leaves that were hiding the two of you. And when he saw you footing off in the direction of the raft, he hoped you weren't up to some treachery, were only slipping off to empty yourself. It took a lot of pretending, he said, to act surprised when you and he later got to the raft and found the canoe gone. And he did his best to ignore the faint shadows of dampness on the raft — your footprints, he decided.

"It warn't no use fer me to do nuffin but t' go 'long wid Huck en t' hide f'om him my mistrust. It warn't easy lettin' on dat I wuz happy to see him when ole Jack led him out t' whar I wuz whilst he wuz stayin' wid de Grangerfords. En when he tole me all 'bout dat feud en de bullits dat dem Shepherdsons wuz shootin' en him perched in dat tree seein' all — well, I knowed agin (but I dassent p'int it out t' *him*) dat he wuz in de bes' place for to warn dat young Misto Buck o' de Shepherdsons circlin' roun' him and his kuzin. I jedged it bes' not to ax him why he didn' warn Misto Buck, why he didn' keep his eye peeled like he awluz did when we wuz on de river."

"James Hawkins! Dat's only spekyulashun! Mebbe dat young'n didn' see dem shepherds' sons one bit. Mebbe he wuz fixin' his eye on dem boys' dads! How 'bout dat? But here you go 'ccusin' him o' treachery. Oughtn't you be hangin' yo' haid fo' shame, awluz thinkin' de wust o' dat boy?"

"Good lan', mammy. Sho' nuff, it *is* spekyulashun. Sum. But I wuz dere, wuzn't I? En I 'members de way old Huck's lip — awluz de lower wun — would stiffen up when he wuz strayin' f'om de truth er 'nittin' bombuls onto de facks. En whilst he wuz tellin' me 'bout dat gun-shootin' dat lip wuz gettin' a good freeze on it. En I doan' think it wuz b'kase de sight o' blood wuz puttin' a chill on it."

Then pappy held forth like one of those Chautauqua talkers, like he had a lecture all worked out, asking first a load of questions and then answering them all himself. He asked us to think over that stretch about the Duke and the King, to reckon up how long you and he had those two scoundrels along. I guessed about three weeks and mammy guessed four while he was gathering up breath for the next questions. He told us to hush. Did we, he asked, believe that he didn't see through those two trash-peddlers? And did we wonder why *you* believed it would have done no good to tell him that they were frauds? More, had we bothered to ask ourselves why you hadn't found a way — early on — to cast off without those rascals so that you and he could continue on your own? Most, could we read the signs of your fascination with that pair of low-down water-rats?

Mammy and I knew that pappy's questions weren't questions at all. Naturally he saw through the Duke and King. After all, before I was five years old pappy had learned me by heart his favorite saying — one I was to recite only to him when we were alone. "De white folks is white," he'd say slowly, speaking like a schoolmaster, "b'kase dey is like glass. En glass," he'd emphasize, lowering his voice to sound sinister, "is what you *sees troo*!"

"Go on, go on, James Hawkins, en answer yo' questions — all 'cept dat wun 'bout wedder you saw troo de trash-pedlars. Dey's glass, o' course."

According to him you needed to believe in the uselessness of telling *him* that the rascals were frauds: You didn't want to be beholden to a nigger for working up a plan to free yourselves from them. He also knew he had to wait for you to signal your disapproval of the rascals, else you'd get uppity at his quicker perception and shorter fuse for moral outrage. Besides, he argued, you didn't want to be free from them. So you made out that you and he were the next thing to hostages, played up the fear that the rascals could catch you or else release the poster with the reward for Jim. Pappy scoffed at this, insisting to us that if you and he were smart enough by yourselves to escape from St. Petersburg and to get yourselves that far down river, then you could surely slip out of the clutches of that pair, cover your tracks to keep them from catching you, and masquerade yourselves well enough to dodge reward-hungry slave-hunters.

All of his answers, he continued, pointed to your fascination with those rascals. Neither their prisoner nor their lackey, you were, he was convinced, their shadow. You liked their adventures, the excitement of running risks and nudging up against danger. You secretly admired their ability to fleece others, the willow way they could bend down and scoop up out of the dirt some far-fetched lie that they could usually get other folks to swallow. You were plumb in awe of their smarts, the warehouse of tricks, pappy called it, that they always seemed to have at hand. But even more, pappy claimed, you liked to watch them hurt people. After all, that was one purpose in all of their pranks — to fool gullible, believing folks who'd be hard put, in most cases, to replace the money and self-esteem that those rascals robbed them of.

"Dem two," he declared, stabbing his forefinger into his thigh to emphasize each word, "dem two give ole Huck de sugar tit he mos' longed fo', de wish to feel sco'n fo' yuther folks. On de wun han' ole Huck looked down his nose on dem sapheads fo' bein' sich simple lam's, so easy to shear de fleece f'om. En on de yuther han' he looked down his nose on dem rascals fo' pullin' sich low-down tricks, fo' fleecin' folks who jis' might have a streak of decency in dem.

"Yes, indeedy. Po' Huck honey. He didn' know hissef. He didn' know dat dem two frauds wuz parts o' hissef, dat dey wuz like his brudders unner de skin, dat dey wuz acktin' out de very t'ings dat he hissef wanted so much to do. On'y he could let on like he wuz jis' wun innercent bystander, sumbody yanked into sumfn he didn' want to 'ticipate in."

"Is you talkin' 'bout dat Huck wid de Duke en de King? Er is you talkin', James Hawkins, 'bout dat Huck wid dat Misto Sawyer at dem Phelps's farm?"

"Dat's de bes' question yet, mammy. Fer if'n I'm talkin' 'bout wun, den I'm sholy talkin' 'bout de yuther as well, hain't I?"

They were both going too fast for me, so I asked pappy to explain the connection that seemed so clear to him and mammy.

"Come, mammy. Le's go back en fetch John. 'Pears we done hopped a crick en lef' him on de yuther side. Chile, doan' you see de link 'tween dem two grow'd-up rascals en dat young 'un, dat Mars Tom? Huck tuck to all t'ree o' dem like a cat to milk 'kase dey 'llowed him to hide de meanness in hissef. Ef'n he could go 'long wid de pranks o' dem fust two, lettin' on like he wuz drug 'long agin his will, den it wuz sholy easy fo' him to go 'long wid de same kine o' pranks o' Mars Tom. Sholy you sees de link, doan' you?"

To my nodding head he continued. "Lemme put sum drippin's on dat co'n bread fo' to salt de taste. Tells me dis, bof' o' you. Duz Huck honey ever try to ruffle eny o' de feathers o' Mars Tom's plans? Even oncet? Duz he quarr'l er protest wid Mars Tom over eny o' dem gashly tricks dat dey plays? Duz Huck show *eny* sign o' bein' axasp'rated wid de blimblammin' foolishness dat wuz plumb wearin' me out en wuz — f'om what Nat tole me — makin' wracks o' de mines o' dat Misto Silas and Missus Sally? All t'roo dat 'hole long ordeal (bof' o' you be pleased to notus) Huck honey shows all de signs dat reveals — to enybody what kin *read* signs — jis' how full o'venom he wuz: *glass,* mine you.

"Now dat Mars Tom, he wuz plumb crazy, dey hain't no question 'bout dat. I knowed him by de back. He wuz bewitched by clap-trap, by de 'style' dat he wuz awluz talkin' 'bout. En so real livin' folks en real thin's didn' matter none to him. He lived in a kine o' dream world like Huck honey's pap arter he'd swill down dat rotgut. Er like me arter dat snake-bite and dat whiskey dat I had to slosh down my belly. Good lan' but dat Mars Tom wuz wun dang'rus boy.

"But dat Huck. He wuz even mo' dang'rus 'kase he let on dat he wuz a pooty good boy what'd got caught in a tight place en had no way to get out o' it. His telling makes it soun' like he wuz Mars Tom's chattel, like dat mean Mars Tom — ef'n Huck didn' do his biddin' — 'd blow up de 'hole show, 'd up en tell dem Phelps 'bout de game dat dey wuz playin'."

Pappy pulled himself out of his rocker, came across the room, and took your book from my hands. He held it, turning it to one side and the other. Then he drew deep at his corncob. Slowly he blew the smoke all over your book. When the smoke rose away he said, "But ef'n you's sumwun's fren', den you doan' skaseley ever treats 'em like Huck en Mars Tom treated me en dem po' Phelps folks."

"James Hawkins, hain't you overlookin' sumfn? Hain't you overlookin' Misto Huck's sentimenterin' over dat Aunt Sally de night arter de 'scape? 'Members him startin' out o' dat house twyste er t'ree times on'y to come back inter de house 'kase he seed dat grievin' Aunt Sally sittin' in de rockin' chair, waitin' fo' news o' dat chile?"

"That was a nice gesture, mammy. I remember it making my voice wobbly when I was reading that scene. But I don't trust pappy's Huck. His swearing he'd never grieve her again reminds me of a couple other changes of heart. Huck's pap conned that fool judge into believing he'd reformed his ways. And at the camp meeting, the King put on that

he was a pirate who'd seen the light. Besides, mammy, pappy's Huck
made his vow only after Missus Sally'd been mothering him. That
must've boosted all his bad feelings about the tricks he'd been helping
that Mister Tom to heap on her head. Huck's vow, I reckon, is a sign
pappy'd read different from most folks. Make a show of repentance or
remorse, and what happens? Folks get all gushy and think well of you
for making those signs, just like you're doing, now, for Mister Huck."

"Dat's right, chile. But dat hain't de ha'f o' it. Dem hain't de on'y
signs to read. Read de res' o' dem. Huck put me in de pickle barr'l, he
did, by sendin' dat doctor 'lone in de canoe. I 'spect'd ole Huck'd
come 'long en give sum sign to 'lert me to up en hide. But de splash o'
de paddle wuz mos' on me fo' I heard it. I skaseley had time to hide.
Later I could see dat de doctor needed help to fix up Mars Tom. I kep'
'spectin' ole Huck to come back. But no sign o' him. I saw dat I had to
help dat doctor or else when I did get foun' I wuz gwinter get mighty
'bused by de white folks. En when Huck doan' show up all de nex' day
en durin' de nex' night, den I knowed dat Huck wuz probly fixin' up
sum 'splanashun fer why he couldn' come back. En I knowed dat dey
wuz mo' to his not showin' up dan jis' his 'splanashun. I could read dat
sign, you bet! Huck wanted dat doctor en me to be in a pickle widout
de stuff to fix Mars Tom b'kase he wuz wishin' fo' de wust to happen to
Mars Tom."

"You mean to make me b'lieve dat dat Misto Huck o' yours wuz
hopin' dat dat Misto Tom would die? Ef'n you duz, den *you* de crazy
wun, a *mighty* sick Arab!"

"Well, mammy, mebbe so, mebbe so. But all de whiles dat I wuz
nussin' Mars Tom wid dat doctor I couldn' get shut f'om my mine how
ole Huck 'membered dat ep'sode in dat town whar dat Sherburn kernel
shot down dat Boggs feller. Ole Huck wuz — what's dat newfangle'
word? yes, mezm'rized — Huck wuz mezm'rized by dat ep'sode en
'specially by dat kernel. Jis' like de way dat Johnny read it, Huck tole
me 'bout dat kernel's speechifyin', tole it like it wuz writ on his mine,
like dat man's words wuz sumfn dat Huck foun' wuth 'memberin, a
Sunny school lesson. En dat kernel! Why dat wuz a man what shot dat
yuther man in cold blood. En den he had de face to skold dem white
folks like dey wuz nuffn mo' dan misbehavin' chillens. Dat wuz wun
mean man, mammy. En Huck? Why Huck honey 'dmired him!

"So when Huck doan' show up fo' mo' dan twenty-fo' hours,
den de meanin' o' dat sign come to me: Huck wanted to 'bandon dat
doctor en me, hopin' dat Mars Tom'd die. Dat way he could get shut

'o Tom. En den I'd be beholden agin on'y to him fo' helpin' me get free.

"I could see dat de only way fo' me to do wuz to help dat doctor all I could, to let on like I wuz snorin' when dem men came on dat skiff, en to give 'em no fight when dey grabbed me and tied me up. It wuz de easiest thin' I ever did to let on like I didn't know Huck when dem men led me, de doctor en Tom — flat on dat mattress — back to de farm."

"En when dey tole you dat you wuz a free man, den how'd you feel? Tell us dat, fo' yo' Huck doan' writes much 'bout what you said er dun when he and Mars Tom went an' got you out o' dem chains."

Pappy laughed long, then said he was sure he bested Mister Tom and the Duke and the King all rolled together for the handbill of roles he played in ten minutes. Believing their news just another mean-spirited prank, he pretended astonishment and began to chant to himself distractedly, "James Alexander Hawkins. You is a free man. You's no mo' a slave. A slave no mo', no mo', no mo'. YOU IS WUN FREE MAN." Then he said he faked his gratitude, fell to his knees on the dirt floor of the hut, raised his arms and thanked the Lord for sending his deliverers, his Moses and his Aaron, to lead him out of bondage. Then he began to dance about, like he was "settin' de flo' wid Jenny," capering like a fool with Missus Sally's calico dress still on and the chains clanging all about. Finally he fell to blubbering on your shoulder, he told us, thanking you for being the old true Huck, the best friend he'd ever had, blessing you and Mister Tom, vowing that he'd always do right by you both, pledging that for the rest of his life never a day would go by without him saying a prayer for the two of you.

"En all dat time I wuz a stoppered bottle o' water come to a bile. Dat low-'count Mars Tom, mo' vishus dan a wild dog wid de frothy mout'. Knowin' all de time dat I wuz already free! Puttin' me t'roo dem trashy tricks! En Huck wuz even mo' disgustin' fo' goin' 'long wid 'em. But did I haff to bite my tongue? Did I haff to hide my wish to thrash de two wid de chains dat wuz on my back? Did I haff to let on dat I wuz jis' a barr'l o' smiles en gladness en joy? Jis' like dat picture o' de t'ree o' us at de beginnin' o' dat las' chapter. Yes. Here. Wid my han's on de shoulders of my two bes' fren's."

Pappy closed the book, held it at arm's length and let it drop to the floor. "Nemmine what I did when I got all by mysef. You bof' gots 'maginashuns to draw you de pictures o' *dat*."

Mammy set her mending aside, went over to pappy's rocker, pulled his head to her, and began running her hand over his head, stroking it, again and again and again. And all the while she repeated, "My Jim. My man. My Jim. My man."

After a bit, mammy tried to break away. But by this time pappy was holding her. And he wouldn't let go.

"Well, James Hawkins," she finally said, "what good's our long evenin' en what we's foun' out 'bout dat book en dat boy ef'n we's de on'y wuns what knows what we knows. Duz you think dey's eny chance dat yuther folks'll see dis story en dat Huck de way we sees it?"

"Like as not, mammy. De story'll get read by whites, mos' likely. En dey hain't gwineter be skwintin' at Huck — 'cept fo' folks in New England, dem genteel folks. But it's like ole Nat, de slave what brought me de vittles, tole Mars Tom en Huck dat fust time dey come to see me in de hut by de ash-hopper. Chile, fine dat place, please, en read it 'loud? Fo' it wun mo' place dat show how smart us folks is, how we kin play dumb b'fo' white folks. It's dat place, chile, whar Nat's axin' Mars Tom en Huck not to tell nuffn 'bout de dad-blame witches singin' out when Huck en Mars Tom come into de hut. Fine it, chile? It's whar Nat's 'splainin' 'bout how hard it is to make Mars Silas b'lieve in witches."

"Here it is, pappy. Nat says, 'I jis' wish to goodness he was heah now — *den* what would he say! I jis' bet he couldn' fine no way to get aroun' it *dis* time.'"

"Now slowly, chile," pappy interrupted.

"'But its awluz jis' so; people dat's *sot,* stays sot; dey won't look into nothin' en fine it out f'r deyselves, en when *you* fine it out en tell um 'bout it, dey doan' b'lieve you.'"

"Hain't dat de truth, mammy," pappy asked as he pulled her into his lap, kissed her hard and buried his head in her neck.

"It sholy is, James Hawkins. It sholy is." They laughed. And I laughed too.

But, Mister Finn, I'm not quite so sure that it is true, now that I've copied out what I wrote down a decade ago. Of course for years after that long evening we'd occasionally pull your book from the cupboard and I'd read aloud a scene or two. Mammy and I'd marvel at pappy's resourcefulness. How quickly he could size up a situation and fall in with it. Like the time you and Mister Tom pretended you didn't know him when the two of you stepped into his hut at the Phelps for the first time and he blurted out your names. And we got many a laugh from his scheming. Like at the Grangerfords, how he got you to follow Jack in hopes of seeing a stack of water-moccasins, only to come upon him instead. We laughed most at all those times he was faking sleep, pretending to snore, knowing full well what was going on and anticipating what he would do.

For many year, then, Mister Finn, I've had a pretty low opinion of you because of the way you exploited my pappy, used him for your adventures, pretending an interest in freeing him. You all but forgot about him when some better adventure came along, like with the Grangerfords, the Wilks, and all through those dupings by the Duke and the King. You treated my pappy like dirt, plain and simple. A sick Arab, outfitted like some outlandish King Lear, whoever he was! You didn't mind seeing my pappy humiliated, ever.

And of course you tried to cover up your abuse of him by pretending moral distress. Several years ago I asked pappy about that, having read again the long passage where you resolve to find and free him from the Phelps. I told him that your moral dilemma, your agonizing, made me sympathize with you. When you chose to "go to hell," to tear up the letter you had written to Miss Watson, then I felt you showed you were capable of responsible human feelings.

"Well," pappy said, "I doan' rule out sich feelin's in Huck. En mebbe it wuz a close place fer him. But, chile, you gots to 'member dat Huck wrote 'bout all o' dem adventures *arter* dey wuz over. En ef'n you think 'bout dem adventures all by demsefs, den mebbe you see dat dey make Huck look like a pooty low-'count dog, jis' goin' 'long wid the bes' adventure dat comes to han'. Well, den, to make hissef look better mebbe he planted dat passage you mentionin', like it wuz a flower bed of moral worryin', jis' de same as he did back when we tho't we wuz near Cairo. Dat way he gets folks to think well o' him, keeps folks f'om trowin' him onter de trash pile wid dem yuther rapscallions dat hain't got so much moral feelin's as a bitch in heat. Mebbe I'm hard on ole Huck. But dat long passage soun' like it wuz writ en re-writ lots o'times, like ole Huck knowed dat he needed to put a gob o' bootshine on de scruffy parts o' his adventure to make de toes o' it shine up fo' de Sunny School folks. I guess, chile, I'd call dat long passage nuffn mo' dan a pair o' moral galluses. Dey keep his pants f'om fallin' down en showin' dat he wuz a bare-rumped boy out fer de wick'dest fun he could fine."

Since pappy's death I've pulled our book from the shelf and read it clean through, twice. For days after each reading, I've found myself repeating Nat's words and asking myself, "Am I 'sot?' Am I so set in *our* way of understanding your book that I can't see it any other way?"

To answer that question I've begun to wonder if, when writing your book, you got a glimmer of pappy's intelligence, his survival shrewdness, his skill in letting on. What makes me wonder *that* is my inability to shake from my mind those words you remember the Duke saying after you led him and the King to think that it was the Wilks' slaves — whom those two had already sold — who had stolen and taken with themselves the 6,000 dollars in gold pieces: "'It does beat all, how neat the niggers played their hand. They let on to be *sorry* they was going out of this region! and I believed they *was* sorry. And so did you, and so did everybody. Don't ever tell *me* any more that a nigger ain't got any histrionic talent. Why, the way they played that thing, it would fool *anybody*. In my opinion there's a fortune in 'em. If I had capital and a theatre, I wouldn't want a better lay out than that — and here we've gone and sold 'em for a song.'"

Of course the Duke's praise is unfounded, for the Wilks' slaves had nothing to do with the disappearance of that money. Still, Mister Finn, by this time — if not then — you must've learned a good deal about the shrewdness that our people are capable of, shrewdness we've been forced by the evil of slavery to learn, shrewdness our wish for survival has mandated.

As I sit here, thinking how to end this, I also wonder if maybe, when you wrote your book, you felt some deep itch, one you couldn't get a finger on to scratch. Maybe some itch of guilt and wish to make amends for the wrongs you did my pappy? Maybe some unruly feelings of love for my pappy? Maybe you realized the truly noble purpose behind all of his actions: to get himself free so that, in turn, he could free his family? If so, I wonder whether those spells of lonesomeness that find their way into your book express lonesomeness for the one man who was as close to a loving father as you would ever have — my pappy. Maybe your regard for him explains your use of *that* pronoun when, rousing him to begin the flight from Jackson's Island, you said, "They're after *us*!"

Maybe I'm wrong. Maybe you'll only laugh and call my notions "sentimentering." But that doesn't matter. What matters is that pappy's "alive," thanks to your book. And maybe, if your book doesn't die, other readers will learn to read signs the way pappy could, the way pappy, bless him, the smartest man I've ever known, taught me to read them, too.

Sincerely yours,
John Isaac Hawkins

JAMES PHELAN

On the Nature and Status of Covert Texts: A Reply to Gerry Brenner's "Letter to 'De Ole True Huck'"

James Phelan (b. 1951) is professor of English at Ohio State University. He received his B.A. (1972) from Boston College and his M.A. (1973) and Ph.D. (1977) from the University of Chicago. He has taught at Ohio State since completing his Ph.D., and served as Department Chair from 1994 to 2002. His books include *Worlds from Words* (1981), *Reading People, Reading Plots* (1989), *Beyond the Tenure Track* (1991), and *Narrative as Rhetoric* (1996). He is the editor of *Narrative*, the journal of the Society for the Study of Narrative Literature, which won the 1993 prize for Best New Journal from the Council of Editors of Learned Journals. Since 1993, he has been coeditor, with Peter J. Rabinowitz, of the Ohio State University Press series on the Theory and Interpretation of Narrative. He is currently working on a book on character narrators, *Living to Tell about It,* and another called *Reading the Twentieth-Century American Novel.* With Rabinowitz, he is also at work on an introduction to narrative theory. This essay was published with Brenner's in 1990 in *The Journal of Narrative Technique.*

Gerry Brenner's "Letter to 'De Ole True Huck'" is appealing for its imaginative and its critical power. By creating a voice for John Hawkins and by giving vibrant new life to Jim's, Brenner constructs a critical text that calls attention to itself as a literary performance. The text's value and success depend in part on Brenner's ability to sustain Jim's voice and to invest the dramatic situations of the letter with a verisimilitude comparable to that achieved in Twain's novel. By succeeding in these tasks, Brenner establishes and maintains the mimetic illusion that the "Letter to 'De Ole True Huck'" is an authentic rival account of the events narrated in *Adventures of Huckleberry Finn.*

Nevertheless, to say, as I now do, that Brenner is admirably successful in establishing the mimetic illusion is not to say that the "Letter" achieves all Brenner's purposes. Establishing and sustaining the mimetic illusion is not sufficient because Brenner's text is finally not so much a rival to as it is an interpretation of Twain's. Brenner's ultimate purpose is to revise the way in which most readers understand the novel, especially the way in which they understand Jim and Huck. Brenner seeks to replace the view of Jim as a simple yet proud and dignified man with one of Jim as proud, compassionate, dignified — and shrewd and sophisticated. Brenner seeks to uproot the notion that Huck is a boy who learns to resolve the conflict between society's values and his ethical instincts in favor of those superior instincts. In its place, Brenner wants to plant the idea that Huck is a seriously deficient ethical creature who resents anyone outdoing him, and who, like the King and the Duke and Tom Sawyer, enjoys conning others to make himself feel better. In the closing lines of the letter, John summarizes the general ends Brenner seeks; John's words are addressed to Huck but they apply to Brenner's text as well: "What matters is that pappy's 'alive,' thanks to your book. And maybe, if your book doesn't die, other readers will learn to read signs the way pappy could, the way pappy, bless him, the smartest man I've ever known, taught me to read them, too" (p. 422 in this volume).

John's remark about "reading signs" points to the key assumption underlying Brenner's performance: The text of *Huckleberry Finn* covertly tells the story that Jim relates. As I wrestle with the virtues and drawbacks, the power and the problems associated with this assumption, I will look not only at the text of Twain's novel but also at some larger theoretical questions about the nature and status of covert texts and about the claims of reader-response criticism based on the uncovering of covert texts.[1]

As John's closing remarks remind us, Jim insists that seeing his version of events is a matter of reading the signs skillfully — and of reading them without being already "sot" in one interpretation. Fair enough. But Jim's way of calling Huck's authority into doubt can be turned back upon himself. What if we read the signs of John's letter without being "sot" in John's interpretation of them? To the extent that Brenner's Jim is persuasive when he claims that Huck distorts the truth in order to make himself look good, Jim is also raising our suspicions of his own version. For we can readily see that Jim has a strong interest in

---

[1]Though I will focus on the way Brenner's resistance works, my sense of the issue is also informed by much of the work in what Elaine Showalter has called the mode of "feminist critique," especially that by Judith Fetterley.

making his wife and son see him in a much more complimentary light than Huck does. Furthermore, if we read the signs of John's letter to Huck skillfully, we can see that Jim's concern with his image in the narrative determines some of his behavior: How else to explain Jim's delay in replying to Huck's story? If Jim just wants to set the record straight, then he should have no objection to replying to the installments of Huck's story. But if he wants to make himself look good, then he needs to know all that Huck has said about him: Waiting until he hears all of Huck's account will enable him not only to fashion rebuttals to local matters but also to work out the details of a full — and coherent — counterstory. Surely that's what Jim's doing when he waits another whole day after the reading of the last installment. Once we skillfully read the signs of John's letter without being set in our interpretations, Jim's story is as subject to charges of "mispropriatin'" and "stretchin'" and "buttuh-spreadin'" as Huck's.

Now notice that what I have just done in reading the signs of John's letter is at least superficially similar to what Brenner does in having Jim read the signs of Huck's story. I look at the signs and try to find a subversive covert text in them. Furthermore, I have restricted myself to the signs in the text more than Brenner does — and his bringing in new signs is a matter I will come back to — and, like him, I have found a coherent new arrangement for them. Thus, like Brenner, I can claim to have uncovered a plausible covert text. In our assessments of these texts, however, Brenner and I part company: He regards his covert text as something that ought to modify the traditional view of the novel whereas I find mine, despite a surface plausibility, singularly unpersuasive.

I don't buy my account of the covert text because I cannot convince myself that this text is really hidden beneath the text that Brenner has constructed. John's letter, like Huck's narrative (indeed, like any narrative), is built out of numerous disparate materials — call them elements of story and elements of discourse.[2] When we break the letter down into these elements, we can see that they can be recombined in numerous — indeed, perhaps countless — ways. Yet Brenner has combined them in only one way, and that combination is what produces his text. In other words, when we encounter the text of John's — or Huck's — narrative, we encounter an already shaped version of the

---

[2]The view that narrative can be easily and simply and adequately divided into elements of story and discourse overlooks some knotty problems. For my purposes, however, the rough distinction will serve. For some useful discussion of the limits of the story-discourse distinction, see Chambers.

narrative materials. In constructing covert texts, we can use two different methods, either separately or in combination: We can disregard the shaping and focus on reconfiguring the material or we can analyze the way that the material has been shaped in order to discover another story told by that shaping that its shaper may not be aware of. When we recombine the material of the text without regard for the shaping, we are, I think, establishing a critic's covert text. When we discover the story beneath the one told by the original combiner, we are establishing an author's covert text. When we use both methods, we are creating a hybrid covert text — part critic's and part author's. As is probably already obvious, I am unpersuaded by my claims about the covert text of Jim's story, because it strikes me as my covert text — not John Hawkins's or Gerry Brenner's or even a hybrid of mine and theirs.

I've taken some of the material of that text — Jim's point about Huck's self-interest and Jim's delay in responding to Huck's narrative — and put them into a new relationship to each other by claiming that the point about self-interest leads to a reinterpretation of the delay and thus leads to my version of the covert text. What I failed to establish is the way in which the shaped version of Brenner's text unwittingly points to this covert text. And the failure is not one of execution: The shaped text is too recalcitrant plausibly to make such a case. In that version, Jim's delay cannot be separated from the other reactions to Huck's story that John reports. Together the delay and the reactions are complicated signs: First, they signify Jim's willingness to be just — he wants them all to hear the whole tale because "this book belongs to Huck." Second, they show his genuine concerns about what Huck has done in telling his story — he worries, he gets lost in thought. And finally, they show his superiority to the tale — Jim doesn't feel compelled to launch into correcting Huck as soon as John is finished but instead he laughs and laughs.

This reaction also has consequences for the way in which Brenner's text shapes Jim's point about Huck's self-interest — as does the difference between Huck's relation to his audience and Jim's relation to his. Huck is writing for strangers; Jim is talking to two people who already know him well. Huck has to worry about the way his audience perceives him in a way that Jim does not. Brenner's text consistently emphasizes the love and respect Jim receives from his wife and son and Jim's way of addressing them shows that he knows he possesses that love and respect. Nor does Jim worry much about what other readers of the book will think of him: Our last view of him is in his wife's arms laughing with her about people "what's sot staying sot." In sum, once we consider the way in which Brenner has shaped his materials to produce John's letter, my version of its covert text must be judged as just that — my version. Its attempt to turn Jim back on himself and its slight creativity in reconfiguring the elements of Brenner's text may give that version a certain appeal, but I cannot claim that it really challenges us to alter our understanding of the text as Brenner has shaped it.

Suppose now that Brenner or some other reader-response critic would say that my worrying the question of whether the covert text is an author's unwitting one or a reader's creative one is just another way of privileging authors over readers and therefore is a refusal to grant Brenner one of the fundamental premises of his project: The reader can be considered as the source of a text's meaning. The first part of my reply is that I too share that premise. Furthermore, any criticism that wants to emphasize the importance of a covert text is a kind of reader-response criticism because it insists on seeing a meaning in the text beyond the one its author is implicitly asking the audience to see. By distinguishing between an author's unwitting covert text and one created by the reader's reconfiguration of a text's basic material, we can see that not all reader-response interpretations make the same kinds of claims on their audience and that not all relate to previous readings in the same way. When I show that the covert text I find in John's letter is not one unwittingly contained within Brenner's shaping, then I must conclude that my interpretation cannot mount a serious challenge to anyone else's reading: The interpretation cannot give someone who disagrees sufficient warrants to adopt my perspective. Consequently, my covert text's interest for others is in its demonstration of how the material could have been shaped differently — and perhaps also in its demonstration of my abilities and idiosyncracies as a reader.

A dyed-in-the-wool reader-response critic might still object that I am privileging authorial reading: No sooner do I say that I accept the premise that the reader can be the source of a text's meaning than I start to appeal once again to the authorially shaped text — and the whole point of reader-response criticism is to rid us of such conceptions of texts. This hypothetical objection forces me to make overt something that has until now been covert in my text: I am operating here as one kind of critical pluralist. Although I accept the premise that the reader can be the source of a text's meaning, that is not the only premise I accept. Accepting the premise that an author can also be considered a source of a text's meaning leads me to differentiate between the two kinds of reader-response criticism — one of resistance to or subversion of that authorially shaped meaning and one of inventiveness.

The pluralist position does not privilege either author-centered readings over reader-centered ones or subversive reading over inventive reading. Instead, it wants to understand the relations among the kinds of claims that the practitioners of each approach can make and then to judge the practice according to how well-suited its methods are to its claims. How successful, then, is Brenner's subversive reading of Twain's novel?

Brenner has his greatest success with Jim. That success is especially impressive because Brenner's innovative means serve his traditional ends beautifully. By giving Jim a voice that is not controlled by Huck, Brenner moves Jim out of his inescapably subordinate — and I use that term in several senses — position in Huck's text. Huck's view of Jim as a slave and a simpleton, albeit one with certain pride and dignity, allows Huck to do such things as easily forget Jim during the shore adventures, and readily acquiesce in the degrading treatment Jim receives from the King and the Duke and from Tom Sawyer. Furthermore, in Huck's version, Jim's situation is important only in relation to Huck's — Jim exists less as a person with his own needs and desires than as either a convenient companion or a problem for Huck to deal with. Brenner's move of giving Jim the authority to tell the tale throws this feature of Huck's narrative into dramatic relief. One consequence of Brenner's ventriloquizing, then, is a powerful ethical criticism that points out the lingering racism in Twain's representation of Jim and implicitly calls into question previous criticism that celebrates that representation.

Notice, however, that this assessment gets at the way Jim's counter-story unmasks the problems of Huck's narrative without actually endorsing Jim's version of the events. To make an assessment of that version we need to look more closely at *how* Brenner constructs the covert text. It is striking that he takes a certain license by having Jim introduce signs into the story that Huck never mentions: To cite just a few, Huck's stiffening lower lip; his footprints on the raft when they lose the canoe; his low chuckling after telling the men hunting the runaway slave that his pap was on the raft sick with smallpox. It is also striking that Brenner extends this license by having Jim directly contradict some of what Huck reports — rather than being unenlightened about the way things are working, Jim sees through everything; the five-cent piece around Jim's neck is not the money Tom left for the candles but a love-token; the incident of Huck and Jim's separation and reconciliation in the fog occurred not two or three days after the arguments about Solomon and about the French language but that same night. These elements of Jim's story may seem to suggest that Brenner's reader-response is more concerned with inventiveness than with subversion, but some reflection on the motivation for these inventions will confirm that his main concern is resistance. The key to the subversive reading is Brenner's analysis of what Huck's text covertly reveals about himself; it is these revelations that provide the warrant for Jim's introduction of new or contradictory material into the narrative. If Brenner can show that the authorially shaped text unwittingly communicates Jim's view of Huck, then it is a short step to accepting Jim's additions and corrections to the tale. And these additions and corrections will contribute to the subversion of Huck's story and to the new understanding of the novel that Brenner seeks. Brenner is constructing what I've called a hybrid covert text, one that arises partly out of unwitting communication in the authorially shaped text and partly out of his own recombining — and even reimagining — the material of the novel in order to alter our understanding of the novel. The crucial question, then, is how well Brenner makes the case for his negative view of Huck's character.

This question cannot be adequately answered apart from a consideration of how Brenner handles the shaper of the narrative — not Huck but Twain. And here Brenner runs into a problem inextricably linked to his innovative means. By using the voices of Jim and John as his way of uncovering the novel's subtext, Brenner must see Huck as the only begetter of the narrative. Once he does that, Huck becomes responsible for all the choices of the narration; consequently, his motivations not just as actor but also as narrator can be scrutinized and questioned. Jim and John's view of a self-conscious, self-interested Huck provides Brenner with an effective way of handling what would initially appear to be the most recalcitrant material for his interpretation. John tells Huck that Jim figures he wrote truthfully about the "fog episode" "to use it as a decoy," so that "by owning up to the cruelty of that prank you [could] put readers off the scent" (p. 413). And John accuses Huck of "cover[ing] up your abuse of [Jim] by pretending moral distress" and reports that Jim views the passage in which Huck records his decision to go to hell as one that was

> re-writ lots o'times, like ole Huck knowed dat he needed to put a gob o' bootshine on de scruffy parts o' his adventure to make de toes o' it shine up fo' de Sunny School folks. I guess, chile, I'd call

dat long passage nuffn mo' dan a pair o' moral galluses. Dey keep his pants f'om fallin' down en showin' dat he wuz a bare-rumped boy out fer de wick'dest fun he could fine. (p. 421)

Now the implication of Brenner's view of Huck in these passages is that Huck must be seen as a self-conscious narrator: Despite the surface appearances of naiveté, he is actually *always* in control of his narrative, *always* aware of how what he says might be affecting his audience. (It must be *always;* since the text does not call attention to Huck as a self-conscious narrator, Brenner cannot be anything but arbitrary if he were to say that Huck is in control in some places but not in others.) In the traditional interpretation of Huck as naive, critics see Twain using him to communicate many things to us that Huck is not aware of. Huck records things without knowing the full import of what he is recording — as in this passage from the first chapter "you couldn't go right to eating, but you had to wait for the widow to tuck down her head and grumble a little over the victuals, though there warn't really anything the matter with them" (p. 33). Huck is also naive in his assumptions about what his audience will believe about himself. After Sherburn faces down the lynch mob until they go "tearing off every which way," he tells us that "I could a staid, if I'd a wanted to, but I didn't want to" (p. 148).

When Brenner has Jim put forth the view that in the passage about his decision to go to hell Huck is trying to throw his readers off the scent of his true character, Brenner is implying that we need to make a steamboat-sized pile of inferences. We would have to infer that Huck would assume that his audience would recognize a confession of wickedness — "It was awful thoughts, and awful words, but they was said. And I let them stay said; and never thought no more about reforming" (p. 201) — as a powerful sign of his virtue. We would also have to infer that Huck would further assume that his audience would not be smart enough to recognize that this confession was completely insincere. If Brenner's Jim is right about Huck in the "go to hell" passage, then Huck would have to be a narrator who knows much more than his audience — including how best to manipulate them. But the bigger number of inferences would come once we recognize that if Huck is in fact operating this way in this passage, then he must be operating in a similar way in all other passages that seem to point to his naiveté. We would now have to see these passages as deliberate deceptions too, for the success of the deception in the passage about going to hell depends on our developing a prior view of Huck as naive.

Now notice what happens once we put Twain back into these considerations. If Huck is deliberately deceiving, then Twain must have created him that way: The notion that Huck is deliberately deceiving and Twain doesn't know it simply doesn't compute. If Twain created Huck as a self-conscious deceiver, then Brenner isn't doing reader-response but intentionalist criticism. Thus, his attempt to handle the recalcitrant material leads him into this paradox. If Brenner's right about the narration, then he's wrong about what he's doing. If he's wrong about the narration, then what he's doing doesn't work.

Could he be right about the narration? Does Twain want us to see Huck as a self-conscious deceiver? Once we start asking about the warrants underlying Brenner's view of Huck's narration, we have a hard time finding them. Furthermore, the view that Huck is a non-self-conscious recorder helps explain the way Twain's irony works at the expense of certain social practices, certain individuals, and occasionally Huck himself. Brenner shows that it is possible to reimagine the relationship that Huck has to his narration and, I think, the interpretive possibilities are exciting once we start thinking of Huck's naiveté as concealing his very deep designs. But just as my reading of John's letter to Huck did not uncover Brenner's subtext so too these readings of Huck are inventive, not subversive.

There is a larger point about the interpretation of first-person narration that I would like to touch on briefly here. Because the first-person narrator is the dominant voice of the narrative it is always possible to see him as in control of the narrative, always possible to read motives into what he tells and how he tells it. Brenner's Jim performs this operation when he argues that Huck is taken with Colonel Sherburn. Huck gives us a very vivid account of the whole sequence of events from Boggs riding drunkenly into the street, through Sherburn's cold-blooded murder of him, to Sherburn's intimidation of the lynch mob. For Brenner that very vividness becomes a sign of Huck's identification with Sherburn. But such an interpretation assumes that everything a first-person narrator tells must also tell us something about that narrator. This assumption, I think, is not warranted in the case of unself-conscious recording narrators. In fact, it seems to me that Huck essentially disappears in the narration of the Sherburn incident: He becomes the all but transparent window through which we look at Twain's depiction of one kind of lawlessness in shore society.

So far I have found Brenner's reading of Huck to be more inventive than subversive but I have not yet dealt with the pattern of action that Brenner sees in the narrative. The rattlesnake incident, the arguments about Solomon and the French language followed by the fog incident, the missing canoe, the support of and identification with first the King and the Duke, and then Tom Sawyer: In Brenner's reading this material shows Huck to be a rattlesnake himself. Brenner's Jim makes a very good case, I think, but the trouble with making it stick is all the recalcitrant material it has to overlook or explain away. Twain's text does leave open the possibility that Huck places the rattlesnake on Jim's blanket for some reason other than to play a good-natured prank and Jim's explanation of Huck's resentment has some plausibility. But after Jim is bitten, Huck reports that he agreed with Jim that he "druther see the new moon over his left shoulder as much as a thousand times than take up a snake-skin in his hand" (p. 73). Furthermore, shortly after this incident, Huck acquiesces in Jim's modification of his plan to go on shore. When Jim says that Huck should wait and go at night and that he should dress up like a girl, Huck comments, "That was a good notion, too" (p. 74). And it is when Huck comes back from that trip ashore that he hollers out his famous warning to Jim, "They're after us!" (p. 80). Twain does make Huck look thoughtless, cowardly, and inconsiderate of Jim in the rattlesnake incident, but the reading of the event as vindictive and in that way emblematic of Huck's character is very hard to sustain.

Similar recalcitrant material clouds the analyses of the other incidents, though the events of the Evasion are more problematic. The fog episode ends with Huck genuinely apologetic — and the attempt to read that as a way to throw readers off the scent takes us back to the question of Huck as self-conscious narrator. The analysis of the missing canoe works only if the analyses of the other incidents are convincing, since Jim has to add the presence of Huck's footprints on the raft to support his story. Huck's working against the king and the duke during the Wilks episode impedes the claim about his identification with them. Furthermore, when Huck decides to go to hell, his meditation about Jim shows how far he has come from the time when he played the thoughtless prank with the rattlesnake skin.

Huck's account of his behavior toward Jim during the Evasion does lend itself more readily to Brenner's reading, but even there the situation is complicated. Brenner wisely leaves the issue personal: Huck has made a decision not about slavery but about one man. Nevertheless, from that man's perspective, "ef'n you's sumwun's fren', den you doan' skaseley ever treats 'em like Huck en Mars Tom treated me en dem po Phelps folks" (p. 417). But the recalcitrant material here is provided by Tom's presence and what we know of Huck's relation to Tom. Huck's acquiescence in Tom's plan is not a sign of his meanness but rather of his sense of inferiority before Tom's book-larnin' and apparent self-confidence. Furthermore, Huck's behavior toward Jim is so striking in large part because it is so different from his previous behavior. This difference doesn't, I think, point to Brenner's covert text but rather to one of the flaws of the ending.[3]

I find, then, that Brenner has much greater success in getting us to rethink our views of Jim than in getting us to revise our views of Huck. His subversive criticism is only partially successful, but that success constitutes a significant piece of ethical criticism.[4] At the same time, Brenner's attempt to carry out the subversive reading leads to an impressive inventive reading. The value of that invention derives not from its ethical commentary on Twain's novel, but from its exposure of the rich possibilities in Twain's material. In other words, my analysis of Brenner's critique of Huck in effect unmoors that critique from Twain's text and reconstitutes it as a separate narrative. This part of Brenner's reading does not comment on Twain's text except by showing that the same material can be used for different effects. Brenner's inventive narrative can itself be the subject of an act of ethical criticism but because the narrative has been unmoored from Twain's text, the force of that criticism will apply to Brenner and not Twain. To put the point another way, we can follow Brenner's lead as we think about other texts (imagine how Lolita would tell Humbert Humbert's story) and we can develop inventive readings for different ethical ends. But as long as we work in the realm of the inventive rather than the subversive, our ethical ends will not include critiquing the original texts. These readings will, however, make us more attuned to the way the material of the original text has been shaped and how it could easily have been shaped differently. What this all means is that I can both keep my sense of Twain's Huck and contemplate the intriguing possibility of Brenner's Huck. What's more, I can be grateful for the creative power of both Twain and Brenner.

One final question: What is the covert text of my discourse here? Or to step back from that direct way of putting it, does the very problem I

---

[3]For an account of Twain's problem with the ending based on an assessment of how he has configured the material of the narrative until Huck's decision to go to hell, see Phelan 112–14. [See also the essays on the ending in this edition by Eliot, Trilling, Marx, Morrison, Margolis, and Bercovitch.]

[4]Compare Wayne Booth's discussion of the novel in *The Company We Keep*.

am grappling with here lead to an infinite regress, since Brenner — or some other astute reader — may come along and uncover my covert text? If so, does that then undermine my argument? It seems to me that these questions, though they need to be faced, are more clever than substantial. Of course someone could uncover a covert text here and of course someone could claim that such uncovering would undermine my argument. But there is no reason to privilege a priori that maneuver over the actual argument I have made. To do so would be to say that because it is always possible to uncover covert texts, it is impossible to sort out the differences and relations among them: Any attempt at sorting is always subject to a recasting — and an undermining — by a reading of its covert message. That conclusion seems erroneous to me because it ignores the way this argument is like most other critical arguments. I have attempted one kind of sorting here, have made a case for my side. Someone could argue from the other side and try to undermine that case by finding one kind of covert text in my attempt. But that person's attempt will not be ensured of success any more than my attempt is ensured of success. Instead, we each make our cases and the debate goes on, as other voices who are interested in the issues make judgments about the merits of our cases and add additional perspectives to these issues. Rather than finding ourselves in a situation of infinite regress, we are, I hope, in a situation of ongoing productive interchange.

WORKS CITED

Booth, Wayne C. *The Company We Keep.* Berkeley: U of California P, 1988.

Chambers, Ross. "'Narrative' and 'Textual' Functions (With an Example from La Fontaine)." *Reading Narrative.* Ed. James Phelan. Columbus: Ohio State UP, 1989. 27–39.

Fetterley, Judith. *The Resisting Reader.* Bloomington: Indiana UP, 1978.

Phelan, James. *Reading People, Reading Plots.* Chicago: U of Chicago P, 1989.

Showalter, Elaine. "Feminist Criticism in the Wilderness." *Critical Inquiry* 8 (1981): 179–205.

Twain, Mark. *Adventures of Huckleberry Finn.* Eds. Gerald Graff and James Phelan. Boston: Bedford, 2004.

JONATHAN ARAC

FROM *Huckleberry Finn* as Idol and Target

Jonathan Arac (b. 1945) is Orlando Harriman Professor of English and Comparative Literature at Columbia University. He received his B.A. (1967) and Ph.D. (1974) from Harvard University, and has taught at Princeton University, the University of Illinois at Chicago, Duke University, and the University of Pittsburgh. The author of *Critical Genealogies: Historical Situations for Postmodern Literary Studies* (1987) and *Commissioned Spirits: The Shaping of Social Motion in Dickens, Carlyle, Melville, and Hawthorne* (1979), Arac has also edited *Postmodernism and Politics* (1989) and *After Foucault: Humanistic Knowledge, Postmodern Challenges* (1988). The following piece is an excerpt from his *"Huckleberry Finn" as Idol and Target: The Functions of Criticism in Our Time* (1997).

Huckleberry Finn is a wonderful book that has been loaded with so much value in our culture that it has become an idol. It is invoked by the upper-middlebrow establishment in endlessly various circumstances to shed its power and elevate the subject under discussion, as I illustrate with a range of instances from the *New York Times*. This idolatry would be a harmless foible, except that it goes along with the novel's required presence in schools, frequently at junior high level, and when parents and children of color complain about the classroom effects of Huck's constant use of the word *nigger,* they are put down with the passion provoked by the defense of an idol. Even though protests are denigrated by asserting the immense good *Huckleberry Finn* does for race relations, in fact the idolatry of the book has served, and — remarkably — continues to serve, as an excuse for well-meaning white people to use the term *nigger* with the good conscience that comes from believing that their usage is sanctioned by their idol (whether Twain, or his book, or Huck) and is made safe by the technique of irony. In this chapter, after illustrating the modes of sanctifying reference in *Times,* I begin tracing some of the controversy provoked by opposition to the book, focusing on the problem of "Nigger Jim" and the difficulties of the argument from irony.

THE IDOL

In the *Times,* the novelist Anne Tyler reviewed E. L. Doctorow's *Billy Bathgate* — a novel that shares with *Huckleberry Finn* an early teenaged narrator-protagonist, living in a violent and morally dubious environment close to the time and place of its author's own youth. All this she did not mention, it was so obvious; all she needed to say was that the plot of *Billy Bathgate* was "almost perfectly constructed," that it was "as tightly constructed as that of *Huckleberry Finn.*" Few other readers have ever found the plot of *Huckleberry Finn* almost perfect, at least since Hemingway drew attention to the ending as a problem, but when a work is an idol, its memory can be used to supply any desired perfection. For Tyler, Doctorow's book was "darker than Huck and Jim floating down a river together," because the gangster Dutch Schultz is a "scary man" who figures as a "powerful but capricious parent." She did not mention Huck's pap — a drunkard who locks Huck up, beats him, and even threatens to kill him. Pap's grotesque violence has disappeared for Tyler, and she has forgotten the weakness of the plot: idolatry means selective memory.

In the *Times,* the theater critic Frank Rich reviewed the Steppenwolf Company production of *The Grapes of Wrath.* He observed that in this performance, Tom Joad and Jim Casy, "who leave civilization to battle against injustice," are historically the "forefathers of the rock-and-roll rebels in Steppenwolf Productions by Sam Shepard and Lanford Wilson just as they are the heirs to Huck and Jim." What is the respect in which they are similar? "They get their hands dirty in the fight for right" — a sentence that makes me imagine Rich was actually thinking of Gene Hackman in *Mississippi Burning,* a film that evidently remained a point of reference for Rich, since he brought it up again in the context of recent debates over the "N-Bomb."

Sometimes it is not necessary to make any comparison at all; the mere invocation of *Huckleberry Finn* is enough to position audience and writer happily on the same good side. When Veronica Geng reviewed Garrison Keillor's *Lake Wobegon Days,* she reached out to her readers, allowing each individually to share a credo, to be "some one who believes, as I do, that the greatest moment in American literature is when Huckleberry Finn says to himself [at least she remembers that he didn't say it to a vigilante posse], 'All right, then, I'll *go* to hell.'"

It's not just a *New Yorker* parodist who so admires a funny novel. Arthur Schlesinger Jr., an important historian, an architect of Camelot, the author of the prophetic 1960 polemic, *Nixon or Kennedy: Does It*

Make Any Difference? shares this belief. Schlesinger not only is an honored historian but has also been for half a century a powerful participant in national political debate, so his voice reaches far beyond the academy. In a *Times* piece titled "The Opening of the American Mind," originally the inaugural address when Vartan Gregorian became president of Brown University, Schlesinger argued, against Allan Bloom's *Closing of the American Mind,* that absolutism is socially dangerous and relativism does much less damage. In his concluding sequence, Schlesinger devoted a half column to the "greatest . . . American . . . of them all," Abraham Lincoln, and then for his finale a quarter column to the "human struggle against the absolute in the finest scene of the greatest of American novels." Schlesinger zeroed in on chapter 31. He recalled Huck's indecision over whether to write to Miss Watson and tell her where she could catch Jim, and Huck's disobedience to the voice of the absolute, speaking as his conscience, which tells him it is wrong to have helped a slave to escape. After quoting the most memorable line of that sequence, "All right, then, I'll *go* to hell," Schlesinger ended, "That, if I may say so, is what America is all about."

Part of what I mean by idolatry is that Schlesinger here joins a long tradition of using *Huckleberry Finn* as the basis for statements proclaiming what is truly American — I have never seen so much use of the term "quintessentially" as in the claims for the Americanness of *Huckleberry Finn.* So to question *Huckleberry Finn* is to be *un*American. For Van Wyck Brooks in the 1920s, as for Bernard DeVoto in the 1930s, as for Lionel Trilling in the 1940s, so for Schlesinger and many others today — whether like Schlesinger combating the "disuniting of America," or like Shelley Fisher Fishkin glorying in "hybridity" — *Huckleberry Finn* figures at the core of what an authoritative "we" takes to be the meaning of America.

Trilling's essay is especially important. In 1948 the newly published *Literary History of the United States* laid out a triumphant nationalist vindication of American literature, and Rinehart published the first college text version of *Huckleberry Finn,* introduced by Trilling, who was to become the most widely respected and influential American critic of the next two decades. Trilling was already known for his sense of nuance and complexity, tempered in the debates of *Partisan Review* over Marxism and modernism, yet his introduction (excerpted on pages 283–84 in this volume) is hyperbolic praise, commonly reprinted under the title "The Greatness of *Huckleberry Finn.*" His essay proved the book's open sesame into college canonicity. Once there was a time, for somewhat more than the first half of the book's century of existence,

when many public cultural authorities argued against *Huckleberry Finn*
for its alleged vulgarity or disrespect for social hierarchy and when an
avant-garde defended it, while it was also widely read by many who
were in neither of these cultural parties. The Second World War
brought the United States to an unparalleled place of world power, and
it also marked the point at which many previously oppositional intellectuals found their way to accommodation.

As part of this movement, Trilling redefined the relation of a book
to our nation at a key moment in its history. Trilling brought to bear on
Huckleberry Finn comparisons drawn from his years teaching the
Columbia College Humanities ("great books") course, and he thereby
authenticated the work as a masterpiece of world literature, elevating
the popular art form of prose fiction to the elite level of epic, tragedy,
and aristocratic verse drama. For Trilling, *Huckleberry Finn* in American culture was like the *Odyssey* in classical Greek culture, a book read in
childhood that grows as its reader does. The recurrent ecstatic passages
on the river were, for Trilling, like the choral odes of Greek tragedy, and
even the ending had the perfect formal aptness of the Turkish masque
that ends Molière's *Bourgeois Gentilhomme*. So Trilling asserted.

Moreover his essay's inclusion in Trilling's collection *The Liberal
Imagination* made its extravagant praises all the more striking, since
Trilling's volume as a whole favored the complex and the "conditioned."
In the volume's keynote essay, "Reality in America," Trilling rescued
Henry James from charges of effete snobbery by placing James's work
at the "dark and bloody crossroads where literature and politics meet"
(8). Likewise, Trilling rescued Twain from Van Wyck Brooks's charges
of moral timidity, by asserting that Huck and Jim form a "community
of saints." Since Trilling's landmark hymn of praise, *Huckleberry Finn*
remains an object for debate and analysis in the academy, but the public
authorities have made it an idol. Just as socially marginal and culturally
avant-garde ethnics like Trilling (who Columbia planned to dismiss in
1936 because as "a Jew, a Marxist, a Freudian" he couldn't be happy
there — see Diana Trilling 274) became authorities, so the book that
was an underdog has become an overlord.

THE PROBLEM

Nowadays the people in the public sphere who are most unhappy
about *Huckleberry Finn* are African American parents and students who
find that the book's established role in the schools creates painful diffi-

culties. The fundamental issue in parents' and children's pain over the classroom prestige of *Huckleberry Finn* has been the 213 uses of the deeply offensive term "nigger." Scholars, following a lead from Ralph Ellison, have been especially concerned with the role of stereotypical minstrel techniques in the representation of Jim. But the core issue may be focused in the phrase with which Robert Penn Warren titled his 1965 volume of exploratory conversations about America in the civil rights era, "Who Speaks for the Negro?" Cold War liberal American culture seemed to find in *Huckleberry Finn* a century-old solution to the race problems that had newly reemerged on the national agenda. Twain's solution would permit an imaginary national first person to trust that, like Huck, in "our" hearts "we" had always been right. In 1944 Gunnar Myrdal's massive study of "The Negro Problem and American Democracy" had defined "the American Dilemma" as "a problem in the heart of the American" (lxix); tragically, Myrdal's perspective made clear that "the" American is white. Many African Americans, inside and outside the academy, have found that answer inadequate, both in the social science scholarship and policy advice following from Myrdal, and in the educational and cultural efforts focused around *Huckleberry Finn*.

Even Ralph Ellison, whose "Fiction and the Black Mask of Humanity" made one of the most powerful affirmations of the greatness of *Huckleberry Finn,* and who was at all times a fiercely committed integrationist, by the later 1960s found it necessary to "insist" that the figure of Jim was "not grounded enough in the reality of Negro American personality" (*Conversations* 171). The reason, Ellison argued, was that Twain's imagined audience was exclusively white:

> I know of no black — Negro — critics (I'm a Negro, by the way) who wrote criticisms of *Huckleberry Finn* when it appeared. It was all a dialogue between, a recreation, a collaboration, between a white American novelist of good heart, of democratic vision, one dedicated to values — I know much of Mark Twain's writing — and white readers, primarily. What is going on is that now you have more literate Negroes, and they are questioning themselves, and questioning everything which has occurred and been written in the country.

Even as Ellison asserted his unpopular principles — he was a "Negro," he had read and valued a lot of Twain, even black separatists were "American" — he underlined the major thrust of Black Power. Because "*everybody* reads now" and "*Everybody* is American whether they call themselves separatists, black separatists, secessionists or what not," therefore "everybody is saying, Damn it, tell it like *I* think it is" (172).

Let me spell out the complexity here, for it is still not widely acknowledged. It was only after the Second World War that *Huckleberry Finn* achieved massive canonicity in the schools, as the great spiritual representative of the America that had become the dominant power in the world, and that aimed to embrace alien peoples with the loving innocence that Huck offered Jim; yet these same years were the time that the assertion of African American civil rights, most strongly symbolized in *Brown V. Board of Education* (1954), brought new voices into play concerning the relations of whites and blacks. African Americans increasingly gained the power to assert their rights to define and judge the terms of those relations, but they were also increasingly subjected to agonizing scenes of interracial good intentions. (Of course, I, too, may prove guilty on this count.) *Huckleberry Finn* served a national and global political function as an icon of integration, and the importance of this cultural work overrode the offense the book generated among many of its newly authorized, but also newly obligated, African American readers.

A letter to the *Times* written during a controversy over *Huckleberry Finn* in 1982 looked back to the writer's schooldays in the 1950s:

> I can still recall the anger and pain I felt as my white classmates read aloud the word "nigger." . . . I wanted to sink into my seat. Some of the whites snickered, others giggled. I can recall nothing of the literary merits of this work that you term the "greatest of all American novels." I only recall the sense of relief I felt when I would flip ahead a few pages and see that the word "nigger" would not be read that hour. (Ballard; also quoted by Henry, p. 386 in this volume)

When a school board or library attempts to act in response to this pain, out come the authorities to defend the book. The standard pattern is for journalists to draw authority from scholars to dump on parents and children. I am disturbed by the structure of debate I have found, and this book is my response. The character of discussion that is still most prevalent emerges from two examples of what seems to me thoughtlessness on the part of journalists who have earned some claim to be taken seriously.

Christopher Hitchens has been a regular columnist for so diverse a set of journals as the *TLS* (London), *Elle*, *Vanity Fair*, and the *Nation*. He is a political and cultural commentator whose work I often greatly admire, but I disagree with his attack on those who wish to "remove *Huckleberry Finn* from the curriculum" because they find it racially offensive. He characterized them as "know-nothings and noise-makers" and, in an astonishing swing of medicalizing normativity, "neurotics." It would seem that if you are an African American child who does not like to go to school because some other students feel empowered to talk like the hero of the assigned book and call you "nigger," that is your sickness, not a matter of public concern.

Fred Hechinger, then education editor of the *New York Times,* sounded the same note in drawing from a pamphlet by Justin Kaplan on the troubles of *Huckleberry Finn* over the century since it was published. Kaplan is a scholar most of whose career has been independent of the academy. He was chosen to introduce the 1996 edition of *Huckleberry Finn* (based on the newly discovered first half of the manuscript), and he has long been a public authority. His biographical study *Mr. Clemens and Mark Twain* won the Pulitzer Prize and National Book Award in 1967, and his pamphlet was sponsored by the Library of Congress and the Florida Center for the Book. From the genteel library committees of the nineteenth century to concerned parents and pained students today, Kaplan saw a continuity in attacks on *Huckleberry Finn* by "official or self-appointed guardians of public taste or morality" (*Born* 14). These are not terms of respectful description for parents and children, and in discussing the recent debates, Kaplan could not have been less respectful. "It seems unlikely," he wrote,

> that anyone, of any color, who had actually read *Huckleberry Finn,* instead of merely reading or hearing about it, and who had allowed himself or herself even the barest minimum of intelligent response to its underlying spirit and intention, could accuse it of being "racist" because some of its characters [Kaplan does not say its narrator and hero] use offensive racial epithets. (p. 378 in this volume)

Yet, I would note, no one seeks to ban Frederick Douglass's 1845 *Narrative of the Life of an American Slave, Written by Himself* even though this work uses the term a few times. Douglass makes clear, however, every time the term is used that it is meant as hostile toward African Americans. "One has to be deliberately dense," Kaplan added, "to miss the point that Mark Twain is making" (p. 379). But what is the point? So any black person who disagrees with Kaplan on this issue is, if not neurotic, at least stubborn and stupid, and probably incapable of "actually" reading. Kaplan used Twain's authority to construct a model of reading in which "the" reader is a white liberal, and a model of race relations that requires blacks to listen to the master-reader's voice, and if you don't take his lesson, it's your fault.

I am not holding Twain solely responsible for such use of his book. For example, ever since *Huckleberry Finn* was first published, readers — not all readers — have referred to Jim as "Nigger Jim," although the book never uses this phrase. Public idolatry of *Huckleberry Finn* lends authority to the continued honorable circulation of this terribly offensive term of racial antagonism. In 1984, to celebrate the centennial of *Huckleberry Finn,* the *New York Times Book Review* commissioned arguably the greatest living American novelist, Norman Mailer, to read *Huckleberry Finn* as if it were a new book, and to write about it not as a monument, but as a piece of living literature. Mailer hymned the book's praises: "The river winds like a fugue through the marrow of the true narrative." What was this true narrative for Mailer? It was "nothing less than the ongoing relation between Huck and the runaway slave, this Nigger Jim whose name embodies the very stuff of the slave system itself — his name is not Jim but Nigger Jim." Rather than refuse to publish Mailer because he had obviously not read the book, the *Times* ran this feature on its front page. Likewise, in a feature article in the Children's Books section of the *Times,* the eminent Czechoslovakian emigré novelist Joseph Skvorecky argued that *Huckleberry Finn* is not racist even though "the second principal character is called Nigger Jim." Evidently no *Times* literary editor recognized the inaccuracy of this statement, because the lesson public authorities wish this book to teach is that even saints say "nigger."

THE WORD

Now I must go on at some length about the word *nigger.* I start at a historic distance, but then move, as so many Americans have found themselves doing recently, toward Detective Mark Fuhrman's role at the murder trial of O. J. Simpson. You recall that many broadcast media bleeped out Fuhrman's use of the term, and *USA Today* would not print the term even in their front-page story revealing the contents of the Fuhrman tapes. So I ask before going on: should people of goodwill unhesitatingly maintain that a word banned from CNN and *USA Today* must be required in the eighth-grade schoolroom?

In 1968 appeared the earliest essay I know on the topic of *Huckleberry Finn* and race by someone still active among senior African American literary scholars. Donald B. Gibson observed a scholarly anomaly. Even though Jim is "frequently referred to by critics as 'Nigger Jim'," actually Jim "is never once called this in *Huckleberry Finn*!" (196).

It is often claimed that Albert Bigelow Paine put this offensive naming into circulation in his authorized biography of Twain (1912). In fact, this pejorative title for Jim was coined in the very first newspaper responses to *Huckleberry Finn,* before its American publication and while excerpts were being published in the *Century* magazine. While the *Louisville Courier-Journal* reprinted the comic account of Jim's misfortunes as a banker, referring to him as "A Colored Citizen," both the *Chicago Herald* and *Cleveland Herald* reprinted the touching episode about Jim and his deaf daughter, referring to "Nigger Jim" (pp. 154–55). The complexities that have accompanied responses to *Huckleberry Finn* over its history are there from the beginning. The paper from a state only twenty years removed from slavery reprints an episode that contributes to the stereotype of African Americans as incapable of effective citizenship in a free economy, while the papers from what had been the "free" states choose one of the most humane representations of Jim but caption it with a name for him that undoes that humanity.

There is little point in detailing the prevalence of this degrading way of referring to Jim during the first half of the twentieth century. It participated in the ethos of segregation that prevailed across the culture. Even Bernard DeVoto used this phrase that Twain never wrote in *Huckleberry Finn* (*Mark* 52, 292). Yet DeVoto emphasized, more than any other scholar for decades before and after, the impact of African American cultural practices on the young Sam Clemens, and he intended that his *Mark Twain's America* (1932) should differ from biographical criticism in the wake of Van Wyck Brooks by virtue of devoting scrupulous attention to "what a great man wrote" (xi). Twenty years later, Dixon Wecter, DeVoto's successor as literary director for the Twain estate, did no better. His posthumously published biographical study, *Sam Clemens of Hannibal* (1952), in tune with polite standards of its time was rather more sensitive than DeVoto had been to the sufferings, and rather less concerned with the cultural contributions, of African Americans in Twain's early milieu. Nonetheless, in proclaiming Jim "Mark Twain's noblest creation" (100), Wecter called him by a name that Twain never used, putting the phrase in quotation marks as if to authenticate it (Wecter also used the phrase without qualification [44]).

The very Sunday after the Supreme Court decision of 17 May 1954 in *Brown vs. Board of Education,* Joseph Wood Krutch wrote in the

New York Times Book Review in praise of the greatness of *Huckleberry Finn*. He set Twain's accomplishment against the procedures of the "problem novelist" which his Columbia colleague Lionel Trilling had been attacking since the later 1930s. Krutch valued "artistically" even the "intellectual" and "sociological" "points" in *Huckleberry Finn* over the whole tradition from *Uncle Tom's Cabin* to "the complete corpus of recent novels about 'prejudice.'" In referring to *Uncle Tom's Cabin,* Krutch more specifically echoed the argument of James Baldwin's 1949 *Partisan Review* essay, "Everybody's Protest Novel," which had polemically placed Stowe at the beginning of the tradition that led to Richard Wright. Yet Krutch's apparent affiliation with the views of Baldwin, in 1954 an increasingly respected African American writer, did not keep him from naming Jim with the term that continues to mark the American history of racial inequality.

A younger and far more flamboyantly transgressive writer than Krutch, Leslie Fiedler first broached in the 1940s a thesis that has been one of the most productive and controversial lines of thought about American literature and popular culture for nearly fifty years. His 1948 *Partisan Review* essay, "Come Back to the Raft Ag'in, Huck Honey!" (a phrase that embodies Fiedler's thesis but is not actually found in the book), boldly argued that the characteristic American act of imagination involves the deeply affectionate but chaste bond between males of different races. It was part of Fiedler's daring that he linked this historical thesis to current American social practices and tensions around both sexuality and race:

> The situations of the Negro and the homosexual in our society are precisely opposite problems, or at least are problems suggesting precisely opposite solutions: Our laws on homosexuality and the context of prejudice and feeling they objectify must apparently be changed in accord with a stubborn social fact, whereas it is the social fact, our overt behavior toward the Negro, that must be modified to accord with our laws and the, at least official, morality they objectify. (p. 520)

Among the postwar critical works that began the idolatry of *Huckleberry Finn,* Fiedler's is the only one I know that actually brought the book into relation to the struggle for racial justice. Yet his essay, it would seem both from intellectual brashness and also to mimic the ethos of popular culture, continued to name Jim not in Twain's words but in those of the long American tradition of racial discrimination (p. 521). And in line with Fiedler's wish to remain the bad boy, even as he became a distinguished senior scholar, holding a chair at SUNY-Buffalo that he had wished to name after Huckleberry Finn, his major book *Love and Death in the American Novel* (584) and so recent a work as *What Was Literature* (70), published in 1982, continued to use the term.

In a 1977 essay polemically entitled — contra Fiedler — "Welcome Back from the Raft, Huck Honey!" the neoconservative critic Kenneth Lynn, who had himself in 1966, as part of his commitment to the civil rights movement, left Harvard for the University of the District of Columbia, looked back over the work produced by his generation of Americanists on *Huckleberry Finn*. Lynn reflected, "Back in the 1950s . . . literary critics were moved to misread *Huckleberry Finn* for a variety of reasons. Americans in the postwar period were gradually coming to the conclusion . . . that the ancient pattern of discrimination against Negroes was morally indefensible. This conclusion precipitated numerous misreadings of *Huckleberry Finn*," including Lynn's own. One importance of Lynn's piece is his acknowledgment that white scholars — not only black parents and children — may err as readers. He admitted: "Critics like myself wanted to believe that Huck was renouncing membership in a society that condoned slavery because they did not wish to live in a segregationist nation" (48). Yet misreading continues: Lynn still used the old misnaming of Jim (42, 48), which is surprising for two reasons. First, the essay appeared in the *American Scholar,* a journal with famously high standards of editorial care, and second, it formed part of a series of essays in which Lynn convicted left-oriented scholarship of tendentious carelessness about documented facts.

But the argument from accuracy is often misused. For example, in the aggressively liberal journal the *Humanist,* June Edwards argued against objections to *Huckleberry Finn* arising in the schools: "*Nigger* is what blacks were commonly called in the South until recent times. It is wrong to censure a novel for historical accuracy. Truth should never be bent to fit an ideology." Edwards's critique of ideologically produced untruth was full of inaccuracy. Her simplified linguistic history may be faulted in at least three dimensions. It erased decades of struggle against the term by many Southern liberals; it forgot that the term was also "commonly" used in the North; and it pretended that in "recent times" the term has ceased to be common. But historiographic debate aside, Edwards was inaccurate in a fourth dimension. For throughout her essay Edwards called Jim by a title that does not appear in the book she was talking about.

What is more surprising and disturbing than Lynn's error in the 1977 *American Scholar,* or — amazingly — twenty years later once more, in 1996 in the *TLS* (London) ("Huckleberry" 4), is that in his own earlier scholarly work, despite its now-acknowledged commitment to a civil rights agenda, he did not allow his wish for racial equality and justice to correct his mistitling of Jim ("You" 409). Even in a textbook that he edited in 1961 for use at quite an introductory stage of literary study, Lynn suggested the following topics for papers: "Nigger Jim: minstrel-show clown, Black Christ, or human being?" and "Compare the description of Uncle Dan'l in *Mark Twain's Autobiography* to Nigger Jim" (*Huckleberry* 217). So the authoritative scholar's pedagogical guidance required students to perpetuate this wounding error. In fact, one motive for John Wallace's 1982 protest was the experience of Rosa Harper: "My child comes home . . . concerned that she had to answer a question on a test about the book by using the word 'nigger' to describe a black character in the book" (Moore 6).

Lynn's teacher and longtime senior colleague at Harvard, the most distinguished intellectual historian active in American studies in the twentieth century, Perry Miller, did not set a better example in his posthumously published lectures entitled "An American Language" of which the third of three is devoted to *Huckleberry Finn* (*Nature's* 230, 238, 240). And to this day, a professionally respected senior figure in Twain studies, Tom Quirk, seems to think that by placing the phrase in quotation marks (64), implying that it is Twain's own usage, he can go on writing as if there were really no cause to worry about offensive language. But Quirk's own language is troubling; he writes of racial issues as if there were not complex issues dividing African Americans, such as those of class and gender, but instead only one single person of color who need be thought about, "the Negro" (65).

British scholars are no more immune than American scholars to this offensive carelessness toward the text they are discussing and the readers they are addressing. In a pathbreaking article that in the wake of American Black Power initiatives rethought *Huckleberry Finn* from Jim's perspective, Harold Beaver argued that "white and black throughout had been mutual pawns, utilizing each other, manipulating each other as *objects* of romance or *tools* of escape." For in "a slave-owning republic, where human labour was bought and sold, human relations too were inevitably turned to strategic devices and men to things" (357). In this context, it makes good sense that Beaver used a dehumanizing term in his own title — "Run, Nigger, Run: *Adventures of Huckleberry Finn* as a Fugitive Slave Narrative" — but it makes less good sense to me that he did not distinguish his own usage from that of the society he condemned, for he too titled Jim "Nigger" (339). An even more distinguished critic and novelist, Malcolm Bradbury, wrote on *Huckleberry Finn* for an international, nonspecialized audience of social goodwill. On every page of his article, on the imagined authority of Mark Twain, Jim was defined by a term that I cannot believe would otherwise have been permitted in the *UNESCO Courier.*

It may be a small professional comfort to literary scholars, but it hardly makes one feel better for either critical standards of reading or politics in the United States that the most admired historians are just as damagingly careless. The most important historian of the American South over the last fifty years, and an important activist and publicist on behalf of the civil rights movement, C. Vann Woodward, in a pained and powerful essay of 1967 referred to Jim by a term that I'm not aware he has elsewhere ever allowed himself to write in his own voice in his published works (*Burden* 181). And in a book that explicitly set out to supplement for our time Woodward's classic *Origins of the New South* (1951) and that won the 1992 Pulitzer Prize, Edward Ayers hauled out this old, mistaken term (538).

This maddening survey suggests that even though *Huckleberry Finn* is claimed as a talisman of racially progressive thought and action, one of its major effects is actually to license and authorize the continued honored circulation of a term that is both explosive and degrading.

Recall the debate at the trial of O. J. Simpson. In a story itself scrupulously sparing in the use of what its headline called the "epithet," Kenneth B. Noble reported that Christopher Darden, "a Deputy District Attorney who is black," said that "what he called the 'N-word' was so hideously pejorative that it would inevitably prejudice the mostly black jury" against Detective Fuhrman, if it could be shown that he had used the term. Darden continued, "It's the filthiest, dirtiest, nastiest word in the English language," so powerful that "when you mention that word to this jury, or any African-American, it blinds people. It'll blind the jury. It'll blind the truth. They won't be able to discern what's true and what's not." Johnnie Cochran, counsel for Simpson's defense, did not claim that the term was any less offensive than Darden had, only that African Americans have to bear so much that they can bear this too and keep their "perspective": "African-Americans live with offensive words, offensive looks, offensive treatment every day of their lives."

Although Judge Ito decided in favor of the defense, he powerfully summarized Darden's argument as maintaining that the epithet is "so vile that it operates as a divisive demand that those to whom or about whom it is said take some action and that its use can cloud the operation of good judgment and common sense."

A powerful illustration of the judge's point comes as a climactic moment in *Uncle Tom's Cabin*. George Shelby, the son of Uncle Tom's original Kentucky master, has been seeking to rescue Tom from the horrors into which he has been sold. But when George finally locates Tom on Legree's plantation, it is too late. Tom has already died from Legree's beating, heroically refusing to reveal anything about the other slaves who have escaped. George threatens to charge Legree with murder. "Snapping his fingers, scornfully," Legree dares him to try: "Where you going to get witnesses — how you going to prove it?" George is stymied by the Southern prohibition against testimony by blacks against whites. Legree in triumph gloats, "After all, what a fuss, for a dead nigger!" Stowe writes, "The word was as a spark to a powder magazine," and George knocks Legree flat (592). So, a major point of *Uncle Tom's Cabin* has been to bring good-hearted white folks to realize that "nigger" is a fighting word, just as Judge Ito said a century and a half later.

A more distressing example of Ito's point occurred in late 1995 in San Francisco. Louis Waldron was charged with first-degree murder after an incident in which he hit a man once. The Irish American who died was on his way home from a bar when a traffic incident with Waldron left him "uninjured but angered." He "called Mr. Waldron a 'nigger.'" Waldron, a college student majoring in criminology, responded with a punch: "the single blow knocked Mr. Hourican, a former amateur boxer, to the pavement, fracturing his skull. He died two days later" (Noble, "A Man"). The charge of first-degree murder makes sense only on the presumption that African Americans form a firm intention to kill anyone who insults them with this offensive term. I don't believe this is true, but it is worth noting that a recent feature in the *New York Times* indicates that in New York street talk, "ethnic slurs" nowadays form the "most taboo language" (Goldberg).

In the Simpson and Waldron cases the fates of several individuals, living and dead, were at issue, but can it be asserted with confidence that the fates of many individuals are not at stake in the classroom? Has any public authority ever defended the decision not to teach *Huckleberry Finn* in a particular class with arguments as powerful as Darden used here? In their different ways, both attorneys crafted arguments that showed high respect for the jurors. Have the discussions concerning *Huckleberry Finn* shown a comparable respect for the citizens — parents or children — who find themselves pained, offended, or frightened by the permission *Huckleberry Finn* gives to the circulation of an abusive term in classroom and schoolyard? The difference is clear enough: in one instance it's a murder trial, in the other instance it's just kids' lives.

In summer 1995, as the Simpson trial continued, Michael Jackson's *HIStory* came out. Here the use of abusively anti-Semitic terms was obviously in the context of an artwork, the speech of a character in a lyric genre, yet neither the widely shared confidence that Jackson did not intend to express an anti-Semitic position nor the aesthetic explanations of impersonation or irony were sufficient to calm a level of outrage that quickly produced not only apology but actual changes in the lyrics for future issues. In February 1996, while relaxing in a hotel room prior to giving a lecture on this material, I was astonished to find, on the five o'clock news, reports from Brazil that Michael Jackson was suspected of having sung his original lyrics. Evidently, he is under ongoing surveillance. By contrast, Twain's greatness not only means that authorities rush to preserve, rather than to urge changing, his words; his greatness also leads authorities to urge that his words be enforced on every schoolchild. How great must artists be before we trust them so much that their words are treated not only as unchangeable but also as obligatory? How much must a slur hurt, and whom, before we decide that it need not be made a compulsory part of what Cochran called the everyday "offensive treatment" that marks the ongoing racial life of the United States?

The fact that *nigger* is widely used in the text of *Huckleberry Finn* has had the effect of encouraging authors, scholars, teachers, and other persons of goodwill to feel that they are doing the right thing when they name Jim in the language of a racism that it is less important to locate in the psyche of individuals — as Myrdal did in *An American Dilemma* — than in the structures of our nation, what since the days of Black Power has been called "institutionalized racism." Over forty years ago, Lionel Trilling praised *Huckleberry Finn* for being a "subversive book," and Hechinger echoed him in his *Times* article, but it seems to me that *Huckleberry Finn* is currently being read and publicly used in support of complacency.

THE ARGUMENTS

When they are not simply denying the specific experiences and charges of wounded and angry students and parents, the authoritative defenders of *Huckleberry Finn* must use arguments, and they do. The arguments used by the public authorities are an especially interesting case of the relations between professional academic critical discourses and the sphere of public life from which academic work is supposedly isolated.

The major lines of analysis used by the public cultural authorities closely correspond to the major lines of interpretation worked out over the forty years following the challenge posed by Van Wyck Brooks. Brooks's *Ordeal of Mark Twain* argued in 1920 that Twain failed to achieve the greatness of which he was capable because he muted his social criticism in favor of pleasing a large popular readership. Current public analyses draw particularly on the period when academic canonical discourse around *Huckleberry Finn* was most intensely in formation, roughly the 1950s, the years from Trilling's introduction to the appearance of Henry Nash Smith's summational *Mark Twain: The Development of a Writer* in 1962 and Leo Marx's *The Machine in the Garden* in 1964 — the years, I emphasize, of the rise and cresting of the civil rights movement.

Decades of revisionary academic work has been done since then. Only a few years after Trilling's edition, Leo Marx challenged what I call the hypercanonizing principle that "once a work has been admitted to the highest canon of literary reputability," critics then must "find reasons . . . for admiring every bit of it" (p. 300). Some thirty years ago, James Cox and Richard Poirier developed critical arguments that cut against the terms by which most recent public discussion has praised *Huckleberry Finn*. Cox found that "Huck's revolt" is not very morally impressive, for he is involved in "a subversive project which has the reader's complete approval — the freeing of a slave in the Old South, a world which, by virtue of the Civil War, had been declared morally reprehensible because of the slavery it condoned" (168). He continued, "if this were all there was to it we would have nothing but the blandest sentimental action" (170). Poirier elucidated an important limitation of Twain's method, which helps to explain why the book runs down. *Huckleberry Finn,* he argued, "cannot dramatize the meanings accumulated at the moment of social crisis because the crisis itself reveals the inadequacy of the terms by which understandings can be expressed between the hero and other members of his society. There is no publicly accredited vocabulary which allows Huck to reveal his inner self to others" (177). This inadequacy of vocabulary, which idolaters take as a truth about Huck's America, Poirier instead treated as a limiting artistic feature of the fictional world Twain has constructed.

The thinking of such revisionists, and many others who have followed, has hardly reached the public authorities. The only new academic development since the early 1960s that has begun to reach the public may be dated from the *Mark Twain Journal* 1984 special issue, for the centennial of *Huckleberry Finn,* edited by Thadious Davis, in which black scholars addressed the book. This special issue, expanded as a book in 1992 (Leonard et al.), began the process that made possible both the accomplishment and the attention won by Shelley Fisher Fishkin's *Was Huck Black?* (1993).

Three major categories organize the decades-long pattern of public critical defense of *Huckleberry Finn:* irony, realism, and historicism. At this point, I will say something about irony, deferring the other topics for later chapters. Within the academy both sophisticated theorists and regretful conservatives tend to assume that stable irony has been superseded since the demise of New Criticism and its technique of close reading of the work in itself without regard to biography or history. But the most insistent public claims made for the value of *Huckleberry Finn* involve its moral stance as an achievement of irony. Hitchens took this position against the noisemakers and neurotics. This comes down to claiming that there is a bad kind of discrimination, practiced by white society in the antebellum South of Twain's novel, and a good kind of discrimination, practiced by readers who are sufficiently sophisticated to understand exactly what parts Twain is criticizing of the world he portrays.

But how does a reader know, and who is "the reader"? In 1971 the sitcom *All in the Family* quickly rose to the top of the charts. Norman Lear, its producer, is now very well known as a liberal, and many liberal viewers at the time understood that in representing the bigoted views of Archie Bunker, the show was subjecting them to satiric criticism, just as critical authorities now hold that Huck's racist language is. But the show reached a far larger audience than the liberal intelligentsia. Many viewers were reported as saying that "they identified with [Archie]." As one of them put it to *Life,* in a formulation that has great resonance for the problems of what *Huckleberry Finn* means in the classroom: "You think it, but ole Archie he says it, by damn" (Patterson 740). Twain and Lear alike provoke different responses from different readers. It is offensive for cultural authorities to grant legitimacy to only a single way of reading.

The one certain basis for a necessary irony in reading *Huckleberry Finn* is that Huck does not know, and every reader the book has ever had does know, that American slavery was historically doomed, and it vanished between the time of the book's action (about 1845) and its publication (about 1885). Moreover, the martyrdom of Lincoln established at least through the North a consensus, which had not existed at the beginning of the Civil War or even at the time of the Emancipation Proclamation, that in the Civil War the North intended not only to preserve the Union, but also to extend freedom to slaves. Everyone who has read the book, therefore, knows enough to understand the irony of "All right, then, I'll *go* to hell."

Here I think James Cox is right and Lionel Trilling and Arthur Schlesinger are wrong. The moral lesson of *Huckleberry Finn* is not relativist or subversive but absolute. As the intellectual historian Perry Miller explained:

> Hell in 1885 was still officially a reality. Even so, Mark Twain's readers were not offended; on the contrary, they loved Huck all the more. . . . Mark Twain enlisted the Protestant conscience on the side of the naive Huckleberry Finn because that conscience was long since assured that slavery had been a sin. The most orthodox of churchmen would smile benevolently over Huck's crisis. All could rejoice in this triumph of instinctive benevolence over the ancient formalities of a crude society and a crude theology — and congratulate themselves upon their sophistication. (282)

Only the universally shared assumption by readers that slavery is morally unacceptable defines the moral significance of Huck's decision to go to hell; all readers recognize that Huck will not go to hell because, contrary to his society's beliefs, he is doing the right thing. But where does the book stand on racism as opposed to slavery? Here many readers have disagreed, and yet here is the crux of the pain for contemporary black readers. If Huck has such moral insight that he is willing to go to hell for Jim's sake, why does he not find new ways of saying his new sense of the world? Why not stop using a word that is part of the system he is, we suppose, rejecting?

I have already referred to Frederick Douglass and Harriet Beecher Stowe. Let me add one more text from the time when the action of *Huckleberry Finn* occurs. In a moment of despair, around 1845, Ralph Waldo Emerson wrote in his journal: "What argument, what eloquence can avail against the power of that one word *niggers*? The man of the world annihilates the whole combined force of all the antislavery societies of the world by pronouncing it" (338). Huck may not mean anything bad by the word, but his continuing usage helps keep it alive and ready to be exploited by those who benefit from the way of the world that denigrates blacks.

I find a further problem with the ironic moral stance. What if we apply the analytic mode, favored by ironizing critics, which involves placing various parts of the book in relation to each other to test their potentially contradictory relationship? Huck, we recall, in the early pages of the book has received a certain amount of religious instruction. Miss Watson tells him "all about the bad place." His response? "I said I wished I was there." And when she tells him about her plans to get to "the good place," "couldn't see no advantage in going where she was going" (p. 33). So from the beginning Huck has been ready to go to hell, and in chapter 31, despite the powerfully affecting rhetorical pressure, there is therefore no actual drama in what is generally referred to as his "crisis." In Aristotle's terms, it is strong in thought not plot, just as the ending of the book undermines what has seemed to be its action by revealing that Jim has already been willed free. As Leslie Fiedler suggested, in terms compatible with my own analysis of Huck as a "sensitive spectator" (the crucial type of character in the mode of writing that I call literary narrative), the "ultimate problem" is whether Huck, "whose role is to suffer and evade," can successfully "take a hand in the affairs of the world, make something *happen*" (*Love* 587). The answer is no.

Or take it another way: Ironizing critics tend to agree that a major structural irony of the book is the exposure of various literary and conventional modes of thought, feeling, behavior, of which slavery may be the most consequential and repellent but is by no means the only one. Tom Sawyer is the exemplary character for this pattern, and Tom's renewed dominance in the book's ending has provoked elaborate critical discussions. But what if Huck's great moment before the return of Tom were itself already only another pose? Is Walter Scott chivalry to be condemned only so that a romantic satanism, like that made famous, and conventional, by Scott's younger contemporary Lord Byron, can take its place? The decision to go to hell was not dominant but was nonetheless widespread across nineteenth-century culture. The same principle of superior knowledge that permits a reader to ironize Huck's fears also allows a reader who knows more to ironize his independence. Readers may recognize its conventionality even if he doesn't, just as we recognize the morality of what he believes is immoral.

Both of these problems that might discomfit public ironizers, but have not, are problems that arise from the narrative structure of *Huckleberry Finn;* they arise from readerly attempts to impose a coherent meaning across a range of differentiated repetitions. Winfried Fluck, over twenty years ago, published what remains the most impressive analysis of the critical literature on *Huckleberry Finn;* it is so iconoclastic that it has never been translated from German and has had accordingly little impact. Yet its critique of unifying attempts to define "pattern" and "rhythm" is devastating. Rather than the coolly dispassionate, ironic love of intricate interrelations, I find a different process at work in readers' idolatry of chapter 31, and their generalization from that to the book as a whole. The critical concept of "the sublime" offers resources that may help us hold onto the thrilling power of chapter 31 while understanding, and thereby perhaps resisting, the extravagance of idolatry.

The crucial treatment of the sublime comes from the Greek critic known as Longinus. What he means by the sublime is, most simply, the greatest moments of literary experience, and it is crucial to recognize that only moments concern him. The sublime does not depend on fancy language, and it does not arise from the unity of a work; like a "whirlwind" it tears up any established pattern or texture, so as to stand out from the context or work in which it occurs. The sublime produces, and depends on, a series of identifications, so that the words of a character, at a sublime moment, seem "the echo of a great soul" that is the author's, and in reading the sublime we are "uplifted," "as if we had ourselves produced" what we hear or read (1.4, 9.2, 7.2). The key Greek term here is *ekstasis,* a getting out of one's place, a "transport" into a new state or position. Such an analysis seems to me appropriately to honor the accomplishment of *Huckleberry Finn* without committing criticism to fruitless and ultimately offensive hyperbole about the excellence of the work as a whole, and it seems to me also to underline why the investments made in the work are so great. Here is the motive for idolatry. Because the structure of the sublime joins reader, character, and author in interlinked identifications, it may lead to narcissistically fixed mirrorings rather than "ecstatic" mobility. Readers may then tend to be highly protective of the characters and authors in which they are invested, and at the same time will feel themselves intimately threatened by anything that seems to criticize or diminish either Huck or Twain. When America itself is added to the system of identifications, the stakes are raised immensely by the "quintessential" linkage of character and author and reader to nation.

WORKS CITED

Ayers, Edward L. *The Promise of the New South: Life after Reconstruction.* New York: Oxford UP, 1992.

Ballard, Allan B. Letter. *New York Times,* 9 May 1982.

Beaver, Harold. "Run, Nigger, Run: *Adventures of Huckleberry Finn* as a Fugitive Slave Narrative." *American Studies* 8 (1974): 339–61.

Cox, James M. *Mark Twain: The Fate of Humor.* Princeton: Princeton UP, 1966.

De Voto, Bernard. *Mark Twain's America.* Boston: Little, Brown, 1932.

Ellison, Ralph. *Conversations with Ralph Ellison.* Eds. Maryemma Graham and Amritjit Singh. Jackson: UP of Mississippi, 1995.

Emerson, Ralph Waldo. *Emerson in His Journals.* Selected and edited by Joel Porte. Cambridge: Harvard UP, 1982.

Fiedler, Leslie A. *Love and Death in the American Novel.* 1960. Cleveland: Meridian, 1962.

Gibson, Donald B. "Mark Twain's Jim in the Classroom." *English Journal* 57 (Feb. 1968): 196–99, 202.

Goldberg, Carey. "Welcome to New York, Curse Capital." *New York Times,* 19 June 1995, B12.

Kaplan, Justin. *Born to Trouble: One Hundred Years of Huckleberry Finn.* Center for the Book Viewpoint Series, no. 13. Washington, D.C.: Library of Congress, 1985.

Leonard, James S., Thomas A. Tenney, and Thadious M. Davis, eds. *Satire or Evasion? Black Perspectives on "Huckleberry Finn."* Durham, NC: Duke UP, 1992.

Lynn, Kenneth S., ed. *Huckleberry Finn: Text, Sources, and Criticism.* New York: Harcourt, Brace and World, 1961.

Marx, Leo. *The Pilot and the Passenger: Essays on Literature, Culture, and Technology in the United States.* New York: Oxford UP, 1988.

Miller, Perry. *Nature's Nation.* Cambridge: Harvard UP, 1967.

Moore, Molly. "Behind the Attack on 'Huck Finn': One Angry Educator." *Washington Post,* metro section, 21 April 1982, 1, 6–7.

Noble, Kenneth B. "Issue of Racism Erupts in Simpson Trial: Prosecutor and Defense Lawyer Clash in Arguments over Epithet." *New York Times,* 14 Jan. 1995, 7.

Patterson, James T. *Grand Expectations: The United States, 1945–1974. Oxford History of the United States,* vol. 10. New York: Oxford UP, 1996.

Poirier, Richard. *A World Elsewhere: The Place of Style in American Literature.* New York: Oxford UP, 1966.

Quirk, Tom. *Coming to Grips with "Huckleberry Finn": Essays on a Book, a Boy, and a Man.* Columbia: U of Missouri P, 1993.

Trilling, Diana. *The Beginning of the Journey: The Marriage of Diana and Lionel Trilling.* New York: Harcourt Brace and Company, 1993.

Trilling, Lionel. *The Liberal Imagination: Essays on Literature and Society.* 1950. Garden City, NY: Doubleday, 1953.

Wecter, Dixon. *Sam Clemens of Hannibal.* Boston: Houghton Mifflin, 1952.

Woodward, C. Vann. *The Burden of Southern History.* Rev. ed. Baton Rouge: Louisiana State UP, 1968.

JANE SMILEY

Say It Ain't So, Huck: Second Thoughts on Mark Twain's "Masterpiece"

Jane Smiley (b. 1949) is the author of the 1992 Pulitzer Prize–winning novel *A Thousand Acres.* Born in Los Angeles and raised in St. Louis, Smiley attended Vassar College, where she earned her B.A. in 1971. After receiving both an M.F.A. and Ph.D. from the University of Iowa, Smiley taught at Iowa State University from 1981 until 1996. Smiley's other works of fiction include *The Age of Grief* (1987), *Ordinary Love and Good Will* (1989), *The Greenlanders* (1988), *Moo* (1995), *The All-True Travels of Lidie Newton* (1998), *Horse Heaven* (2000), and *Good Faith* (2003). She is also the author of numerous magazine essays. The essay included here, "Say It Ain't So, Huck," first appeared in the January 1996 issue of *Harper's Magazine.*

So I broke my leg. Doesn't matter how — since the accident I've heard plenty of broken-leg tales, and, I'm telling you, I didn't realize that walking down the stairs, walking down hills, dancing in high heels, or stamping your foot on the brake pedal could be so dangerous. At any rate, like numerous broken-legged intellectuals before me, I found the prospect of three months in bed in the dining room rather seductive from a book-reading point of view, and I eagerly got started. Great novels piled up on my table, and right at the top was *Adventures of Huckleberry Finn,* which, I'm embarrassed to admit, I hadn't read since junior high school. The novel took me a couple of days (it was longer than I had remembered), and I closed the cover stunned. Yes, stunned. Not, by any means, by the artistry of the book but by the notion that this is the novel all American literature grows out of, that this is a great novel, that this is even a serious novel.

Although Huck had his fans at publication, his real elevation into the pantheon was worked out early in the Propaganda Era, between 1948 and 1955, by Lionel Trilling, Leslie Fiedler, T. S. Eliot, Joseph Wood Krutch, and some lesser lights, in the introductions to American and British editions of the novel and in such journals as *Partisan Review* and *The New York Times Book Review*. The requirements of Huck's installation rapidly revealed themselves: the failure of the last twelve chapters (in which Huck finds Jim imprisoned on the Phelps plantation and Tom Sawyer is reintroduced and elaborates a cruel and unnecessary scheme for Jim's liberation) had to be diminished, accounted for, or forgiven; after that, the novel's special qualities had to be placed in the context first of other American novels (to their detriment) and then of world literature. The best bets here seemed to be Twain's style and the river setting, and the critics invested accordingly: Eliot, who had never read the novel as a boy, traded on his own childhood beside the big river, elevating Huck to the Boy, and the Mississippi to the River God, therein finding the sort of mythic resonance that he admired. Trilling liked the river god idea, too, though he didn't bother to capitalize it. He also thought that Twain, through Huck's lying, told truths, one of them being (I kid you not) that "something . . . had gone out of American life after the [Civil War], some simplicity, some innocence, some peace." What Twain himself was proudest of in the novel — his style — Trilling was glad to dub "not less than definitive in American literature. The prose of *Huckleberry Finn* established for written prose the virtues of American colloquial speech. . . . He is the master of the style that escapes the fixity of the printed page, that sounds in our ears with the immediacy of the heard voice, the very voice of unpretentious truth." The last requirement was some quality that would link Huck to other, though "lesser," American novels such as Herman Melville's *Moby-Dick,* that would possess some profound insight into the American character. Leslie Fiedler obligingly provided it when he read homoerotic attraction into the relationship between Huck and Jim, pointing out the similarity of this to such other white man–dark man friendships as those between Ishmael and Queequeg in *Moby-Dick* and Natty Bumppo and Chingachgook in James Fenimore Cooper's *Last of the Mohicans.*

The canonization proceeded apace: great novel (Trilling, 1950), greatest novel (Eliot, 1950), world-class novel (Lauriat Lane Jr., 1955). Sensible naysayers, such as Leo Marx, were lost in the shuffle of propaganda. But, in fact, *Adventures of Huckleberry Finn* has little to offer in the way of greatness. There is more to be learned about the American character *from* its canonization than *through* its canonization.

Let me hasten to point out that, like most others, I don't hold any grudges against Huck himself. He's just a boy trying to survive. The villain here is Mark Twain, who knew how to give Huck a voice but didn't know how to give him a novel. Twain was clearly aware of the story's difficulties. Not finished with having revisited his boyhood in *Tom Sawyer*, Twain conceived of a sequel and began composition while still working on *Tom Sawyer*'s page proofs. Four hundred pages into it, having just passed Cairo and exhausted most of his memories of Hannibal and the upper Mississippi, Twain put the manuscript aside for three years. He was facing a problem every novelist is familiar with: his original conception was beginning to conflict with the implications of the actual story. It is at this point in the story that Huck and Jim realize two things: they have become close friends, and they have missed the Ohio River and drifted into what for Jim must be the most frightening territory of all — down the river, the very place Miss Watson was going to sell him to begin with. Jim's putative savior, Huck, has led him as far astray as a slave can go, and the farther they go, the worse it is going to be for him. Because the Ohio was not Twain's territory, the fulfillment of Jim's wish would necessarily lead the novel away from the artistic integrity that Twain certainly sensed his first four hundred pages possessed. He found himself writing not a boy's novel, like *Tom Sawyer*, but a man's novel, about real moral dilemmas and growth. The patina of nostalgia for a time and place, Missouri in the 1840s (not unlike former President Ronald Reagan's nostalgia for his own boyhood, when "Americans got along"), had been transformed into actual longing for a timeless place of friendship and freedom, safe and hidden, on the big river. But the raft had floated Huck and Jim, and their author with them, into the truly dark heart of the American soul and of American history: slave country.

Twain came back to the novel and worked on it twice again, once to rewrite the chapters containing the feud between the Grangerfords and the Shepherdsons, and later to introduce the Duke and the Dauphin. It is with the feud that the novel begins to fail, because from here on the episodes are mere distractions from the true subject of the work:

Huck's affection for and responsibility to Jim. The signs of this failure are everywhere, as Jim is pushed to the side of the narrative, hiding on the raft and confined to it, while Huck follows the Duke and the Dauphin onshore to the scenes of much simpler and much less philosophically taxing moral dilemmas, such as fraud. Twain was by nature an improviser, and he was pleased enough with these improvisations to continue. When the Duke and the Dauphin finally betray Jim by selling him for forty dollars, Huck is shocked, but the fact is neither he nor Twain has come up with a plan that would have saved Jim in the end. Tom Sawyer does that.

Considerable critical ink has flowed over the years in an attempt to integrate the Tom Sawyer chapters with the rest of the book, but it has flowed in vain. As Leo Marx points out, and as most readers sense intuitively, once Tom reappears, "[m]ost of those traits which made [Huck] so appealing a hero now disappear. . . . It should be added at once that Jim doesn't mind too much. The fact is that he has undergone a similar transformation. On the raft he was an individual, man enough to denounce Huck when Huck made him the victim of a practical joke. In the closing episode, however, we lose sight of Jim in the maze of farcical invention" (p. 295 in this volume). And the last twelve chapters are boring, a sure sign that an author has lost the battle between plot and theme and is just filling in the blanks.

As with all bad endings, the problem really lies at the beginning, and at the beginning of *Adventures of Huckleberry Finn* neither Huck nor Twain takes Jim's desire for freedom at all seriously; that is, they do not accord it the respect that a man's passion deserves. The sign of this is that not only do the two never cross the Mississippi to Illinois, a free state, but they hardly even consider it. In both *Tom Sawyer* and *Huckleberry Finn*, the Jackson's Island scenes show that such a crossing, even in secret, is both possible and routine, and even though it would present legal difficulties for an escaped slave, these would certainly pose no more hardship than locating the mouth of the Ohio and then finding passage up it. It is true that there could have been slave catchers in pursuit (though the novel ostensibly takes place in the 1840s and the Fugitive Slave Act was not passed until 1850), but Twain's moral failure, once Huck and Jim link up, is never even to account for their choice to go down the river rather than across it. What this reveals is that for all his lip service to real attachment between white boy and black man, Twain really saw Jim as no more than Huck's sidekick, homoerotic or otherwise. All the claims that are routinely made for the book's humanitarian power are, in the end, simply absurd. Jim is never autonomous, never has a vote, always finds his purposes subordinate to Huck's, and, like every good sidekick, he never minds. He grows ever more passive and also more affectionate as Huck and the Duke and the Dauphin and Tom (and Twain) make ever more use of him for their own purposes. But this use they make of him is not supplementary; it is integral to Twain's whole conception of the novel. Twain thinks that Huck's affection is a good enough reward for Jim.

The sort of meretricious critical reasoning that has raised Huck's paltry good intentions to a "strategy of subversion" (David L. Smith) and a "convincing indictment of slavery" (Eliot) precisely mirrors the same sort of meretricious reasoning that white people use to convince themselves that they are not "racist." If Huck *feels* positive toward Jim, and *loves* him, and *thinks* of him as a man, then that's enough. He doesn't actually have to act in accordance with his feelings. White Americans always think racism is a feeling, and they reject it or they embrace it. To most Americans, it seems more honorable and nicer to reject it, so they do, but they almost invariably fail to understand that how they *feel* means very little to black Americans, who understand racism as a way of structuring American culture, American politics, and the American economy. To invest *Adventures of Huckleberry Finn* with "greatness" is to underwrite a very simplistic and evasive theory of what racism is and to promulgate it, philosophically, in schools and the media as well as in academic journals. Surely the discomfort of many readers, black and white, and the censorship battles that have dogged *Huck Finn* in the last twenty years are understandable in this context. No matter how often the critics "place in context" Huck's use of the word "nigger," they can never excuse or fully hide the deeper racism of the novel — the way Twain and Huck use Jim because they really don't care enough about his desire for freedom to let that desire change their plans. And to give credit to Huck suggests that the only racial insight Americans of the nineteenth or twentieth century are capable of is a recognition of the obvious — that blacks, slave and free, are human.

Ernest Hemingway, thinking of himself, as always, once said that all American literature grew out of *Huck Finn*. It undoubtedly would have been better for American literature, and American culture, if our literature had grown out of one of the best-selling novels of all time, another American work of the nineteenth century, *Uncle Tom's Cabin*, which for its portrayal of an array of thoughtful, autonomous, and passionate black characters leaves *Huck Finn* far behind. *Uncle Tom's Cabin* was published in 1852, when Twain was seventeen, still living in Hannibal and contributing to his brother's newspapers, still sympathizing with the South, nine years before his abortive career in the Confederate Army. *Uncle Tom's Cabin* was the most popular novel of its era, universally controversial. In 1863, when Harriet Beecher Stowe visited the White House, Abraham Lincoln condescended to remark to her, "So this is the little lady who made this great war."

The story, familiar to most nineteenth-century Americans, either through the novel or through the many stage adaptations that sentimentalized Stowe's work, may be sketched briefly: A Kentucky slave, Tom, is sold to pay off a debt to a slave trader, who takes him to New Orleans. On the boat trip downriver, Tom is purchased by the wealthy Augustine St. Clare at the behest of his daughter, Eva. After Eva's death, and then St. Clare's, Tom is sold again, this time to Simon Legree, whose remote plantation is the site of every form of cruelty and degradation. The novel was immediately read and acclaimed by any number of excellent judges: Charles Dickens, George Eliot, Leo Tolstoy, George Sand — the whole roster of nineteenth-century liberals whose work we read today and try to persuade ourselves that *Huck Finn* is equal to. English novelist and critic Charles Kingsley thought *Uncle Tom's Cabin* the best novel ever written. These writers honored Stowe's book for all its myriad virtues. One of these was her adept characterization of a whole world of whites and blacks who find themselves gripped by slavery, many of whose names have entered the American language as expressions — not only Uncle Tom himself but Simon Legree and, to a lesser extent, little Eva and the black child Topsy. The characters appear, one after another, vivified by their attitudes, desires, and opinions as much as by their histories and their fates. Surely Augustine St. Clare, Tom's owner in New Orleans, is an exquisite portrayal of a humane but indecisive man, who knows what he is doing but not how to stop it. Surely Cassy, a fellow slave whom Tom meets on the Legree plantation, is one of the great angry women in all of literature — not only bitter, murderous, and nihilistic but also intelligent and enterprising. Surely the midlife spiritual journey of Ophelia St. Clare, Augustine's Yankee cousin, from self-confident ignorance to affectionate understanding is most convincing, as is Topsy's parallel journey from ignorance and self-hatred to humanity. The ineffectual Mr. Shelby and his submissive, and subversive, wife; the slave trader Haley; Tom's wife, Chloe; Augustine's wife, Marie; Legree's overseers, Sambo and Quimbo — good or evil, they all live.

As for Tom himself, we all know what an "Uncle Tom" is, except we don't. The popular Uncle Tom sucks up to the master and exhibits bovine patience. The real Uncle Tom is both a realist and a man of deep principle. When he is sold by Mr. Shelby in Kentucky, he knows enough of Shelby's affairs to know that what his master asserts is true: it's Tom who must go or the whole estate will be sold off for debt, including Tom's wife and three children. Later, on the Legree estate, his religious faith tells him that the greatest danger he finds there is not to his life but to his soul. His logic is impeccable. He holds fast to his soul, in the face of suffering, in a way that even nonbelievers like myself must respect. In fact, Tom's story eerily prefigures stories of spiritual solace through deep religious belief that have come out of both the Soviet Gulag and the Nazi concentration camp in the same way that the structure of power on Legree's plantation, and the suffering endured there, forecasts and duplicates many stories of recent genocides.

The power of *Uncle Tom's Cabin* is the power of brilliant analysis married to great wisdom of feeling. Stowe never forgets the logical end of any relationship in which one person is the subject and the other is the object. No matter how the two people feel, or what their intentions are, the logic of the relationship is inherently tragic and traps both parties until the false subject/object relationship is ended. Stowe's most oft-repeated and potent representation of this inexorable logic is the forcible separation of family members, especially of mothers from children. Eliza, faced with the sale of her child, Harry, escapes across the breaking ice of the Ohio River. Lucy, whose ten-month-old is sold behind her back, kills herself. Prue, who has been used for breeding, must listen to her last child cry itself to death because her mistress won't let her save it; she falls into alcoholism and thievery and is finally whipped to death. Cassy, prefiguring a choice made by one of the characters in Toni Morrison's *Beloved*, kills her last child so that it won't grow up in slavery. All of these women have been promised something by their owners — love, education, the privilege and joy of raising their children — but, owing to slavery, all of these promises have been broken. The grief and despair these women display is no doubt what T. S. Eliot was thinking of when he superciliously labeled *Uncle Tom's Cabin* "sensationalist propaganda," but, in fact, few critics in the nineteenth century ever accused Stowe of making up or even exaggerating such stories. One group of former slaves who were asked to comment on Stowe's depiction of slave life said that she had failed to portray the very worst, and Stowe herself was afraid that if she told some of what she had heard from escaped slaves and other informants during her eighteen years in Cincinnati, the book would be too dark to find any readership at all.

Stowe's analysis does not stop with the slave owners and traders, or with the slaves themselves. She understands perfectly that slavery is an economic system embedded in America as a whole, and she comments ironically on Christian bankers in New York whose financial dealings result in the sale of slaves, on Northern politicians who promote the capture of escaped slaves for the sake of the public good, on ministers of churches who give the system a Christian stamp of approval. One of Stowe's most skillful techniques is her method of weaving a discussion of slavery into the dialogue of her characters. Especially interesting is a conversation Mark Twain could have paid attention to. Augustine St. Clare and his abolitionist cousin, Ophelia, are discussing his failure to act in accordance with his feelings of revulsion against slavery. After entertaining Ophelia's criticisms for a period, Augustine points out that Ophelia herself is personally disgusted by black people and doesn't like to come into contact with them. He says, "You would think no harm in a child's caressing a large dog, even if he was black . . . custom with us does what Christianity ought to do, — obliterates the feeling of personal prejudice." When Ophelia takes over the education of Topsy, a child who has suffered a most brutal previous upbringing, she discovers that she can do nothing with her until she takes her, literally, to her bosom. But personal relationships do not mitigate the evils of slavery; Ophelia makes sure to give Topsy her freedom.

Stowe also understands that the real root of slavery is that it is profitable as well as customary. Augustine and his brother live with slavery because it is the system they know and because they haven't the imagination to live without it. Simon Legree embraces slavery because he can make money from it and because it gives him even more absolute power over his workers than he could find in the North or in England.

The very heart of nineteenth-century American experience and literature, the nature and meaning of slavery, is finally what Twain cannot face in *Adventures of Huckleberry Finn*. As Jim and Huck drift down Twain's beloved river, the author finds himself nearing what must have been a crucial personal nexus: how to reconcile the felt memory of boyhood with the cruel implications of the social system within which that boyhood was lived. He had avoided this problem for the most part in *Tom Sawyer*: slaves hardly impinge on the lives of Tom and the other boys. But once Twain allows Jim a voice, this voice must speak in counterpoint to Huck's voice and must raise issues that cannot easily be resolved, either personally or culturally. Harriet Beecher Stowe, New Englander, daughter of Puritans and thinkers, active in the abolitionist movement and in the effort to aid and educate escaped slaves, had no such personal conflict when she sat down to write *Uncle Tom's Cabin.* Nothing about slavery was attractive to her either as a New Englander or as a resident of Cincinnati for almost twenty years. Her lack of conflict is apparent in the clarity of both the style and substance of the novel.

Why, then, we may ask, did *Uncle Tom's Cabin,* for all its power and popularity, fail to spawn American literature? Fail, even, to work as a model for how to draw passionate, autonomous, and interesting black literary characters? Fail to keep the focus of the American literary imagination on the central dilemma of the American experience: race? Part of the reason is certainly that the public conversation about race and slavery that had been a feature of antebellum American life fell silent after the Civil War. Perhaps the answer is to be found in *The Adventures of Huckleberry Finn:* everyone opted for the ultimate distraction, lighting out for the territory. And the reason is to be found in *Uncle Tom's Cabin:* that's where the money was.

But so what? These are only authors, after all, and once a book is published the author can't be held accountable for its role in the culture. For that we have to blame the citizens themselves, or their teachers, or *their* teachers, the arbiters of critical taste. In "Melodramas of Beset Manhood: How Theories of American Fiction Exclude Women Authors," the scholar Nina Baym has already detailed how the canonization of a very narrow range of white, Protestant, middle-class male authors (Twain, Hawthorne, Melville, Emerson, etc.) has misrepresented our literary life — first by defining the only worthy American literary subject as "the struggle of the individual against society [in which] the essential quality of America comes to reside in its unsettled wilderness and the opportunities that such a wilderness offers to the individual as the medium on which he may inscribe, unhindered, his own destiny and his own nature," and then by casting women, and especially women writers (specialists in the "flagrantly bad best-seller," according to Leslie Fiedler), as the enemy. In such critical readings, all other themes and modes of literary expression fall out of consideration as "un-American." There goes *Uncle Tom's Cabin,* there goes Edith Wharton, there goes domestic life as a subject, there go almost all the best-selling novelists of the nineteenth century and their readers, who were mostly women. The real loss, though, is not to our literature but to our culture and ourselves, because we have lost the subject of how the various social groups who may not escape to the wilderness are to get along in society; and, in the case of *Uncle Tom's Cabin,* the hard-nosed, unsentimental dialogue about race that we should have been having since before the Civil War. Obviously, *Uncle Tom's Cabin* is no more the last word on race relations than *The Brothers Karamazov* or *David Copperfield* is on any number of characteristically Russian or English themes and social questions. Some of Stowe's ideas about inherent racial characteristics (whites: cold, heartless; blacks: naturally religious and warm) are bad and have been exploded. One of her solutions to the American racial conflicts that she foresaw, a colony in Africa, she later repudiated. Nevertheless, her views about many issues were brilliant, and her heart was wise. She gained the respect and friendship of many men and women of goodwill, black and white, such as Frederick Douglass, the civil-rights activist Mary Church Terrill, the writer and social activist James Weldon Johnson, and W. E. B. Du Bois. What she did was find a way to talk about slavery and family, power and law, life and death, good and evil, North and South. She truly believed that all Americans together had to find a solution to the problem of slavery in which all were implicated. When her voice, a courageously public voice — as demonstrated by the public arguments about slavery that rage throughout *Uncle Tom's Cabin* — fell silent in our culture and was replaced by the secretive voice of Huck Finn, who acknowledges Jim only when they are alone on the raft together out in the middle of the big river, racism fell out of the public world and into the private one, where whites think it really is but blacks know it really isn't.

Should *Huckleberry Finn* be taught in the schools? The critics of the Propaganda Era laid the groundwork for the universal inclusion of the book in school curriculums by declaring it great. Although they predated the current generation of politicized English professors, this was clearly a political act, because the entry of *Huck Finn* into classrooms sets the terms of the discussion of racism and American history, and sets them very low: all you have to do to be a hero is acknowledge that your poor sidekick is human; you don't actually have to act in the interests of his humanity. Arguments about censorship have been regularly turned into nonsense by appeals to Huck's "greatness." Moreover, so much critical thinking has gone into defending Huck so that he *can* be great, so that American literature can be found different from and maybe better than Russian or English or French literature, that the very integrity of the critical enterprise has been called into question. That most readers intuitively reject the last twelve chapters of the novel on the grounds of tedium or triviality is clear from the fact that so many critics have turned themselves inside out to defend them. Is it so mysterious that criticism has failed in our time after being so robust only a generation ago? Those who cannot be persuaded that *Adventures of Huckleberry Finn* is a great novel have to draw *some* conclusion.

I would rather my children read *Uncle Tom's Cabin,* even though it is far more vivid in its depiction of cruelty than *Huck Finn,* and this is because Stowe's novel is clearly and unmistakably a tragedy. No whitewash, no secrets, but evil, suffering, imagination, endurance, and redemption — just like life. Like little Eva, who eagerly but fearfully listens to the stories of the slaves that her family tries to keep from her, our children want to know what is going on, what has gone on, and what we intend to do about it. If "great" literature has any purpose, it is to help us face up to our responsibilities instead of enabling us to avoid them once again by lighting out for the territory.

SEYMOUR CHWAST

Selling *Huck Finn* Down the River: A Response to Jane Smiley

An internationally recognized graphic designer and illustrator, Seymour Chwast (b. 1931) is the author or illustrator of more than thirty children's books. After studying design at Cooper Union School from 1948 to 1951, Chwast cofounded Push Pin Studios with Milton Glaser in 1954. Push Pin became well known for its eclectic approach to graphic design. Chwast's children's books include *The Alphabet Parade* (1991), *The Twelve Circus Rings* (1993), *Mr. Merlin and the Turtle* (1996), and *Harry, I Need You!* (2002). He is also the author of *Graphic Style: From Victorian to Digital* (with Steven Heller, 2000), and is coeditor of *The Art of New York* (with Heller, 1983). The following response to Smiley's essay, headlined "Selling *Huck Finn* Down the River," first appeared in the March 10, 1996, book section of *The New York Times.*

In the January issue of *Harper's Magazine,* the novelist Jane Smiley writes that she's "stunned" by the notion that *Adventures of Huckleberry Finn* "is a great novel . . . even a serious novel." She attributes its canonization to a propaganda initiative by a small group of literary critics, among them Lionel Trilling and T. S. Eliot, soon after World War II. She sees this as part of a longstanding cultism that assigns a dominant position to "white, Protestant, middle-class male authors" — Emerson, Hawthorne and Melville, for example — while relegating women authors, especially authors of best-selling novels, to the kitchen middens of Parnassus. Citing Ernest Hemingway's famously unhesitating assertion that "all modern American literature" comes from *Huckleberry Finn,* Ms. Smiley argues that American literature would have been better off if it had grown instead out of *Uncle Tom's Cabin,* one of the few novels that may be said to have had a pronounced effect on events.

Harriet Beecher Stowe's novel portrays "thoughtful, autonomous and passionate black characters," Ms. Smiley writes, while Mark Twain's Jim is merely a sidekick for Huck, who, moreover, fails to take Jim's quest for freedom seriously. *Huckleberry Finn* promotes a "simplistic and evasive theory" of racism as a problem to be alleviated through feeling rather than action. A truly responsible writer, she seems to be saying, would not have been satisfied with Huck's recognition of Jim's humanity and dignity but would have evolved Huck into John Brown and Jim into Nat Turner, two people who, indeed, "did" something about racism instead of just having a feeling about it.

The issue here, in part, is whether you want certainty or conflict in the literature you value — closure or risk, instruction or exploration, right-mindedness or free-mindedness. Writing *Uncle Tom's Cabin* in 1850–51, a decade before the argument about slavery boiled over into the Civil War, Stowe was dealing with a clear and present evil for which, as she believed, abolition and an aroused public were the sole remedy. In *Huckleberry Finn,* started in 1876, by which time slavery was no longer a present fact, Mark Twain was writing a historical, not a reformist, novel. Instead of being issue-driven, a cry for action, as Stowe's book was, his was autobiographical and nostalgic. Perhaps he had set out to do something not altogether possible, to meld a tenderly remembered boyhood with a profoundly troubled adult recognition that the same white, riverine society that allowed Huck his brief rafting idyll was also heartless and greedy, a league of swindlers, drunks, hypocrites, lunkheads, bounty hunters and trigger-happy psychopaths. To praise (as Ms. Smiley does) Stowe's reformist novel for its "clarity of both . . . style and substance" while faulting Mark Twain's quite different sort of book for its conflictiveness and "secretive voice" is to sell stylistic innovation, humor and imaginative literature down the river.

Inevitably, given the rhetorical thrust and focus of much discussion these days, the issue comes down to one of "correctness," but even on this dismal level Ms. Smiley's praise of the one book to the virtual stigmatization of the other doesn't make much sense. *Huckleberry Finn* is in constant trouble with teachers, librarians and parents because of its iterations of "nigger," a word that has a pre-emptive force today that it did not have in Huck Finn's Mississippi Valley of the 1840s. As far as I can tell, there have been no comparable objections to the frequent use, again by black characters as well as whites, of the word in *Uncle Tom's Cabin*.

For all its undisputed power, moral outrage and a literary brilliance too easily overshadowed by message, Stowe's novel comes with serious problems of attitude for contemporary readers: the same "deeper racism" Ms. Smiley finds in *Huckleberry Finn*. This begins with the stereotypical portrayal of Uncle Tom presiding over a family evening in his cabin and affects lesser characters like Black Sam, so called from his being "three shades blacker than any other son of ebony on the place," and shown hitching up his pantaloons, "his regularly organized method of assisting his mental perplexities." Other problems that afflict this book are organic and structural, reflecting the belief, held by Stowe and other abolitionists, that blacks were genetically unadaptable to both the climate and the advanced society of the United States. Repatriation to a gentler haven far away appeared to be the only answer. Lucy, one of Stowe's black characters, commits suicide; Prue becomes a drunk and a thief; George Harris and Eliza leave for Liberia; Tom is beaten to death. This generalized hopelessness, in Stowe's vision representing the tragedy inherent not only in slavery as an institution but in blacks as an uprooted race, is alien to *Huckleberry Finn*, where Jim's future as a free man reunited with his family at least remains an open question.

No other major American book has been so vigorously challenged, and over so many years, as *Adventures of Huckleberry Finn*. Yet it manages somehow, through its humor, lyricism and distinctive, even revolutionary narrative voice, not only to survive but to transcend its author's definition of a classic: "A book which people praise and don't read." Since it was first published in this country in 1885, "Huckleberry Finn" has been read in some 65 languages and almost a thousand editions. This spring Random House is publishing yet another edition, for which I have written an introduction. This one incorporates material from Mark Twain's original manuscript, the first part of which, presumed lost or destroyed, was recovered in 1990 in a trunk in a California attic. For all its enduring popularity, Mark Twain's novel is the book many Americans love to hate and wish had never happened, but we're now as bonded to this nettlesome work as Brer Rabbit was to Tar-Baby. Like Huck, after Pap Finn "got too handy with his hick'ry," the book is "all over welts."

By now its early trials are almost as familiar as the story the novel tells. A month after publication, the trustees of the Concord (Mass.) Public Library expelled the book from its shelves. It was "trash and suitable only for the slums," they said. "It deals with a series of adventures of a very low grade of morality; it is couched in the language of a rough dialect, and all through its pages there is a systematic use of bad grammar and an employment of rough, coarse, inelegant expressions." Over the next quarter-century other libraries — in Denver, Omaha, Brooklyn and the New York State Reformatory — fell in line, claiming the book was "immoral and sacrilegious," put "wrong ideas in youngsters' heads" and set "a bad example." Within the bounds of pure literalmindedness, the people making these judgments had a point. Son of the town drunkard, Mark Twain's hero-narrator steals, lies, consorts with swindlers and violates both the law and the prevailing social code by helping a slave to escape and recognizing him as an equal. Huck's story ridicules the work ethic, the Bible, prayer, "missionarying," preaching and pious sentiments in general — "tears and flapdoodle," "soul-butter and hogwash." Even Mark Twain's wife and daughters, the audience whose approval he most wanted for a book that came out of his deepest imperatives, acknowledged "dear old Huck" only as someone to be let in through the back door and fed in the kitchen.

It's no longer ethical and social transgressiveness that drives controversy but "racism," a mainly invisible issue in the book's earlier career. Mark Twain's characterization of Jim allegedly stereotypes black people as ignorant, superstitious, passive, indiscriminately affectionate and infantile. This ignores the fact that at crucial junctures Jim is Huck's adult guide and protector and throughout lives on a higher ethical level than anybody else in this book, including Huck.

John Wallace, a black educator who has long been on the warpath against *Huckleberry Finn,* calls it "the most grotesque example of racist trash ever given our children to read. . . . Any teacher caught trying to use that piece of trash with our children should be fired on the spot, for he or she is either racist, insensitive, naïve, incompetent or all of the above." The novel figures prominently on the American Library Association's list of books most frequently challenged in schools and libraries.

Here the attack on grounds of racism and "negative stereotypes" joins a more literary sort of objection to the last quarter of the book for reducing Jim to a prop for Tom Sawyer's boyish theatrical ingenuities.

Even Hemingway told readers, "The rest is just cheating." "The last 12 chapters are boring," Ms. Smiley writes, "a sure sign that an author has lost the battle between plot and theme and is just filling in the blanks." I don't disagree with this, but at the same time I'm happy to settle for any novel that, like *Huckleberry Finn,* may be only 75 percent great.

The Controversy over Gender and Sexuality: Are Twain's Sexual Politics Progressive, Regressive, or Beside the Point?

Few readers of *Huckleberry Finn* will be surprised that the novel's treatment of race and the merits of its ending have been objects of controversy. Both issues seem clearly to be "there" in the book: the race question is explicitly at the center of the story and the problem of the ending is equally conspicuous. By contrast, for many readers, the bearing of issues about gender and sexuality on *Huckleberry Finn* will seem far from obvious. For these readers, critics who focus on these issues will seem to be imposing an agenda on the book rather than following the agenda in the book; furthermore, these readers are also likely to claim that such critics are attempting to enlist Twain's book in the service of their own politics. The objections of these readers lead us to the following question: Will an effort to explore issues of gender and sexuality in *Huck Finn* inevitably force on the book concerns that are not actually in it?

We would like to offer several answers. First, *Huckleberry Finn* was considered the preeminent "boy's book" in American literature long before the emergence of feminist criticism or gay studies. To classify a text as a boy's book is implicitly to underscore the issue of gender. If gender was not considered an issue by early readers who called the novel a boy's book, this was only because the definition of what a boy is or should be was then assumed to be uncontroversial. The critic Steven

Mailloux has pointed out, however, that at the time of the novel's publication, the apparent rise of adolescent delinquency and rebellion had become a major concern of American social authorities. As Mailloux shows, many of the first reviewers of the novel read it as a contribution to this cultural discussion of the suddenly alarming problem of the "bad boy" (indeed, the early sentiment for banning the book reflected these alarms). Insofar as *Huckleberry Finn* addresses the question of what a true boy is — and much of the byplay between Huck and Tom represents an attempt to negotiate this question — it would seem that gender roles are very much "there" in the novel itself.

Second, separating what is obviously there in a text from what seems imposed by critics and readers is less easy than it first appears. Mailloux has noted that while the issue of race seems obviously there in *Huckleberry Finn* to readers today, earlier critics were curiously silent about it and seem not to have noticed it at all. For Twain's contemporaries — or at least the white readers and critics who responded publicly to the book — the just-mentioned problem of the "bad boy" evidently appeared far more central than the problem of race, which, presumably, in the eyes of these readers and critics, had been settled by the abolition of slavery twenty years before the novel's publication. It seems to have taken the civil rights struggles of the post–World War II era to condition readers of *Huckleberry Finn* to see the centrality of the racial theme to the novel. Was the race theme there in the 1880s and 1890s? Is the "bad boy" theme still there in the 1990s? Is one more "there" than the other?

Pointing to how drastically interpretations shift from one period to the next, some recent reader-response theorists (most notably Stanley Fish and Jane Tompkins) have argued that "thereness" is not determined by the text but rather by the interests that readers and critics bring to it. For these theorists, it makes no sense to speak of what is objectively "there" in the text itself or to try to distinguish it from what is "attributed to" the text by readers or what Fish calls "interpretive communities" of readers. According to this theory, the features we think we find or discover in texts are always in fact imposed on them by our perceiving apparatus — though the word *imposed* is misleading, since, if the text itself is never available to us independent of our interpretations of it, it does not exist to be imposed upon.

One does not have to go as far as these theorists, however, to acknowledge that what we notice in texts depends to some degree on what we have been trained to notice by our culture and education. If Twain's (white) contemporaries read *Huckleberry Finn* as a book about juvenile delinquency rather than a book about race, this presumably was not because race was absent from the book, but because their cultural mind-set did not dispose them to attend to its presence. In the same way, questions about gender and sexuality have arguably always been present in *Huckleberry Finn*, but it is only recently, with the rise of women's and gay movements, that our cultural lenses have prepared us to notice these aspects of the book.

Third, insofar as literature deals with the doings of men and women it is inevitably "about" gender and sexuality (just as it is inevitably "about" social class, psychology, religion, and an infinite number of other aspects of human behavior). When Macbeth and Lady Macbeth debate whether murdering King Duncan is a manly or unmanly thing to do, Shakespeare's play can be said to be opening the question of manliness for its audience. This is not to say that *Macbeth* is a feminist play (though some feminist critics have seen a critique of traditional ideas of masculinity in it), but only that, like other works that deal with the relations of the sexes, it invites gender analysis.

This conclusion touches on the second half of the "thereness" problem: the objection that reading *Macbeth* or *Huckleberry Finn* in such a way as to emphasize issues of gender involves a misdirection of the reader's proper attention in the interests of advancing the critic's political agenda. This is the charge that Frederick Crews here levels against Myra Jehlen's essay "Reading Gender in *Adventures of Huckleberry Finn*" (pp. 496–509 in this volume). Jehlen argues that the Judith Loftus scene, in which Huck masquerades as a girl and is caught out by Judith, works to dramatize the way in which conventional male and female identities are a product of nurture not nature. In "Walker versus Jehlen versus Twain" (pp. 509–16), Crews contends that Jehlen's essay is part of her own political agenda, not Twain's, and he contrasts what he regards as Jehlen's imposition of her politics on the book with Nancy Walker's recognition that there is a significant gap between her feminism and Twain's representation of women. (Walker's essay "Reformers and Young Maidens: Women and Virtue in *Adventures of Huckleberry Finn*" appears on pp. 476–96.) Crews's objections to Jehlen may seem incontrovertible to many readers, because it is hard to believe that the problematizing of gender roles could have been part of Mark Twain's purpose. However, as Martha Woodmansee points out in her "Response to Frederick Crews" (pp. 516–18), texts can have effects that are not part of the purpose for which they were designed. Woodmansee argues that though Crews may be right that questioning conventional gender roles was far from Twain's mind, the effect of the Judith Loftus scene is indeed to raise questions about how we tell boys from girls.

In "Come Back to the Raft Ag'in, Huck Honey!" (pp. 519–25), a similar range of issues is raised by Leslie Fiedler's famous claim that the bond between Huck and Jim on the raft in *Huckleberry Finn* suggests an unconsummated homosexual relationship or "chaste male love" (p. 521). This claim is part of a broader argument on Fiedler's part that much American literature harbors a "regressive" nostalgia, typical of the culture at large, in which American males long to recover the lost innocence of childhood. Noting that many celebrated American novels involve a friendship between a white male and a black or American Indian companion who is presented as close to nature in some way, Fiedler argues that this pattern expresses an unconscious desire on the part of American males to flee from the responsibilities of adult work and the entanglements embodied in relations with women. For Fiedler, Huck epitomizes this homoerotic escape pattern in his flight from women like Miss Watson and Aunt Sally who want to "sivilize" him.

Some of Fiedler's contemporaries reacted to his conclusions much as Crews has reacted to Jehlen. Irving Howe, in a review of *Love and Death in the American Novel*, writes:

> Indeed, [Fiedler's] strategy is not that of a literary man at all. He engages not in formal description or historical placement or critical evaluation but in a relentless and joyless exposure. The work of literature comes before him as if it were a defendant without defense, or an enemy intent upon deceiving him so that he will not see through its moral claims and coverings. And the duty of the critic then becomes to strip the American novel to a pitiful bareness and reveal it in all its genital inadequacy.
>
> Now this is a method that works at least as well with tenth-rate books as with masterpieces, and Fiedler is not less illuminating on *Charlotte Temple* than on *Huckleberry Finn*. It is a method that disregards the work as something "made," a construct of mind and imagination through the medium of language, requiring attention on its own terms and according to its own structure. A Twain or Melville or Hawthorne becomes a "case" at the mercy of his repressions while he, Leslie Fiedler, speaks with the assurance of maturity. . . .
>
> What matters about [many of Fiedler's claims] is not merely that they are inaccurate, absurd, or sensational, but that they have little to do with literature and even less with that scrupulous loyalty to a work of art which is the critic's primary obligation. (152–53)

Whereas Howe and some of Fiedler's other contemporaries found Fiedler's suggestion of homoeroticism in the novel so unconventional as to be farfetched, Christopher Looby, in his essay "'Innocent Homosexuality': The Fiedler Thesis in Retrospect" (pp. 526–41), maintains that Fiedler's argument does not go far enough in challenging conventional assumptions about homosexuality. Looby, who works in the emerging field of gay studies, credits Fiedler with a significant breakthrough in seeing and calling attention to the presence of a homosexual subtext in *Huckleberry Finn* long before such concerns had become permissible in literary criticism. Nevertheless, Looby complains that, for all its innovative courage, Fiedler's account remains tied to the assumption that heterosexuality alone is "normal" sexuality. Taking up phrases of Fiedler's like "innocent homosexuality" (which appears in another version of Fiedler's argument from the one reprinted here), Looby asks, "[i]nnocent, one wants to know, as opposed to what? The implication is that there is some other, 'guilty' form of homosexuality" (p. 529). In other words, Looby finds homophobic implications in the suggestion that homosexuality is perverse or deviant when it is "overt" instead of "chaste." Thus, for Looby, Fiedler's essay finally reflects and supports rather than challenges a system in which heterosexuality defines itself as normal by "stigmatizing the homosexual as deviant" (p. 532).

What, then, are we to make of the bond between Huck and Jim? Does it contain a homosexual aspect or not? Looby argues that the question itself assumes a twentieth-century distinction between heterosexual and homosexual behavior that was only beginning to rigidify in the late-nineteenth-century world of Mark Twain — or in the earlier period in which the novel is set. That is, the novel "requires us to suspend our modern social categories" and "try to imagine what it was like for these two outcasts to devote themselves to one another, having never heard that it mattered whether their love was 'innocent' or 'guilty'" (pp. 529–30) according to laws of heterosexual normality that had not yet been invented.

In answering our initial question by arguing that criticism attending to gender and sexuality in *Huckleberry Finn* does not automatically impose an alien political agenda on the text, we do not mean to resolve the particular controversies represented in the essays in this section. Instead, having pointed out the relevance of the general controversy to *Huckleberry Finn*, we now turn the particular controversies over to you: Has Jehlen, as Crews maintained, gone beyond the boundaries of what *Huckleberry Finn* can reasonably be said to be about? Or has Crews, as Woodmansee argues, posited a too narrow boundary for the novel's concerns? If you side with Woodmansee, will you accept or find fault with Crews's more positive assessment of Nancy Walker's feminist essay? If you side with Crews, will you find that both Fiedler and Looby are unconvincing? Or is Looby's historicizing of Twain's text actually bringing us closer to its representation of sexuality? Alternatively, are both Fiedler and Looby too tame in their readings, too constrained by some concern for Twain's probable intentions and not sufficiently open to the effects created by his representations?

WORKS CITED

Howe, Irving. *Celebrations and Attacks.* New York: Horizon, 1979.

Mailloux, Steven. *Rhetorical Power.* Ithaca: Cornell UP, 1989.

FURTHER READING IN THE CONTROVERSY

Crews, Frederick. *The Critics Bear It Away.* New York: Random, 1992.

Fetterley, Judith. *The Resisting Reader.* Bloomington: Indiana UP, 1979.

Sedgwick, Eve Kosofsky. *Epistemology of the Closet.* Berkeley: U of California P, 1990.

Showalter, Elaine, ed. *The New Feminist Criticism.* New York: Pantheon, 1985.

Skandera-Trombley, Laura E. *Mark Twain in the Company of Women.* Philadelphia: U of Pennsylvania P, 1994.

Warner, Michael, ed. *Fear of a Queer Planet.* Minneapolis: U of Minnesota P, 1993.

NANCY A. WALKER

Reformers and Young Maidens: Women and Virtue in *Adventures of Huckleberry Finn*

Nancy A. Walker (1942–2000) received her B.A. (1964) at Louisiana State University, her M.A. (1966) at Tulane University, and her Ph.D. (1971) at Kent State University. She taught at Stephens College before moving to Vanderbilt University in 1989, where she was professor of English and director of women's studies. Her books include *"A Very Serious Thing"*: *Women's Humor and American Culture* (1988) and *Feminist Alternatives: Irony and Fantasy in the Contemporary Novel by Women* (1991), which won the Eudora Welty Prize given jointly by the Mississippi University for Women and the University of Mississippi Press. Walker is also the author of *The Disobedient Writer: Women and Narrative Tradition* (1995), *Shaping Our Mothers' World: American Women's Magazines* (2000), and *Kate Chopin: A Literary Life* (2001). This essay first appeared in *One Hundred Years of "Huckleberry Finn"* (1985), edited by Robert Sattlemeyer and J. Donald Crowley.

Mark Twain considered it "another boy's book." The Concord, Massachusetts, public library, in 1885, regarded it as "the veriest trash."[1] Daniel G. Hoffman has called it "the most universal book to have come out of the United States of America."[2] The object of praise, banning, and veneration during the hundred years since its publication, *Adventures of Huckleberry Finn* has not commonly been considered a novel about women in nineteenth-century American society. Men occupy center stage in *Huck Finn;* women stand toward the back and sides of the novel, nagging, providing inspiration, often weeping or hysterical. Indeed, Twain's masterpiece would seem a likely reference point for Judith Fetterley's blunt statement: "American literature is male. To read the canon of what is currently considered classic American literature is perforce to identify as male. . . . Our literature neither leaves women alone nor allows them to participate."[3]

As one of several novels commonly thought to address the formation of American attitudes and values, and therefore a "classic" part of the American literary tradition, *Huck Finn* is indeed a "male" novel in several senses. The narrative voice, the specific angle of vision from which the events of the novel unfold, is that of a young boy. Moreover, as a deliberate bildungsroman, the novel traces the moral development of Huck Finn: the traditional passage of the young man from youthful innocence to maturity. Most significantly, the thematic core of the

---

[1]Reported in the *Boston Transcript*, 17 March 1885, reprinted in Thomas Asa Tenney, *Mark Twain: A Reference Guide* (Boston: G. K. Hall, 1977) 14.

[2]*Form and Fable in American Fiction* (Oxford University Press, 1961) 317.

[3]*The Resisting Reader: A Feminist Approach to American Fiction* (Bloomington: Indiana University Press, 1978) xii.

novel embodies a dream of escape to freedom that is both peculiarly American and identifiably masculine. Historically, the political and physical experiences of exploring and settling a wilderness have required a power to initiate and lead social movements that has commonly been granted to men rather than to women. In mythic terms, the typical American hero has, like Huck, resisted the "civilizing" efforts of women and has struck out boldly, often iconoclastically, for a new "territory." For Fetterley, as for other recent critics, the exploitation of the land has come to be seen as analogous to the suppression of women, who are traditionally regarded as both desirable and dangerous. In Fetterley's terms, "America is female; to be American is male; and the quintessential American experience is betrayal by a woman."[4]

Although it would not be accurate to say that Huck Finn is "betrayed" by a woman, Miss Watson's decision to sell Jim down the river — certainly a betrayal of Jim — sets the novel in motion. Were it not for the relationship between the slave and the boy, much of Twain's social commentary would be impossible, and Miss Watson's action allows their relationship to develop, making her a vital element of the plot. Nevertheless, for most readers, the significance of *Huck Finn* requires the male characters to occupy the foreground, leaving the female characters as part of the scenic backdrop. Virtually all readings of the novel, from Leslie Fiedler's assumption of a homosexual relationship between Huck and Jim[5] to discussions of the novel's roots in Southwestern humor,[6] reflect its origins in a male-dominated culture. Even the controversy about the role Tom Sawyer plays in the last seven chapters of the novel centers on the conflict between Tom's romantic swagger and Huck's tenuous moral supremacy: a boy's games versus adult responsibility.

Without detracting from the central role that Huck Finn plays in the novel that bears his name, it is possible to re-view *Huck Finn* as embodying a basic tension between male and female values and roles — a tension that bears directly on Huck's moral growth. Most of the female characters are derived from traditional — usually unflattering — stereotypes of women common to nineteenth-century authors and read-

---

[4]Ibid., xiii.

[5]"Come Back to the Raft Ag'in, Huck Honey!" *Partisan Review* 15 (1948): 664–71. (This article is reprinted on pp. 519–25 of this volume. — Eds.)

[6]See especially Walter Blair, *Mark Twain and Huck Finn* (Berkeley: University of California Press, 1960).

ers; indeed, the novel could serve as an index to common attitudes toward women as reflected in these stereotypical images. Those few women in the novel who are not merely stereotypes, such as Judith Loftus and Mary Jane Wilks, have more to do with Huck's development than is normally acknowledged. Finally, Huck's ambivalence about women — whom he tends to view as either nagging moralists or paragons of virtue — demonstrates the limited nature of his maturity by the end of the novel. The virtues that Huck begins to develop — honesty, compassion, a sense of duty — are identified in the novel as female virtues. Yet Huck's maleness requires that he ultimately emulate men, that he see women as "other"; and in the end he tries to run from the civilizing presence of women, unable to make the distinction between essential humanity and what society incorrectly considers virtue.

Discussions of Twain's male characters' attitudes toward or relationships with women seem inevitably to address the attitudes of Twain — or, rather, Samuel Clemens — toward women in his own life. Clemens's relationships with his mother, Jane Clemens, and with his wife, Olivia, particularly as they appear to be sources for the female characters in his works (and, in the case of Olivia, to be a "censor" of his work), have been the subject of much biographical and critical study. Although such an approach can invite a confusion of character and author, it may be useful to consider briefly Clemens's view of womanhood, since it is likely that, as the creation of a nineteenth-century male imagination, Huck mirrors some of Clemens's conceptions of the nature and role of women.

Mary Ellen Goad has defined the role that Clemens wished women to play in his own life in order to illuminate his creation of female characters. Goad contends that Twain created patterns of female behavior to which even the actual women in his life were expected to adhere, and that his fictional women were designed as models for the real women in his life:

> Twain viewed the role of the female in a particular, and, to the modern mind, strange way. He operated on the theory that the male of the species was rough and crude, and needed the softening and refining influence of a woman, or, if necessary, many women. The primary function of the women was thus reformation of man.[7]

[7]"The Image and the Woman in the Life and Writings of Mark Twain," *Emporia State Research Studies* 19:3 (March 1971) 5.

This view of woman as the reformer of inherently brutish man was not unique to Twain and had been enhanced by the Victorian insistence on female purity. Ann Douglas argues that between 1820 and 1875 middle-class women and Protestant ministers turned simultaneously to the promulgation of "the potentially matriarchal values of nurture, generosity, and acceptance."[8] Both groups felt powerless to exert influence in overt ways — women because of the removal of key economic activities from the household to the factory, and clergymen because of the legal disestablishment of the church — and therefore adopted the moral suasion of others as their sphere of influence. The fact that this position resulted in women remaining in a real sense powerless coincided with society's efforts to oppress them, according to Douglas, who states: "The cruelest aspect of the process of oppression is the logic by which it forces its objects to be oppressive in turn, to do the dirty work of their society in several senses."[9] The Victorian definition of woman's role as moral guide would account for such characters as Miss Watson and Aunt Sally, part of whose function is "civilizing" recalcitrant boys. In addition, the persistence of this figure in Twain's life and art is explained, Goad says, by the habit that Twain and some of his male characters had of not remaining long in a reformed state. "The business of reform became a game in which one made promises, then suffered periodic relapses, as a sort of recreation."[10]

When Goad discusses the female characters in Twain's work, however, she argues, as so many others have done, that they are merely flat and stereotypical — that in fact they represent one of Twain's failures as a writer. "Twain," she says, "was simply unable to create a female character, of whatever age, of whatever time and place, who is other than wooden and unrealistic." She continues:

> He had evolved over the years a narrow, specialized role for women, and although none of the women he knew fit the ideal, Twain continued to hold it in the abstract. Livy refused to become the narrow, moralizing, reforming shrew that Twain seemed to want, and it is no doubt well that she did, for Twain could not have lived with such a woman. When he was creating a female character in a work of fiction, however, Twain was not troubled by either a refusal to fit a role or the problem of living with someone

[8] *The Feminization of American Culture* (New York: Alfred A. Knopf, 1977) 10.
[9] Ibid., 11.
[10] Goad, "Image and Woman" 5.

who did fit the role. He could make a character do exactly what he wanted her to do, and what he wanted was an idealization.[11]

In *Huck Finn*, however, the relationship between Huck and women is more complex and dynamic than a simple response to idealized figures. Changes in our perceptions of the realities of women's lives during the last one hundred years allow us to see that, although Twain may have used idealizations of women as the basis for many of his female characters, those characters play a vital if underrated role in the society of which they are a part; although they may be perceived by the male characters only as occasions for rebellion or opportunities for heroic action, they represent both positive and negative values of that society. For all Twain's mockery of middle-class "respectability," without the real human virtues represented primarily by the women in *Huck Finn* there would be little opportunity for Huck to grow.

With few exceptions, the male characters in the novel are far from admirable by the standards of either conventional or actual morality. They tend to be degenerate, selfish, greedy, and vengeful and are just as stereotypical as are many of the female characters. Pap is an exaggerated version of the "natural man" on the frontier, an illiterate alcoholic such as inspired the temperance movement of the nineteenth century. Though a figure of broad comedy at times, he lives outside society's rules and rejects even its positive values, such as education. Huck's description of Pap in chapter 5 underscores his subhuman status:

> There warn't no color in his face, where his face showed; it was white; not like another man's white, but a white to make a body sick, a white to make a body's flesh crawl — a tree-toad white, a fish-belly white. (p. 46)

The Duke and the Dauphin are far more human; they are — initially, at least — rogues rather than bestial villains despite their dishonest schemes. Twain clearly admires their rascality; they are vehicles of satire rather than subjects of horror. Also satirically treated are the Grangerfords and the Shepherdsons, to whom a half-forgotten lawsuit and murder are sufficient to maintain a multigenerational feud. Though Huck describes Colonel Grangerford as a "gentleman all over" (p. 114), we are meant to see the irony of the term "gentle," and Huck is eventually

[11]Ibid., 56.

glad to leave his house. Similarly, Colonel Sherburn, for all his insight into the cowardice of a lynch mob, is the cold-blooded killer of the drunken Boggs.

Not all the men in the novel are this recklessly violent, but none except Jim exhibits maturity and virtue. Uncle Silas Phelps is the stereotype of the bumbling, absentminded man married to a woman with a tart tongue; the couple is in the tradition of Rip and Dame Van Winkle and Harriet Beecher Stowe's Sam Lawson and his wife. Tom Sawyer, the classic "bad boy," turns from youthful prankster early in the novel to cunning — if not malicious — torturer during the "freeing" of Jim at the end.

When Huck and Jim lie and steal, they do so to survive, and this behavior seems therefore excusable. Huck's numerous false identities and Jim's posing as a "sick A-rab" are ways of avoiding detection and thus contribute to rather than detract from the moral thrust of the novel. The same is true of their habit of stealing, or "borrowing," as Huck prefers to call it:

> Pap always said it warn't no harm to borrow things, if you was meaning to pay them back, sometime; but the widow said it warn't anything but a soft name for stealing, and no decent body would do it. Jim said he reckoned the widow was partly right and Pap was partly right. (p. 81)

Jim's morality thus mediates between the socially unacceptable element, represented by Pap, and the acceptable behavior represented by the widow. Because Jim and Huck steal food and other necessities, rather than the Wilks girls' inheritance, as do the Duke and the Dauphin, this habit, like lying, seems justified to the reader. Huck's most flagrant "sin" is helping a slave to escape, just as Jim's is running away from his owner; ironically, of course, these acts are in Twain's view their greatest moral triumphs, even though they are not sanctioned by the society Twain describes. Only Jim, among the male characters in the novel, exerts a positive influence on Huck. Jim's position outside white society allows him freedom from — if nothing else — both the moralizers and the rascals of that society, and he teaches Huck morality by example rather than by precept.

In contrast to the male characters in the novel, the female characters largely conform to what society — and Mark Twain — expects of them, and this conformity is the source of their often flat, stereotypical presence. Whether stern moralizers, like Miss Watson, or innocent young girls, like Boggs's daughter, the women have been molded by social pressure into representations of several kinds of womanly virtue. As members of the gender responsible for upholding the moral and religious values of civilization, even when those values sanction slave-owning, the women make possible the lawlessness and violence of the men. If we accept the fact that Twain saw men as naturally "rough and crude," then women were either reformers one could tease by temporarily conforming to their rules, or innocent maidens who could restore one's faith in decency and goodness.

Including the deceased Emmeline Grangerford, there are twelve women in *Huck Finn* aged fourteen or older. Of these, some are merely walk-on characters; for example, Emmeline's sisters, Charlotte and Sophia, and Mary Jane Wilks's sisters, Susan and Joanna. Sophia Grangerford, who Huck says is "gentle and sweet, like a dove" (p. 115), is one-half of the Romeo-and-Juliet couple whose elopement triggers a renewal of the feud between the Grangerfords and the Shepherdsons. Twain describes her as the stereotypical young woman in love, blushing and sighing and always "sweet." With Charlotte Grangerford and the younger Wilks sisters Huck has little to do, and Twain seems to use them all merely as parts of his portrait of Southern gentility.

The most obvious "reformers" in *Huck Finn* are the Widow Douglas, Miss Watson, and Aunt Sally Phelps. The widow and Miss Watson are Huck's unofficial guardians at the beginning of the novel; it is their insistence on prayers and clothes that makes Huck feel "all cramped up" (p. 32), and it is from Aunt Sally that Huck runs at the end, with his famous concluding statement, "But I reckon I got to light out for the Territory ahead of the rest, because Aunt Sally she's going to adopt me and sivilize me and I can't stand it. I been there before" (p. 263). Huck's comment that he's "been there before" points to the pattern of reform and backsliding that Goad discusses and suggests that, having escaped the clutches of the Widow Douglas and Miss Watson at the beginning of the novel, Huck has, at the end, endured another period of civilizing at the hands of Aunt Sally. The repetition of the pattern of reform and escape might lead one to believe that all these women are instances of the same stereotype, whereas in fact they represent three different popular images of women in the nineteenth century. There is no doubt that Twain had different models in mind when he created these three characters, and Huck's responses to them emphasize their differences.

The key to the differences among these three female reformers is their marital status. No matter how devoutly some women of the time clung to a state of "single blessedness," marriage was the only widely sanctioned state for an adult woman. American humor in the nine-teenth century is filled with satiric portraits of husband-hunting spin-sters and widows, and both humorous and serious literature describes the older single woman as straight-laced and narrow-minded. The nov-elist Marietta Holley, for example, has her persona, Samantha Allen, describe her spinster neighbor, Betsey Bobbet:

> She is awful opposed to wimmin's havein' any right only the right to get married. She holds on to that right as tight as any single woman I ever see which makes it hard and wearin' on the single men round here.[12]

Widows had a somewhat better time of it than spinsters in the public eye, as was pointed out by another female humorist, Helen Rowland: "Even a dead husband gives a widow some advantage over an old maid."[13] The spinster, presumed to be unwanted, is presumed also to have ossified. The image of the widow, at one time a wife and probably a mother, is somewhat softer; even as a "reformer," she has a kinder heart. The married woman, assumed to be in her proper element, pro-vides the most contented image of the three and thus is likely to be the mildest reformer of all. The three principal reformers in *Huck Finn* rep-resent each of these three states.

Walter Blair has suggested that the prototype for Miss Watson might have been a spinster schoolteacher who visited the Clemens fam-ily in Hannibal. Twain remembered this woman, Mary Ann Newcomb, as being a thin woman and a strict Calvinist.[14] Miss Watson has both of these qualities. Huck describes her as "a tolerable slim old maid, with goggles on" (p. 33), and she threatens Huck with hellfire for his sins. It is not surprising that when Huck, Tom, and the other boys are forming their gang, and Huck has no family to be killed if he reveals the gang's secrets, he offers to let them kill Miss Watson. Miss Watson is a constant nagging presence who is particularly concerned with Huck's manners and his education. It is she, Huck says, who "took a set at me . . . with a spelling-book" and "worked me middling hard for about an hour" (p. 33). She is eternally watchful of his demeanor: "Miss Watson would say, 'Dont put your feet up there, Huckleberry;' and 'dont scrunch up like that, Huckleberry — set up straight'" (p. 33). In the matter of reli-gion she seems to Huck prissy and sterile. The heaven she describes to

---

[12] *My Opinions and Betsey Bobbet's* (Hartford: American Publishing Co., 1872) 27.
[13] *Reflections of a Bachelor Girl* (New York: Dodge, 1909) 35.
[14] *Mark Twain and Huck Finn* 106.

him is unappealing: "She said all a body would have to do there was to go around all day long with a harp and sing, forever and ever. So I didn't think much of it" (p. 33). The subject of heaven is one of several on which Huck distinguishes between the Widow Douglas and Miss Watson:

> Sometimes the widow would take me one side and talk about Providence in a way to make a body's mouth water; but maybe next day Miss Watson would take hold and knock it all down again. I judged I could see that there was two Providences, and a poor chap would stand considerable show with the widow's Providence, but if Miss Watson's got him there warn't no help for him any more. (p. 40)

Dedicated to duty rather than pleasure in a life that apparently has given her little of the latter, Miss Watson imagines an afterlife inspired by her Calvinist background, one ill-suited to the imagination of an adolescent boy.

Although Huck resists Miss Watson's bleak vision, he recognizes that she merely wishes to make him a "good" person according to her definition of that concept, and Twain suggests that Huck understands that Miss Watson is filling a role determined for "old maids" in American society. Huck's offer to let the gang kill her if he betrays them may be read in two ways. On the one hand, she may be an expendable person in his world, but the gang members have specifically required that he have a "family" to kill, and, by naming Miss Watson, Huck suggests that he accepts her as such. More telling is the famous episode in chapter 31 in which Huck wrestles with his conscience about helping a slave to escape and ultimately decides that he will go to hell. Jim is Miss Watson's property, and the morality he has absorbed — partly from her — tells him he is stealing from her. As his argument with himself gradually builds from practical to humanistic considerations, he fears sending Jim back to Miss Watson because "she'd be mad and disgusted at [Jim's] rascality and ungratefulness for leaving her" (p. 199). When his "conscience" overtakes him, however, he agonizes about "stealing a poor old woman's nigger that hadn't ever done me no harm" (p. 199). Despite the syntax of the sentence, it is clear that Huck means that Miss Watson has "done [him] no harm." Although the reader can easily see the harm done by the spurious morality of people like Miss Watson, Huck merely sees her as a "poor old woman," as indeed she is.

Twain makes a clear distinction between Miss Watson and the Widow Douglas. The widow is a far more gentle reformer than her unmarried sister and often intercedes between Huck and Miss Watson to mitigate the latter's severity. Although Twain based the character of the widow on a popular nineteenth-century conception of widowhood, he omitted several of the least desirable characteristics of that image. The most negative presentation of the widow in American humor is Frances M. Whicher's Widow Bedott, a gossiping husband-hunter who was the pseudonymous author of sketches in *Neal's Saturday Gazette* in the 1840s. Despite her protestations to the contrary, she is always on the lookout for eligible men, whom she smothers with terrible poetry and home remedies.[15] Twain's notes about his immediate prototype for the Widow Douglas, Mrs. Richard Holiday, suggest that he originally regarded her as a target of similar satire:

> Well off. Hospitable. Fond of having young people. Old, but anxious to marry. Always consulting fortune-tellers; always managed to make them understand that she had been promised three husbands by the first fraud.[16]

Aside from the fondness for young people, the Widow Douglas is considerably modified from this model.

Huck does not resent or pity the widow as he does Miss Watson. He is quick to excuse her behavior toward him, as he does early in the first chapter: "The widow she cried over me, and called me a poor lost lamb, and she called me a lot of other names, too, but she never meant no harm by it" (p. 32). He finds her attitude toward tobacco hypocritical, but is more amused than angry:

> Pretty soon I wanted to smoke, and asked the widow to let me. But she wouldn't. She said it was a mean practice and wasn't clean, and I must try not to do it any more. . . . And she took snuff, too; of course that was all right, because she done it herself. (p. 33)

The widow's method of reforming is to request or explain rather than to scold or nag. Whereas Miss Watson's "pecking" makes Huck feel "tiresome and lonesome" (p. 34), he responds favorably to the widow's kind heart. When Huck stays out all night with Tom and the gang, the two women react quite differently:

---

[15] *The Widow Bedott Papers* (New York: J. D. Derby, 1856).
[16] Quoted in Blair, *Mark Twain and Huck Finn* 106.

> Well, I got a good going-over in the morning, from old Miss Watson, on account of my clothes; but the widow she didn't scold, but only cleaned off the grease and clay and looked so sorry that I thought I would behave a while if I could. (p. 39)

By chapter 4, Huck has become accustomed to being civilized. When he slips into his old habits, such as playing hooky from school, he welcomes the ensuing punishment: "the hiding I got next day done me good and cheered me up" (p. 43). He retains a fondness for his old life but is pleased by the widow's praise of his progress:

> I liked the old ways best, but I was getting so I liked the new ones, too, a little bit. The widow said I was coming along slow but sure, and doing very satisfactory. She said she warn't ashamed of me. (p. 43)

Huck's response to the Widow Douglas's kindness is important to understanding his later reaction to Jim's essential humanity. From the first pages of the novel, Twain presents Huck as a basically decent boy who is able to respond to loving discipline, and it seems likely that he altered the stereotype of the widow — removing her more laughable traits — in order to allow her to have a positive influence on Huck's moral development. Before Huck sets out on the raft with Jim, Miss Watson and the Widow Douglas are the only representatives of decency in his world. Despite her implicit approval of slavery, the widow has a coherent view of what Huck needs in order to be a "respectable" citizen — a view involving education, cleanliness, and Christian virtues. Were it not for the events that propel Huck into his trip down the river with Jim, he could grow up in the mold of the Horatio Alger hero. The other two major models for Huck's development at this point are Tom Sawyer and Pap; Tom, as the eternal child, would have Huck remain irresponsible and unrealistic, and Pap, in his complete rejection of society's rules and forms, would have him descend into barbarism. It is, after all, from Pap and not from the Widow Douglas that Huck flees in chapter 7.

The most important lesson that Huck learns from the widow is that it is possible — even desirable — to place another human being's welfare before one's own. Not only has the widow taken the unpromising Huck into her home; she has also demonstrated that she cares about him, that his escapades make her not so much angry as sad. When Huck responds favorably to the widow's efforts to alter his behavior and values, he does so because he realizes his actions have an effect on others.

It is this same principle that motivates Huck's final decision to help Jim escape regardless of the consequences for himself. As he is struggling with his conscience, he recalls first the good times he and Jim have had, then the favors Jim has done for him, and finally "the time I saved him by telling the men we had small-pox aboard, and he was so grateful, and said I was the best friend old Jim ever had in the world, and the *only* one he's got now" (pp. 200–01). In his realization of his responsibility for another human being, Huck builds upon the example the widow has set for him; in fact, he surpasses the widow in moral integrity by recognizing a black man as a fellow human being.

Yet Huck's experiences with the third "reforming woman," Aunt Sally Phelps, show the limits of his maturation. The effectiveness of the final chapters of *Huck Finn* has been debated for decades. Those critics who find Huck's acquiescence to Tom's romantic game-playing disturbing in light of his previous maturation on the river probably have the stronger argument, and this objection is strengthened by the presence of Aunt Sally. If Huck ever needs a reformer, it is during the torture of Jim in these final chapters, but Aunt Sally, because of the particular stereotype upon which she is based, is an ineffectual reformer, though reforming is clearly her function.

Aunt Sally and Uncle Silas are a familiar pair in American humor: the harmless nag and the befuddled husband. Aunt Sally is a warm, gregarious woman who whirls around the still center of Uncle Silas. Hers is far from the strict, staid demeanor of Miss Watson; though Uncle Silas is a part-time preacher, Aunt Sally is untouched by the Calvinist gloom that characterizes Miss Watson's outlook. Apparently happily married to the good-hearted Silas, and the mother of several children, she has a far sunnier disposition than the Widow Douglas and is more likely to be understanding of youthful pranks. When Tom Sawyer kisses her while she still thinks he is the stranger William Thompson, she calls him an "owdacious puppy" and a "born fool," but once she thinks he is Sid Sawyer, she enjoys the joke: "I don't mind the terms — I'd be willing to stand a thousand such jokes to have you here" (p. 213).

But when Huck and Tom — disguised as Tom and Sid — embark on the activities that Tom feels appropriate to freeing a prisoner and begin stealing sheets and spoons and filling the Phelps house with rats and snakes, Aunt Sally shows her temper. Twain's gift for comic exaggeration is nowhere more apparent than in some of these slapstick scenes, and the descriptions of Aunt Sally are strikingly similar to those of Livy, his own "reforming woman," that he included in letters to friends and relatives early in their marriage. In February 1870 he wrote:

But there is no romance in this existence for Livy. She embodies the Practical, the Hard, the Practical, the Unsentimental. She is lord of all she surveys. She goes around with her bunch of house-keeper's keys (which she don't know how to unlock anything with them because they are mixed,) & is overbearing & perfectly happy, when things don't go right she breaks the furniture & knocks everything endways. You ought to see her charge around. When I hear her war whoop I know it is time to climb out on the roof.[17]

Just as the dignified Livy becomes a comic figure in such descriptions, so Aunt Sally becomes comic and nonthreatening even as she attempts to discipline Huck and Tom. To cover their theft of a spoon, the two boys confuse Aunt Sally as she attempts to count:

Well, she *was* in a tearing way — just a trembling all over, she was so mad. But she counted and counted, till she got that addled she'd start to count-in the *basket* for a spoon, sometimes; and so, three times they come out right, and three times they come out wrong. Then she grabbed up the basket and slammed it across the house and knocked the cat galley-west; and she said cle'r out and let her have some peace, and if we come bothering around her again betwixt that and dinner, she'd skin us. (p. 233)

Most of the time Aunt Sally's threats are idle, but even when she punishes the boys it has little effect. When the snakes they have collected to put in Jim's cabin get loose in the house, Aunt Sally takes action:

We got a licking every time one of our snakes come in her way; and she allowed these lickings warn't nothing to what she would do if we ever loaded up the place again with them. I didn't mind the lickings, because they didn't amount to nothing; but I minded the trouble we had, to lay in another lot. (p. 242)

Huck's response to Aunt Sally's discipline is to ignore it — it "didn't amount to nothing" — whereas his reaction to the Widow Douglas's disappointment in his backsliding early in the novel had been to try to "behave a while" if he could. The widow touched Huck's humanity; Aunt Sally merely touches his backside with a hickory switch.

It is difficult, therefore, to take seriously Huck's fear of being "sivi-lized" by Aunt Sally at the end of the novel. Not a true "reformer," she

[17]Dixon Wecter, ed., *Mark Twain to Mrs. Fairbanks* (San Marino, CA: Huntington Library, 1949) 123.

is a harmless comic figure similar to the Livy of Clemens's letters. Given Twain's insistence on the conflict between Huck's innocence and the corruption of civilization, it is important that Huck thinks he can escape at the end and that the reader knows he cannot — knows, that is, that the "Territory" is simply another civilization. But it seems odd to posit Aunt Sally as a major representative of civilization — instead of, say, Miss Watson or the Widow Douglas — unless we understand that Twain's view of women as the reformers of young men was a product of his own youthful fantasy, formed in part by the Victorian culture in which he lived. In attempting to claim legitimate — if ultimately ineffectual — authority and self-esteem in a society that had made them powerless, Victorian women willingly acceded to a "cult of motherhood," which, as Ann Douglas points out, "was nearly as sacred in mid-nineteenth-century America as the belief in some version of democracy." Douglas quotes Lydia Sigourney, who, writing to young mothers in 1838, urged them to realize their potential influence on their children: "How entire and perfect is this dominion over the unformed character of your infant. . . . Now you have over a new-born immortal almost that degree of power which the mind exercises over the body."[18] All three of the women who attempt to make Huck conform to society's rules are derived from traditional stereotypes of women who may superficially be seen as mother figures from the same societal mold; but Huck's more complex and ambivalent relationships with them point up the different social realities they represent and his own boyish immaturity at the end of the novel. The fact that Huck can ignore Aunt Sally's female authority testifies to both his own lack of significant maturity and Mark Twain's awareness of the final ineffectuality of women in his society.

What growth Huck does achieve comes largely from his perception of qualities in others that he wishes to assume himself. With the exception of Jim, all of Huck's important models of decent human behavior are female. Though the "goodness" of both the reforming older women and the young girls in the novel is exaggerated for comic or satiric effect, several of the women display qualities that Huck begins to adopt as his character develops before the final chapters. In addition to the Widow Douglas, whose kindness and sincerity are apparent to Huck even as he chafes at the restrictions of his life with her, Mrs. Judith Loftus and Mary Jane Wilks are important influences on his self-

[18]Douglas, *Feminization* 74–75.

definition. Both characters are more than mere stereotypes, and both demonstrate intelligence and courage that Huck does not find in most of the men he knows.

Mrs. Loftus, whom Huck encounters just before he and Jim begin their trip on the raft, is the shrewd, garrulous woman who sees through Huck's disguise as a girl. She shares with common stereotypes of women a love of gossip, but it is her common sense and kindness to which Huck responds. In terms of her age, Mrs. Loftus belongs to the category of "reforming" women; Huck thinks she is "about forty year old" (p. 74). But her advice at this point in the novel (unlike the moralizing of Miss Watson and the Widow Douglas) is the practical sort that Huck needs for survival, and Huck perceives her as strong and intelligent. His clumsy efforts to thread a needle and catch a lump of lead in his lap call forth Mrs. Loftus's scorn, but Twain also emphasizes her kindly attitude toward the boy she assumes to be a runaway apprentice:

> I ain't going to hurt you, and I ain't going to tell on you, nuther. You just tell me your secret, and trust me. I'll keep it; and what's more, I'll help you. . . . Bless you, child, I wouldn't tell on you. (p. 78)

Huck cautiously responds with another lie about his identity, but he is clearly impressed with Mrs. Loftus's perspicacity. When he returns to the raft and reports on his conversation with Judith Loftus, Jim says she is a "smart one" (p. 81).

More importantly, Mrs. Loftus confirms Huck in his maleness early in the novel. Not only does she quickly see through Huck's female disguise; she also outlines for him the male behavior that has betrayed him:

> Bless you, child, when you set out to thread a needle, don't hold the thread still and fetch the needle up to it; hold the needle still and poke the thread at it — that's the way a woman most always does; but a man always does 'tother way. And when you throw at a rat or anything, hitch yourself up a tip-toe, and fetch your hand up over your head as awkard as you can, and miss your rat about six or seven foot. . . . And mind you, when a girl tries to catch anything in her lap, she throws her knees apart; she don't clap them together, the way you did when you catched the lump of lead. (p. 80)

Instead of following Mrs. Loftus's advice, Huck never again pretends to be a girl. He rejects his female disguise after he leaves the Loftus house by taking off his sunbonnet, "for I didn't want no blinders on" (p. 80).

A few paragraphs later, at the end of chapter 11, he joins his fortunes to those of Jim when he says, "There ain't a minute to lose. They're after us!" (p. 82). The male identification forecasts the American male adventure, at the end of which Huck will assume Tom Sawyer's identity and his behavior.

Later in the novel, in anticipation of Huck's final capitulation to Tom's boyish romanticism, comes Huck's rescue of the "damsel in distress," Mary Jane Wilks. Huck's response to Mary Jane is not merely that of the gallant knight to the damsel, however; he is at this point (chs. 24–30) still on his way to the real moral stature he will achieve in chapter 31, and Mary Jane is more complex than the traditional damsel. Twain makes her simultaneously weak and strong, so that she in some ways embodies the paradox that Ann Douglas points to in Victorian women who "lived out a display of competence while they talked and wrote of the beauties of incompetence."[19] Though Mary Jane in part matches the sentimental stereotype of the pure, innocent young woman, Huck's view of her includes admiration as well as protectiveness. She combines the piety of the older reforming woman with the absolute innocence of the ideal young girl, but it is finally her intelligence and courage that Huck finds most appealing.

Twain was apparently fascinated with young girls, and he idealized them in both his life and his art. His deep attachment to his daughter Susy and his intense interest in Joan of Arc are only two examples among many of this preoccupation, and portraits of young female characters in his fiction are often suffused with reverence for their beauty and spotless virtue. Albert E. Stone, Jr., explores Twain's devotion to "young maidens, hovering on the edge of adult experience," and quotes from a fragment that Twain wrote in 1898, describing a recurrent dream of adolescent love:

> She was always fifteen, and looked it and acted it; and I was always seventeen, and never felt a day older. To me she is a real person not a fiction, and her sweet and innocent society has been one of the prettiest and pleasantest experiences of my life.[20]

Most of the young girls in *Huck Finn* are versions of this romantic ideal, including such minor figures as Boggs's daughter, glimpsed

---

[19]Ibid., 93.

[20]*The Innocent Eye: Childhood in Mark Twain's Imagination* (New Haven: Archon Books, 1970) 207–09.

grieving over her father's body: "She was about sixteen, and very sweet and gentle-looking, but awful pale and scared" (p. 145). Here an object of pity, the young girl can also be an object of satire, as in the well-known portrait of Emmeline Grangerford. Apparently modeled on Julia A. Moore, a sentimental poet known as the "Sweet Singer of Michigan,"[21] Emmeline represents the common stereotype of the morbid female poet, and Twain uses her to satirize sentimental art and the execrable taste of the Grangerford family.

However, it is precisely for her *lack* of sentimentality that Huck admires Mary Jane Wilks. At nineteen, she is the oldest of the three Wilks sisters, undoubtedly older than Huck. The only drawback to her beauty is her red hair, but Huck forgives that: "Mary Jane *was* red-headed, but that don't make no difference, she was most awful beautiful, and her face and her eyes was all lit up like glory" (p. 160). Mary Jane is indeed innocent and trusting. She gives the inheritance money to the Duke and the Dauphin to prove her faith in them and defends Huck when her younger sister accuses him — accurately — of lying:

> "It don't make no difference what he *said* — that ain't the thing. The thing is for you to treat him *kind,* and not be saying things to make him remember he ain't in his own country and amongst his own folks."
> I says to myself, *this* is a girl that I'm letting that old reptle rob her of her money! (p. 170)

Mary Jane's goodness bothers Huck's conscience sufficiently that he decides to foil the Duke and Dauphin's scheme by recovering and hiding the money, but he does not tell her what he has done until he realizes that she is upset about the slave family being broken up. In his effort to comfort her, Huck inadvertently tells her the truth, and in a passage that closely prefigures his later decision to help Jim escape, he wrestles with the necessity for truth, still in Mary Jane's presence:

> she set there, very impatient and excited, and handsome, but looking kind of happy and eased-up, like a person that's had a tooth pulled out. So I went to studying it out. I says to myself, I reckon a body that ups and tells the truth when he is in a tight place, is taking considerable many resks, . . . and yet here's a case where

---

[21]See L. W. Michaelson, "Four Emmeline Grangerfords," *Mark Twain Journal* 11 (1961): 10–12.

I'm blest if it don't look to me like the truth is better, and actuly *safer*, than a lie. (p. 179)

The passage describing Huck's parting with Mary Jane in chapter 28 marks the penultimate step in the moral development that culminates in his decision to risk his soul to help Jim. He is impressed by her willingness to go along with his plan to save the girls' inheritance — a plan that, though involving lies and deceptions, is a model of decency compared with Tom's plan to free Jim — and particularly by her offer to pray for him. Contrasting his sinful nature to her goodness, he thinks:

> Pray for me! I reckoned if she knowed me she'd take a job that was more nearer her size. But I bet she done it, just the same — she was just that kind. She had the grit to pray for Judas if she took the notion — there warn't no backdown to her, I judge.
> (p. 183)

By putting himself in a category with Judas and emphasizing Mary Jane's virtues, Huck is playing a game with his reformer: Though drawn to the innocence and purity she represents, he simultaneously insists on his unregenerate nature. Mary Jane represents the female principle of virtue, always coupled with beauty. "And when it comes to beauty," Huck says, "and goodness too — she lays over them all" (p. 183). Huck, on the other hand, is the sinful male, unworthy of but longing for the redeeming power of the woman.

However, Huck is not merely playing a game at this point. His praise of Mary Jane Wilks is couched in terms that show he has an adolescent crush on her. She has, he says, "more sand in her than any girl I ever see," and though she disappears from his life at this point, Huck's memory of her testifies to her effect on his values: "I reckon I've thought of her a many and a many a million times, and of her saying she would pray for me; and if ever I'd a thought it would do any good for me to pray for *her*, blamed if I wouldn't a done it or bust" (p. 183). Twain combines here the terms of a boy's admiration — "grit" and "sand" — and the desire to help another person that marks the maturing human being. Given Huck's uncomfortable relationship with religion, his willingness to pray for Mary Jane Wilks is a true gift of love. Huck's feelings for Mary Jane and Twain's depiction of her strength and determination raise her above the level of stereotype and allow her, like other women in the novel, to be a significant influence on Huck's developing conscience. His offer to pray for her if it "would do any good" suggests that the idea of self-sacrifice is becoming natural to him and prepares for his ultimate "sacrifice" of his own soul to help Jim. A close look at the part women play in Huck Finn's life thus makes clearer the extent of his moral regression at the end of the novel. In his relationships with his principal female mentors — the Widow Douglas, Judith Loftus, and Mary Jane Wilks — he has achieved an appreciation of those virtues that begin to separate him from the hypocrisy and violence of the society in which he lives. But his contact with these women has also confirmed that he is in fact male and must remove himself from what he perceives as a "female" world of conformity to certain standards of behavior. With the Widow Douglas and Miss Watson he plays the part of the unruly boy; with Judith Loftus he tries to be a girl and fails; and with Mary Jane Wilks he assumes the role of the male protector of female innocence. Finally, with Jim, he arrives at a mature friendship with another man, one for whom he is prepared to risk eternal damnation. But his acquiescence to the adolescent behavior of Tom Sawyer in the final chapters demonstrates just how tenuous and fragile his maturity has been, and his desire to "light out for the Territory" is youthful escapism rather than a mature rejection of a corrupt society.

Twain's use of nineteenth-century stereotypes of women as the basis of his female characters in *Huck Finn* allows the reader to understand some of the ways a male-dominated culture perceived woman's place and function. Both the men and the women in the novel illustrate the values of a society that has little regard for human dignity, but the female characters also embody virtues that could redeem that society if the women were empowered to do so. The male characters, even the rascals and thieves, are allowed the freedom to accept or reject these values, whereas the women, as members of a subservient group, are obliged to preserve and transmit them. Whether as innocent young girls or as middle-aged reforming women, the female characters are for the most part creations of a male imagination that requires them to inspire men with their goodness or "save" them from their undesirable tendencies. Huck is both inspired and "saved" or "sivilized" in the course of the novel, but finally he exercises the male prerogative of rejection — not of the values of his society, but of the "female" virtues he has struggled so hard to attain. By accepting the limited roles for women that his culture promoted, Twain effectively limits the extent to which Huck Finn can be a moral force in his society. Though they are frequently inspirational or influential, the women in *Huck Finn*, viewed from the male perspective of the novel, are finally powerless — as Aunt

Sally Phelps demonstrates — to change the adolescent dreams of the American male.

MYRA JEHLEN

Reading Gender in
Adventures of Huckleberry Finn

Myra Jehlen (b. 1940) is professor of English at Rutgers University, where she holds the Board of Governors Chair of Literatures. She earned her B.A. (1961) from the City College of New York and her Ph.D. (1968) from the University of California, Berkeley, and began her career as a teacher and scholar at New York University in 1966. She moved to Columbia University in 1968, and then to the State University of New York at Purchase, where she was promoted to associate professor and professor. Jehlen taught at Rutgers from 1985 to 1989 and moved to the University of Pennsylvania in 1989, where she spent several years before returning to Rutgers. A very active and visible scholar, Jehlen has received fellowships from the National Endowment for the Humanities, the Woodrow Wilson Institute, and the Guggenheim Foundation. Her books include *Class and Character in Faulkner's South* (1976), *American Incarnation: The Individual, the Nation, and the Continent* (1986), and *Readings at the Edge of Literature* (2002). She has also contributed a major section to volume 1 of the five-volume *Cambridge History of American Literature*. This essay first appeared in *Critical Terms for Literary Study* (1990), edited by Frank Lentricchia and Thomas McLaughlin.

Like Molière's bourgeois gentleman who discovered one day that all the time he thought he was only talking he was in fact speaking prose, literary critics have recently recognized that in their most ordinary expositions of character, plot, and style they speak the language of gender.[1]

---

[1]Webster's *New World Dictionary,* second college edition (New York: World, 1968), defines gender as follows: "The formal classification by which nouns and pronouns (and often accompanying modifiers) are grouped and inflected, or changed in form, so as to

The terms of critical analysis, its references and allusions, its very structure, these critics now find, incorporate assumptions about the nature of sexual identity that organize and even suggest critical perception. When we describe certain verse cadences as "virile" while naming some rhymes "feminine," when Boswell explains judiciously that "Johnson's language . . . must be allowed to be too masculine for the delicate gentleness of female writing," the conventional meanings of "masculine" and "feminine" shape the sense of literary phenomena that have no intrinsic association with sex. Posited as analytical terms rather than the objects of analysis, these meanings go unexamined and with them aspects of literature that they seem to explain but actually only name. It would not have occurred to Boswell to reverse the direction of his definition and, instead of invoking the conventional attributes of masculinity to define the limits of Johnson's language, cite Johnson's language to define the limits of conventional masculinity. But just such a reversal has been going on in recent critical practice where literary analysis is reflexively querying its own sexual rhetoric. The terms "masculine" and "feminine," which the eighteenth-century biographer assumed were standard measures, have become for twentieth-century readers the first objects of critical measurement.

Boswell taking masculinity as a given expressed a traditional conviction that the differences between men and women arise from natural causes to organize the cultural order. Himself "too masculine . . . [for] female writing," Johnson declared women in turn too feminine for masculine pursuits; "'Sir,'" he famously addressed Boswell, "'a woman's preaching is like a dog's walking on his hinder legs. It is not done well; but you are surprized to find it done at all'" (Boswell, 327).

Perhaps because upright dogs remain relatively rare while more and more women are taking the podium, Johnson's view that the appurtenances of sex are as distinct as those of species and as surely rooted in biology has lately had to be rethought. The insurgent view that gender

---

control certain syntactic relationships: although gender is not a formal feature of English, some nouns and the third person singular pronouns are distinguished according to sex or the lack of sex (*man* or *he,* masculine gender; *woman* or *she,* feminine gender; *door* or *it,* neuter gender): in most Indo-European languages and in others, gender is not necessarily correlated with sex." This last specification underlies the choice of "gender" over "sex" as the critical term that designates sexual identity and its associated characteristics. For as the discussion below will explain, the argument implicit in analyzing literature from a "gender" perspective is that sexual identity is not "necessarily correlated with sex"; in other words, that biological sex does not directly or even at all generate the characteristics conventionally associated with it. Culture, society, history define gender, not nature.

is a cultural idea rather than a biological fact shares the ground that it has been gaining with parallel arguments about other identities — of class, of race, of national or religious association. Denaturalizing the character of women is part of a larger denaturalization of all the categories of human character, which emerges as both a social and a linguistic construction.

Implicating literature in the making of society has a reciprocal implication *for* literature. If gender is a matter of nurture and not nature, the character conventionally assigned men and women in novels reflects history and culture rather than nature, and novels, poems, and plays are neither timeless nor transcendent. This reciprocal historicizing extends to criticism which comes to read in the character of Hamlet, say, instead of a portrait of universal manhood, let alone of universal humanity, an exceptionally resonant but still particular depiction of aristocratic young manhood in Renaissance England (featuring among other characteristic attitudes, the assumption that young men of the dominant class are universally representative). If literature speaks gender, along with class and race, the critic has to read culture and ideology. It turns out that all the time writers and critics thought they were just creating and explicating transcendingly in a separate artistic language, willy nilly they were speaking the contemporary cultural wisdom.

Not all critics have been as delighted as Molière's Monsieur Jourdain to learn that the way of speaking they took for granted constituted a statement in itself. The aspiring bourgeois thought his conversation much enhanced by its participation in the ambient culture, but some critics fear that talk of gender, as of class and race, will rather diminish literature. They worry that reading literature in relation to society will, by rendering literature's meaning more particular, reduce it *to* the particular. But it is possible to argue just the opposite, that uncovering the social and cultural assumptions of literary language actually complicates reading. For when we take fictional characters to be universal, they subsume the particular traits and attributes of different kinds of people — as a character like Hamlet does when he is taken as embodying the general human condition. Ironically such transcendent characterization works reductively to submerge the complexities of human difference; while in order to explicate the particular, a critic needs to focus precisely on distinctions and qualifications, on the complexities of human difference. Against the fantasy of transcendence, a criticism conscious of literature's and its own sexual politics affirms the permanent complexity of engagements and interactions.

This should suggest what it is useful nonetheless to say explicitly: that speaking of gender does not mean speaking only of women. As a critical term "gender" invokes women only insofar as in its absence they are essentially invisible. And it brings them up not only for their own interest but to signal the sexed nature of men as well, and beyond that the way the sexed nature of both women and men is not natural but cultural. In this sense, gender may be opposed to sex as culture is to nature so that its relation to sexual nature is unknown and probably unknowable: How, after all, do we speak of human beings outside of culture? From the perspective of gender, identity is a role, character traits are not autonomous qualities but functions and ways of relating. Actions define actors rather than vice versa. Connoting history and not nature, gender is *not* a category of human nature.

Uncovering the contingencies of gender at the heart of even the most apparently universal writing has been a way of challenging the view that men embody the transcendent human norm, a view to which the first objection was that it was unjust to women. But in proposing gender as a basic problem and an essential category in cultural and historical analysis, feminists have recast the issue of women's relative identity as equally an issue for men, who, upon ceasing to be mankind, become, precisely, men. Thus gender has emerged as a problem that is always implicit in any work. It is a quality of the literary voice hitherto masked by the static of common assumptions. And as a critical category gender is an additional lens, or a way of lifting the curtain to an unseen recess of the self and of society. Simply put, the perspective of gender enhances the critical senses; let us try to see how.

Adventures of Huckleberry Finn is a man's book about a boy, and just as likely an object of gender criticism as writing by or about women. Mark Twain's best-known work is a classic or . . . canonical text. This story of an adolescent who undergoes a series of trials on the rocky road or the river voyage to adulthood is a central work in the American tradition, a work that articulates and helps define dominant values and ways of seeing the world. Such works and their central characters claim to represent the universal human condition. So one prevailing critical view that *Huckleberry Finn* is "a great book" because it champions "the autonomy of the individual" (Smith 1958, xxix), assumes that "the individual" is generically a self-sufficient being able to define himself autonomously, meaning apart from society. Note that in the preceding sentence one could not substitute "herself" and "her" nor indicate that the representative individual is black or Asian because specifying an alternative and subcategorical sex or race invokes limits on individual autonomy. On the other hand, not to specify alternative categories of identity subsumes them in the white male norm, when it does not exclude them from it altogether. Huck's individuality transcends all the particularities of his class and generation.

A little like Hamlet, except that Huck is no prince but in fact the antithesis of a prince, occupying the very bottom rung of his social ladder. It has been suggested that in Hannibal society Huck ranks below the slaves, who at least play a useful role in the community, whereas "poor white trash" like him are at best useless and most times a nuisance. The son of the town drunk, almost illiterate, dirt-poor, and innocent of ambition for either education, property, or shoes, Huck seems to lack all conventional worth, but this only makes him the better embodiment of individual values. For Huck's missing social attributes and graces dramatize his separation from society and make him an emblem of individualism. Huck personally transcends his abjection (as Hamlet, the unsuccessful prince, his loftiness). From the beginning of the story, he is headed out. He starts by leaving the home of the Widow Douglas and the village itself. This places him on the threshold of more radical departures, as Huck opposes his universal principles to the fundamental tenets of both his class and his race. He achieves heroism by renouncing genteel hypocrisies as Hamlet does by denouncing the rot at the Danish court.

For all its systematic extraction of its hero from social categories and roles, however, the novel actually reaffirms one category and role, paradoxically appropriating its terms to depict transcendence. By rejecting the false values of his society, Huck eventually becomes a man of integrity; and whatever else in our culture defines a man's integrity, not being feminine, being un- and even antifeminine is key. In fact Huck's first passage, once he leaves village society, takes him into a limbo of gender.

Huck's voyage out begins on the island in the middle of the Mississippi where he comes upon the runaway Jim. Having joined forces, the outcast boy and the escaped slave deem it prudent before proceeding with their journey to freedom to see whether they are being pursued. Huck will have to return to the shore to reconnoiter and, to avoid being recognized, he will need a disguise. A deep bonnet such as is worn by local girls seems ideal for the purpose. Dressed therefore in bonnet and gown, Huck sets off, concentrating hard on remembering that he is a girl. Fortunately the first house he comes to is inhabited by a stranger in town, a middle-aged woman to whom, introducing himself as Sarah Williams, he spins a tale about a sick mother for whom he is seeking help. As they sit comfortably chatting, the woman mentions that the entire neighborhood is astir with rumors about Huck Finn's disappearance and probable murder. At first, she reports, everyone assumed that the murderer was the runaway Jim but now folks are inclined to believe that it was Huck's own "white-trash" father, who has also disappeared. Still, a reward of $300 has been posted for the slave's capture and the woman herself has great hopes of earning it; for she has seen smoke rising on the island where in fact Huck and Jim are camping, and that very evening her husband is to row out there.

Agitated by this ominous news, Huck cannot keep still and, as an occupation appropriate to his disguise, attempts to thread a needle. His hostess, who is named Judith Loftus, watches his maneuvers with astonishment and a short time later, on the pretext that she has hurt her arm, asks him to throw a lead weight at a rat that has been poking its nose out of a hole in the wall. Naturally Huck throws brilliantly, where-upon she retrieves the weight and tosses it to the seated boy who claps his knees together to catch it. With this, Mrs. Loftus announces tri-umphantly that she has not been fooled: He is not a girl but a boy apprentice run away from his abusive master. Huck breaks down and confesses to this new identity and, giving him much good advice, Mrs. Loftus sends him on his way. In a panic, he hastens to the island, and arriving, calls out to Jim to hurry, they have to get off at once: " 'There ain't a minute to lose. They're after us!' " (p. 80).

This last exclamation deserves all the critical attention it has received. "They" Huck cries to Jim are "after us," but of course "they" are only after Jim. Indeed, in racial and even class terms, "they" include Huck, who at that moment disengages from all his kind to identify with a black man and a slave. Earlier, hearing about the magnificent sum to be had for turning Jim in, Huck was so far from being tempted that Judith Loftus had to explain to him that although her neighbors no longer thought the slave was a murderer, the money was incentive enough to continue the chase. " 'Well, you're innocent, ain't you!' " (p. 76) she teases Huck who at this moment has become literally inno-cent, redeeming himself in these passages from sins of racism and of greed.

This episode culminates Huck's moral and political ascension; he will not rise higher in the rest of the novel but rather slide back. There is an archetypal, typological dimension in this situation of a boy discard-ing his given identity and recreating himself more just and good. But what is the role in all this of the feminine disguise? Why and to what effect does Huck pass through the crisis of rejecting his born identity dressed as a girl?

We should note first that the plot does not require this costume. Since Mark Twain makes Judith Loftus a stranger, there is no reason why Huck cannot pretend to be a runaway apprentice in the first place. One explanation could be that turning Huck into a girl gives Twain the opportunity to ridicule femininity — something he does intermittently throughout the novel, making fun for instance of female sentimentality in the tear-filled story of Emmeline Grangerford, young poetess, deceased. But if this was the inspiration for the masquerade, it effectively backfired. For the ridiculous figure in the Loftus kitchen is Huck himself, while in lecturing him on his ineptitude in impersonating the feminine, Judith effects a temporary but nonetheless radical reversal of the very nature of gender. What should have been Huck's saving grace, that he is too boylike to imitate a girl successfully, cannot redeem his discomfiture; when Mrs. Loftus dispatches him at the end of the scene she is clearly skeptical about his ability to get on even in masculine guise: "If you get into trouble you send word" she offers, "and I'll do what I can to get you out of it" (p. 80). On the strength of this short-lived turnabout, womanhood even develops a maternal aspect all but unknown in the rest of Mark Twain's writings. "Keep the river road, . . . and next time you tramp, take shoes and socks with you" (p. 80) must sound an unaccustomed note to a boy whose experience runs more commonly to scolding aunts than to nurturing mothers.

The motherly Judith Loftus is in command of the scene and of Huck; but most unexpectedly, she is in command of herself, making this explicit when she takes command of femininity itself. In explaining how she has penetrated Huck's disguise, through his inept rendering of girlness, she analyzes feminine behavior as if from outside, herself standing apart as much "the individual" as Huck is when he stands apart from his "white-trash" ignorance, or Jim, briefly, from his "black" superstition. For the interval from that speech to the end of the chapter a few paragraphs later, conventional femininity is a social construction equally with the novel's account of organized religion or the cavalier ethic.

As a social construction femininity has its standard parts. A girl, Judith Loftus tells Huck, can thread a needle, she spreads her lap to catch things which thus land in her skirt, and she cannot throw straight. The precision with which Mrs. Loftus describes how a girl does throw necessarily implies equal knowledge of how boys do it. She can detail femininity because she sees it as a role, which must mean that masculinity is also a role. The logic of this is that anyone who knows the rules can play, boy or girl, man or woman. For instance she has just been playing, pretending not to be able to hit the rat, thus *pretending* to be feminine in order to force Huck to reveal his masculinity. In her criticism of Huck's feminine acting, Judith Loftus labels it just that, acting.

The chapter's opening inaugurates the notion that femininity is a situation by placing us on its threshold: " 'Come in,' says the woman, and I did" (p. 75). No sooner has Huck taken on the role with the name Sarah Williams than he gets his first lesson in how to act as a girl. For while he had meant just to gather information and leave, the good Mrs. Loftus will not hear of the ostensible Sarah's wandering the roads at night alone. To be a girl is to be unable to move about freely: Sarah-Huck will have to wait for a man, Judith Loftus's husband, to return and escort her-him. In this scene displaced to the wings, men wait to act out their parts. Although Mrs. Loftus is the one who has discovered Jim's hiding place, properly, she will send her husband, "him and another man," to effect the capture.

The culminating moment in the reversal of femininity from nature to nurture — from sex to gender — comes toward the end of the episode when after warning Huck not to go among women pretending to be one of them Judith adds kindly, " 'You do a girl tolerable poor, but you might fool men, maybe' " (p. 80). This is the final blow not to male authority but to the authority of gender itself, for if women recognize femininity better than men that can only mean that femininity is a performance and not a natural mode of being.

Sexual orthodoxy is not self-contained but dualistic, a matter of relations. This interdependence between self-definition and the definition of the opposite gender is especially true for women, whose more restricted horizon is entirely spanned by masculinity. Taken to be rooted in biological propensity, femininity reveals itself, as it refers, first or at least equally, to men, who represent its reason and its rationality and who possess the key to its code as an essential component of their masculinity. If women are born and not made women, men should be the best judges of femininity.

When Judith Loftus tells Huck that women will recognize his absence of femininity but that he may fool men, she posits, on the contrary, a femininity that, instead of reflecting order, generates it, whose original impulse is therefore not biology but ideology. The femininity Mrs. Loftus deploys in restricted travel, sewing, knitting, and maladroit pitching represents its oppositional relation to masculinity as a series of actions that are anything but spontaneous or natural. These actions enact a stance that is willful if not consciously willed. Bring the thread to the needle, she instructs Huck, not the needle to the thread; hold your arm "as awkard as you can" and above all "miss your rat about six or seven foot" (p. 80). Missing rats is what a girl *does*. Let us say the obvious: When it is an action rather than an accident, missing implies the theoretical ability to hit. Nor can we interpret this to mean that, as a boy, Huck can choose to hit the rat or miss him but that a girl could only miss, because all of it, the way to hit and to miss and above all the necessity of choosing between them, is being explained by a woman who controls the entire situation: " 'I spotted you for a boy when you was threading the needle; and I contrived the other things just to make certain' " (p. 80).

Femininity, as Judith Loftus has here defined it, is something women *do,* a composite activity made up of certain acts they perform well and others they as skillfully perform badly, or perhaps most skillfully not at all. Masculinity is the equal and opposite condition: She spots Huck for a boy when after lacking the skill of threading needles — threading is what men skillfully do-not-do — he reveals that he usually wears trousers by clapping his knees together to catch the ball. One suspects, it is true, that sharp-eyed Mrs. Loftus would spot a girl in boy's clothing more quickly than her husband would, but this does not negate the implication of her warning to Huck, that gender is nurture rather than nature. In part this is because the performance of femininity includes observing more shrewdly, especially the performance of gender.

But the other reason for her likely superiority at catching out fraudulent boys as well as girls lies precisely in her ideological stance. At the close of the preceding chapter, before the trip to the village, Jim criticizes Huck, who is practicing walking about in a dress: He "said I didn't walk like a girl; and he said I must quit pulling up my gown to get at my britches pocket" (p. 74). Jim's instructions are negative, as is the entire disguise, whose intent is to hide and not to project, to conceal "real" masculinity. What Huck learns from Judith Loftus, however, is that concealment is not the issue but projection: projection, meaning construction. Extrapolating, masculinity also becomes a construction and in renaming Huck a boy, Mrs. Loftus returns his masculinity to him not in the old absolute terms but as *his* way of performing.

It is this experience, effectively a revolution in the way Huck defines himself in the basic area of gender, that sets the stage for the revolution to come in his sense of himself in the equally basic area of race. The move involved in both transformations is the same, from essentialist to cultural and political definitions of gender and race, from nature to history. When Huck, in that epiphanic cry " 'They're after us!,' " casts himself as an object of his own race's persecution, he does not mean that he now considers himself black. Rather he has come to see that in the cavalier South the blackness of an enslaved black man refers not to a set of inherent attributes but to a situation, to an oppression such as can also torment a poor white boy.

The sequence — Huck and Jim on the island as white boy and escaped slave; Huck pretending to be a girl in the Loftus kitchen; Huck and Jim fleeing the island to escape white slavers — places the middle episode in the role not only of catalyst but of mediator. It is in the context of a temporary displacement of his gender identity, and of the questions Judith Loftus raises about gender identity as such, that Huck moves permanently into a new social identity in which, resuming an unquestioned maleness, he questions the other conventions of his culture far more radically than he ever has before. At the moment when he associates himself fully with Jim, Huck Finn and his story might be said to touch bottom in the contemporary culture and ideology and to spring back to an antipode that marks not transcendence but the outer limits of the culturally and ideologically imaginable.

Such moments are not easily sustained. Many students of Mark Twain and *Huckleberry Finn* have noted that after a dazzlingly iconoclastic first half or so, the novel retreats toward a disappointingly conventional conclusion; and that on the way, with Huck's complicity, the character of Jim is returned to a black stereotype. The subject here, however, is not *Huckleberry Finn,* but the uses of gender as a critical term that can illuminate not only the literary treatment of associated topics like romantic love and the family but thematic and formal concerns that are not obviously involved with sexual identity at all. We could have fruitfully examined the treatment of the Widow Douglas, for instance, or of Emmeline Grangerford and the contemporary tradition of women's writings which Twain mocks through her, and related these examinations to the novel as a whole. But the issue of gender arises in the Judith Loftus episode in a more generally paradigmatic way, at once overtly, in that Huck pretends to be a girl, and as a deep structure whose ramifications Twain himself may not have fully understood.

These ramifications have to do with the overall theme of the early part of the novel which traces Huck's passage out of his society into a liminal state in which not only his moral philosophy but his very identity is in flux. It is no coincidence that he enters into a state of aggravated mutability by stepping into the woman's sphere of Judith Loftus;

nor that her exposition of the inessentiality of femininity immediately precedes his extraordinary identification with a black slave. In this process, race and sex are not wholly analogous: Huck emerges from the encounter with Judith Loftus, indubitably and forever, a boy, whom one cannot imagine actually identifying with a girl, only protecting her. Conversely, the final lesson he learns from Judith Loftus is not the one she means to teach him, since she herself is hell-bent on catching Jim and returning him to slavery. But these complications are precisely the point in manifesting the fundamental or axiomatic character of gender in the organization of thought and writing: By plunging Huck into the deepest possible limbo of identity, this very brief eclipse of his masculinity, even rectified by his inability to maintain the pretense, opens him and Mark Twain's imagination to rethinking the basic principles of personal identity and social ideology both. Through Judith Loftus, the novel speaks as it could not through Huck himself. It is as if the novel itself had found a female voice and the language to say things its male vocabulary could not articulate and therefore did not know, or did not know it knew. The term "gender" can empower criticism in the same way, enabling it to pose new questions and thus discover new levels of interpretation. In reading the Judith Loftus episode, raising gender as an issue affects one's interpretation in a widening circle that finally encompasses the whole novel. At the center of the circle, the very fact of Huck's female impersonation becomes charged with a new energy when it is seen not so much to conceal or erase his masculinity as to render it problematical. So long as masculinity is considered literally organic, Huck's calico gown and bonnet could at the extreme signify his castration without thereby raising questions about masculinity as such. Castration as we know, is the classic stuff of anxiety, but it also allows for total reassurance. In that regard, the episode is entirely reassuring: Huck fails at being a girl because he is so thoroughly a boy. When the issue, however, is not the possession of masculinity but, precisely, its provenance — whether biological or ideological — no such reassurance can be had. On the contrary, the more explicitly the characteristics of masculinity are described, directly or as the reverse of Mrs. Loftus's account of femininity, the more they become contingent, possibly arbitrary, and certainly disputable.

With Huck sitting in Mrs. Loftus's kitchen got up like a girl, nothing any longer is given, anyone can be anything. The certainty of gender provides for literature generally and for the rest of *Huckleberry Finn* an anchor for the kinetic self. Lifting that anchor even briefly accentuates all the instabilities of Huck's other identifications. The early part of the boy's journey out of town moves toward an indefinite horizon. How indefinite or infinite a horizon is dramatically evident in the explosion of his cry "They're after us!" Joining an escaped slave in the first person plural, he has traveled a cosmic distance which the additional critical perspective of gender helps both measure and explain by bridging the opening of the chapter, in which Huck passes into the world apart of women, and the close, which propels him right out of his culture and society. In the end, while discarding the accoutrements of "white-trash" ideology, he will certainly retain the panoply of conventional masculinity. But the fact that he has temporarily put off even that gauges the radical reach of his alienation, and plumbs the depths of its terrors.

In other words, gender is both an embedded assumption and functions as a touchstone for others. It is logically impossible to interrogate gender — to transform it from axiom to object of scrutiny and critical term — without also interrogating race and class. The introduction of gender into the critical discussion multiplies its concerns and categories by those of historiography to produce a newly encompassing account of cultural consciousness that is also newly self-conscious.

From the perspective of gender, then, a critic sees both deeper and more broadly. But the view may also appear more obstructed, exactly the enhancement of critical vision seeming to hinder it, or to interpose a new obstacle between critic and text. In analyzing the ways gender concepts complicate the Judith Loftus episode, this discussion has invoked some issues and ideas which Mark Twain probably did not consciously consider when he wrote it. In a much later story, describing a boy and girl each of whom behaves like the opposite, Twain expresses a clear understanding that gender is a matter of ideology. Or as he puts it more vividly: "Hellfire Hotchkiss [the girl] is the only genuwyne male man in this town and Thug Carpenter's [the boy] the only genuwyne female girl, if you leave out sex and just consider the business facts" (cited in Gillman, 109–10). Indeed "the business facts" of sexual identity is about as good a definition of gender as one could offer and Judith's exposition of how girls are made girls and boys boys can certainly be read as an early draft. But within *Huckleberry Finn* itself there is little to indicate such understanding and in fact evidence to the contrary. When the narrator describes women directly they seem rather the incarnation of femininity than its practitioners, innately either sentimental sillies like Emmeline Grangerford or, like the Widow Douglas, pious hypocrites. On the whole in this story, being a woman is not a proud thing.

That Judith Loftus is anomalously admirable is not a problem but that we have read her as defining herself and the scene she dominates in terms for which there seems to be no other reference in the book could be one. The apparent absence within the text of these critical terms suggests that the reading has introduced its own notions into the writer's world. One of the ways the term "gender" alters the entire enterprise of criticism is by responding positively to such suggestions, though in relation to a revised understanding of the interactions between reading and text. Because an ideology of gender is basic to virtually all thought while, by most thinkers, unrecognized as such, gender criticism often has a confrontational edge. One has to read for gender; unless it figures explicitly in story or poem, it will seldom read for itself. On the other hand "interpretation" is an ambiguous word meaning both to translate and to explain. Literary interpretation does both inextricably, and when critics limit themselves to the explicit terms of the texts they read their interpretations can be more congenial yet not less (re) or (de)constructive. They also interpret who only think to explicate. Literary criticism involves action as much as reflection, and reading for gender makes the deed explicit.

The exhilarating discovery of Molière's bourgeois gentleman, that when he talked he talked prose, has a counterpart in the rather inhibiting epigram that when you speak you have to use words. The term "gender" in literary criticism refers to a set of concerns and also to a vocabulary — what Mark Twain might have called a business vocabulary — that contributes its own meanings to everything that is said or written.

SUGGESTED READINGS

No short list of titles can do justice to the rich variety of recent works in gender criticism. Moreover, for an understanding of the general significance of the term it seems as important to develop a sense of its possibilities as to explore these individually in depth. The following are five anthologies that among them offer a wide survey of the field and can provide an excellent introduction to it.

Christian, Barbara, ed. *Black Feminist Criticism*. New York: Pergamon, 1985.

de Lauretis, Theresa, ed. *Feminist Studies, Critical Studies*. Bloomington: Indiana UP, 1986.

Hull, Gloria T., Patricia Bell Scott, and Barbara Smith, eds. *All the Women Are White, All the Blacks Are Men, But Some of Us Are*

Brave: Black Women's Studies. Old Westbury, NY: Feminist, 1982.

Keohane, Nannerl O., Michelle Z. Rosaldo, and Barbara G. Gelpi, eds. *Feminist Theory: A Critique of Ideology.* Chicago: U of Chicago P, 1982.

Miller, Nancy, ed. *The Poetics of Gender.* New York: Columbia UP, 1987.

WORKS CITED

Boswell, James. *Boswell's Life of Johnson.* London: Oxford UP, 1960 [1799].

Gillman, Susan. *Dark Twins: Imposture and Identity in Mark Twain's America.* Chicago: U of Chicago P, 1989.

Smith, Henry Nash. Introduction to *Adventures of Huckleberry Finn.* Boston: Riverside, 1958.

FREDERICK CREWS

Walker versus Jehlen versus Twain

Frederick Crews (b. 1933) is professor emeritus of English at the University of California, Berkeley. He received his B.A. (1955) from Yale University. After receiving his Ph.D. (1958) from Princeton, he began teaching at UC Berkeley, where he has remained ever since. Crews is well known for both his early efforts to develop an effective psychoanalytic literary criticism (*The Sins of the Fathers,* 1966) and his later repudiation of psychoanalysis (*Out of My System,* 1975; *Skeptical Engagements,* 1986). His other books include *The Tragedy of Manners* (1957), *E. M. Forster: The Perils of Humanism* (1962), and *The Critics Bear It Away* (1992). He has also edited *Unauthorized Freud: Doubters Confront a Legend* (1998) and *Postmodern Pooh* (2002). *The Pooh Perplex* (1963) is an entertaining and instructive send-up of the various modes of literary criticism current at the time of its publication. Crews wrote "Walker versus Jehlen versus Twain" for the first edition of this Case Study of *Adventures of Huckleberry Finn.*

The preceding essays by Nancy Walker and Myra Jehlen both constitute responses not just to *Huckleberry Finn* but to a general dilemma facing feminist critics of American fiction. The dilemma was most memorably posed by Nina Baym in her essay of 1981, "Melodramas of Beset Manhood: How Theories of American Fiction Exclude Women Authors."[1] In brief, an androcentric critical tradition has redoubled an androcentric bias already established in our "classics" the selves, leaving women critics as well as women authors disenfranchised in both blatant and subtle ways. As Baym proposed, one straightforward corrective lies at hand: Stop treating a narrow range of rebellious-adolescent-male themes as the "quintessentially American" ones and expand the canon accordingly. Walker and Jehlen, however, are wrestling with the far trickier issue of how to adjust our apprehension of the "classics" themselves, now that some of the most blithely celebrated features of those texts have come to appear problematic and possibly even offensive. If the gender biases of both Mark Twain and his "universalizing" male critics require explicit challenge, on what terms, if any, can we retain a sense of the permanent importance of *Huckleberry Finn*? Here, suddenly, nothing is simple anymore.

On the surface, at least, Myra Jehlen and Nancy Walker are taking quite similar approaches to Twain's novel. Without harboring illusions about Twain's conscious partiality toward a liberalizing of gender roles, each critic attempts a limited feminist "rehabilitation" of *Huckleberry Finn* by highlighting a feature of the book that mitigates its overt masculinism. In their execution, however, these two essays differ radically, and in a way that corresponds to a deep division not just within feminist practice but also within the literary academy as a whole. Whereas Nancy Walker writes as if constrained by the manifest narrative facts of *Huckleberry Finn*, Jehlen feels entitled to distort or override those facts wherever they might trouble her thesis. In her case, methodology becomes a steamroller that flattens the contours of Twain's plot, making room for wholly wishful "findings." In a word, then, these essays epitomize the widest of all academic chasms — the one between empirical and aprioristic approaches to inquiry.

This is not to say that Nancy Walker's essay rests at all times on uncontestably solid ground. "[I]t is possible to re-view *Huck Finn*," Walker writes, "as embodying a basic tension between male and female values and roles — a tension that bears directly on Huck's moral growth" (p. 478). Fair enough, but isn't Walker oversimplifying when

---

[1]See *American Quarterly* 33 (1981): 123–39.

she claims that "the virtues that Huck begins to develop — honesty, compassion, a sense of duty — are identified in the novel as female virtues"? Aren't these also the virtues of Jim, a male whose ability to shame and reshape Huck is far greater than that of any woman character? Although one could argue that as a slave Jim is socially "feminized," Walker does not do so.

Moreover, Walker errs when, coming to terms with the novel's unsatisfactory ending, she characterizes Huck as fleeing from "the 'female' virtues he has struggled so hard to attain." Huck never "struggles to attain" *any* virtues, unless one counts his attempt to be "washed clean of sin" by betraying Jim. His struggle is always for survival, and his halting, half-conscious, partly revocable moral education comes about as a result of his finding himself swirled like river driftwood from one vortex of crisis to the next. In general, the contest between male and female value systems in the novel appears to be somewhat less sharply drawn than Walker would have us believe.

On the whole, however, Walker's article remains admirably faithful to the *Huckleberry Finn* that every reader can recognize. At the same time, it enriches our grasp of the novel by estimating how the impressionable Huck must be affected by his encounters with female characters, especially the Widow Douglas, Mrs. Loftus, and Mary Jane Wilks. To be sure, a skeptical reader might want to ask whether Huck is really *changed* by every such episode; in some cases, perhaps, he is merely afforded opportunities to manifest preexisting traits of his character. There is no easy way to resolve such doubts. But if, as Walker establishes, the Widow Douglas has had an avowedly softening effect on Huck prior to his adventures on the river, it is a reasonable extrapolation to suppose that he is similarly affected by the other women who test him later.

Walker shrewdly perceives that Huck, in his capacity as an outlaw adolescent, both absorbs and resists "female" socialization. In this sense, his retreat into boyish adventure seeking at the end falls well within the decorum of his portrait. It also presents Walker with a disappointment that she squarely faces: a recognition that all of the novel's strong females together, limited as they are by Twain's stock notion that women exist only to inspire their men, are powerless to enlighten Huck about the evil of slavery. *Huck Finn* cooperates very imperfectly with Walker's feminist hopes for it, and the strength of her article derives in large part from her refusal to dodge that fact.

Although *Huckleberry Finn* is not the primary object of her attention, Myra Jehlen's claims about it are significantly more ambitious than Walker's. That is because she sets out to use the novel as an object lesson in the necessity of radical gender analysis — analysis, that is, showing that "gender is a cultural idea rather than a biological fact." If her discussion of *Huck Finn* runs into serious trouble, it is not because that proposition is untrue. On the contrary, it is true by definition; if "sex" belongs to biology, "gender" belongs to acculturation. The problem is rather that Jehlen wants Twain's novel not just to show itself amenable to gender study but to *speak* her own ideological position. That is a good deal to ask of a book emerging from the relatively benighted 1880s. As the tortuousness of Jehlen's reasoning suggests, you can't really get there from here.

Jehlen's discussion is scarcely under way before it displays the most fundamental misconstrual of Huck's depicted character. Huck, says Jehlen,

> opposes his universal principles to the fundamental tenets of both his class and his race. He achieves heroism by renouncing genteel hypocrisies as Hamlet does by denouncing the rot at the Danish court. . . . By rejecting the false values of his society, Huck eventually becomes a man of integrity. . . . (p. 500)

Could this be the same Huck whom Mark Twain himself famously characterized as possessing a "sound heart" in conflict with a "deformed conscience"? The whole moral irony of *Huckleberry Finn* depends on Huck's inability to adopt abolitionist "principles" that could render him a conscious critic of the antebellum South. He is quite unaware of his "class," which in any event is hardly given to "genteel hypocrisies." (Pap Finn's?) Nor, a fortiori, does he finally become "a man of integrity"; he remains an impressionable boy, and never more so than in the trivial "Evasion" at the end. The entirety of Twain's brilliantly rendered internal dialogue between Huck's humane impulses and his unreflective acceptance of slavery passes Jehlen by.

Stranger still is Jehlen's claim that Huck's visit to Judith Loftus's house in chapter 11 "culminates Huck's moral and political ascension; he will not rise higher in the rest of the novel but rather slide back." Considering that Huck's anguished, obviously climactic, declaration of willingness to "go to hell" for Jim does not occur until chapter 31, this is an exceedingly eccentric judgment. And as we will see, Jehlen's attempt to justify it by viewing the Loftus episode through ideologically tinted lenses produces assertions that are flatly incredible.

The scene in which Huck's disguise as a girl is unmasked by the observant Judith Loftus, who tells him where his impersonation is ama-

teurish and then unwittingly allows him to return to Jim with the news
that they are facing imminent capture, figures largely in both of the critical essays under review. For Walker, as we recall, Mrs. Loftus is one
among several exemplars of "female virtues" who humanize but also
fortify Huck's soul, preparing him to resist the male slaveholding ethic
at least for a brief period. But the very thought of "female virtues" is
alarming to the antiessentialist Jehlen. For this reason, perhaps, Jehlen
finds it easy to acknowledge, as Walker does not, that the "virtuous"
Mrs. Loftus has already dispatched her husband across the river to earn
the reward money for returning a fugitive slave. In this respect — but
in this respect alone — Jehlen is more faithful to the text than Walker is.

The reason Jehlen is not discomfited by Mrs. Loftus's thoughtless
racism is that she is after bigger game: the very deconstruction of gender as a natural category. Since that is her own aim as a didactic critic in
1990, she would be pleased to conclude that it had been anticipated
more than a century earlier by *Huckleberry Finn*. Therefore she does so,
wildly inflating the importance of Huck's amusing dress-up scene.
Judith Loftus, Jehlen says, "effects a temporary but nonetheless radical
reversal of the very nature of gender" (p. 502), and Huck momentously
"pass[es] through the crisis of rejecting his born identity dressed as a
girl." Thus poor Huck, who wants and receives from Mrs. Loftus only
one piece of hard information about his and Jim's plight, is treated by
Jehlen to an altogether fantastic trip through the transvestite psychic
underworld.

As Nancy Walker pointed out, Huck does learn something from
Mrs. Loftus besides the key fact that he and Jim are being pursued; it is
that he had better not try to disguise himself as a girl again. Girls, Mrs.
Loftus shows him, reflexively perform certain actions — threading a
needle, throwing and catching an object — in telltale ways that Huck,
precisely because he is "all boy," cannot hope to mimic successfully.
Huck readily gets the point, but Jehlen gets it backwards.

For Jehlen, Mrs. Loftus's lesson is that male and female traits are
just an act — that, really, "anyone can be anything" in a world liberated
from sexual stereotyping. What a revelation this must be, thinks Jehlen,
for the Huck who used to take his maleness for granted! "This very
brief eclipse of his masculinity . . . opens him and Mark Twain's imagination to rethinking the basic principles of personal identity and social
ideology both" (p. 506).

No, it doesn't. If Mark Twain happened to be privately fascinated
by the pliability of sex boundaries — and there is plenty of suggestive
evidence that he was — the ground rules of fiction nevertheless forbade

him to impart such sophistication to the provincial characters of his novel. Mrs. Loftus does *not* warn Huck, as Jehlen maintains, "that gender is nurture rather than nature"; she assumes that males and females do things differently by virtue of their inherent constitution. And Huck himself remains an ignorant if natively canny frontier boy, not a social-constructionist philosopher à la Jehlen.

In order to turn the relatively minor Loftus episode into the pivotal moment of *Huckleberry Finn*, Jehlen must labor to improve Twain's actual plot. It is quite clear, for example, that Huck has already formed an emotional tie with Jim when he goes to the trouble of reconnoitering for him in girl's clothing. Never once does Huck, found out in his disguise and subliminally wooed toward "sivilization" by Mrs. Loftus's kindly maternal behavior, contemplate abandoning Jim and saving his own white skin by confiding in her. Rather, he arrives at her house as a dissimulator on an espionage mission, and he departs in exactly the same role. For Jehlen, however, it is an ideologically retooled Huck — the beneficiary of "a revolution in the way [he] defines himself in the basic area of gender" (p. 504) — who returns to Jim. Moreover, it is *solely because* of this intellectual breakthrough, Jehlen fancies, that Huck can now *perceive* that "in the cavalier South the blackness of an enslaved black man refers not to a set of inherent attributes but to a situation, to an oppression such as can also torment a poor white boy" (p. 505).

The ludicrousness of this attempt to shovel contemporary academic dogma into Huck's practical and theory-proof brain ought to be apparent by now. So, too, Jehlen will have a hard time convincing anyone that Huck's cry to Jim, "They're after us!," could not have been uttered without the expansion of his sympathies wrought by Judith Loftus. That warning is exactly what we would already have expected from the plucky boy who paddled ashore and, for the sake of his black friend, risked exposure and delivery to Pap's vengeful fury.

Beyond any sum of distortions on Jehlen's part lies a global refusal of empathy with Twain's moral daring in *Huckleberry Finn*. For her, the *Huck Finn* awaiting her feminist makeover must be apprehended as a drably conformist work that merely "articulates and helps define dominant values and ways of seeing the world." This is to say that, like the other critics I have elsewhere called New Americanists,[2] Jehlen empties *Huck Finn* of its reformist energy in order to award her own transformational reading a monopoly on whatever rectitude the book can be

---

[2]See Crews, *The Critics Bear It Away: American Fiction and the Academy* (New York: Random House, 1992) chs. 2, 3.

shown to possess. In particular, her assimilation of the novel to "dominant values" tacitly dismisses Mark Twain's flawed but nevertheless fervent attempt to dissociate himself from the barbarism not just of slavery but also of Jim Crow. On Jehlen's account, the fact that *Huckleberry Finn* has struck so many observers as contributing to interracial understanding becomes an unfathomable mystery. Indeed, her campaign against "apparently universal" values and "the fantasy of transcendence" could cause a reader to wonder whether racial justice itself isn't a phony "universal" from which we ought to withhold our approval.

"In reading the Judith Loftus episode," Jehlen remarks, "raising gender as an issue affects one's interpretation in a widening circle that finally encompasses the whole novel" (p. 506). How true, in Jehlen's case at least! But before celebrating this outcome, we ought to ask whether Jehlen's *Huckleberry Finn* bears much resemblance to the original. When Jehlen infers Huck's putative "castration" from his mere wearing of a disguise; when she turns a good-humored exposure of that disguise into a "plunging [of Huck] into the deepest possible limbo of identity"; and when she says that this minor scene "gauges the radical reach of [Huck's] alienation, and plumbs the depths of its terrors," she is all in a sweat, as Huck might have put it, to make the troublesomest fuss about nothing.

Interestingly, the same point appears to have occurred to Jehlen herself. "Through Judith Loftus," she queasily asserts, "the novel speaks as it could not through Huck himself. It is as if the novel itself had found a female voice and the language to say things its male vocabulary could not articulate and therefore did not know, or did not know it knew" (p. 506). The novel's "female voice" is of course Jehlen's own, ventriloquized. And in her three final paragraphs she all but retracts her thesis, worrying aloud that she may have "obstructed" a clear view of the novel and "interpose[d] a new obstacle between critic and text." Still, she is undeterred. Although her reading "has introduced its own notions into the writer's world," the die is cast. To avoid ending up a timid critical Hamlet ("Literary criticism involves action as much as reflection"), she steels herself to become a critical Macbeth ("reading for gender makes the deed explicit") (p. 508).

In Gerald Graff's model university, I gather, feminist critical discourse would be featured in the curriculum alongside other "isms," and students would receive educational benefit from the open clash of methodologies that ensued. But "feminist critical discourse," we have been seeing here, encompasses rules of analysis that are flatly incompatible with one another. Who will be chosen to speak for feminism, the party of Nancy Walker or the party of Myra Jehlen? Wouldn't the more radical-sounding voice drown out the more rational one?

My own principles make me believe that the need for empirical accountability in literary study is more urgent than any arraying of rival schools. Beyond loyalty to one approach or another, or even to the unexceptionable notion of tolerant eclecticism, we ought to be teaching a loyalty to literary fact. The extent to which such a proposal sounds hopelessly archaic and "positivistic," I would say, could serve as a rough measure of the extent to which our field now falls short of constituting an authentic discipline.

MARTHA WOODMANSEE

A Response to Frederick Crews

Martha Woodmansee (b. 1944) is associate professor of English and comparative literature at Case Western Reserve University. She received her B.A. (1968) in English and German literature from Northwestern University, her M.A. (1969) in German literature from Stanford University, and her Ph.D. (1977) in English and German literature from Stanford. Since 1990, she has been the executive director of the Society for Critical Exchange. She has written *The Author, Art and the Market: Rereading the History of Aesthetics* (1993), translated Peter Szondi's *Literary Hermeneutics* (1994), and coedited three books: *Erkennen and Deuten* (with Walter F. W. Lohnes, 1983), *Intellectual Property and the Construction of Authorship* (with Peter Jaszi, 1994), and *The New Economic Criticism: Studies at the Interface of Literature and Economics* (with Mark Osteen, 1999). This response was written for the first edition of this Case Study of *Adventures of Huckleberry Finn*.

Frederick Crews concludes his assessment of two recent feminist considerations of *Huckleberry Finn* by calling for "empirical accountability in literary study" (p. 516). For Crews, gender analysis of the novel is viable only when it proceeds empirically rather than "aprioristically" — that is, only when the critic recognizes that texts have their own independent meanings and purposes and thus restricts herself to such "literary facts."

Accordingly, for Crews a good feminist critic like Nancy Walker respects those independent purposes and meanings as they are revealed by the empirical facts of the text, while a zealous ideologue rides roughshod over such textual facts in order to advance the particular ideological agenda she brings to the text. Crews regards Myra Jehlen's discussion of *Huckleberry Finn* as just such an aprioristic intervention because she turns this product of "the relatively benighted 1880s" into a realization of her own feminist agenda — a veritable object lesson in the social construction of gender. To accomplish this conversion, according to Crews, Jehlen has had to distort all manner of "literary fact," and he devotes much of his essay to identifying the most egregious misreadings and distortions.

But how vulnerable is Jehlen to such criticism? I share Crews's view that literary critics should be held accountable to the "empirical facts" of the text, but I think Crews is operating with an extremely narrow conception of what counts as an empirical fact. Are not the facts of which Crews speaks interpretations, and thereby open to challenge by appeal to different facts? Indeed, the chief point of Jehlen's essay would seem to be that by considering literary works in the light of gender we will come to see facts that we would otherwise miss, facts that will then lead us to new, or significantly revised, interpretations.

Jehlen's reading of the Judith Loftus episode is designed to work in just this way. Attending primarily to the way gender roles are played out in this scene, Jehlen finds that the scene dramatizes the socially constructed nature of gender — that is, the fact that the accepted definitions of male and female in our culture (boys and girls catch balls and hold yarn in different ways) are products of social conditioning rather than reflections of the way boys and girls "really are." Though Judith Loftus, and perhaps Twain himself, thinks that boys will be boys and girls girls, the very reassertion of this commonplace by the scene has the effect of making us wonder if it is really true; furthermore, the manner of the reassertion — through reference to learned behavior — raises the possibility that boys can be girls and girls boys, or, in other words, calls attention to the social construction of gender.

Jehlen then uses this conclusion, along with the interpretive convention that successive scenes in a novel may be related, to argue that Huck's famous cry to Jim in the next chapter, "They're after us!" has been influenced by Huck's exposure to this lesson about gender. In this way, Jehlen makes her larger point that attention to gender in *Huck Finn* can shed new light on the book's treatment of race. Such a procedure would seem to be no less empirical than the one that underlies Crews's interpretation.

In other words, though Crews repeatedly invokes the "literary facts" of the text, he never addresses the question of how we decide which of the virtually infinite number of facts that might be turned up in a text are actually relevant in a given interpretive situation. Jehlen's argument is that if we foreground gender in our reading of the novel, a different set of facts come into view than those we are accustomed to seeing in a conventional reading. Indeed, a chief aim of feminist criticism is to show how new and different facts emerge when gender provides the context for analysis.

It also seems pertinent that even though Crews castigates Jehlen for ignoring the empirical facts of Twain's text, he himself ignores a rather obvious empirical fact about her text, namely that it was originally written for a textbook of literary-critical terms entitled *Critical Terms for Literary Study*. Seen in this context, Jehlen's interpretation of the Loftus scene has little to do with an attempt at politically "rehabilitating" the novel; instead, its purpose is to illustrate for students how the term and concept of "gender" can be relevant to reading texts that are not explicitly about issues of gender.

Let me put this last point more bluntly. One of the major "empirical facts" that Crews seems to ignore is the fact that texts very often have effects that are different from the purposes for which they were intended. The reason for this lies not in the mysteries of the unconscious mind (though these may play a role), but in the fact that everything we say contains implications and assumptions that we cannot possibly be fully aware of. Jehlen makes this point by referring at the very beginning of her essay to the well-known bourgeois gentleman of Molière's play who suddenly becomes aware that he has been "speaking prose" all his life without recognizing it. If most of us would agree that Molière's gentleman could indeed have been speaking prose with-out knowing he was doing so, then why is it so farfetched for feminist critics to say that Twain in *Huckleberry Finn* spoke "the language of gender" without necessarily having this as his conscious purpose?

WORK CITED

Lentricchia, Frank, and Thomas McLaughlin, eds. *Critical Terms for Literary Study*. Chicago: U of Chicago P, 1990.

Come Back to the Raft Ag'in, Huck Honey!

Leslie Fiedler (1917–2003) received his B.A. (1938) from New York University and his M.A. (1939) and Ph.D. (1941) in English from the University of Wisconsin. After teaching at Montana State University from 1941 to 1963, Fiedler became professor of English at the State University of New York at Buffalo in 1964. In 1973, SUNY-Buffalo created the Samuel L. Clemens Chair in English for Fiedler, a position he held for the remainder of his career. A creative writer as well as a consistently provocative critic, Fiedler wrote more than twenty-five books, including *An End to Innocence* (1955), *Love and Death in the American Novel* (1960, rev. ed. 1966), *No! In Thunder* (1960), *The Collected Essays of Leslie Fiedler* (1971), *Freaks: Myths and Images of the Secret Self* (1978), *What Was Literature?* (1982), *Fiedler on the Roof: Essays on Literature and Jewish Identity* (1991), and *Tyranny of the Normal* (1996). This essay originally appeared in *Partisan Review* (1948).

It is perhaps to be expected that the Negro and the homosexual should become stock literary themes, compulsive, almost mythic in their insistence, in a period when the reassertion of responsibility and of the inward meaning of failure has become again a primary concern of our literature. Their locus is, of course, discrepancy — in a culture which has no resources (no tradition of courtesy, no honored mode of cynicism) for dealing with a contradiction between principle and practice. It used once to be fashionable to think of puritanism as a force in our life encouraging hypocrisy; quite the contrary, its rigid emphasis upon the singleness of belief and action, its turning of the most prosaic areas of common life into arenas where one's state of grace is symbolically tested, confuse the outer and the inner and make among us, perhaps more strikingly than ever elsewhere, hypocrisy *visible,* visibly detestable, a cardinal sin. It is not without significance that the shrug of the shoulders (the acceptance of circumstance as a sufficient excuse, the vulgar sign of self-pardon before the inevitable lapse) seems in America an unfamiliar, an alien gesture.

And yet before the underground existence of crude homosexual love (the ultimate American epithets of contempt notoriously exploit the mechanics of such affairs), before the blatant ghettos in which the cast-off Negro conspicuously creates the gaudiness and stench that offend him, the white American must over and over make a choice between coming to uneasy terms with an institutionalized discrepancy, or formulating radically new ideologies. There are, to be sure, stop-gap devices, evasions of that final choice; not the least interesting is the special night club: the fag café, the black-and-tan joint, in which fairy or Negro exhibit their fairyness, their Negro-ness as if they were mere divertissements, gags thought up for the laughs and having no reality once the lights go out and the chairs are piled on the tables for the cleaning-woman. In the earlier minstrel show, a negro performer was required to put on with grease paint and burnt cork the formalized mask of blackness.

The situations of the Negro and the homosexual in our society pose precisely opposite problems, or at least problems suggesting precisely opposite solutions: Our laws on homosexuality and the context of prejudice and feeling they objectify must apparently be changed to accord with a stubborn social fact, whereas it is the social fact, our overt behavior toward the Negro, that must be modified to accord with our laws and the, at least official, morality they objectify.

It is not, of course, quite so simple. There is another sense in which the fact of homosexual passion contradicts a national myth of masculine love, just as our real relationship with the Negro contradicts a myth of that relationship, and those two myths with their betrayals are, as we shall see, one.

The existence of overt homosexuality threatens to compromise an essential aspect of American sentimental life: the camaraderie of the locker-room and ball park, the good fellowship of the poker game and fishing trip, a kind of passionless passion, at once gross and delicate, homoerotic in the boy's sense, possessing an innocence above suspicion. To doubt for a moment this innocence, which can survive only as *assumed,* would destroy our stubborn belief in a relationship simple, utterly satisfying, yet immune to lust: physical as the handshake is physical, this side of copulation. The nineteenth-century myth of the immaculate Young Girl has failed to survive in any *felt* way into our time; rather in the dirty jokes shared among men in the smoking-car, the barracks, or the dormitory there is a common male revenge against women for having flagrantly betrayed that myth, and under the revenge, there is the rather smug assumption of the chastity of the group as a masculine society. From what other source could that unexpected air of good clean fun which overhangs such sessions arise? It is this self-congratulatory buddy-buddiness, its astonishing naiveté, that breeds at once endless opportunities for inversion and the terrible reluctance to admit its existence, to surrender the last believed-in stronghold of love without passion.

It is, after all, what we know from a hundred other sources that is here verified: the regressiveness, in a technical sense, of American life, its implacable nostalgia for the infantile, at once wrongheaded and somehow admirable. The mythic America is boyhood — and who would dare be startled to realize that two (and the two most popular, the two most *absorbed,* I think) of the handful of great books on our native heritage are customarily to be found, illustrated, on the shelves of the Children's Library. I am referring of course to *Moby Dick* and *Huckleberry Finn,* splendidly counterpoised in their oceanic complexity and fluminal simplicity, but alike children's books, or more precisely, *boys'* books.

Among the most distinguished novelists of the American past, only Henry James escapes completely classification as a writer of juvenile classics; even Hawthorne, who did write sometimes for children, must in his most adult novels endure, though not as Mark Twain and Melville submit to, the child's perusal; a child's version of *The Scarlet Letter* would seem a rather far-fetched joke if it were not a part of our common experience. On a lower level of excellence, there are the Leatherstocking Tales of Cooper and Dana's *Two Years Before the Mast,* books read still, though almost unaccountably in Cooper's case, by boys. What do all these novels have in common?

As boys' books we would expect them shyly, guilelessly as it were, to proffer a chaste male love as the ultimate emotional experience — and this is spectacularly the case. In Dana, it is the narrator's melancholy love for the *kanaka,* Hope; in Cooper, the lifelong affection of Natty Bumppo and Chingachgook; in Melville, Ishmael's love for Queequeg; in Twain, Huck's feeling for Nigger Jim. At the focus of emotion, where we are accustomed to find in the world's great novels some heterosexual passion, be it Platonic love or adultery, seduction, rape, or long-drawn-out flirtation, we come instead upon the fugitive slave and the no-account boy lying side by side on the raft borne by the endless river towards an impossible escape, or the pariah sailor waking in the tattooed arms of the brown harpooner on the verge of their impossible quest. "Aloha, aikane, aloha nui," Hope cries to the lover who prefers him above his fellow-whites; and Ishmael, in utter frankness tells us:

"Thus, then, in our heart's honeymoon, lay I and Queequeg — a cosy, loving pair." Physical it all is, certainly, yet of an ultimate innocence; there is between the lovers no sword but a childlike ignorance, as if the possibility of a fall to the carnal had not yet been discovered. Even in the *Vita Nuova* of Dante there is no vision of love less offensively, more unremittingly chaste; that it is not adult seems sometimes beside the point.

The tenderness of Huck's repeated loss and refinding of Jim, Ishmael's sensations as he wakes under the pressure of Queequeg's arm, the role of almost Edenic helpmate played for Bumppo by the Indian — these shape us from childhood: We have no sense of first discovering them, of having been once without them.

Of the infantile, the homoerotic aspects of these stories we are, though vaguely, aware, but it is only with an effort that we can wake to a consciousness of how, among us who at the level of adulthood find a difference in color sufficient provocation for distrust and hatred, they celebrate, all of them, the mutual love of *a white man and a colored*.

So buried at a level of acceptance which does not touch reason, so desperately repressed from overt recognition, so contrary to what is usually thought of as our ultimate level of taboo — the sense of that love can survive only in the obliquity of a symbol, persistent, archetypical, in short, as a myth: the boy's homoerotic crush, the love of the black fused at this level into a single thing.

I hope I have been using here a hopelessly abused word with some precision; by myth I mean a coherent pattern of beliefs and feelings, so widely shared at a level beneath consciousness that there exists no abstract vocabulary for representing it, and (this is perhaps another aspect of the same thing) so "sacred" that unexamined, irrational restraints inhibit any explicit analysis. Such a complex achieves a formula or pattern story, which serves both to embody it, and, at first at least, to conceal its full implications. Later the secret may be revealed, the myth (I use a single word for the formula and what is formulized) "analyzed" or "allegorically interpreted" according to the language of the day.

I find the situation we have been explicating genuinely mythic; certainly it has the concealed character of the true myth, eluding the wary pounce of Howells or of Mrs. Twain who excised from *Huckleberry Finn* the cussin' as unfit for children, but left, unperceived, a conventionally abhorrent doctrine of ideal love. Even the writers in whom we find it, attained it, in a sense, dreaming. The felt difference between *Huckleberry Finn* and Twain's other books must lie surely in the release from conscious restraint inherent in the author's assumption of the character of Huck; the passage in and out of darkness and river mist, the constant confusion of identities (Huck's ten or twelve names — the questions of who is the real uncle, who the true Tom), the sudden intrusions into alien violences without past or future, give the whole work for all its carefully observed detail, the texture of a dream. For *Moby Dick*, such a point need scarcely be made. Even Cooper, despite his insufferable gentlemanliness, his civilized tedium, cannot conceal from the kids who continue to read him the secret behind the over-conscious, stilted prose: the childish impossible dream. D. H. Lawrence saw in him clearly the kid's Utopia: the absolute wilderness in which the stuffiness of home yields to the wigwam and "My Wife" to Chingachgook.

I do not recall ever having seen in the commentaries of the social anthropologist or psychologist an awareness of the role of this profound child's dream of love in our relation to the Negro. (I say Negro, though the beloved in the books we have mentioned is variously Indian and Hawaiian, because the Negro has become more and more exclusively for us *the* colored man, the colored man par excellence.) Trapped in what has by now become a shackling cliché: the concept of the white man's sexual envy of the Negro male, they do not sufficiently note the complementary factor of physical attraction, the mythic love of white male and black. I am deliberately ignoring here an underlying Indo-European myth of great antiquity, the Manichaean notion of an absolute Black and White, hostile yet needing each other for completion, as I ignore more recent ideologies that have nourished the view that concerns us: the Shakespearean myth of good homosexual love opposed to an evil heterosexual attachment, the Rousseauistic concept of the Noble Savage; I have tried to stay within the limits of a single unified myth, re-enforced by disparate materials.

Ishmael and Queequeg, arm in arm, about to ship out, Huck and Jim swimming beside the raft in the peaceful flux of the Mississippi, — it is the motion of water which completes the syndrome, the American dream of isolation afloat. The Negro as homoerotic lover blends with the myth of running off to sea, of running the great river down to the sea. The immensity of water defines a loneliness that demands love, its strangeness symbolizes the disavowal of the conventional that makes possible all versions of love.

In *Two Years Before the Mast*, in *Moby Dick*, in *Huckleberry Finn* the water is there, is the very texture of the novel; the Leatherstocking Tales propose another symbol for the same meaning: the virgin forest.

Notice the adjective — the virgin forest and the forever inviolable sea. It is well to remember, too, what surely must be more than a coincidence, that Cooper who could dream this myth invented the novel of the sea, wrote for the first time in history the sea-story proper. The rude pederasty of the forecastle and the Captain's cabin, celebrated in a thousand jokes, is the profanation of a dream. In a recent book of Gore Vidal's, an incipient homosexual, not yet aware of his feelings, indulges in the apt reverie of running off to sea with his dearest friend. The buggery of sailors is taken for granted among us, yet it is thought of usually as an inversion forced on men by their isolation from women, though the opposite case may well be true, the isolation sought more or less consciously as an occasion for male encounters. There is a context in which the legend of the sea as escape and solace, the fixated sexuality of boys, the dark beloved are one.

In Melville and Twain at the center of our tradition, in the lesser writers at the periphery, the myth is at once formalized and perpetuated; Nigger Jim and Queequeg make concrete for us what was without them a vague pressure upon the threshold of our consciousness; the proper existence of the myth is in the realized character, who waits, as it were, only to be asked his secret. Think of Oedipus biding in silence from Sophocles to Freud.

Unwittingly we are possessed in childhood by the characters and their undiscriminated meaning, and it is difficult for us to dissociate them without a sense of disbelief. What! These household figures clues to our subtlest passions! The foreigner finds it easier to perceive the remoter significance; D. H. Lawrence saw in our classics a linked mythos of escape and immaculate male love; Lorca in *The Poet in New York* grasped instinctively the kinship of Harlem and Walt Whitman, the fairy as bard. Yet in every generation of our own writers the myth appears; in the gothic reverie of Capote's *Other Voices, Other Rooms*, both elements of the syndrome are presented, though disjunctively: the boy moving between the love of a Negro maidservant and his inverted cousin.

In the myth, one notes finally, it is always in the role of outcast, ragged woodsman, or despised sailor (Call me Ishmael!), or unregenerate boy (Huck before the prospect of being "sivilized" cries, "I been there before!") that we turn to the love of a colored man. But how, we must surely ask, does the vision of the white American as pariah correspond with our long-held public status: the world's beloved, the success? It is perhaps only the artist's portrayal of *himself,* the notoriously alienated writer in America, at home with such images, child of the town drunk, the survivor. But no, Ishmael is all of us, our unconfessed universal fear objectified in the writer's status as in the sailor's: that compelling anxiety, which every foreigner notes, that we may not be loved, that we are loved for our possessions and not ourselves, that we are really — *alone!* It is that underlying terror which explains our almost furtive incredulity in the face of adulation or favor, what is called (once more the happy adjective) our "boyish modesty."

Our dark-skinned beloved will take us, we assure ourselves, when we have been cut off, or have cut ourselves off from all others, without rancor or the insult of forgiveness; he will fold us in his arms saying "Honey" or "Aikane!", he will comfort us, as if our offense against him were long ago remitted, were never truly *real.* And yet we cannot really forget our guilt ever; the stories that embody the myth dramatize almost compulsively the role of the colored man as victim: Dana's Hope is shown dying of the white man's syphilis; Queequeg is portrayed as racked by fever, a pointless episode except in the light of this necessity; Cooper's Indian smolders to a hopeless old age conscious of the imminent disappearance of his race; Jim is shown loaded down with chains, weakened by the hundred torments of Tom's notion of bullyness. The immense gulf of guilt must be underlined, just as is the disparity of color (Queequeg is not merely brown but monstrously tattooed, Chingachgook is horrid with paint, Jim is shown as the Sick A-rab dyed blue), so that the final reconciliation will seem more unbelievable, more tender. The myth makes no attempt to whitewash our outrage as a fact; it portrays it as meaningless in the face of love.

There would be something insufferable, I think, in that final vision of remission if it were not for the apparent presence of a motivating anxiety, the sense always of a last chance; behind the white American's nightmare that someday, no longer tourist, inheritor, or liberator, he will be rejected, refused — he dreams of his acceptance at the breast he has most utterly offended. It is a dream so sentimental, so outrageous, so desperate that it redeems our concept of boyhood from nostalgia to tragedy.

In each generation we *play* out the impossible mythos, and we live to see our children play it, the white boy and the black we can discover wrestling affectionately on any American street, along which they will walk in adulthood, eyes averted from each other, unwilling to touch. The dream recedes; the immaculate passion and the astonishing reconciliation become a memory, and less, a regret, at last the unrecognized motifs of a child's book. "It's too good to be true, Honey," Jim says to Huck. "It's too good to be true."

CHRISTOPHER LOOBY

"Innocent Homosexuality":
The Fiedler Thesis in Retrospect

Christopher Looby (b. 1957) is professor of English at the University of California, Los Angeles. He received his A.B. (1979) and his M.A. (1981), both in literature and history, from Washington University in St. Louis, and his Ph.D. (1989) in English and comparative literature from Columbia University. He worked for several years at the Library of America, first as a research assistant and then as an associate editor. His books include *Voicing America: Language, Literary Form, and the Origins of the United States* (1996) and *The Complete Civil War Journal and Selected Letters of Thomas Wentworth Higginson* (2000). Although Looby wrote this essay for the first edition of this Case Study of *Adventures of Huckleberry Finn*, it is part of his ongoing project on masculinity, sexuality, and race in nineteenth-century America with the working title "The Sentiment of Sex."

Leslie Fiedler's famously scandalizing claim, articulated first in his June 1948 essay in *Partisan Review,* "Come Back to the Raft Ag'in, Huck Honey!,"[1] that the classic literature of the United States formulated a "national myth of masculine love" (p. 520 in this volume), may be the most controversial statement in the whole archive of criticism of American literature. Fiedler's "full development" of this thesis, in the wake of what he called the "shocked and, I suspect, partly willful incomprehension" with which it was first greeted, led him to elaborate his argument in *Love and Death in the American Novel,* a long study first published in 1960. It is in this later book that he used the curious phrase "innocent homosexuality" to describe the "archetypal image" of a loving male interracial couple that he discovered insistently in the novels he discussed.[2] My wish is to salvage from the essay what is gen-

---

[1]Leslie Fiedler, "Come Back to the Raft Ag'in, Huck Honey!" *Partisan Review* (June 1948).

[2]Leslie Fiedler, *Love and Death in the American Novel* (1960; rev. ed. 1966; New York: Stein and Day, 1975) 12. Although Fiedler plainly meant "innocent" here to mean

uinely useful, but that salvage operation requires that it initially be conceded that the essay does its thinking from within a deeply homophobic and gay-baiting structure of assumptions. This is true in spite of the fact that Fiedler signals his progressive belief, for instance, that the "laws on homosexuality and the context of prejudice and feeling they objectify must apparently be changed to accord with a stubborn social fact" (p. 520). Such a sentence proclaims a liberal position on the issue of homosexuals' civil rights, but its weird language vitiates the political commitment. Why describe the "social fact" of homosexuality and homosexuals as "stubborn," except to imply that one would erase it if one actually could? Why qualify the claimed necessity of law reform as only "apparent," except to hint that although one wearily concedes that the legal harassment of homosexuals has failed to eradicate the "stubborn social fact" it vainly opposes, one retains the hope that this necessity will prove to be illusory?

There *is* something critically significant in the prominence of such interracial male pairs as Huck and Jim, Ishmael and Queequeg, Natty and Chingachgook in the canonized literature of nineteenth-century America, and Fiedler was the first to bring this significance to the attention of the critical community. The subsequent reinvention of this "archetypal image" in countless artifacts of American popular culture testifies to its inexhaustible resonance. The partners Andy and Bobby in television's *Hill Street Blues,* the Mel Gibson/Danny Glover pairing in the *Lethal Weapon* movies, Chris the (white) DJ in *Northern Exposure* and his (black) brother Bernard, and the protagonists in countless other interracial buddy narratives, all fit the pattern Fiedler discerned. (The story enacted by Tom Hanks and Denzel Washington in the movie *Philadelphia* achieved some kind of culmination in this tradition: the black attorney as savior of gay white AIDS sufferer.) Fiedler's thesis

---

sexually chaste and therefore morally blameless, the root sense of "innocent" as *unknowing* or *uncomprehending* might serve here to reference the range of issues discussed by Eve Kosofsky Sedgwick in *Epistemology of the Closet* and other works: The sense that homosexuality in our culture is largely constituted by relations of knowing and unknowing. See Fiedler also at 349n for another swipe at critics who, despite his care to "be quite clear that I was not attributing sodomy to certain literary characters or their authors," persisted in thinking that he had done so. By way of contemporary contrast to Fiedler in another direction, see James Baldwin, "Preservation of Innocence," *Zero* 1.2 (Summer 1949), 14–22, where the "innocence" in question is the willful ignorance of the American tough guy, purchased often in violence against women and homosexuals, with which he preserves his "immaculate manliness" (20) against the depredations of both, and keeps himself from "discover[ing] the connection between that Boy-Scout who smiles from the subway poster and that [gay] underworld to be found all over America" (22).

opened the difficult question of the intricate historical coimplications of male homoeroticism and interracial feeling in America in a way that was deeply enabling, even if (in retrospect) intensely problematic. The essential insight — that male homoeroticism and love between non-white and white were "fused . . . into a single thing" (p. 522) in the texts he discusses — remains powerfully suggestive but still largely neglected.

It is only fair to specify that Fiedler deserves credit for the risk he took in publishing such an essay when he did, and for the obviously decent intentions it imperfectly realized. January of 1948 saw the publication of Alfred Kinsey's *Sexual Behavior in the Human Male*, with its revelation that, as John D'Emilio has winningly put it, "95 percent of white American men had violated the law in some way at least once along the way to an orgasm,"[3] 50 percent of men admitted homosexual desires, 37 percent admitted to postadolescent same-sex orgasmic experience, and 4 percent were exclusively homosexual in orientation throughout adulthood.[4] Kinsey was widely vilified, and his information had no immediate effect on the massive ordinary oppression of gay people by the criminal justice system, the medical establishment, educational institutions, and other disciplinary apparatuses — except perhaps to alert them to intensify their apparently inadequate oppressive measures. Kinsey's statistics did, however, have a decided effect on the postwar process of formation of gay identity and community, making public a "stubborn" fact (the widespread existence of homosexual passion and behavior, and the numerous existence of self-identified homosexuals) that had a positive value for gay self-identification even as it stimulated official paranoia.

Simply for Fiedler to utter, in 1948, in the pages of *Partisan Review*, the name of the unspeakable love, took some bravado. The simple transgressive power of this utterance should not be casually underestimated (the many horrified reactions to his thesis attest to its violation of a taboo), and my analysis of the problematic qualities of the form that utterance took is not meant to detract from the real service Fiedler performed in opening a discussion on some important questions. The fact remains, however, that Fiedler's dense, elliptical essay is

[3]John D'Emilio, *Sexual Politics, Sexual Communities: The Making of a Homosexual Minority in the United States, 1940–1970* (Chicago: Univ. of Chicago Press, 1983) 35. These figures, and the survey methodology that produced them, have been subject to strong challenge since then; my point, however, has to do only with the context of scholarly and public opinion to which they contributed in 1948.

[4]Loc. cit.

one that doesn't altogether know what it is saying. "Come Back to the Raft Ag'in, Huck Honey!" at once flaunts the scandalous claim that classic American books are full of erotically charged interracial male same-sex relationships, but also solemnly warns against misunderstanding the nature of those relationships. It is "innocent" homosexuality only that is present in Cooper, Melville, and Twain. Innocent, one wants to know, as opposed to what? The implication is that there is some other, "guilty," form of homosexuality.

Readers of the essay have tended to forget the overwhelmingly normalizing force of Fiedler's reassurances. The wish to employ the rhetoric of scandal — to exploit the force of the gesture of uncovering a secret truth — coexists uneasily in Fiedler's essay with a countervailing wish to justify Jim and Huck et al. by showing that *there is nothing scandalous,* after all, about their relationships. Ralph Ellison observed that when Fiedler "named the friendship homosexual" he had merely "yelled out his most terrifying name for chaos," having been unable to unsnarl the ambiguities of the relationship.[5] Fiedler brings Huck and Jim forcibly out of the closet (to use an anachronistic expression) only to tell us that they weren't in the closet to begin with: They were normal males all along. The incoherence (and, possibly, the bad faith) of this critical project is manifest. What's so interesting about claiming that, after all, Huck and Jim are just good pals?

The interesting thing about Huck and Jim is that their relationship can't be mapped onto our late-twentieth-century system of affectional relationships, a system in which loving friendship and sexual involvement are crisply distinguished from each other, and "homosexual" and "heterosexual" people are thought to be separate and well-defined groups. The world in which Huck and Jim lived (the 1840s) did not maintain these categories with the rigor later generations would do, although the world Twain lived and wrote the novel in (the 1880s) was beginning to observe these distinctions more consistently. Thus understanding Huck and Jim requires us to suspend our modern social categories, and try to imagine what it was like for these two outcasts to

[5]Ralph Ellison, "Change the Joke and Slip the Yoke," *Shadow and Act* (New York: Random House, 1964), 51. Ellison argues that Jim is a figure out of the blackface minstrel tradition, whose "dignity and human capacity" only partially emerge from behind that "stereotype mask"; lacking adult dignity, "Jim's friendship for Huck comes across as that of a boy for another boy rather than as the friendship of an adult for a junior; thus there is implicit in it not only a violation of the manners sanctioned by society for relations between Negroes and whites, there is a violation of our conception of adult maleness" (50, 51).

devote themselves to one another, having never heard that it mattered whether their love was "innocent" or "guilty" according to as-yet-uninvented laws of heterosexual normativity. And it requires us to imagine how Twain, when he wrote the novel, may have been harking back to a prior era in which sexual and gender identities were not so rigidly defined. Fiedler's essay sometimes suspends these modern concepts of sexual identity in an effort to retrieve this historical moment, and at other times reinforces modern sexual categories and consequently presents an ahistorical account of Huck and Jim.

That Fiedler may have soon realized that this dual rhetorical strategy was incoherent and perhaps dishonest may be inferred from the kinds of revisions he made to the essay when he included it in his collection *An End to Innocence* in 1955.[6] For example: "the underground existence of crude homosexual love" (p. 520) in the 1948 version was rewritten as "the continued existence of physical homosexual love" in 1955 (142). Fiedler's reference to "the fag café" in 1948 became "the 'queer' café" in the revised essay of 1955 — one epithet (perhaps slightly less invidious?) substituted for another, and the apologetic gesture of inverted commas around the word *queer* holding the new name at arm's length. The underlying conceptual structure is unchanged, however, despite the cosmetic attempt to tone down the abusive rhetoric: It is a structure in which "infantile" and "homoerotic" are equated (p. 522), and an ideal of "chaste male love as the ultimate emotional experience" (p. 521) is held to be unfortunately "compromise[d]," "destroy[ed]," and "contradict[ed]" by "overt homosexuality" (p. 520). These expressions represent Fiedler's attempt to paraphrase, as it were, the homoerotic myth as he believed Cooper, Melville, Twain, and others had created and elaborated it; but Fiedler doesn't challenge the queer-hating assumptions with which, on his account, the myth was framed. On the contrary, he tacitly endorses the opposition between chaste and unchaste, carnal and pure, "ideal [male-male] love" (p. 522) and its debased and debasing physical realization. At the same time as he reinscribes these tired binaries, he describes this idealized "chaste male love" as "not adult" (pp. 521, 522), a "child's dream" (p. 523), and so forth, with a rather quaint confidence in Freudian psychosexual developmental norms.[7]

[6]Leslie A. Fiedler, "Come Back to the Raft Ag'in, Huck Honey!," *An End to Innocence: Essays on Culture and Politics* (Boston: Beacon Press, 1955) 142–51.

[7]See Joseph Allen Boone, *Tradition Counter Tradition: Love and the Form of Fiction* (Chicago: U of Chicago P, 1987), ch. 5, for a fairly comprehensive critique and revision

In Fiedler's view, homosocial phenomena like "the camaraderie of the locker-room and ball park, the good fellowship of the poker game and fishing trip" exemplify an "astonishing naiveté" on the part of their participants because, he believes, the "smug assumption of the chastity of the group as a masculine society" is unwarranted (pp. 520–21). Don't they know that sex is lurking? But this "smug assumption" is unwarranted not simply because there is physical passion "latent," as psychologists would have said at the time, just beneath the veneer of normal male bonding, and certainly not because this libidinal energy is a harmless variant of human erotic desire. Rather, the *smugness* is the problem: For Fiedler such smugness is a dangerous relaxation of a necessary vigilance, a fearsome ignorance "that breeds at once endless opportunities for inversion and the terrible reluctance to admit its existence" (p. 521). A hostile paraphrase of Fiedler's reasoning would go something like this: We're kidding ourselves if we pretend there aren't fags everywhere (and if we don't guard against turning into fags ourselves), and unless we chuck this happy myth of chaste male love and admit the real existence of real homos they'll multiply endlessly.

The implication, quite clearly, is that healthy suspicion rather than guileless innocence will help us to stop breeding inverts and, consequently, enable us to preserve the "good clean fun" of male homosociality. We won't then have to "surrender the last believed-in stronghold of love without passion" (p. 521). What Fiedler doesn't say is why he would have us preserve this "believed-in" myth of chaste male passion when he has already characterized it as a juvenile dream. The answer, it seems, is that the alternative is worse: He flinches at the prospect of recognizing physical homosexual love as a simple (albeit "stubborn") social fact, a fact that doesn't compromise, destroy, or contradict anything except the homophobic fantasy on which male heterosexual identity in modern American society is precariously built.[8]

---

of Fiedler. Boone observes that "Fiedler often betrays a biased view of 'normal' or 'correct' male development, one rooted in the psychoanalytic milieu of America in the 1950s: for, in his eyes, the freedom sought by the male protagonist 'on the run' from society *necessarily* constitutes an arrested adolescent avoidance of adult identity and of the mature love embodied in marital responsibility" (228). It is evident even from this brief quotation that Boone's analysis emphasizes issues of male gender identity over questions of sexuality.

[8]See George Chauncey, *Gay New York: Gender, Urban Culture, and the Making of the Gay Male World 1890–1940* (New York: Basic Books, 1994) 111–26. Chauncey argues that in the early twentieth century, as pronounced heterosexuality became the hallmark of middle-class masculine style, the "fairy," i.e., the effeminate homosexual, was "the primary pejorative category against which male normativity was measured" (115).

My rearrangement of Fiedler's rather inchoate prose, in the interest of bringing its fundamental paranoia into focus, should not obscure the fact that the most prominent effects of the rhetoric of the essay are directed against the "hypocrisy," "naiveté," and "smugness" of those who fail to see the "gross" potential latent in the "delicate" homoerotic impulses of such pairs as Natty and Chingachgook or Huck and Jim. Those impulses are only "homoerotic in the boy's sense" (p. 520), and must be carefully distinguished from the gross version, presumably homosexual in the adult's sense, to which they may unwittingly lead. This is a tense rhetorical balancing act, at once maintaining the distinction between benign juvenile homoeroticism and harmful adult homosexuality and yet threatening it with imminent collapse. It trades, as I have said, on the shock value of exposing the scandalous while insisting that the scandalous is actually harmless.

Such rhetorical tension runs through "Come Back to the Raft Ag'in, Huck Honey!," surfacing for instance in such statements as Fiedler's decrying of "the regressiveness, in a technical sense, of American life, its implacable nostalgia for the infantile," in his nostalgia for the boyish homoerotic passion that is "at once gross and delicate," nostalgia that is "at once wrongheaded and somehow admirable" (pp. 521, 520, 521). *Somehow* admirable, but *how?* Under a show of being unable to decide, Fiedler remains a partisan of the orthodox Freudian paradigm of psychosexual development, according to which a child naturally must pass from immature polymorphous desire to mature heterosexual genital performance. This paradigm of "normal" psychosexual maturation depends, as many theorists (including Freud himself) have shown, on a paranoid suspicion of lurking homosexuality. The normality of the heterosexual depends on stigmatizing the homosexual as deviant.

Thus Fiedler is demonstrably *not* saying that Huck and Jim, Ishmael and Queequeg, and Natty and Chingachgook are "queer as three-dollar bills," as he would later recall was said by those who heard of his essay "at second or third hand." But he *is* saying that American writers unwittingly and unfortunately privileged a form of love that was dangerously mutable, potentially transformable into outright queerness. He trades on the scandalous power of his claims even as he denigrates the unworldliness of those who would be scandalized. He pushes Huck and the others to the brink of the abyss of homosexuality only to pull them back to "this side of copulation" (p. 520). Fiedler wants at once to be an iconoclast and a defender of heterosexual propriety.

Scholarship has recently begun to emerge that presents fragmentary evidence that sexual relations between black and white men in nineteenth-century America did not in fact always stop "this side of copulation," but until further research provides more information one is limited to provisional speculation in this area. Although it has become a commonplace, for instance, that female slaves had an especially traumatic experience of enslavement because they were subject to the sexual abuse of their masters, the tacit assumption that male slaves were not sexually abused is, at the very least, unproven and therefore unwarranted. The historian Martin Duberman has published a pair of letters that bear indirectly on this issue, written in 1826 by Thomas Jefferson Withers (a twenty-two-year-old law student at South Carolina College in Columbia, later to become a judge of the South Carolina Court of Appeals and a leading nullifier) to his friend James H. Hammond (later a governor, congressman, and senator from South Carolina, as well as a leading pro-slavery polemicist). Withers coyly writes, "I feel some inclination to learn whether you yet sleep in your Shirt-tail, and whether you yet have the extravagant delight of poking and punching a writhing Bedfellow with your long fleshen pole — the exquisite touches of which I have often had the honor of feeling?"[9] The letters are playful, coy, and lack any sense of a strict demarcation between carnal and platonic affection. "Sir, you roughen the downy Slumbers of your Bedfellow — by such hostile — furious lunges as you are in the habit of making at him — when he is least prepared for defence against the crushing force of a Battering Ram."[10] The second letter features Withers's elaborate dream image of Hammond in quest of sex: "I fancy, Jim, that your *elongated protuberance* — your fleshen pole — your [two Latin words; indecipherable] — has captured complete mastery over you — and I really believe, that you are charging over the pine barrens of your locality, braying, like an ass, at every she-male you can discover."[11] These letters may suggest that within the libertine sexual culture of upper-class white men in the South, homosexual acts were relatively uncontroversial. We know from countless sources that slave masters frequently used their female slaves sexually; there is little reason

---

[9]Martin Bauml Duberman, " 'Writhing Bedfellows': Two Young Men from Antebellum South Carolina's Ruling Elite Share 'Extravagant Delight,' " *About Time: Exploring the Gay Past* (New York: Gay Presses of New York, 1986) 7.

[10]Loc. cit.

[11]Op. cit. 8.

to assume that they did not sometimes use their male slaves in this way also. The sociologist Orlando Patterson, author of *Slavery and Social Death* and *Freedom* among other studies of the ideological world of slave societies, has remarked that "anyone acquainted with the comparative ethnohistory of honorific cultures" like that of the antebellum South would know that "homosexuality is pronounced in such systems, both ancient and modern. Southern domestic life most closely resembles that of the Mediterranean in precisely those areas which are most highly conducive to homosexuality."[12] These provocative suggestions remain to be substantiated definitively by detailed historical research, but in the meantime a certain intuition seems to have been shared by imaginative witnesses as various as William Faulkner and Toni Morrison. In *Absalom, Absalom!* (1936) Faulkner described Thomas Sutpen's fondness for naked fighting with his negroes in the stable, a strange ritual in which by this temporary status equalization ("both naked to the waist and gouging at one another's eyes as if their skins should not only have been the same color but should have been covered with fur too") Sutpen secures "supremacy, domination" — the compound status of white, masculine, and respectable of which he is so desirous.[13] In *Beloved* (1987) Morrison imagines how male slaves, chained into a coffle in the morning, would be made to kneel before the sadistic guards whose "whim" it might be to offer their prisoners some "breakfast" in the form of their penises to fellate. "Occasionally a kneeling man chose gunshot in his head as the price, maybe, of taking a bit of foreskin with him to Jesus." One slave escapes this humiliation only because he retches as he witnesses the sodomization of the man next to him, and the guard consequently skips him for fear of his clothing getting "soiled by nigger puke."[14]

Indeed Harriet Jacobs in her celebrated slave narrative had intimated that violent homosexual domination was not unknown in Southern slave culture. Toward the end of *Incidents in the Life of a Slave Girl* Jacobs tells about a fugitive slave named Luke, whom she met in a New York street soon after his escape and warned about the slave-catchers who might menace him there. Luke's master, Jacobs recalls, had been prey to unspecified "vices" that made him, "by excessive dissipation,"

---

[12]Orlando Patterson, "The Code of Honor in the Old South," *Reviews in American History* 12 (1984): 29.

[13]William Faulkner, *Absalom, Absalom!*, in *Novels 1936–1940* (New York: The Library of America, 1990) 23, 47.

[14]Toni Morrison, *Beloved* (1987; New York: Plume, 1988) 108.

finally a "mere degraded wreck of manhood" whose whim it was to keep Luke naked except for a shirt, "in order to be in a readiness to be flogged." The bedridden young master "took into his head the strangest freaks of despotism," Jacobs avers; "Some of these freaks were of a nature too filthy to be repeated."[15] The traditional horrified designation of homosexuality by tropes of unnameability — "the sin that cannot be named," "the unmentionable vice," and "the love that dare not speak its name" — makes it presumable that Jacobs was intimating that Luke's master abused him sexually. A Confederate private wrote home to his sister in 1865 that his fellow soldiers "rode one of our company on a rail last night for leaving the company and going to sleep with Captain Lowry's black man."[16] Although it can't be positively stated that "sleep with" denoted sexual activity in 1865, certainly what was being punished was taboo physical intimacy — though it seems that the race (and perhaps the social class) rather than the gender of the participants was what made this intimacy punishable.

In other regions of the United States homosexuality in a variety of social forms was not unknown, although again the available evidence is as yet scattered and partial. Provisionally one can say that there seem to have been emergent homosexual subcultures in the streets and taverns of various metropolitan areas; these subcultures often overlapped considerably with communities of sailors and other socially marginal working-class groups, some of which were distinctly racially diverse.[17] (Fiedler himself mentions the "rude pederasty of the forecastle and the Captain's cabin," but predictably calls it "the profanation of a dream" [p. 524].) In the popular blackface minstrel shows of antebellum America, as Eric Lott has shown, the general atmosphere of racial and gender inversion frequently licensed expressions of homoerotic desire.[18] Frontier communities were another site of homosexual emergence, probably both because these locations (mining camps, ranches) were often populated only by men and what is called "situational homosexuality" prevailed, and because men with pronounced homosexual inclinations

[15]Harriet A. Jacobs, *Incidents in the Life of a Slave Girl, Written by Herself,* ed. Jean Fagan Yellin (1861; Cambridge, MA: Harvard UP, 1987) 192.

[16]Thomas P. Lowry, M.D., *The Story the Soldiers Wouldn't Tell: Sex in the Civil War* (Mechanicsburg, PA: Stackpole Books, 1994) 112.

[17]Perhaps the best source to date on the (homo)sexual life of American seamen in the nineteenth century is B. R. Burg, *An American Seafarer in the Age of Sail: The Erotic Diaries of Philip C. Van Buskirk, 1851–1870* (New Haven, CT: Yale UP, 1994).

[18]Eric Lott, *Love and Theft: Blackface Minstrelsy and the American Working Class* (New York: Oxford UP, 1993) 27, 53–55, 86, 117, 120–22, 152, 161–68.

found the frontier's relative lack of social discipline to their taste. Thus the unmistakably homosexual writer Charles Warren Stoddard was drawn toward the bohemian artistic circles of San Francisco in the 1860s, where he met Mark Twain among others. Twain, who later employed Stoddard as his secretary in London during a time when Stoddard was actively exploring that city's homoerotic venues, referred to Stoddard as "such a nice girl."[19] Recently a Twain biographer, Andy Hoffman, and other Twain scholars have suggested that during his early years as a bohemian journalist in the American West Twain's relationships with his intimate male friends may well have had an erotic dimension.[20]

It has long been known that Twain's sexual subjectivity was complex and unusual in several respects; the issue is woefully miscast, however, if it is reduced to the mere question of whether or not Twain (or any other writer, or any literary character) actually had sex with another man. The crucial point is that Twain lived through a dramatic transformation in the late nineteenth century of what cultural theorists call the sex-gender system, the set of rules and norms that governs the social organization of the related phenomena of gender identity and sexual orientation. The specific historical transformation here is the one that brought about the emergence of distinct categories of sexual identity (homosexual and heterosexual, i.e., sexualities defined by their same-gender or different-gender preferences) where such sexual identities had not been distinctly recognized before.[21] That Twain came into close contact with various effects of this massive transformation — effects on others among his acquaintance and on himself — cannot be doubted.

These and other stray indications of the presence in the United States during Twain's lifetime of *non*chaste homosexuality, sometimes

---

[19]Roger Austen, *Genteel Pagan: The Double Life of Charles Warren Stoddard* (Amherst: U of Massachusetts P, 1991) 39, 65–68. Robert K. Martin in "Knights-Errant and Gothic Seducers: The Representation of Male Friendship in Mid-Nineteenth-Century America," in *Hidden from History: Reclaiming the Gay and Lesbian Past*, ed. Martin Duberman, Martha Vicinus, and George Chauncey, Jr. (New York: Meridian, 1990) 169–82, notes that Stoddard and a number of other contemporary writers "seem to have located their erotic fantasies in the South Seas" (171). The ways in which sexual and racial transgressions interanimate one another in such circumstances needs further exploration.

[20]Liz McMillen, "New Theory about Mark Twain's Sexuality Brings Strong Reactions from Experts," *Chronicle of Higher Education* (Sept. 8, 1993): A8, A15.

[21]The influential standard account is Michel Foucault, *The History of Sexuality, Volume I: An Introduction,* trans. Robert Hurley (New York: Vintage, 1980). See esp. 43.

interracial, may suggest that the relationship between Huck and Jim as Twain portrayed it represents a deeper and more pointed reflection on real social conditions than Fiedler would have us believe. In 1881 in the *St. Louis Medical and Surgical Journal* Dr. William Dickinson discussed a case of sodomy in Mark Twain's hometown of Hannibal, Missouri, a case that involved one eighteen-year-old who was "known to the police as an abandoned character" and a thirteen-year-old "street gamin" (roughly the age and condition of Huck Finn) who was partly per-suaded and partly coerced into anal intercourse. "This is a crime which however frequently committed, is rarely brought to the knowledge of the police," Dickinson observed.[22] Historians of sexuality refer to the 1860s and immediately subsequent decades as the period of the inven-tion of the homosexual as a recognized social type; the mere temporal coincidence of this emergence of a distinctive homosexual identity with the charged racial atmosphere of these same decades in the United States (violent controversies over the social relationships between the races that underwrote the Civil War and Reconstruction) would be enough to suggest that the analytically distinct categories of racial and sexual identity interacted in everyday lived experience and in the public consciousness in complicated and potentially explosive ways. But it seems possible that what Fiedler was sensing was something more than a contingent intersection of sexual and racial categories in this period. We may at least hypothesize that the dominant form of subjectivity in this period in America — white heterosexual manhood, whose pre-scribed object of desire was white heterosexual womanhood — was constituted by perpetually disavowing its homoerotic desire for black men. What is at stake then, in the "national myth of masculine love," is not, as Fiedler would have it, boyish or asexual desire for the black male other, but a fully sexual desire, a desire on the repression and punish-ment of which dominant white masculinity was historically founded.

In a society like ours, characterized generally by patriarchal domina-tion of women, theorists like Gayle Rubin and Eve Kosofsky Sedgwick have maintained that the fundamental social bonds are those between men, and that women function as mediators of those primary bonds. But because such approved forms of male bonding as "friendship, men-torship, admiring identification, bureaucratic subordination, and het-erosexual rivalry" entail degrees of libidinal investment that make them "remarkably cognate" with and "not readily distinguishable from"

[22]Jonathan Ned Katz, *Gay/Lesbian Almanac* (New York: Harper & Row, 1983) 179.

male homosexual bonds, in Sedgwick's words,[23] such male bonds are chronically under pressure to guarantee their own heterosexual status, to ward off the threatening possibility that they are not, after all, so very different from directly homosexual bonds. (This warding-off is, essentially, the effort Fiedler's nervous rhetoric collaborates in.) This is often accomplished by casting male same-sex bonds as relations of rivalry or competition for a female object of desire rather than as directly desirous relations between men.

Now, in nineteenth-century America, white men thought frequently of black men as their erotic rivals in the competition for white women; popular culture was full of images of hypermasculine black men as sexual predators with an all but irresistible attraction to white women. If in the psyches of white men the most charged homosocial rivalry for women was with black men (or, more accurately, with an imaginary black sex fiend), one result would be that the bonds between white men and black (as aversive as they ordinarily were) would then be the bonds at most risk, so to speak, of mutating into homoeroticism. To borrow from the logic of Freud's account of how paranoia in men is produced by their repression of their homosexual desire, white men's exaggerated sense of the sexual threat posed to them by black men might well be understood as a defensive response to a wish-fantasy of loving a black man.[24]

These speculations, altogether too sketchy, may nevertheless suggest why I think Fiedler's essay was prescient in its identification of homosexuality and race as interrelated features of *Adventures of Huckleberry Finn*. It is important that critical attention to sexuality not be displaced by interest in gender in this novel and in others that Fiedler identified as participating in the "national myth of masculine love." Gender analyses like that of Myra Jehlen tend to obscure the presence of the homoerotic in the text because, to the extent that the gender binary (masculine/feminine) governs their conceptual apparatus, same-

---

[23]Eve Kosofsky Sedgwick, *Epistemology of the Closet* (Berkeley: U of California P, 1990) 186, 185. Sedgwick draws on Gayle Rubin, "The Traffic in Women: Notes on the 'Political Economy' of Sex," in Rayna E. Reiter, ed., *Toward an Anthropology of Women* (New York: Monthly Review Press, 1975) 157–210, and idem., "Thinking Sex: Notes for a Radical Theory of the Politics of Sexuality," in Carole S. Vance, ed., *Pleasure and Danger: Exploring Female Sexuality* (Boston: Routledge & Kegan Paul, 1984).

[24]The canonical analysis is Sigmund Freud, "Psychoanalytic Notes upon an Autobiographical Account of a Case of Paranoia (Dementia Paranoides) (1911)," in *Three Case Histories,* ed. Philip Rieff (New York: Collier, 1963) 103–86.

gender relations fade from view. To advert to Sedgwick once more, "It may be . . . that a damaging bias toward heterosocial or heterosexist assumptions inheres unavoidably in the very concept of gender."[25] Thus while the scene of Huck's masquerade as "Sarah Williams"[26] may indeed, as Jehlen argues, demonstrate Twain's sense of the arbitrariness or constructedness of social gender roles, the possibility that gender inversion has something to do in the novel with sexuality (recall Twain's remark that Charles Warren Stoddard was "such a nice girl," quoted earlier) is effectively foreclosed. And the other scenes of transvestism in *Huckleberry Finn* remain unexplored by Jehlen — the King's performance as Juliet in "night-gown" and "ruffled night-cap" (p. 134); the King's naked performance in particolored paint in "The Royal Nonesuch" (p. 151); Jim's masquerade as a "Sick Arab," painted a "dead dull solid blue" and wearing "a long curtain-calico gown" (p. 155); Tom Sawyer's plan for Huck to dress in the "yaller girl's frock" and for himself to wear "Aunt Sally's gown" and then give it to Jim to wear during their "rescue" of Jim from bondage (pp. 243, 244) — in all of these, gender masquerade provides an alibi for potentially transgressive male-male encounters.

In Twain's later fragmentary story, "Hellfire Hotchkiss" (1897), which Jehlen invokes as a work in which "Twain expresses a clear understanding that gender is a matter of ideology [rather than biology]," to support her assignment to Twain of a gender-constructionist viewpoint in the earlier *Huckleberry Finn,* it strikes me that issues of sexual identity are again at least as salient as those of gender. Jehlen misascribes to Twain the startling judgment in that text that "Hellfire Hotchkiss [the girl] is the only genuwyne male man in this town and [the boy] Thug Carpenter's the only genuwyne female girl, if you leave out sex and just consider the business facts."[27] But in the extant draft of

[25]Sedgwick 31.

[26]Mark Twain, *Adventures of Huckleberry Finn,* ed. Walter Blair and Victor Fischer (The Mark Twain Library; Berkeley: Univ. of California Press, 1985) 66ff.

[27]Myra Jehlen, "Gender," in Frank Lentricchia and Thomas McLaughlin ed., *Critical Terms for Literary Study* (Chicago: U of Chicago P, 1990), 272. (Jehlen's essay is reprinted as "Reading Gender in *Adventures of Huckleberry Finn,*" see p. 496.) Jehlen cites Susan Gillman, *Dark Twins: Imposture and Identity in Mark Twain's America* (Chicago: U of Chicago P, 1989) 109–10, as her source for the gender-switching Hellfire Hotchkiss quotation. The fragmentary tale can be found in Mark Twain, *Satires & Burlesques,* ed. Franklin R. Rogers (Berkeley: U of California P, 1968) 172–203. Jehlen's/Gillman's quotation is on page 187. Further page references will be given parenthetically in the text.

"Hellfire Hotchkiss," this observation on the paradoxical genuine maleness of the girl and femaleness of the boy is made by Jake Thompson, the town baker, who quotes it from Puddn'head Wilson, the eccentric expounder of counterintuitive apothegms who was revived here by Twain after he had been depicted in his own eponymous novel in 1894. It is a remark thus at least twice removed from Twain the author, and explicitly marked as an excessively clever satirical bon mot. It cannot be taken simply to reveal Twain's "clear understanding" of the constructedness of gender; it might even plausibly be construed as his rejection of such an understanding. But Twain's rendering of Thug as a sissy and Hellfire as a tomboy might plausibly be taken as recognizing the role gender inversion played then in constituting male (and female) homosexuality as social types.

Oscar "Thug" Carpenter is an embarrassment to his father, who avers that his disappointing son "ought to put on petticoats" (178). When skating on the river one late-winter day the ice breaks up and Thug is left isolated and adrift on an ice-cake, paralyzed by fear and unable to act to save himself. Rachel "Hellfire" Hotchkiss rescues the "unmanned" boy by swimming through the icy waters and pulling Thug to safety (189). This "tomboy" (195) likes the racy company of boys and the challenge of masculine pursuits in preference to girlish things, but vicious town gossip eventually forces her to a dismayed realization:

> Oh, everything seems to be made wrong, nothing seems to [be] the way it ought to be. Thug Carpenter is out of his sphere, I am out of mine. Neither of us can arrive at any success in life, we shall always be hampered and fretted and kept back by our misplaced sexes, and in the end defeated by them, whereas if we could change we should stand as good a chance as any of the young people in the town. (199)

And indeed Rachel "Hellfire" Hotchkiss consequently resolves to "do ungirlish things" no longer (200). Twain's text is an unfinished fragment, so it would be unwise to assume that his story has any decisive final position on how gender or sexuality "ought to be." But at the very end of the nineteenth century, in a society in which gender inversion is widely taken to be the distinguishing mark of an emerging social category of (homo)sexual deviance, Twain's story seems at the very least to be not only about gender styles but about the social stigmatization and painful subjective confusion of two gay kids.

The loving relationship between Huck and Jim in Twain's novel is misunderstood when the reductive question, gay or straight?, is addressed to it. It cannot be saved for heterosexuality by establishing that it was not a genital homosexual relationship. Aside from the vulgarity and parochialism of taking genitality as the measure of the eroticism of a relationship, it is also an error to think that because the relationship was not homosexual it was therefore heterosexual. Neither of these categories was readily available in their twentieth-century form when Twain wrote the novel, much less during the antebellum time period when the action of *Huckleberry Finn* is set. These categories were *in formation* during that time period; the reorganization of collective affectional life that the emergence of those categories entailed was *in process;* relations between men were coming to be governed by normative heterosexual imperatives at the same time as relations between the races were undergoing stressful new reorganizations. The ways in which these historical processes of sexual and racial transformation influenced each other had to have been many and various and inscrutable, and probably were not readily understandable to those who lived through them then, much less to those like Fiedler who examined them retrospectively in the 1940s. And it would be unwise to claim that they are fully legible now, when such events as the beating of Rodney King and the arrest of O. J. Simpson have generated such swarms of charged representations in which the issues of race and sex continue to be intricately knotted together. What we can say is that Twain portrayed a loving interracial male same-sex bond in all of its dense affectional complexity, with all of its social inscrutability, and portrayed it within the ambiguous and tragic historical circumstances that made it so hard to understand and represent.

Appendix:
Writing about Critical Controversy

In our introductory essay, we discussed why it makes sense to study critical controversies and, in doing so, suggested that such study can increase your engagement with literary texts and with the world of literary criticism in which your teachers and many other readers live. In this essay, we offer some suggestions about *how* to contribute to the debates yourselves. We will focus our advice primarily on how to write about controversies because, if you are like most people, you will find writing more challenging than speaking, but we believe that our advice can also be useful for participating in class discussion. Our advice will cover some general principles and some specific techniques not just for managing an argument but for doing so in response to the arguments of others.

GETTING DIALOGIC

Let us suppose that your teacher, after discussing with you and your classmates the essays in this book on the controversy over race, gives you an assignment to write a five-page paper making your own contribution to that debate. How should you proceed? Consider the following responses to the assignment by two different students. (1) Student A decides that the most important thing to do is say something original; therefore, she declares her opinion early in the paper and then spends the rest of the paper presenting the textual evidence that supports her opinion. Along the way she drops in footnotes that indicate which critics in this text agree with her opinion and which do not. (2) Student B decides that the most important thing to do is to show the complexity of the debate and so he spends most of the paper summarizing what others have said, saving his own opinion for the last few paragraphs. Indeed, to impress the teacher, Student B goes to the library to find more essays on the novel so that he can include their views in his summary.

Although each approach has some merit, each, in our view, has a major flaw. Student A's, which we will call the *solo flyer model,* mentions and occasionally quotes or summarizes several critics but does not really grapple with their ideas. Her references to that debate are not integral to her argument, but something added on, because she has learned that English teachers like footnotes. Since the solo flyer paper does not respond to the debate, the chances of its being recognized as a substantial contribution are very low, even if it does have original things to say. Student B's approach, which we will call the *shrinking violet model,* does not give enough emphasis to his own contribution to the debate. Instead, the paper is dominated by the opinions of others. Consequently, although student B's approach is likely to require more hours of work than student A's, his paper, too, is unlikely to be a substantial contribution to the debate.

Although the solo flyer and the shrinking violet models are, in one sense, very different, they both are insufficiently *dialogic,* by which we mean that they both do a poor job of relating the writer's ideas to those of others. Critical debates are like conversations, and to be a good conversationalist you need to do two interrelated things: (1) make what you say responsive to what others in the conversation have been saying; and (2) have something worthwhile to say. In fact, listening closely to others or closely reading their texts and attempting to be responsive to their arguments is the best way to find something worthwhile to say. We suspect that you've had the experience of joining a conversation on a topic that you did not think you had much of an opinion about, only to discover to your surprise, after listening to others offer their views, that you actually have a strong opinion and are interested in expressing it. Of course not all conversations, critical or otherwise, work in exactly that way, but the experience does underline the point that an excellent way to find something worthwhile to say is to work dialogically. To put the point another way, making a good argument of your own entails situating your ideas in relation to others'.

CHOOSING A POSITION: AGREEING, DISAGREEING, DOING BOTH

In one sense, the process of making a critical argument is very simple. If you think about situating your ideas in relation to others' along a spectrum from complete agreement to complete disagreement, you can see that there are a limited number of general positions to take: strongly agree, strongly disagree, and partially agree and partially disagree. We think you'll be helped if you decide which of these three options you want your essay to conform to and stick to that plan as you write it. If you find yourself shifting to one of the other options, no problem; just revise your essay so it sticks to that one.

At the same time, each of these three simple positions — agree, disagree, do both — is open to an infinite number of variations and complications. To illustrate, here are the main responses and a few of their variations. The variations are rarely mutually exclusive; almost all of them can be combined within a single response.

1. You can strongly disagree with another critic's argument. You can go on to develop the disagreement by (a) arguing for an opposing interpretation of the critic's main evidence; (b) arguing that there's significant relevant evidence that the critic's argument neglects and that leads to another conclusion; (c) arguing that the context within which the critic reads the evidence is not appropriate. Justin Kaplan's essay "Born to Trouble: One Hundred Years of *Huckleberry Finn*," for example, strongly disagrees with the charge that the novel is racist and argues that, if read in its appropriate historical context and with due attention to its ironic tone, the novel is clearly "a savage indictment" of racist attitudes.

2. You can disagree and explore what you find to be a tension or even a contradiction in the other critic's argument. You can develop your case by arguing that, despite the critic's best efforts, there's still an underlying issue that needs to be addressed and that addressing it leads to a different conclusion. Martha Woodmansee's "A Response to Frederick Crews" uses this strategy, as Woodmansee contests the key concept Crews uses to

argue against the efficacy of Myra Jehlen's feminist criticism of *Huckleberry Finn:* the concept of "literary facts." Woodmansee argues that Crews's understanding of this concept is too narrow, that there are good reasons for working with a broader understanding, and that doing so leads to a far more positive assessment of Jehlen's essay.

3. You can say "Yes, but"; that is, you can partially agree and partially disagree. You can develop the agreement by (a) pointing to positive features of the critic's argument such as the use of evidence or (b) extending the critic's argument to some issue or part of the text that the critic has not addressed. You can develop the disagreement by using the strategies in number 1 or by arguing that the critic's case is good as far as it goes but it does not go far enough. Christopher Looby's essay " 'Innocent Homosexuality': The Fiedler Thesis in Retrospect" provides an excellent example of this strategy. Looby praises Fiedler for making the argument that there is a significant homoerotic dimension to the Huck-Jim relationship, but Looby also objects to the way Fiedler's essay "does its thinking from within a deeply homophobic and gay-baiting structure of assumptions" (p. 527 in this volume).

4. You can say "yes, and"; that is, you can agree and develop the agreement along the lines in 3 (b). In this response, you want to show both that you're building on the previous critic's case and making your own contribution to the debate through the skillful analysis of the material that has been neglected or not sufficiently explored by the previous critic. Stacey Margolis's essay "*Huckleberry Finn;* Or, Consequences" provides a fine example of this strategy. Margolis agrees with both Jane Smiley and Jonathan Arac that the novel must be assessed in light of its effects on readers (its consequences) rather than its intentions, and goes on to argue that in making this case Arac and Smiley are indebted to the novel itself. They owe this debt, Margolis contends, because *Huckleberry Finn* is part of a cultural shift in the nineteenth century that led Americans to decide that the consequences of one's actions were more important than the intentions of those actions.

DEALING WITH MULTIPLE OTHERS

As the examples indicate, these options are available to you whether you are situating yourself in relation to just one other critic or to more than one, but there are also some common strategies for dealing with more than one. Here are four such ways:

1. After summarizing the other critics' positions, you can identify and focus on something significant that they have in common: a view of a certain part of the text, an assumption about what is important in the novel or the criticism of it, or some other such issue. You can be explicit and straightforward about the underlying issue and your relation to it: "Despite their different concerns, X and Y identify Z as a crucial element of the text, and their views of it are largely the same. However, by considering evidence of the text that both essays neglect, I will argue for a different view of Z." Leo Marx's essay "Mr. Eliot, Mr. Trilling, and *Huckleberry Finn*" provides an excellent example of this strategy. Marx begins the essay by noting that both Trilling and Eliot (a) praise Twain's novel but find it necessary to defend the unusual ending and (b) discuss that ending in purely formal terms. Marx then turns to argue that the ending cannot be successfully defended, and his case includes his contention that the form of the novel is inseparable from its content or "moral insight."

2. After summarizing two or more other critics' positions, you can point out that underneath a surface similarity is an underlying difference or disagreement and then turn to your position on the issue. You can summarize your case with a sentence such as the following: "Although X and Y seem to agree about Z, a close look at their essays indicates that they actually have quite different views of Z, and that difference is significant in the following ways." Frederic Crews's essay "Walker versus Jehlen versus Twain" provides a very clear illustration of this strategy. In his second paragraph, Crews writes, "On the surface, at least, Myra Jehlen and Nancy Walker are taking quite similar approaches to Twain's novel. . . . In their execution, however, these two essays differ radically, and in a way that corresponds to a deep division not just within feminist practice but also within the literary academy as a whole" (p. 510). Crews identifies this division as one between interpretations like Walker's that are accountable to the text and those like Jehlen's that he thinks are not.

3. After summarizing two or more other critics' positions, you can suggest that a new approach to the issue will recontextualize those positions — perhaps making some stronger and others weaker — and offer a more adequate treatment of the issue. Toni Morrison's essay "Jim's Africanist Presence in *Huckleberry Finn*" provides an excellent example of this strategy in relation to the ending of the novel. After noting multiple posi-

tions on the efficacy of Twain's ending, Morrison points out that "[w]hat is not stressed [by previous critics] is that there is no way, given the confines of the novel, for Huck to mature into a moral human being *in America* without Jim" (p. 309). From there she goes on to argue that, with Jim's Africanist presence, "the book may indeed be 'great' because in its structure, in the hell it puts readers through at the end, the frontal debate it forces, it simulates and describes the parasitical nature of white freedom" (p. 310).

4. After summarizing other critics' positions, you can argue for what theorists call a meta-position, that is, one that does not try to resolve the debate but comments on it in another way. Peaches Henry's essay "The Struggle for Tolerance: Race and Censorship in *Huckleberry Finn*" provides a fine example of this strategy. After offering an insightful survey of the debates about Twain's treatment of race, Henry does not side with either the defenders or detractors of *Huck* but shows that both are persuasive about different aspects of the novel. She then builds on this analysis in her concluding comments on the potential value of the controversy: "Though the problems of racial perspective present in *Huckleberry Finn* may never be satisfactorily explained for censors or scholars, the consideration of them may have a practical, positive bearing on the manner in which America approaches race in the coming century" (p. 405).

As with any art, the best way to develop skill in critical argument is through practice. As you get accustomed to situating your ideas in relation to those of others, you are likely to find yourself becoming better at both reading and writing critical arguments. Your reading skills will develop because you will be more attuned to the moves other critics make, and this greater awareness will enhance your own ability to make similar moves in your writing. Furthermore, the more you practice, the more you will realize that, whether you agree or disagree with others, your engagement with their ideas is crucial to the development of your own.

Acknowledgments

Jonathan Arac. Excerpt from *"Huckleberry Finn" as Idol and Target.* © 1997. Reprinted by permission of The University of Wisconsin Press.

Sacvan Bercovitch. Excerpted from "Deadpan Huck." Originally published in the *Kenyon Review* 24 (2002): 90–134. Reprinted by permission of the author.

Gerry Brenner. "More Than a Reader's Response: A Letter to 'De Ole True Huck." From *Journal of Narrative Technique* 20 (1990): 200–34. Reprinted by permission of the *Journal of Narrative Technique.*

Seymour Chwast. "Selling Huck Down the River." From *The New York Times* book section, March 10, 1996. Copyright © 1996 by *The New York Times.* Reprinted by permission.

Frederick Crews. "Walker versus Jehlen versus Twain." Reprinted by permission of the author.

T. S. Eliot. "The Boy and the River: Without Beginning or End." Excerpted from the introduction to the 1950 Chanticleer edition of *Adventures of Huckleberry Finn* by Mark Twain. © The T. S. Eliot Estate. Reprinted by permission of Faber and Faber Ltd.

Leslie Fiedler. "Come Back to the Raft Ag'in, Huck Honey!" First published in the *Partisan Review* 15 (1948): 664–711. Reprinted by permission of the Estate of Leslie Fiedler.

Ernest Hemingway. Excerpted from *Green Hills of Africa* by Ernest Hemingway. Copyright © 1935 by Charles Scribner's Sons. Copyright renewed © 1963 by Mary Hemingway. Reprinted with permission of Scribner, an imprint of Simon & Schuster Adult Publishing Group.

Peaches Henry. "The Struggle for Tolerance: Race and Censorship in *Huckleberry Finn.*" From *Satire or Evasion? Black Perspective on "Huckleberry Finn."* Copyright © 1992 Duke University Press. All rights reserved. Used by permission of the publisher.

Myra Jehlen. "Reading Gender in *Adventures of Huckleberry Finn.*" From *Critical Terms for Literary Study* edited by Frank Lentricchia & Thomas McLaughlin. Copyright © 1990. Reprinted by permission of the University of Chicago Press.

Justin Kaplan. *Born to Trouble: One Hundred Years of "Huckleberry Finn."* A Lecture sponsored by the Florida Center for the Book and presented in Fort Lauderdale, Sept. 11, 1984. Copyright © by Justin Kaplan. Reprinted by permission of Sterling Lord Literistic, Inc.

Julius Lester. "Morality and *Adventures of Huckleberry Finn.*" Copyright © 1969 and 1991 by Julius Lester. Reprinted by permission of the author.

Christopher Looby. "Innocent Homosexuality: The Fiedler Thesis in Retrospect." Reprinted by permission of the author.

Stacey Margolis. "*Huckleberry Finn;* or Consequences." Published in the March 2001 issue of *PMLA* Copyright © 2001. Reprinted by permission of the Modern Language Association of America.

Leo Marx. "Mr. Eliot, Mr. Trilling, and *Huckleberry Finn.*" From *The American Scholar* 22 (1953): 423–40. Copyright © 1953 by Leo Marx. Reprinted by permission of the author.

Toni Morrison. "Jim's Africanist Presence in *Huckleberry Finn.*" From *Playing in the Dark: Whiteness and the Literary Imagination.* Copyright © Toni Morrison. Reprinted by permission of International Creative Management.

James Phelan. "On the Nature and Status of Covert Texts: A Reply to Gerry Brenner's Letter to 'De Ole True Huck.'" First published in the *Journal of Narrative Technique* 20 (1990): 235–44. Reprinted by permission of the *Journal of Narrative Technique*.

Jane Smiley. "Say It Ain't So, Huck: Second Thoughts on Twain's 'Masterpiece.'" Copyright © 1995 by *Harper's Magazine.* All rights reserved. Reproduced from the January 1996 issue by special permission.

Lionel Trilling. "A Certain Formal Aptness." Excerpted from the introduction to the 1848 Rinehart edition of *Adventures of Huckleberry Finn* by Mark Twain. Introduction copyright 1948 by Lionel Trilling. Introduction renewal copyright © 1948 by Lionel Trilling. Reprinted by permission of The Wylie Agency.

Nancy A. Walker. "Reformers and Young Maidens: Women and Virtue in *Adventures of Huckleberry Finn*." From *One Hundred Years of "Huckleberry Finn": The Boy, His Book, and American Culture,* edited by Robert Sattlemeyer and J. Donald Crowley. Copyright © 1995 by the Curators of the University of Missouri. Reprinted by permission of the University of Missouri Press.

Martha Woodmansee. "A Response to Frederick Crews." Reprinted by permission of the author.